HOMECOMING

A NOVEL

HOMECOMING

VILLA VISTA 1920 HIGH SCHOOL

FRANK WINTER

HOMECOMING

Copyright © 2021 Frank Winter

For business inquiries, contact:
frankwinterfiction@gmail.com

Or find additional information at:
www.frankwinterfiction.com

Book and Cover design by Frank Winter.
White bricks wall texture by Mrsiraphol (Freepik.com).
ISBN: 978-1-7376232-2-9 (Hardback)
ISBN: 978-1-7376232-0-5 (Paperback)
ISBN: 978-1-7376232-1-2 (eBook)

Library of Congress Control Number: 2021914629

BISAC category code: FIC031070 FICTION / Thrillers / Supernatural

First Edition: September 2021

10 9 8 7 6 5 4 3 2 1

Dedicated to my loving parents, who supported all of my endeavors.

PROLOGUE

This is NEWS10 Alexandria, coming to you with an emergency announcement. A massive explosion has occurred at Villa Vista High School. The Alexandria Police Department has ordered the evacuation of homes within five miles of the campus, fearing critical damage to natural gas lines could cause secondary explosions.

Pacific Gas and Electric have shut off and are now bleeding the lines of the Oceanside neighborhoods, which they believe are still feeding the blaze. Additional support has been requested of the San Rafael and Marin County fire departments to keep the flames from spreading beyond school grounds.

Villa Vista High School was hosting its annual Homecoming dance during the explosion. Search and rescue is ongoing, and the Fire Marshall has requested friends and family not to approach the school. The fire is not contained.

If you know someone in the affected area who is unaccounted for, please dial 311. You will be put in contact with the proper officials and provided information as soon as it becomes available.

ONE

TIME ON THE CLOCK

VV (claps) HS (claps)
Villa Vista is the very very best! (claps)
VV (claps) HS (claps)
The Jaguars strike, you go down like the rest! Rawr!

THE CHEERLEADERS WARMED UP the crowd with one of their most common chants. It was familiar and repetitive.

The alliterative usage of "...very very..." popped up all too often among teachers and students. Whoever helmed the school intercom were more than happy to make use of the wordplay, especially with such phrases as "... a very very wonderful Villa Vista morning." The sing-songy aspect was very exploitable and sometimes it felt like every new announcer tried to invent their own variant.

The less *cheer*-ful among the student body had grown *very very* sick of it over the years. But to those students one thing about the cheer always irked them more, that was the iconic "Rawr!" at the end of the chant.

The cheerleaders always enunciated the "Rawr" as they struck their final pose. At some point, someone must have pointed out that it rhymed with "Jaguar" and it had stuck ever since. Most of the crowd at the games, football and basketball especially, would default to a more intimidating and realistic growl or just an ambiguous shout.

Despite the naysayers, the cheer was popular and fun, so it appeared quite often throughout Varsity Football season.

That night in particular, the Jaguars needed all the crowd enthusiasm the cheerleaders could muster. The annual Homecoming game happened to be up against the school's biggest rival, the John Muir High Mountaineers.

Both schools kept a running tally on how many games they had bested the other throughout the years in what had become known as the "Coastal Classic". While the administrations of each tried to maintain a good-natured spirit to the rivalry, the students and faculty that gave a damn about sports took it very seriously.

While Villa Vista held the all-time win record since the competition began in the 1950s, John Muir High had been on a winning streak the past few years thanks to a new coach they poached from Marin City.

The Jaguars hadn't won a Coastal Classic since Joe Torelli entered high school. However, as the new starting quarterback for the Jaguars, he intended to change that.

Standing at 6'-3", and having reached that height as early as his sophomore year, Joe was scouted to try out for basketball very early on.

But, possessing the broad shoulders and physical endurance that a full-contact sport required, Joe very quickly settled into JV Football as soon as his freshmen year began.

He wasn't out of place among the other Torellis, his whole family placed high importance on athletics. The tradition went back nearly a century to his great-grandfather, Giuseppe Torelli. He played defense on the New York Giants during their historic seasons in the 1930s.

Everything was falling into place for Joseph Emiliano Torelli to join his great-grandfather as a great player in the NFL ... everything except for this one very important game.

At halftime, the score was 7-14, with the Mountaineers leading.

Joe tore his helmet off like he was about to smash it against the concrete.

While most of the crowd were unwinding, going to the restroom, or heading up to the concession stand, Joe stewed on the bench, drinking the last drops of Gatorade from his squeeze bottle.

More than anything Joe wanted to vent his rage at someone from the defensive line or one of his receivers, but he was forced to bite his tongue. He knew it was ultimately his fault.

Just five minutes earlier, Joe threw what he thought was a clear shot to his wide receiver #83, Jimmy O'Shaughnessy.

It took only moments to see that he'd overshot Jimmy by almost 10 yards and the ball was intercepted by the Mountaineers' #66.

That gigantic mistake would lead to their second touchdown right before the end of the second quarter.

After making a few rounds to the other players for individual comments, Head Coach Scott Kelley kneeled down and handed Joe a fresh sport bottle.

"Alright Torelli, so-"

"You don't have to say it," Joe said as intensely as he could without drawing attention. "It was a shit throw."

"Language ..." Kelley said. "It was long, yeah, but defense should have stopped that drive."

"Yeah, they should have!" Joe fumed, taking advantage of the opportunity to redirect his anger.

"But you need to stop showing off ..." Kelley continued. "No more artillery throws, we're going to run the ball up the middle in short passes, where the offensive line is strongest. We don't need a big spectacle; we need to win."

Coach Kelley stood up and moved on to the next player.

If Joe were in his shoes, he would have pulled him from the game for such a mistake, but unfortunately that wasn't really an option right now.

The second-string quarterback, Bill Mansley, went out joyriding in his dad's Corvette a few weeks back and slammed it into the center divider of a boulevard. Luckily his girlfriend was okay, but Bill's left knee had been messed up badly in the crash. They had to re-center the patella after it was knocked out of place and stitch up some other torn ligaments around it. He'd be out the rest of the season at least.

Joe was pretty familiar with knee injuries. In his opinion, Bill's football and sports career was over. He'd better figure out something else to do with his life now ... before the bitterness sets in.

The only other quarterback, third-string Howard Boychick, had only started playing football this season. He didn't have nearly the experience, or throwing arm, that Torelli did.

There were no substitutions, Joe had to win this game.

After a few minutes, he pulled his helmet back on and grouped up with the others around Coach Kelley as they planned out the third quarter.

***

In the stands, Niles Koh watched as they cleared the field for the halftime show. The line for concessions almost reached the bottom row of the bleachers but he really didn't care much about whatever the Color Guard were doing anyway.

While they were flipping their flags and plastic rifles, Niles kept one eye on the parked parade of floats at the far side of the stadium.

He could see Laura toiling away on some ribbons on the corner of their Junior Class float.

The theme that year was "High Society", as voted on by the members of the Student Council.

The administration was hesitant to approve it, considering the optics on social media and the cost of living of their zip code. Luckily those like Laura Nakano, the Junior Class Treasurer, were able to convince them that it was more about parody than parity.

They promised they were poking fun at the rich and the famous of days gone by, not flaunting the deep pockets of their own parents.

The theme carried into the Homecoming Dance too and Laura really wanted to dress up in some kind of historic dress.

With the faculty convinced, the themes were decided on by each class. The Senior Class reps on the Student Council selected Victorian England, the Junior Class reps selected French Bourbon Restoration, the Sophomore Class reps selected Italian Renaissance, and the Freshman Class reps selected American Roaring Twenties.

While not actually riding on the float, Laura was by far its biggest contributor, having pulled all the right pieces together to make the plywood backdrop look like the interior of the Palace of Versailles.

The line shifted and Niles walked forward, closing in on the snack counter.

Niles first saw Laura when she joined the school at the start of their sophomore year. They shared a homeroom together, Mrs. Jefferson's English class.

Niles was not very talkative outside of his friend group, but he often found himself watching her from the back row, even when Barry was trying to plan their next game night. Laura Nakano had completely captured his heart.

She stood around 5'-3", with jet black hair and a slender frame. He'd be lying to say that her physical beauty hadn't caught his eye first, but as time went on, he learned more about her from the small interactions they had or seeing how she was with her friends.

Laura was driven in ways that Niles was not. She actually seemed to *like* high school, likely because she was good at it … or perhaps it was the other way around. She walked away with straight A's after putting in seemingly no effort at all. Of course, that was an outsider's perspective, but she never really seemed to "sweat it", as it were.

Her real zeal showed up in her extracurriculars and chief among those was the Student Council. She got as much fulfillment out of planning dances and student body events as she did actually attending them.

Niles was in every way her opposite.

High school was that thing that consumed too much of his day before he went home and actually did the things he enjoyed. That included gaming with friends from all around the world. Having to show up to a brick-and-mortar building for eight hours a day blocked off a window of time that he otherwise could have been playing with his friends in Europe. Their clan was only four million credits away from buying a *Galaxy*-class ship in *Intrepid*, a space MMORPG.

Niles applied himself enough to get a C average and that was sufficient as far as he was concerned.

Villa Vista was just the place he was forced to go to by the California Board of Education, it didn't actually give a damn about him or his future, just that he was a conforming citizen.

His real dream was to get a job with Kladivo Studios and work on *Intrepid* (and games like it) full time. Not to mention, Prague seemed like a much cooler place to live than the Bay Area.

Somehow though, his long pursuit of Laura had changed his outlook on high school. By the time winter break rolled around, Niles' C average grades had risen to B's. Villa Vista suddenly seemed like an alright place to spend the day.

When they returned in January, Mrs. Jefferson began grouping up the class for a Shakespeare project they would be developing over the entire Spring Semester.

Working up four months of courage, Niles went right up to Laura and asked her if she wanted to be in a group. To his utter shock, she had said yes, on the contingency that her friend Anne Kirkpatrick could join them as well. Barry came along too, becoming the fourth member of their group.

Niles, Barry, and Melvin had been close friends since elementary school, clearly standing out as the geekiest among Mr. Olowe's third-grade class.

Barry Owens had not been too happy to see Niles "slobbering after Laura" all year ... his words. However, he too had a new perspective on school now that he'd be working opposite Anne for their English project.

Mrs. Jefferson began assigning stories to the other groups, *Twelfth Night, Midsummer Night's Dream, The Comedy of Errors,* and for Niles' and Laura's group ... *Macbeth.*

The project gave Niles the excuse for face time that he needed until eventually making his second big play, asking her to the Spring Formal.

The Spring Formal at Villa Vista High was essentially the end of the year dance for freshmen and sophomores. It was something for them to do as a substitute for Prom, which the juniors and seniors would attend two weekends later.

It had just the right amount of informality, ironically. It wasn't seen by anyone as majestic or romantic like Prom or Homecoming. It was the "Practice Prom", a chance for fun and a dance without the great expectations of the older, more historic institutions.

Niles Koh did not consider himself attractive at all, but he cleaned up as well as he could to finally pop the question one day after school. He knew effort was something she would appreciate, so he put together a display of balloons with a frame outside by her car. The balloons spelled out "SPRING FORMAL LAURA?" He timed it so he would be filling up the question mark balloon right as she walked out.

Based on Anne's reaction standing next to her, Niles felt pretty confident he had pulled it off, which was confirmed by a big hug from Laura.

The line shifted forward and the man at the counter asked for his order. Niles picked up two Diet Pepsis and a large basket of chicken strips and fries for them to share. He gazed for a moment at the chili cheese dog at the bottom of the menu but was terrified by the idea of spilling anything on her.

He walked off with the food and returned to their place on the bench.

Barry and Anne were there, as well as Melvin and a couple of Laura's other friends. Seeing Melvin Mueller show up to a school sporting event was something he still could not believe was actually happening, but it had been a pretty strange year all around.

The Spring Formal went as well as Niles could have hoped, and he and Laura spent the summer sort-of-dating and getting to know each other on a much more personal level.

Laura walked back to the bleachers once the final changes had been made to the float. It was in the best state she was going to get it, after the two of them put in the lion's share of the effort. She waved when she saw Niles getting back at the same time.

He still didn't understand what Laura saw in him, but he hoped more than anything that she wouldn't come to her senses. Homecoming had to go perfectly, for both of their sakes.

If it did, maybe he could make it official, maybe they could be boyfriend and girlfriend.

Before the float parade would start, the choir was up to perform. A hundred students filtered onto the field from behind the home stands.

***

"I hate it," Blaire said, as Elise began adjusting the buckles on the decorative vest.

"You're supposed to hate it," Elise said with a smirk. "I'd be worried about you if you didn't hate it."

The Villa Vista Choir & Drama department always performed a musical medley during the Homecoming game halftime show.

It mostly served as advertising for the program and their upcoming shows for the rest of the year. Students could transfer classes until the end of October, giving them two more weeks to be wooed into joining by the spectacle. Although the truth was that most people who transferred this late were in pursuit of a crush or to spend time with friends.

That's how it went with Blaire, who would otherwise be voted the student least likely to join the C&Ds. Rather than "Choir & Drama", they would be the "Cheerful & Dimwitted" in her eyes.

Unfortunately, Blaire knew Elise too well to consider her dimwitted. Her cheerful disposition was spot on though and separated the two like water and oil.

Elise on the other hand knew Blaire well enough to recognize that she was a strong mezzo-soprano.

After playing the long game for two years Elise had finally captured Blaire like a fly in a web and dragged her right into the rafters of the school's Lawrence Murphy Performing Arts Center.

Blaire Tidwell came from a family filled with people like Elise, who rose to greet the day as though life were a river of endless possibilities.

Blaire greeted the day with a scowl. As a borderline nocturnal creature, the sunrise was her mortal enemy.

She was a troubled child. Even from a young age, most of her youthful indiscretions came from a lack of knowing about herself.

Everyone in her family got on her nerves in one way or another and none of them seemed to understand her.

That would all change when she was nine years old and her father's father came to live with them.

Edward Tidwell was a tall and imposing man, who used to command the newsroom at the San Francisco Chronicle in his younger days. The Assignment Editors below him used to call him "The Statue" because of the way he would stand and peer out over the floor while they worked.

Decades later however, his standing was not as strong as it used to be. After one too many falls, he relented to his son's invitation to come live with them.

In the mornings, when the rest of the family were buzzing about the house in their daily routines, Blaire would find her grandfather standing in the study at the rear of their cliffside estate. With a cane grasped tightly in his left hand, he stood statuesque and stared out at the fog rolling in off of the ocean.

He sipped on coffee as thick as molasses and as hot as lava, greeting the morning with a comforting silence which became infectious to the young girl.

Blaire would join him every chance she could, eventually equipped with a mug of mud-like coffee of her own, to her mother's dismay.

But the caffeine did not tweak her out like one of her brothers. Instead, she and Edward would eventually take a seat and her grandfather would read to her from the stack of morning papers that came in from all over the country.

Blaire listened intently, asking questions whenever they came to her in the same way Edward had once grilled his editors for story details.

At one point, Blaire had seriously considered whether or not she was adopted, but her grandfather was the anchor she needed to make sense of herself.

His passing was the hardest day of her life, but she was eternally grateful for the years she did have with him. For a brief window of time, she felt like she wasn't alone.

That didn't make interacting with these daywalkers any easier though.

Blaire naturally had chocolate brown hair, but she would frequently blacken it with a charcoal wash or some other organic hair dye. It was a striking contrast to Elise Gosselin, who had bright, naturally red hair from a Danish-Norman ancestry.

Her clever and conniving personality had her greeting each morning not with dread, but determination. Every day was her own personal Battle of Hastings, with similar results.

That also applied to her love life. Basically every dance was a Sadie Hawkins as far as she was concerned.

"Raf, safety pin." Elise snapped her fingers and like a magic butler, Rafael Herrera produced a medium-sized pin.

Blaire was now standing in fifth position like a ballerina, blushing through her foundation make-up as Elise cinched up the sides of the vest after one of the buckles broke to pieces.

While the girls were offered midi-length skirts to wear, the yellow sequin tops were unisex monstrosities which really didn't seem to fit anyone well.

Most of the choir girls took in the sides beyond the simple adjustment of the buckles to give a more flattering look. The Homecoming game was packed and they wanted to look their cutest.

The team colors were black and yellow, so the black pants, skirts, and shirts were actually quite striking and versatile. Then they were given the skins of murdered traffic signs to cover their torsos, so the effect was a bit mixed.

Blaire was regretting the fact that she'd chosen the skirt. There were no pockets, there were never pockets ... and it's not like anyone would have stopped her from going with pants. But the sleek black skirt actually looked pretty good on her and she realized all too late that she had chosen to suffer for fashion.

"Pin," Elise said again, as Rafael pulled another one from the deep, spacious pockets of his choir pants.

Elise was the kind of girl who took what she wanted, but she was a teenager, so what she wanted changed on a regular basis.

After Paul Maxon spent half of their sophomore Spring Formal talking to his Cross-Country friends, Elise had decided that it was time for an upgrade.

Rafael had been openly flirtatious with her for all of their time together in Choir & Drama, so she decided to throw him a bone, see if he could prove himself worthy.

At the very least, he proved to be a good purse.

He was one of the tenors, a chatty and vivacious boy that spent entirely too much time breaking out into Top 40 Hits. It surprised Blaire that the C&Ds didn't cast him out as some kind of heretic long ago.

His opposite was Andrei Tunnikov, one of the basses, who stood nearly 6'-8" tall.

Blaire was not a short girl, but Andrei towered over her and almost everyone else.

Unlike Raf, he was ... quieter, when he needed to be anyway. His voice naturally carried far, with a deep timber, so he spoke softly in normal conversation.

When he wanted to however, his pipes could thunder to a frightening degree. His voice stood out most distinctly among the 18 basses in the choir. He was often set aside for solos or small ensemble sections.

Elise was the kind of girl who knew what she wanted, and when provided an opportunity, tried to help Blaire find what *she* wanted.

When they were talking randomly one day, Elise brought up the new senior who had joined the choir and immediately Blaire began to blush. Not missing the chance, she began to grill Blaire for information. After that, it was just one more game for Elise, who refused to let her miss out on another Homecoming.

Blaire had successfully outmaneuvered her the previous year by getting sick. The boy she'd lined up for Blaire had to find a backup.

There wasn't really much potential there anyway ... Maurice Gellman was just kind of, well, available. Andrei Tunnikov was another story.

Blaire had gotten visibly flustered in a way she rarely ever did. At the very least, there was a spark. After some careful whispering in Andrei's ear, the match was made ... for the dance anyway.

"Yo, we probably need to go soon, they're almost lined up," Raf said to Elise as she finished patching the broken buckle.

Still standing at relevé, Blaire looked up to Andrei and said, "I should have gotten the pants."

A smile cracked the corner of his lips and he pulled out a thin powdered foundation compact.

She smiled back; it was just what she needed. Around him, it was hard to hide her blush.

***

The choir assembled on the field and began their medley in earnest, singing in their adorable little bumblebee costumes.

Mr. Melkonian sat in the announcer's booth while a handful of other faculty ate their dinners at the back of the room.

He actually liked the school colors, but they were hard to get across sometimes. The school mascot was a black jaguar, so the yellow highlights were meant to represent the subtle rosettes of the creature's fur pattern, as well as the intimidating yellow eyes.

There's no way they were going to put a bunch of teenagers in that kind of fabric though, so whenever pep rallies were concerned, they had to get more abstract with the color scheme. Still, he couldn't help but see the choir kids as drones swarming around Cynthia Donovan, the Choir & Drama Director, as their queen bee.

There was only one student allowed to actually wear jaguar print in an official capacity ... and he had to wear the felt mascot head to go with it.

Down at one corner of the field, Melkonian could see Harold Cordelia in the Jackie the Jaguar costume. He was taking a break by the cheerleaders, most likely chatting up Shawna Guthrie again.

He shook his head and sipped on some hot chocolate.

Robert Melkonian's main job at Villa Vista was serving as the biology teacher. He cut up more frogs in a given year than your average French restaurant and he loved every minute of it.

"Mr. Mel" always had a passion for teaching. He really loved being able to properly introduce new generations of kids to the life sciences, even if a few animals had to die in the process.

At the same time, he really enjoyed working at a high school. It kept him young. Even though his daughter had graduated a couple years back, he could see putting in another decade at least before retiring.

After proving himself at corralling the youngsters in and out of the lunchroom, he was given the chance to help out with announcements too. Now, years later, he'd become the voice of VVHS.

"Bob, you wanted onions, right?"

Richard Wallace sat back down next to Melkonian, holding two large chili cheese dogs.

"Rick, I'm allergic to onions," Bob said, putting on a convincing face of distress.

Rick furrowed his silver walrus mustache and quipped, "well there's got to be an epi-pen around here somewhere."

Rick Wallace was in his mid-seventies, two decades senior to the biology teacher. His official capacity was as the school's guidance counselor, but he'd served as a coach of some kind for almost every sport the school played.

He was the Bob Melkonian of the previous generation. While he wasn't a coach anymore, no one in the school wanted him to retire, least of all Bob. Their back-and-forth banter was a highlight of the VVHS varsity sports programs.

While Melkonian could provide snappy second-to-second commentary on plays, Wallace was at the ready with some story or comparison from his 46-year tenure that made him sound like the school historian. More often than not, a parent would stop by after a game, surprised that Rick had reminded them of a story from their own life that they'd forgotten.

"So, what do you think," Bob asked, as Rick took a large bite from the chili dog, "do our boys have a chance of turning this around?"

Rick Wallace searched his archives, zoning out over the field while the choir's medley broadcast in the background.

He finally swallowed the bite and turned back to Melkonian. "The closest situation I can think of is the '89 game. Woody Thompson was our quarterback and we were losing at halftime. Woody was a bit of a showboat, but Pierce ... I don't know if you remember him, Coach Pierce Leighford ... He sat that boy down on the bench and he yelled at him, just hollered so hard I thought they'd hear him in the stands.

"I was the Defensive Coordinator at the time and I was about to intervene. But when I turned from the linemen to look at Woody, he was okay. Leighford had put the fear of God into that boy, and it was just enough to focus him on the task at hand."

"And we won that game?" Bob asked, only vaguely remembering Coach Leighford, let alone the year 1989.

"We did ..." Rick confirmed, but there was a hanging hesitation to his words which he only answered after taking another bite. "Woody Thompson had a much different personality than Joe Torelli though.

"Coach Kelley could have yelled at Bill Mansley like that and gotten similar results. Maybe then Bill wouldn't have banged up his dad's car or his knee. Not sure Scott could get away with 'coaching' like that these days though.

"Regardless, that wouldn't help Joe. If I were to guess, Joe's already been yelled at enough."

"What do you mean?" Melkonian asked.

"I've met Joe's old man," Rick continued. "Salvatore Torelli is the kind of guy that only has two volumes, loud and sleeping."

Bob thought back on if he'd ever met Sal Torelli, but couldn't place a time. Joe was far from an honor's student, but he was capable of maintaining a B- in Melkonian's class. Nothing low enough that would have called for a meeting with his parents.

Bob would have remembered a father like that. He'd known too many fathers like that.

"Luckily ..." Rick continued, "Kelley's the kind of guy who can give Joe what he needs, a firm hand on the shoulder and a wave in the right direction.

"It's not the end of the world if we lose this game. Joe needs to know that, even if it might feel that way."

The choir were completing their piece, which concluded on a choral arrangement of "Shooting Star" by Owl City.

On the final note, the pyrotechnics guy fired a mortar with an eruption of fireworks right over the middle of the field.

The crowd erupted into applause and Melkonian flicked on his microphone.

"Another *amazing* performance by the Villa Vista Choir. Just a small sample of what's to come with this year's Winter Pageant, 'Radio Rat Pack'! If you want to throw your voice into the mix there are still spaces available. See your homeroom teacher for more details."

Rick picked up after that. "That's right Bob, it's gonna be a night to swoon and croon, but first we have to focus on the here and now. After a week of hard work from so many dedicated students, it's time to kick off the float parade!"

***

The Freshman Class float slowly rolled out of the side parking lot, being pulled by a classic Cadillac owned by one of the parents. It was the only "High Society" float where the tug car was actually period-appropriate for the theme. The others had to use their closest approximations.

Jennifer Maxwell scoffed. She knew that the century-old car was one of the reasons they had selected that theme in the first place.

The float was decorated like the party scene from *The Great Gatsby*, with Enrique Rodriguez and Ellen Taylor representing their class on the Homecoming Court.

The Freshman Class was always a wild card when it came to school spirit events, but the Homecoming Court nominations followed a particular pattern. The classmates chosen were usually among the oldest or most mature. "Maturity" was highly valuable currency in the hormone economy.

Enrique was on the swim team, which gave him a muscled and toned body with less than 2% body fat. Ellen Taylor had a bit more body fat, but it was in all the right places.

The float began its slow loop around the football field before it would eventually stop at the far end of the home team bleachers. Mr. Mel and Mr. Wallace were already reading their prepared scripts talking about the theme and recapping the Freshman Class highlights from the Spirit Week events, including when Enrique beat the other boys by being first to finish eating a caramel-covered onion.

The Sophomore Class float looked almost clownish in comparison to the other three. They arguably took the biggest gamble on their theme of "Italian Renaissance". The float was covered in reds, oranges, and yellows as though they'd raided the wardrobe of the Pontifical Swiss Guard. It was being pulled by a rather nice cherry-red Ferrari though.

Still, Jennifer knew their float would win the "Most Creative" prize, but that wasn't her department to worry about.

Chelsea Morton and Greg Henshaw were actually pretty sweet kids and on top of that they were a couple. It wasn't often that the Homecoming King & Queen were both sophomores, but when it did happen it was usually because of something like that.

They had the reputation of being "everyone's friends", which seemed sincere. Couple that with a genuine romance and they easily had the second-best odds of winning.

The Junior Class float was boring. For all the vivid and tumultuous history behind the Bourbons and nineteenth century France, their float didn't even look like it was worth putting in a guillotine.

Jennifer knew she didn't really have much competition from the royalty either. Melissa Levitt had a notorious reputation for being a snobby bitch. She broke the same rule of High Society that the Bourbons did ... don't play the part too well. If all 500-ish students decided to greet her in the hallway one day, she'd maybe respond to only 70 of them.

It was unfathomable why the juniors voted her as princess, but there was no way she'd be rising above that.

Liam Connelly didn't have an air of infamy about him, but it didn't help being paired with Melissa during the Spirit Week events. His "Rebel Without a Cause" personality couldn't shrug off the toxic shock of being in her presence for too long.

It was pretty funny that their French float was being pulled by a Porsche though.

Finally, there was the Senior Class float.

Jennifer Maxwell had been quite sincere early on in the week when she praised the Student Council seniors for picking Victorian England as their class theme. It seemed like there was no contest invoking thoughts of *Downton Abbey* rather than *Les Misérables*.

Jennifer was self-aware enough to understand her own popularity and not spoil it by rubbing it in the faces of others. What was the point of "biting the hand that feeds you?"

She was naturally attractive, dirty blonde hair, baby blue eyes, an enviable cup size … but she put the work in to earn her looks as well.

She'd been on the tennis team, swim in her sophomore year, and full-time cheerleading all throughout. She'd be out there doing the "Jaguar Rawr" cheers if she weren't the centerpiece on the class float.

She tried to accept the nomination for Homecoming Queen with as much humility as she could, but deep down this had always been a dream of hers.

Prom Queen was one thing, but it almost seemed like the consolation prize. You're only competing against one other class, and considering the state of the Junior Class it would be an easy sweep if she was already ranked highest among the seniors.

Homecoming Queen was an honor bestowed on you by the whole school. The politics are trickier and you actually have to prove your merit during the pep rallies.

Luckily for her, the Senior Class Prince could handle the competition.

Marcus Johnson, the center on the Men's Varsity Basketball team, was the clear choice to be selected. He was athletic, he was cool, and was pretty chummy with everyone.

He absolutely dominated most of the Spirit Week games. The "Top Hat Sprint" alone put their class 10 points above the sophomores.

At one point in her life, Jennifer wouldn't have minded sealing their royalty chances like the sophomore couple, but unfortunately Marcus was happily hitched to Janice Short, a junior.

Jennifer had a bit of a rough start to the year when she found her boyfriend, Blake Samuels, uncoupling the bra of some bitch who didn't even go to their school.

Of course, when the news spread that she was available, the buzz around her for Homecoming rose dramatically.

She glanced over at the field where the players were still listening to the coach give some new game plan for the second half. On the edge of the crowd was one of the running backs, #38 Darren Clark.

He'd been keeping his eyes on Jennifer as well and raised his hand in a subtle wave when he saw her turn.

Darren was a safe choice. They'd known each other since middle school, when their moms used to carpool. They had been sort of friends, but didn't really run in the same circles. They'd seen a lot more of each other over their junior year though, when he joined Varsity Football. She'd always be there, cheering from the sideline.

They'd have fun. Fun is what she needed right now; Blake had broken her heart far more than she cared to admit.

"Ready to go?" Marcus extended a hand to help her up onto the float.

Jennifer tweaked his bow tie, then adjusted the crease on her gloves. "Ready," she said.

Marcus waved at the driver, and the Aston Martin slowly rolled onto the track, pulling the Victorian Gothic float behind it.

***

Halftime felt like it took forever, but in contrast, the second half of the game seemed to fly by.

Joe Torelli walked back onto the field a team player. He followed every play and direction Coach Kelley set out for them.

Short passes up the middle tied them with the John Muir Mountaineers, but it would end up being an offensive struggle. They came right back, trading another set of touchdowns.

With only two minutes left on the clock, the score was now 21-24. The Jaguars defense were able to hold the Mountaineers to a field goal during the last drive. Villa Vista needed a touchdown to win.

It was up to Torelli now.

Joe moved the ball down the field until they reached the 50-yard line. In a worst-case scenario, they could kick a field goal now and send the game into overtime. Their kicker, Trey Devall, could pull that off from the 50 if they really needed him to.

Joe didn't want it to come to that though. He wanted that touchdown, and there was still 45 seconds left on the clock.

Joe faked out their defensive line by handing the ball off to Darren Clark. He made the 1st down, but was tackled at the 36-yard line.

After a bad handoff though, it was now 3rd down. He was throwing it for real this time.

Following the hike, the field scrambled. The Mountaineers were just as determined to win this game as Joe was.

He looked to his left then made a quick pivot right, snapping around to where his receiver #87 Álvaro Pérez should be waiting.

Pérez was moving where he was supposed to, so Joe sent the ball flying.

Then, what seemed like a ghost materialized between the ball and Álvaro.

The Mountaineers colors were forest green and white (for the trees and snowy mountains), so their dark green away jerseys blended into the trees in the background very easily, even with a lit field and other colors from surrounding buildings.

Villa Vista had a similar advantage with the jet black of their away jerseys, but this was their stadium and their Homecoming game. They were wearing their gold jerseys with black accents.

The Mountaineers' defensive back #27 leapt into the air and snatched the ball seven yards away from where Pérez could have easily caught it.

Time seemed to slow down for Joe as #27 was downed at the 40-yard line and the referees affirmed the interception.

All the world went quiet and he couldn't move from where he stood. It was as though his brain had stopped all operations and thought processes.

There was an audible gasp from one side of the field, and a dull roar from the John Muir High fans in the other bleachers.

Torelli felt a slapping sensation on his shoulder pads, which finally snapped him out of the shell shock. It was Darren Clark, trying to pull him off of the field before it became a spectacle ... well, before it became a bigger spectacle.

The Mountaineers' quarterback took to the field, and as soon as the whistle was blown, he fell to one knee.

The rest of their team rushed to pile on him, while the last seconds of the clock trickled away to zero. The Coastal Classic was over, the John Muir High School Mountaineers had won 24-21, getting one step closer to taking the all-time win record.

Even worse though, they had beat the Jaguars at Villa Vista, during their own Homecoming game. They wouldn't even have the chance to return the favor for a Mountaineers Homecoming for at least three years.

When that chance came around, Joe Torelli would not be there to see it.

TWO

SETTING THE STAGE

SATURDAY STARTED LATE for most of the VVHS students, because most of them slept in.

Of course, that applied to most Saturdays, but this one especially as all the students expected (and very much hoped for) a late night after the dance.

Blaire and Elise had left the game after the halftime show. They really didn't care to stay either way and Elise had a bout of paranoia after the vest buckle incident. She wanted to go home and make sure everything on her dress was as it should be.

After assuaging her fears, Blaire was freed to head home and get a good night's sleep.

It might have been a long sleep, but it was far from good. Her whole slumber was riddled with nightmares.

Blaire dreamed quite often, probably more than most, but usually it was a peaceful world, her own private garden of contemplation.

She thought of it like a mutation, a coping mechanism her body had developed since it was so hard to find peace and quiet in the waking world, even in their rather spacious house.

The only time in her life she didn't dream as much was when her grandfather lived with them. Since his death a few years earlier, things had returned to the way they were.

Blaire faded in from the blackness, feeling a tightening around her waist. She reached down for the vest buckle, but did not find it. Instead, she was wearing a corset which began to tighten with every breath.

She reached out into the darkness trying to feel for a knife or scissors, but there was nothing there.

Soon a powerful white light turned into view, slicing through the darkness like a greatsword.

Blaire looked down and found a planked wooden deck extending beyond her heels.

The corset, which continued to squeeze her, was part of a full Victorian dress.

The powerful white light turned away from her before circling around again. Now the whole night sky had been revealed by the turning beams of a lighthouse.

Blaire was standing on the deck of a nineteenth century wooden schooner. The deck was empty and the sails had been furled. The ship was by itself, anchored in a nameless harbor.

She searched the shore but could not find anyone to help.

Finally, she saw a figure, a silhouetted shadow in front of the spinning beacon. It was her grandfather, standing statuesque, looking down at her.

She reached the railing and tried to call out to him, but her chest was too tight and the words left her lips like a whimper.

That is when she heard the noise.

She looked down the side of the ship, below the wooden railing. There was a row of things extending beyond the hull where the cannons should be. Instead of black iron, large-bore guns facing the shoreline, the sixteen gunports on the ship's starboard side held the spouts of oversized tea kettles.

Each kettle was made of a smooth brass surface and every one of them was now whistling. Soon the whistling grew loud enough that Blaire decided to focus on turning them off rather than free herself from the corset.

She stumbled away from the railing and made her way for the lower decks.

She glanced down at her hands and found them covered in a fine layer of powder. She touched her face and found more of the powder. It was not make-up, but felt almost like salt, coarse and abrasive to the touch, like it was digging into her skin. The frilled sleeves of her dress were covered in it, as was the bodice, the skirt, and her hair.

She stepped faster down the stairs.

When she reached the bottom, she saw what was causing the distress. The lower decks were on fire, burning slowly. It wasn't noticeable from the top, but the soot was everywhere and the flames had licked at the kettles long enough that they were now whistling as loudly as they could.

There was nothing Blaire could do. She knew her only hope was to jump overboard and swim for shore.

The corset tightened once more and she fell on all fours, crawling for the stairwell. As she was about to reach the top, a silhouette stepped from the shadows. It grabbed the edge of the hatch and threw it down on top of Blaire, sealing her below deck.

The sound of the wooden thud caused Blaire to jump and she quickly began to crawl backwards. Her travel was short and she found herself gripping the decorative metal rails of her bed's headboard. The burning deck of the ship had been replaced with lavender walls and a soft, carpeted floor.

She quickly reached down, patting around her navel, ready to tear open the corset. There was nothing there, except for the oversized shirt she wore as a nightgown.

The fear continued to grip her. She hugged her sides while her body shuddered uncontrollably. The adrenaline surged through her veins as she breathed deeply, trying to relax. Slowly, her body tipped sideways down onto one of the pillows.

It took a minute for her heart rate to calm down to a normal rhythm.

Once she felt comfortable, she slid to the edge of the bed and pulled her phone off of the nightstand.

9:32 a.m.

The lock screen showed one new message from Elise. Blaire flicked her thumb in a pattern and unlocked it to the messenger app.

Saturday · 8:47 a.m.

TODAYS THE DAY!!;! Ugh, I could hardly sleep a wink. Need cafe b4 we meet at Madisons

Also guess we lost the game last night, boo :P

Blaire answered her while kicking off the last of her covers.

Saturday · 9:33 a.m.

Oh really? That sucks could use
the extra java too. How about
NeuBreu on Palisades?

Blaire brushed over the pale skin on her arms, feeling around for any powder, but there was nothing there.

Her phone buzzed.

Saturday · 9:35 a.m.

Sounds good see you at 11!

Normally Blaire showered at night, but she still couldn't shake the feeling of being covered in all that soot. She decided to shower again before meeting up with Elise. They were going to the Madison Lane salon to get their hair done ... after a stop for some coffee.

Blaire scrubbed for several minutes in the hottest water she could stand before slipping on some casual clothes and lurching out into the rest of the house.

"One side!"

Blaire found herself taking evasive maneuvers, pressing up against the wall of the hallway.

"Chris!" she yelled at the fourteen-year-old as he careened through the house like it was a running track.

She would have recentered in the hallway, but Blaire knew that every comet had a tail.

Tommy, the youngest at eleven, also darted past her, wielding a foam mallet.

"Morning Blaire!" he said as he disappeared down the next bend.

The multi-level house had a lot of twists and turns, which made it a perfect circuit for the various competitions her brothers would invent.

The latest one was a modified form of tag. If you get bashed with the foam hammer, it's your turn to chase the other. Whoever spends the least amount of time holding the hammer in a session wins. If you break something, you automatically lose.

"Brats," she hissed to herself while making her way down a safe avenue for the kitchen.

"Good morning sweetheart," Jack Tidwell said as Blaire reached for the handle of the coffee pot. "Everything work out with Elise?"

"Yeah, turns out her clothes don't fall off of her like mine do." She cracked a snide smile while taking a sip of the thick mud coffee.

Jack eyed her over the morning paper. "Well, that's why we keep Elise around."

Blaire knew that the easiest way to push her dad's buttons was by reminding him of her impending womanhood.

He was the kind of father who ran a background check on anyone Blaire dated.

Blaire settled into one of the chairs at the kitchen table. The kitchen was at the back of the house. Just beyond Jack's shoulder was the hallway that led to the study in the far corner. It had the best view of the ocean, but this wasn't bad either.

She gazed out the window and was surprised by how much fog still covered the beach. It was going to be a festive Halloween.

"Did you stay for the rest of the game?" Blaire asked.

Her parents were thrilled that Elise had dragged her into the Choir & Drama program. They were all right at the center of the crowd cheering her on during the halftime show. However, they likely would have gone anyway, because Chris was thinking about joining JV Football next year and wanted to watch the Coastal Classic.

"Yeah, what a shame ..." Jack said. "One bad throw is all it takes sometimes. It got your brother all fired up though, he's already plotting revenge if he can make it to Varsity in a few years."

Blaire sipped the coffee without responding. While NeuBreu was better than most of the trendy cafes, they still basically served milkshakes compared to what she was used to.

Jack took a sip from his own mug.

After Edward died, Jack continued making coffee the way his father liked it ... the way Blaire liked it. Her mother always had a full container of half-and-half to draw from if it was too bitter and Jack would water it down sometimes, but it was worth it.

He knew how hard Edward's death would be on Blaire. He'd done a lot of learning from the elder patriarch and tried to reach out to Blaire wherever he could.

Then she became a teenager.

He didn't have any framework on how to handle things. The truth was, Jack and his father didn't get along until he was an adult. By then Jack had learned more about raising a family of his own and some of

Edward's harder edges had softened after he retired and after Jack's mother died.

But then to see that same cold stare manifest in his baby girl was hard for Jack to get used to. He had taken very much after his mother, and now had to reverse engineer all the coping mechanisms he'd called a relationship with his father into something healthier with Blaire.

Even still, there was more of Edward in Jack than even he realized.

One day in eighth grade, Blaire was telling her mother about a boy she met. Suddenly, something woke up inside of Jack and he began grilling her for information like it was about nuclear waste being dumped offshore.

Of course, this gave thirteen-year-old Blaire all the ammunition she'd need to terrorize him throughout her adolescence.

While probably overbearing in its own way, Jack didn't try to repress the instinct. It was probably the only part of his father he could see in himself. He probably missed Edward as much as his daughter did. He wished he could still seek his guidance on raising Blaire, if nothing else.

One other blessing was that if anyone really did threaten Blaire, Elise would draw blood before Jack could even arrive on the scene.

He took one more sip of the watered-down coffee, then noticed her getting up to leave.

"Heading out already?" he asked after her, wishing he had more time to just chat.

"Elise wanted to meet up before Madison's," she said, dropping the mug onto the drying rack.

"Alright, well have fun ... and don't forget the limo arrives at four-thirty," he reminded her.

"I got it. Bye, Dad," she said, disappearing into the hallway.

"Love you ..." he said meekly, but she was already gone.

Jack sighed, then returned to the paper.

***

Niles woke up like he usually did, shaped vaguely like a pretzel with his head at the foot of his bed.

He sometimes wondered what progression of tossing and turning had to take place to shift position so radically every night, but he ultimately didn't care.

Really it wouldn't even become a concern until he was sharing the bed with someone else.

That thought snapped Niles out of his stupor and he rolled to the floor.

It was Homecoming, the big night!

He wandered through his bedroom door for the bathroom.

There was a time not too long ago that his bedroom was not so easily navigable.

Niles didn't consider himself a "slob" back then ... but a lot of other people probably would have, and his mother *definitely* did.

He never crossed the line of leaving old take-out boxes or soda bottles lying around, but it would be fair to say that he was comfortable with clutter.

With the exception of a pathway between his bed and computer desk, a lot of the room would just accrue stuff. He really didn't notice it happening, but eventually every piece of clothing he wore would end up on the floor in various piles. A stack of old CDs and other obsolete hardware seemed to shift places every few months.

It was stuff that he didn't really want to get rid of. It wouldn't be worth anything on like eBay or something. Plus, it could be useful. On more than one occasion he needed a strange adapter after salvaging used electronics for something of real value.

At one point his mother started putting on conspicuous episodes of *Hoarders* when he got home from school just to make a point.

His dad was a bit more understanding. He spent most of his career in QA Testing at Sun Microsystems before accepting a golden parachute retirement during the Oracle merger. Probably half of his coworkers were like Niles in one way or another.

However, Niles did face a shock to his system the first time Laura was coming over to his house. He actually postponed the family dinner to meet his parents so he could do some quick-fixing.

This started with buying a new dresser, twice the height of his old one. It was literally overflow containment. Nothing seemed to stay in the closet for long, so he just gave up on using the closet.

Instead, he arranged his old computer parts, surplus cases, boxes of mixed physical media, and rat's nest of cords into the emptied closet. Like a losing game of *Tetris*, everything was precariously balanced against each other in such a way that nothing would fall out without a certain amount of effort. He then slid the closet door closed and sealed it like a crypt.

A quick vacuuming and bottle of air freshener later and the room was back within normal high school boy parameters.

Needless to say, Judy Koh fell in love with Laura for this reason alone. Any girl who could inspire this much positive change in his life was daughter-in-law material in her book.

Luckily, the dinner the next weekend went just as well. The only awkward moment came when his dad began bragging about his fancy Lexus coupe in the driveway.

Niles had to listen to them talk about it along with the Mercedes that Laura's parents let her drive.

With every minute that stretched on, Niles wanted to drive his Honda Civic off a cliff and collect the insurance money.

That was the last time they had dinner with his parents.

Niles couldn't help reflecting back on that story now, because that polished red Lexus was his royal chariot for the evening.

Despite being years old, it looked like it rolled right off of the factory floor.

It had been a custom order to celebrate Andrew's retirement, and he cared for it like it was the Crown Jewels.

He saved it for taking weekend trips with Judy to various places up and down the California coast. The car spent more time on the Pacific Coast Highway than it did on the streets of Alexandria. Tonight, however, was the exception.

Laura's friends were either being picked up by their dates, or were in limos with different groups of friends. Niles' friends, Barry and Melvin, didn't have dates and thus weren't going to the dance.

Niles immediately told her he'd pick her up, despite not having a solid plan in place. He had a pretty average car for one specific reason. As his mother used to say, "A teenager's first car is a bumper car."

He then considered renting a fancier car to take her in, but most car rental agencies held a similar perspective to his mother's.

He could've rented a limo of some kind for just the two of them, but that would get expensive very quickly. Niles had already spent most of his budget on regular dates and outings with Laura over the past year.

Niles was beginning to fear a situation of her picking *him* up in her Mercedes, and was trying to decide if that would be worse than the Honda.

Before panic could truly settle in about what to do, Andrew stepped through the doorway and tossed him the keys to the Lexus. Niles hugged him tighter than the time he got the brand-new PlayStation 3 for Christmas.

He spent all Saturday morning going over every inch of the car, making sure everything was shiny and smooth. Luckily his own outer polish had already been Laura selected and approved.

As the Junior Class Treasurer, Laura was dead set on dressing to their class theme. What exactly she was wearing however would be a surprise for Niles. To make sure their wardrobes matched, Laura went with him to pick out the right set of formal attire.

Niles had only briefly tried searching for what French fashion was like during the Bourbon Restoration, but the word "Dandy" came up a lot and he was beginning to fear what she had in store.

To his relief, by the end of the fitting he was wearing something mostly normal. There were no piles of frills everywhere. There wasn't an excess of feathers or robes or anything else strange. And the best part was that his pants went all the way down to his ankles. But of course, it was historic, so everything was topped off with a silk top hat.

He looked like a cross between Abraham Lincoln and Jean Valjean, but it worked.

Laura only vaguely alluded to what her dress was like, so Niles really was going to have to wait.

Now, a month later, the day was finally here.

Niles opened up the wardrobe bag and made sure all the pieces were still present. The top hat came with its own special box which was both ridiculous and practical. There was no way he was risking wearing the hat with the roof down and it wouldn't fit on his head otherwise.

Even after checking everything, his nerves began to fry again.

He decided to have a big lunch, just in case the banquet food was really messy.

***

The Homecoming game had not ended well for the Jaguars.

It was already the fourth quarter by the time Jennifer Maxwell returned to the stands to watch Darren for the rest of the game.

She sat in a group with Isabella Carrizo, Joe Torelli's date for Homecoming.

"Come on baby, you can do it!" Isabella shouted while clapping for emphasis.

Villa Vista was only down by three points and the Jaguars had the ball. The cheerleaders inserted another round of:

VV (claps) HS (claps)
Villa Vista is the very very best! (claps)
VV (claps) HS (claps)
The Jaguars strike, you go down like the rest! Rawr!

They looked like they were getting close, they were already most of the way down the field. Then, they hiked the ball and Joe threw to the right. Within moments, one of the Mountaineers jumped into the air and caught the ball, running it back a little before being tackled.

Jennifer winced her eyes in pain. After four years of cheerleading, she had a pretty good handle on football. If that Mountaineers interception cleared and they took control of the ball it was all over.

"What's going on?" Isabella asked, as Darren struggled to pull Joe off of the field.

"It's over," Jennifer mumbled in disappointment.

"What do you mean, can't they just steal the ball back?" Isabella asked.

As soon as the ball was hiked, the Mountaineers' quarterback fell to one knee and was subsequently dogpiled by the rest of his team.

"What? No ..." Isabella pouted, watching the game clock tick down to zero. "Oh, Joe must be so upset."

Joe and Isabella were not necessarily dating, but had been going out exclusively since the late summer. He seldom stuck with any one girl for too long though. He wasn't a cheater like Blake, but that was mostly because he never really made commitments.

Isabella more or less had an annual boyfriend, a trend which started in middle school. Unfortunately, the first boy had cheated on her, which perhaps started the vicious cycle. While she could fall hard and fast for someone, the longer they stayed together, the more critically she would examine the details of their relationship.

They were usually cast aside sometime in the spring, and she would go on a series of dates with prospective classmates until being truly wooed by someone over the summer.

When Isabella first mentioned that she was seeing Joe, Jennifer really didn't see a future for it beyond Christmas. Then Isabella would most likely accept someone's invitation for Winter Banquet and end up dating them through graduation.

The pile of Mountaineers on the field shifted position as their coach came out carrying the "Coast Board".

The novelty trophy was a log of coastal redwood which had been smoothed into the shape of a paddleboard by the ocean. It was almost large enough to become a surfboard, but not quite. Even still, it was a beautiful piece of driftwood with a nice color pattern to the distinctive red heartwood.

Charles "Chuckie" Baker, the Villa Vista quarterback at the time, kept it mounted to the roof of his station wagon with his actual surfboards. It probably would have ended up a bar counter in a beachside surf stand if not for the ensuing school rivalry.

Following a contested football season, both Villa Vista and John Muir High spent a very long summer in 1957 egging each other on, each promising to finally prove who the better team was.

The term "Coastal Championship" was used informally to represent the first game they would play together in the fall. It wouldn't be a Homecoming game, but it was held at Villa Vista.

As Rick Wallace had repeated through the years, it was a completely defensive struggle. There was only one score the entire game, when Chuckie Baker himself ran the ball into the end zone in the third quarter.

As everyone on the field was celebrating, Chuckie carried the piece of driftwood onto the field and carved a notch into the far-left side. He promised to add a new notch every time the Jaguars beat the Mountaineers in their first game each season ... and thus it began.

When the Mountaineers beat them in the third year, they were given the Coast Board and the tradition was formalized. They would mark the notch of the winner of their first matchup each season, then paint it to represent the winning school, gold for the Jaguars and green for the Mountaineers.

Decades later, the colored notches covered a large part of the board. Some formal lettering was punched into the top of the face to mark the trophy, as well as the years added beneath each notch.

With a pocket knife in hand, the Mountaineers quarterback carved yet another notch into the sequence. Their defensive back #27, who'd intercepted that last ball from Joe, was handed the paint brush to add the green at the end.

Joe silently watched all this take place from the sidelines.

After some pictures and showboating, the teams finally lined up for the "good game" high fives. It was a bitter walk for the losing team of any game.

It looked like a struggle to drag Joe back onto the field at all. Jennifer bit her lip, half expecting him to take a swing at Darren or someone else.

The line moved and they completed the walk without incident, but after that Torelli walked toward the home bleachers and disappeared into the locker room below the stands.

Jennifer and Isabella circled around to where the players exit and waited for the boys.

The bleachers emptied first, as the fans and faculty left for their respective destinations. Once most of them were gone, the cheerleaders filtered out from the girls' locker room.

Most of them said hi to Jennifer on the way out, with the seniors wishing her luck tomorrow on the Homecoming Court.

After a few more minutes, the Mountaineers left on their bus. The Jaguars slowly trickled out too, licking their wounds. It wouldn't be long until the stadium was nearly empty. Only two players had yet to leave.

Finally, Darren came out, walking alone. He was sliding his phone into a pocket with a disgusted look on his face.

"Good game, Darren," Jennifer said, hugging him around the large duffel bag slung over his back.

"Where's Joe?" Isabella asked, the three of them standing under one of the walkway lights.

"I don't know," he said with an annoyed shrug, eyebrows furrowing in anger. "I called and texted him, but he didn't pick up."

Isabella said nothing, apparently left alone as the third wheel in the group.

Jennifer put her hand on Isabella's shoulder, guiding her toward the parking lot. "I'm sure he just has to cool down. He wouldn't want you to see him like that."

"Yeah …" Isabella said, not really agreeing with her but not really having a choice.

Darren walked them down the long stretch to the main parking lot, past two of the baseball diamonds, the shot put field, and a storage building.

Villa Vista High School was not a religious, private, or charter school, but it looked like it had the revenue stream of all three combined. Marin County had a notoriously high cost of living, but most of that notoriety came from locales within San Francisco Bay. Everything that made the greater Bay Area noteworthy lay beyond the Golden Gate.

Alexandria was more of a satellite community, nestled 30 miles north of the world-famous bridge. In most cases, its residents were natives who had a strong attachment to their roots, and thus never left. Everyone else ended up in the coastal community because they enjoyed the relative peace and quiet, while still being within commuting distance to downtown San Francisco.

Recreationally, Alexandria didn't have much to offer besides a small local surfing scene. Most surfers prefer the warmer beaches of Southern California. Even those that don't mind a little cold tend to go north to the more famous Bodega Bay. Still, the culture persisted.

Historically speaking, that part of the coast was home to a little-known Russian settlement in North America. With the exception of Alaska, there were two small encampments that the Russian-American Company built on the continent which came to be known as Fort Ross and Alexandria. In the case of Fort Ross, the actual wooden fortress remains as a historic curio.

Alexandria was the trading post town set up to buy and sell to the denizens of the Bay Area, the Spaniards and later the Mexicans. Then, during the Mexican-American War, the last Russian traders in the area surrendered to Stockton and Freemont's forces when the Americans occupied the bay.

That was the last exciting thing to happen in Alexandria for over a century and a half.

As time passed, it slowly grew in population. One major surge followed the big earthquake of 1906.

The area provided a gorgeous view of the Pacific Ocean, which would fog regularly due to wind currents from nearby Drakes Bay.

Eventually, enough people settled in the area that two schools formed to educate their children, Villa Vista and John Muir.

Their relative isolation from the rest of the San Francisco Bay Area meant rivalry was destined from the outset. The Coastal Classic was simply a manifestation of said rivalry for the teenagers of the respective attached high schools.

The Villa Vista High School building was separated from the elementary and middle schools by a parking lot and decorative lawn. The building itself was a giant complex separated into roughly three proportional sections.

Villa Vista was at the end of a series of remodels. Something had been changed or added every year the three seniors had been in high school.

The changes were kicked off when remodeling began on the southern third of the complex, the newly named "Lawrence Murphy Performing Arts Center".

Lawrence Murphy was an alumnus from the 1970s who went on to become a Broadway producer. He donated millions of dollars to the school following his death, attributing a large part of his success to the Choir & Drama department for fostering his creativity.

While a capable theatre, the Murphy Center also doubled as the school's lunchroom and dance hall. It was very versatile for hosting a wide variety of events, including Homecoming.

The northern third of the complex (which actually made up 60% of the total square footage) was the school building proper. The angular trapezium shape held two stories of classrooms, lockers, and miscellaneous other staff rooms ... all arranged around a central atrium.

The middle section of the complex was the gymnasium, which hosted the basketball programs, volleyball, indoor pep rallies, and a litany of other events.

After all the efforts, they were finally finishing the renovations just as Jennifer was about to graduate. She'd maybe enjoy one semester of not attending school at a construction site.

The gymnasium was the last piece of the puzzle. It had been sealed off all year, but at this point they were literally just waiting for the paint to dry.

There was a big grand opening planned to kick off basketball season in November. The cheer squad had been working on a number of new routines to accompany the opening night.

The different positions danced in Jennifer's head while she stared off absentmindedly at the gym entrance. It still had a small construction fence blocking the doors.

There hadn't been much small talk in the slow walk from the football stadium.

Darren took them to Isabella's car first. She broke the silence while fumbling for her keys.

"Anyway, sorry about what happened." Her words held a clear double meaning.

"It's alright," Darren said, saving her from feeling like she had to go on. "We'll get 'em next year."

"We'll see you tomorrow Iz," Jennifer said.

"You too ... Later," she said. She then pulled the door closed and quickly slipped out of the parking lot.

"He's such an asshole," Darren said, stomping against the pavement. "Do you know how hard all the rest of us trained for this too? He's acting like he was the only one that mattered, that our win or loss was entirely because of him."

Jennifer looked down sheepishly, there really wasn't much else to say.

Not wanting to end the night on Torelli's unsurprisingly short fuse, Darren quickly changed the subject.

"Whatever … he'll get over it. Besides, we have so much to look forward to." He put his hands on her shoulders. "You've got a crown to win. It's going to be a great night."

Jenny looked up at him. His charcoal black hair was combed loosely to one side, reaching down just beyond his ears. The permanent five o'clock shadow contrasted his tanned face as he stared back at her with an alluring set of blue eyes.

All the time spent outside playing football had given Darren a rougher, more chiseled look. He definitely wasn't the boy from eighth-grade carpool anymore.

She was really happy that things had turned out this way.

"A night good enough for a princess?" Jenny asked.

"A night good enough for a queen," Darren answered.

He then pulled her close and they kissed there in the empty parking lot. He held her for what felt like an eternity before they finally departed in their own cars.

She could still feel his lips the next morning, making her way to the salon to get her hair done.

Madison Lane had a full lobby of almost exclusively teenage girls. High school banquets always pushed them beyond capacity.

Taking a glance over the other girls in the chairs, Jennifer was pretty happy with what she saw among the braids, weaves, and perms.

Every Homecoming had some kind of theme to it, but it was mostly for the decorations and Spirit Week games … things like that. When it actually came to the dance itself, beauty took priority over all else.

They weren't putting on a musical, there wouldn't be ridiculous wigs or costumes. Most of the girls were going to wear something mostly contemporary or timeless, with a few subtle colors or accessories to make it theme appropriate.

Of course, that was Jennifer's perspective as one of the princesses. Half of the girls probably didn't consider the theme at all.

She was happy with the approach she'd decided on. She had a *navy*-blue dress picked out that was not only regal, but very fitting to represent Victorian England at the height of their naval supremacy. The dress also had an *empire* waist which was not only period-appropriate but another form of wordplay.

Otherwise, the dress was fairly modern, so she'd also be incorporating a removable accessory, a gorgeous cream-colored shawl which had frills, tassels, and a thread pattern that looked perfectly turn-of-the-century. It could be taken off and hung on a chair whenever they were dancing.

She'd come to Madison's to get some highlights and touch-up work done before pulling all of her hair together into a voluminous braid to rest on her collar.

Absent from the salon was Isabella. Her mother was a fairly gifted hairdresser in her own right and she probably wasn't getting any coloring done, but Jenny was still hoping she might see her. She wanted to know if Joe had pulled his head out of his ass and apologized for ghosting her last night.

Jenny was really, really hoping he wouldn't cause a scene at the dance. At the same time, she was also glad they weren't in a limo together.

When everyone was making their arrangements for the evening a few weeks back, Joe said they'd be driving separately. He was planning on borrowing his cousin Tito's Camaro.

It was a blessing in disguise because all four boys in their limo were varsity players. Luckily, the other three were like Darren. They probably wouldn't bring up the loss at all except maybe to say they were still the all-time champs. It was not really smart to spend all night telling your date about how you lost the big game.

All of them did play really well, and almost won, but that one bad throw cost them everything.

Jenny couldn't even imagine how much it was eating away at Joe.

THREE

TOO LATE TO TURN BACK

BLAIRE FOUND HERSELF in quite an unusual position. Instead of staring contemplatively out over the ocean, her gaze was fixed on the circular driveway in front of her house.

"Girl, you really need to relax," Elise said, fiddling with the left strap on her dress.

It was 4:30 p.m. and the others would be arriving at any time. The limo had pulled up a few minutes earlier and was now waiting in a picturesque location by the decorative lanterns.

Despite how she teased her dad, Blaire had a known antipathy toward the more formal dances and the high expectation relationships that could blossom from them. The only Homecoming she'd been to was when they were first starting out as freshmen and they just went as a group of girls at the time.

She didn't even remember what she wore. The only clear memory she had from the dance was seeing Mr. Melkonian, who was already wearing a suit and tie, put on a coconut bikini top for the entire night. That was what a "Tropical Getaway" theme resulted in. She was already mentally preparing herself for his countless shifts between *Titanic* and *Blackadder The Third* references.

Aside from that Homecoming, she'd been to one of the Winter Banquets, which are just talent shows that serve food, and one Spring Formal. She'd actually had a fun time at the latter with Mark Harrison.

He really didn't want to go alone and made his intentions clear that he wouldn't pester her with unwelcome flirtations or anything similar throughout the night. They went as just friends and that was perfectly fine with Blaire.

Of course, that was an opportunity granted to Elise Gosselin, who had been expanding her practice as a love doctor for many years. As meddling as Elise was sometimes, Blaire knew she'd been getting soft treatment. Elise was like the sister she never had while everyone else were mice in an experimental habitat called high school.

Most of her work focused on knocking sense into boys who were too dense to realize that a certain girl liked them and was waiting for them to make the first move. She would give them a few tips on how to make that move based on the girl.

"Trisha is really skittish, so just begin by saying hi to her in the hallways."

"Martha sits in the far corner of the lunch room and that's the best time to have a good conversation."

"Heather wants to feel like the one in control, so start by asking for her help on a homework question."

Blaire was witness to all of these experiments and feared the awesome power that Elise held, because so far, she proved to have a 75% success rate.

Following that not-so-formal Spring Formal, Blaire had let her guard down and been convinced by Elise to join her in Choir & Drama.

Musical theatre was something she'd always enjoyed, but secretly and from afar. For the most part, her audience had been the faucet head in her shower. Even then she had to be careful because her brothers had overheard her singing a few times. Each incident resulted in a week-long period of them breaking out into song whenever they saw her. Those were weeks she got her own use out of the foam mallet.

Things changed though when she turned sixteen in April and began driving herself to school. Suddenly she had a slice of time every morning in total solitude. Soon she'd begin to take the long way home after school, cruising a few miles on the PCH before turning off toward her house. She began to understand why so many people settled down in Alexandria.

Eventually she was able to sing a whole album to herself during her daily commute. When her parents asked her why she wasn't getting home until almost four o'clock, she would make up excuses about talking with Elise after school or asking someone questions about homework.

Every new album, every Broadway or West End cast recording, gave her a bit more confidence in her own voice. She could no longer live in denial that deep in her heart she was a theatre kid. She didn't seek the spotlight, but the stage of the newly remodeled Murphy Center was much more attractive to her than it had been before.

What she didn't expect was just *how* attractive Choir & Drama would be.

On the first day of class Elise marched her up to the hidden second floor of the Murphy Center. It served as more than just access to the rafters above the stage. A hallway circuit bordered the entire open space of the auditorium, connecting the stage control room on one end to a large rehearsal room and costume storage space on the other side.

Beyond the rehearsal room door were six rows of seats forming a shallow arc around the front of the class. Elise took her toward the front row. Blaire prepared herself for the impending introduction to the C&D Director.

Cynthia Donovan stood at the front of the room talking to Mr. Jan Richter. He was one of her assistants in the department. He organized the musicians and orchestra for shows while she focused on the cast and choir. On a regular school day though, he was just the piano man.

He was a German expat with salt and pepper hair and round glasses. He was very fluent in English, but a trace of an accent was still present.

Mrs. Donovan was on the more colorful side. What Mr. Richter might find funny with a reserved chuckle would leave her in stitches. She had strawberry blonde hair and a slender face. Her most distinctive feature though was a scarf draped around her neck that was so vibrant it looked like it had been torn from Joseph's amazing technicolor dreamcoat.

Elise pulled Blaire forward before stopping at the second row. It was labeled "M-S" while Elise stepped forward into the front row, labeled with an "S" on the chairs.

A small twitch surged through Blaire. Her fight-or-flight response really wanted her to consider whether or not she was *really* committing to this.

That is when Mrs. Donovan turned from Mr. Richter and said hi to Elise.

"Good morning Elise, welcome back."

"I'm glad to be back." She wore an ear-to-ear smile.

"And who might this be?" Mrs. Donovan looked over her shoulder at Blaire.

"It's too late to turn back," Blaire thought to herself.

"This is Blaire Tidwell." Elise bounced as she announced her victory.

"Hi," Blaire mumbled, sliding down into a chair.

"Well, it's nice to meet you Blaire, I'm Cynthia Donovan and this is Jan Richter."

"Hallo," Mr. Richter said, closing the book of sheet music he'd been reviewing.

"I see that you've been placed as a mezzo-soprano," Mrs. Donovan glanced at Elise. "Ms. Gosselin usually does have a good ear, but we'll be testing out your range later on in class, once everyone has warmed up."

Mrs. Donovan then flipped like a switch from teacher mode to performer mode. "But until then ... welcome to Choir & Drama! We have an incredible year ahead."

She then zipped away after sighting some more new members of her esteemed department.

Blaire's gaze turned toward Elise, the same cold, penetrating glare she used to greet each morning.

Elise was still smiling like the Cheshire Cat.

"What have you done?" Blaire accused her, feeling the bars of the songbird cage.

"It is going to be so fun!" Elise reassured her.

Blaire sank lower in the chair, already exhausted.

The class seemed to fill up quickly after that, as a hundred or so students populated the chairs. Blaire didn't pay mind to most of them, she was reading through the syllabus, which doubled as a schedule for the major shows that year.

In early December, they held what had become known as the "Winter Pageant" ... even though it didn't take place in the winter. It made a lot more sense when it was still called the "Christmas Pageant". Even though it had always been a bit of a variety show, Christmas and holiday music made up at least half of the program.

This year was called "Radio Rat Pack". It wouldn't be limited to Sinatra, Dean Martin, and Sammy Davis Jr., but was just a catchy name for that era of swing and big band music in general. There were quite a number of songs listed, and it looked like Mrs. Donovan would be casting for the choir's own Andrews Sisters, Nat King Cole, Peggy Lee, Bing Crosby, and etc.

Outside of the soloists, quite a few of the songs had a prominent choir, which is where the rest of them would come into play.

That was the large performance that capped off the Fall Semester, but the real show was always the Spring Musical. The last few years they had done *Cats, Mama Mia!,* and *Spamalot,* but were going back to a proper drama this time ... *The Phantom of the Opera.*

"That ... could actually be fun." Of course, that was contingent on how well the C&Ds could handle the material. She was a bit of a Michael Crawford purist and did not want to be an accessory to murder.

That is when her thoughts of the Andrew Lloyd Webber classic were interrupted with "Get Lucky" by Daft Punk & Pharrell Williams.

Rafael Herrera sang as he danced into the front of the room. After wrapping up the chorus he did a little spin and planted himself down next to Elise.

"Hey babe," he said. For a moment it looked like he was going in for a peck on her cheek, but caught himself when he saw Mrs. Donovan's watchful eyes glance over at him.

Only scripted romance was allowed as far as Choir & Drama were concerned. "Keep it offstage" was her common refrain. Of course, by the nature of the department there were a lot of chances to fool around. More than once, students had been caught having sex on the catwalk above the rafters.

Blaire didn't think Elise and Raf would do something that stupid though. Elise was far too careful and wouldn't jeopardize getting expelled for a boy. Plus, Elise was still a virgin, at least as far as she'd told Blaire. Raf was very openly flirtatious, but it was all very performative. She'd even mentioned a time she gave him a chance at second base and he didn't make the move.

After a bit of chit chat between the two of them, he turned to her. "So, she finally reeled you in, ey Blaire?"

"I know where all the emergency exits are," Blaire responded, gesturing toward the windows.

"I don't know ..." Raf said. "The drop is like forty feet. I don't think that Redwood Sorrel would provide enough cushion."

Raf also had an unexpectedly large amount of knowledge in botany. Blaire could unironically see him running a flower shop or nursery one day.

"I'll be the judge of that," she said.

"Trust me," Raf said, "It's gonna be great, you want to stick around. Not to mention, you know how many classes and things we get to cut out of for all the little random shows?"

In truth, that had been one of the selling points. Blaire wouldn't mind spending time with Elise rather than suffer more Precalculus than she was legally required to.

That is when Mrs. Donovan tapped on a music stand with her conducting baton and brought the class to order.

While her words had a chirpy quality to them, her voice could carry quite far. All the returning students had been well tamed, things grew silent almost immediately.

She introduced herself again and began going over the syllabus for the next year, including the audition process for the various ensemble and solo roles, which would also include acting rehearsals and doing test scenes before being selected.

Once all the details were out of the way, Mrs. Donovan began leading them in a vocal warm up.

At first it was mostly just a series of neck exercises. They rolled their heads left and right and began dipping their chins up and down like they were doing a meningitis test. In fact, a medical exam was what the whole procedure reminded her of most.

Then they began the mouth vibrating.

At least that was how her embarrassment interpreted it. They had to purse their lips and blow through them like they were making a motorboat noise. While they vibrated their faces like that, they began doing vocal steps, like "Do-re-mi-fa-so-la-ti-do". She was probably spitting on the back of Elise's neck and just knew she'd hear about it later.

Only then did she realize there were sixty or so kids standing behind her, watching her do all of these ridiculous things. She felt her cheeks flush and could not imagine doing this for another 180 days.

Luckily, the exercises did not last long and they moved on to some actual singing. They were given instruction by rows, and their assumed vocal ranges, on what parts to sing.

All throughout the lesson, she felt like Mrs. Donovan looked her way more than a lot of the others, and her confidence wilted even further. She was only squeaking out the words now, trying to disappear behind the nineteen other mezzo-sopranos.

With only ten minutes left in the class period, the other students were allowed to stay or leave while the new students would be tested on their exact vocal range.

With free time handed to them on a platter, the room quickly emptied until only sixteen students remained. Elise likewise disappeared, being dragged off by Rafael.

Blaire glanced around the room and noticed that most of those left were freshmen. They were the ones backfilling the slots from the seniors who had graduated in the spring. Then about five of them looked to be older, including three boys spread among the back sections.

One by one, names were called up to the piano where Mr. Richter started them out at a comfortable note for the range they'd been singing in all day. He would then move them high and low on the white keys. Mrs. Donovan listened along, having paid special attention to each of them to see how well they were doing in their assumed range.

"So that's why she was giving me the stink eye during class," Blaire thought to herself.

They were going in alphabetical order, starting with Lindsey Anderson.

"Great ... I'm going to be the last one out."

The freshmen slowly trickled out of the room, including the occasional older girl or boy, until it was her turn.

"Blaire Tidwell," Mrs. Donovan called.

She took a deep breath, then walked up to them at the piano. She made an "ahh" sound and slowly followed the notes down. Once her low range bottomed out, Mr. Richter stepped her up the octaves until she reached her last comfortable note at A5. Everything after that began cracking.

"Well would you look at that, mezzo-soprano," Mrs. Donovan chirped. "Seems Ms. Gosselin was right again."

"Of course," Blaire thought to herself in resignation.

Donovan continued, "... and a very bright quality to your voice."

"Bright? Is that a joke?" Blaire almost said that out loud but caught it at the last second, instead letting out a quick, "B-Great."

"We'll see you tomorrow," she said.

"Yeah, thanks." Blaire started to pivot on one heel.

"Andrei Tunnikov."

Blaire stumbled on her pivot, thinking that Mrs. Donovan was still talking to her. It took a moment for her brain to catch up.

She thought she was the last one, but noticed one more boy sitting in the back row by a cabinet. His dark grey shirt blended in with it almost perfectly. As he stood up, Blaire saw that he was almost as tall as the cabinet too.

He had chestnut hair, trimmed low and neat, with stern and intimidating eyebrows. He had brown eyes which looked tired, but Blaire would soon come to realize they were his normal disposition. He didn't have facial hair, but he did have a jaw like it had been chiseled on a statue.

When he caught her looking, they locked eyes for just a moment and Blaire immediately dropped hers to the floor.

She gathered up her things into the backpack as quickly as she could without appearing like she was rushing. The process took much longer than it should have as the binder for her music stuff was acting like a USB plug, refusing to bypass the zipper no matter which way she flipped it.

Only when Andrei sang that first note did it finally slide in.

Blaire crept toward the door, trying not to draw any attention to herself. His voice and its deep, earthy timbre dropped down smoothly and naturally before bottoming out just below G1. Even so, he could hold that final note with such clarity that he could definitely pull it off on stage.

Blaire took another glance back at him as she closed the door.

She was alone in the dark hallway and his voice began to rise to its highest registers, seeping through the cracks of the door like a bursting dam.

That is when she realized that when he left, it would be just the two of them standing out there. She darted for the stairwell and down into the single-stall bathroom by the front entrance.

That was the first time they saw each other, but it would be far from the last.

The following weekend, Elise was talking absentmindedly about the new students added to the choir. That's when she then brought up "the tall boy".

"I'm pretty sure he's new, I haven't seen him around before. It's not like you'd miss him in a crowd." Elise sipped on a bubble tea in the mall's food court.

Blaire could feel her cheeks redden. It was infuriating. Despite her make-up and her usually dispassionate personality, she simply could not help herself.

"Wait a minute ..." Elise raised an eyebrow.

And now Blaire was caught.

"Are you blushing?" Elise asked.

Blaire shifted in her chair. She was not the best liar, especially not to Elise.

"It's really hot out today," she said, not even really committing to the excuse.

Following the exchange, Elise was able to force the whole story of that first day out of her. After having to expose her tortured gothic soul, she demanded that Elise not say anything to him.

After an annoyed sigh, Elise agreed. "Okay Blaire, if you don't want me to say anything, I won't say anything ..."

"Thank you." Blaire relaxed her shoulders, taking a large sip from the cold tea.

She got Raf to do it.

Admittedly she should have seen it coming, but Blaire really wasn't thinking straight at the time.

The next week, Mrs. Donovan and Mr. Richter were running late for class. Everyone was scattered around the classroom, just talking or mingling.

Blaire was leaning against the window ledge by the piano. There was a steady rain outside, and fog filled most of the parking lot. Only the tops of the trees were clearly visible.

She was tuning out the rabble in the classroom, letting the sound of the pounding rain on the roof and windows wash it away.

Then, a familiar voice spoke, and it was close to her.

"Do you mind if I sit down?"

She turned and found Andrei Tunnikov on the other side of the piano.

"N-no," she mumbled, turning back towards the rain. She buried her face in her left hand, hiding the cheek that faced him.

He put his hands on the keyboard. His arms were long enough to travel all eighty-eight keys with ease.

He began to play.

The music was soft, peaceful, fitting for the storm outside. As the piece played on, Blaire was inching toward him without noticing, her ear trying to determine if she recognized it.

When it became too obvious that she was listening, she asked him, "What is that?"

"Tchaikovsky. 'The Seasons, No. 10.' It's not as famous as *The Nutcracker*, but probably more fitting."

"It's nice."

"Of course, if you wanted both fitting and famous ..." he transitioned into the title song of *Singing in the Rain*.

That actually got her to chuckle.

"I'm Andrei by the way," he added nonchalantly.

"I'm Blaire," she replied.

With that, the ice was broken and Elise's success rate ticked a little higher.

"Blaire is really reserved, words probably aren't your best approach, introduce yourself another way."

After that they would try to chat whenever they could. Him being a senior and Blaire being a junior, they didn't share any classes together ... except for Choir & Drama. So, they stopped whenever they caught each other in the hallways.

Blaire invited him to sit with the rest of them at lunch, and that increased their face time dramatically. The small talk became more substantive and their conversations grew deeper.

Andrei's musical upbringing came from his father, Vasily Tunnikov. His great-grandparents had emigrated during the Russian Civil War, abandoning what little land they owned. They and their children worked in factories most of their lives, but in the 1960s they were finally able to give Vasily and his siblings a true education in whatever they wanted. Vasily chose music and eventually worked as a concert pianist in various venues around Los Angeles. Then in the last year, he accepted a position with the San Francisco Symphony.

After spending most of his life in Pasadena, Andrei was still settling into the area. He was the youngest of three. His sisters were both older. Only one of them was still in college, down at UCLA.

He still wasn't sure what he wanted to do in life, but he had been the sibling most interested in music compared to his two sisters. Since he enjoyed his old school's choir, he made sure to join Villa Vista's performing arts department.

Then, after some unsolicited advice from one of the tenors in that C&D class, Villa Vista High School was turning out to be pretty great.

With Homecoming on the horizon, Andrei held Blaire one day after class. There was a new piece he was practicing and he wanted her to listen for if anything sounded off.

She agreed and met him by the piano as everyone else disappeared out the door, including Mrs. Donovan and Mr. Richter.

Andrei took a deep breath then began to play the piece.

It was slow and melodic, just like that first Tchaikovsky piece he'd introduced himself with. Then it began to change movements. The tempo picked up, becoming faster as Andrei added in more complexity and weaving harmonies. After a few short minutes all of those sounds fell away and he tapped on a single chord.

"That's the one that doesn't sound finished yet ..." Andrei said, pressing his ear against the panel of the upright piano.

"What do you mean 'finished' ... did you write this?" The realization was beginning to settle over her.

"Could you see if I'm playing the right strings?" Andrei asked, still putting on the act, but choosing his words carefully.

Blaire hesitated and Andrei tapped the chord three more times, motioning toward the top of the piano.

She lifted the lid, and found a meticulously decorated banner covering the bottom: "Homecoming, Blaire?"

The blush came in full.

Andrei swiveled on the piano bench, but stayed seated. He didn't want to loom over her when making a proposal of any kind.

It didn't take her long to answer. "Yes, absolutely!"

She leaned down to hug him. Even when he was seated, she only stood taller by a few inches.

Then a flash appeared out of seemingly nowhere.

Blaire turned toward the source, finding a black rectangle hidden behind one of the decorative plants in the window sill.

Elise popped her head in from just behind the classroom doorway. She held a small black remote in her hand.

This time Andrei was the one to blush. "She threatened to torture me if I didn't warn her in advance."

Blaire stared daggers at her, but Elise had built up a total immunity over the years.

"Of course you would resort to war crimes!" she yelled theatrically as Elise pranced into the room and pulled her cell phone out of the plant.

"You'll thank me one day ..." she whispered, basking in the moment.

She pulled up the picture and her face began to melt.

"Oh, it turned out perfectly! You two are s-o-a-d-o-r-a-b-l-e," she cooed.

Blaire reached for the phone, but in a single swift motion Elise dodged her and flipped the screen around to show them. The sign and hug were both perfectly framed and lit.

That hadn't even been three weeks ago, but Blaire felt like she'd looked at the picture a thousand times.

"So, what do you think?" Elise asked.

Blaire snapped out of her phone to look back at her.

She had finished performing whatever last fix she was making to her left strap. The rose-pink dress hung down to her ankles. The floral pattern grew more detailed and elaborate from bottom to top, culminating in the straps.

Elise got straight to the point. "Are my boobs even?"

Blaire began to smile, a big smile, almost holding back tears.

"Definitely," she said.

She walked over and hugged her.

"Thanks Elise. I'm really looking forward to tonight."

Elise gladly accepted the hug. She may have had some fun with the part she played, but in the end, Blaire really deserved this.

***

The handling on the Lexus was *way* different than Niles' Honda Civic.

He'd driven it a few times before, but with his blood pressure running as high as it was, Niles was not operating at peak performance.

The Lexus felt like it was the one in control, turning the curves in the road before Niles could even put forward the thought. Still, it would be a smooth ride so long as Niles could hold his own cool.

There had been a slight upset in his "Perfect Homecoming" plans ... their Junior Class float lost Spirit Week. He was afraid that might happen.

Their class was the smallest of the four currently attending Villa Vista High. And even worse, it had the highest percentage of students like Niles. They were people so apathetic about high school that they put in the bare minimum amount of effort to avoid having to talk to a truant officer.

That reflected very starkly in the turnout of students who actually showed up to build the float. Except for Laura, Niles was the only one to show up for all four days ... and of course he wouldn't have shown up at all if Laura wasn't a factor.

He felt an indescribable kind of group guilt, like he had passively contributed to the disinterest of all the others. That was a main factor that drove his perseverance in building the float.

They'd ride over after school and Niles would basically just do whatever Laura told him to. He nailed wood and frames together, hung drapes, painted, and duct-taped certain decorations to their correct position.

Overall, he was really proud of the effort the two of them had put in ... but in a lot of ways it was just the two of them. Every other class had at least a dozen people helping out every day of the week. The most people that showed up for them was on Wednesday, and that was eight.

They just ran out of time. They could only build so much in the available time slots.

Not to mention, the tug car was a bit of a haphazard choice. It was the nicest car they could procure which already had a tow hitch on it. It was a Porsche 911 that Sean Northam's dad would use to take their boat when they went camping.

He actually felt fairly confident that they would at least get the "Most Creative" award. Then the Sophomore Class float appeared and was so insancly colorful compared to the other three that it just stood out too much to not win the de facto silver medal.

The surprise winner was actually the Freshman Class float. They had been smart choosing their "Roaring Twenties" theme, because the new *Great Gatsby* movie was still fresh in everyone's minds. They even had a fish tank mounted behind the stage of the float to simulate water out one of the windows. On the other side of the tank was a bright green bulb to wrap up the memorable moments from the F. Scott Fitzgerald story.

Topping all that off was Gershwin's "Rhapsody in Blue". They snatched the "Best Float" recognition with ease. Although Niles thought that their use of "Do You Hear the People Sing?" was the second-best song from the parade.

Laura was a good sport, but the whole ordeal had really dampened her spirits by the end of the night. Five nights of work and they walked away empty-handed.

Niles would avoid the subject at all costs if he could, but a good portion of his subconscious was already working on the right words to say if she brought it up.

The Lexus made a final loop up one of the mountainous roadways, ending at a house that bordered a private lake.

Niles slid the door open, grabbing the hat box that was sitting behind his head rest. He pulled the top off and carefully removed the black silk accessory. He pressed it firmly around his head before it could escape his grasp and bounce on the asphalt.

Resting below the hat box, he grabbed a vanity mirror that matched their outfits. It had been a surprisingly cheap find on Amazon, just a cheap prop that could still fulfill the essential function of a mirror.

The hat rested fine. Niles inspected every corner of his face, looking for oversights. His teeth were also fine, which wasn't a surprise because he had brushed them twice since lunch. Finally, he popped in a fresh wintergreen mint, cracking it into pieces so he'd get all the freshness out of it immediately.

He dropped the mirror and hat box down on the driver's seat and grabbed the third accessory, the corsage. It was a very full arrangement highlighting the center flower, a purple and white sweet iris … which of course was theme appropriate.

Niles bumped the car door shut and strolled up the footpath toward her house. He rang the doorbell and stood waiting.

After an anxious fifteen seconds, someone finally opened the door. It was her father, Mr. Nakano. His first name wasn't important because Niles never dared use it.

He was a stern man who only spoke when there was something to be critical of. Of course, this was Niles' impression of him as the guy who was sort-of-dating his daughter.

They hadn't actually made anything official, the words "boyfriend" or "girlfriend" not being used, but Niles was hoping Homecoming would change that.

Since the Spring Formal they had spent a lot of time talking on the phone, especially in the evenings. On maybe a dozen occasions since then, they had actually gone out. Most of those were daytime outings to lunch or the mall. A handful were actual dinners with higher stakes.

One of those was the uncomfortable dinner with Niles' parents, but a month after that was the dinner here with the Nakanos.

Laura's mother Phoebe was actually fairly nice, similar to Laura in many ways. She had worked in the finance department at Industrial Light & Magic for a good portion of her career.

She would probably still be working there if not for a car accident which happened when Laura was young. Mrs. Nakano ultimately had to retire, still suffering from some long-lasting side effects caused by the accident.

Many of their family friends were former coworkers of hers at ILM, so Laura grew up around many creative personalities.

Laura's father, Maro Nakano, had a quite different temperament. He worked for Transamerica Corporation in the iconic pyramid tower that defines the San Francisco skyline. Let's just say he had the kind of personality that made him an excellent insurance executive. People like him were the reason why that tower had overshadowed everything else for over forty years.

He did not like Niles. Even when he was on his best behavior, Mr. Nakano seemed to always see him as the slob computer gamer barely holding a C average.

When Mr. Nakano saw Niles at the door, he said the best thing that he could have ... which was nothing at all. In any other dance scenario, Niles was sure he would have found and exploited some kind of issue with the way he was dressed. Unfortunately for him, he was aware that

Laura had picked out Niles' entire wardrobe. So, he was forced to bite his tongue while Niles took a seat in the front room.

After a few minutes, Phoebe Nakano came down, clutching a camcorder firmly but discreetly in one hand. After her, followed Laura.

She gripped the railing with one hand while her purse and a decorative folding fan hung from the other. Her dress was a bright crimson gown which sat just below her shoulders. There were velvet frills on the arms with a matching cream-colored lace shawl. There was also a gold necklace with a noticeable fleur-de-lis symbol dangling from the end.

Laura herself smiled through subtle make-up. Her hair was done up in a series of inch-wide curls which framed both sides of her face.

Niles was totally stunned, a single line ran through his mind on a loop, "I can't believe I'm this lucky."

"Y-you look great ..." he said aloud, stumbling on the words. When her father leered from one of the shadows, he added, "... so historic!"

"Do you like it? It's Princess Louise-Marie of Orléans! I think I covered all the essential parts of the wardrobe, but I dropped the headpiece. I figured the curls are enough."

"The curls are enough," he parroted her.

When she noticed the corsage, her face lit up even more so.

"That turned out beautifully!"

"Oh, yes." He opened the plastic clamshell. "It took some searching, but this place off the Embarcadero was able to make one."

He slipped the arrangement onto her left wrist.

"Oh really? I found this at a place in San Rafael," she said, presenting the boutonniere.

They posed for some still images her mom began to take at different angles.

"Oh, we should get a few by the car," Niles interjected after a dozen or so. They moved toward the door.

"Midnight," Maro Nakano said, without another word.

"It'll be fine dad," Laura said, her eyebrows furrowing for the first time that night.

He didn't leave the house, instead closing the door behind her mother.

Niles didn't think of the fact that she might wear a red dress. The Lexus was enough of a save that he didn't want to push his cosmic luck.

Fortunately, the crimson color of the velvet was much darker and richer than the primary red of the convertible.

They posed for a few more pictures, then Laura hugged her mom and Niles opened the passenger door for her.

"Have a good night," Phoebe Nakano said, waving them off.

Niles opened the driver's side door and slipped his hat securely into the box, before sliding it behind his seat.

"What's that?" Laura asked, looking at the mirror.

"Exactly what it looks like," he said, handing it to her so he could sit down.

"Not an accessory I expected you to have," she teased.

"What can I say, beauty requires constant upkeep." He pivoted her wrist and inspected his teeth in the mirror.

She laughed, and he adjusted the car's rear view mirror in a similar way.

The car roared to life and pulled out of the cul-de-sac.

The drive started out peacefully. Niles took the long way along Shoreline Blvd., bypassing the highway for the scenic views of the ocean.

Laura was going on about some more background details in her costume: "You think the Bourbons were bad enough, but she was also the mother of Leopold II of Belgium ... yikes. Like, can you imagine having all that power, all that wealth, and still bringing about so much evil to maintain it?"

"Still had an eye for fashion." Niles complemented her while ignoring the history lesson.

"By the way," she added. "I'm sorry if my dad was worse than usual."

"Oh no, it's fine." Her dad really didn't stand out too much to him. Most adults in his life saw him as the same waste of place and potential. Maro Nakano was just more honest about it.

"Like, sometimes I just don't know what my mom saw in him. They couldn't be more different." She fiddled with her necklace.

That was a feeling Niles could definitely relate to.

"Guess it doesn't matter how new or old the money is. It always just gravitates together, leaving everything else empty."

Laura had a tendency to wax philosophical sometimes.

She reminded him a lot of the Xendathu character from *Intrepid*.

Whenever they were starting a new mission, Xendathu, the star priestess, would usually have a paragraph or two of poetic-sounding dialogue that gave the mission some added emotional meaning. Of course, she was just a one-dimensional NPC meant to hide loading times when they were in lightspace.

Barry would usually slash at her with his sword during the soliloquies in a fruitless attempt to either shut her up or speed along the loading time.

Of course, Laura wasn't like that. She had a lot of deep convictions. While she did originally join the Student Council as a creative outlet to help plan the dances and rallies, it was having a different effect on her. She'd mentioned during one of their lunch-sort-of-date-things that she was seriously considering becoming a Political Science major in college.

At the time Niles had deflected her question about what major he was considering.

He didn't really want to go to college, despite his parents' best attempts to push him in that direction. He hated regular school enough, he didn't want to spend $100,000 of his own (or his parents') money just to gain validation from another apparatus of the state. The universities were filled with the kind of people Laura seemed to dislike the most, people with too much money and no self-awareness.

"They don't appreciate hard work either! After all the time we put into the float, to get nothing?!" Laura had jumped over to talking about the floats. Niles tried to follow along and remember his prepared responses.

"The sophomores should not have won the Most Creative prize. Their float was not the most creative, it was just colorful. And the freshmen winning by just ripping off a more recent movie? If we wanted to play that game, we could have done *Elysium*." Laura's gaze drifted off toward the setting sun.

She was still pretty upset about what happened.

Niles had totally forgotten all of the things he was going to say, so instead he tried the change of subject route.

"So, what kind of songs will they be playing at the dance?"

Laura continued on as though she didn't hear him. "... and why else did they win? Because they had more people to donate supplies and resources too. Money is the death of creativity. Heck, it's the death of everything. It just consumes, leaving no focus on love or care for the things that really matter! Everything of beauty gets bled dry for fleeting power."

Niles refocused on the road, a small pit forming in his stomach. He really hoped this would pass and that the night would end on a better note.

FOUR

LOVE & LONGING

BOB MELKONIAN STOOD over the bathroom sink, adjusting the layers on his button-on cravat. The white frills looked like a regular bow tie that decided to blow up like a pufferfish.

The blonde, poofy wig slipped easily over his admittedly thinning espresso-colored hair. Aside from that he donned a frilly shirt, vest, cloak, sash, some white pants, and to top it all off, powdered make-up.

It was a surprisingly simple costume to put together, but he knew he'd be able to use it to great effect.

Once he was satisfied with the cravat's positioning, he stood upright practicing a few faces in the mirror that he'd use to greet people. Only when he looked beyond his reflection did he see Angelina in the doorway.

He twisted around, still in character. "I say, do you have my socks?"

His wife smiled, shaking her head. She replied back with a bit of theatrics, but not nearly to Bob's degree. "You've lost them again?"

"It's not like they could have just walked away on their own!" He improvised the scenario.

"Well, who has access to your socks?" Angelina shrugged.

He thought expressively for a moment before squinting. "Only myself ... and you."

"What contrafibularities are you accusing me of? Why would I show interest in your wardrobe?" She crossed her arms.

"Well, I don't know, but it sounds damn saucy!" He smiled.

She finally cracked, laughing to herself as she sat down on their bed.

"I swear, you enjoy this more than the kids."

"I should hope so," he said, finally breaking character. "Could you imagine an M.C. less enthusiastic than their audience?"

"So, why George, Prince of Wales?"

"Why not? He's as silly as a 'High Society' theme could call for."

"I just wish Monika were here to witness this in person."

"She wouldn't get the references," he said with resignation in his voice. Bob considered it a personal failing that he couldn't hook their daughter on *Blackadder*.

"Most of the other kids aren't going to either," she said in a sing-songy way.

"Angie, it's a school ... I am educating them," he said with mock seriousness.

"Bob, it's a Saturday, they won't be receptive to a lesson." She adjusted the pillows on her side of the bed, picking up one of the novels from her nightstand.

"Kids are always learning, whether they know it or not. Comedy can be a great teaching tool." He spoke with real sincerity.

"You mean like Monika's last Homecoming?"

"Exactly! When our seventeen-year-old little girl brought home a coconut bikini top that she wanted to wear to a school dance, we could have easily yelled or made a big deal out of it, but the simple fix was staring us in the face."

"So, you put it on yourself." Angie thought back on the night.

"And she had to pick out an actual top instead." He smiled triumphantly.

"Any idea what Rick's wearing?"

"No, but I have a theory."

"Oh?" she asked, thumbing to the next page.

"He tends to dress according to the Freshman Class theme, since they usually get drowned out by the older students. So, I'm thinking ... Mr. Monopoly."

"You're just saying that because he's bald."

"I mean, you gotta play to your strengths. Maybe he'll be Daddy Warbucks from *Annie*."

"Didn't you say the Freshman float *won* this year?"

"Yeah ..." He started tying the dress shoes. "They did really well this year. It's great seeing that much effort and enthusiasm at such a young age."

Once finished, he stood up.

"Alright, final inspection, how do I look?"

"Like a clown." She rested the book in her lap.

"Perfect. 'All the world loves a clown.'"

"A lot of people are scared of clowns ..." she warned.

"Well, what's comedy without a bit of drama?" He then leaned over her on the bed. "Boo."

She kissed him goodbye, being careful not to disturb his make-up.

"Say hi to Rick for me," she called after him.

"I will!" He slipped through the door into the garage.

***

"What's up assholes?" were the first words Jenny and Darren heard as they got out of his truck.

"Oh, I'm sorry ..." Their host walked up to them. "I didn't realize we had a lady present."

He looked at Darren as he said "lady", then offered a hand.

"Hello, Jimmy." He rolled his eyes. He took his hand in for a pat on the back.

As soon as they separated Jimmy got a slap to the back of his head.

"You're the only asshole here," Camellia said. She then turned to Jennifer, "Oh sweetie you look great!"

"Hi Camellia, so do you!" Jennifer said, marveling at her satin magenta dress.

They were standing in the extensive driveway of Jimmy O'Shaughnessy's house, which was large even by local standards. Aside from him and his girlfriend, Camellia Latifi, Darren and Jenny were apparently the first to arrive, even beating the limo.

Jennifer never understood the "fashionably late" axiom. Being late usually caused her more problems than not. Darren had been kind enough to pick her up a little early. Besides, Camellia was always very chatty and she was sure Darren would be kept entertained as well.

"Darren, come on, I gotta show you the spread for tonight," Jimmy said, almost on cue.

He gave a quick wave to Jenny as he was pulled away. She waved back as her and Camellia followed them in at a much slower pace.

For the fourth year in a row, Jimmy was hosting a big afterparty following the dance.

He led Darren through the opening atrium and past a curved staircase. A great room with several couches bordered a long glass wall facing the forest. Opposite the glass wall was a bar counter with fully stacked shelves behind it. Jimmy pulled one of the bottles off of the top shelf.

"You ever had a drink of $8,000 dollar whiskey?" Jimmy popped off the top.

"Are you serious?" Darren looked at the finely decorated glass bottle.

"Maybe ..." Jimmy played coy while pulling out two shot glasses.

"Bro, I can't tell the difference at all, don't waste the good stuff on me." Darren was really trying to pass on the offer.

"Don't give it another thought, my guy!" He poured up a finger for each of them.

He knew if he didn't accept this now Jimmy could get more belligerent later in the night.

"To the good life." Jimmy raised his shot glass.

"To the good life," Darren repeated, downing the shot. He placed the glass top down on the counter to keep Jimmy from pouring him any more.

Jimmy added another finger to his glass, taking it in a slow sip.

His dad, Cillian O'Shaughnessy, was an executive in the Global Operations department of Qualcomm. He spent more of his life in China alone than in California, and that didn't include the three dozen other countries he would transit regularly as he expanded the portfolio of the microchip giant.

Spending most of his life in modern office buildings or luxury hotels, he bought a house to reflect the trappings he'd become accustomed to. Plus, their remote but accessible villa could be used strategically to host parties when foreign executives were visiting the Bay Area. It was a party in the woods just over the Golden Gate Bridge.

During all the months he was gone, roughly a dozen contractors were on some form of regular rotation for landscaping, cleaning, food deliveries, washing windows, home repair, and other tasks.

Except for them, there was one live-in nanny who would help schedule and organize those tasks. Mostly however, her job was to care for Jimmy.

Inka Jirásek was a Czech woman who still possessed a very thick accent. She was mostly fluent in English, but certain idioms and metaphors would need explanation.

Darren had bumped into her a few times at some of Jimmy's parties in the past, but for the most part she stayed hidden in her room until everyone was gone. She took a "see nothing, say nothing" approach when it came to Jimmy's obvious misdemeanors.

She'd reappear the next day after "some of Jimmy's friends" went home and mobilized the other contractors to return the house to pristine condition.

Darren had met Cillian O'Shaughnessy once and knew instantly that all this performance wasn't for his sake. Even if he were fully knowledgeable about what took place at Jimmy's parties, he probably wouldn't do much to change it. Jimmy wasn't the only one who used illicit substances to entertain his guests.

Cillian would just play dumb and if somehow the law became involved, there was a sacrificial lamb for just such a scenario.

Inka maintained the lie because Cillian did pay her well. Not to mention she wanted to stay in good standing with her nanny agency and U.S. Immigration Services.

"So, where's Inka?" Darren mentioned nonchalantly.

"Inka?" he said in surprise. "Bro, you were at my party in August. I'm eighteen now, I don't need a nanny. Never needed one before either. Pops cut her loose."

He poured a third finger of the expensive whiskey.

"Tonight, we have the house all to ourselves ... nine bedrooms plus the den." He gestured toward the girls sitting on the opposite side of the room.

Darren fought the temptation to turn over his own shot glass again.

He had known Jenny since they were in middle school, during what he considered to be the worst time of his life. Between the ages of twelve and fifteen puberty hit him like Apollo Creed hit Rocky Balboa. Things worked out eventually, but there was a lot of pain and suffering in between.

He was among the last boys in his class to start growing taller, but when it finally happened it was a rapid change. He grew six inches a year between the end of eighth grade and the end of tenth grade. By the time he was starting his junior year, he had finally topped out at an even 6'-0" tall.

Now he was among the tallest boys in his class. There were only a few significant outliers, including Joe Torelli, Marcus Johnson, and that new Russian guy.

Unsurprisingly, Jennifer had stopped talking to him when they started high school. His maturity, in every sense, needed time to catch up with everyone else. At the same time, her mom had retired from work and started driving her to school. He didn't even see her circumstantially in the carpool anymore.

Darren was a pretty angry kid for those two years. It felt like his hormones were running a marathon against all the other kids in the class.

By the end of his freshman year, he was getting into a lot of mischief, though not necessarily in the same ways as Jimmy. Rather than deal with his problems through reckless hedonism, Darren had begun to lash out in anger in any way he could.

One bigger difference between the two was that Darren had parents who were not only there but gave a damn. His dad started setting aside more time to spend together. During his rough sophomore year, they even went to three San Francisco Forty-Niners games.

In addition to that, Rick Wallace scheduled them for a weekly one-hour session. Darren hadn't even told anyone where he was going in that time slot. There were so many electives that the few friends he had during those years didn't notice where he went during that period.

It was never even a lecture or interrogation by the guidance counselor. Sometimes they would just sit quietly and Darren would read from notes or a book. Sometimes they'd listen to music on Mr. Wallace's old 1980s cassette boombox. Then, every few weeks, Darren would actually open himself up to a real discussion. Those are what really counted for him, really helped him navigate those two years.

Jimmy probably had a similar opportunity with Rick Wallace, but with no support structure at home, it wasn't enough. He had gone into football mostly to fill up his schedule. It must be lonely sitting in such a large, empty house. If it weren't for all the carpets and sound paneling, the manor would echo like a cave.

Darren had gone into football to do something that he loved. He would watch the Niners with his dad and brother a lot when he was growing up. His dad would often tell them stories from the Joe Montana years. It was a passion that they all shared and it motivated him enough to go into a training camp at the end of his sophomore year.

When the varsity tryouts started that fall, Darren was able to make the cut as one of the Jaguars' new running backs. By the end of the season, he'd become their starting fullback, positioned right next to Joe Torelli for most of their games.

He'd settled into the new clique. On or off the field, all the varsity jocks were usually hanging around together in one form or another.

Of course, that hadn't excluded him from Jimmy's parties before. Jimmy really wasn't very selective. It was more about the general air of peer pressure to keep the "nice" kids out. Every time something was planned, the word-of-mouth would spread quickly until all the right people knew about it.

A hundred or so kids would pass in and out of the mansion as a night would drag on. They were the ones who knew not to spoil a good thing. They kept the details of the bashes a secret from their parents and more importantly, the school faculty.

Villa Vista was not a massive school, there were only 500-600 high schoolers at any given time. On top of that, Alexandria was not a large town. Snitches usually got snitched out themselves, and would spend the rest of their adolescence in social isolation until they went away to college.

That almost never happened though. For one reason or another, everyone wanted to protect the little pockets of escape that were available to them. Jimmy's place was a great escape.

Maybe high school just sucks for everyone. The occasional illegal party was a much-needed pressure-release valve to keep everyone sane. That was Jimmy's guiding principle anyway.

Over his junior year, not only had Darren cemented himself into a new friend group, but he had reconnected with Jenny too.

Before and after the games he tried to chat up all the cheerleaders at least a little bit. He had a newfound confidence after finally settling into his adult body.

He noticed as time went on his conversations with Jenny got longer and longer. Not only were they talking about recent events, but even diving back into near-forgotten stories from their freshman and sophomore years. It felt like bridge-building, filling in the two-year-long gap in their friendship.

Unfortunately, for most of her junior year, Jenny was coupled with an absolute waste of flesh named Blake Samuels. He was the kind of guy who saw everyone as a commodity to be consumed and disposed of. He had all the personality traits of a Hollywood producer, someone that groomed and exploited child actors until they grew too old and were cast aside for "fresh talent".

Darren's skin would crawl whenever he heard Blake talk, in the same way a dog might bark at a serial killer.

Jennifer would have to learn of his true nature the hard way, when she discovered him "sizing up" some "fresh talent" over the summer. Darren was one of the first to hear about what happened.

A few days afterwards, he bumped into Jenny at a coffee shop. She could barely put on a face for two minutes of small talk before breaking down crying in his arms. He led her away to someplace more private, taking her behind one of the rear patios at the outlet mall.

Once they were seated, she came out with the whole story about what happened, including some little events that had occurred throughout their relationship that she was now seeing in a clearer light.

She still didn't see him as quite the monster that Darren characterized him as, but she was a lot closer to the truth now that she was set free from his silver tongue.

August had been a long month for her, but as the school year got into full swing, she seemed determined to push through the pain.

In their intermittent conversations, Jenny had mentioned not-so-subtly that she wondered how Homecoming was going to go this year. In one way she was talking about her campaign for Homecoming Queen, but Darren read the other signals mixed in with it loud and clear.

After cheer practice one day, Darren enlisted some of the other cheerleaders to add one more special routine at the end of their next practice. They were a few girls he knew he could trust to keep the secret.

When the time came, they unfurled a custom banner, and broke out into a modified version of the "Jaguar Rawr".

DC (claps) JM (claps)
For a girl who has always been a gem! (claps)
DC (claps) JM (claps)
On Homecoming night, you can't go wrong with him! Yay!

When Jenny turned around, Darren was there holding a small bouquet of roses.

Not only did she accept the roses, but she completely surprised him with a peck on the lips. It was their first kiss, and definitely not their last.

Things were moving faster than he expected. He wasn't even sure what they were right now.

Darren tilted the overturned shot glass, dancing it on the rim back and forth. Jimmy was still going on mindlessly about all the foods and overpriced liquors he'd be breaking open at the afterparty.

A nagging voice at the back of Darren's mind was pointing out the obvious. "She's rebounding hard after Blake, she's vulnerable right now, clinging for something ... someone ... stable."

If they really had a future together, then there would be more time for that later. They wouldn't be staying the night and he'd be sober enough to drive her home later.

He took his finger off of the shot glass, letting it come to a rest definitively on the wooden counter.

"So, where the hell is Trey?" Darren said loud enough to bridge both conversations. He got off of the barstool and crossed the room. He sunk down into the couch next to Jenny.

"Oh, it's not Trey, it's Ashley for sure," Camellia said, apparently referencing an earlier part of the girls' conversation. "She was *still* deciding between three different dresses ... *this morning.*"

Jimmy hopped over the bar counter to join the others on the couch. "She probably waited for Trey to pick one for her, which means the clock started whenever his lazy ass actually showed up at her house."

"I told her, 'Just pick the green one!'" Camellia clapped for emphasis. "'You have green eyes; you can't go wrong with the green one.' But then she sends me four different texts complaining about the lacing on the back or some shit. I pity the man."

"I do too," Jimmy broke out into a wry but serious laugh. "Because if he's not here by five-thirty, we're leaving without him."

"I still bet Brendan and Sheena will be last ..." Darren said, rounding out the fourth couple in their limo arrangement.

"Really, why?" Jenny asked. "He's usually on time to practice."

"That's because he's already at the school when practice starts," Darren explained. "As soon as a car enters the equation his ETA can range anywhere between ten minutes and two hours. He'll forget to get gas, he'll get a flat tire, he'll have to double back for his wallet ... *Sheena* should have picked *him* up."

Camellia laughed and Jimmy followed after. The three fingers of whiskey were already bubbling up his personality more than usual.

Jenny slid closer to Darren and they all settled down.

The night had truly begun.

***

"You have arrived at your destination."

The navigation app on his phone spoke aloud as Andrei Tunnikov pulled up in front of the Tidwell residence.

He wasn't quite sure where to park. A few cars were scattered around the edges of the circular driveway, but most of it was completely occupied by a forty-foot-long stretch Cadillac Escalade.

The limousine was pearl white with a neon light pattern glowing around the undercarriage. Its hue shifted back and forth between green and blue, covering every shade of mint, aqua, turquoise, and etc., in between.

The heavenly chariot had distracted him so much that it took him a moment to see a pair of waving hands ahead of him.

It was Rafael Herrera, stepping out of a blue Mazda 3.

Andrei gave an acknowledging wave through the windshield, but Raf continued signaling, pointing to an empty spot on the road behind him.

He nodded and spun his grey Toyota 4Runner around, lining up right behind the Mazda.

Raf was wearing a white suit and shirt with a scarlet red vest and tie. It was a perfectly normal dress suit, without any of the Spirit Week themes weaved into it.

No one Andrei knew was actually going to dress to the theme, although that was mostly going off of what he'd overheard in the hallways.

Blaire hadn't given him a dress code or anything, she had just mentioned that her dress was all black. That was easy enough to match. He suggested that he wear something monochrome and she agreed that would work fine.

Andrei had been to quite a few black-tie concerts that his dad had performed in, so he'd worn a wide selection of suits over his life. Most of them were rentals though. Even if he still had them, they probably wouldn't fit anymore.

He hadn't even thought of going to the Homecoming dance in the first place. He didn't think he'd find a friend group so quickly, let alone a girl who'd want to go with him.

Andrei had dated someone back in Pasadena, but she was becoming way too "Hollywood" for his taste. The move was the perfect opportunity to break things off.

Really, the move was a lot less uprooting than he expected. He still had a few friends down there, but most really didn't expect to stay in the area anyway. With none of his friends left, the only person he'd know was his older sister. Andrei had no intention of joining Katya at UCLA though. Even if he did, they'd only share two or three semesters on campus and she'd be off finding a job elsewhere.

She was getting a degree in Political Science, so her first destination for job searching was going to be up in the state capital, Sacramento. She'd actually be living a lot closer to them in Alexandria.

At this point, Pasadena was just a place he used to live; it held no real anchoring importance for Andrei.

Well, there was one thing that connected him to Pasadena, but he didn't visit the grave often enough.

When they were in the process of moving, he had begun considering East Coast music schools for after graduation. He basically just wanted to explore somewhere new, outside of Southern California.

He was already out of Los Angeles now though ... and there were other factors to consider.

Looking over the roof of the Toyota at Blaire's house, he thought to himself, "The San Francisco Conservatory is pretty nice too ..."

He pulled the suit coat off of its hanger and slid it over his shoulders.

The coat and pants were black with a white shirt and silver vest. Topping it off was a silver ascot tie and handkerchief, both of which had thin black stripes. The style was overall fairly simple, but it had enough details to not be plain.

Considering they'd both be in greyscale, he thought of them getting an especially colorful combination for the corsage and boutonniere. She ended up loving the idea, and they settled on the Paradiso Pink Chrysanthemum. It had a pinkish-purple coloring that was just colorful enough without being flashy or out of place.

"Hombre, you are looking fresh!" Rafael said, locking his car with a key fob.

"Thanks, so are you." He closed the car door.

"Woo, I am so excited. Nervous as hell though. This' my first dance with Elise. After Paul messed things up last time, I am *not* making the same mistake. She gets my one hundred percent focus, *all* night."

"I'm a bit nervous myself," Andrei admitted.

"What? *Phsst*, homie you don't got anything to worry about," he said as they approached the limo. "You keep treating Blaire like you have been already, and you can't go wrong."

Andrei was inclined to agree, considering Raf had played assistant matchmaker to Elise.

Blaire had initially caught his eye during their first week of C&D class. They were the last two to get their voice ranges tested so they could be placed appropriately in the choir.

Andrei was the last one out and couldn't help but notice her when she was leaving class. She was wearing this long-sleeve, dark grey top with cutouts on the shoulders. She also donned a black belt and skirt which went down to just below her knees.

There was a certain energy she gave off that was very attractive, that wasn't even including her voice, or her hair, or her eyes. He caught a glance at them once before she left. They were striking, almost like an old-fashioned portrait. In just a single glance he felt like they peered right through him.

After that, he couldn't help but notice her a lot more often.

She usually hung around with one of the soprano girls, and one of the tenor guys would orbit around the two of them.

Andrei wasn't the best at making first impressions. He knew that his height intimidated people, so he'd usually introduce himself circumstantially. Most of his old friends back in Pasadena were made when getting put into a study group for a book report, or on his ski and snowboard team, or in the men's ensemble of his old choir class.

He was not quick to make friends and mostly expected to find a few new ones in the Choir & Drama class over the course of the year. Maybe if he was lucky, he'd find a date for Prom.

That timetable accelerated suddenly when that tenor guy stopped him after class one day.

At first, he thought it was going to come to blows. Raf had introduced himself by saying. "Hey, I saw you looking at Blaire."

"I don't know what you mean," he had said. He really didn't think he'd looked at her inappropriately at any point, leering too long or in the wrong places. He just ... noticed her ... when she came to class. Besides, he thought this guy was dating the redhead.

Andrei took a step backwards, about to slip out through the door if this really was heading for violence.

That's when Raf finally dropped the act and told him to relax.

"Maybe you should look a little harder," Raf said. "She's the one sizing you up on the regular."

This caught Andrei by surprise. Only after a bit more explanation did Raf finally reveal the full situation as it was, namely, that Blaire was also crushing hard.

"Elise knows what she's talking about. You just gotta break the ice."

It was Raf's last line that really had him considering his approach though.

"Blaire is really reserved, words probably aren't your best approach, introduce yourself another way."

It took an act of God, a stormy day and the teachers being late, for him to find an opportunity with her by the piano.

Everything was a blur after that. Here he was, not even three months later walking up to her house with a corsage in hand.

"Marky, my man!" Raf said as they reached the limo. It was Mark Schlesinger, one of the baritones from the choir.

The other two guys were seniors, like Andrei, so at least he wasn't both the tallest and oldest. They weren't from the choir, just the dates of some of Elise and Blaire's other friends.

"Andrei." Paxton Bannister shook his hand. They both had Calculus 1A as their homeroom, so they'd talked a few times in the mornings.

Rounding out the five dates was Jeremy Wilson.

Two more men were talking near the front of the limo. Once they exchanged the last of their information, the driver broke off to put some forms away.

The other man approached the group. He wore black-rimmed glasses, which contrasted with some streaks of silver over his temples. He had a stern look and carried himself accordingly.

This must be Jack Tidwell, Blaire's father. Andrei recognized him from some of the pictures on her Facebook page.

They were meeting at Blaire's house mostly because of its central location between everyone else. The limo had actually been paid for by Amanda Burke's parents. She was a friend of the girls and also Paxton's date.

As he turned away from the driver, Jack noticed Andrei and began approaching him.

"Mr. Tidwell." He extended his hand. "Andrei Tunnikov."

"Good to meet you Andrei," Jack said, taking a firm grasp.

"Sounds like Amanda has the limo rented until 2:00 a.m. Going to be a late night?" Jack didn't hide the vague air of intimidation in his voice.

"I had no idea." Alarm bells sounded in the back of Andrei's head. He scrambled for an explanation based on what he'd heard the girls discuss. "I think she'd mentioned a drive down through the city. Stop by the Wharf, Market Street, the Embarcadero. I can call us a cab earlier than that, if-"

"No, no, that's fine," Jack conceded.

He'd scared this poor boy who was half a foot taller than him. It was a good feeling. Perhaps there was still some of Edward left in him after all. However, he'd already done a bit of investigation into Andrei. He seemed like a good kid, from a good family.

Plus, renting a limo for the longest possible window, regardless of what the kids did, was very much something the Burkes would do "just in case".

"No, you all have a fun night. Just … stay with the group," was Jack's blessing and warning. The kids coming back late was better than the two of them breaking off on their own.

He also didn't want to actually ruin the night for Blaire. Forcing her to come home earlier than her friends was a recipe for serious retaliation.

Besides, for all of her taunting, Blaire had mostly stayed clear of boys. Jack had to trust that her mother, Milly, would warn him if she actually did get too close for comfort with someone.

"Absolutely." Andrei nodded. "We'll be with the others in the limo … and we'll call if there are any delays."

Blaire's dad seemed satisfied, so Andrei breathed a sigh of relief and straightened out his jacket.

That's when they heard the creak of the front door opening. The girls came out in a line, Amanda leading the group with Elise and Blaire at the back.

The others paired off with their respective dates, leaving just Andrei and Blaire.

Her dress looked like it was made of two layers. There was a silk black dress as the foundation, which was strapless and came down to her knees. On top of it was a layer of elaborately-patterned black lace shaped like rose vines. That lace layer ran from her calves up to her shoulders, with very short sleeves.

Her hair was worn down in wide curls with a decorative silver pin holding the left side back behind her ear. It accentuated one of the silver earrings which matched the pin. On the other side of her face, the bangs almost covered her right eye. She wore more eyeliner than usual, which bordered an eye shadow that transitioned from black to subtle silver near her brows.

She stood there smiling on medium length heels. The extra height closed the gap between them, at least by a few inches.

Blaire looked stunning, gazing at him expectantly with her vivid hazel eyes.

There was a slight pause as he searched for the right words to say. Yet for every compliment that came to mind, one other thing sat there first and foremost.

"I thought you were going to wear the pants?"

Not expecting that, Blaire began chuckling. She pulled on a thin strap hanging from one shoulder and a small purse swiveled into view.

"I didn't need to." She pulled out the make-up clamshell from last night's game. She then swapped it with a small Ziploc bag of other items. Safety pins showed clearly through the transparent plastic.

Playing on the moment, Andrei presented his own accessory, the plastic container fresh from his refrigerator. He opened it, revealing the chrysanthemum corsage.

"You look incredible," he said, lifting her left hand and sliding the flower arrangement onto her wrist.

"So do you," she agreed, but she was careful not to stare too long. After all, they had an audience.

Blaire waved a hand at her mother, who was watching the whole exchange.

She moved in with a perky spring in her step and handed over the boutonniere.

"Andrei, this is my mother, Millicent. Mom, this is Andrei."

"It's nice to meet you Mrs. Tidwell."

She shook his hand with both of hers.

He didn't expect her to be like the father, with that edge of father-daughter protectionism, but the woman also threw off his expectations a bit.

Blaire had told him a lot about her grandfather, and about how little her dad took after him, but she really hadn't gone into much detail about her mother at all.

Millicent Tidwell didn't even look like Blaire's mother, she looked like she could be Elise's. With the exception of Elise's natural red hair, her disposition seemed very similar in an almost uncanny way.

"So nice to finally meet you Andrei," she said as Blaire began pinning the boutonniere to his lapel. "Boy that silver vest sure is dashing, we need to remember that for your brother next year."

Blaire had mentioned her brothers much less sparingly than she did her mother, but none of what she said had been particularly positive.

They were both on the edges of middle school, one starting and one finishing. The two of them were always screwing around, playing obnoxious games. Their favorite game, of course, was how much they could annoy their big sister.

He remembered telling Blaire about the inverse experience he'd had with his older sisters. To them he was a wind-up toy to be played with. He was much more reserved than either of them, who had very extroverted personalities. Luckily, they had all grown out of that phase before Andrei started middle school. It had been for a number of reasons, including tragedy. Everyone had to grow up a little faster.

"Can you believe he didn't want to go?" Millicent asked Andrei, as though he had been present for the conversation. "Even Blaire went to her freshman year Homecoming."

"Mother." Blaire took her eyes off of the boutonniere pin to stare her down.

"Their first chance to be there together and Chris decides to stay home." She tisked, shaking her head.

"There is a God," Blaire mumbled in relief while smoothing out the lapel.

Andrei cracked a smile, catching her glance.

The three heard a clicking sound behind them. They turned to see Elise clipping her phone into a camera tripod.

Despite that, Milly was armed with a camera of her own. She also recruited Jack into taking pictures with his phone. By the end, the kids felt like their faces had frozen into permanent Joker-esq smiles.

Blaire was the first one to break, feeling overwhelmed with every snap of her parents' cameras.

"I think we'd better get going."

"True, we don't want all the best tables to get taken," Elise agreed, clicking once more on her remote.

"You kids have a good time. Let us know if anything comes up," Jack said, as the couples piled into the stretch Escalade.

"Yeah, yeah, we will. Goodbye." Blaire darted through the door, trying to escape the situation.

The driver pushed a button, closing the gull wing door of the passenger section. The tires pivoted in the driveway, turning tightly until the vehicle was out onto a flat, straight road.

The lights of the undercarriage appeared brighter by the minute as the glow of daylight faded. The sun touched down onto the calm waters of the Pacific Ocean, twilight fast approaching.

The evening fog seemed thicker than usual, sweeping over the beach and creeping through the streets of Alexandria.

When the limo had disappeared from view, Jack felt a surprising and indescribable sensation of unease. He looked down at Milly as she cheerfully clicked through the pictures they'd just taken.

"Milly, you think things will go okay?"

"Oh of course Jack," his wife said. "Did you see the way she looked at that boy? That was no Mark Harrison, I think she's really falling for him."

Somehow that didn't put Jack at ease, but it did set his mind to thinking that it was his paternal instincts that were tapping at the door of his subconscious.

He once more deferred to Milly. She and Blaire might have had some rough patches, but he had to trust her mother's intuition.

He pushed the feeling out of his mind, turning toward the front door. His wife followed after, already formulating the ways she would work the details of the evening out of Blaire, as well as Elise of course.

Unknown to both of them, that had been the last time they would see Blaire alive ever again.

FIVE

DANGEROUS ROADS

WITH THE DOOR OF THE LIMO CLOSED, Blaire could finally breathe a sigh of relief that she was no longer under a lens ... for the most part.

Elise was a fervent photographer. Beyond the shallow or glammy stuff, like posting selfies on social media, she actually had a decent eye for shot composition. One particular picture in Blaire's phone was proof enough of that.

She knew Elise would get plenty of pictures of her and Andrei throughout the evening.

"Man, look at all this!" Raf marveled. "Looks like *Tron* up in here!"

The roof of the limo, as well as some side panels, were decorated with prismatic shapes glowing in different patterns. As they entered, the lights staggered between deep purple hues and seafoam green.

The left side of the passenger compartment contained a full bar area with ice boxes for drinks of any variety. Of course, those containers were filled with sparkling ciders, sodas, waters, and other non-alcoholic beverages so that North Bay Limousine Services didn't get sued for providing alcohol to minors.

The right side of the passenger cabin had three of the five luxury seats. The other two seats were at the front and back of the space. While each of them had enough emergency seat belts for four, the couples spread out, turning each bench into a loveseat.

Blaire & Andrei were on the back seat bench, adjacent to the door. Next to them were Elise & Raf, followed by Amanda & Paxton, Raquel & Mark, and finally Dina & Jeremy.

"Sorry about all that," Blaire whispered to Andrei, once the limo had pulled away from the house. "Did my dad say anything to you?"

"No." Andrei played down how things had actually come across. "He just said to 'have a fun night.'"

"Okay, good." She breathed a sigh of relief. "He can sometimes get kind of, ah ... never mind."

There was a sinking feeling in the pit of her stomach, like she had to explain herself to Andrei about what her mother had said.

"With the last Homecoming I just ... I had like this bronchitis thing ... and there was no, ahh ..." She trailed off. Her rational mind fought for control against her intrusive endocrine system. She was just making it weird by talking about it more. The other couples were off on their own conversations and here she was discussing old dates and abandoned dances.

"Would you like some cider?" he asked, seeing that she wanted to change the subject.

"Yes, please." She smiled, grateful for both offers.

He pulled a bottle opener from the little shelf and popped off the cap. The Sparkling Apple-Grape Martinelli's fizzled out, but he was quick to catch it in one of the glasses. He then poured a second glass with a cleaner flow.

"Keep the bottle moving." Raf extended a hand.

Andrei passed it over then turned back to Blaire. He gave her the second, less foamy glass.

"You know," he whispered. "I wasn't originally planning on going to Homecoming either. What's the point if you don't have someone great to go with?"

He lowered his glass toward her. Blaire smiled and tapped it with hers. They both took a long sip of the cider.

"Good thing they're done renovating the Murphy Center," Mark Schlesinger said to the group. "You remember last year's dance, when one wall was all taped off with sheets like it was wearing a diaper?"

"I remember them covering over the construction signs with *Spamalot* posters," Raf added.

"When's the gym supposed to be done?" Jeremy Wilson turned to Paxton. Paxton was one of the point guards on the Varsity Basketball team, if anyone would have news on its current status, it would be him.

"Supposedly soon," Paxton responded. "Coach says we'll have maybe a week or two to practice there before the first game."

"They're sure cutting it close." Amanda raised an eyebrow.

"That's construction for you," Jeremy Wilson quipped. "There was that three month delay on the upstairs classrooms too. I got really sick of walking to the middle school for labs."

"The real question is how long the new locker rooms will stay fresh," Raquel Perry said.

As one of the cheerleaders, she'd seen everyone using the locker room and showers in the stadium during the gymnasium renovation. The stadium had been built in the late seventies, so the ventilation was a lot older, and the rooms had four decades worth of smells and funk that hung in the air. She knew that as soon as the new indoor lockers were open, all of the sports players would swarm to them immediately.

She answered her own question. "They're going to smell like ass in no time."

Dina Petrakis followed with, "I just want the rear parking lot back. I'm sick of fighting for the good spaces."

One of the main construction staging areas had been in the secondary parking lot between the mechanical yard and the northernmost baseball diamond. The school administration determined it would be less disruptive than a shifting column of pallets and materials bisecting the front parking area.

Of course, a lot of teachers and students with homerooms on the east side of the building ended up getting displaced. That was another hundred or so cars added to the west lot. It was now filling up almost every day, sending the final stragglers to the middle and elementary school parking lots.

Elise spoke up while Raf poured her a second glass of the cider. "This is a fantastic limo selection Amanda."

"Hell yeah it is," she said with a look of satisfaction. "And even better, we can take it anywhere we want until 2:00 a.m."

"Anywhere?" Jeremy Wilson asked. "We could always stop by Jimmy O'Shaughnessy's. Word is that it's going to be crazy, his biggest bash to date."

Paxton looked down at Amanda, raising an eyebrow. Amanda looked back at him, taking a slow sip from her cider glass.

Andrei had been sitting quietly for a few minutes. Blaire was resting her head on his arm, which stretched over her on top of the leather seat cushion. He didn't want to disturb her, break the serenity of the moment. He was really taking in the experience.

An electronic music playlist had been pulsing just below the volume of conversation. One of the subwoofers was beating right behind the two of them.

When the others started talking about the afterparty, his ears perked up. The exchange with Jack Tidwell was still fresh in mind.

He'd heard the name Jimmy O'Shaughnessy before. He shared exactly one period with him. The dude was a bit of a hyena, always cackling at the back of their Government & Civics class. He also might be one of the football players. Otherwise, Andrei knew nothing about him.

"Whew, I don't know man," Raf responded to Jeremy. "Think the driver might say something?"

"Why would he?" Amanda asked. "It's just one more stop ... and he stays outside."

Blaire had also tuned in closer when Jimmy's place was brought up, eyeing the reaction of the other girls. Despite not attending most of the dances, she had heard quite a bit about past events at the hillside mansion.

Jimmy's parents were non-existent. His mom was a total unknown and his dad was always working. He basically had free reign of the house like it was his own private club. Not to mention, he had enough booze and drugs to fully supply such an establishment.

That was all secondary however. There was one main reason why Jimmy's place stood out amongst the other party houses. It was why students were quick to enforce its secrecy whenever parents or school faculty were concerned. That reason was the size.

Jimmy's place might as well have been an Embassy Suites, because there were plenty of *private* spaces spread throughout the estate. It had become a common locale for many Villa Vista couples to experience their first time together.

Homecoming was unfolding like a dream come true for Blaire. For years she had been apathetic toward the rituals and traditions of the various school dances. Nevertheless, something was definitely different this time and she knew exactly what that something was, or rather who that someone was.

Another part of her tried to assert itself, force her to consider the scenarios and risks.

She and Andrei weren't even officially a couple. They'd only known each other for a few months. Heck, they hadn't even kissed yet.

"There's a simple fix for that," she thought, as the flame inside of her grew.

Her cautious self made one more attempt at reason. "You don't even know what Andrei thinks about Jimmy, or the reputation his parties carry."

"I'm game," Dina said, interrupting Blaire's internal debate.

"Mhm, me too," Raquel agreed, cozying up to Mark.

"I don't know, we've got a limo!" Elise retorted. "Do we really want to waste the night parking it somewhere?"

She glanced over at Blaire, offering this as an out. She wanted Blaire to come to the dance, but this was not part of her shrewd calculations. Elise tried to keep her from feeling pressured into going by the others.

Blaire turned toward Andrei. She could see immediately in his face that he was completely ignorant to the context. There were no preconceptions or judgements … no signs of hesitation.

"Whatever you want to do," he said.

Andrei had been so sweet to her. He was the first date in all of high school that she'd ever really felt something deep for. It stirred something in her that she didn't want to run away from … something she couldn't ignore. She was going to follow that flame and let the waltz of passion lead them to their night's crescendo.

She turned back toward Elise and the others. "I mean, we'll have the limo for a long time …"

Rafael and Elise both looked shocked by her answer.

"Hell yeah!" Jeremy said from the far bench.

Amanda bit her lip, turning toward Paxton.

"I'll give him the heads up at the dance," he told the rest of them.

Andrei didn't fully understand what had just happened, but the energy in the limo noticeably shifted. He couldn't quite interpret the expressions he was seeing from Raf and Elise.

Blaire scooted closer into the crook of his arm. It felt nice … he decided that he wasn't going to question it.

Once more they got lost in the music, as the subwoofers pounded behind the two of them.

***

"How about a little something for the princess?" Brendan Jensen offered, revealing a selection of travel-sized liquors he had smuggled aboard the Hummer limousine.

"I think I'm good for now," Jennifer declined.

She could already see a scenario where the overly genial Melkonian or Wallace caught the smell of alcohol on her breath and disqualified her from winning. She couldn't risk it. Mr. Mel in particular always stood too close to their microphones when he was doing some kind of character.

"She doesn't need to relax," Sheena Gilquist, Brendan's girlfriend, said. "She already has Homecoming locked up tight."

"Oh, I don't know about that ..." Jennifer waved her hand.

"Are you serious?" Camellia asked. "You dominated the rally games."

"Oh my god, yes," Ashley Stillwell agreed. "Like with that flower hat game, when you just dead sprinted across the field."

The "Top Hat Trot", as the Student Council had called it, involved the competitors putting on oversized pieces of headwear and racing back and forth between the 30-yard lines. The boys wore top hats and the girls wore oversized sun hats with flower arrangements.

Jenny was by far the most athletic of the bunch. None of the other girls were in a single sport, or cheerleading, or Color Guard, or even the band.

Among the boys, Marcus Johnson was by far the fastest. Sprints are par for the course for Varsity Basketball, they're like half of the requirements for the sport. The freshman, Enrique Rodriguez, came pretty close though. He was very fit thanks to the swimming team, but Marcus was eight inches taller than him. Every step covered more ground.

The Homecoming Court did have a bit of a *Hunger Games* angle to it. While it was primarily a popularity contest or beauty pageant, a noteworthy portion of the student body would vote for someone they wanted to put through the gauntlet of the Spirit Week games.

They were always goofy or ridiculous challenges, such as eating strange things or embarrassing competitions. The students had a lot of fun watching the princes and princesses compete not only for their class's glory, but also for the sake of entertainment. "All the world's a stage", after all.

That was Jenny's leading theory on the juniors, Melissa Levitt and Liam Connelly. A large percentage of the Junior Class probably just wanted to metaphorically put them in a dunk tank.

While Liam didn't explicitly belittle anyone, he did have a certain "bad boy" edge which was equally unapproachable to the "lower status" boys and alluring to a large contingent of girls.

True to form, he didn't look like he cared whether he won or not. Melissa, on the other hand, was playing for keeps.

During the tomato toss, she was aiming almost exclusively for Jenny, trying to nail her in places that would leave lasting welts through the dance. Luckily, Jenny was too fast for her.

"Whew, that freshman girl sure took a tumble though, didn't she?" Trey Devall added.

Ellen Taylor had slipped during the tug-of-war and landed face-first in the mud. She did *not* take it well either. The mud left a bustier pattern on her shirt which got the whole stadium laughing, with quite a few hoots and wolf whistles. She turned red immediately, storming off the field toward the girls' locker room.

For the last two days of rallies, it was clear she wasn't really trying to win, just trying to avoid unwanted attention. Enrique did his best to pull the extra weight, but ... they were freshmen. This early in the year they were still basically middle-schoolers, while the senior team were almost adults.

In their case, Marcus' 18th birthday was next month and hers was in December.

Then the sophomore couple, Chelsea Morton and Greg Henshaw, had performed fairly well for sophomores.

The faculty never let on exactly how much the Spirit Week games affected the final decision, but the sophomores hadn't performed poorly enough that it would impact them.

That didn't matter anyway, because their support would be strongest during the popular vote of those that showed up for the dance. Real life couples always did well.

They had these really adorable posters done up too. They posed for a picture in Burger King crowns with a "dream bubble" Photoshopped above them. In the bubble was a picture of them wearing more realistic looking plastic crowns and formal clothes.

There was a chance they didn't get voted together though. Technically the Homecoming King and Homecoming Queen were separate votes. In Jennifer's sophomore year, the king was the Senior Class boy and the queen was the Junior Class girl. That was the first time Jennifer had been on the Homecoming Court, as the Sophomore Class Princess.

It really kicked off her own dream of eventually winning one day. Perhaps it was a bit shallow and she'd be upset if she lost, but she had some perspective too. She certainly wasn't going to act like Joe Torelli and throw a huge bitch fit over it. The temptation was definitely there though.

Social validation was the best drug there was. Jennifer knew that most students, most people, spent a large part of their lives chasing that dragon. If they couldn't fill that void with real affection from their peers, they filled it with cocaine, booze, pot, work, thrill-seeking, and any number of other vices that patched over the biggest desire of the soul ... love.

Jenny felt a twinge inside of her. For all the joy winning Homecoming Queen might bring her, it wouldn't fill up the deeper wound she'd felt recently.

She turned toward Darren. He had just told some joke to the boys, which left Jimmy in stitches.

After Blake, Darren had been there when no one else had.

There were a dozen other guys who might have asked her to the dance if she dropped hints that she was interested. Someone probably would have asked her eventually regardless.

Darren was different though, he wasn't just a date, he was an old friend. They were friends first, and that was a stronger foundation than anything.

She rested one hand on his, which caught his attention. He curled his fingers gently around hers.

He met her eyes as she pulled him in close. He could smell the luscious perfume drifting off of her neck. He thought she was going for a kiss, when instead she rested her cheek against his.

"Jimmy's drunk already," she whispered in his ear.

Darren did his best to hold in the laughter. He dropped his forehead to her shoulder.

***

"Dammit. Dammit. Dammit. Dammit. Dammit. Dammit ..."

With every tick of the dial, Niles cursed himself internally.

All the preparation, all the polish, getting the suit, getting the corsage, grooming himself top to bottom for every errant hair, and putting cover-up over every noticeable blemish ... and what did he forget?

Gas.

He forgot to get gas for the stupid Lexus.

They were just returning to city streets from the scenic Shoreline Blvd. when the low fuel light popped up in his display. Thus began a level of calculus he had not implemented in a long time. "Do I get gas now or after the dance?"

He felt like he had turned into a waterfall of *Matrix* code as a thousand different variables were considered.

"What if after the dance we are having a great time and the stop kills the mood?"

"What if things are actually going terribly and she uses the gas station as an excuse to end the night early?"

"What if we stop now and that makes her think I'm unreliable for the rest of the night?"

"What if we stop now and she gets all weird like I need a full tank of gas for afterwards and starts expecting a big drive with a lot of stops?"

"What if I just ignore the light and try to get us back to her place before the car dies?"

"What if the car does die?"

"What if her dad calls at some point and convinces her to come home early, could stopping for gas buy time to convince her to stay longer?"

"What if I sneak away during the dance to use the 'bathroom' and fill it up really quickly at the Chevron down the street from campus?"

These questions and dozens of others seemed to occur simultaneously as Niles struggled to weigh the options.

That is when the blinking gas pump signal disappeared and was replaced with a "miles remaining" counter. There were only twelve miles on the counter. Villa Vista High School was twenty miles away from their scenic detour, and all of those miles were uphill.

"Dammit. Dammit. Dammit. Dammit. Dammit. Dammit ..."

Laura didn't seem to mind the stop, but Niles felt like a starter-level Borthian Crawler at the moment. As a creature with the lowest level of intelligence in the entire game, in this case the game of life, Niles was just trying not to swallow his tongue.

Out of a reflection in the gas pump, he saw that Laura was on her cell phone.

"Oh god, she's texting Anne, isn't she?" he thought.

Her best friend, Anne Kirkpatrick, was not exactly an advocate for her relationship with Niles.

Barry had made an ass of himself trying to make a move on Anne over the summer, and that rejection had a ripple effect on Niles' own chances with Laura.

"Bad Company" was the refrain that often came to mind ... in part because it was one of his dad's favorite songs.

Niles had no idea if Anne had actually tried to poison the water for him, but it was one more set of variables cycling recursively in his brain's overtaxed code compiler.

Seeing Laura checking her phone, he pulled out his own. At the very least he could distract himself with Twitter for a minute.

That's when he saw a text message from Barry Owens.

Saturday · 6:06 p.m.

How goes the date loverboy?

Speak of the devil ...

Saturday · 6:17 p.m.

Fukd.

Saturday · 6:17 p.m.

Damn, already? Thought you hadn't even kissed

Saturday · 6:17 p.m.

Yeah I wish. No, forgot to get gas

Saturday · 6:17 p.m.

LMAO, YOU DUMBASS

Saturday · 6:17 p.m.

Fuck off.

Saturday · 6:17 p.m.

So the dress is staying on then?

Saturday · 6:17 p.m.

Sigh

Saturday · 6:17 p.m.

What about afterwards?

Saturday · 6:17 p.m.

Have a few options on the table

Saturday · 6:17 p.m.

Well remember, she's big on the whole theme thing. U don't want to cut out early. might as well stay as long as the staff since she acts like one

Saturday · 6:17 p.m.

Don't plan to split early, unless her dad shows up to chop my balls off

Saturday · 6:17 p.m.

Could be a net gain, keep you from humping the furniture

Saturday · 6:17 p.m.

Pfft, I'm not your mom's terrier

There was a pause in the otherwise instantaneous back and forth they were having, until Barry finally replied.

Saturday · 6:18 p.m.

Good luck Niles

Niles wasn't sure how to read that last message. "Good luck" with what, not getting his balls chopped off? Text messaging could be frustrating sometimes, because it stripped a lot of nuance out of language. That's why he preferred voice chat when they were playing online.

The pump finally clicked. Niles flicked the app closed and pocketed his phone. He tugged hard on the pump trigger, strangling out another tenth of a gallon of 93 Octane.

Once the tank was sufficiently topped off, he put away the nozzle and screwed on the gas cap. With a click, the cover was closed and flush with the body of the car again.

Niles slid back into the driver's seat.

"All set," he said.

An uncomfortably long pause passed as Laura completed and sent her final text message.

She then locked her phone screen and turned to acknowledge him. "Great, let's go."

"So has Anne arrived yet?" Niles asked her, making an educated guess.

"Yeah," she said, with only a hint of annoyance to her voice. "But it should be fine, they're saving us seats."

After things went south with Barry, Anne wasn't around as much whenever he and Laura were hanging out. They no longer had a common destination like Mrs. Jefferson's sophomore English class anymore.

Lunches had become just as awkward. Most of the time, Niles would sit by Laura at a table with Anne and their other friends. Then, on increasingly rare occasions, he would sit with Barry and Melvin, in which case it was usually just the three of them.

That's how it had been for the first year and a half of high school, not to mention a large chunk of their elementary and middle school days.

Then during the English project, Niles had been successful in asking Laura to the Spring Formal. That had been encouragement for Barry, who eventually worked up the nerve to ask Anne out at some random point over the summer.

Barry never explained how exactly he asked her, or how terribly the conversation went, but regardless the answer was the same. It was a step too far for her, and she had to clarify her feelings that they were "just friends".

It was an incredibly loaded term, and often really meant "former acquaintances". You simply get filed to the back of that person's Dunbar Rolodex. They technically have a social relationship with you, but it's the smallest one their brain can retain without forgetting about you completely.

In the case of Barry and Anne, they were "just classmates" again. It was back to square one, exactly as they were the same time the previous year.

This was the Sword of Damocles that Niles imagined was hanging over his own head. At any moment the string could snap and he would go back to just being a face in the crowd with Laura.

With the Lexus sufficiently fed, the machine rolled them up the slope of Fremont Street back toward the highway.

Niles wanted to get conversation going quickly, to hopefully help Laura forget the pit stop.

"So, what are Anne and Liam wearing?" he asked her.

"Well Anne has this really cute broach to go with her dress, but Liam refused to wear anything historical." Laura crossed her legs. "He's just got like a white tie or something."

"He just can't appreciate the finer things," Niles scoffed, straightening out the arms of his white shirt.

"Right? So pedestrian ..." Laura bounced the curls hanging by her left ear.

Liam Connelly was a bit of an antithesis to Niles and his friends. He had a similar sort of detachment and apathy in regards to anything having to do with the school. This manifested much differently in the eyes of the students though.

Everyone saw him as too cool to care about school, rather than too geeky to focus on anything except one's outlets of escapism. It also helped that he was really fit, handsome, and had a decent fashion sense.

Laura hadn't really gone into details about how he ended up being Anne's date for Homecoming, but Niles had seen enough fragments that he believed he had a workable model.

First, Liam was elected as Junior Class Prince for the Homecoming Court. It was a position he was not campaigning for and definitely wasn't expecting. It turned out that a word-of-mouth campaign led by a group of popular girls was what made it happen.

The group strategically placed themselves around him when the announcements were made and were able to peer pressure him into begrudgingly accepting.

In a small way, it was almost a humanizing moment. He actually seemed like a real person to Niles rather than just another popular kid. No matter how cool he acted, when enough hot girls told him to do something ... he did it.

It was also amusing watching him struggle through some of the Spirit Week games in his gym clothes, often wearing some other ridiculous game-related items.

At one point the Sophomore Prince kid, Greg ... something ... accidently hit him in the back of the head when they were playing one of the sophomore/junior vs. freshman/senior games. Already riled up by the competition, Liam turned around and almost decked the guy.

Since he was now representing their class in the Homecoming events, Laura had to talk to him a few times for planning and organizing purposes. During one of those times, Anne was there and apparently put on her A game. She flirted enough to lure him into asking her.

When Niles formally asked Laura to Homecoming, it was this elaborate thing where he set up a surprise cake to be delivered after they grabbed dinner one night. The cake read "Danse De Retour Avec Moi?" which he was pretty sure said "Homecoming Dance With Me?" in French.

The cake itself had three layers. The top was lemon, but dyed blue with food coloring, the middle layer was vanilla, and the bottom layer was red velvet. It was like the French tricolor flag. That wasn't technically the flag during the actual Bourbon Restoration years, but Niles thought it was good enough. Plus, the cake itself had white icing with the gold fleur-de-lis around it.

Laura seemed to like it, and obviously she said yes.

Liam Connelly's invitation was something plain, essentially just saying: "How about Homecoming, you and me? I've got to show up anyway."

That tidbit did come from Barry though, so Niles assumed a bit of bitterness was filtering through. The bitterness wasn't exactly unfounded though. Liam didn't need to do anything like buy a $50 custom, three-layer cake for two.

"So, out of curiosity," Niles asked. "Did you ever actually see *Les Mis*, like, on stage?"

"No," Laura said, "Just the movie, which was ... okay."

"Would you like to?" Niles asked. "Like next time it's down in San Fran or something?"

"Yeah, that would be fun," Laura said.

Niles smiled; it was another opportunity opened up for the future.

If everything went well tonight, it'd be a future as a real couple.

***

It had been a very scenic limo ride. The sunset was incredibly colorful, a splendor of purples, pinks, and oranges lit up the sky as the star sunk below the horizon.

Blaire and Andrei had shifted seats a few times, taking pictures with the others in the limo. But now everyone was back where they started, mostly talking with their dates.

Rafael had been very chatty throughout the trip. He'd been telling Elise a series of stories related to his cousin José's wedding.

The first story was centered around the bachelor party they threw for him. They accidentally locked José in a closet and ended up spending an hour getting him free. It came down to them having to pull the pins out of the door hinges.

After that, the saga progressed to having to find a replacement jacket for his other cousin. He had drenched his suit with soy sauce when they were getting an early lunch at a Chinese restaurant.

At least the misadventures had a happy ending and they were able to send José and his new bride to their honeymoon without further incident.

Andrei was impressed, this was clearly a series of tales Raf had saved for just this occasion. Elise definitely seemed to be entertained.

He and Blaire had a less focused conversation, drifting from one topic to another.

"I didn't even know there was someplace to snowboard near Pasadena." Blaire found the idea amusing.

Northern California had a very rich winter sports community because of the Sierra Nevada mountains. The resorts around Lake Tahoe were especially popular. Southern California was known for some very different locales, namely the Mojave Desert, Death Valley, and Malibu.

"Yeah there's a few good places," Andrei reminisced. "At Pasadena North High we'd usually end up doing practices at Mt. Baldy. It's just north of Rancho Cucamonga, maybe an hour's drive in regular traffic. It was kind of fun."

"Yeah, but you were surrounded by a bunch of beaches and warm weather, yet you chose Ski & Snowboarding instead? Why not, like, volleyball?"

"No, no way. Anastasia played volleyball … for *three* years. If I had even shown a hint of interest as a kid, she would have conscripted me into her own kind of boot camp."

"She was *that* committed?"

"No, she's just always been competitive," he elaborated. "In a weird way she thought of it as being supportive. She wouldn't have even *allowed* me to be mediocre."

"Was Katya any better?"

Andrei snickered. "Oh no."

"What was her sport then?" Blaire asked.

"Karate," Andrei said ominously, as though he were experiencing Vietnam flashbacks.

He turned to Blaire. "Let's just say I learned how to take a punch ... and kick ... and elbow ..."

Blaire was holding back laughter behind a face of genuine pity. She imagined Katya bursting into his room at random hours to put new routines to the test.

Andrei had told Blaire a bit about his sisters over the past few months, but they were so busy with their own lives they hadn't been on his mind much. He hadn't seen either of them for most of the year.

Katya had stopped by the new house over the summer, once they had settled into Alexandria. Then the whole family had visited Anastasia and her husband back in April.

They lived in Virginia, closer to his family. She had met him at Duke University in North Carolina when they were in the Business program together.

"So they were always looking out for their 'little' brother?" Blaire prodded, affecting a cutesy voice.

"Maybe a bit ..." He thought back on those early years. "But I was still young when Anastasia started at Duke ... Katya was the real gatekeeper."

When Andrei was just a kid, their mother had died of cancer. Until she went off to college, Anastasia had really stepped into a maternal role. She was the eldest, seven years older than him, so there felt like a more mature separation between her and the others.

Katya on the other hand was only three years older. In retrospect, she was the one that really took an involved approach with him. She was the pestering big sister, keeping just enough tabs on Andrei to make sure he stayed out of trouble. Even though, in Andrei's opinion, she was the one who was generally more reckless. But, that's family.

"Do you think she'd approve of me?" Blaire asked. She had said it nonchalantly, but there was a much deeper hope of acceptance lying just beneath.

Andrei smiled and pulled out his phone. He began scrolling through his text messaging app until it reached back a few weeks.

He had sent Katya the picture that Elise had taken. He showed Blaire the reply she sent:

September 28th · 1:38 p.m.

Ooh, she's cute ... congrats Andrei! You better be on your best behavior, treat that girl right.

Andrei pocketed the phone as he said, "Nothing would have changed if she'd said otherwise, but in this case, I tend to agree."

"Well, that's encouraging ..." Blaire crossed a leg toward him, her heel brushing against his pants.

Time seemed to slow. It felt as though their lips were coming together ... but they were interrupted when the limo took a hard pivot to the left.

The stretch Escalade turned through one of the open gates into the main parking lot of Villa Vista High School.

There were three other limos parked on the south side near the football stadium. The drivers were making small talk between the Lincoln and Chrysler limos.

Some multicolored spotlights were crossing back and forth over the front wall of the Murphy Center. A banner over the entrance read: "HAPPY HOMECOMING VVHS!"

"Party time!" Raquel shouted from the far back seat.

The gull wing door began to open. Everyone looked at Andrei and Blaire. They were anxiously waiting for the pair to exit first.

The two glanced at each other ... the moment had passed.

Andrei shifted his legs, stepping out onto the asphalt. He then extended a hand to help Blaire through the door.

The others dismounted, making their way for the entrance.

Blaire took Andrei's arm and they followed the group through the parted doors.

SIX

CROWNS & CURSES

"WELL, IF IT ISN'T the little bumblebees!" Bob Melkonian said as he spotted a group of Choir & Drama kids stepping into the ballroom. "Then again, maybe not so little."

It was really easy to pick out the tall one. He was one of the new boys at the school, "Andrei Totenkopf" or something like that. The boy rolled his eyes when he heard Mr. Mel's acknowledgement, but his partner found it quite amusing.

Bob recognized the girl instantly, Blaire Tidwell. She'd been at Villa Vista since kindergarten. Kind of a quiet girl, maybe a bit moody … but then again dissecting animals isn't for everyone.

She'd made it out of Mr. Mel's biology class with a solid B. Her redhead friend did most of the cutting, while Blaire documented the organs, holding back a look of disgust throughout each lab.

"Everyone find yourself a place at a table. It is *very very* improper to dawdle on the edges carrying unnecessary accessories," Melkonian continued.

He did his best to incorporate as much silliness into the general announcements as he could, but there were only so many memorable quotes that fit the circumstances. He was the Prince of Wales more in spirit than substance.

He stood atop the stage carrying a wireless mic as he trounced back and forth, giving general direction to those entering. Some pop dance music was playing in the background, a modern playlist to get everyone (else's) energy going.

Melkonian was not a purist for the Homecoming themes, case-in-point his own British-themed costume was a century off. He understood that most kids just wanted a generally fun atmosphere. While this year they could do a lot with tunes from the Jazz Era, almost none of the kids wanted to hear Renaissance-period Italian folk music at a school dance. Plus, there would be plenty of waltzes and classical dance music later on in the night.

The performing arts center had been arranged very nicely as a ballroom. There was an open egress forming a walkway around the outer edges of the main floor. To the right and left of the stage were columns of dinner tables, with ten seats at each. Between those columns of tables, in the very middle of the auditorium, was the actual dance floor. It extended from the front wall of the stage apron all the way to the back wall adjacent to the gymnasium.

They'd sold a lot of tickets for the night, there'd be over 300 students. Not all of them were students from Villa Vista, of course. A few kids would have dates from John Muir High, and others would come from more remote schools in the area. It should be a good time.

To help patrol that many youngsters, there were about two dozen faculty attending the dance as well, including Melkonian and Wallace.

Principal Leonard McDouglas was against one of the back walls, talking to Ms. Harriet, the Freshman English teacher, as well as Mr. Guzmán, the Algebra 2 teacher. In a few other pods he could see Reynolds, the U.S. History teacher, Moll, the Chemistry teacher, Van Gaal, the Classics teacher, and others still.

The faculty basically took shifts walking around the floor, making sure everyone was properly supervised. They'd take turns eating their dinners in the cafeteria throughout the night.

Melkonian more or less owned the stage, which is a position he reveled in. He felt like a live set piece, adding to the atmosphere for the event.

Finding a lull in time, Bob unfolded the program brochure from his pocket. It included a rough schedule for the evening.

From 6:00 to 6:30 p.m. would be introductions and seating everyone. People could mingle, dance a little, or take pictures.

From 6:30 to 6:45 p.m. would be the announcements of which class won Homecoming. This included a number of factors.

First there was student participation in the Spirit Week days.

That measured what percentage of each class dressed up for each theme day. Monday, everyone dressed for the American Roaring 20's, Tuesday, Italian Renaissance, Wednesday, French Bourbon, and Thursday, Victorian England. On Friday, it was about how many students wore Jaguars or Villa Vista gear to show support for the Varsity Football team.

From what Melkonian knew of the tallying, the Juniors had done the worst during the week and the Seniors had done the best.

The next category of points was based on how well each float did during the Homecoming game. In this case, it was a surprise victory by the Freshman Class. Finally, there were the points based on how each class's prince and princess did during the rally games.

It was important that the class results were called first, because that could influence how people would vote for the Homecoming Royalty. If your classmates didn't pull their weight, then maybe you would end up voting for someone else.

Melkonian liked that factor of the competition. At least then the kids weren't just voting for who was the most popular or attractive, there was a real sense of earning your victory through some semblance of merit.

Following those announcements, the attendees would cast their votes for Homecoming King & Queen. Then they'd be set loose to cut loose, maybe even to some "Footloose". Unfortunately, that only happened during the "Back to the 80s" Homecoming a few years ago.

From 6:45 to 7:30 p.m. they would be free to dance or go up to the photographer to have an official picture taken before dinner.

From 7:30 to 8:00 p.m. they'd serve the meals.

From 8:00 to 8:15 p.m. they would announce the Homecoming Royalty. After basking in the celebration, those students would go to the photographer and have their own special pictures taken for the yearbook. They could bring their dates in for some shots too.

From 8:15 to 9:00 p.m. there would be time for final official pictures by the late stragglers and there would be another set of songs.

The ones after dinner were on the slower side, since everyone had just eaten. Of course, that usually meant they aired on the more romantic side too. The faculty had to watch out for that, make sure the students didn't get carried away.

On too many occasions Melkonian had to recruit a female faculty member to help him break up a couple that were getting too "touchy" on the dance floor. They'd usually get one warning, then get kicked out if they continued.

At 9:00 p.m. the dance was officially over. When the last formal song was finished, they'd switch back to the walk-in playlist. The service staff would clean everything up and return the ballroom back to its default "lunchroom" layout. Over half of the attendees would be gone by that point anyway.

After a few of the slow songs, by around 8:30 p.m., a good third of the students would start to leave. They would head to their *hopefully* PG-13 afterparties.

For her senior year Homecoming, Bob and Angie's daughter Monika was going with a boy she'd been dating for several months.

Bob was very proud of his appropriation of the coconut bikini top. However, he otherwise had to promise not to specifically call her out or embarrass her intentionally at the dance. He'd held to his end of that bargain, but was sweating when the two of them disappeared in their limo for a friend's party.

According to Angie nothing unseemly had happened, but Bob knew firsthand how crafty teenagers could be.

There were at least three party houses popular among the students because of a lack of supervision. Even then, Bob only knew so many details. He was pretty sure that some of what he'd been told was intentional misdirection.

Bob casually scanned the edges of the ballroom and could already see a few hands where they shouldn't be.

He sighed to himself.

That is when he heard a surprising stir in the crowd as some students hooted and whistled at the stage.

Bob twisted to one side, following their attention. He saw a familiar figure stroll in from stage left. It was none other than the 26th President of the United States, Teddy Roosevelt. At the very least, it was a damn good look alike.

Rick Wallace had subverted Bob's expectations by donning a simple but believable wig. His head had been shine-bald for the last decade. He usually trimmed the crown line down to only a fraction of an inch. But now he had a brown carpet combed over to one side.

Rick had also applied a light hair dye to his already fitting mustache to cover the silver whiskers. After all, Teddy Roosevelt was the youngest president to take the oath of office. At forty-two years old, he had even beaten John F. Kennedy. Of course, that young tenure was due to the assassination of President McKinley, his predecessor, but that's a detail most forget.

The wig and mustache dye might not have erased thirty years off of Rick Wallace, but it came surprisingly close. He also wore a pair of fake round spectacles. In contrast to Teddy, Rick always had excellent vision. After that, it was just the clothes and a pocket watch to help top off the character.

"Well, isn't this a man out of time?" Melkonian announced through the microphone. "Seems the colonies really pulled themselves together in the end."

Rick revealed his own microphone from the suit pocket without a watch in it.

"And how are you tonight, 'Mr. President?'" Melkonian asked, setting Rick up for any introduction he wanted.

"Why I'm feeling quite bully!" Rick announced.

The same contingent of guests cheered again.

"I don't think I know you though," Rick asked him.

"Why I am George, Prince regent of Wales." Melkonian posed.

"Whales? My boy, we have electric light now! No more need for whale oil," Rick replied.

"Not the fish," Melkonian responded in mock offense. "Wales, of mighty Britannia!"

"That strip of shoreline west of Birmingham?" Rick asked, with a disregarding tone.

"I am not some lord of the beach; I shall be reigning monarch of the entire British Empire one day!" Melkonian responded.

"That's nice," Rick answered. "While you play in daddy's shadow, I have a canal to dig."

"Insolent colonist!" Melkonian huffed.

By that point, the students were no longer paying attention to the improv.

Rick signaled to Bob to turn from the crowd for a moment. They faced the back wall and Rick turned off his microphone, motioning Bob to do the same.

"What's up?" Bob asked, speaking in a low tone even though the ambient music easily drowned out their voices.

"Just wanted to give you a heads up on something," Rick said, becoming very serious all of the sudden. "It's about one of the royalty, the freshman girl, Ellen Taylor."

"Okay." Bob wasn't sure where he was going with this.

"I just wanted to warn you to go easy on her during the announcements and stuff tonight," Rick began. "Whether or not she wins, keep the bits to a minimum."

"Yeah of course, I wasn't going to mock the girl or anything-" Melkonian was a bit wounded.

"I know, I know," Rick said. "It's just a unique situation right now. Do you remember what happened during the rally game on Wednesday?"

"You mean when she fell?" Bob asked. He remembered the crowd laughing at that, and her running to the lockers, but he figured that was just because she wanted to change her shirt. The mud left an *unflattering* print on her.

"Yes." Rick's head dropped a little. "That afternoon she was brought to my office. She didn't show up to her fifth-period class after lunch. When they finally found her, out behind the storage building, she was in tears."

"What?" Bob said in shock.

"It took fifteen minutes to get anything out of her about what happened," Rick explained. "I had to bring Barbara in."

Barbara Fletcher was the school's Vice Principal. She didn't have any direct interaction with students on a regular basis, so they didn't see her as much of an authority figure, despite her position. Usually when serious punishments or consequential discussions were being held, it was Principal McDouglas in the judge's seat. He was the one that carried the air of intimidation.

In those instances, Ms. Fletcher was usually seen as the "good cop", the advocate for the student, if she was present at all. This gave her a kind of separation in the minds of the kids. Most of her tasks were purely administrative, directing staff or teachers, handling office affairs or scheduling.

In most cases that she bumped into a student, it was just to greet them in the hallway or answer a question if they had one for her. The kids really felt like they could talk with her. It helped that she was one of the youngest faculty at the school. They saw her more as an older sister.

She was very helpful when Rick Wallace had a sensitive matter at play.

Despite being an experienced and credentialed guidance counselor, there were certain situations where a woman's touch was needed. Despite Rick's own grandfatherly persona, when a feminine issue was one of the concerns, Barbara Fletcher was easier for them to open up to.

In Ellen Taylor's case, the situation at the Spirit Week rally was only the latest and most conspicuous. As a freshman, she was new to the student body. Rick had little knowledge about her deeper emotions or history. Even after contacting his colleague in the middle school, Rick found that she was unaware of anything specific where Ellen was concerned.

Ellen eventually revealed to Barbara that a lot of the freshmen were now calling her "Mudbra" after the mishap at the rally. She wouldn't name anyone specifically however.

They offered to let her out of the rally games, but she quickly shot them down.

She was very concerned about the repercussions of stepping down, that the others would only mock her worse. Her absence would draw more unwanted attention.

It was one of the broader issues Rick dealt with as part of his job. Middle school kids are often the most emotionally tumultuous. Much of that early pubescent angst still remained present among the freshmen and sophomores. It's a hard time in life for everyone, but for some it's worse than others.

After she was no longer crying, Ellen began to retreat emotionally, telling Rick and Barbara that she was fine. Eventually she convinced them to release her for her seventh-period class.

Despite what they talked about, Rick could see that there were clearly many other problems just under the surface. He would need to follow-up eventually once he decided on the right approach.

It was a tricky calculus, because you can't just call a kid's parents and ask them what's wrong. There's a high likelihood of shutting them down from ever talking to you again. It may also be the case that one or both parents are part of the problem. Calling them could make the kid's life tremendously worse.

He was already considering asking her to sit down with him and/or Barbara again at some point in the future, to try to establish an ongoing dialogue. She may open up more eventually.

Rick Wallace explained all of this in simple and discretionary terms for Bob Melkonian, the bottom line being to leave her out of the limelight. Even if she wins Homecoming Queen, make her celebration short and sweet.

Bob was extremely moved and saddened by the situation. He felt ashamed of his shortsightedness, not realizing the accident at the rally might have had a longer chain of effects. He couldn't help but imagine

Monika going through such a situation and Bob being totally obtuse to it until she broke down one day.

"So that's all I'm asking," Rick ended his explanation.

"Yeah Rick, of course." Bob crossed his arms. "Poor girl, I had no idea."

***

Darren and Jennifer were settling in at one of the banquet tables. It was on the far side of the column, just one row back from the staircase to stage right. She'd be getting called up at least once this evening, so she suggested a table where she could easily move without bumping into anyone.

The others agreed readily, in part because their table was also one of the closest to the kitchen, meaning they'd probably get served first.

Despite Brendan and Sheena, they didn't arrive late. Only about half of the tables were filled up when they walked in.

Jennifer had gotten more than a few whistles when the ballroom noticed her. Her dress was regal and she filled it out quite beautifully. Darren wore a tie and vest that matched the navy blue. The color scheme worked well for their baby blue eyes too.

She removed the Victorian-looking shawl and hung it carefully over her seat. In truth, the accessory only had to last through the yearbook photo (if she won). Otherwise, it would live on the chair through most of the night, especially when they were dancing.

She pulled on Darren's hand, saying they should mingle. A little extra face time wouldn't hurt with the voters. Darren agreed, and they began networking, stopping by various groups of people scattered around the ballroom.

It really didn't feel too much like campaigning, Jenny was fairly personable when she passed people in the halls. At the same time, Darren didn't think she needed to go through the effort. Many of the dancers they bumped into overtly mentioned they'd be voting for her.

Early on they found Marcus and Janice. She wore a soft bubblegum pink dress, and he was matching her with the vest and tie. As an "on theme" accessory though, he flipped out a top hat and placed it on his head. Janice rolled her eyes.

"I just know he is going to toss it at me at some point." She eyed the hat like a proximity mine.

"Who knows what could happen?" He bobbed his head toward her. "You just gotta be sure to catch it."

"He means on my head, like this is Vaudeville or something," she elaborated.

"Mhm, and you can do it too," he agreed.

"You're going to land it in a punch bowl or salad dressing, goofy ass." She shook her head.

"You going to be catching something too?" Janice asked Darren.

"Probably not." Darren chuckled. "You can't throw a shawl that far."

"The only place I'm throwing it is in the back of my closet." Jennifer scratched a shoulder as though it were still bothering her. "Basically until the next time I need it for a costume party."

"The real party isn't starting until nine though, isn't it?" Janice asked them.

"I think so?" Jennifer turned to Darren.

"We'll be back to open the doors by nine, for sure," he confirmed. "Whether or not Jimmy's passed out."

"Just get that boy a hamburger," Marcus said. "I'll probably need one too depending on how much of the 'fancy' food they give us."

"Same." Jennifer chuckled. "Well, I'll see you soon."

"You too." Marcus snapped a finger and they turned back to their table.

After a bit more mingling, Jenny and Darren bumped into the competition, Chelsea Morton and Greg Henshaw.

"Hey guys, how's it going?" Chelsea had a perky grin on her face.

"Going well," Jennifer returned the pleasantry.

"Great job last night," Greg said to Darren. "You guys were so close."

"Yeah." Darren waved a hand. "They can have it. We'll probably go farther than them in the finals this year anyway. They just got a few lucky catches."

"You guys look really great," Jennifer marveled at their wardrobe.

"Oh, I know." Chelsea laughed. "So glad *that's* over."

The clothes everyone wore on the floats were usually more on the costume side of the continuum rather than actual clothes you might actually wear to a school dance.

The time period that Chelsea and Greg had to pay tribute to was so much more medieval than everyone else. Rather than go back one or two centuries, they were dressed half a millennium out of date. They (quite fittingly) looked like they'd escaped from a Renaissance fair ... or perhaps an insane asylum.

Now they were wearing something much more normal. To pay light homage to the theme, they'd chosen apricot orange as their main color. Similar to Jenny, Chelsea was wearing a high waist dress with thin straps. She wore her sable-colored hair up.

"Oh, I've got to show you my earrings." Chelsea pressed one forward with the back of her hand so that she could tilt it under the lights. The light green gem sparkled brilliantly with its complex cut. They matched her eyes.

"Oh, peridot. They're lovely," Jennifer said.

"They're my birthstone." Chelsea squeezed Greg's arm. "He got them for me back in August."

"Good selection." Darren nodded, seeing how genuinely happy she looked. Greg had clearly done something right.

"It was the least I could do." Greg shrugged.

"Well, we're going to keep mingling," Jenny said. "Great seeing you two."

"Later," Chelsea said as they strolled off in the other direction.

"'Least he could do?'" Jennifer whispered to Darren. "Talk about setting a high bar."

"Those earrings definitely didn't look cheap," Darren said.

"G-o-l-d-d-i-g-g-e-r." Jenny sang the words.

Darren chuckled to himself as they moved on through the dance hall.

That's when he noticed something out of the corner of his eye. Someone was entering through the left doors and moving loosely in their direction.

"Son of a bitch," Darren growled under his breath.

It was Blake Samuels. Not only had he shown up to the dance in the first place, but he had brought along the girl he had cheated on Jennifer with.

Darren had a small debate with himself on what they should do. Blake wouldn't actually walk up to them, would he?

He clenched a fist. They were going to be stuck in the same place together for a few hours no matter what.

Jenny had actively ignored his existence over the past few months, but he still went to Villa Vista. He was always lurking around someplace, like mold clinging to the walls.

This was the first time the girl was here though. Whether or not she had known Blake was already a thing with someone, she found out when Jenny discovered them. That betrayal clearly didn't seem to matter to her.

Darren had to at least give Jenny a heads-up first.

He put his hand on her shoulder, leading them to one of the side hallways.

"What is it?" she asked him.

"I want to show you something," he said, thinking on his feet.

At the very least, they could avoid the asshole until everyone was seated.

He led her through one of the connection corridors that bordered the gym. There was a temporary plastic wall covering over the doors that led out onto the basketball court. To their right were the new locker rooms and bathrooms.

While the locker rooms were not technically usable, since the new locker cabinets hadn't arrived yet, everything else was available. Having the gym bathrooms open again had significantly cut down the lines for all the other toilets in the school.

They passed through the other set of double doors. They were in the school atrium. Hallways branched out in four directions on each floor. No one was around, the classroom section of the building was almost empty.

"Have you ever been here at night before?" Darren asked her.

She rolled her eyes. "I guess only during football games or school dances."

"No, no," Darren elaborated. "Not at the school as a whole, but here by the classrooms."

Jennifer thought back, but no specific instance came to mind.

"Maybe once after cheer practice?" she said. "Like if I forgot a book in my locker or something."

Darren guided her up one of the stairwells.

"But it wasn't *that* late," he continued. "They lock up this side by 6:00 p.m. on most nights."

"Why do you know that?" She raised an eyebrow.

"Would you believe me if I told you I'd broken into the school before?" Darren asked her.

"You broke into the school?" she repeated, thinking this was the set up for a joke.

"It's true." He looked down at her from the top step, waiting for her to catch up.

She reached his level, then smiled.

"Go on." She was intrigued by this sideline.

"You don't want me to." He strolled forward. "Because it was for a really dumb reason."

"No, I definitely want to hear this now." She walked past him, beating him to the railing of the atrium.

"Well ..." he said. "It was in our freshman year, during like March or something. It was right before the midterm report cards got sent out."

"Okay," she said, placing herself back in that time.

"I wasn't doing too well in Mr. Bernard's Geometry class. I'd pulled a C- in the Fall Semester and really needed to boost my grades or I'd have to take summer school."

"Ugh." Jennifer shuddered in disgust. She wasn't the best at math in general, but Mr. Bernard in particular was a terrible teacher.

"I know, he sucked," Darren agreed. "But what was the one good thing about his class that helped everyone survive it?"

She thought hard, un-repressing memories she'd filed away.

"He let you bring a cheat sheet," Darren answered.

"Oh, that's right. One piece of printer paper, and you could write as small as you want to fit any tables or formulas or graphs or notes."

"And I had done just that. For two weeks I worked on the most densely packed quick reference guide that my stupid fifteen-year-old mind could assemble. It was the third version and I kid you not, I got the thing laminated."

"No you didn't." She shoved him a little.

"I absolutely did." He blushed. "My biggest fear was that I was going to spill water or Coke or Mountain Dew or something and completely destroy it before Mr. Bernard's midterm test."

"Not only would it help me during the test," Darren continued. "But it was also my study tool. The cypher through which all the mysteries of math would be revealed to me."

"Oh my god ..." She chuckled.

"It's true." He led her to one of the Freshman Class hallways on the northwest side of the building.

"The test was on Monday, and I had all weekend to study. But on Friday, when I opened up my backpack after dinner, the cheat sheet was gone. I had left it in my locker."

"You went through the trouble of laminating it but you didn't make copies?" Jennifer asked.

"Jenny, I was almost failing math, obviously there was some flawed logic at play."

"And with that flawed logic, you decided that the only solution was to break into the school and retrieve it from your locker ..."

"Yes," he had to admit.

"So, it was later, maybe eight-thirty or nine," Darren began. "I got to the school fence on my bike, but left it there out of view of the cameras. I walked into the faculty parking lot wearing a USF hoodie with some khaki pants and dress shoes."

"You just had those lying around?"

"My brother almost went to USF. He got the hoodie and everything, but then Uncle Sam got to him. I don't think he's ever worn it."

"And all the other stuff?" she asked.

"It was so I would look like one of the faculty, at least on shitty surveillance cameras. Remember, they hadn't done most of the renovations yet."

"But what about your face? I'm sure the cameras were still good enough to see that."

"You mean *Johnson's* face."

"Who?"

"President Johnson, LBJ. We went as the *Point Break* characters for Halloween one year, I've got all the masks. Johnson's looked the least cartoony."

"Okay, now I don't believe you again."

Darren stopped halfway down the Freshman Class hallway. He offered her his hand.

"Sit down."

She folded her dress and they sat against the lower lockers, facing Mr. Nordquist's World History classroom.

"So, I walked through the parking lot and did a little performance where I felt against the door handle of one of the parked cars, like it was *my* car and I left my keys inside. After that I headed for the building. It's important to remember that this is before the remodels, because most of them have been fixed now."

"Most of what?" Jenny asked, invested again.

"The door frames," Darren said. "The old door frames were just wide enough that you could squeeze a metal coat hanger down and pop the latch, even if the door was locked."

Jenny's eyes opened a bit wider, trying to remember how they were. She looked over at him.

"You're being serious," she said in amazement. "It was *that* easy to break in?"

"Well, I had to put on a good show outside."

"What about the new doors?"

"It doesn't work on those. The frames are different and they have a double latch. At the time though, that only kept me out of the Performing Arts Center, and the doors between wings of the building were still the old ones."

"Wow," she said, still a bit shocked.

"So, I popped the door by the gymnasium, because there were the least number of cameras. There was only one angle I had to hide the coat hanger from. After that, I only had to pop the connecting door between the gym hallway and atrium, the same one we just walked through."

"Okay." She rested her head on her knees.

"I only had one obstacle left. I had to cover up the camera, so they couldn't see which locker I was opening."

"They would have caught you red-handed."

Darren pointed to their left. Up near the corner of the hallway was a black dome security camera facing down the length of the corridor. There was another one just like it on the other side of the hallway.

"That used to be where the only camera was. And it was an older model, the plastic box with a lens on the front," Darren explained. "I used the same coat hanger, but tied one of those drawstring cinch bags to it, so it would hang over the camera."

"Wow," Jenny said, impressed but also a bit curious why he was telling her any of this.

Darren looked down between them, at locker #463. He tapped the door. It made a soft metal thud as it pressed against the frame.

"This was it. Once I got the cheat sheet, I recovered the bag and coat hanger and slipped out the way I came."

"And no one stopped you?" Jenny asked.

"I was pretty familiar with the guard rotation." Darren glanced away from her.

"Why is that?" she asked, her voice quieter.

"Because it wasn't the first time I'd broken into the school," he admitted.

"That seemed obvious, considering how smoothly the operation went."

Darren rested his head back against the metal locker. "To be honest, I was pretty angry about a lot of things that year.

"Whenever someone pissed me off, like really did something to mess with me, I'd break into their locker and steal some stuff. After a few days,

I'd return it discreetly. I'd leave a typed-up note with some stupid edgy shit like 'play nice' taped on the outside."

Jenny chuckled a bit.

"When did you stop?" she asked.

"The last time was in our sophomore year, right at the beginning, like September. It was just once to this kid who'd been telling lies about me to some of the others in our class. But I didn't like it, and I never did it again. It was just too much."

There was a long pause as he waited for Jenny to give any final judgments for his confession.

"We all make mistakes," she told him. "At least you were able to undo some of yours."

Darren turned his head toward her, his old locker being the only thing that separated them.

"I really wish you hadn't left the carpool."

"Me too," she whispered. They joined in the middle with a tender kiss, then leaned against each other.

They sat there for a long minute before Darren spoke up again.

"I should warn you. I saw Blake ... he brought that girl with him."

A heavy sigh left Jenny and she sunk down a little bit.

"I know."

"I've done a lot of bad things in my life. But I would never do that."

"I know." Her voice lifted a bit.

"Oh, I almost forgot to show you!" Darren perked up.

"Another locker?" she joked.

"No, no ..." Darren helped her to her feet.

He led her down the rest of the hallway, away from the atrium, to the far corner of the building. There was a window at the end of it, separating the north-facing classrooms from one of the west-facing rooms.

"Whenever I did come up here, for whatever reason, I would always stop at this window at least once."

Jenny followed him up to the glass and immediately saw what he meant.

From their vantage point on the second floor, they could look out over all of Alexandria. The slope of the town dropped down into Drakes Bay. At the far extent of the peninsula was the Point Reyes Lighthouse. The houses and street lights glowed peacefully in the evening fog, creating pools of illumination. The historic beacon shining above it all was like the star atop a Christmas tree.

"It's beautiful." Jenny leaned toward the glass.

"It's one of the best views of the town. There are too many trees by the highway to see it all any better."

"I'm glad you shared it with me," she said, a double meaning to her words.

"Me too," Darren agreed.

They gazed over Alexandria, taking in the view before finally turning back for the atrium.

As they left the hallway, and that part of their conversation, Jenny had to ask one more question about Darren's escapades.

"So, did you come up with the coat hanger thing all on your own?"

"What?" he said in surprise. "No, I wish I were that clever. My brother told me about it when he was still in high school. A few people knew about it back then too, so it wasn't the biggest secret."

Darren chuckled. "Probably one of the reasons they've been replacing the doors, and adding more cameras."

That did reassure Jennifer. The renovations were basically done, all the doorframes should be corrected now.

They walked into the gymnasium corridor, through a new set of double doors. The fire escape to their left was also brand new. It had a panic-bar door handle, but with a modern frame.

"So, any idea how much food we're getting with our dinners?" Darren asked. "I don't think we can fit the limo in a drive-thru."

"No idea." She smiled. "You'd have to ask someone on the Student Council."

As Darren and Jennifer entered the ballroom once more, a familiar voice rose above the Daft Punk music playing in the background.

On the other side of the table, Camellia pointed toward the couple and the voice went silent.

He stood up from his chair, with his date following after.

Even without football pads, the black suit hung on broad shoulders. A red tie accented a charcoal grey vest. A simple red rose boutonniere was pinned to the lapel.

His shoulder-length black hair was washed and trimmed, the curls neatly combed back behind his ears. His dark brown eyes looked at the couple as a smile crossed his face.

"There he is." Joe Torelli took Darren into a big bear hug. Darren hugged him back, really having no other choice in the matter.

Joe slapped the side of his neck, something he usually only did when they were wearing their gear.

"You two starting the night early?" He winked. It seemed like Joe meant to whisper that to Darren, but he didn't change the volume of his voice at all. Luckily Jenny was distracted, talking to Isabella.

"No, nothing like that," Darren played off.

"Well good. You gotta save something for the afterparty. Don't want to end up whiskey-dick like Jimmy."

Darren wasn't even going to follow that line of conversation.

"Everything work out with the Camaro?"

"Oh yeah! Tito came through, the ride was amazing. We took a quick trip to Bodega Bay."

"Whew, fifty miles around."

"Yeah, and the ride handled it beautifully. 45th Anniversary edition, all new features, it was a thrill." Joe was buzzing. "Iz, wasn't the ride great?"

Isabella turned towards them, connecting the conversations. "Oh my god, yes. We drove so fast, my head was spinning!"

The fast driving made sense, Joe being in this good of a mood after what happened last night did not.

Before Darren could say any more, Mr. Mel and Mr. Wallace walked back to center stage and told everyone to take their seats.

Joe threw an arm over Isabella and the other one over Darren's shoulders. Darren looked down and noticed that Joe's fingers and knuckles were covered in deep cuts. They weren't old scars. These wounds were new, barely scabbed over, let alone healed.

"Woo, time to celebrate!" Joe said, as he walked them back to their table.

SEVEN

ONE LAST DANCE

THE TOP OF THE LEXUS was still retracted when Niles and Laura pulled into the VVHS parking lot. One of the far corners had not one, but four limousines parked in waiting.

The more affordable limousine packages usually booked a "to trip" and "return trip" time slot for their customers. To literally reserve them for the entire night, where they were parked waiting through a whole dance, was quite the purchase.

A slight sense of embarrassment passed through Niles. Maybe he should have saved up more to join some limo group. He felt better when they actually pulled into a space and the polished red Lexus drew a few eyes.

He got out and circled around to Laura, opening the door for her. With a gentle hand, he guided her out of the car nice and formal-like. As she composed herself, he went back to the driver's side and pulled his top hat out of its dedicated box. He then picked up the decorative vanity mirror and held it up to make sure the hat was sitting right.

Once Niles was satisfied, he dropped the mirror into the half-seat and pressed the "lock" button on the key fob. The hard-top roof slid back into place and the doors clicked. A satisfying blink of the tail lights confirmed that the car was secure.

"Please be okay, please no one back into you," he prayed, somewhat to the car and somewhat to a higher power.

After that, he offered his arm to Laura and they walked into the Murphy Center.

The ballroom was a bit busy, but there were still a few open tables. Of course, their seats should already be saved.

A girl stood up from one of the tables near the entrance doors. It was Anne Kirkpatrick. She was wearing a royal blue dress. Laura walked ahead of Niles to hug her. They then marveled at what each other was wearing.

In contrast to Laura, Anne's dress wasn't anything historical at all. After a cursory glance over the dance floor, Niles could see that most people weren't wearing anything different than any other dance.

He sighed to himself. Even his somewhat subtle approach stood out. Maybe not as much as Mr. Mel or Wallace, but on the floor itself, he felt silly.

He approached the table, pulling out what was presumably his chair. With Anne and Laura chatting, he greeted Liam Connelly.

Liam was wearing a royal blue vest, similar to Anne's dress. The suit itself was black, as was the dress shirt. To accent those, he wore a white tie with a subtle herringbone pattern.

"Hey," Niles said, taking his seat.

"Nice hat," was Liam's response.

"Of course," Niles thought to himself.

The worst part about the hat was that there wasn't really anyplace he could put it. Either it remained on his head or he'd have to take it back to the car. If he put it on the table, it was 100% going to get spilled on or ruined somehow and Niles would lose his deposit. Same thing if he tried to hang it on the chair and it inevitably fell off.

Liam turned back to the others at the table, reengaging with some conversation they were already having. One of the guys leaned back in his chair, revealing that they had another special guest with them, Melissa Levitt.

"Great," Niles thought to himself. They had both of the royals to deal with.

Melissa was talking to no one in particular. She just spoke and expected others to listen to her. Her own date, Ryan Lewis, was just sitting along with the others, listening to Melissa yammer on about how much she hated the Spirit Week games.

"It is just so stupid that we need to play at all," she complained. "Shouldn't there be like an all-star team that the classes pick? Not, ugh, us."

Liam shrugged in detached agreement.

"Like, Liam had to eat a caramel-covered onion and do that stupid crab walk."

"Took forever to brush the taste out," he muttered.

"The whole setup for Homecoming is dumb," Ryan Lewis added. "Like, why even do the float thing either?"

"I know, they were so lame," Melissa said.

Niles winced; he glanced over to see if Laura had heard that. She and Anne still seemed to be wrapped up in their own discussion.

Melissa also glanced at Laura and Niles. The next thing she said was whispered to Ryan, which gave him a good laugh.

Niles started to steam, thinking back on all the painting he did, all the nails he drove into the wooden frame to make Laura's best approximation of the French palace.

He sat back in his chair. He didn't have to engage with these people. They were only sitting there circumstantially anyway. Once the dance was over, Liam would probably slip out to Jimmy's place or likely to some smaller, more private party.

A weight hung over Niles that he didn't really have a fleshed-out plan for the afterparty. He assumed Laura would want to go wherever Anne was going. So, he may be stuck with all of them for quite a while regardless.

Laura was his bridge into their world anyway, he just needed to wait for her to engage in the conversation and things would be smoother.

***

Raf and Elise's limousine group had found a great table on the east side of the ballroom, just adjacent to the dance floor.

It was perfect, Raf thought to himself. He could sweep Elise off her seat and get moving to a song whenever the moment was right.

Elise had been such a breath of fresh air for him. He'd always liked chatting up the ladies, but his last real relationship was just a train wreck of poor decisions.

Mary Green was a caustic person who was never satisfied with anything. If he got her the wrong flowers, she was upset about it. If he took her to the wrong restaurant, she'd be sour the rest of the day. No matter how many times he tried to get it right, she always found fault somewhere.

Raf didn't think he was a bad guy. He lived to please, but she was never happy!

Elise was the complete opposite. When she wanted something, she said it in plain, direct language.

She wanted peacock feathers in her corsage? Bam, done.

She wanted to get lunch at Surf'N'Bird to try out their new teriyaki chicken sandwich? Delicious, great day.

She wanted to double date with Blaire and Andrei to hit up a movie? Planned. *Wizard of Oz*, 3D, Emerald City, life was a yellow brick road.

And after all of that, what does she do?

"Thank you, Raf, I love it!"

"We definitely have to come back here next summer when it's beach weather."

"That was so crazy and colorful!"

Always happy, always smiling, always appreciative.

If the girls weren't doing their own thing, he'd be talking with her right now, making her smile some more. But he wasn't lying dormant either.

Elise had given him a mission, some fact finding. Because she may have had an Icarus moment and played a little too close to the sun. Luckily, Raf was up to the task.

"And so, my brother Danny is just making a total ass of himself," he continued, all the guys of their limo group were off to one side of the table. "He thinks he's going to be all clever and get Rosa to stand in front of the pool so he can bump her in. But he pulled that same trick at my party last year!"

"Uh oh!" Mark Schlesinger said, gearing up for the payoff.

"So, Rosa, who is not only smarter than him, but vindictive as hell, gets *him* to go grab the cooler instead. Then as soon as he turns the corner, BAM, right in his head with the foam noodle."

Jeremy Wilson burst out laughing.

"Now the whole cooler, and a bag of ice, and dumbass Danny were all in the pool. You know who had to run to the store to get more ice? It sure wasn't Rosa."

"Awe man." Paxton chuckled.

"That's the great thing about having a summer birthday," Raf said. "Everyone goes in the pool, one way or another."

"Better than me," Mark said. "You can't do anything in April. Everyone's stressed out about end of the year finals, or they're too busy with sports or the Spring Musical."

"What about you Andrei?" Raf asked.

Andrei swallowed the water he'd been drinking. "Oh, me? February. It's okay, I guess. I never really threw any big bashes like that anyway."

"So, you're eighteen now?" Raf raised an eyebrow.

"No, seventeen," Andrei corrected.

"What? No way." Raf waved a hand. "So, we're the same age, plus or minus six months?"

"I guess so?" He chuckled at the absurdity.

Raf took a sip from his own water.

Finally, the girls were done with their talk about make-up or something, and the couples started going out to jam a bit on the dance floor.

Andrei led Blaire off into the fray.

He had really good moves, surprisingly good for someone more on the classical side of the music spectrum. Guess Los Angeles had left some kind of mark on him. A bit of Sunset Boulevard was in there somewhere.

Raf and Elise were the only two left at the table.

"So?" she asked as soon as they were alone.

"Seventeen," he answered.

"Shit!" Elise said, almost loud enough to draw eyes. She adjusted her volume. "So much for technicalities ..."

"You really think Blaire would take things that far ... and tonight?" Raf asked.

"I mean ... I wouldn't have thought so an hour ago. But I didn't expect her to agree to Jimmy's place either! Are you picking up any vibes from Andrei?"

"Are you kidding? Dude is like a statue. Unless he says something explicitly, I have no idea what he's thinking."

"Ohh ..." Elise moaned, burying her face in her hands.

"Hey, hey, it's okay." Raf put his hand on her back.

"I did go too far," Elise lamented. "Blaire was a sweet innocent child and I dragged her into a candy store. Now she's all whacked out on sugar and I can't stop what's happening!"

"Wait, but, just ..." Raf searched for the right words. "Do *you* want to go to Jimmy's place?"

Elise blushed, looking both embarrassed and confused.

"W-what?"

"No, wait," Raf corrected, backtracking. "I mean, literally, if you don't feel comfortable going to Jimmy's we don't have to."

"Oh no, I absolutely have to go now. We cannot let her go in there alone! Who knows what could happen?"

"Well, that's my point. What could happen?"

Elise seemed uncertain of his meaning, so he continued.

"Blaire is a big girl. What you did-" he corrected himself, sharing the blame that Elise was feeling. "What *we* did was the right thing. So far Andrei has proved himself to be a good guy. He's a friend, we need to have some faith in both of them to make the right decision for themselves."

Elise stared out over the centerpiece on the table.

Raf put his hand on her cheek and turned her head toward the dance floor. "Look at them."

Blaire and Andrei were full on clubbing to "Alive" by Empire of the Sun.

Her face had one of the biggest smiles Elise had ever seen on it.

"You did that for her," Raf said. "Not only did you bring her here tonight, but you found someone who genuinely seems to care about her as much as she cares about him."

It really *was* an unbelievable sight.

"Now, I agree that we should probably go with them to Jimmy's. Because things can get crazy, and neither of them have been there before."

Jimmy O'Shaughnessy was sitting just two tables away and he already looked absolutely wasted. Although that was sort of his natural state to begin with. It was easy to get him drunk, but a lot harder to get him to pass out. Plenty of people had tried, some for fun and others to swipe stuff from the house. Jimmy never really seemed to care either way, and he'd always outlast them.

The song died down, changing into something else. Blaire and Andrei stopped moving, struck by a short wave of self-consciousness. Then the next song came on.

Raf touched Elise's hand and she turned away from the two.

"That all sound okay?"

She nodded.

"You wanna dance?"

She smiled, standing up with him.

***

"Alright, alright, enough with this industrial bongo banging." Mr. Melkonian walked back to center stage in his ridiculous British aristocrat getup.

"That's right," Mr. Wallace agreed, wearing a Teddy Roosevelt costume. "Welcome one and all to the Villa Vista High School High Society Homecoming Dance!"

Darren began to tune out while the two went on into some kind of bit, talking about the four class themes and some obvious jokes between their characters. Most of the actual content they were communicating was in the little programs left at each of their seats anyway, such as the schedule for the evening.

Darren couldn't help but glance over at Joe a few times. He covered this by making it look like he was looking at Jenny. She was sitting next to Isabella, and Torelli was next to her.

Joe was talking to Isabella almost non-stop, cracking little jokes in her ear and keeping her laughing. Darren tried to inconspicuously glance over her too, make sure she didn't show any marks or bruising.

The scratches on Joe's knuckles were more than a little worrying.

He had seen Joe dry-knuckle a punching bag before. That's where many of the older scars came from in the first place. These didn't look the same though. The cuts were more pronounced, not just split skin from a body bag. Could he have been punching trees?

Isabella didn't seem wounded at all, so the tree theory was rising in rank.

So, was that it? He spent the night punching trees until his knuckles were bloody, pumping enough endorphins into his system to blot out losing the game?

"Maybe," Darren thought to himself, but even then, he didn't feel satisfied by the explanation.

On stage, Mr. Melkonian, still affecting a silly British accent, said it was time to announce the results of Spirit Week.

"All of you did extremely well this year," he opened. "Each class shined brilliantly in certain portions of the competition. Please understand that the point totals were close."

It was an unusually ingratiating leading statement, Darren thought to himself. After mostly playing the mean foil to Mr. Wallace all night, Melkonian now sounded like he was protecting someone's feelings. The fourth-place class must have done *really* badly.

"In fourth place is the Junior Class," Melkonian announced, dropping the British accent as much as he could without abandoning the character completely.

An audible groan washed over the floor. It wasn't really a shock, but more begrudging acceptance.

He whispered in Jenny's ear: "Damn, even *they* knew it went that badly."

Jenny nodded in agreement.

The class behind them was not very spirited in any sense. They came in last place when Jenny was the Sophomore Class Princess too. Of course, at the time, she thought it was because they were freshmen. The class usually ranked low in the games just by nature of being the "rookies".

"In third place," Melkonian continued. "We have the Sophomore Class."

There was much more surprise in the noise that filled the ballroom.

Even with their ridiculous Renaissance float, and a decent showing during Spirit Week, it wasn't enough to elevate them.

"Our first and second place classes came neck-and-neck," Melkonian announced, his accent getting thicker again as the news was more positive. "While one class showed off their creativity during the float parade, the other class proved themselves in the fires of competition."

"Don't you mean the *mud* of competition?" a voice said from the crowd, filling the dramatic pause that Melkonian had left silent.

"Ooh ..." Jenny shuddered, as more than a bit of laughter rose up in the room.

"No. No more of that!" Melkonian yelled, dropping the British voice completely.

The crowd quieted down.

Someone from the sound booth followed his cue, playing a drum roll sound effect to move past the interruption.

"The winner of this year's Spirit Week is ... The Senior Class!" he announced.

"Yeah!" Joe yelled from the other side of the table as the Murphy Center erupted into cheering.

On the far side of the room, Marcus Johnson's table encouraged him to stand up. After just a bit of nudging, he did, striking poses for the tables around him.

"Get up," Darren said to Jenny.

"What? No." She shook her head.

"Stand up girl!" Ashley Stillwell said. Now the whole table and several others nearby were looking at her.

Jennifer rolled her eyes and stood up. She matched Marcus' current pose, putting one heel on the chair and flexing her biceps.

The noise in the room doubled as everyone faced her. Of course, her table was cheering the loudest, much of that coming from Darren and also Joe for some reason.

The flex she gave was more than a little impressive, her biceps and traps really tightening up. Darren sometimes forgot how physically demanding cheerleading was. Jenny was often one of the bases when they were doing formations. She was picking up chicks all the time and the results showed.

Once the noise died down, Marcus and Jennifer took their seats again.

"Don't get too comfortable," Mr. Wallace said to them in his Teddy Roosevelt voice. "You'll be joining us in just a moment, because now it's time to bring up this year's Homecoming Court!"

He pulled out a set of notes.

"First up, we have the Freshman Class Prince, Enrique Rodriguez!" Wallace announced.

A decent amount of applause rose in the room as he walked onto the stage. One table in particular chanted, "Ricky, Ricky, Ricky, Ricky!"

"Next, we have the Freshman Class Princess, Ellen Taylor."

A similar amount of applause greeted her, but there was a slight hesitation. Over on stage left, Melkonian was giving a stink eye to the crowd, just waiting for someone to pull another stunt.

Jennifer felt bad for the girl. Ellen really didn't look like she wanted to be on stage at all. She was dressed in an emerald green gown and had worn her hair down for the night. A lot of it covered her face.

"For our Sophomore Class Prince, we have Gregory Henshaw."

A much larger group of people cheered as Greg walked on stage.

"With him as Sophomore Class Princess, we have Chelsea Morton."

Again, the group cheered as she joined him from stage right. As soon as she took position, she leaned in and kissed him on the cheek.

The crowd went crazy, followed by hoots and whistles.

Melkonian leaned in from stage left, eyeing them as a warning.

"She's good," Jenny whispered to Darren.

"Oh, I doubt that," Darren replied. "I'm sure you're a *much* better kisser."

Jenny flicked his chest with the linen napkin.

"Now we have the Junior Class Prince, Liam Connelly," Wallace continued.

Liam stood up from a table on the other side of the room and strolled into place from stage left. A small, but vocal cluster of cheering rose from a certain batch of tables.

"With him is the Junior Class Princess, Melissa Levitt."

The same group cheered as Melissa got up from apparently the same table and followed him on stage.

"Finally," Mr. Wallace continued, still using his Teddy Roosevelt voice. "We have the Senior Class Prince, Marcus Johnson."

A big portion of the crowd cheered again, same as when they were flexing.

"With him is the Senior Class Princess, Jennifer Maxwell."

"Good luck!" Darren said, helping her lay the Victorian shawl over her shoulders.

Jenny climbed the short flight of stairs onto the stage. She did her best approximation of a runway walk, swinging her hips just a bit more than usual. As she passed in front of Marcus, he put his hand up. Without missing a beat, she high-fived it with a hard slap.

A chant of "SEN-IORS, SEN-IORS, SEN-IORS," echoed through the crowd.

Darren thought to himself, "She should have left the shawl, showing off her arms would have even better results."

"I don't think there's much more to be said," Mr. Wallace closed. "Please check your selection for Homecoming King & Queen and your votes will be collected."

There were two cards located on everyone's bread and appetizer plate. The spares had been picked up with empty place settings when the announcements began. They tried to minimize the chances of ballot stuffing.

Darren marked the boxes for Jennifer and Marcus on their respective cards, then dropped them in the container one of the waiters was holding.

The princes and princesses deposited their own cards as they exited the stage and returned to their seats.

Jennifer stopped in front of her chair, pulling the cream-colored fabric from her neck.

"And that is the end of Mr. Shawl." She draped it over the backrest. It was condemned to sit there for the remainder of the night.

"He's not showing up in any pictures?" Darren asked.

"I don't think so." She shook her head. "Too itchy."

"Are we getting in line for pictures?" Camellia asked the group.

"What? No," Joe groaned in disappointment. "The music is just starting, let's dance a bit!"

"I don't know about you guys," Sheena added, "but I want to get the pictures done now in case my dress gets messed up."

"She's got a point," Brendan agreed. "Let's take the pics now, then we can jam."

"That alright with you?" Darren asked Jenny.

"Yeah, Sheena's right," she replied.

Isabella turned to Joe, "We'll be back down soon."

"It's fine," Joe snapped, several decibels above where he should have been talking.

Isabella turned away, putting on a fake expression and following the other girls.

Darren guided Jennifer over to the other side of him as they trailed to the back of the group.

"Hey, something's up with Torelli," Darren warned her. "Keep your distance from him, alright?"

"I need your help to watch out for Isabella too," Jenny said. "Did you see his knuckles?"

"I know." Darren nodded.

***

Blaire had already gotten quite a bit of dancing time out of the actual dance. In fact, in retrospect she looked absolutely ridiculous. She didn't even recognize anything she was dancing to, she was just grooving back and forth to the beat, trying to match whatever Andrei was doing.

Andrei, though modest in setting expectations, picked up the rhythm as soon as they were in the crowd of people.

Blaire needed a cool down after watching all that, so she jumped at the idea of taking pictures first when Amanda suggested it. That way it was all taken care of and she could focus on ... other things ... the rest of the night.

It was a bit surreal actually, the photographer was set up in the Choir & Drama Rehearsal Room on the second floor. In the hallway, they could still hear the music coming through the floor and walls from the ballroom below.

They were in a pretty good position in line, there were only a few groups ahead of them. A lot of people were making the same wise choice of getting pictures before the meals came.

Blaire & Andrei were at the back of the line, behind Elise & Raf and the others from their limo.

A few minutes after they arrived, a second group lined up behind them. It was composed mostly of other juniors. Two of them in particular had gotten a lot of attention during the dance, Melissa Levitt and Liam Connelly.

On the list of fellow juniors that Blaire talked to, they were probably right down at the very bottom. Melissa was this obnoxious creature of plastic and silicon who never seemed to have a nice word for anyone. It made a lot of sense that everyone else in their group looked miserable too.

Liam Connelly was famously high and mighty, too good for the rest of them, let alone the school as a whole. This was less annoying than Melissa, who did think she was above it all, but was also vainglorious enough that she needed everyone else to acknowledge her superiority.

Neither of their dates seemed to be taking any pleasure in their company either. Melissa's date, Ryan Lewis, was zoned out, looking through his phone. Meanwhile, Anne Kirkpatrick kept staring at the back of Liam's head expecting him to talk to her.

Behind them were Laura Nakano and this other kid Blaire had seen around. She couldn't place the name. "Neil", maybe? He must have been Laura's date because they were the only two wearing some kind of weird period-piece cosplay.

Laura was particularly cross, giving off this body language like she had caught Neil kissing someone else.

That's when it came to Blaire, Laura was on the Student Council. She was dressed that way because the theme might have been her idea, and the Junior Class completely bombed in the competition.

Blaire didn't remember voting for anyone when they did the Prince/Princess thing in homeroom a few weeks back, but if she did it definitely wasn't for Liam or Melissa. Neither of them looked like they would either give a damn or be capable of succeeding at the Spirit Week games. That proved to be so true. To them it looked like torture having to perform at all. They couldn't just stand there and look cool and have everyone love them.

The Neil guy standing next to Laura seemed to be in a bad mood mostly because she was. He was now at the back of the line instead of Andrei. Occasionally he would open his own phone or try to say something to Laura, but she would give a clipped response and go quiet again.

No one in their group was really speaking to each other at all. It was funny because they hadn't even announced the Homecoming Royalty yet, but Liam and Melissa already seemed to know that they would lose.

After another few minutes, everyone shifted forward. The line was bending around a corner now, so they were actually closer to the people in the back. That's when another group showed up behind Neil.

It was a bunch of jocks and their dates. One jock in particular couldn't be ignored, because he was always so damn loud. Joe Torelli was chatting up the other Varsity Football guys, talking about some random nonsense that she didn't pay attention to.

Among the group was Jimmy O'Shaughnessy, the prince of the party palace himself.

Upon seeing him, Paxton cut out of line and walked up to him. The boys greeted each other with some kind of dude-bro chest bump thing and Paxton let him know that their limo of ten would be on the way over after the dance.

Blaire couldn't believe how real everything felt. She was like a vampire that had been cured, stepping out into sunlight for the first time in ages.

She glanced up at Andrei, who had been listening to something that Raf was telling him.

A slight sense of guilt ran through her. Does Andrei really know what she had gotten them into? What if she was rushing this, would that make him feel uncomfortable? Could that mess up the chances for them down the road?

"You haven't even kissed yet," a nagging voice repeated from the back of her mind.

"That's right," Blaire thought to herself. "One step at a time."

As Paxton walked back to Amanda, the broken-up huddle of varsity jocks revealed who one of the girls was. It was Jennifer Maxwell, the Senior Class Princess.

She had been a killer in the competition during Spirit Week. She was one of the cheerleaders, and had done some other sports too, if Blaire remembered correctly. She probably had the best chance of winning Homecoming Queen in Blaire's opinion.

Even though she was a peppy cheerleader-type, she wasn't a bitch like a lot of the others that ran in those cliques. That alone put her above Melissa Levitt.

Blaire had chosen differently though. For how little she paid attention to the social Olympics that was Homecoming, one thing had stood out to her. The adorable sophomore couple tugged at her heart strings just a little bit. Blaire had a hard time not picturing herself and Andrei when Chelsea kissed Greg on stage.

Her thoughts were interrupted by an obnoxious jock voice. She noticed Joe Torelli take a few steps toward them. He was standing in the crook of the hallway now, addressing everyone that had lined up around the corner.

"... isn't that right everyone?" he said, continuing some conversation he was having. "We've got a knock-out winner on our hands!"

Joe Torelli gestured toward Jennifer, who was now hiding her face in her hand. Her date looked pissed.

"What about you new guy?" Joe said, taking a step toward Andrei. "You voted for Jenny, didn't you?"

"Of course," Andrei said in a calm tone.

Joe's eyes then dropped to Blaire.

There was a reason Joe was quarterback of the Jaguars. They might not win every game, but Joe was a slab of solid muscle. If he didn't play football, he probably could have succeeded in any other sport he set his mind to. He had that kind body and that kind of focus ... except for now that is.

The first thing Blaire noticed when they locked eyes was how bloodshot his were. He had dark eyes, which usually made him look very expressive contrasted against the white. Now though, there were so many visible veins creeping in from the edges that he looked like he just needed to sleep for like twelve hours.

He probably hadn't slept at all the night before, after blowing the Homecoming game.

"And you," he asked. "You voted for Jennifer too?"

"Y-yeah," Blaire agreed. She desperately wished she could put on a poker face like Andrei.

Luckily, Joe's critical thinking was severely impacted at the moment and he accepted her answer at face value.

While everyone was a bit dumbstruck by what Torelli was doing, two people at the front of the line were already making fun of the situation.

"I was going to vote for her," Jeremy said, although not directed at Joe. It was just quiet enough that everyone could hear. "But my vote got intercepted."

Something cracked inside of Torelli and the crazed smile disappeared from his face, turning into a snarl.

Mark Schlesinger, whom Jeremy was actually addressing, was laughing to himself. The two continued their back and forth at a slightly lower volume, seemingly unaware of the fury building inside of the quarterback.

Blaire felt something touch her stomach and almost jumped in surprise.

It was Andrei's arm; he was nudging her back toward the wall. She complied without hesitation. Andrei now stood between the two of them, even though Joe's anger was clearly directed at Jeremy.

Before anything could happen, one of the other girls stepped up and put a hand on Joe's chest. It was apparently his date. She pulled him gently to the back of the line. It took five full seconds before he would take a step backwards, relenting to her.

None of the other jocks said anything to Joe. He just stood there at the back while his date rubbed his chest a bit, trying to calm him down.

Once it seemed like the tension had passed, Andrei turned back toward Blaire.

"Well, that was fun," he said in a quiet voice.

"It's a good thing you voted for Jennifer ..." Blaire whispered back.

Andrei reached into his pocket, revealing two blank voter cards.

"I've only been here a few months," he said. "Didn't think I knew any of them well enough."

"Maybe you could've spent more time getting to know them," Blaire offered.

"My time's better spent elsewhere." He smiled at her.

After an uneventful few minutes, it was finally their turn for photos.

They did the couple shots first. Jeremy & Dina posed, then Mark & Raquel, then Paxton & Amanda. Following them, Elise & Raf were up. They took two normal shots, followed by a silly one where Raf had materialized two pairs of hip-hop style sunglasses, like they were posing for a *Billboard* magazine spread.

Andrei stepped up to the photographer's assistant.

"So, standard package," the man explained. "You get three final shots right away, as well as access to the touched-up files next week, once those have been edited. Everything will have that nice, professional look. You're guaranteed the digital files with your purchase to do with as you wish, but there is the caveat that they will be in the yearbook as well. So just be aware of that."

The guy motioned to something he'd had Andrei download as he was paying for the pictures.

"They'll be on our app as soon as you walk out of here," he explained. "You can download them whenever you want. Then tonight or tomorrow, or next week, you can pick out the prints or commemorative items you'd like to order."

Andrei looked down at Blaire.

"Sounds good," she agreed.

"We'll take it."

Elise and Raf were looking at a computer screen, confirming their shots for the photographer.

Blaire pulled the make-up clamshell out of her purse to make any necessary touch-ups. She certainly didn't want to leave that completely in the hands of the photographers.

"So, what do you want to do for the poses?" Andrei asked.

Blaire thought for a moment, then settled on three she really liked.

Following the flashes, she and Andrei reviewed the little screen.

The first was fairly standard. Blaire put her left hand on his chest, accenting the pink chrysanthemums of their corsage and boutonniere. They added the right flare of color to the center of the frame. For the other two, she wanted to have a bit more personality.

In the second shot, Andrei was leaning her back, with her left hand on his arm. It was like a pose taken in the middle of a waltz.

Finally, a bit of a sillier, if somewhat conventional shot. She was taking hold of his tie, and pulling him down to her level.

"Perfect," Andrei said, more than happy with how they'd turned out.

With that done, the other couples came back into frame. They posed for a picture with all ten of them.

Because of his height, the photographer placed Andrei and Blaire in the center. Elise and Raf were on one side of them and Amanda and Paxton were on the other. It was the Burkes paying for the shot after all.

With that done, they filed out into the hallway to return to the ballroom.

As they passed by, Blaire caught a glance at Joe Torelli. He was no longer at the tail end of the line, but he noticed them regardless. He eyed the group until they were totally out of view.

Blaire sighed. She really wished Jeremy had kept his mouth shut.

EIGHT

WHEN LIGHTNING STRIKES

"THAT WOULD BE my luck," Niles thought, arms crossed over his chest.

Last place. It somehow seemed fitting.

Laura had stood up right after Melkonian made the announcement and disappeared into one of the bathrooms. Curiously, best friend Anne didn't run after her at all.

Niles was now standing in the entrance lobby of the Murphy Center. The nearest restrooms from their table were the ones by the front.

The worst part was that even Mr. Mel seemed to pity them when he announced that they'd come in fourth.

After a very long few minutes, Laura finally appeared. After a bit of crying, she had re-applied some fresh eyeliner.

"Hey," Niles said, walking up to her. "I'm really sorry about what happened."

"Not one of them helped us," Laura said. "The float could have been so much better."

She squeezed the decorative handkerchief she'd brought along.

"Forget them. We did great on our own. We put in the most effort of anyone, we just had to do it alone."

"And look where it got us!" Laura snapped back at him.

"Okay, she's still upset," Niles thought to himself. "As the night goes on, it'll get better."

He followed her back to the table. They were sitting down just as Melissa and Liam were being called on stage for the Homecoming Royalty voting.

Niles pulled out his ballot cards, concealing the writing with his hand. No way in Hell he was voting for those two assholes. He checked the boxes for the seniors, Jennifer Maxwell and Marcus Johnson.

Niles had interacted with them a few times over the years.

Did they know his name at all? No. But when they had a sophomore/junior game last year, Marcus picked Niles for their team, saying "Yo legs, what about you?"

Niles was scrawny, which made him just limber enough for the 100-meter sprints they were doing for a relay race. Niles pulled his weight that day. They won the game, in part because Marcus gave him a chance.

In the case of Jennifer, it was a bit less dramatic.

He had to run back to his locker after forgetting his wallet for the lunch line. It was Pizza Friday and he knew that if he had to get back in line they would only have cheese and vegetarian left.

Jennifer was in front of him, and on a whim, he asked her if she would hold his place in line. Surprisingly, she agreed and Niles booked it.

When he got back, just in time, the lunch lady was about to chastise him for cutting. But true to her word, Jennifer spoke up and vouched for him.

It was so stupid that he even remembered those otherwise insignificant moments, but he had literally zero such interactions with Liam or Melissa ... so fuck 'em.

Niles dropped the ballots into one of the waiter boxes.

After that was done, Anne said that she wanted to get the official pictures before dinner. No one really disagreed with her, so they sauntered upstairs, following the arrows.

"Yeah, I really want to commemorate this moment," Niles thought to himself.

The negative energy the others were giving off was really starting to drag him down. He felt like he was in the presence of a Goryyk Sink.

The alien device fed off of the lifeforce of your *Intrepid* characters until they were too weak to battle. They survive, still consuming your resources, but any energy they recover is sucked out of them again. It's like a parasite.

The thought crossed his mind what Barry and Melvin were doing. At this time of night, they were probably meeting up with Clan Roterhai. It was a starship of Australians on their server. They would do quests together if they happened to be online at the same time.

Niles pulled out his phone to see if he had any more texts from either of them.

Nothing.

He was tempted to send them one, but was way too embarrassed to basically admit defeat this early in the night.

He put the phone away and turned back to Laura, who was sulking.

"So where did you say you found that clock again?" Niles asked, referencing this antique looking timepiece they had mounted on the back wall of the float.

"Oh, uh, I don't know," she said. "I think eBay."

There was no follow-up statement.

"Okay," Niles thought to himself, "nothing about the float."

"So which dinner did you end up choosing?" he asked.

"Ugh …" Laura sighed. "The French pork in apple cream sauce."

"Of course she did."

For dances, they always have four menu options offered to the attendees. Each of them loosely correlated to one of the class themes. Laura chose the option correlating to theirs.

Niles had gone with the roast chicken and potato wedges, which was the Victorian England inspired dish. After that there was steak and green beans. That was the American dish. Then finally, the sophomores were the ones connected to the "special diet" option. It was vegan, gluten-free pasta with spinach and mushrooms.

It was good that they offered it for people who wanted or needed such a selection, but it definitely didn't sound appetizing to him.

Niles made a few more attempts at initiating small talk, but they all fell on deaf ears.

He gave up and just leaned against the wall, waiting for the line to move forward.

That's when a group of varsity guys and their dates showed up behind them. One of the girls was Jennifer Maxwell. She was talking with her date. Niles thought his name might be "Clark", or that could be his last name. He recognized it from matching the face to the image of a football jersey.

Clark made some joke and she laughed, and so did one of the other girls who was standing next to the quarterback guy.

Niles sighed. They looked like they were having so much fun. Why is life so easy for the jocks?

The quarterback was even in a good mood, despite tanking the Homecoming game just the night before.

One of the guys ahead of them walked out of line and approached the football jocks. That's when Niles recognized someone, it was Jimmy O'Something, the party house guy.

The first guy hugged Jimmy then said that they'd definitely be there at his afterparty. Niles looked back at that guy's group.

He recognized some of them, the ones who were in his class anyway. There was Rafael Herrera, Elise Gossamer, Blaire Tidwell, and Mark Schuler.

Maybe this was the answer, maybe he should be encouraging them to go to Jimmy's. Problem was, how does he suggest that idea without sounding creepy? His place sort of has the reputation of being a hook-up hotel.

But really that wasn't even on Niles' mind, he just wanted to get some weed or something so everyone would chill the fuck out and have fun.

He began working out a way to broach the subject when all of the sudden the quarterback guy started talking to them.

Niles was at the back of the group, so he was the first one that Torelli addressed.

"Jennifer here is a class act, right? You voted for her, didn't you?"

"Yeah," Niles said, without taking stock of the situation.

"You did what?" Melissa growled under her breath. Niles could see one of her eyes staring him down through Laura's hair curls.

"Of course you did, because she's the clear winner. Isn't that right everyone?" Torelli was now talking to like two dozen people in the corner of the hallway.

He glanced back at the six of them and Niles actually got a good look at his face. The dude had a few screws coming loose.

Even Melissa, who had a hard time not shutting her face hole, stayed quiet when she saw just how manic the quarterback was being right now. After that, the pressure got out of control.

Some guys further up in line made a joke about him losing the game. Torelli was furious, and looked like he was about to charge them. Luckily, his date came up and pulled him back.

After that, she spent the next ten minutes rubbing his chest with her hand.

That just made Niles feel worse. Jocks can literally get away with anything and the girls will be all over them.

The line shifted forward and Niles went through the motions. It was the most hollow experience he'd ever felt. It was like he had gotten a date for Homecoming, but only by wishing on a monkey's paw or something.

He didn't even remember what pictures they had selected, they felt standard, routine.

Niles may not know a lot about love, or even *like*, but he was pretty sure it didn't feel like this.

***

Once they got back down to the dance floor, there was finally a way for Joe to let off some steam.

Darren was pretty sure Joe was going to beat the shit out of the two guys who made the "interception" crack. He focused on protecting Jennifer and Isabella. Then Iz got away from the two of them and was able to calm Joe down.

At least they got the pictures done without any actual violence.

Now Joe was back to being overly excited, really going all out to the music. That is when Darren finally put the pieces together.

Mania, mood swings, aggression, excitability ... Joe was wired on Addys.

Adderall is a very common drug prescribed for certain attention deficit disorders and other legitimate medical needs. However, its potential for abuse is limitless.

It is commonly used as a performance enhancer to help kids focus for studying, sports, or other activities. It's a stimulant, medical meth.

Villa Vista had a crackdown a few years back when half of the Varsity Baseball team came up positive for Addys during one of their winningest seasons in a decade. There were still regular drug tests, but the "crackdown" phase had passed.

It wasn't like you could just remove the drug. Probably 10% of kids at Villa Vista had a legitimate prescription.

Darren knew that he could probably crack open a dozen lockers and find a month's worth of pills if he ever wanted to. Luckily, Addys were never his thing.

He communicated his theory to Jennifer, but it didn't change the circumstances. Their goal was still to keep an eye on Isabella and keep Joe from doing anything *else* stupid.

At the same time, Darren had to try to keep Jenny's mind on enjoying the evening too. She deserved it; she'd been incredible. If she won

Homecoming Queen and they could keep Joe from punching someone out, it would be a storybook ending.

Then when they got back to Jimmy's, they could put him in a room somewhere and he could sleep off the Addys.

They settled back into the atmosphere of the ballroom. The music was really great. Despite how goofy some of the Homecoming themes had been over the years, the AV guys always did a decent job of putting a mix together.

Especially in the first half of the evening, they'd include a few eclectic songs along with the normal hits. At one point, the crowd were dancing to an EDM remix of some old sea shanty. It was just the right amount of variety to break up the playlist, give it some dynamics and flavor.

Darren had a hard time taking his eyes off of Jenny. She was absolutely gorgeous, from top to bottom. No matter how much drama happened that night, she made everything worth it. He wished he could go back in time three years and show this to his younger self. How different things might have been.

Everyone else seemed to be having a good time too. There weren't many people hiding against the walls or moping in their seats.

Before long, it was 7:30 p.m. and dinner was served.

Darren had done the risky thing and gambled on the steak. The fact that they were serving steak at all was too good to pass up. Maybe it would be terrible, maybe he'd be hungry again in an hour. But what the heck, why not?

Surprisingly, the meals they were delivered weren't too shabby looking. A lot of the guys at the table had taken the chance with the steak, as did Ashley Stillwell. They were given 10 oz T-bone cuts grilled to medium, which seemed like a fair compromise for those who preferred rare or well done.

Darren took his knife and carved into it. The outside was crisp and the inside was juicy, much better than he was expecting. The green beans had some seasoning and a hint of lemon.

Jennifer selected the roast chicken and potato wedges. The chicken came with a cranberry sauce and gravy that could be dipped or drizzled. The potato wedges were sliced thin and spiced.

"Damn," Trey Devall said from one side of the table. "The food's not bad."

His girlfriend Ashley was already halfway through her steak.

"I don't know," Joe said. "Mine's a bit dry."

He offered his fork to Isabella, who had the chicken. She finished his bite, then gave an approving look.

"It's alright," she said.

Joe slid the plate closer to her. "Have all you want."

Trying to keep things positive, Darren said, "Yo Joe, what if we grabbed some Casa Gordita after dropping Jimmy off? I could go for some Mexican."

"Guys we can order-in whatever we want," Jimmy offered. "You kidding me? Not to mention, the fridge is full of party platters, wings, all sorts of shit."

"Yeah, yeah, it's fine," Joe said.

Despite his offer, Isabella didn't touch any of his food. She looked like she wanted it to be there in case he suddenly got his appetite back.

Jennifer was enjoying the chicken while the boys were already talking about their next meal. She only paid attention so much as it concerned Isabella and Joe.

She hadn't spoken directly to Joe since he did the embarrassing spectacle in the hallway. Something like that would have cost her votes if the ballots weren't already in. He had a serious problem.

Loss of appetite was textbook Addys also.

She took a closer look at his knuckles again. It really looked like those cuts hurt. There could be something else mixed in his system. Maybe he had doubled up with some kind of Vicodin or Oxy too.

That's when he did something that she hadn't noticed before.

Joe was wearing a watch. Almost no one wears watches anymore. Unless it's a fancy watch or a smart watch, you just use your phone.

It was a nice watch, definitely part of the wardrobe, but he tugged back his sleeve and checked it very fluidly. Only when thinking back did she remember seeing him do it a few other times during the evening.

Maybe it was just a distraction. He was fidgeting because his brain chemistry was so whacked out at the moment. It's not like he had a plane to catch.

Jennifer continued eating her chicken, chatting with everyone casually. Joe checked his watch three more times before 8:00 p.m.

By that point, most people had finished their meals, and were starting to stir.

Mr. Melkonian and Mr. Wallace returned to the stage.

"That was delicious," Mr. Mel said in his British accent. "Finally, a meal worthy enough for royalty."

"Mhm," Mr. Wallace agreed, having added a cowboy hat to his Teddy Roosevelt costume. "Nothing like home grown All-American beef."

"We hope you are all thoroughly satisfied," Mr. Mel said, revealing a plastic sceptre. "Because we have a coronation to proceed with."

"Once more," Mr. Wallace explained. "The competition was close, only a few votes different between all the prospective nobles."

"But with that said," Mr. Mel continued. "We are proud to honor this year's Homecoming King and Homecoming Queen."

Jennifer glanced back at the other tables. On the far side of the room behind them, she could see Enrique Rodriguez. At one point in the evening, Ellen Taylor was sitting two tables away from him, but she wasn't at her seat.

In the other column of tables, Melissa and Liam were still seated with their dates. The table looked like a wake, the only person who wasn't sad was Melissa, who was anxious.

Back behind them a few tables was Marcus, who looked like he was having a great time with Janice and their friends.

In the middle of the column were Chelsea and Greg in their bright orange outfits. They were huddled close, anticipating the moment.

She was still looking at them when Melkonian called the winners.

"Congratulations to our seniors, Marcus Johnson and Jennifer Maxwell!"

The look on their faces dropped, and Jenny remembered feeling bad for them before even realizing that she had won.

She felt Darren's hand on her shoulder and looked over at him.

"Jenny, Jenny you won!" he said. It finally clicked for her and she stood up.

Marcus was already halfway to the stage, high-fiving dozens of people on the way.

Jenny reached the staircase and climbed up on stage right.

Melkonian was waving the plastic sceptre over Marcus, after placing the crown on his head.

Mr. Wallace had the Queen's tiara.

Reveling in the moment, she curtseyed in front of him, so he could place the tiara easier.

"Great job, kiddo," he said in his regular Rick Wallace voice.

"Thank you so much!" Jennifer could hardly contain her joy.

She walked to center stage, where Marcus was offering her a hand.

She took it and he raised them both up in the air.

The room was cheering. Darren and the rest of her table were standing in applause.

She looked back at Marcus, then raised her right arm in a flex. He did the same with his left arm, although the muscle wasn't as visible beneath the suit coat.

As Jenny scanned the crowd, she saw Melissa burst through one of the doors, abandoning the ballroom completely.

"Well, what did you expect?" she thought to herself.

Ellen Taylor was still nowhere in sight.

Looking at Chelsea and Greg was a bit of a downer. Chelsea was crying and Greg was trying to console her.

"If they're still together next year, they'll take the crowns easily," Jenny thought to herself.

"Alright everyone," Mr. Mel said to the crowd. "With the formalities taken care of, it's time to get back to the festivities."

With that, the music turned back up to dance volume again. "All of Me" by John Legend began playing out of the Murphy Center's pristine new sound system.

Melkonian and Wallace switched off their wireless mics, dropping the characters.

"Alright," Mr. Wallace said to them. "You kids ready for your royalty pictures?"

"Can we bring our dates too?" Jennifer asked.

"Yeah, of course," Mr. Mel said. "We'll get a few of the two of you and then you can each have some shots with your special someone."

"Great." Jenny walked forward on the stage and signaled to Darren to join them.

Marcus eyed his table and Janice began shaking her head.

With a flick like a frisbee, Marcus sent his top hat twirling over the crowd. Janice leapt to her feet and chased it. She didn't quite catch it with her head, but she did grab the rim with her hand, taking it back on stage with her.

Darren climbed the few steps and hugged Jenny.

"Congratulations, you earned this," he whispered in her ear.

"I'm so glad you could be here with me." She kissed him on the cheek.

Before Darren could respond they heard Mr. Mel clear his throat.

"Ehem," he warned. "Might not be smart to smear lipstick, for pictures ..."

The four of them followed the announcers up the stairwell backstage.

**

"Bullshit. Fucking bullshit!" Melissa screamed, but her yells were drowned out by the ruckus applause around them.

She stood up and stormed away from the table, smacking Niles in the side of his face as she walked by.

"Ow," he yelped in surprise. "Bitch ..."

"Great going," Anne said to him.

"You've got to be kidding," Niles responded, no longer maintaining any social graces. "You aren't dumb enough to believe that it was one vote difference, are you?"

Anne raised an eyebrow in shock.

"You know who didn't vote for Melissa?" Niles continued, letting the vent pour out. "Me and probably 280 others who weren't part of the stupid cliques that got her selected in the first place."

Anne turned toward Liam, expecting him to defend her or something.

"He's probably right." Liam shrugged. "I didn't vote for her either."

"I don't believe this." Anne threw up her hands. "No wonder our class came in last, when it's filled with idiots like you two."

Laura was quiet, unsettled by what was unfolding.

Ryan Lewis, Melissa's date, was still seated at the table. He hadn't even made an attempt to go after her.

"Who *did* you vote for?" Ryan asked Liam.

"Sophomore couple," he said. "I was really hoping they'd tongue on stage and get Melkonian to freak out."

Anne stood up from her chair and left, walking off in a different direction than Melissa.

"I voted for Marcus and that freshman girl," Ryan added.

"Who, Mudbra?" Liam asked.

"Yeah," Ryan responded. "The trip was funny, but she's got a nice rack."

Liam started laughing, putting his feet up in Melissa's chair like an ottoman.

Laura also got up and began walking off in a third direction.

"Laura, wait!" Niles yelled, following after her.

She burst through the east-facing doors of the building.

There was an outdoor seating area and some open pavement separating the school building from the faculty parking lot. There was still a construction fence around the parking lot, with a few miscellaneous cranes, CONEX boxes, and some open-air pallets of unused building materials.

"Don't talk to me Niles," Laura said, coming to a stop at one of the outdoor tables.

"Wait," he said, his filters dropping away again. "You're mad at me?"

"Of course I'm mad at you," she said, a few tears trickling out of one eye.

Niles stood dumbfounded for a moment before answering. "Why?!"

Laura turned to look at him, not expecting the outburst.

"No, really," he said. "How on earth could *you* be mad at *me*? I spent twenty-five hours this week building that float. Do you think I would have done that if not for you?"

He continued, before she could respond. "Did you see anyone else there for even a fraction of that time? Liam wasn't there for one second, we're lucky he even showed up for the float parade. Same for Melissa."

Laura was still staring at him, eyes wide and her arms crossed.

"How about this, or this?!" he said, tugging at the coat and top hat. They were completely out of place in the sea of modern suits the other guys were wearing. "I wouldn't have worn this normally, but I did it for you, because you really wanted something historic to match your outfit."

He continued, "And I *like* your dress, I think you look beautiful in it, and I mostly don't care what anyone else thinks about us. But it would have been nice not being judged so much by the other people at our own table …"

"I'm sure they weren't judging," she tried to interject.

"Laura, they were mocking the float behind your back," he admitted. "I heard at least a bit of it, but they've probably been saying more out of my earshot too. They think the theme is a joke."

"Are they saying that Niles, or are *you* saying that?" She was still trying to deflect.

Once again, Niles pulled the top hat off of his head. He flicked it with his fingers.

"I'm not big into history. I prefer the future, sci-fi, stuff like that. But I was happy, thinking it'd make you happy. But instead, how do you spend the night? Not talking to me, not joking around with someone who was happy to indulge in your interests."

He pulled the top hat back on.

"Instead, you wasted the night trying to impress a bunch of people who don't care about it at all, which includes all your other 'friends'."

"A three-layer cake ..." Niles added, not clearly connecting the non-sequitur to the rest of his chain of thought.

This time he left ample space for her to respond, but she didn't. Instead, she stood there in shock, as though Niles had sprouted a third arm.

"Look, I'm going to go back inside," he said. "If you want to dance, have a little fun, I'll be waiting."

With that, he turned his back on her and returned to the Murphy Center through the same doors.

When Niles got back to their table, it was empty. He saw Liam on the dance floor, having been dragged away by some of his groupies. Ryan Lewis was back by the punch bowls, talking to Mrs. Donovan for some reason.

As Niles sat there, the full gravity of everything that happened collapsed over him. He slouched back in his chair, as though the Sword of Damocles had dropped down through his collar bone.

He was mentally and emotionally exhausted. He felt worse than he did last year, when he just sat home during Homecoming and played *Intrepid*.

"Just fucking kill me," he muttered to the ceiling.

It was 8:21 p.m.

***

Dinner had been surprisingly delicious. Back in Pasadena North High, the food they served at school banquets was usually bland and flavorless.

After every dance Andrei attended, the group he was with would inevitably make a 10:00 p.m. food run to a Taco Bell or some other late-night fast-food joint.

Andrei could still taste a bit of the steak and green beans, despite his best efforts to wash away the flavor and get his mouth "minty fresh" again. The last thing he wanted was for Blaire to smell latent dinner odors.

Homecoming had already been quite an experience, especially when the evening took an unexpected turn, coloring his expectations.

Early on in the night, before they'd even voted for the royalty or anything, Andrei had to use the restroom. He hadn't gone since before he left for Blaire's house and he'd had more than a little cider in the limo.

As Andrei was stepping up to one of the urinals, he crossed paths with someone else, who was flipping on the sink. It was none other than Jimmy O'Shaughnessy himself.

"Hey," Jimmy said.

Andrei glanced over his shoulder, expecting to see feet beneath one of the stalls.

"Yeah, you." Jimmy nodded, addressing him. "You're Andrew, right?"

"Uh, Andrei," he said.

"Nice to meet you," Jimmy said, extending a hand.

Andrei hesitated for a second before Jimmy pulled back.

"Just kidding." He wiggled his fingers. "Don't want to wash twice."

He dried his hands with one of the paper towels.

"I was hoping I'd bump into you," Jimmy said. "Couldn't really find a time to stop you the last few weeks."

"What's up?"

"I don't know if you've heard, but I have this thing going on after the dance at my place. My dad has a really nice pad that he is almost never around to live in."

"Really?" Andrei was unaware of the family dynamic.

"Anyway ... it's a bit hush-hush. I let people 'live it up' however they want, if ya get me. 'See nothing, say nothing.'"

"I get ya." Andrei nodded. Some of the parties he'd been to back in Los Angeles had their various back rooms and less-than-legal escapes.

"Cool, cool." Jimmy breathed out in relief. "Since you're the new guy, I wanted to mention it. It's my last year, and I want everyone to have the chance to make the most out of their night. My address is 1830 Crestmore ... trust me, you can't miss it."

"Actually, I was already planning on showing," Andrei said.

"Oh really?" He raised an eyebrow.

"Yeah, I sort of got invited," Andrei explained.

"By who?" Jimmy prodded, a strange smile curving up one side of his face.

"My date," Andrei said.

Jimmy lit up. "Boy or girl?"

"Girl," Andrei confirmed.

"My man!" Jimmy clapped his hands. "You are getting lucky tonight!"

"What?!" Andrei almost turned from the urinal in shock.

"Look, I don't mean to brag," Jimmy explained. "But my place has been a bit of a destination for some time. If a girl asked *you* over ... be sure to wash up."

Jimmy winked, opening the door to leave. "Don't worry, I've got eight bathrooms!"

With that, Andrei was alone.

He zipped up and washed his hands.

He began replaying the conversation in the limo, examining the details with this new perspective.

"He can't be serious," Andrei said to himself.

"*She* can't be serious ... can she?"

That conversation happened nearly two hours ago, but all the signals he'd been picking up from Blaire since then only seemed to be proving the theory.

"Hey ... you still with me?"

Andrei snapped out of his thoughts.

Following a few slow pop songs, the music had shifted into full on classical waltz.

They were moving back and forth in perfect form. The dance floor had spread out a bit, seeping into the hallways. Everyone was giving each other a bit more privacy.

Blaire looked up at him with her bright hazel eyes.

"What are you thinking about?" she whispered.

Andrei searched for the right words to say. He was never good at the intricate subtleties in relationships.

"I bumped into Jimmy," he admitted.

Blaire's countenance dropped and a look of fear washed over her.

Andrei continued, not wanting to let her mind race.

"Do you really want to go to *the afterparty*?" he asked.

Blaire searched his face, her eyes full of panic.

"Because I do ..." he whispered back.

Everything else seemed to disappear. A million emotions flooded between them like the rising tides.

Blaire wrapped her arms around Andrei's neck and their lips came together. Her kiss was like nothing he'd ever felt before, full of passion. He pulled her closer, losing himself in the moment.

There was no Homecoming anymore. There was nothing else at all. It was just the two of them and everything that the future had in store.

On the other side of the room, Elise caught notice of what was happening.

"Look," she said to Raf.

He followed her nod.

Andrei and Blaire were entwined in the center of the dance floor, not even moving to the music anymore.

Elise turned back to him. "We did the right thing."

"I told you," he assured her. Then they too came together in a kiss.

The waltz carried the couples onward in an almost dreamlike state.

It was 8:23 p.m.

***

Jennifer and Marcus posed for a variety of funny pictures. All of their flexing had gone over well with the crowd. Mrs. Lathrop was standing with the photographer to make sure they got some good ones for the yearbook.

Once she was satisfied, Darren and Janice were able to hop in for a free set of pictures with the Homecoming Royalty.

Darren was pretty happy with the shots he and Jennifer took. In one picture, he went down on one leg and she used his knee like a throne. In another, he picked her up like she was being carried through a threshold. Mr. Mel let them use the plastic sceptre as a prop.

Once they were done reviewing the pictures, Melkonian and Wallace said they could return to the dance.

Darren stepped out into the hallway, holding the door open for her.

"So, what's it feel like to be a queen?" Darren asked her now that they were alone.

"It feels pretty good," Jenny said. "I'm glad you kept your promise."

"Oh, I didn't stuff the ballot box or anything." He waved a hand away, thinking she was referencing the locker thing. "You won totally because of your own worth, as a competitor and a person."

"But that wasn't what you said last night," Jenny said, becoming more serious. "You couldn't promise me something you didn't have control of."

She stopped him in the hallway.

"You promised an evening that *you* would treat me like a queen ... and you did."

She took off the plastic tiara.

"This is just an accessory. It didn't matter whether or not I won anything. People could have voted for me for one reason or another, but that wouldn't have made a real difference."

"*You* treated me like a queen." She started to tear up. "Thank you, Darren."

She wrapped her arms around him.

Darren returned the embrace. Tears began streaming out of his eyes too, the emotions were impossible to hold back.

"I love you, Jenny," he admitted, an old yearning of his heart finally expressed.

She pressed her face into his shoulder.

"I love you too, Darren," she whispered.

They stood in that hallway for many minutes, until there were no more tears left to shed.

Once they'd composed themselves, Darren set the tiara back on Jenny's head. After all this, she had to at least wear it through the rest of the dance.

They walked toward the stairwell and climbed back down into the main lobby of the building. Their fingers were intertwined and a certain peace filled them up.

It was a feeling Darren had prayed for, for a long time. He'd spent years living in doubt, regret, and sorrow for the time he felt like they'd lost. None of that mattered now.

This was a new start, a new forever for both of them.

But for all the joy they felt in their hearts, the world came crashing in around them once again.

"No, I'm done! I'm fucking done, Iz!" Joe Torelli yelled. A security guard walked him through the door with Principal McDouglas in tow.

Behind McDouglas was Trey Devall, nursing a massive purple welt on the left side of his jaw.

"Prince-pull McDoug-iss, peas ..." Trey tried to mouth through the swelling. "We wuh juss messen arouw."

Isabella was next to Trey, and the rest of their group trailed behind.

"Brendan, what the fuck happened?!" Darren asked Jensen.

Brendan got closer to Darren and Jennifer so no one else could hear them. "Joe and Iz got in an argument. He was flipping out on her over some dumb shit, like her taking too long to get ready or something. Trey stepped in to try to cool him down and he decked him."

Jennifer was horrified, she went to Iz, who had started crying.

"Don't call me!" Joe yelled as the guard took post on the sidewalk.

"Get in your car and leave, son," the guard said.

"We'll be talking about this on Monday, Torelli," Principal McDouglas called after Joe.

Joe flipped him off with his left hand, then unlocked the doors of the black Camaro.

Principal McDouglas turned back to the rest of them.

"Go back inside, kids," he said, ushering them in.

That's when a call came on the guard's radio, and he started jogging back toward the baseball diamonds.

Principal McDouglas didn't notice this, he was focused on getting the others back into the building.

"Does Isabella have a way home?" McDouglas asked Jennifer, who was still holding the heartbroken girl.

"Yes, we'll take care of her," Jenny told him.

She was still wearing the plastic Homecoming Queen tiara. McDouglas felt like he should congratulate her, but this was the worst possible opportunity. He decided to find her in the hallway on Monday.

Once they were in the lobby, Isabella broke free of Jenny's grasp and ran for the single-stall restroom, locking it behind her.

"You guys go get some ice for Trey," Darren said to the rest of the group. "We'll take care of Iz."

Brendan, Jimmy, and the girls led Trey back inside.

"Iz," Jenny said, knocking on the door. "Darren and I are just outside, please come out when you can, everything's going to be okay."

Darren noticed some empty chairs, and dragged them over by the restroom door. He offered one to Jenny, sitting down next to her. There was a third one available for Isabella, whenever she decided to come out.

Jenny leaned her head down on Darren's shoulder. The weekend had been a rollercoaster of emotions, but through thick and thin Darren was still right there.

It was 8:29 p.m.

***

"Heaven. This is Heaven."

As they had been dancing, Blaire noticed Andrei start to zone out for a minute. He was very deep in thought, and it took some encouragement for him to come back to her.

"Hey ... you still with me?" she asked him.

He snapped back.

"What are you thinking about?" she whispered.

His eyes drifted off and Blaire thought she was losing him again.

Then he spoke, "I bumped into Jimmy."

"What?!" the voice in her head exclaimed. "What do you mean 'bumped into'? What did Jimmy say?!"

Andrei shifted his hand on her back and the sensation broke her chain of thought.

"Do you really want to go to *the afterparty*?" he asked.

Blaire felt like she was dying inside, collapsing like an ancient house rotted hollow by termites. But before she could put the worries into words, he spoke again.

"Because I do ..." he whispered to her.

In an instant, her whole body erupted in flame.

Her mind had gone silent, unable to narrate the countless feelings and sensations that raced through her.

Her body seemed to move on its own as she wrapped her arms around Andrei's neck.

She felt his lips touch hers and nothing else. He wrapped her in a loving embrace for what felt like an eternity.

She didn't even know when it stopped. At one point, she realized that her head was resting against his chest and they were swaying to the orchestra.

Eventually the waltz died down and another modern pop song came on. The tempo was just a bit out of place for the mood, so she asked Andrei if he wanted to take a break.

They stopped by the drink table and each got a tall glass of ice water, finishing them in just a few sips.

After that, they retreated to the far side of the dance floor, leaning against the back. The whole stage was in front of them and they could feel the beat of the subwoofers reverberate through the wall.

Once they were comfortable, Andrei began to chuckle.

"What is it?" she asked, mock worry in her voice.

"I just realized," he said, glancing down at her. "That's why you didn't wear the pants."

"Oh my god." She buried her face in her hands.

"I should have worn the skirt too," he said.

Blaire whopped him with a hand.

Andrei turned, leaning his right shoulder on the wall so he could face her.

"This has been a great night."

Blaire shifted as well, her left shoulder against the wall.

"The night's not over, sport." She stared longingly into his eyes.

Andrei leaned in again, sharing a gentler kiss.

"Do you think Elise will figure it out?" Blaire asked him.

Andrei's eyebrows flexed in realization.

"Raf asked me how old I was."

"You're kidding." Blaire's shoulders slouched.

"No, it was just a few hours ago," Andrei confirmed.

"Of course she figured it out, why would I expect otherwise?" Blaire winced from embarrassment, facing into the wall.

"I'm not old, I'm just tall," Andrei moped.

Blaire rested her head against the surface. Elise was going to grill her for weeks. And now Raf knows too, which means Elise was going to feel weird around him. So, it'd be awkward with just the four of them for a while.

Blaire took a breath, letting those thoughts drift away from her. The subwoofer was shaking through the wall. It was a nice steady pulse, calming down her racing heart to a better rhythm.

But there was something else there.

Blaire furrowed her brows, pressing her ear flat against the wall.

Andrei noticed her expression change.

"What is it?" he asked.

Blaire listened closely. Beyond the *thump-thump, thump-thump* of the song, was a single, high-pitched noise.

A whistling.

Blaire's eyes opened wide in horror. The nightmare she endured last night flashed through the front of her mind in an instant.

"Blaire."

Andrei put a hand on her shoulder, growing concerned.

"Let's go, I want to go." Her mouth was trembling.

"Yeah, sure," Andrei stammered. "We'll grab your purse and-"

"Forget the purse, we need to go now!" she screamed, tugging at his arm.

"Wait, why?" His adrenaline was spiking from Blaire's panic.

It was 8:34 p.m.

The steady pounding of the subwoofer seemed to be wiped away. A much larger pulse rippled through the concrete wall.

His senses heightened, Andrei reacted in an instant. He straightened his arm, pushing away from the wall, while pulling Blaire with the other.

They leapt away in a single motion. The wall, however, was not getting any further. The new concrete blocks, and the old bricks that lay below, followed the couple into the air.

Andrei brought his arm around, pulling Blaire in tight.

The pieces by their feet were moving the fastest. They pressed on his dress shoes, tilting the couple until the soles of their feet were almost facing the stage.

That's when they felt the heat.

Between each crack in the pieces, a warm air blew through.

Then hot air.

Then fire.

With what little momentum he could control, Andrei tucked his body like a cat, trying to put himself between Blaire and the wall.

Between every broken brick were yellow and red wisps of flame, reaching toward them.

The pain doubled with every passing moment.

Blaire held close to Andrei as they continued to soar through the air, being carried forward on a bed of fire.

Something hard slammed against Blaire's back, then it was gone.

Then it slammed, then it was gone.

A third time it slammed, before pulling away.

She and Andrei were tumbling across the floor.

Soon they felt one final slam, which gripped them and would not let go.

The pain was like millions of flaming hot pins stabbing into her skin from all sides.

Blaire opened her eyes, but saw nothing. She was enveloped in total darkness. She glanced around wherever she could, but the lighthouse beam never came.

She tried to scream, but the corset was fixed in place.

With every breath, it gripped her tighter.

She could not pull air into her lungs, only darkness.

Soon the darkness filled her completely ... and all went silent.

NINE

THE AFTERPARTY

BLAIRE WAS NOT SURE how long her slumber lasted, but eventually, sensation returned to her.

She began to stir, feeling stiffness and aching in every muscle. It was as though she'd fallen asleep on a hardwood floor.

Finally, she opened her eyes.

The first thing she saw was better than she could have hoped for. It was Andrei's face, only inches from hers. His eyes were closed.

His right arm was resting over her left elbow.

"Andrei." She shifted her left arm to touch his cheek.

His arm fell away lifelessly as she moved.

Blaire could feel her heart begin to race.

"Andrei ..." she said, slapping his cheek.

"Andrei!" she yelled, tugging hard against his shoulder.

"Ugh ..." He let out a groan.

"Andrei?" she asked him, on the verge of tears. "Are you still with me?"

"Yes," he said, the word barely audible.

"Oh, thank God ..." she answered, pulling him in close.

Blaire kissed his cheek.

He was slow to move, and that had her worried the most. She wanted him awake, she wanted him talking to her.

"Come on," she said, "let's sit you up."

Andrei's back was pressed against a short wall of some kind. Blaire was able to get him upright, leaning against the wall.

She began looking over his face, neck, and hands, anything that was exposed, that she could inspect. As far as she could tell, there were no cuts or bruises, no bleeding or burns. Except for being creased from laying on the floor, his suit didn't even look like it had been torn or pierced in any way.

Satisfied by Andrei's condition, Blaire began looking over herself. She was also basically unharmed. Her hair bent in a few weird ways after sleeping on it, but that was it.

She looked back down at Andrei, and had to blink her eyes a few times. It almost looked like Andrei's suit was moving.

Blaire looked closer at the shoulder, where the movement was most obvious. It wasn't the coat itself; it was the white particulate trickling down onto the coat. A fine powder was settling out of the air.

Blaire brushed at it and a patch of the coat turned a darker shade. She brushed Andrei in a few more places as he was starting to rouse.

Then she looked down at herself. After brushing against the bare skin of her arm, a puff of white powder rose back into the air.

The only thing Andrei had heard out of the darkness was Blaire's voice. When he opened his eyes, she was panicking, brushing herself everywhere she could, trying to shake the dust off.

"Whoa, whoa, take it easy."

Andrei shifted to rest his right hand on her back. But as soon as he did, a sharp pain shot across his shoulder.

"Agh," he grunted.

Blaire calmed down a bit, placing her hand on his shoulder.

"What ... happened?" Andrei asked.

Blaire looked around at where they were. The short wall Andrei was seated against was the stage apron.

Andrei looked past Blaire at the north wall of the ballroom. It was where they had been standing beforehand. They'd been thrown at least a hundred feet.

They glanced around the rest of the room, taking in their surroundings. It appeared to be morning. The glow of daylight was filtering through the windows on the east wall. With the exception of the fine white dust hanging in the air, there didn't appear to be any damage.

The students were scattered around the room at their own unique angles. Some had been pressed up against the stage apron like Blaire and Andrei were. Many more were lying on top of banquet tables or crumpled awkwardly among the chairs. Some were lying against the walls on the far sides of the room, and others still were lying on the stage itself.

Blaire stood up, scanning from body to body. Eventually she saw Elise and Raf.

"Elise!" she yelled, stumbling through the dance floor. She tried to avoid some of the other dancers lying about.

Seeing her move, Andrei scrambled to his feet and followed her. Every muscle and joint in his body ached, but he did his best to shake the stiffness out of his legs.

Elise was lying in the seat of a chair. It was like she had fallen asleep in it and then slid off of the side. Her head and an arm were crumpled on the cushion.

Rafael was on the floor, between two other chairs which his body had knocked into the table.

Andrei paused for a moment before touching him. He'd heard several times while on his old snowboarding team that you shouldn't move someone after an accident unless you were sure that you could do so without harming them.

He gazed back over the ballroom, at how far he and Blaire had tumbled across the dance floor. If they rolled that far and were still standing, then Raf was probably okay to move.

Andrei pulled his body away from the chairs. He straightened Raf out, trying to wake him up.

Blaire carefully pulled Elise's hair off of her face. She put her ear down by Elise's mouth, listening for breathing. She felt a shallow puff of air and a murmur.

"Elise?" she said, folding her arm into a more comfortable position. "Elise, wake up. Say something …"

"Blaire?" she whispered.

"It's okay, we're here. Andrei's got Raf." She turned back toward him, seeking confirmation.

Andrei had him sitting upright. Raf was groaning, but he was conscious. Andrei nodded at Blaire.

"Come on," Blaire said. "Wake up, we're okay."

Elise tensed, and her head inched up off of her arm. Blaire eased her down as she twisted. She was now sitting cross-legged against one of the chair legs.

"It hurts," Elise muttered.

"What hurts?" Blaire asked, scanning her body for injuries.

"Everything," Elise muttered again.

"But nothing specific?" Blaire asked. "No sharp pain, or numbness?"

Elise shook her head. She then shifted her legs. The ankle-length dress pulled away from her feet. She kicked off her left heel, then the right.

Seeing her do this, Blaire looked down and noticed that her own shoes were gone too.

She looked over at the wall where she and Andrei woke up, but didn't see them.

Some of the other dancers were beginning to awaken also, sitting upright, looking around.

"What was that light?" Raf said, trying to stand to his feet.

"Light?" Andrei asked him.

"Yeah, like a camera flash." He rubbed his eyes.

Blaire helped Elise to her feet and walked her back over to their table. Elise and Raf hadn't landed too far away from it.

"I didn't see a flash," Elise said. "Raf and I were dancing and I thought someone had tripped and fallen into us. They hit my back hard."

The four of them sat down in their original chairs. The table looked more or less how they left it. The centerpiece was still there and a few scattered dessert plates remained with half-eaten rolls or chocolate torte.

Andrei's linen napkin was still folded the way he left it, an old habit from past black-tie events he'd attended. Blaire's purse was still hung over one corner of her chair, hiding in the shadow of the table cloth. She unzipped a hidden pocket, which still held her driver's license, cash, and emergency credit card.

Elise pulled the cell phone out of her own purse, unlocking the screen.

Sunday, 8:17 a.m.

A silence hung between them. They remained a bit shell-shocked by whatever had just occurred.

Their minds did not have long to ponder.

A blood-curdling scream echoed down one of the hallways. It was a shrill, high-pitched cry which Blaire had heard before.

"That's Dina!" she said, jumping up from her chair.

"Blaire, wait!" Andrei followed after her. "It could be dangerous!"

They entered the hallway, where a few other students were recoiling from the source of the sound. It was coming from the girls' bathroom.

Andrei hesitated for a second, but Blaire pushed open the door. The scream poured out at full volume and Blaire ran in. He wasn't going to let her go in alone, so he stepped through.

Dina Petrakis was pressed up against the wall of stall doors, frozen in absolute fear. Her mouth was almost unhinging. She was looking at the sinks. Blaire and Andrei stepping into view snapped her out of whatever mental loop she was caught in. She bolted past them, shoving Andrei back against the door.

Despite her screams, Dina didn't look physically injured at all. Blaire continued walking into the bathroom, turning the corner of the privacy wall. Andrei was right behind her.

The image that gripped Dina in fear was not something in the sinks, it was something in the mirrors.

The mirrors did not reflect the remodeled bathroom stalls at all. Instead, the world they showed was one where the plastic material of the doors and dividers had melted down into bulbous piles, clinging to the metal frames. The back wall behind the toilets was blown open completely, revealing a nighttime sky. Billows of smoke poured out of the building, blotting out most of the stars.

However, the most horrifying thing was not the destroyed building beyond, but Blaire and Andrei's own reflections standing to face them.

In contrast to the harsh amber and red light of the world inside the mirror, the two forms were illuminated in what appeared to be fluorescent, white light. It looked like it came from the ceiling fixtures just above the 'real world' pair. While Blaire and Andrei saw each other as unscathed, the mirror revealed a harsher truth.

Blaire's soft hazel eyes were glazed over in a sickly grey film, concealing a red pulp just beneath. There was no white left, every blood vessel had boiled and burst. Her left iris was torn open. There was no distinct pupil, just a mess of fibers which only barely held their color in the pool of red blood, beneath a grey sclera.

Her eyelashes and eyebrows were completely gone, singed in an instant. The left side of her face was grey and discolored, with an old, leather-like quality. Beneath the surface, every vein looked like a pale blue line, spider-webbing beneath every bit of skin that was visible. The lifeless grey was only interrupted by harsher colors, miscellaneous spots that were more severely burned. Her left elbow was particularly carbonized.

The hair on the left side of her head was mostly seared away, her decorative silver hair pin was missing. The matching earring was still present, but was charred black.

The right side of her face fared a bit better, but the eye was just the same and the skin was just as grey. What remained of her hair looked like doll hair, dry and coarse.

Most of the lace layer of her dress had burned away completely, leaving a branding-like pattern on her skin where it once was.

After what felt like hours staring at the ghoul beyond the glass, her eyes drifted over to the reflection of Andrei. He had fared far worse.

The shirt and suit coat covering his right arm were missing, as was most of the flesh. Only thin strands of sinew held the bones in place. He raised his right arm closer to the mirror. The reflection beyond held up a hand of charred black bones.

All of the hair on his head was gone and the right side of his face showed little more than skull. The right eye was missing, leaving only the void of the empty socket. The ear and cheek were gone and the tip of his nose had melted off.

His right shoulder, clavicle, and five ribs were visible. Beyond that, enough strands of shirt or flesh remained to conceal the rest.

The left side of his face looked more like Blaire's. The eye was similarly flash-boiled, with greyed, leathery skin.

The rest of their clothes were in tatters. Various tears in the fabric revealed cuts in the grey, seared skin. These were marks of the different bits of shrapnel that struck their bodies. The exposed tears were the worst on their backs.

Andrei's right shoulder blade was completely exposed, the boney plate covered in visible scratches from some of the flying debris. Much of Blaire's back was also exposed. The tears in her dress hung open at strange angles, as though she had suffered forty lashes in a medieval punishment. The cuts were deep, yet bloodless.

Staring at this corrupted form of herself was unnerving enough, but for Blaire the real disturbance came when the bodies moved. The way the corpses mimicked their every motion made her stomach turn in knots.

Andrei was silent, looking at what had become of them. The fingertips of his skeletal right hand pressed against the glass.

Blaire finally freed her attention away from their other selves. She looked up at the Andrei standing next to her. He was handsome and whole, as he had been when the night began.

He met her eyes, taking his hand off of the mirror. Her eyes were as beautiful as ever ... but were filled with tears.

"Andrei ..." she whispered, her voice breaking. "Are we dead?"

Her words sounded as though she were looking for one last possible strand of hope, some truth Andrei could reveal to her that would explain everything.

As much as he wished he could give meaning to this, he had no other answer.

He pulled her close as she cried into his chest. He rested his head on hers, glancing back one more time at what lay beyond.

The burns on their bodies lined up like two pieces of a puzzle. He was holding her this same way when the fire consumed them.

He led her back outside, where a small group of people were staring at the door. A few of them were hunched down near Dina, including her date Jeremy, trying to get her to talk. She was in a fetal position, hyperventilating.

As they saw Andrei walk out with Blaire, one of the kids asked them what was in there.

Andrei said only one word: "Mirror."

Rafael and Elise were still sitting at their table. When Elise saw Blaire crying, she got to her feet and closed the gap between them. Andrei handed her off to Elise and she cried into her shoulder.

Elise led her down to their chairs.

"Bro, what is it, what happened?" Raf said, confused.

Andrei did not answer him, instead he turned to the table, picking up Blaire's purse. Only one question crossed his mind now and he had to see for himself.

He pulled the make-up compact out of her purse and opened it. Inside the clamshell was the application pad and on the top hatch was a small mirror.

One grey, lifeless eye stared back at him.

"Andrei, talk to us!" Raf shouted.

He looked up from the clamshell.

Elise was trying to get Blaire to calm down, but couldn't get her to speak coherently.

Andrei turned the small mirror toward Raf.

"The hell are you-" Raf's voice cut out as he took the clamshell from Andrei's hand.

"What the fuck?!" he said in shock. He moved the mirror around at different angles.

Rafael's entire face and much of the front of his chest had been scorched away. Both eyes were missing and his nose and lips had been seared off, leaving an emotionless row of teeth "grinning" back at him.

Another scream echoed from the hallway where Andrei and Blaire had come from.

"It's every mirror," Andrei said, sitting down in the chair next to Blaire.

Elise looked at Raf. "Show me."

He hesitated, the implications starting to settle into his mind.

"Raf, give it to me!" she demanded, her nerves starting to fray.

He did, passing the compact to her outstretched hand.

She looked into the small circular disc and a visceral gasp erupted from her chest. The shock of the sight caused her to drop it to the floor.

She still held Blaire on one shoulder, so Raf bent down and picked it up.

After a few deep breaths, Elise extended her hand again.

Once more, he handed it to her.

Elise's face was grey, with boiled eyes and cuts across her shoulders. That did not hold the most focus of her attention though. Instead, her stare was fixed on an unnatural lump. While the reflection in the mirror matched her movements, a bulge pressed out of the right side of the corpse's neck.

She leaned her head towards her left shoulder, resting it against Blaire. The angle was closer to how she was when she woke up. The bump seemed to invert, now becoming a thin crater where part of her muscle should be.

She reached up with a grey hand and pressed into the crater. Almost two fingers were able to slip into the crease of skin.

A memory from Health class floated to the front of her mind. It was a mostly useless piece of knowledge she'd learned for a test on the human skeleton. However, it helped explain just how bad the damage really was.

Of the cervical vertebrae in her neck, the C4 and C5 were no longer connected, at all. The term for it was "internal decapitation". The harsh angle the bones were at suggested that the spinal cord within had snapped at the same instant. She had probably died of that before she could feel the pain from the fire or suffocate from the smoke.

Blaire calmed down enough to see Elise's reflection in the clamshell. She turned away from the dark window, retreating into Andrei's embrace again.

Raf pulled his chair around, taking a closer look at what had become of her. When she saw the reflection of his exposed skull, she closed the clamshell.

Tears trickled from her eyes. She looked at Raf, who was also welling up. Their foreheads touched as they sobbed quietly together.

***

The first thought that came to Jenny was that she had fallen asleep on Darren's shoulder as they waited for Isabella.

Little by little, she took hold of her senses again.

She noticed things were very quiet, the heavy beats of the dance music were not playing at all. She only heard what she could guess was static, like turning to an old FM radio station that was off the air now.

Her sense of touch returned to her next. At this point she became aware of the fact that she had not been sleeping on Darren's shoulder. Her body was splayed out in a very strange way and she didn't feel like she was sitting upright. It was more of an angle, like a steep hill.

She tried to tuck herself into a more modest composure, but as soon as she moved her limbs a bolt of pain answered her back.

"Ah!" she yelped, ceasing the attempted motion.

Taking a different approach, she focused on just one arm, her left. She bent her fingers and slowly rotated her wrist. It didn't even take one rotation to feel her brush against something. She pivoted her elbow, feeling the object. It was some kind of linen, or a tablecloth maybe? She followed one of the seams until the texture changed. She felt skin.

Her hand twisted more, finding another hand.

Finally, Jenny summoned enough strength to move more of herself. She slid sideways, pulling herself toward the hand. There was a sudden drop. She fell backwards a few inches. Rows of hard teeth bit into her back.

The shock was enough to jumpstart the rest of her.

She spun, trying to twist away from the teeth. They took hold of her arm instead. Now she felt herself pressed against a wall.

Her eyes opened; a grey blur began to come into focus.

It was Darren.

He was collapsed against a stairwell and so was she. She had been lying on top of him when she woke.

She looked around, trying to regain awareness.

They were in the stairwell that led up to the Choir & Drama room. Their feet had landed about five risers above the ground floor. The three chairs they had been sitting in were knocked over. They were about thirty feet from the door of the single-stall bathroom.

Darren started coughing.

"Darren?" Jenny asked. "Can you hear me?"

"Yeah," he said, through the last of his coughing.

He turned over onto his stomach, using his elbows and knees to rest more comfortably against the hard stairs.

"I feel like I just went through Hell Week," he grunted.

"What are we doing in the stairwell?" she asked him.

"I don't remember. We were talking and then ... nothing."

A scream got their attention.

"We're dead! We're all dead!" Some younger looking kid collapsed to her knees in the middle of the entrance lobby. Her yells became more incoherent.

Scattered around the lobby were a couple dozen other bodies, pressed against the doors or lying in strange arrangements.

"What is going on?!" Jenny asked him. She then turned toward the single-stall bathroom. "Darren, Isabella!"

Darren turned and they jogged up to the door. He pounded on it with his fist.

"Isabella?!" he shouted.

He tried the handle, but it was still locked.

"We've got to check on her!" Jenny said, panicking.

"Okay," Darren replied, looking around the lobby, forming a quick plan.

He picked up one of the chairs they were sitting on. They were stackable chairs with straight steel legs that angled outward.

He slid one of the metal legs through the gap in the bathroom's lever handle. He then jumped and brought the full weight of his body down on the chair.

The hard steel frame busted the handle fixture off of the door. Long scrapes tore down the wood face and wall finishing as the chair came to a rest on the ground.

Darren fiddled around with the exposed pieces, but couldn't get the latch to trip.

"Iz," he shouted at the door. "If you can hear me, get away from the door handle."

He picked up the chair again, shoving one of the metal legs into the exposed mechanism of the door lever.

He then tackled it like it was a football practice dummy. The inside handle was knocked off of the door.

Darren reached inside and jostled the guts of the key latch until the door finally pulled open.

A cloud of white powder exploded outward from the rush of air. Darren and Jennifer were dusted head to toe as though someone had torn open a giant bag of flour in front of them.

"What the hell?!" Darren said, sputtering and wiping the powder off wherever he could.

"Iz?" Jennifer said, looking into the room.

It was empty.

"Isabella!" Jenny shouted.

She walked in and there was more of the white powder everywhere, covering the sink, toilet, and garbage can.

She looked up at the ceiling. There was no air conditioning duct she might have crawled in, just an exhaust fan that you couldn't even pass a baseball through.

"Is this some kind of joke?!" Darren asked, addressing the whole room.

The other bodies lying around the corners were starting to stir, roused by the commotion.

The freshman girl in the middle was hugging her knees, no longer screaming.

Jenny stepped into the bathroom. Spitting out the last of the powder that had gotten in her mouth.

It almost felt like baby powder, but not exactly. It was basically flavorless. The texture also reminded her of chalky antacid tablets. The stuff was everywhere.

She figured she must be covered in it, so she went up to the mirror to help wipe it off.

The mirror was also dusted in the powder, so she pulled a few of the paper towels.

With one swipe, she brushed away a layer at eye level.

Darren heard Jenny scream and darted toward the bathroom. He ran up to the door.

Jenny had locked eyes with something that looked through the mirror from the other side.

In the thin strip that was visible through the powder, only one eye was looking back at her. The baby blue coloring of her left iris was surrounded by deep blood red, and all of it was covered in what looked like a giant cataract. Where her right eye should be, there was nothing but darkness staring back at her.

She wiped off another layer of dust.

Her normally vibrant blond hair looked dry and frayed, like the bristles on an old broom. The left side of the creature's face was grey and cracked. The right side was burnt nearly black.

She wiped off another layer of dust.

The creature seemed to snarl at her. Several teeth were showing on her right side, where the flesh of her cheek should be.

She wiped off the bottom of the mirror.

The gradient of black ash went all the way down her body, almost bisecting her in two. On her right side, the dress had fused to her skin. The hand, arm, shoulder, the right side of her neck, right side of her stomach, and her right breast had all taken on the texture of cooked charcoal.

The left side of her body was bloodless and grey.

Jenny was covering her mouth, almost unable to comprehend the creature staring back at her.

Behind the monster was another, standing in the doorway.

Darren's body was just as grey as her left side, with patches of hair burned away and ghastly, bloody eyes. One thing that distinguished his undead form were the half-dozen breaks in the bones of his arms and legs. The corpse in the mirror should not be able to stand at all, and yet it did. Its first priority was to mimic the motions of its twin.

Jenny turned away from the monstrous reflections.

Darren stood in the door frame, seemingly unharmed, covered in a dusting of the white powder.

He tried his best not to lock eyes with his double in the mirror.

"Come on," he said, offering her his hand. "Come out of there."

She took it, and he pulled her through the door, away from the restroom. She began sobbing into his shoulder.

Darren walked them away from that portal of death, sitting down against a nearby wall.

A clear gradient was now visible as the powder in the bathroom mixed with the rest of the air in the space. Darren noticed that the dust didn't just come from the bathroom, it was everywhere. It collected as a thin layer on his arms, his clothes, the walls, the floor, and the furniture.

He stroked Jenny's hair, keeping any more dust from settling in it. It seemed to relax her, and it distracted him.

Darren glanced over at the stairwell, besides their original chairs. Sitting on the first riser of the staircase was Jenny's Homecoming Queen tiara.

***

"Ow. Ow. Ow. Ow. Ow. Ow."

As Niles faded in, a dull throbbing pulsed through his body, but the sharpest pain came from just above his left eye.

"Stupid migraines," he thought to himself.

He didn't realize how tired the night had made him. After his fight with Laura, he sat down in his chair and must have fallen asleep.

His eyes fell open and all he could see was the ceiling. It also looked like they had been running the fog machine too long.

The back of Niles' chair was on the floor, but he was more or less still sitting in it. He had slid off of the seat a bit and was now straddling it like a horse.

Niles pulled his legs in, kicking the right one over the seat and rolling to his knees.

He began flexing every muscle, trying to shake out the random pains he was still feeling. He was used to stiffness like that based on how erratic his sleeping habits were. He'd woken up on the floor of his room more than once in recent years.

Niles reached into his pocket, pulling out a small medicine bag. He pulled out a Maxalt tablet and popped it in his mouth. It worked well enough at killing migraines.

He stood to his feet and the first thing he saw was the top hat being crushed by another chair.

"Shit!" he said, flinging the chair off. The hat had been flattened sideways, so the creases didn't even look uniform. It was only fit for a hobo costume now.

Niles tossed it on the table, then pulled his own chair upright.

Looking out over the ballroom, he could see bright beams of light pouring in from the east-facing windows.

"Wait, what?" he said aloud.

He pulled out his phone.

Sunday, 8:17 a.m.

"It's Sunday?!" he thought to himself, scrolling through the notifications on his phone.

There was nothing new. The last message he received was that text from Barry when he was at the gas station.

Niles pulled up Laura's contact card in his phone and pressed "Call".

He put it up to his face while he started looking around the rest of the room.

Ring.

The whole ballroom was filled with fog, everything had a whitish-grey haze over it.

Ring.

He looked back at the table, none of the others were there, but there was a sophomore kid lying between Liam's chair and the table next to him.

Ring.

In fact, the closer he looked, there were kids sleeping everywhere. About half of them were starting to sit or stand up like him.

Ring.

"What happened last night?" he thought to himself.

Ring.

Niles pulled the phone from his face. After four rings it usually went to Laura's answering machine.

That's when he looked closer at the icons at the top of his phone screen.

No signal.

That couldn't be right, Villa Vista High usually had pretty good cell service, it was only in the woods scattered around Alexandria where the bars might drop.

Niles checked his settings and confirmed that the "Mobile Service" icon was switched on.

The GPS had no signal either. Now *that* was weird.

The GPS satellites could connect to phones deep in remote areas of the Congo or the Australian Outback or the Amazon. The only way to really stop GPS service was to shoot a bunch of U.S. military satellites out of orbit.

Niles pulled up the navigator application to see if the GPS would reset.

No map showed up. There was only the "You Are Here" icon in the middle of a blank screen.

"What?" Niles thought, moving the image around with his thumb. Nothing new came into view.

He lowered the phone. It was only giving him more questions than answers.

That's when a loud scream rang out from the other side of the room.

Niles looked up.

He could see Blaire Tidwell and the tall guy run off toward the hallway. Niles followed them, curious about the noise.

The further he walked through the ballroom, the more scattered bodies he walked past. Niles' stomach was beginning to sink. Something was very wrong.

He pulled out his phone again, deciding that he needed to capture this on video. He tapped the camera application, but the only thing that appeared was a black screen.

Niles tilted the lens, pointing it in all directions. Then he tried using the front-facing camera. Nothing appeared.

As he passed by the second column of tables, he saw Liam wrapped around the legs of one table near the dance floor. The metal bar was pressed into his back. He still hadn't woken up yet.

Niles kept walking.

He entered the hallway where the screaming had come from. A couple of students were huddled around one of the girls from Blaire's group. He didn't know her name but assumed she was one of the seniors.

She was having a full-on panic attack, hyperventilating and shivering while tucking her knees into her face. Her date was trying to get her to talk to him, but she was staring straight ahead, at the door of the girls' bathroom. It was like she was expecting Jason Voorhees to walk out and hack her to pieces with a machete.

"What happened?" Niles asked one of the bystanders.

"Don't know," the sophomore said. "She just ran out screaming then collapsed on the floor like this."

Niles looked back at the door. There were a half dozen others there with them, and not one of them approached it.

It was a shock when he saw Blaire walk out with the tall guy. She was crying.

"What's in there?" the sophomore guy asked him.

The tall guy was new, he was a senior that had only come to Villa Vista this year. He had this really intimidating presence to him. Like whenever you locked eyes with him, he had this cold stare, like he could kill you if you tried to mess with him. He didn't look that way right now.

Instead, his eyes were open wide, full of fear.

He turned to the sophomore kid and only said one word: "Mirror."

The bystanders all exchanged glances. None of them wanted to take the first step.

Niles was briefly reminded of how badly he felt before he blacked out.

"Why not?" he thought to himself. "The day couldn't get any worse."

He stepped forward, passing by the circular girls' bathroom sign.

The bathroom was really nice and clean. The set had only opened a few months ago with the new school year, after they had been remodeled. The girls had apparently kept theirs in excellent condition.

Niles turned the corner of the privacy wall.

What he saw stunned him so suddenly that he stumbled backwards, almost falling through one of the stall doors. He caught himself on the corners and stood upright.

The bathroom in the reflection looked like a war zone ... fire, smoke, and rubble everywhere.

Only one entity stood to face Niles. It followed his movements perfectly, but it was such a distortion that it took him a moment to recognize his own likeness.

Niles stepped forward, squinting to get a closer look.

His doppelganger still wore the ridiculous Lincoln/Valjean outfit, but the clothes were completely trashed. Tears and burns were scattered across the body like craters on an asteroid. The larger holes exposed patches of grey, wrinkled skin, often with a deep cut in the center.

Most of that still looked relatively like him though.

The thing that didn't, the thing that made himself hard to recognize, was the "head" which sat atop the torso.

A massive crater was crushed into the left side of the reflection. There were no distinct eyes or nose to the figure at all. The jaw was only attached on his right side, the left of the reflection.

From the creature's perspective, the crater was on its right side. However, as Niles raised his hand, it mirrored his actions.

He pressed on his forehead, just above his left eye, where a subtle migraine still persisted. The creature's hand continued to move, only stopping once it was touching the mash of white matter.

Niles pulled open his left eyelids, as though an optometrist was doing an exam. The creature matched his motions, but there were no eyelids to take hold of. Its right hand pressed down against the detached side of the jaw. The left hand took hold of a piece of solid skull at the back of its head.

"You're a terrible reflection," Niles said aloud, dissociating from the reality of the experience.

A girl walked into the bathroom behind him. Her reflection was charred over most of the surface. You couldn't even tell what color her dress was originally.

She screamed at the top of her lungs staring at her other self.

Niles scrambled to leave, driven by a juvenile fear of being caught in the girls' bathroom.

He was still following an old set of rules, but as he was beginning to discover, a lot of old rules didn't apply anymore.

TEN

NO SPLITTING UP

ONE THING THAT YOU become more attuned to as a parent is the sound of crying children.

When she was young, Monika was a very colicky baby. Bob Melkonian spent almost three years waking up at such odd hours to calm her down. She was their only child, he and Angie loved her more than anything, but ... he never got used to the crying.

It was like nails on a chalkboard. He only answered Monika so much at night because Bob knew Angie would have her all day, at least until she started school.

A few sleepless nights were fine with Bob. Teenagers, in an odd way, were easier to understand.

Of course, there were instances where teenagers would cry too. That was usually where Bob's limit of understanding was drawn. After that, Rick Wallace would take over, he always knew what to do.

Bob and Rick had become fairly good friends over the years. Rick and his wife Mary had invited the Melkonians over for holidays on occasion, and they'd tried to return the favor. There was no one quite Monika's age, Rick's three kids were in their forties and the grandchildren ranged from three to ten.

Of course, none of the families still lived in Alexandria. Most of them had settled down elsewhere with their spouses. The holidays were the chance for Rick to really see them all together. Because of that, the only time they came to the Melkonians' was when none of the kids could make it into town.

Bob was pretty sure that was one reason why Rick was so good with the Villa Vista students. He saw them a lot more than his own grandkids, and in many ways, he loved them just as much.

The first sensation Bob felt was coughing. He coughed almost twenty times in a row, until a pestering sensation finally disappeared from his lungs.

Every cough was painful and by the end he was clutching his chest.

He rolled to his side, tearing off the cravat and opening the top two buttons of the dress shirt. With the frilly tie cast aside, Bob noticed that his wig had fallen off too. It sat next to where he'd been lying.

He pressed his hand down, feeling commercial carpeting. Every bone in his body was aching. Had he really fallen asleep on the ground?

Bob felt the area around him and found some kind of hard railing. With it, he pulled himself to his feet.

Even the coat and sash felt like they weighed down on his shoulders, so he shed them. The George, Prince of Wales costume lay in a rough pile on the floor. All that remained were the white vest, dress shirt, knickers, socks, and black dress shoes.

Bob blinked his eyes a few more times until things came into focus.

He was in the landing at the top of a stairwell. Specifically, it was the backstage stairwell that led into the costume room on the top floor. It held a boys and girls changing room within, as well as the costume storage space. Adjacent to that was the Choir & Drama Rehearsal Room.

The last thing Bob remembered was talking to the official photographer and Mrs. Lathrop, the Yearbook teacher.

He walked into the costume room and then exited to the second-floor hallway. The C&D Rehearsal Room doors were still propped open for kids getting final pictures.

"Hello?" Bob called inside. "Mrs. Lathrop?"

There was no response.

Bob entered the room. Both the photographer and his assistant were gone.

"Eveline?" Bob asked, using her given name.

"Mrs. Donovan?" he tried, seeing if the Choir & Drama Director was around. He had seen her earlier in the night. "Cynthia?"

He doubled back to the costume room, calling for both of them again. The rooms were empty. Well, not completely empty, a strange new presence had filled them.

Quite a bit of fog, from the machines, had settled on the second floor. It must have been sucked up by the HVAC system by mistake.

Melkonian returned to the stairwell. He kicked the costume pieces into the corner, but otherwise left them there like dirty laundry.

He started walking down the stairwell, taking the same path backstage that they'd been using all night.

When he looked up from the handrail, he was shocked by what he saw.

"Rick?!" he yelled.

Rick Wallace was lying on his stomach. His arms and legs were dangling over the edges of one of the lighting trusses. He was at least eighteen feet off of the ground. The fall could kill him.

Bob ran to the edge of the middle landing, getting as close as he could to Rick's arm.

"Rick, can you hear me? Stay still, or grab hold of something."

He heard a groan leave Rick's mouth.

"Rick, come on, I need you to wake up," Melkonian said. "I'm gonna get you down, but I'll need your help."

The old man started coughing, which caused the lighting truss to bounce a bit on its anchor wires.

"Rick, be careful or you'll fall!"

Wallace's eyes peeled open. He could see the nervous expression on Bob's face. Quickly after that he must have noticed the movement of the truss. He latched onto the metal bars like he was trying to hang onto a runaway horse.

Bob extended his hand as far as he could, the other hand gripping the metal railing.

"What the-? How?" Rick stuttered. "What's going on?"

"You tell me," Bob said. "How'd you get up there?"

Rick looked down at the ground, disoriented by the rocking motion.

"I can pull you in," Bob said, "but you'll have to jump just a little closer to the landing."

Rick took a few breaths to calm himself. "Okay, I'll count to three."

He propped himself up on top of the truss. The landing was about six feet below him, but two feet away from where the truss hung.

"One ... two ... three!" He flexed his legs, springing like a frog.

He cleared the railing and Melkonian grabbed his arms, softening the impact.

Rick slumped down, resting his back against one of the glass panels beneath the handrails.

They both sat in the landing, waiting for the adrenaline to pass.

Melkonian spoke first. "Now ... you're a *real* Rough Rider."

Rick didn't answer, too confused to entertain the joke.

"How on earth did you end up there?" Melkonian asked.

"I tell ya, I don't know!"

"I woke up on the stairwell," he explained. "On that top landing by the changing rooms."

"What's the last thing you remember?" Rick asked him.

Bob tried to call the scene back to mind.

"I was following you. We had finished up with Marcus and Jennifer's pictures and we were heading down to the stage to keep an eye on the students. I was right behind you, but then Mrs. Lathrop stopped me for a second to point out that my wig was crooked."

"It's very crooked," Rick said, regaining some humor. "It's so crooked that it's gone."

"Oh, I know," Bob said. "I took it off."

"I do remember something," Rick whispered.

His eyes zoned out on the backstage wall as he focused on the memory. "I heard, like a 'whoosh!'"

"A whoosh?" Melkonian repeated.

"Yeah," Rick said. "I thought one of the new stage speakers had just blown. That happened to one of the old ones too when they spliced it into the wrong power supply."

"Did the old speaker literally blow you into the rafters?" Bob asked, half-joking, half-serious.

"No." Rick's eyebrows furrowed in worry. "What happened to the speakers? The music's off."

Once he pointed it out, Bob realized it too.

The speakers were not turned off, but rather emitted an electronic feedback of static. It was like they had been switched to an open analog input. The volume was still fairly loud too, Bob couldn't hear any ambient noise from the ballroom below.

"What time is it?" Bob asked.

Rick pulled out the Teddy Roosevelt pocket watch.

"Eight forty-five."

Everything felt wrong, they couldn't have been out for only a few minutes. To Bob, it felt like hours at least.

"Come on," he said to Rick. "I don't like this."

They hustled down the stairwell to the back of the stage, then pushed aside the red theatre curtain.

They were blinded with daylight. Melkonian put his arm up, blocking the unexpected white glow.

Wallace took off the fake spectacles and blinked.

Now that they were far enough from the ceiling-mounted speakers, they heard only one sound filling the ballroom.

Crying.

A grey haze hung over everything in front of them, but the shapes were obvious enough. Small clusters of students were seated at tables, huddled against walls, or retreated into other places, such as the window sills.

A murmur rose from the scattered crowd when they noticed Melkonian and Wallace appear. A few of the cries became louder, and a handful of students stood up. They ran toward the stairwells on either side of the stage. Three of them huddled around Wallace, sobbing.

Bob assumed they were all freshmen. They were very young and he didn't know their names, which meant they hadn't passed through his class yet.

One of them was not though, she was a sophomore. Trisha Forrester was in Melkonian's fourth-period biology class. She clung to Bob, and began crying into his white vest.

"I'm sorry ..." She said through the tears. "I'm sorry, I'm sorry, I'm sorry."

"Trisha, it's okay," Bob said, putting his hands on her shoulders. "You didn't do anything wrong."

"Yes, I did ..." She continued sobbing. "I'm the one who was supposed to be watching Buster, not Johnny."

"What?" Bob asked. He felt like he'd been dragged into the middle of a conversation.

"I knew they would blame him anyway, so I stayed quiet." She continued to sniffle between sentences.

Bob glanced over at Rick who was trying to decipher three different stories which were even less intelligible.

"That's why I'm here," Trisha stepped away from him, almost scared of the touch. "I'm to blame for Buster getting hit by that car."

"Trisha," Melkonian said, "you should talk to-"

But before he could finish his platitude, she finished her confession.

"I'm the reason why Buster died ... that's why *I* deserved to die."

Her final sentence chilled Bob to the bone.

"That's why I'm in Hell."

Bob's mouth was agape, not sure if he had heard her correctly.

Overwhelmed by the admission, Trisha ran off.

Bob looked at Rick, who met his eyes.

He had heard her say the same thing.

Two more students walked up to them on stage, Chelsea Morton and Greg Henshaw. There was a hollowness behind both of their eyes, their faces hung low, contrasting the vibrant orange they were still wearing.

"Guys, come on." Chelsea pulled the freshmen off of Wallace. "Give them time to adjust."

She then addressed Melkonian and Wallace. "In the bathroom, in the mirror ... you'll understand."

She led the freshmen away, with Greg right behind her.

A rather large group had formed around the sophomore couple. They gathered in the west column of tables, near their original seats. The kids offered what little comfort they could provide.

Neither Bob nor Rick had words as the fifteen-year-olds shepherded the others offstage.

Bob peered over the ballroom and felt dozens of eyes watching them. For the first time in a long time, he hated the limelight.

Wallace began walking to stage left. The large men's bathroom was just off of the entrance lobby. He dropped the wig and glasses to the ground.

Once they entered the lobby, the dozen or so kids scattered around the walls took notice.

Wallace pushed open the door, rounding the privacy wall. The shock hit him as it hit everyone else. When Melkonian saw his horrified expression, he ran up next to him.

Both of their bodies appeared to be burned and broken.

Bob Melkonian's reflection still wore the coat and cravat, but they were both sliced full of holes by flying debris. His chest was caved in. Every rib had been shattered and flattened by the force of him striking the costume room door. What remained of his natural hair had been scorched away, leaving charred, leathery skin with red and grey eyes.

Rick Wallace had all the common forms of damage, but instead of a crushed rib cage, his spine was broken in at least three places. The corpse in his reflection looked like a severe scoliosis patient.

While Melkonian's expression was one of confusion and horror, it disturbed him how quickly Wallace seemed to acquiesce to his fate.

Rick's eyes lowered without a word, then he turned and exited the bathroom.

"Rick?!" Bob called after him, unable to process the creatures in the dark beyond.

When he didn't return, Bob followed him out of the bathroom. "Rick, wait!"

The kids scattered around the lobby still eyed the men from afar. However, two in particular had approached the door to wait for them.

Darren Clark and Jennifer Maxwell were standing there, a look of surprise breaking through their despondence.

"Darren, Jennifer?" Melkonian asked. "No, no, no, don't tell me that you ..."

He motioned toward the mirror.

Jennifer's eyes darted away from them and she crossed her arms in front of her chest. Darren nodded, sliding his hands into his pockets.

Rick closed his eyes and shook his head. He was trying to force away the idea that these two kids had met the same fate as him.

"Where are the others?" Bob asked them, clinging to details to distract himself from the broader truth.

"Others?" Jennifer glanced between them.

"Yes," Melkonian said. "The other teachers ... Principal McDouglas, Mrs. Lathrop, Mrs. Donovan, Guzmán, Reynolds, Van Gaal?"

"There are no others," Darren answered. "You're the first adults we've seen since the explosion."

A pause hung in the air ... drifting among the dust.

Denial still gripping his mind, Melkonian echoed, "Ex-plosion?"

Darren pulled out a triangular-shaped mirror. It was about as long as his hand. Melkonian recognized it as having come from one of the decorative entrance tables. They were used to display school papers, fliers, and other handouts for students to grab.

Darren held it up between the two of them. As he adjusted the angle, Bob caught a glimpse of the boy's reflection. A twinge of despair passed through his heart.

The mirror pointed northeast, toward the gym. A column of black smoke poured out of the basketball court like it was the mouth of an active volcano.

"The remodel ..." Jennifer pointed out. "No one's been in there for months ... except for the contractors."

"As far as we know ..." Darren growled under his breath.

"Darren," she said, trying to stop him.

"What are you saying?" Bob pivoted away from the fire and rubble in the small mirror.

"I'm saying that something made the gym go Chernobyl ... and it happened as hundreds of people were partying right next door."

Tears were trickling off of Jennifer's face.

"Everyone's thinking it," Darren continued. "The explosion wasn't an accident. Someone blew up the school on purpose, right when everyone would be here for Homecoming."

Bob stumbled backwards, feeling faint. Rick caught him before he could fall.

"And if this is Hell ..." Darren concluded. "Then the killer could be here too."

VRRRRGT. VRRRRGT.

Two distinctive growls of an engine thundered through the relative silence.

A bright set of lights flashed through the glass doors of the Murphy Center.

***

Blaire hadn't moved from their table since she and Andrei returned from the girls' bathroom.

All four of them had remained mostly silent. No one knew what to say, no one knew how to even begin.

Are they really dead? Is this really Hell? Is she having some awful coma dream and can't wake up?

Andrei stroked her shoulder with his hand ... his right hand.

The sensation was comforting. He was warm, he felt alive, his fingertips had a practiced strength to the way they moved. It was like she was the piano, and the music he played was beautiful, if melancholy.

But no matter how much visceral relief she experienced, one image could not leave her mind ... the skeletal right arm.

Whenever she looked at Andrei's hand, in every other glimpse she'd see the black, charred bones reaching out to grab her.

No matter how much the thought disturbed her though, she fought the urge to recoil or flinch at the sight. She could tell that he was taking as much comfort from the simple touch as she was.

Every few minutes, Blaire glanced around to see who else was joining them for their eternal damnation. A little over a hundred people remained in the ballroom. If they spoke at all it was too hushed to carry beyond their immediate circles. Most of them were huddled into groups of three to five, clinging to the closest loved ones they could find.

At one point Paxton, Amanda, Mark, and Raquel stopped at the table to grab their things. They were helping Jeremy watch Dina.

Once she broke free from her trance, she started screaming wildly again, often with her jaw clenched tight.

Blaire checked a box in her mind. "Confirmed: gnashing of teeth."

She couldn't be around that right now.

The other girls were nice, they were friends, but they weren't like Elise.

Blaire was not in the mood to help the others build a DIY padded cell for Dina. They might not even need to do that anyway. Eventually one of them would find some chill-pills in someone's locker. It shouldn't take them long to dig up some Xanax or Zoloft.

A thought crossed Blaire's mind ... scarcity.

Are those pills going to be all that's left? Is the food going to run out? Is that when the red guys with pitchforks roll in?

"Hey, Blaire ..." Elise spoke up suddenly.

They all turned toward her.

"Are your gym shoes in your locker?"

Blaire thought back. Despite everything, school seemed so far away.

"Yes," she replied.

While they waited for the new lockers to be installed in the gym, some of the athletes were keeping their things in the football stadium lockers.

That was way too far of a walk just to get clothes for P.E., so a lot of people just kept their gym bag in their regular lockers.

"Then let's get our shoes," she said, before whispering the second part, "and get out of here."

"What do you mean?" Raf asked, a slight flutter of hope in his words.

"I mean, I want to go home," Elise said. "Let's just leave."

It struck the three of them that it had taken so long to think of the idea. The images in the mirror were so haunting they had been sort of trapped in their own thoughts.

"Okay," Blaire agreed. "Let's go."

Andrei nodded and they all got up carefully, trying not to attract attention.

They shuffled toward the gym hallway.

Blaire could feel the cold, laminate floor against her feet, beneath the thin layer of her nylon leggings.

"Isn't Hell supposed to be hot?" she thought to herself.

Most other groups didn't even turn to look at them, they were lost in their own depression.

Blaire could see a wall of darkness in the back of her own mind too. Depression was an ever-present experience for most of her short life. She was still equipped with an arsenal of coping mechanisms to keep the pain from leaking through.

They passed through another set of double doors, walking out into the atrium of the classrooms section.

Andrei stopped. "I have some stuff to grab in my locker too."

Blaire turned to Elise and Raf. "We'll meet you there in a second."

She took Andrei's hand. "No splitting up."

"Agreed." He smiled.

Each class had lockers on the first and second floors. The ground-floor lockers were normally claimed first because it meant less walking time on average. Then again, some people preferred the top floor lockers. It depended on whose classes you had in a semester and where their classrooms were located. There was a bit of personal preference at play, of course. It was just like people who chose the top or bottom of a bunk bed.

She and Andrei entered the ground-floor Senior Class hallway.

The first classroom they passed was the Yearbook room. The name "Eveline Lathrop" was still posted on the door.

Blaire remembered seeing her in the corner when the photographer was taking pictures. It struck her that none of the teachers were down there with them. Did they all make it to the "Good Place"?

A leak of sadness began pouring through her wall of darkness.

Blaire took a deep breath. She had cried enough for one day. Besides, she had an eternity to spread out her suffering.

Andrei spun the number dial back and forth. With a tug on the lever, the metal door swung open. He pulled out the duffel bag crumpled on top of the stack of books. Unzipping it, he revealed the generic P.E. clothes with the Villa Vista Jaguars logo plastered on the front.

"What do you think," he said, laying the shirt over his dress suit, "business or casual?"

"Is there a third option?" she asked, pulling the shirt off of him.

"I sure hope so," Andrei said, stuffing the gym clothes back into the duffel bag.

Flirtations aside, Andrei was just happy to see her in a better mood.

He scanned the locker, retrieving some other random items.

Blaire didn't really have any opportunities to linger by his locker like this when they were alive. Their classes were so far apart that the paths never crossed. Normally they'd talk in one of the empty corners of the atrium.

"Nice and basic?" she asked him, marveling at what little he had in his locker.

"I kept some other stuff in my 4Runner," he said, a neutral expression on his face. He flipped it to positive. "Hopefully we can get there before nightfall."

Andrei slid his Physics textbook off of the metal shelf.

"Maybe some light reading for the road?" he asked, cocking an eyebrow.

"I'm pretty sure *Science* is dead." She leaned against the lockers, glancing up at wherever the "Big Guy" might be watching them from.

"Good point," Andrei replied, dropping it back on the shelf.

He slammed the locker door shut and spun the padlock out of habit.

Back in the Junior Class hallway, Raf had his gym bag slung over his shoulder. He was holding Elise's bag while she dropped things inside.

They went up to Blaire's locker and she dialed in the combo.

She slid the gym bag out from one of the shelves, handing it to Andrei. The zipper pulled away and she removed the tennis shoes.

Blaire slid some ankle-length socks over her nylons, then stepped into the plain white shoes with black stripes. Once they were laced up, she stood.

"Feel better?" Andrei asked.

"Well, I feel like I can run now … if I have to," she said.

Andrei's expression dropped. It was a cold reminder of whatever demonic forces may end up chasing them in this underworld.

Blaire winced. She wished she could take back the words, but she didn't have some line to cover them up with.

Returning to the locker, she pulled out anything that felt useful.

"Oh, here we go." She revealed a box of Nutri-Grain bars. It was still mostly full, so she poured them out into the bag then tossed the cardboard box back into the locker.

Just behind the Nutri-Grain bars was her sweatshirt jacket. She added it to the bag.

Tucked over on one side of a shelf was her spare cell phone charger. She dragged it out of the compartment like she was presenting a dead snake to Andrei.

"I guess this is useful?"

Their eyes drifted upward. The rows of fluorescent bulbs in the ceiling fixtures continued to glow a bright, even white.

"Good thing someone's still paying the power bill," Andrei observed.

"It wouldn't surprise me if PG&E had an office in Hell," Blaire quipped.

Andrei chuckled.

Blaire dropped the phone charger into the duffel bag.

Something else occurred to Andrei. He pulled out his own cell phone. "I have a full battery."

"You do?" Blaire raised an eyebrow.

"I was down to like fifty percent when we were dancing," he said.

Blaire pulled out her own phone.

100% battery.

"Ugh, I don't want to know." Blaire slid it back into her purse. "Let's just go, I want to go."

Andrei's eyes opened wider.

"You said that before ..." he whispered. Andrei glanced over his shoulder.

Elise and Raf were still cleaning out her locker, otherwise the four were alone.

A look of dread returned to Blaire's face.

"I'll explain later." She met his eyes, begging him to let it go for now.

"But what did you mean?" he asked, those final moments vivid in his mind. "You knew it was coming."

She stared into her locker, wondering how to put it into words.

Elise closed her own locker and started approaching them with Raf.

"I'll explain later, I promise."

Andrei glanced from her to the other two, then nodded.

She did not know how to explain it at all. Blaire needed more time before she told Andrei about the nightmare.

There was one thing she wanted to clarify first though. Placing a hand on his arm, she whispered, "I didn't do it."

"That feels *so* much better!" Elise tapped her pink sneakers together like they were Dorothy's ruby slippers.

"I'm glad," Raf said. "The heels must really dig in after a while."

"Let's go," Blaire said, slamming her locker.

They circled around the bend which connected to the main corridor. The doors of the front entrance were just ahead, with the Administration offices to one side.

Raf pushed on the handle and they all walked out into the main parking lot.

"I think your house is closest, Blaire," Elise said. "We'll go there first."

They crossed through the security gate, which was still propped open for the dance.

The main road in front of the high school was Westmont Street. It intersected with Mitchell Avenue, which led toward the middle school.

Blaire was pretty sure that's what the signs still read.

While there was hanging dust inside the school building, the outside was covered in a thick blanket of fog. The differences between the two were subtle, but they were noticeable. For the most part, the dust stayed inside and the fog stayed outside.

At the edges of campus, the fog was so thick, they could barely see beyond an arm's length.

Blaire was still holding Andrei's hand. He placed the other firmly on Raf's shoulder.

"Can we even walk through this?" Raf asked. "I can't see anything at all."

"We've got to try," Elise said, leading the pack.

They continued walking, crossing into the intersection of Westmont and Mitchell.

At some point, the crunching of their tennis shoes on asphalt seemed to soften.

"We should have hit the other sidewalk twenty or thirty feet back," Blaire thought to herself.

"I see something!" Elise exclaimed.

Indeed, the fog was starting to thin. They were approaching some sort of shape.

When the crunching sound died out, Elise looked down.

"Guys, we're on grass now," she announced.

"Grass?" Blaire pressed her feet harder to confirm for herself.

Westmont Street separated Villa Vista High from the Oceanside housing edition. There should have been a sidewalk, then the twenty-foot hedge wall that the builders installed as a noise barrier. She was planning on following that hedge wall for at least the first mile.

Elise squinted through the fog, trying to figure out the shape. It was kind of rectangular, maybe a gate or a frame.

After another few steps Elise stood still.

"What is it?" Raf jostled her hand a bit to get her attention.

The rest of them caught up next to her. They all witnessed what had stopped Elise in her tracks.

Jackie the Jaguar was staring at them through frightening yellow eyes. He hissed, bearing four large, sharp fangs. His claws were extended, digging into an oversized baseball like it was a captured boar.

The image was painted on the back of the school's home team dugout. They were at the baseball diamonds on the east side of campus.

"No." Elise's composure dissolved. "No, no, no, no!"

Her knees gave out as fresh tears began to stream from her face.

Raf caught her, kneeling down next to her in the grass.

Blaire looked up at Andrei. "What do we do now?"

His normally stoic expression had cracked more and more since they awoke in this netherworld, but the face he wore now was perhaps the most disheartening ... resignation.

"We'd better get comfortable," he said. "Looks like this is our home now."

ELEVEN

JAGUARS

THE SHAMPOO BOTTLE WAS NEARLY EMPTY and most of what was left was collected around the sides.

Joe Torelli unscrewed the cap and tossed it out of the shower to land in some random spot on the bathroom floor. He shook out every last drop from the bottle until a small puddle of lather filled his hand. Then the bottle was tossed out too.

He scrubbed his hair, then everything else. For almost half an hour the quarterback sat under the burning hot water of the faucet until he was sure he'd removed a layer of flesh.

The hair dryer was put to work teasing the natural black curls until everything was as coiffed and uniform as possible.

Joe pulled out his razor, examining his face. Enough shadow had grown back since shaving for the game that he felt the need to give it another pass.

Eyes open wide, he examined every inch of his face. Errant hairs were plucked and small patches of cover up were applied. Eventually, the only problems were the eyes themselves. Like bolts of lightning, a dozen red lines creeped in toward the pupils.

He pulled an eye drop bottle from the drawer which guaranteed "Extra-Strength Red Eye Relief!"

Joe squeezed several drops into each eye, blinking until the fluid was evenly applied.

The bathroom rituals complete, he walked over to the closet. The bottle was dropped into one of the front pockets of his dress pants. Then he began to pack.

The DVR built into the cable box cycled through a playlist of football highlights as Joe finished the last of his tasks.

Once almost everything was done, he returned to the TV.

A short clip had been saved earlier in the day.

Joe hit play.

And as we're going into Week 7, let's take a look back at last week's games, specifically the Giants/Bears matchup. The game looked like the Giants were going to come from behind for a clutch victory, when Eli Manning threw his third interception for the night right at the Two Minute Warning. It was picked up by Chicago's Tim Jennings, and ended any chance for a Giants victory.

Joe replayed the clip and replayed it again.

He had listened to it perhaps a hundred times by this point.

"You see?!" he yelled to the empty house, "even Manning!"

Joe played the clip again.

Eventually, his hands began shaking, the fingers twitching involuntarily.

He slid a plastic bag out of his pocket, unzipping the seal.

Joe plucked out three tablets, one oblong, one shaped like an oval, and a round yellow one. He couldn't remember exactly what the round yellow one was, but it was an upper, and that's all that mattered right now.

He swallowed all three at the same time and zipped the bag shut. It was returned to his pocket as he stood up.

Walking over to the refrigerator, he retrieved the elegant rose corsage. The suit coat was slung over his back on its hanger. He placed both of them in the car's half seat behind the driver.

A single important letter was placed in the outgoing mailbox.

Joe pulled back his sleeve, comparing his watch to his cell phone's clock.

They were synchronized, both showing 4:33 p.m.

Almost everything else was taken care of.

He flipped on the air conditioning to max to keep the house nice and cool. Then Joe returned to the bedroom.

His football kit bag had been repacked. It had just about everything he thought he needed to pull this off.

He put the kit bag in the Camaro's trunk, right next to the five gallon can of premium gasoline.

"One last dance," he said to himself, before closing the lid.

Joe knew Isabella was going to be upset about last night. It was really unfortunate, because Joe loved how last night turned out, at least the parts of it he could remember. He never used to mix the oblong and oval pills. But Isabella would find out soon enough. All that mattered to him now was that he could give her one truly great night before it was over. That's what the round yellow pill was for, that extra burst of energy. It would get him more talkative, more fun!

They were going to drive, they were going to dance, they'd probably make out a bit, and then he had to break her heart.

He wished things could have ended differently, but in all honesty, he was surprised he didn't do this earlier.

Joe sat behind the driver's seat of the 45th Anniversary Edition Camaro. The entire body of the car was metallic black, except for two silver racing stripes. One of the racing stripes had a bright red accent to it.

He felt bad about screwing over his cousin Tito. But at the same time, Tito wasn't totally blameless in all this.

Joe pulled back his sleeve to check the watch again.

He could make it to Tijuana by sunrise and then further down into the rural Sonoran Desert by Sunday night. He'd be able to sell the Camaro somewhere, eventually.

Joe turned the key. The 3.6-liter V6 engine roared to life.

He wrapped his knuckles around the wheel and pressed the gas pedal to the floor. Four hours seemed to just disappear in a haze.

The most recent memory he could recall featured Iz, who was already upset. Joe felt like he was watching himself on a television screen, replaying the clip over and over again.

"So much for 'talkative,' the mix of pills didn't keep me quite as stable as I'd hoped.

"Fuckin' Trey is going to step in now, like he's Mr. Savior Complex. He's been spending too much time around Darren.

"Oh, there was his mistake, he put his hand on my shoulder."

Without hesitation, Joe wound back his right fist and made solid contact with Trey's jaw.

"Dumbass, he should have seen that coming.

"And right on cue, there's the guard stepping in to throw me out.

"Ha! Of course McDouglas is going to trail after him so he can feel like a big man too.

"Ugh, I shouldn't have yelled at Iz quite so much, she was really crying.

"Okay, I was in the Camaro, and ... Well? ... What are you doing? Turn the key. Come on! What are you waiting for? Turn the key!"

The gaps in Joe's memory felt very familiar to him, but this was something else entirely.

To his mind's eye, this moment was like the screen had been paused. His fingers were wrapped around the key, but he would not turn it.

Joe was breathing heavy, but every breath was shallow. He did not have the strength to pull air into his lungs. His head rested on the steering wheel. He was waiting for the episode to pass.

He sat in the expensive, stolen sports car, facing the Lawrence Murphy Performing Arts Center. The stimulants in his system had depressed his heart rate so much that he could not gather the strength to begin his escape.

It was 8:34 p.m.

Darkness seemed to envelop him in an instant.

The last thing he remembered was that single thought, that single command his body refused to carry out. "Turn the key!"

VRRRRGT. VRRRRGT.

Two distinctive growls of an engine thundered through the relative silence.

Headlights flooded the Murphy Center lobby with each failed attempt to get the engine to turn over.

Joe Torelli opened his eyes.

Painful sensations needled him all over his arms, chest, and face.

A wall of figures were pressed up against the glass of the entrance, their silhouettes backlit by a glowing haze.

Joe's heart began pumping quickly. He turned the key once more.

The Camaro growled, but refused to roar. The high-performance engine, which had never failed to start in the past, would not turn over now.

Joe checked for the "low battery" light. It was turned off.

He smacked the steering wheel with his fist. His eyes darted around for any other indication of why the car wouldn't start.

In his outrage, he caught a glance of himself in the rear-view mirror.

The quick flash scared him so much that he pulled open the door handle and stumbled out of the driver's seat.

Behind the glass of the Murphy Center entrance, everyone was drawn to the spectacle of one of the cars in the parking lot suddenly awakening. Regardless of how hard it struggled though, the car didn't seem to be able to gather the strength to actually move. The internal combustion of the engine wouldn't ignite. The "heart" could not beat on its own.

Darren and Jennifer were among the onlookers, as were Bob Melkonian and Rick Wallace.

Darren turned to her, "Go get the guys."

She nodded and slipped away from the window.

The image flashed in front of Joe's vision as he struggled to get up off of the asphalt. His eyes continued glancing back at the rear-view mirror, where the thing had appeared.

After a few deep breaths, he found sure footing and stood, creeping toward the open car door.

The figure appeared in and out of view as he moved in and out of the mirror's reflection.

Finally, he grabbed the fixture with both hands and stared it down.

The only monster Joe could see was himself.

The face which looked back at him was torn open with hundreds of small cuts, shredding the flesh as though he'd taken a round of birdshot. Yet with all of the deep tears, there was no trickling blood anywhere. It was as though he'd been shot then immediately spit-roasted over an open fire, drying out all the juices.

The creature's eyes had been peppered by several pieces of debris, destroying the round shapes. What remained looked like fleshy, dried apricots in the back of his skull.

The black billows of curly hair, which normally poured from his head, were all gone. Deep scorches and pieces of melted flesh formed a loose circle around his crown line. The discoloration made it look like he was wearing a priest's zucchetto.

Joe leaned back in the driver's seat. The billows of hair, which he could still feel, pressed into the leather headrest of the sports car. In the reflection, the line of seared flesh matched, as the creature's skull slotted into the melted seat cushion.

He brought his hands to his face. The mirror showed them to be charred and grey. Joe could feel the whole, undamaged flesh of his cheeks. His face was fine and his hair was fine. Who was this creature that stared back at him?

Further down, Joe could see that the shredding and tearing stopped just around his navel. Beyond that, the burns and destruction were more uniform.

He turned from the mirror for the first time, pressing his hand on the windshield. He called back a memory of his uncle Tony getting put through the glass when he T-boned someone. Some of the cuts on his face were quite similar to those that now appeared on Joe.

Beyond the windshield, Joe could see five shadows approaching the car.

It was the guys ... Brendan, Trey, Jimmy, Darren, and Mr. Mel for some reason. They looked like themselves, more or less, not some shambling grey zombies.

Joe looked at the mirror again, and a surge of rage pulsed through him.

In one swift motion, he ripped the deceitful looking glass from its mount. He stepped out of the Camaro, not stumbling, but in full control. His arm wound back and spiked the rear-view mirror into the ground. The plastic assembly exploded into a hundred pieces as soon as it impacted the pavement.

"Joe," Brendan said, being the first to approach him, "what the hell are you doing here?"

Joe looked up at him. "What time is it?"

"That doesn't really matter anymore," Jimmy threw up his hands.

Joe remembered his watch and tugged back the shirt sleeve.

9:02 a.m.

"What's going on?" Joe asked them. He glanced at Melkonian, somehow expecting him to be more informed, but his face looked more lost than the rest of them.

"We thought you had made it out," Trey said, the welt on his jaw was gone.

"Joe ..." Darren said, taking a step towards him, "something's happened ... we're dead."

"The hell are you talking about?" Joe laughed. "You're standing right here."

"It's true," Brendan said, walking up next to Darren. "You saw it yourself, didn't you?"

He kicked at the smashed rear-view mirror.

"Dead how?" Joe mocked him, acting like the guys were doing a poorly executed bit.

"Boom!" Jimmy said from the back, wiggling his fingers down like falling debris.

Darren bent down to the rear-view mirror. He brushed away the smashed plastic, loose metal screws, and electronics. He then lifted up from the ground ... the mirror itself.

It was perfectly intact. Its shape remained, there were no scratches, and no chips of any kind had broken off.

Joe's brows tightened. The glass should be in a dozen pieces after how hard he threw it.

Darren flipped it over. Black smoke and distant orange glows were visible from all angles.

He stepped past Joe a little, aiming the mirror at the front of the gym.

Melkonian watched all of these interactions from the back. He listened to the explanation again, as though he had somehow misunderstood something the first time.

Joe saw the gym, burning. The inferno as a whole spread much further though. Fires extended in all directions. The open field by the middle school, the baseball diamonds, even the football stadium on the far end of campus was alight in wisps of flame.

Joe was silent.

After being dilated for the last twenty-four hours, his pupils were now pin-pricks.

His hands had begun shaking, so he balled them into fists, trying to keep the others from seeing.

"It *wants* us to see ..." Darren said, tilting the mirror so Joe could see the broken and burned bodies of the rest of them. "That's why you can't destroy any of the mirrors."

Darren copied Joe's motion, spiking it into the ground.

After making contact with the asphalt, the mirror flicked upwards. It landed a few feet away, by the others. Trey picked it up and walked it over to them.

Once more they found it to be totally without damage.

A very long pause held in the air while Joe took all of this in.

He dropped the mirror to the ground.

"Where's Iz?" he finally asked.

Trey and Brendan looked at each other, then looked to Darren to answer.

"She's not here Joe." He sighed.

"What do you mean she's not here?!" Joe exploded.

Darren took a step backwards as his ears began ringing.

"She must have made it to the other side," Darren guessed. "We should be happy for her."

"Happy?" Joe said, frothing again. He grabbed Darren's lapels with both hands and almost picked him up off of the ground. "You think I should be fucking happy that someone killed Isabella?!"

Darren grabbed his wrists, wrestling for control.

"You think I should be happy that I can't see her?!" he yelled again.

After watching everything from afar, Melkonian finally stepped up.

"Torelli, stop." Bob put an arm between the two of them.

Joe looked at Melkonian with a scowl, then he noticed four more figures in front of the glass doors.

It was the girls ... all the girls except Isabella. Jennifer stood at the front, looking like she was coming to intervene. But having heard the contents of the conversation, she was struggling to hold back her own tears.

Joe let go of Darren's lapels.

Jimmy stepped up, joining the huddled group.

"Come on," he said. "There's quite a bit of food left. You want some microwaved steak?"

Joe said nothing, but he relented, walking with them.

They left behind a parking lot full of dozens of vehicles, including Joe's.

The keys remained in the ignition of the Camaro, and the trunk remained closed.

***

After a short jog away from the screaming, Niles found himself standing in the atrium of the school's classrooms section.

He raised his hand to his forehead, feeling the solid section of skull that was still there.

Niles started laughing, longer and harder than he had in a long time ... and it was for all the wrong reasons.

He laughed as he strolled through the hallways, stumbling like he was drunk, which he desperately wanted to be at the moment.

"Yes ... yes!" he screamed to the empty section of the building. "How perfectly appropriate that the worst day of my life should end with my head getting caved in and the rest of me burned to a crisp!"

Niles walked into the ground-floor Junior Class hallway, where his locker was.

"Thank you, thank you, Lord Xenu? Or whatever fifth-dimensional alien child is running this shitty simulation." Niles' mind fired wildly, overwhelmed with the stress and emotions he was ill-equipped to process.

"Not only that, but I get to wear this two-century-old monkey suit for all of this level." He laughed again, tearing off the frilled necktie and tossing it into one of the trash cans. "You going to put me in a fucking diaper next time?! I was never that cruel to any of my video game characters!"

He stumbled past the door of Mr. Reynolds' U.S. History classroom.

The dial for his locker spun and the latch pulled open. On the bottom shelf of the locker were six cans of Axon energy drink.

Niles popped one open and immediately chugged half of the 24 oz can. He then slammed the locker door shut and slid down to the floor.

He sat there for a while, talking out loud to the empty halls as he sipped down two more Axon energy drinks.

Eventually though, he noticed some slight movement down the hall. The door to Mr. Reynolds' classroom was opening.

"Niles," a voice called from it.

"Barry?!" Niles answered in surprise.

"Yes." He didn't step out into the light, or view of the cameras.

"What are *you* doing here?" Niles asked, walking over to the door.

"Just get inside!"

Niles walked into the dark room and felt the door close with a whoosh of air.

Two cell phone lights came on.

"Melvin?" he added, before asking again, "what are you guys doing here?"

Barry Owens and Melvin Mueller were dressed head to toe in black. Black t-shirts, black sweatshirt jackets, black sweatpants, and black shoes.

"What is this a stick-up?" Niles commented.

"This is serious," Melvin whispered, more nervous than he usually sounded.

"Look," Barry said, "we just need you to find us some spare dress clothes to put on so we can blend in and get out of this stuff."

"Why are you wearing that stuff in the first place?" Niles asked. "How did you guys get into the school without Homecoming tickets?"

"Well," Barry said, "we kind of broke in."

"I might have swiped the spare key Reynolds keeps in his desk drawer ..." Melvin said.

"What?" Niles replied. "You better not be going where I think you're going with this. Have you looked in a mirror?"

"Yes, we've looked in a mirror!" Melvin stammered. "We were hiding in one of the bathrooms when it happened!"

"So, you two?" Niles accused them.

"No!" Barry said. "We did not blow up the school!"

"Then what the hell are you guys doing here?" Niles asked.

"Ahh ... ahh ..." Melvin was making the same grunts he usually did when he took too long to think of something.

"A prank!" Barry said. "We were going to play a prank."

"Like the truck full of fertilizer kind of prank?" Niles retorted.

"On you," Melvin mumbled.

Niles was silent, looking at their faces lit up by the cell phone LEDs.

"Well, it was a great prank," Niles said, "wanna see what *I* look like in a mirror?"

"It was my idea," Barry admitted. "We were going to trip the fire alarm so you and Laura would have to leave the dance. I was still pissed about the Anne thing ..."

Niles pulled out his own phone.

"So that's what this 'Good luck Niles' shit was about?" he spit back.

After thinking for a minute, he said, "I don't believe you."

"What?! No, you have to believe us!" Melvin begged.

"How were you going to trip the fire alarm?" Niles asked.

Both of them remained silent.

"Is there some bag of wire cutters and other electrical tools hidden somewhere?" Niles asked.

Again, they both remained silent.

"Nope, I am not getting involved in this." Niles turned toward the door.

Melvin moved between, blocking the exit with his body. Barry went up and put his hands on Niles' shoulders, trying to convince him.

"I swear," Barry said, "it's the truth."

Right as Niles was about to make another move for the door, they heard a group of voices outside.

"Lights off!" Melvin whispered, clicking the phone's LED. He slid his head lower on the door.

There were no windows in the classroom doors, so Melvin had his eyes locked on the shadows moving around on the bottom.

They stayed quiet.

There were too many voices, and they were too far away for Niles to distinguish anything. It just sounded like muffled noises.

They waited for a few minutes, until the rambling died away.

"Holy shit," Melvin said, still in a hushed tone.

"What is it?" Barry asked.

"I think they were talking about the bomb!" Melvin answered.

"Who?" Niles asked, crossing his arms.

"I don't recognize the voices ... some girl and some guy."

"Yeah, bullshit." Niles shoved Barry aside.

"At least leave us your stupid overcoat," Barry pleaded.

"They'd immediately recognize it as mine," Niles said in a low tone. "No one else wore fucking cosplay to the dance."

"So the date went well then?" Melvin mocked.

Niles shoved Melvin's head into the wall and pulled open the door.

He turned back toward them to say one last thing.

"Good luck Barry."

Then he slammed the door behind him.

***

Elise felt like she had cried harder in the last hour than she ever did when she was alive.

Seeing her broken neck had been morbid. Even worse, it was simply the cherry on top of how hellish her death had been. Thanks to the sadistic designs of this world, she would no longer be able to see herself as anything more than an animate corpse.

She had sobbed with Raf and Blaire and Andrei over all that was taken from them, the separation from their families, and the long, beautiful lives they would never have.

Somehow though, the leering, painted-yellow eyes of Jackie the Jaguar cut her much deeper. Those eyes didn't represent loss, things she wouldn't experience. They represented terror, things she would have no choice but to experience.

The fangs and open mouth, the claws dug into the baseball, she saw those as promises for the near future ... the eternal torment which would show up when she least expected it.

That's how her death was, it showed up when she least expected it.

At the time, her thoughts had dwelled on the music she was hearing as they danced. She was taking internal notes on what songs she wanted to download to her phone for her own playlists.

She was thinking about how handsome Raf looked in his white suit and scarlet vest, how kind he had been in helping her process the situation with Blaire.

Elise had already begun formulating new schemes on how they'd navigate Jimmy's afterparty, including exit strategies for if things got too wild or they needed a believable excuse to get the others to leave.

She knew Mark & Raquel could disappear together for long stretches of time, and she did not want to get stranded at the hillside party palace.

Then, Elise had felt something slam hard into her back.

For the split second she had to think, she had assumed some overly spirited boy had spun his girl right into her and Raf.

Rather than falling to the ground though, she remembered seeing that she was flying much further than seemed possible.

Then there was nothing.

Like a popped circuit breaker, everything went totally black in the fraction of a second.

Now she knew that the thing which popped ... was her spinal cord. It snapped cleanly against the seat of a chair, pressed by the force of flying bricks and a wave of fire.

The next thing she felt at all was the sensation of Blaire whispering in her ear, begging her to wake up.

Fear had paralyzed most of the kids who had woken up in this ghost world, but Elise was a fighter. As soon as the initial horror and depression wore off, her mind immediately set itself on solutions. At the very least, she wanted to feel out the boundaries of this place.

A large part of her was hopeful that there was a shadow of the entire town for them to live within. They could go to each of their respective houses and gather what belongings they could find.

She would want to stay together of course, pick a house and all of them share it. Most likely that would have been Blaire's. It was the nicest and most scenic. Then again, she'd never been to Andrei's place.

But all of those hopes had been dashed so quickly. Their world appeared to end at the limits of the real fire which had consumed their real school.

They explored a bit more of the boundary, finding that the same approaches would return them to the same antipodes.

So if they entered the fog from the baseball diamonds, it would dump them out at the intersection of Westmont and Mitchell. If they crossed the grass toward the middle school, it would move them by the tennis courts on the far south side of campus, beyond the football stadium.

At the end of this walking in circles, Elise begged them to make one more attempt as they had at the beginning.

They walked through the fog at the intersection of streets ... and once more arrived at the dugout of Baseball Diamond #3.

Fully understanding the walls of their prison, Elise resigned from her explorations.

She led the three past the painted image of Jackie the Jaguar. They slowly approached the main school building. Along that route were two smaller buildings.

One of them was for outdoor storage. It held all the sports supplies, lawn mowers, tree trimmers, and anything used to maintain the various athletics fields. The second building was the snack stand.

While the football stadium had its own concessions counter for games of football, soccer, and other stadium sports, this snack stand supported the baseball fields and gymnasium sports. The stand also had a set of bathrooms attached to the back.

Very few of the students had ventured outside yet, so she wondered if they would find someone huddled in either building, also too paralyzed to leave their immediate surroundings.

It turned out, they didn't even have to go *that* far.

As soon as the group passed the dugout for Baseball Diamond #2, they heard whimpering.

Despite Raf trying to stop her, Elise turned the corner.

At first, Elise thought she was seeing a real ghost. Well, perhaps 'real' wasn't the right word, considering the circumstances.

Elise was seeing a stereotypical nineteenth century noble lady ghost. She looked like countless spirits featured on melodramatic romance shows that played during this time of year. After all, they had died less than two weeks before Halloween.

The girl had a series of very old-fashioned curls framing both sides of her face. Below those, she wore a richly-colored red gown with lace and frills and other "High Society" looking ostentatious elements. She also appeared to have a cream-colored shawl which she had folded up to use as a makeshift pillow.

The girl was laying sideways on the dugout bench, weeping to herself.

"Hello?" Elise called out to her.

The girl's head snapped around in an instant. She hadn't heard them approach.

Once Elise got a good look at her face, she recognized her. It was Laura Nakano, the Junior Class Treasurer.

She scooted backwards on the bench pressing into the wooden corner of the dugout.

"Whoa, it's okay," Elise said, trying to comfort her. "We're in the same boat."

Laura's eyes scanned them up and down, apparently looking for cuts or tears or burns or other ghoulish damage.

Elise thought Laura's eyes lingered a bit too long on Rafael.

"It's only in the mirrors," Blaire said from the back.

"I ... I ... I ..." Laura had a hard time speaking. It appeared to be the first time she'd tried to speak aloud since she woke up.

"Bathroom," she finally said.

The snack bar bathroom was about thirty feet away from the dugout.

"You mean in the mirrors, right?" Elise asked. "Or is it something else?"

Laura just shook her head sideways, an answer which wasn't satisfying.

"Just wait here." Elise sighed, moseying over to the bathroom.

"Whoa, wait up!" Raf followed close behind. Blaire and Andrei stayed with the girl.

Creating small tasks like "getting shoes from my locker," or "exploring the fog border", or "seeing what scared the Student Council girl" helped to distract Elise's mind from thinking about bigger picture stuff.

The doors were propped open, probably as overflow for the Homecoming attendees. Sometimes service staff would use them too, because they were the closest lavatories to the cafeteria without having to cross through the ballroom area.

Elise walked into the girls' room. Her first impression was that the bathrooms were surprisingly clean.

When the staff did special preparation for the football stadium ... like for the Homecoming game ... they would usually clean the baseball snack bar bathroom at the same time, just to maintain a consistent schedule.

Another thought crossed Elise's mind. Even though she'd been awake for a few hours now, she hadn't needed to "go" at all. Do ghosts even need to use the bathroom?

She passed the sinks, and it was enough to give her pause.

This was the largest mirror she'd seen herself in so far.

The mirror in her locker had given her a brief, but sobering look at her upper body. With the exception of her broken neck, much of the damage had been similar to the others.

This mirror was large enough for her to get a full view of her back too.

The same intense lick of flame which washed over Raf's face and chest had also terribly scorched her upper back. Just below the bones that were broken in her neck was a large patch of skin with the top layers burned away to muscle. Most of her thoracic and lumbar vertebrae were now partially visible.

Health class had taught her that the "points" on the outside of the spine, that you can feel with your fingers, are called spinous processes. Most of those were now exposed to air, standing out against the larger patch of seared away skin. They featured on her now backless pink dress.

The sight was surprisingly not as horrible as Elise expected.

The gruesome gore that the mirrors mocked them with was not even an ounce as terrible as the existential dread she felt for whatever the future held.

It was only when Raf entered the bathroom too did she turn away from the reflection. She chose instead to look at his normal, unburnt face.

Raf was distracted by this unseen side of what had happened to them.

He walked up and took Elise in his arms, standing as they were when they danced.

She accepted the embrace, leaning close to him as he looked.

The missing flesh on his chest ended right where the missing flesh on her back began.

He stared at the vacuous sockets for only a few seconds before closing his eyes.

"I'm so sorry this happened to us," he whispered to Elise.

"Me too," she said to him.

They held each other in silence for a minute, before Elise opened her eyes.

She was now facing the stalls. In the very last stall, the large one meant for handicapped patrons, she could see a set of black shoes.

"Hello?" Elise called.

Raf let go of her as she walked deeper into the bathroom.

The shoes were flats, rather than heels or wedges. They seemed rather plain for a school dance. They looked more like something you'd only wear for church on Sundays ... or maybe to a funeral.

A pair of pale white legs were attached to them. They were legs which seldom saw sunlight at all, not from skirts, not from shorts, and not from the beach.

This was California and they had just wrapped up a rather hot summer. Elise's legs were still a healthy tan from all the time she and Raf had spent swimming the last few months.

Once she was close enough, Elise pushed open the stall door ... and shrieked at the top of her lungs.

Rafael caught up to her, placing one hand on her hip to pull her away from whatever she'd seen.

The girl was wearing an emerald green dress, which had been pulled back into a bunched pile so that her thighs were exposed.

There were long, deep cuts in the muscle of her inner legs. Above them were two pale arms resting on the girl's knees. Both forearms had been badly sliced open. Strips of skin and muscle dangled off the sides.

Elise could see the ulna and radius bones of the girl's arms.

This was not in a mirror; this was not some facsimile of the way they'd died. These were her real, actual arms.

An X-Acto knife was still lodged deep in the muscle of her left arm. It was propped upright, like chopsticks standing vertically in a bowl of rice.

All of this carnage should have left the girl sitting in a pool of her own blood ... literally all of her blood, considering how much her femoral arteries had been shredded. However, there was not a drop of blood to be found anywhere. Instead, she sat in something else entirely ... dust.

Enough fine particulate had collected in a pile between her legs that she could have filled a punch bowl. Even more of the powder remained in the wounds themselves.

Despite all this mutilation, the girl turned her head to look up at Elise and Raf.

It was Ellen Taylor, the Freshman Class Princess.

"There's no way out." Her face was full of anguish and rage.

"There's no way out!" She stood to her feet, hot tears trickling from her chin.

Elise was hyperventilating now, all reason and sanity plastered over by images of Ellen's bloodless, butchered flesh.

Raf had both arms around her waist, pulling her out of the bathroom. She was too scared to move otherwise.

Ellen stood in the door of the handicapped stall, wild eyes staring back at them.

"Just leave me alone!" she cried.

As Raf turned the corner, Elise got a glimpse of the girl in the mirror.

Her body was mangled and broken, almost not retaining a human form at all. She looked as though she'd been buried in a pile of heavy concrete blocks, like the kind which formed the dividing wall between the bathrooms and the snack counter.

"There's no way out," Elise whispered to herself, fear digging into her like fangs and claws.

TWELVE

NOWHERESVILLE

BOB MELKONIAN PLODDED SLOWLY behind the football players and their girlfriends as they guided Joe Torelli back into the Murphy Center.

He had now heard Darren Clark's explanation of events twice, and seen half a dozen walking cadavers appear in the glass of mirrors ... including himself. The sheer amount of mutilation everyone had suffered were images he struggled to shake from his thoughts.

A small voice whispered in the back of his head to really process what Darren had said, but a much louder portion of his mind was in a state of total denial.

He was now working under the theory that he had tripped and fallen down the backstage stairwell. This was all a horrific coma dream. He would wake up in a few days in the hospital with Angie on one side and Monika on the other.

Bob paused, taking another look around from the front of the building.

A thick wall of fog seemed to lie just beyond the school's security fence. He could barely see the closest yellow line of the turning lane on Westmont Street. Of course, the white haze was everywhere else too.

None of it felt quite like fog though. There wasn't a wetness to it. You couldn't wave your hand around and feel dew. It seemed closer to smoke from a wildfire. However, it didn't have a smell to it, and he wasn't coughing from the particulate.

Bob would have recognized smoke instantly, because his father was a heavy smoker.

He turned back toward the front door and saw Darren and Jennifer holding it open for him. He walked through the passage, with a simple: "Thanks."

They disappeared into the ballroom, following the others.

Bob remained in the lobby, his eyes drifting over to one of the decorative entrance tables. The wood frame of the table had been smashed in by one of the metal stackable chairs. On the floor below the table top were the other dozen or so decorative mirror shards, perfectly intact.

Melkonian bent down and picked one up, locking eyes with his decayed duplicate on the other side.

He pivoted the mirror around himself, glancing over the images of the other dozen or so kids huddled against the walls. All of them were just as broken, often with their own unique misshapen features.

"Is this about Monika?" he thought to himself, interpreting the nightmare as a personal message from God. "Did I not take her to church enough as a girl?"

Bob thought that he and Angie had actually done a pretty good job with her. They even attended one of the few Armenian Apostolic churches in the area just to have that extra value of their cultural heritage. Armenia after all was the first kingdom to adopt Christianity as its official religion. Modern Armenian Christians were proud of that fact.

Sure, they might not have gone *every* weekend, but it was more than half, especially when Monika was young.

Monika, who was now going to school at the University of Southern California, did say she went to church occasionally with one of her Armenian friends. How true that was, Bob didn't know. But the girl was 400 miles away now, and almost twenty years old, how much could he really do?

Bob slipped the mirror into his pocket and walked back into the ballroom.

The group Greg and Chelsea were talking to had doubled. They seemed to have kicked off a sort of group therapy session. Their collective took up almost half of the tables on one of the two columns.

Among the crowd was the Homecoming King, Marcus Johnson. He was doubled over in his chair, a broken man. Some of the other Varsity Basketball players were next to him, trying to help keep him together.

The one person notably absent was Janice Short, his long-time girlfriend.

While many of the other teens were still scattered around the edges of the room, they began trickling toward the group with each passing minute.

Bob listened in for a while from the side. They were going one by one, each kid telling their personal stories. They talked about people they missed, things they wished they could have done, and eventually, what they thought they did to deserve Hell.

The kids were doing this on their own. Bob felt a nagging guilt from within. That's something that he and Rick should be a part of, or even leading.

Melkonian was still coming to these conclusions based on a kind of dream logic. He was going about his routine, regardless of the circumstance most kids thought that they were in.

These were figments of his imagination, keys to some riddle about a shortcoming in his own personal morality that he had to solve in order to wake up. Real or not however, he needed help.

Bob set out, looking for where Rick Wallace disappeared to. After a sweep of the ballroom and backstage, he decided the best bet was Rick's office. He made his way to the hallway that passed by the gymnasium.

While the kids had scattered in strange places around the school building, every one of them avoided even touching the wall of the gymnasium. It was like an animalistic instinct, that it was radioactive, smelled of rotting flesh, and glowed in strange colors.

The truth of course is that they could all see the endless column of black smoke rising up out of the basketball court. Every single mirror showed that image.

Bob kept to the other side of the hallway as well, not even coming within arm's length of the construction wall covering the doors.

He made it through the passage and walked into the middle of the atrium.

CRUNCH.

Bob heard a very unnatural sound. It startled him and he instantly turned to face the source, right as it made a second noise. A pair of dress shoes bounced off of the decorative stone floor tiles, until the senior's body came to rest.

A boy had just dived off the railing of the atrium, forty feet above.

"Oh my god!" Bob jumped back in horror.

After a moment of hesitation, mentally processing the situation, he approached the kid. There were a few other students who had migrated to different parts of the atrium. They circled up as spectators.

Melkonian was too afraid to touch him. The angle his head was twisted at guaranteed that he was already gone.

Bob's heart raced and his stomach began to churn. He whirled around, stepping only a few feet away before vomiting.

A lighter set of pops sounded from the body. Bob braced himself before glancing back, expecting something even worse.

The neck and the body had straightened out a bit. The kid now looked like he was just lying on his stomach on the ground.

The boy coughed up a handful of white dust ... like he had drunk a cup of powdered coffee creamer. He then began to scream.

"W-what?" Melkonian whispered to himself. He ran back to him.

"It hurts, it hurts!" the jumper cried.

"Don't move, Sid." Melkonian recognized him as Sidney Lee from a past biology class.

His head darted from side to side, trying to come up with a plan. He looked up at the railing where Sid had jumped from, and the corridor just behind it.

"I'll get the first aid kit in my classroom," Bob told him, rushing off towards the stairwell.

His biology lab was in the second-floor Sophomore Class hallway.

Not having time to fiddle with keys, he punched in the four-digit numerical code and tugged open the handle.

The kit was sitting on the middle shelf of the front cabinet. Mr. Mel pulled down the white plastic box with a red cross on the front.

As he reached the bottom of the atrium, he found Sidney Lee lying on his back. His head was righted to the center of his chest, looking at the ceiling.

"Who moved him?!" Melkonian snapped at the small, gathered group.

"None of us, Mr. Mel," one of his sophomores said. "He flipped over, himself."

Bob kneeled down next to the boy, opening the kit.

"Sid, what were you thinking?" He tried to keep his voice comforting but still a bit chastising.

The kid was no longer screaming in pain, but he was crying.

"I can't do it," Sidney moaned. "I want to go home."

Melkonian found a basic neck brace among the contents of the kit and wrapped it around the boy. He then pulled out some of the extra strength ibuprofen tablets.

"Can you swallow?" Bob asked.

"Yes," Sid answered.

Bob dropped a few in his mouth. He took the pills without water.

"We really are stuck here forever," one of the onlookers said.

The crowd began to scatter.

"Are you paralyzed?" Bob asked him. Sid's head was bending clear in the other direction just a minute ago. He should be dead.

Sid looked down and Bob followed his eyes. His feet were tapping left and right like he was riding a bicycle.

"No, I'm fine." He sounded as shocked as Bob was.

"What about the pain?"

"It's not too bad. Once I straightened out, most of it went away."

After a few more basic questions, Sidney Lee said he was just going to lay there for a while, but that Melkonian could go.

Bob stood to his feet in a stupor, continuing his journey toward Rick Wallace's office.

His eyes scanned the walls and ceiling with every step, expecting some other nightmarish manifestation to pop out at him. The first aid kit dangled between three fingers.

Soon, he reached the front lobby and turned left towards the school's Administration offices.

One of the doors had been unlocked already. Bob followed it, staggering down a small, secluded hallway.

The hallway had two single-stall restrooms, which kids often used as an excuse if found in the office by friends. Although most students were given a chance to talk to Mr. Wallace at one point or another, they didn't want to admit it and open up a world of speculation to their classmates.

Many others would come up with a "boring" excuse. The seniors, for instance, also received college and career counseling from him. Just being near his office didn't necessarily mean you were getting therapy for depression or bullying.

Bob reached the back of the hallway, where a thin beam of light trailed out of the open door.

He knocked on the door frame.

"Rick, mind if I come in?" he asked.

There were a few seconds of silence, then some noise as he opened and closed desk drawers.

"Sure, Bob," he said.

Melkonian pulled the door open.

Rick was slouched in his desk chair. It was leather and ergonomic, an exceptional piece of designer office furniture. It had been a Christmas present from his wife a few years back.

Bob sat down on one of the couches meant for students.

There was a long moment of silence. Rick was acting just as strange now as he was when they looked in the bathroom mirror.

"Twenty," Rick finally said.

"What?" Bob responded.

"That's how many teachers and faculty were at the dance besides us." Rick stroked his mustache. "I'm not sure how many cooks and staff were still around."

Bob zoned out, mentally counting faces that he'd seen himself.

"That includes Principal McDouglas." He then let out a sigh of relief. "Thank God Barbara wasn't there. She's probably the most senior Villa Vista official to survive.

"God, she'll have to attend so many funerals, give so many speeches of mourning, handle so many media and press appearances. Hundreds are dead, this is probably already international news. It's gonna haunt her for the rest of her young life."

Bob nodded along, staring at a potted plant as he listened.

"Bob, could I ask you something personal?" There was a heavy misery in Rick's voice. "Why are *you* here? Why are you in Hell?"

A fresh wave of fear swept over Melkonian as he looked back at Rick. The cold sincerity in Wallace's eyes was impossible to interpret any other way. Coming from him made it sound so much more horrible than one of Bob's students.

Even still, the question played into the script that this was all a parable God was weaving into Bob's comatose brain.

His first instinct was diversion.

"I thought you were Catholic? This could be Purgatory, or some kind of Limbo ..."

"Limbo is still Hell," Rick Wallace corrected him, "the First Circle ... you should have chatted with Van Gaal more."

Timothy Van Gaal's "Classics" course was essentially a high school introduction to Western Civ. It was a popular elective, mostly because Tim was very animated about the subject matter.

He was also keen on using "modern embodiments of classic myths" in his lessons ... which amounted to watching a movie or TV show once a month.

"This can't be Hell!" Bob exclaimed, as though he were arguing with his own subconscious. "I don't think I've ever done anything so bad that I deserve damnation."

"Well, I have ..." Rick muttered.

A cold chill ran through Bob and he was afraid to respond.

Rick continued on his own.

"I was finishing up my degree at Berkeley in the spring of 1960. Mary and I just had our wedding the previous fall.

"Some of the guys in my dorm wanted to do a road trip down to San Diego to celebrate graduation. Mary said it was fine, 'have a good time.'

"We spent a few days on the beach, and eventually the rest of them disappeared, hooking up with some of the locals."

Melkonian could see where this was heading.

"I didn't bump into a local ..." Rick continued, "I bumped into an old friend, my high school sweetheart, Gillie Wisbeck.

"She had gone abroad for college, Cambridge. She found herself a nice English guy and was married herself.

"She was in San Diego visiting extended family. It was a total fluke that we should be in the same place at the same time.

"The night started out very nostalgic and friendly, but something came over us.

"By the next morning, we both thought we'd ruined the rest of our lives.

"I couldn't just go home to Mary and tell her I'd been unfaithful in the very first year of our marriage. She was already pregnant with Georgie. It would destroy her life, his life, and rightfully destroy mine.

"Living half a world away, the odds that I'd ever see Gillie again were almost zero. We made a pact to say nothing ... take it to our graves.

"I guess I held up my side of the bargain."

Bob was stunned. He was maybe two years old when all that occurred.

"My whole life is a lie." Rick put his head in his hands. "I shouldn't even be here; I should be in a lake of fire."

"She really never found out?" Bob asked.

Rick shook his head.

"I always thought I'd tell her eventually," he continued. "Maybe after the last kid moved out or something like that. But by that point it had been thirty years. It would have still ruined Mary's life; the whole family would be blown to pieces. I also didn't know what became of Gillie. I knew that if I did tell, it would get back to her eventually, and do untold damage."

Bob was shocked, but he was also still interpreting everything as some kind of moral conviction of himself. Once more, he didn't see a connection.

He'd always been faithful to Angie. He was lucky to have found her ... gorgeous, smart, and funny. The worst thing about the idea of actually being dead was not spending another thirty years with her and Monika.

When Bob looked back at Rick, he didn't even seem like a person. His face was so hollow and empty that he looked like a Halloween mask on a Styrofoam head.

"You're the first person I've ever told that to." Rick's voice shook.

"Don't worry. I'm not going to tell the kids. It's not my place."

Rick breathed a heavy sigh.

"So, that's why *I'm* here. What about you?"

Rick asked this of him, seeking any kind of parity he could find. If they were the only two adults sentenced to this place, then Bob must have a similar skeleton hidden deep in his past.

"I'm sorry," Bob replied, dumbfounded. "I really don't know."

He was hoping this personification of Rick would give him more hints on what lesson he should be learning from this experience.

Instead, Rick said nothing, staring at the black, powered-down computer screen.

Surprisingly, he saw a reflection of his "normal" self in the glare of the monitor. It was faint, nigh unusable for any real function, but at least it wasn't one more vision of his crushed spine and burnt body.

Rick imagined the feeling of those injuries if they suddenly appeared and assaulted him with eternal pain at some point.

After the distraction of Rick's confession, Bob returned to the real reason he had come down there.

"Rick, we need to do something to help these kids. One of them dove off the atrium railing and broke his neck, right in front of me."

Rick was stirred out of his self-flagellation. His eyes locked with Bob's as though he was looking to replay the images he'd witnessed.

"I thought he was dead, but then his neck seemed to just pop back into place. I even went and got this for him."

Bob held up the first aid kit.

"Was there pain, can he walk?" Rick asked, turning his eyes to his other couch.

"There was a lot of pain for a minute." Bob set the box down on one of the end tables. "But then he said it died down once his head had straightened out again."

Rick's eyes were wide, drifting off toward the wooden file cabinet.

"Rick, he tried to kill himself!" Bob yelled, as though he weren't listening. "He probably isn't the only one either. If anything, the mirrors are showing what kind of pain everyone is feeling on the inside.

"Chelsea and Greg have been leading some kind of meeting for everyone to vent their feelings and emotions. They're just kids too. That's something *we* should be doing."

Rick seemed to be dwelling on what he'd said, but then his eyes sunk down again.

"It doesn't matter." Rick leaned back into his chair.

"What do you mean 'doesn't matter'?!"

"We failed them, Bob. They're already dead. There's nothing we can do to change that ... and they know it."

"So you're not even going to try?"

"I'm telling you. Unless they find out who actually killed all of us, they're going to hold you and me responsible. They were under our care and protection."

Rick got up from his chair.

"So you'll come?" Bob asked.

"I'll face their judgement," Rick replied.

Bob hated that answer, but at least Rick was following him back to the ballroom.

They needed to get a handle on the situation, who knows what else could happen in this nightmare world.

***

Jenny was sitting with Darren at the back of the column of students on the west side of the room.

Their original table was on the east side, near stage right, but none of the group had specifically returned to use it ... especially since Joe appeared.

If they had grouped up around the table now, Isabella's vacant seat next to Joe would send him into another rage. Jenny didn't really want to sit by the vacant seat either.

The others had been in the cafeteria when the gym exploded. They were filling up a bag of ice from the soda fountain to put on Trey's jaw.

After getting some random snack items from the cafeteria (to balance out the drugs in Joe's system), they were now listening to Chelsea and Greg lead an AA meeting of sorts ... "Afterlife Anonymous?"

Word got around quickly after a couple of students tried to kill themselves that there was no "second death". Their bodies would snap back together and they would slowly wake back up again.

Another disturbing thing was learning that no one had blood anymore. If you cut yourself, you looked like an over-baked chicken stuffed with white flour. After coughing up or "bleeding" some of the powder, the dust in the air would settle in the wound and eventually heal you back to normal.

As soon as Jenny had made that connection to the dust they found in the bathroom, she had dry-heaved for five minutes. The dust in the single-stall bathroom *was* Isabella.

"Dust to dust" was apparently a very literal phrase, especially for those righteous enough to make it to the other side. The bodies they left behind had filled the building. All of the dust in the air came from the 200+ other people who were at the Homecoming dance that night.

Then, for the rest of them, their damned souls were anchored to this place. If they tried to destroy their own bodies, it would just put them back together again, with some added pain just for good measure.

One of the most heartbreaking stories given at the therapy session came from Marcus Johnson, her fellow Homecoming Royalty.

Janice had made it to the other side and she was everything to him. He had screamed, he was crying, he had run around every corner of the school looking for her. But when he returned, the other Varsity Basketball guys found a shell of his former self.

Just hours ago, he was one of the happiest guys in the world, taking pictures with her and Darren. She knew he and Janice were close, but this was a step beyond. He really loved her.

Jenny had been holding Darren's hand since they sat down again.

They had confessed their own love for each other only minutes before their bodies were crushed and set ablaze in hellfire.

Occasionally, one of the other students would talk about a separation from their significant other. That's when Darren would subtly lift up her hand and kiss it. She had been leaning against him since Marcus gave his story.

Jenny realized that she had been positioning herself behind Darren's left side all day, hiding the burned part of herself. Every mirror showed her ashen, near-naked flesh, and it unsettled her that everyone else could witness it too.

She was not vain enough to be distraught by the idea of her corrupted beauty, like she was some "Picture of *Daria* Gray". The image of her dead self was disturbing, but she could bear that. Darren still saw her for what she really was anyway. However, that every errant glance in a mirror revealed her exposed right side and the charred, nipple-less flesh of her breast, made her feel stripped and vulnerable.

Somewhere behind them, the others from their group were sitting as well.

It just seemed like the thing everyone was doing, gathering around to have a couple of sophomores call on their names and ask them to share something about themselves.

These kids were two years younger than her and Marcus, but they were acting more mature.

Jenny had put away the Homecoming Queen tiara some time ago, as soon as they woke up in this corner of Hell.

The last thing she wanted was for anyone to be looking at her right now - and wearing a novelty crown? ... essentially a fancy party favor from the event where everyone *died*? - no way, that was staying in the purse.

She could see someone like Melissa Levitt make that mistake and end up getting called "Persephone" for all eternity.

Jenny wasn't actually sure where Melissa disappeared to. She definitely showed up down here, as did Liam Connelly, but neither of them seemed like the "group therapy session" types anyway. They were the rare exception though.

People were obviously alone and afraid and desperate for any kind of structure and companionship. The conversations went on for a while.

At some point, Jenny realized that Mr. Mel and Mr. Wallace had slipped into the crowd too. Mr. Mel was moving seats to get closer and closer to Chelsea and Greg. Meanwhile, Mr. Wallace remained against the far wall.

It was a sad sight to see and almost everyone must have noticed. Mr. Wallace's usual warmth and grandfatherly demeanor was completely gone. He looked totally devoid of life, like someone who had spent decades on the streets because of a crippling meth addiction.

Him just sitting there, giving off that aura, was starting to bum people out again. More than a few whispers passed through the crowd.

Not to mention, a lot of people were noting the stark reality of ... why is it just the two of them?

All of the other teachers apparently made it to the other side. It made sense, they came from an older, more religious time ... but so did Melkonian and Wallace.

The raw math would suggest that 1 in 3 students ending up here reflected worse on them than 1 in 12 teachers ... but it was still super weird.

After a few hours of Melkonian awkwardly trying to inject himself into the conversations, the crowd reached the bottom of their energy and tolerance.

The scenario unfolded when Greg Henshaw began a sort of closing statement:

"I think this has been a really good talk. I know *I* needed this," he said. "I'm sure all of you needed this too. We don't know how long we're going to be here; it could very well be forever. Everyone's going to need someplace they can get away from the crowds, and we also can't keep sleeping against the walls of the Murphy Center ... where we died.

"So, my suggestion is that we turn the classrooms into apartments. Divide them up among groups of people, two or four or however many you want to dorm with."

A general mumbling of approval came from the crowd ... but that's when Mr. Mel made a big mistake.

He saw the idea, rightfully so to be fair, as a way for all the remaining couples to carve out their own personal bedrooms.

While Mr. Wallace had sunk into a bottomless depression, Mr. Mel looked manic, disoriented, very *One Flew Over the Cuckoo's Nest.*

Somehow, after hearing a bunch of testimonies from people trying to make sense of why they were sent to Hell, he had a knee-jerk moralizing reaction.

"Now hold on a minute," he said. "We can't just turn the school into some kind of hotel."

"Why the fuck not?!" someone yelled from the crowd.

Jenny didn't even have to turn around to know it was Jimmy who said it.

He was met with a rumble of agreement.

"Where the hell were you when the gym blew up?" another kid asked.

After that, the condemnations only got louder and uglier.

Mr. Mel began retreating from his seat at the tables when Mr. Wallace walked up and pulled him away, leaving the ballroom.

There was applause as they disappeared through the doors.

Moving back to the subject at hand, one of the seniors took a school map off the wall and brought it to one of the center tables. People began picking classrooms with their roommate groups. There were only a few noteworthy conflicts, which ultimately got settled with dice rolls.

It wasn't too long until everyone was happy enough with the arrangement.

The next step was actually getting the classrooms open. That was one way the remodels were going to work in favor of the damned students of Villa Vista High School.

Each of the new locks on the classroom doors had a built-in numerical keypad. Once an access code was set, you didn't need a key to unlock the room at all. Changing the code was an easy process too (made that way to accommodate substitute teachers, TAs, temporary reassignments, and etc.).

On the side of each numerical pad was a small, round keyhole. It turned like the ignition of a car, but the master itself was only about the size of a mailbox key.

Once engaged, the new owners of the "apartment" could punch in their entry code and press "#" to save it. Once disengaged, that combo would be set until it was overwritten.

Obviously, this feature put high security importance on the number pad master keys. There weren't many floating around. But there was an obvious place where one might be and one obvious person who would know how to find it.

It was time to have another conversation with Mr. Wallace and Mr. Mel.

***

Elise's determination had led the four of them across all of the edges of their tiny little slice of Hell.

Blaire wasn't surprised that she would be among the early trailblazers to try to lead them out of bondage into the "Promised Land".

Blaire had moved on to distracting her inner fears by singing songs from musicals.

She was hoping the others didn't hear her soft humming, but she also found it amusing. Elise was wearing her pink shoes and a pink dress, guiding them through walls of fog like Moses parting the Red Sea. All the while, Blaire quietly sang "Deliver Us" from *The Prince of Egypt*.

At one point she heard Andrei chuckling, having noticed what she was doing ... and that made her smile. Any amount of joy she could squeeze out of this situation was worth it.

Eventually they'd crossed basically every boundary there was, popping in and out of the mist like they were using portals.

Elise was disappointed, but satisfied, so she began walking them back toward the school building. She took a wide berth around the Jackie the Jaguar painting. Something about it had really freaked her out.

Blaire could relate in one sense; she was scared of baseball too ... because it was so boring. She was glad that her hyperactive brothers had preferred sports like football and basketball.

Another twinge of sadness gripped Blaire inside. She suddenly missed Chris and Tommy more than she ever did in life.

Chris had just started taking an interest in girls too. She was looking forward to messing with him and watching the adorable drama of his teenage years. Tommy was still basically just a kid. She'd never get to see what kind of man either of them became, once they grew out of their bratty years.

Blaire shook the train of thought from her mind.

As they traveled past the middle baseball diamond, Elise heard a noise and headed for the dugout. The rest of them followed her, right as she made contact with the girl.

Blaire recognized the dress immediately.

"Hello?" Elise called out to her.

Laura Nakano almost jumped from the bench. She looked shocked to see more people. Had she been alone out here since the explosion?

"Whoa, it's okay," Elise said to her. "We're in the same boat."

Laura started weirdly ogling them, almost like she expected them to be the animate corpses.

"It's only in the mirrors," Blaire said, trying to get her to stop.

Laura then stammered a bit before eventually saying: "Bathroom."

She glanced through the wooden walls of the dugout toward the baseball snack bar.

"You mean in the mirrors, right?" Elise asked. "Or is it something else?"

Laura was basically mute, not giving Elise an answer.

She huffed in frustration before walking off to investigate.

"Just wait here," Elise said, with Raf following closely behind.

Laura's eyes were now searching back and forth between her and Andrei.

Blaire really didn't like it. She really didn't like *her*.

The last time she saw Laura, she was making Neil's night a miserable disaster. Unless of course he really did cheat on her or something, but

Neil didn't seem like the type. He looked like he was really trying to talk to her and she was just brushing him off repeatedly.

As someone who had a newfound appreciation for great dates to school dances, Blaire almost took it personally.

"Hey Laura," she said, probably meaner than she intended, "what happened to your date?"

Laura froze up for a moment, thinking. She then dropped her eyes to the ground, tearing up a bit.

"Well?" Blaire asked, demanding an answer.

Andrei looked down at her with a curious eye.

"Don't have Liam and Melissa around to distract you anymore?" Blaire pushed.

"I don't know, okay!" Laura yelled.

"Have you looked?" Andrei added, feeding Blaire's righteous indignation.

Laura turned away from them and didn't answer.

"It's not a big place to search," Andrei continued, "we're basically trapped on school grounds."

"He was the last date of your life," Blaire said. "Was he really *that* bad?"

She really wanted more substantive answers from Laura, but that's when she heard a horrible noise.

Elise was screaming at the top of her lungs.

Andrei was already a step ahead of Blaire. They reached the door of the snack bar bathroom right as Raf was dragging her out.

"Elise, what is it?" Blaire asked, unnerved.

She'd never seen Elise like this before.

"There's no way out. There's no way out. There's no way out," she kept whispering to herself.

Everything must have snowballed, really hitting her all at once.

"What did you see?" Andrei asked.

"I'll tell you later," Raf said, then turned to Andrei, "could you carry these?"

He handed him both of their gym bags.

"Yeah," Andrei said, slinging them on opposite shoulders.

"We've got to get someplace quiet for a while, away from all this shit." Whatever had broken Elise had also badly pissed off Rafael.

"I have an idea," Blaire said.

They walked back into the Murphy Center, Raf more or less had to drag Elise.

Opening the side doors drew a few eyes, but everyone was pretty distracted. They were all huddled in one batch of dining tables, talking or something.

Blaire led the four of them onto the stage, then through the back curtain.

Elise was still too zoned out to climb the stairs.

"Yo, walk behind me," Raf said to Andrei.

He then picked Elise up below her knees and back and walked them up the flights of the backstage stairwell.

Andrei stood by to catch them both in case he slipped or lost his balance.

Once they reached the top step, Blaire gave a sigh of relief. The Choir & Drama Rehearsal Room was still open. They went inside and found it empty.

Once they were in, they closed the two sets of doors behind them. As soon as the last exit was latched, a quiet stillness washed over the room. There was special sound paneling in the walls, considering the room's daily purpose.

Andrei dropped all of their gym bags in a corner and went back to the choir chairs. He turned a dozen of them around to face each other so the seats formed a sort of makeshift cot.

Raf laid her down across the seats, but didn't seem satisfied.

"Ooh, I know what this needs," he said, disappearing through one of the doors.

"Should I follow after him?" Andrei asked Blaire.

She froze up at the question ... she really didn't want him to go.

Before she could give an answer, Raf popped the door back open, arms full of clothes.

"What is all this?" Blaire asked.

"Costumes from the storage room," he said.

Looking at Blaire, he asked, "Could you stand her up?"

"Yeah." She picked Elise up carefully, pulling one arm over her shoulder.

Raf laid out an arrangement of softer costumes. There was some foam, some cotton, and a bit of artificial fabrics too. They now had the closest approximation of bedding they could muster.

"Okay, down we go," Raf said, helping Blaire lay her back on the chairs.

Elise was still whispering "There's no way out," over and over again.

It was really starting to scare Blaire.

Once Elise seemed comfortable, Raf walked away toward the door, covering his mouth with some costume wig. He yelled into the muffling fabric, anger and frustration pouring out of him.

Blaire knelt down on something feathery and slowly stroked Elise's hair, trying to get her to calm down.

It took almost an hour for her to finally pass out.

Once she was asleep, Raf had also calmed down enough to explain what happened.

They had discovered Ellen Taylor in the back of the stall, cutting herself to pieces with an X-Acto knife. He mentioned the fact that she wasn't bleeding, but was leaking powder, like the same powder that was covering everything else.

That caused Blaire to look down at her arms again, brushing away the bit of dust that had resettled on her. She began to cough and gag. Andrei quickly passed her the garbage pail.

Despite all this self-mutilation, it wasn't killing Ellen Taylor, at all.

Raf also mentioned seeing her reflection, and how it looked like she had died in that bathroom, getting crushed by the wall.

Andrei was the first to point out something neither of them had yet considered.

"Did she already have the knife?"

This was the girl who had been mocked by the whole school for the past week. And who knows what her life was like before all that? Was she the bomber and had used the knife to cut wires or something? Then she decided to try to kill herself again when she woke up in this place?

"Whoever bombed the school is gonna fucking pay for what they did to Elise," Raf said through gritted teeth. "They'll pay for what they did to all of us."

Blaire could feel a voice at the back of her own mind agreeing wholeheartedly with Raf. Someone really deserved Hell for all this death and suffering.

She glanced at Andrei, but he wasn't holding back the same fire in his eyes as Rafael. Instead, they looked much more sad.

He had cried the least of the four of them. In that first hour after they woke up, he had mostly held Blaire in stoic silence. A few tears had trickled to the sides, touching the top of her head as he embraced her.

Technically it was still early in the afternoon, but Blaire was very tired. Sunday had been full of nonstop emotional turmoil. She felt worse than she did on the day of her grandpa's funeral. She'd gone to bed early that day too. She barely left her room for a week.

"Maybe it'd be a good idea for all of us to get some shuteye," she suggested to the others.

"Yeah," Raf agreed, the last of his anger cooling down.

They didn't have keys, so they spent a few minutes setting up barricades against the doors.

The rehearsal room doors opened outward, so they used some chairs, cabinets, and other things to completely seal up one of the entrances. Luckily, there were a lot of light stands and equipment brought by the photographer that they could use. Once the second entrance was thoroughly blocked, they worked on the first.

They put some simpler items in place to bar the door handle from turning, and keep the crash bar from pulling away from the frame. The metal framework of the photographer's backdrop stand and some zip ties came in really handy for that.

While the boys were finishing that up, Blaire slipped into the small storage closet at the back-center of the room.

Raf returned to the costume storage room and came back with another large handful of fabrics. He set up a pile for himself, on the ground near Elise's head, then he left a large pile for Andrei and Blaire. After that, he lay down and was passed out in minutes. A light snoring sounded from their side of the room.

Andrei pulled off his suit jacket, vest, and shirt, as well as the accessories, like his belt and socks. Only his white undershirt and pants remained.

Blaire eventually opened the door of the closet, zipping up her gym bag. She'd changed into her P.E. clothes, as well as removed the last of her jewelry from the dance.

"Not exactly my regular pajamas." She shrugged.

The school's gym clothes consisted of black athletic shorts with a light grey t-shirt. The black and yellow Villa Vista logos covered the front and back of the shirt.

"Same," Andrei agreed.

She saw that he had spread out the last of the costume pieces into two distinct piles about an arm's length apart.

He lay on the pile closest to the piano, between Blaire and the door.

Blaire knelt down, pushing the loose fabrics together until they formed a single spread.

"Might be nice to cuddle without having to pay the ultimate price." She lay down next to him.

She knew Andrei was just trying to respect her space and feelings regarding everything that happened. It hadn't exactly been a romantic day. Blaire really preferred it this way though, and she could see in his face how much he preferred it too.

She nestled backwards into his chest, and clutched his left arm between hers.

Andrei felt strong. From his forearms to his bare shoulders, he was muscled and toned. She felt safe with him. His strength, inner and outer, had been a rock to lean on. His presence helped hold her together. Otherwise, she would probably be in a worse state than Elise.

While at first she planned on talking with him a bit, now that they had some alone time, Blaire found that she was much more exhausted than she realized.

Within minutes, Andrei felt her grip on his hand loosen as she fell asleep.

He could still smell some of the perfume on the back of her neck. The scent was almost gone, the final remnants of joy from their ill-fated night were fading away.

He thought back on every moment of that evening, every moment of the months that had passed since that first day in this very classroom.

Andrei wondered what his dad might have thought of Blaire.

She didn't want their parents to get involved yet. She seemed worried that hers would be overbearing and scare him away. As soon as they had entered the limo, it felt like she was in damage control mode.

It was a bit sweet. She'd said she wanted to keep things special, just between them for a little while. But her parents were perfectly fine, she had nothing to worry about. Still, to respect her feelings, he hadn't introduced her to his dad yet either.

He was very understanding. Like Blaire, neither he nor Andrei were particularly sociable either.

After the halftime show, Blaire and Elise left and he returned to the stands to watch the rest of the game with his dad.

That was the last night Andrei would ever spend with him. In a way, he was glad he had a few hours with just the two of them.

Andrei also thought of his sisters, Katya and Anastasia. He would have worried in the same way as Blaire if they lived close by. There were so many embarrassing childhood stories they would have told her behind his back. But that was just the way they were.

After a bit of time, if things went well, they would have grown to love Blaire as much as he did. They would have adored her as a sister-in-law.

Andrei wondered what their mother might have thought of Blaire, what she might have thought of him ... in these last years since her passing.

Then he realized that if he were a better man, he might have known by now. She was not trapped in this cold and desolate place. An ever-faithful Orthodox woman, she was with the Lord in whatever paradise that Andrei had fallen short of.

He would spend an unimaginable eternity apart from all of them, waiting for every new form of suffering that tomorrow might bring.

Andrei covered his mouth with his free hand, to keep from waking Blaire.

He sobbed for a very long time before he could finally slip away into rest.

THIRTEEN

LORDS OF LIMBO

BOB MELKONIAN LAY on the sofa in Rick's office, covering his face with his hands.

The door cracked open and Rick walked back into the room. He was carrying a small bottle of Jack Daniel's whiskey and two shot glasses.

"Where did you get that?" Bob eyed the booze.

"McDouglas keeps this in the back of his storage cabinet." Rick set down both glasses. "Barbara used to tell me about the one night he was always guaranteed to break it out, after they finished the end-of-year financial reports."

"I don't really drink much," Bob admitted.

"Me neither," Rick answered.

He then poured up two fingers for both of them.

Bob picked up the shot as soon as Rick was done pouring.

They held the glasses for a moment, a space in time where someone might have declared a toast. However, there was nothing to toast, there was nothing to celebrate at all.

They sipped the shots in silence.

"You were right Rick." Bob set the glass on the table. "We failed those kids. I don't know what I was thinking."

Rick said nothing, he just poured himself another shot.

Perhaps it was the alcohol working through him, or replaying his embarrassing attempts to reach out to the students in the ballroom, but Bob finally thought of something.

"I know," he said to Rick.

Rick eyed him while putting down the bottle. "Know what?"

"I know why I'm here," Bob said.

Over the next few minutes, he narrated the whole story to Rick.

He finished with another shot of his own.

"So, what happens now?" Bob asked him.

"What do you mean?" Rick replied.

"I mean ... no pearly gates, no standing in judgement, no lake of fire. What exactly is happening?"

"We've already been judged." Rick lifted a hand mirror off of his desk.

He set the mirror back down, glass facing the table top.

"If I were to guess," Rick stroked his mustache, "this is part of the process."

Bob shifted his knees. Rick had already been thinking about this.

"Just like with Christmas, just like with your wedding, just like with your wedding night, anticipation is a critical piece of your enjoyment. It's basic psychology. Being randomly surprised by any of the three may hold their own immediate pleasures, but the feeling is carnal and fades quickly."

Bob nodded.

"Pain works the same," Rick whispered. "Waiting for a court date to arrive, anticipating a hard conversation with a loved one, seeing if someone is going to survive a cancer diagnosis, those are all the fear of the unknown. The waiting, without knowing how long, the smaller samples of pain along the way, it's all part of the suffering. It leaves a deeper impression, that you can't forget, that you can't escape."

Bob considered his words.

"It's an eternity," Rick reminded him. "For all we know it's like this most of the time. Then every few months we do wake up in a lake of fire, feeling untold burning and torment. Maybe we relive the pain of what killed us, but remember it, feel it, repeat it. Then we'll end up back here, wondering every day when the next one will come. It's the most ancient form of torture."

Bob put his head down between his knees. Either the alcohol or Rick's description of Hell was beginning to turn his stomach.

"What would Van Gaal say?" Bob asked him, referencing their conversation about Limbo.

"Well ..." Rick began. "*The Divine Comedy* was an allegory, a narrative poem. It's not Scripture. But Dante Alighieri was heavily influenced by proper Church philosophy of his era, especially *Summa Theologica* by Thomas Aquinas.

"Not to mention, if this is Hell, then we could experience every form of suffering ever conceived of by Man, alongside everything else alluded to in actual Scripture."

"There was a period of time I was really hoping this was all just a coma, or a bad dream," Bob said. "But it's not, is it?"

Rick shook his head.

There was another long silence between the two men.

"I can't stop thinking about Angie and Monika," Bob muttered. "I'm terrified of forgetting them, of having them slip away into the haze."

"I don't think you have to worry about that," Rick said with confidence.

"Why?" Bob was surprised by his assurance.

"The most basic description of Hell is separation from God," Rick explained. "Since 'God is Love', you could more broadly apply that to everyone you might love. Eternal separation from your spouse, your children, your family, your friends ... missing those that you love, that grief, is a powerful pain.

"You can't grieve for something you can't remember."

Bob leaned back against the couch, realizing that he could still see Angie in great detail, every hair on her head, every dimple, the crook of the smile on her left cheek. He could paint a portrait of her if he had any art skills to speak of. Same thing with Monika.

It was actually a bit of a relief.

That is when a soft knock sounded from Rick Wallace's door.

Bob stood up in surprise.

"I'll get it," Rick said, walking around his desk.

He pushed the door open and found Greg Henshaw and Chelsea Morton standing in the hallway.

"Hi Mr. Wallace, Mr. Mel," Chelsea said, with as genial a voice as she could put on.

"We were hoping one of you knows where a number pad master key might be found," Greg said.

He technically addressed both of them, but the sophomores were looking at Mr. Wallace.

Rick nodded. He had been expecting this ever since they first proposed the idea of turning the classrooms into dormitories.

"Of course," Rick said. "This way."

Rick walked past them, heading down the hallway into the main space of the Administration offices.

Melkonian was curious and trailed behind the sophomore couple.

Rick walked up to the two offices at the back of open floor space.

As Bob left the secluded hallway, he glanced to his right and saw beyond the glass into the school's entrance foyer.

Dozens of students had gathered, staring into the offices. Near the front of the group were several of the larger Varsity Football and Basketball players, including Joe Torelli and Marcus Johnson.

Torelli locked eyes with Melkonian, causing him to flinch. The kids were going to get what they wanted one way or another.

Bob swallowed his fear, catching up to Rick.

The two offices were labeled "Principal Leonard McDouglas" and "Vice Principal Barbara Fletcher".

Rick pulled out his keychain. One key in particular fit perfectly in her office door.

"We appreciate your help," Greg said. "Considering how often you worked with Vice Principal Fletcher, we figured you might have a key."

"Of course." Rick was totally submissive, not arguing at all.

They entered her office.

Rick pulled up a different key from his chain, unlocking the bottom file cabinet in her desk.

Melkonian noticed a rolled-up set of construction drawings sitting on the top of her bookshelf. It was a heavy packet of blueprints, almost three feet long. Even rolled up tightly, it was as thick as a basketball.

With the file drawer open, Rick tugged harder on it, pulling the drawer out of the desk frame.

Taped to the back side was a small key with a plastic orange tag on the keyring.

Mr. Wallace handed it to Greg Henshaw.

"Thank you," Chelsea said. "Since we are trying to put at least two to a room, we were hoping that you would stay with Mr. Mel, in his biology classroom."

"We're going to need your keychain too," Greg added.

Rick glanced out of the open doorway. He could see the varsity players lined up in front of the glass. He knew every last one of them by name, having cheered them on and announced their successes for countless games over their high school careers.

Same as Bob, he knew they would get the keys one way or another.

"Of course," he said again, dropping his keychain into Greg's hand.

"I don't have a key for McDouglas' office." Rick put his hands in his pockets. "You might have to break a window."

Bob paused at that line, his already morose face hiding his thoughts.

Rick had just retrieved McDouglas' whiskey from there half an hour ago.

Rick turned to face Melkonian, meeting his eyes.

"Guess we're roommates," he said aloud. The knowing expression behind his eyes helped to keep Bob quiet.

"Yeah … of course," Melkonian said.

Greg and Chelsea led them out of the Administration area, evicting Wallace from his Guidance Counselor office.

Melkonian followed him. The one time he looked at the students, he saw only scorn. It was just as Rick had said … "Hell is eternal separation from those you love."

Bob really loved those kids. He even loved them now, as they stared at him like Jaguars stalking their prey.

**

After abandoning Barry and Melvin in Mr. Reynolds' room, Niles heard something loud coming from the parking lot.

He exited through the front of the classroom section to see a bunch of jocks huddled around this black sports car. They were having some kind of conversation with the quarterback.

At first it looked like a fight was breaking out. The quarterback grabbed one of the other guys, but Mr. Mel was able to calm him down and they took him inside the Murphy Center.

After seeing the commotion around the race car, Niles thought to check his dad's Lexus. The red convertible was still sitting there, undamaged.

Niles pulled the remote from his pocket, triggering one of the buttons. The hard top receded into the car's trunk, and the doors unlocked.

Niles could see the decorative vanity mirror sitting on top of the hat box in the back seat. He lifted it up and stared at the empty cavity where his face used to be. He then angled it around, looking at the Lexus.

There was no red left on the car. The paint and primer had all been burned away, leaving only scorched steel behind. The tires had melted into puddles on the pavement and all of the fabric and leather of the car's interior had burned away to ashes.

Niles tossed the mirror into the passenger seat. Then he picked up the hat box and kicked it like a soccer ball. It bounced awkwardly a few times before landing in an empty parking space.

He pulled out the key to the Lexus and turned it in the ignition. The car usually turned over right away, but it struggled several times before he gave up and let go.

Niles glanced over at the black sports car and assumed that the quarterback had similarly failed with his car.

The headlights of the Lexus were still powered on, the key was engaging the car's battery.

Niles put on the high beams, which illuminated the front of the car parked across from him.

Then he decided to try the radio, spinning the dial across the A.M. and F.M. spectrums. There was nothing but white noise.

Niles thought to himself, was this more or less the lobby to whatever the next game of life might be? Was he in, like, a holding zone before being reincarnated or transported to some new form of existence? What was the point of keeping him awake and sentient in the first place?

If he were the one running the simulation, he would have deleted a character like Niles a long time ago.

What a wasted life.

He tasted a few brief months of what felt like real happiness before having it all ripped away from him on the night he'd anticipated the most ... and that was all before he actually died.

After trying her phone at the start, Niles had scanned around the ballroom a bit for Laura, but didn't see her. He did see Anne, Melissa, and Liam though.

That figures.

After coming face to "face" with himself in the mirror, he had more or less given up on everything. He felt totally alone, regardless of the other hundred or so people stuck there with him.

Bumping into Barry and Melvin was a surprise. A small part of him was really wondering if they had blown up the school. If that were true, he wasn't even sure whether he wanted to beat the shit out of them or thank them.

He wondered what his parents would say if he were somehow able to wake up back in the living world.

Would they be happy he was alive? Maybe.

After everything that had happened with Laura though, Niles knew that he would only spiral deeper into the parts of himself that his mom hated and his dad pretended to tolerate.

He'd probably be brain-damaged from the explosion, removing any possibility of being able to work for Kladivo Studios. He probably wouldn't be able to do anything with technology at all.

He'd have to live off of his parents and eventually the government until the day he died, again.

Niles gripped the steering wheel harder.

He had changed so much for Laura, cleaned himself up, made better choices in school, focused more, and ate better. He put so much energy into her interests, in physically building that stupid fucking float and all the smaller things along the way.

And what had all that done for him? Put him within the blast radius of some Oklahoma City shit.

Hell, if Barry and Melvin really did it because they were jealous of his disastrous relationship with Laura, then that was even worse.

All the others would torture them *and* Niles for as long as they were stuck here.

Most of them actually had a real future, something to live for.

Niles could see something coming out of the fog from the corner of his eye.

It was Blaire Tidwell and her tall boyfriend. They were with Elise and Rafael.

During the dance, Niles had been sulking at his table, alone, when he noticed the two of them waltzing to one of the slow numbers.

Blaire had been making out with that senior guy for so long that Niles thought she was going to rip his clothes off right there on the dance floor.

Why couldn't he find that? Was Niles so terrible of a person that even the idea of love was only used to torture him before blowing him to pieces?

He wouldn't have even been at the stupid dance if it weren't for Laura.

And what about those who hadn't appeared here at all? Had they all moved on to some new Paradise, like a new Garden of Eden for each of them? Even in a perfect world, Adam had needed someone like Eve.

They were literally made for each other, completed each other. That perfect existence meant they each had someone to be with for all time, since it was before death had entered the world. Otherwise, there was something missing from each of them, a void.

It was a void Niles knew all too well.

Blaire and friends disappeared into the fog again. They popped out further away by the middle school lawn then turned back into the fog a third time.

"It's a small world," Niles thought to himself.

As soon as he first saw the fog outside of the glass doors, he had a deep, sinking feeling that there was no place to run.

There were either untold monsters in the mist that would tear them limb from limb or they would just pop in somewhere else on school grounds. Looks like the latter was proving true.

A few other students began making their way into the parking lot, checking their own cars, trying their ignitions, and gathering supplies.

Niles didn't have any possessions to speak of. The Lexus was his dad's. There was quite a bit of random stuff in the trunk of his Honda Civic, including extra clothes. That was all at his house. The only other stuff he had were the gym clothes in his locker.

It was a bit cold though, even inside, so he decided to stay in the cosplay.

Niles clicked on the car's heating, closing the convertible roof and the windows.

Most of the heating worked off of warmed air from the engine block, but the coil itself should provide some of its own heat if the battery still had juice.

It took a bit of time for the temperature to rise, but eventually it did.

Niles leaned the seat back, taking some comfort in the heat.

Before he realized it, he was fast asleep.

***

Darren watched from one side of the group as Melkonian and Wallace were marched upstairs to the biology classroom.

The science classrooms were determined to be the least comfortable when everyone began staking their claims.

Cushions of any kind, or sheets, or pillows were already in very short supply. The science classrooms had cold tile floors and often cold plastic tables or sinks that were bolted into the ground.

You couldn't really move furniture around and you couldn't really make a bed out of the tables. They were very inflexible.

Most of the crowd were happy to consign Wallace and Melkonian to such a room.

Darren couldn't believe how quickly the crowd had turned on them.

He felt bad for Wallace. The man looked severely depressed. After everything he'd done for Darren, for so many kids at Villa Vista, he was now basically an outcast.

Melkonian on the other hand seemed to be having a hard time even coming to terms with the fact that they were dead. He was acting dumb and confused, not mean.

On top of that, a good portion of students genuinely seemed to consider them suspects in blowing up the gym. That seemed crazy to Darren. If they were really responsible for that, they'd have to be better liars than even the most famous serial killers. He really didn't see that as possible, especially in Melkonian's case.

Mr. Mel was always exactly what you expected. There never seemed to be double meanings to his words, angles or games. He was very honest and forthright with students. That was one reason the kids used to like him. He didn't bullshit them or talk down to them like toddlers. Everyone sensed he was telling it exactly as it was, even if he acted a bit silly in the way he said it.

Maybe that's why people were reacting this way now. The idea of so much trust being broken all at once was making people angry ... very angry.

The group reached Melkonian's classroom. He and Rick slipped inside without turning back to face any of them.

Once they did, Greg Henshaw turned the small key in the side of the numerical keypad. He typed in a new access code, which only he and Chelsea could see, then disengaged the key.

Part of the plan for the master key was a vote among students for whom they trusted to hang onto the key. The results were obvious.

Even still, Greg and Chelsea promised that the students could hold a snap vote at any time if they wanted the key to go to someone else.

The sophomore couple weren't super athletic. Greg was a decent second-baseman on the JV Baseball team, but that was about it. If they really tried to hold the keyring against everyone's wishes, Darren felt pretty confident that he could wrestle it away from the two of them by himself.

As the fullback on the Varsity Football team, Darren was Joe's last line of defense. He took the hardest hits to give Joe the precious seconds he needed to get the ball in the air.

He was a bit of an intimidating force by himself. Maybe not as tall as Marcus, or as scary as Joe, but Darren felt like he could hold his own.

The rest of the students were gathered in the middle of the main atrium.

Paxton Bannister, one of the Varsity Basketball guys, had the map of agreed-upon room assignments. He began calling up the groups of people as Greg and Chelsea let the students into their new living spaces.

Continuing from Melkonian's room, they started with the second-floor Sophomore Class hallway.

They let each dorm group pick an entry code, then saved it, disengaging the key. The kids would then disappear inside, to begin rearranging the room into someplace livable.

Greg and Chelsea's own dorm was on that floor. It was across from their lockers and just a few doors down from Melkonian and Wallace.

Most of the students had already pulled some supplies from their lockers, stuffing their gym bags full of anything they thought might make the domestic situation more comfortable. Darren and Jenny had done the same.

His gym bag was strapped sideways over his back. He really didn't have much stuff in there beyond the basics. Most of Darren's extra supplies were either in his truck or in his football kit bag, which was in his truck. It was probably still parked in front of Jimmy's house.

Darren wondered how long it would take for Jimmy's dad to hear the news and come home. It was probably a global news story. Even in Taipei, Cillian should hear about Villa Vista. Alexandria was never in the news otherwise; it would probably shock the hell out of him. Would he try to come home? Would he even care?

Darren was sure his own parents were devastated. His brother had probably already driven down. He missed them all so much.

Jenny was holding her gym bag in front of her, clasping it like a body pillow.

It was hard not to notice how much she was trying to cover herself up. Darren wished he could somehow go back in time to when they were alive, before the explosion. If he could change nothing else about their fates, he would have switched seats with her as they waited outside the bathroom for Isabella.

At the very least, he would be the one to take the brunt of the fire, having an eye melted out of his skull. Her body would be a bit broken when he crushed her in the stairwell, but at least it would be *him* with scorched, skinless muscle flesh covering his right side.

The way the fire had melted Jenny's dress was very revealing. It was obvious how self-conscious it had made her. She acted like she was walking around topless and hoping people wouldn't catch on. In a distorted way, it was sort of true.

The dormitories were a good idea. Everyone was on edge as it was. They'd benefit a lot by having a place to retreat to when they needed to get away from it all.

Not to mention, Darren couldn't stand the idea of waking up in the Murphy Center every morning, the same exact place where they'd been cooked alive.

Every time he saw the dust in the air, or felt it on the railings, he thought of Isabella. He could tell it was the same for Jenny. She had been gagging all day, like she was getting seasick on a cruise ship.

They followed Greg and Chelsea down to the ground-floor Sophomore classrooms, then over to the Junior Class hallway.

Joe and Marcus were some of the biggest supporters of the little township Greg and Chelsea had been organizing. They were also very effective muscle.

The two Varsity teams had sort of been pulled into service with them. It's not like the teams had any real meaning anymore, but the groups were still friends too. There was an indefinable feeling to stick it out with them. Not to mention, the masses really seemed to be supportive of the idea as well.

You couldn't have organization without order and you couldn't have order without law enforcement. If Darren had backed down from his new obligation to help make things work, then he and Jenny could suffer long term consequences for it.

But still, shit. Darren couldn't believe he'd become some kind of police officer. A cop was one of the last things on his list of potential careers.

The top thing he'd actually been considering for a college major was a business degree with a sports or entertainment specialty.

He would have loved to work in some kind of finance or marketing department for the Forty Niners in the new Levi Strauss Stadium they were building.

But no, instead he was dead ... stuck in the hell that is high school ... forever ... and his new job for all eternity was being a glorified hall monitor.

Greg and Chelsea reached the door of Mr. Reynolds' U.S. History classroom. They turned the master key, letting the new occupants punch in an access code.

The door latch pulled open and they flipped on the light.

"Alright, you guys can head in," Chelsea said to a junior couple.

The girls thanked them, then stepped inside excitedly.

Darren could see Joe's eyes following them.

As hard as Isabella's passing had been on Jennifer, Joe really did seem messed up about it too. They hadn't even dated that long, but he had been very emotional since waking up.

Darren wondered how much effect the Addys had in the afterlife. It wasn't zero, that's for sure. He thought he was going to have to fight Joe by the car earlier.

The group moved through the classrooms in the second-floor Freshman Class hallway.

Jenny walked away from those gathered. Darren could tell where she was headed.

The small window faced northwest. It once provided the best view of Alexandria, but that was all gone now. A curtain of white nothingness was draped barely a hundred yards away from the wall. There was no lighthouse, no lights, no town below ... only oblivion.

Jenny placed her hand against the cold glass. Darren hugged her from behind, resting his head against hers.

"I can almost still see it," she whispered to him.

"Me too," Darren responded.

They didn't look too long, because there was nothing left to look at.

Eventually, most of the students had been let into their new dorms. They were in the last section of classrooms, the Senior Class hallway on the second floor.

Greg and Chelsea turned the lock for the number pad.

"You can pick whatever," Joe mumbled.

Marcus Johnson thought for a second then punched in a four-digit combo.

Joe nodded at Darren and Jennifer then shut the door behind the two of them.

Brendan and Trey had both offered to let Joe stay with them, but Joe refused. After a look at Sheena and Ashley respectively, he decided to stay away from the couples.

In the case of Joe and Marcus, it would seem that misery loves company.

Since Paxton Bannister had been handling the dormitory map, Darren wasn't paying close attention to who actually went where. He had been distracted by his own muddled thoughts. He *died* yesterday. Now he was in some kind of Limbo getting an apartment with Jennifer.

At the end of the day, he was just tired. His wits and emotions were hanging from a string.

He supposed that he should be happy that things were as good as they were. He could be in much worse torment, getting flayed alive for all eternity. But in a place like this, some spooky recreation of the school that got blown up, they didn't even have demons to worry about.

"Hey Jen," a reptilian-like voice hissed from behind them.

The hair on Darren's neck stood up, like he'd heard the scratching of a chalkboard.

They turned to face the noise.

It was Blake Samuels.

Jenny clammed up, hugging the gym bag tighter.

Darren did his best to bottle his anger. He hadn't even seen this little shit around all day. He was hoping he'd ended up in a much worse Circle of Hell.

"Stay the fuck away from me," Jenny spat.

"That's going to be hard," Blake said, with mock regret in his voice.

"You wanna bet?" Darren asked, taking a step closer to him.

Blake looked over at Paxton Bannister, who had joined the remains of the group.

"Well, it looks like we're neighbors." Blake shrugged.

Kyle Moreno, another senior, was standing next to him. He was apparently his roommate. Darren had seen the two talk a few times in the past, but they never seemed like close friends.

"No way." Jennifer stomped her foot. "I want a different room. I am not living next to this cheating slime bag."

"Look, I'm very sorry," Chelsea said, sounding tired. "But everyone's turning in, we'll figure something out in the coming days."

Greg put the key into the number pad of Darren and Jenny's room.

Darren stood in front of it, blocking Blake's leers as Jenny punched in the combo.

She slipped into the room as soon as it was open.

Darren glowered at the greasy waste of flesh. "Come within twelve feet of us and I'll throw you off the atrium."

"Goodnight," Blake said with a smile, ignoring Darren's threat.

He disappeared into his own room with Kyle.

Darren fumed for a minute, then kicked one of the metal lockers. He closed the door behind him and flipped the lock.

Jenny stood in the middle of the room, her gym bag on the ground, her face buried in her hands.

Darren set down his bag too and walked up to her.

"Forget him," he said. "We'll find someone to swap rooms with soon, I promise."

"It's not that." She turned to look at him. "For everything Blake has done, lying to me, cheating on me, toying with me like I was just some dumb animal, he ends up in the same place as you and me?"

Darren was at a loss for words.

"Were we really so bad?" she asked him.

"No." Darren hugged her. "Whatever we were, we were not the same as him."

Jenny sniffled as they stood there for a moment. They would probably never get an answer anyway. Cosmic justice seemed as blind and intangible here as it was in the last life.

"Well ..." she said, "do you want to tell me why we chose Mr. Ziegler's Government & Civics room?"

"Oh, yes!" Darren said, happy to lateral over to a more positive topic. "First, let's clear some of the desks."

Following the remodel of the classrooms a few years back, Villa Vista purchased new and modern furniture. The desks and chairs were not attached, like the kind which flourished decades earlier. The desks themselves were rectangular, with lightweight but sturdy metal frames and shaped plastic surfaces. The chairs were constructed the same. Both design features were meant to make them more portable and easier to stack.

Darren and Jenny started with the chairs, placing them in a back corner in two columns. They spread out the student desks a bit more, forming a sort of counter or divider separating the main space of the classroom from the door.

It created an entrance vestibule. It wasn't quite finished yet, but with a thick enough tarp, or maybe the white boards, they could close off the space for the added privacy.

The only desk not part of the entry barrier was Mr. Ziegler's teacher desk. It was L-shaped, with the computer tucked into one corner against the wall. Aside from his own leather office chair, there was a second rolling desk chair across from the main tabletop for talking one on one with students.

Darren sat down in Ziegler's chair and Jenny took the student seat.

"Well, at least we have a lot of comfortable office carpeting to stretch out on." Jenny sighed.

Darren had a very proud look on his face and it was helping to cheer her up.

"Okay ... what?" She smiled.

"As you might remember," Darren opened. "After Mr. Wallace retired from all of his assistant coaching duties, Ziegler became our new Defensive Coordinator."

"Maybe?" she said. She definitely remembered seeing him down around the field during practices. Kris Ziegler had a very iconic jet-black goatee which had become his trademark look.

"Anyway," Darren said. "One time I overheard him talking to Coach Kelley before a game. Coach wanted to know what his secret was for being so spry and alert going into late games."

Darren swiveled in the chair, opening up the back-bottom drawer of the large desk. He pulled out a backpack-sized black canvas bag with a pull-tie on one end. There was a strange bulgy shape to the thing contained inside.

"As it turns out," Darren finished, "Mr. Ziegler would take naps over lunch."

He pulled out the object, revealing an inflatable air mattress.

"No sleeping on the floors for us."

"Yes!" Jenny was surprised and grateful.

She picked up the mattress and walked it over to the far corner in the room. It was the most private corner, partially concealed by a large cabinet and part of their student desk privacy wall.

She unraveled the power cable and plugged it in. With a click, the fan motor whirred to life and the mattress began taking shape. It was a Full-size, which was better than Darren expected. Once it was completely inflated, the mattress elevated them a comfortable twelve inches off of the ground.

They lay down to test it out and were instantly relaxed by the soft cushion.

"This is way better than the stairwell," Jenny said, kicking off her heels. She and Darren were still dressed more or less in their dance clothes. Their gym bags sat idle against one wall and they were far too tired to get up again.

Jenny pivoted to her side, facing him. "Ziegler wasn't at the dance, was he?"

"Naw. He always said he wouldn't take his wife to any party that didn't serve alcohol."

"Was he joking or naive?" Jenny cracked a smile.

"Joking." Darren turned to her. "I think it was just his way of warning us to take it easy."

"His real classroom is totally destroyed, isn't it?"

"I guess so. Who would have thought we'd get to take something with us?"

"The ancient Egyptians, I think. Probably some others too." Jenny tried to summon memories from Van Gaal's class.

"You think there's some kind of Netherworld copy of the pyramids, or Pompeii?" Darren asked.

"Could be. Maybe we'll get two weeks of vacation per year to visit other parts of Limbo."

"If I work hard enough, I can get promoted to school police chief, get us a *King-size* air mattress."

Jenny chuckled.

"I wonder." Darren lowered his voice, becoming more serious. "You think all this means that ghosts might be real too?"

"Like we'd get a chance to interact with the living?"

"Maybe? Although I doubt too many people will come by the school anymore. It'll probably get turned into a memorial or something. Who would send their kids there now? Even the middle and elementary schools will have to close. Villa Vista *as a whole* is dead."

"We weren't the first ones to die on school grounds. Do you remember April Hudgins?"

"Oh, yeah." A wave of memories came back to Darren.

April Hudgins was a senior when he and Jenny were freshmen. Her parents had been going through a really rough divorce. One afternoon, when most of the school parking lot was empty, she was still sitting in her car.

She had done that for many weeks, trying to avoid having to go home to the fighting. That day, she had decided she didn't want to go home at all. She had taken a full bottle of her mother's sleeping pills, swallowing them all at once.

The night guard found her when he was going to lock up the parking lot, but it was already too late.

She wasn't the only death on campus either. After nearly a century in operation, the high school had seen a small share of suicides and accidents.

"Maybe she went to a better place," Jenny posited, "... like Isabella."

"Or, maybe we won't end up staying in a place like *this* forever ..." Darren offered.

He lifted up a hand between them, stroking her cheek.

"... But I don't mind if we do for a while."

They kissed tenderly, then fell asleep in each other's arms.

FOURTEEN

SECOND CHANCES

NILES SLEPT FOR WHAT FELT like a long time, but when he opened his eyes, nothing looked different.

He pulled his cell phone out of the cup holder, checking the time.

Sunday, 10:04 p.m.

"What the hell?" he thought to himself, the daylight fog hadn't changed at all.

Tap. Tap. Tap.

Niles turned toward the sound, apparently the same sound that had just woken him up. It was coming from his passenger window.

It was Laura.

Niles was stunned, he wasn't even sure if she'd shown up in this fake Villa Vista.

He shifted his seat upright and pressed the button to roll down her window.

"Hey," she said in a faint voice.

"Hey," he answered back, unsure of what else to say.

"Do you mind if I sit down?" she asked.

Niles wanted to be angry. Part of him really wanted to yell at her or roll the window up and tell her to get lost. But a bigger part of him was just happy to see her face again.

"No," he mumbled, unlocking the passenger door.

She pulled it open and stepped into the car. She had to pick up the vanity mirror off of the cushion to sit.

"Careful," Niles said. "You don't want to see me."

Laura closed the door, then lifted the mirror, facing herself. She pivoted it in her wrist until they were looking at each other.

Niles winced.

Her reflection was completely skeletal … just charred, black bones. Her beautiful dress, the way she had done her hair, her soft, round face … everything had been totally consumed by the fire.

Laura lay the mirror face down in her lap.

"Where were you when it happened?" she asked him.

"I was at our table, waiting for you."

She nodded.

"Where were *you*?" he asked.

"I decided to take a walk, think about what you said. I was strolling through one of the baseball fields when I heard some commotion."

"Commotion?" Niles repeated.

She nodded again; her eyes full of fear.

"There was a scream and some girl ran out of the snack bar bathroom shouting for help. A couple of guards ran into the girls' room with her. I started walking closer to see what was going on … then the explosion happened."

She looked up at Niles, reliving the horror of the experience.

"I felt it … I felt it all.

"Pieces of the building were everywhere and in seconds literally everything was on fire. The grass was still really dry from the summer and the drought.

"The flames burned for almost a whole minute before everything went numb."

"I'm so sorry," Niles said, picturing how stark of a difference that was compared to his own death.

"I don't remember mine," he admitted. "I think I fell asleep. Some piece of the roof must have crushed my head right when it happened."

"I should have been there with you," Laura said.

She shifted closer in her seat, facing him.

"Niles … I am so sorry." Tears welled up in her eyes. "You were right about everything. I was so caught up in my own insecurities, my own obsession with the class theme, that I completely missed out on enjoying the night with you."

A tear trickled from his eye too.

"I'm sorry it turned out to be our last," he said.

She put her hand on his. "It doesn't have to be. We're still here, somehow. Want to go back inside? See if there's any dessert left?"

A smile came to his face for the first time since he died.

"Yeah, that sounds good."

He turned the key in the ignition and the Lexus powered down.

Once the car was locked, she took his hand again and led him inside the Murphy Center.

As they stepped into the ballroom, Niles found it to be empty.

"What the ... where is everyone?" he asked.

"I think they went to the classrooms a few hours ago. Someone must have found a master key. I fell asleep for a while myself."

They walked into the school cafeteria. There was a bit of a mess around the various shelves and counters, but in one of the refrigerators, several plates of chocolate torte were still sitting there, untouched.

Laura grabbed one for each of them.

Niles noticed a bottle of sparkling cider and brought it with two untouched glasses.

They crossed the empty ballroom again, sitting down at their original table.

"Oh no ..." Laura pushed aside the crushed top hat that was laying by her place setting.

"Oh yeah." He chuckled. "It must have been blown under someone else's chair, which just flattened it."

"You look better without it anyway," she said, setting down the plate in front of him.

"No wonder hats fell out of fashion. I felt like I had to babysit it all night."

Niles pulled out the bottle opener attached to his keys and popped off the cap of the sparkling cider. He poured the Martinelli's Apple-Pomegranate, filling both of their glasses.

She picked up her glass and paused for a moment, unsure if there was anything worth toasting to.

"To new beginnings," Niles said, moving his glass toward hers.

"To new beginnings," she agreed, tapping it.

They both took a long sip of the cider.

"So, what do you think this place is?" she asked him, gazing into the seemingly infinite fog that surrounded them.

"A lobby," he said, without much hesitation.

She raised an eyebrow at him.

Niles did something he had actively suppressed the entire time he'd known Laura Nakano ... he talked about video games.

"In this game Barry and I used to play ..." he began.

"*Intrepid?*" she asked, taking a bite of the chocolate torte.

Niles didn't have a perfect score in containing that side of himself.

"Yeah." He blushed. "In between missions to different planets, we would have to wait in a lobby until everyone was ready to start the new quest. Sometimes it would just take a few minutes, but other times it could take up to an hour. We had these friends in Australia we used to play with called 'Clan Roterhai'."

"'Roterhai'?"

"It means 'red shark'." Niles chuckled. He couldn't believe he was talking about this with her. "They were crazy. They would always rush into battle while we would stay near the back of a ship squadron and snipe with our railgun."

He could tell he was losing her. He got back on topic.

"Anyway ... The point is that they had a slow connection, so we had to wait for their servers to load the new world before the mission could start. In the meantime, we would just wait in the lobby."

"So, you think we have to wait in this ghostly version of the school until the 'next world' loads?" She was not quite connecting with his metaphor.

"We have to wait for everybody to be ready to move on," he put it more broadly. "After the school burned down, no one seemed to wake up for about twelve hours, but a bunch of people were already gone. Maybe they were just ready to move on right away, or they woke up hours before us."

"So, sort of like Purgatory?" Laura asked.

"I don't know." Niles shrugged. "My family was Baptist."

Laura took another bite of her torte. She wasn't sure whether the idea that they were stuck in Purgatory or a video game lobby was more unsettling.

"I know one thing I'm not going to miss about the old world," Niles said, trying to keep the conversation lighthearted. "Taxes."

Laura chuckled.

"Really, *Mr. Franklin?*" she joked. "What taxes did you have to pay before your untimely demise?"

"European VAT tax was like fifteen percent!" Niles said, not even joking. "Every time stupid Barry wanted to change the color of the ship, we had to pay that fee for the new skin."

She shook her head, then took the final bite of her torte.

After wiping her lips with the linen napkin, Laura turned serious again. She was beginning to regret a lot of things from over the past few months.

"It was sad what happened with Anne. At least Barry wasn't at the school when everything exploded."

Niles could feel a bead of sweat grow on his forehead. He wasn't going to lie to Laura, not when everything was going so well.

He lowered his voice as he told her. "He *was* here at the school, both him and Melvin."

"What?"

"I bumped into them after I woke up. They said that they had come to the school to play a prank on us."

"On *us*?"

"Barry was jealous. They were going to do something stupid like pull the fire alarm or trip the sprinklers."

Laura was more accepting of the story than Niles had been.

She sighed. "Anne should have been nicer about breaking things off."

"It's not your fault and it's not Anne's either. They were just in the wrong place at the wrong time, like the rest of us. The only difference was that they had a pettier reason."

"Imagine if they *had* pulled that fire alarm and we were all away from the building ..." she wondered aloud. "Where are they now?"

"I don't know," Niles said. "They were a bit freaked out that people would blame them for the bombing."

Laura paused, considering the idea.

"They wouldn't do that, would they?"

"I don't think so," Niles said, but he added a disclaimer. "I really haven't talked to them much the last few months though."

Laura didn't want to dwell on the darkness.

"Did you still want to have that dance?" she asked him.

"I'd love to," he said, "but I don't think the music works anymore."

They listened to the static that was quietly trailing out of the stage speakers.

"We don't need that."

She offered her hand to Niles, and he took it, going along with whatever she was doing.

She walked them out into the middle of the dance floor. Then she began to hum.

It sounded loosely like a waltz, but there were some breaks with different time signatures. Niles picked up the rhythm and moved them whenever the movement felt right.

Laura was not a Choir & Drama person, but she could hold a tune well enough.

Only after a minute or so of dancing did he finally recognize the melody. They had listened to it on and off all week while building the float.

It was "Castle on a Cloud" from *Les Mis.*

She repeated the main sections for a few minutes, not able to think of any other music at the time. Even still, it was nice. The curls of her hair bounced along to their movements. Niles felt confident in his steps because he already knew the song incredibly well. It was something special that was long overdue for the both of them.

After humming a final bar, they came to a stop.

"I wish I had been able to take you to a show," Niles whispered.

"Me too." Laura stepped closer to him. "It would have been a wonderful date."

Niles leaned in and they shared a long kiss.

Despite how wonderful the moment was, a small voice of doubt wondered from the back of his mind. "Would she have come around like this if we hadn't been immolated last night? Or would things have worked out regardless and we had a long, happy life together stolen from us?"

Just below the throbbing passion he felt in his heart, there was a deeper and hotter fire ... an anger he felt for whoever did this to them. If Barry and Melvin really were responsible, he would be first in line to torture them.

Their lips separated and Laura was blushing.

Niles had no idea what to say. Regardless of what he might have come up with, the afterglow was interrupted anyway.

The sound of chuckling began to fill the room.

Laura's face turned pale. They followed the echo as it bounced around the acoustics of the theatre. It led them to the source.

Joe Torelli was hidden in the shadow of the stage curtain, sitting against the inner wall. He had apparently been there the whole time, but without making any noise they hadn't noticed him.

He stood to his feet and walked off the stairwell on stage right. He entered the hallway which led back to the classrooms section of the building.

"What the hell was that all about?" Niles asked, still holding Laura.

"I don't know."

"Do you want to go back to the car?" he asked her.

She nodded.

***

Andrei and Blaire slept peacefully for a long time. It had been much more restful than the night before, lying on the cold, hard floor of the Murphy Center, where their dead bodies had landed.

Unfortunately, this sleep ended with a rude awakening.

KER-CHOONK.

The sound was loud and sudden.

Andrei's eyes popped open and he reflexively pulled Blaire closer. In doing so, he had accidentally cupped one of her boobs.

Blaire smiled, though he couldn't see it from behind.

"Sorry," he said, pulling his hand away.

"Forget it," she replied, peeking over his arm at the entrance.

KER-CHOONK.

Raf had jumped to his feet by this point.

"Who the fuck is it?!" he yelled, plodding toward the door they had barred.

"It's Greg," a faint voice came through the sound paneling.

Elise was starting to stir on the cot they had assembled out of chairs.

Blaire went over to her.

Andrei rose to his feet and walked up behind Raf. They took the stopping mechanism off of the handle.

Cracking open the door, they found Greg Henshaw with Chelsea Morton a few steps behind him. Marcus Johnson was leaning against the back wall, wearing a Golden State Warriors hoodie.

"Sorry if we woke you," Chelsea apologized. "We were just exploring the rest of the second floor, seeing who might be around."

Greg glanced at the complex rig they had set up to bar the door, even though it opened outward into the hallway.

"Are you guys staking a claim on the C&D Rehearsal Room?" Greg asked.

"The fuck are you talking about?" Raf asked, his patience having yet to wake up.

"We're setting up a system so everyone can have their own personal spaces, essentially turning the classrooms into dorms," Chelsea explained.

"How many are in there with you?" Greg asked.

"Four," Andrei said.

"Four, total?" he clarified.

Andrei and Raf just stared at him.

"Okay, four total." He wrote it down in a notebook.

"That should be fine, right?" He turned back to Chelsea.

"I think so," she agreed. "We'll mark you down."

"Whatever," Raf said, disinterested.

"One last thing," Chelsea asked. "Do you have any personal items in the costume storage room? We're going to be distributing the rest for bedding."

"No, we've got everything," Andrei replied.

"Great!" Chelsea said. "We're trying to make the transition easier on everyone, so just come to us if you have any issues and we'll get it worked out."

She made a subtle gesture toward Marcus Johnson.

He nodded at Andrei, the only guy in their netherworld that was taller than him.

"Thanks guys," Greg said, leading the trio off toward the costume storage room.

Andrei closed the door and put the locking bar back in place.

"Who was that?" a familiar voice called from inside the room.

Raf lit up at the sound and turned the corner into the main space.

Elise was sitting upright on a chair at the end of the makeshift cot.

"Just the sophomores," Raf said, trying not to stress her with the unusual situation. "They were checking in to make sure everyone was okay."

"That's nice of them," Elise replied, not fully awake or aware.

Blaire glanced up at Andrei and he gave her a knowing look. The conversation was definitely not so innocent or straightforward.

"Are you feeling better?" Blaire asked her, standing by one of the chairs used to make the "bed".

Elise rubbed her eyes, still coming to.

"I think so, that was just a lot to-"

She shrieked as she turned toward Blaire.

Glancing down, she realized that Jackie the Jaguar posed aggressively on the front of every gym shirt.

Blaire ducked down, hiding the apex predator behind the back of the chair.

"Hey," she asked Andrei, "can you pass me my hoodie?"

"Yeah." Andrei pivoted toward her gym bag. He pulled it open a bit wider and retrieved the jacket. It was all black, except for some white line detailing on the seams.

He passed it to Blaire and she slid it on, caging Jackie the Jaguar behind the zipper.

"Hey ..." Raf knelt down next to Elise. "I know it's tough right now, but there's going to be a lot of gym shirts out there and other pictures of the jaguar."

Elise nodded.

"There's no rush, but we do need to get you back to being okay."

"I know," she said, squeezing her eyes shut.

Andrei began buttoning up his dress shirt again. He figured the suit was still fine for the time being. He left the vest and tie on the floor by his gym bag though. No real point wearing those anymore.

He noticed his boutonniere lying beside the pile too. It was a bit dry, but surprisingly not wilted.

"Want to go see if there's breakfast?" he asked Blaire while sliding on the suit coat.

"Sure," she said, her hands buried deep in the hoodie's front pockets.

"We'll bring something back for you," she said to Elise and Raf.

"Thanks," Elise said, shrinking down into one of the chairs she had slept on.

Andrei unbarred the door and pushed it open.

"We've got to find a key or something," he said to himself.

A lot of the new doors had fancy locks with numerical keypads, but that was only done for the classrooms in the north section of the building. The Murphy Center, the first section that was remodeled, still only had conventional interchangeable core locks on steel lever handles.

The rigging they'd set up worked well, but someone had to be inside at all times to operate it.

Once they were out in the hallway, Blaire could see a crack of light coming from the costume storage room.

"So, who was at the door?" she asked him, now that Elise was out of earshot.

"Greg, Chelsea, and Marcus Johnson," he said. "Sounds like the others started calling dibs on classrooms for some kind of dormitory situation. We're probably stuck with the rehearsal room now."

"I can live with that," Blaire said. Then she realized the figure of speech she'd used. "I mean, I can ... uh, I don't even know."

"It was pretty weird though," Andrei said. "I think we missed some kind of town hall or constitutional convention, because they were talking like they were McDouglas and Fletcher."

"Great." Blaire sighed. "One day into the afterlife and we already have netherworld politics to deal with."

They passed by a water fountain. Curious, Andrei walked up to it, pressing on the lever. A stream of normal looking water began flowing out. He leaned down and tasted it.

"Is it poison?" Blaire asked.

"Doesn't taste like poison," Andrei said, "but I haven't really sampled many to know for sure."

Blaire took a sip too. It just tasted like normal school water. It even still had that weird metallic aftertaste.

"Assuming that all the water works, at least we have a way to do laundry." Andrei brushed some dust from his coat sleeve.

"That'll be great for the two entire outfits in my wardrobe," Blaire replied.

"I think you're forgetting the colorful closet-full of costumes that make up our bed."

"That's perfect. On laundry days I can pick which *Cats* character I want to spend the time dressed as."

They chuckled.

Andrei followed up with, "Good thing none of the cats are jaguars."

"I know." Blaire sighed. "I hope we can snap her out of that soon. She can't get stuck in that room forever. The school grounds are confining enough."

They walked down the stairwell and ended up in the front lobby of the Murphy Center. The white daylight fog glowed just as brightly as when they fell asleep.

"What time is it?" she asked him.

Andrei pulled out his phone, "Monday, one twenty-two in the morning"

"What?" Blaire groaned. "So there isn't even day and night anymore?"

"I wonder if the time's the same?" Andrei asked, bending his head back in thought. "You think it's past midnight back home?"

Blaire shrugged, a slight gloom coming over her.

Andrei dropped the subject. It's not like they knew a way to go over and check. Not to mention, it was just depressing to think what their loved ones were doing, now that it was thirty hours after the massacre.

There weren't too many people scattered about. About two dozen were talking in four or five groups, sitting at tables.

There was one group in particular that put a smile back on Blaire's face.

She nudged Andrei, nodding toward one of the tables in the closest column. A familiar old-timey crimson red dress adorned one of the girls. Sitting next to her was a guy in a similar period-piece costume. They were both laughing together.

Blaire and Andrei walked by them as they entered the cafeteria, but she kept them in her periphery the whole time.

"Can you believe it?" she said to Andrei, excited.

"You did well," he congratulated her. "Looks like you really picked up something from Elise."

Blaire blushed. "I took a bit of a harsher approach than she would have."

Andrei smiled. "Hey, whatever works."

"Do you mind if we sit with them for a few minutes?" Blaire asked. "I don't want Laura to think I hate her. We're all going to be sharing a roof for a while."

"Sure," Andrei said.

They looked around the cafeteria for what was available. Quite a bit of food was still sitting out in the open, untouched.

One of the regular snack shelves still had plenty of individually-wrapped muffins. Blaire grabbed four; they could bring two back to Raf and Elise.

Andrei grabbed four bottles of orange juice from one of the mini-fridges.

They walked by the check-out counter.

"Shoot, forgot my wallet in the room." Andrei stopped at the register.

"Ah, me too." Blaire groaned.

She snapped out of it right as Andrei walked past her.

"Ha-ha, very funny." She caught up to him.

As they approached the table, they recognized the two other people sitting there. It was the late Prince and Princess of the Junior Class, Liam Connelly and Melissa Levitt.

"Hey," Blaire said, stopping at the table. "Mind if we sit down?"

"No, go ahead," Neil said, without hesitation.

Laura had a bit of a worried look on her face, but she didn't object.

"What's up goth girl?" Liam said, in an unusually affable mood. "We were just talking about stuff we're happy to see in the rear-view mirror."

"Not literally mirrors though," Melissa mumbled.

Streaks of eyeliner were still visible all over her cheeks. She looked like she'd handled the news worse than most.

"Right," Liam continued. "So, Niles just submitted an easy one ... homework."

"Shit, 'Niles' ... that was his name," Blaire thought to herself, really glad she hadn't said it out loud yet.

"We just going in a circle?" Andrei asked, opening his orange juice bottle.

"Yeah, something like that," Niles said.

"Alright," Andrei thought for a moment. "How about getting older? Seventeen's not a bad age to be stuck at."

"Oh, I like that," Melissa said, stroking a few locks of hair. "I hope that turns out to be true."

"Forever young ..." Liam agreed. "At least a lot of the beautiful people showed up down here. Hell is full of hotties."

He nudged Melissa, trying to cheer her up. It seemed to be working, but very slowly.

The group turned to Blaire. Laura still had an uncertain look on her face.

"How about drama?" Blaire proposed, then she met Laura's eyes. "Might as well make the most of a fresh start."

Laura smiled.

"Definitely," Niles agreed. "No more of the day-to-day nonsense which really seems dumb when you're six feet under."

"Hmm ..." Liam wondered aloud. "You think they've buried anyone yet?"

There was a pause as everyone considered what might be going on in the living world.

"Ugh, I hope they bury me first," Melissa groaned. "Because right now I'm buried under the stalls in the girls' bathroom."

Liam chuckled, breaking the momentary melancholy.

"Oh, that's my next submission!" she exclaimed. "Going to the bathroom."

A few people at the table had a curious look, only now realizing the same thing.

"I used to have to pee like ten times a day because I had a stupid chihuahua bladder," Melissa complained, "but now I don't feel anything at all!"

Blaire looked down at her muffin, which she'd already eaten half of. She swallowed the bite.

Liam was next in the circle.

"I'm going to go with damage recovery," he said.

"What do you mean by that?" Laura wondered.

"Well ..." he said. "I might have taken things pretty hard yesterday. I was one of the jumpers who tried the easy way out in the atrium."

Blaire raised her eyebrows, a bit stunned. Laura didn't know how to respond.

"I tried one of the steak knives," Melissa admitted nonchalantly. "But all that happened was more of the baby powder or whatever ... so I just gave up."

She stroked the inside of her forearm. There were no visible scratches or scars at all.

Laura had to take a breath for a moment before continuing. She decided to take it back to something less serious.

"Kind of like Niles said," she began. "But I'm glad there's no more S.A.T.'s or college prep to worry about."

The table nodded in agreement.

The six of them spent some time finding every silver lining they could think of on the otherwise oppressive storm cloud that surrounded them.

***

Bob Melkonian was awoken to the sound of a metal chair clattering on the hard tile floor of his biology classroom.

He was still lying where he had started the night before, on one of the larger prep tables between two back cabinets. He'd set up just enough stuff around him that he wouldn't roll to the floor. Even if he did, it's not like it would kill him.

No matter how many animals he'd dissected, something about the table still seemed softer and preferable to the bare ground. He'd scattered some loose papers and old files over the top to add just a bit more cushion, almost like a bird's nest.

He turned his head to see Rick Wallace putting his shoes back on. Bob had let him sleep in his desk chair, someplace a little more comfortable.

"Where are you going?" Bob asked him.

"I'm going to see if the kids will let me have *my* desk chair," he said. "I can't let you spend another night up there."

"It could have been worse," Bob said, but a pain shooting down his spine disagreed.

"I'll figure something out," Rick said. "Please, take your chair."

Rick opened the door and headed down the hallway toward the atrium. A bright daylight glow continued to fill the building.

Bob looked at his watch ... 3:04 a.m.

He shuffled over to the chair, stretching out along the backrest to try to get his muscles to loosen.

He must have fallen back to sleep, because the next time he opened his eyes it was almost 6:00 a.m.

There was a knocking at the entrance, which caused him to stir. He stood up and walked over.

"Were you able to get the chair?" Bob asked as he pulled open the door.

It wasn't Rick on the other side, it was Trisha Forrester.

"Hi Mr. Mel," she waved.

"Hi, Trisha," he said. "What are you doing here?"

"Can I come in?" she asked.

"Uh, sure."

Bob pushed the door a bit wider, then walked back to one of the lab desks.

She sat down on the chair opposite him.

"Yesterday," she began, "I told you why I thought I was here. I was hoping that you could tell me ... why are *you* here, Mr. Mel?"

Bob turned his eyes down to the floor.

"Okay," Melkonian said. "I'll tell you."

She shifted in the stool, listening closely.

"When I was young," he began, "much younger than any of you are now, I was playing around in our family car.

"It was parked in the driveway of our house, but I had left some toys in the back. At some point, I accidentally kicked the gear shift and the car was put into neutral.

"It rolled about twenty feet down the driveway of our old house, and backed right into a fire hydrant."

Trisha tilted her head; she had expected the situation to turn out similar to what happened with her dog Buster.

"When my father saw what happened," Bob said, "he ran down the driveway and pulled me out of the car as the hydrant poured pressurized water into the street.

"His first instinct as a father wasn't to see if I was okay, wasn't to check for wounds, or check to see if I was scared. His first instinct was to punish me for the accident.

"He took off his belt and he beat me for over an hour, until the fire department came to shut off the flow of water to the hydrant."

Trisha was stunned, covering her mouth.

"That is the earliest memory I have of him," Bob said. "He was a cruel man, who knew only violence. Every memory I have of him plays out more or less without change. I may be a bit bigger, he may be a bit older, but the beatings were all the same."

"Oh my gosh ..." Trisha sat forward.

"When I turned sixteen," Mr. Mel continued, "I was finally old enough, finally strong enough, to fight back. I caught my father's hand, caught his belt, and turned them both back on him.

"I left him bleeding in a hundred places, covered with more lacerations than someone who'd been thrown out of a glass window.

"My mother stood by, as she always did. She never had the will or fortitude to stop what he did to me; she didn't even have the *desire* to stop what I did to him."

"Did he die?" Trisha asked.

"No," Bob said. "I believe he spent a few days in the hospital, but I don't know for sure. That was the last day I saw either of my parents. I ran away and lived with friends until I was financially stable enough to live on my own.

"The last words I said to both of them were that I wished them 'eternal fire and damnation for all time'."

Trisha looked confused.

"Good," she said. "They deserved it."

"Maybe," Bob said. "But I never renounced that curse, and was fully committed to that feeling until the day that I died."

"How is that bad?" Trisha asked. "It doesn't mean you deserve the same."

"I'm not the one to judge," Bob said. "God is. Holding onto that hatred for all those years corrupted me more than any of my father's beatings. I turned away from all the rest of my family, not just him, not just my mother.

"I burned every bridge with everyone I was related to, blaming them for their failure to protect me. I have no idea what damage that caused to the rest of my family.

"That's why I think I'm down here. I never gave them a chance at forgiveness, I treated them all the same as the man who had abused me so terribly.

"I don't even know how long he lived. My father could have died of a heart attack a year later; I could have spent nearly 40 years back in contact with all of them. They might have been genuinely sorry, but now I'll never know.

"Hatred is a dangerous fire. When you feed into it, it can easily destroy you and so many others."

Trisha still looked confused, but she looked deep in his eyes.

He wasn't lying. At least, he didn't *think* he was lying.

"Mr. Mel," she said, getting to the real point of her visit. "Tell me the truth, were you involved in blowing up the school ... at all?"

"No!" he replied without hesitation, his eyes filling with grief. "I would absolutely never have done anything like that.

"Trisha, I loved you kids. For all the anger and hatred that my father showed me, I tried to do the opposite with my dear Monika and with all of you!

"I would have taken that explosion alone, in a heartbeat, if it meant saving your lives."

Trisha looked touched.

"I believe you," she said. "But I had to hear you say it out loud."

She composed herself.

"You were always my favorite teacher Mr. Mel. You *were* always kind to us ... That's why I want to be there to speak on your behalf."

A silence hung in the air.

"Be where, Trisha?" he whispered, feeling the walls close in.

"At your trial," she answered.

A gentle knocking sounded on the door, but it was simply a formality. There were four beeps as a numerical combo was entered into the lock.

"Trisha," Bob said, looking in her eyes. "Where is Mr. Wallace?"

There was an electronic click, and the door latch popped open.

FIFTEEN

UNCAGED BEASTS

DARREN AND JENNY HAD BEEN fast asleep when they were suddenly awoken by the sound of knocking.

"I'll get it," he said.

Darren stumbled to his feet while Jenny curled up then extended her back, stretching to help wake herself up.

He pulled open the door and saw Paxton Bannister.

"Morning Darren," he said. "We've got a meeting happening in about fifteen minutes in the ballroom. Everyone's being summoned."

"Shit, okay," Darren said. "We'll see you there."

Paxton nodded, then moved on to the next room.

Darren pulled out his phone.

Monday, 2:44 a.m.

When he turned around, Jenny was on her feet. She was pulling bobby pins and other accessories out of her hair.

"I can't believe I slept in this," she said. "I need to change into something fresh. Would you mind going to my locker and getting the scrunchie on the top shelf?"

"Sure," he said.

Darren pulled open the door and then closed it behind him, making sure that it latched.

Mr. Ziegler's room was only about fifty feet from their lockers, which was convenient backup storage.

He dialed in the combo to hers and grabbed the only scrunchie he could see. It was royal blue, a few shades lighter than her Homecoming dress.

He closed it and walked back to their room.

Blake Samuels was leaning against the wall in front of his own door, about thirty feet away.

"Morning sunshine." He grinned.

Darren took a deep breath.

"Why don't you be a good person for once and leave for the meeting now?" Darren asked. "So she doesn't have to wake up to this."

Blake chuckled. "You're already power tripping after barely a day as a glorified guard dog?"

"This isn't about me," Darren said. "It's about Jenny."

"Actually, it's about both of you." The humor had dropped from his voice. "Do you know what you are, in this fragile new order the airhead sophomore kids are trying to put together?"

"No, Blake," he said, exasperated. "What?"

"You're one of Cerberus' heads," he said. "The dumb one."

Darren took a step closer to him.

"You already know who the middle head is. You realize that your fate is tied to Joe Torelli?"

This gave Darren pause.

"Think about it," Blake said. "You have a mob of a hundred furious, dead teenagers who want nothing more than to find the person that killed them and shove them asshole-first down a pike."

Darren's eyes widened.

"You and I both know who the killer is," Blake said. "He was spinning on so many Addys Saturday night, I was surprised he didn't drive that car of his through the ballroom."

"We don't know if he did it."

Blake gave him a piteous look. "Come on Darren ... It's only a matter of time until some evidence turns up proving it."

Darren could feel his heart beating faster.

"When they have that," Blake said, "they're going to assume all four of you were somehow complicit. There's going to be five pikes. You'll be up there for months, maybe years, unable to die. Every day someone will walk by and slice pieces off of you until there's no more sand left inside."

"If Joe really did it, I'd be the first to turn him in."

"You sure anyone would actually find that convincing?"

Darren could feel sweat running down his neck.

"And when you are all serving your eternal punishment," Blake hissed. "Someone will have to be there for Jen."

Fury ignited within Darren. He began marching toward Blake, planning out his route to the atrium.

That's when he heard a door open and stopped in his tracks.

"Did you find the scrun-" Jenny said, cutting out when she saw Blake.

"Morning Jen," he said. "See you guys at the meeting."

He then walked off for the stairwell.

"What was all that about?" Jenny asked.

Darren walked with her inside, closing the door behind them.

She was now in her gym clothes. Her dirty blonde hair hung naturally, the braid fully undone.

Darren handed her the scrunchie and she pulled her hair into a ponytail.

"Do you know if Joe did it?" Darren asked her.

"What?! You mean if he blew up the school?"

"Yes," Darren said. "If you have any evidence, you need to tell me right away."

"What's going on?" Jenny grabbed his arm. "What did Blake say?"

"He seems really sure that Joe did it," Darren said. "He wants the rest of us football players to go down with him."

"What?! No!" Jenny exclaimed. "I *know* you had nothing to do with it."

"Blake doesn't care," Darren said. "He wants me out of the picture ... he wants you."

"Never!" She spat venom from her lips. "I'll never let them take you."

"He is right about one thing though. If the rest of them believe we worked with Joe, then we'll all go down with him. As soon as we have any proof Joe may be responsible, we need to turn him over to the others."

"What? I mean ... I think he's really hurting from Isabella. That doesn't look like an act. He has a lot of demons, but Joe's our friend. We can't just toss him to the wolves if he didn't do it either!"

Darren took her hands.

"I can't let you suffer because of him though. If they try to convict us along with Joe, and you reject Blake-"

"Of course I reject him. I hate that scumbag!"

Darren continued, "And *when* you reject Blake, he'll try to pin you to the bombing along with the rest of us."

Darren pulled her closer, "I can't let that happen."

"Okay." She nodded. "I'll tell you if I do see anything. If he really did it, then he has to pay."

***

Blaire and Andrei found themselves having a fun time with Niles and Laura. Even Liam and Melissa had been enjoyable to talk to.

After about half an hour, they returned to the C&D room to give Raf and Elise the breakfast items they picked up.

They were having some kind of heart-to-heart talk, so Andrei suggested they go back down for a while.

Raf seemed grateful as the two of them left.

Downstairs, all of the remaining costumes from the storage room were piled to the side of the stage.

Chelsea and Greg decided to call for some kind of group meeting to pass them out and talk about some other business.

They sent out some of the Varsity Football and Basketball players to knock on people's doors.

Andrei wasn't sure if they'd sent anyone up to Raf and Elise, but if they did, the two had ignored the summons.

Soon, a hundred or so students were scattered across the banquet tables, facing the stage.

"Good morning everyone!" Greg said. "It's a very lovely-"

He checked his phone.

"Three a.m." He chuckled. "So much for sunrises and sunsets."

"Did everyone sleep well enough?" Chelsea asked.

There was some mixed murmuring from the crowd.

"Well, we hope to change that," Greg said, putting on a big smile. "As you can see behind us, we've raided the wardrobe of the C&D Department."

"It's not exactly Bed, Bath, & Beyond ..." Chelsea said, "but at least it's something that can make the tables or floors a little bit more comfortable. 'Nesting' might be the appropriate term."

There was a positive chuckle from the crowd.

Andrei could see Joe Torelli and Marcus Johnson standing at guard positions by stage right and stage left respectively. All this organization had happened far too quickly in his opinion. Something didn't feel right about any of this.

"We would ideally like to hold a meeting like this once a week," Greg continued. "We want everyone to have a place where they can voice ideas, air grievances, or offer suggestions for how we can improve our lot in this small little world."

"We are all stuck here together," Chelsea said. "It's only going to work if we help support each other."

"How can we support each other when the bomber could be here with us?" someone called from the crowd.

There was a sudden clapping in agreement.

"We need to find the killer!" a girl shouted from the other side of the room.

Andrei could feel Blaire grab his hand.

The shouts from the crowd were getting louder.

"It's got to be the teachers!" someone else yelled. Several other voices raised in agreement.

"Everyone, calm down," Chelsea said. "One at a time."

"They can't get away with it!" another voice cried.

The crowd was getting away from the mousy sophomores. They were in way over their heads.

"So, you're saying you want trials?" Greg asked. "For Wallace and Melkonian?"

A loud yell of agreement sounded from the crowd.

Andrei, Blaire, Niles, and Laura had been silent through all of these exchanges.

"Who else?" Greg asked.

"Joe Torelli!" one voice cried from a corner.

Andrei looked over at the Jaguars' quarterback. He was incensed and began walking up to center stage.

"Who the fuck said that?!" he yelled over the crowd.

Blaire clutched Andrei's hand tighter.

He started scanning the doors, looking for the best exits if this turned into a riot.

Greg and Chelsea backed up and Marcus watched the exchange in curiosity.

"You think I did this to us?!" he yelled again.

"Interception!" someone taunted from the left side of the room.

"Ha-ha-ha," Torelli mocked in response.

The rumble in the crowd was growing though, whispers floated between tables.

"You want to know where I went that night?!" Torelli asked them. "See what I did after the game?!"

The noise of the mob shifted.

"I'll fucking show you." He began walking offstage toward the front doors of the Murphy Center.

Andrei whispered to Blaire. "Walk carefully, don't draw suspicion, then we head back up to the room."

She nodded.

Half of the ballroom stood up and started following Torelli. The second half trailed back further, curious to see where this was going.

The other Varsity Football players were right behind him, as were Marcus, Paxton and the two other Varsity Basketball players that had appeared in this place. Greg and Chelsea were left in the third row.

Joe marched into the parking lot, approaching the black Camaro.

Andrei and Blaire moved closer to the stairwell, but before they could break free from the crowd, another group of kids poured through a second door.

Blaire was caught up in the rush, their hands getting pulled apart.

"Andrei!" she yelled.

He reached up, catching her again, but he was pulled along just the same. Soon they were outside, standing next to one of the decorative planters. To their left was the Homecoming Queen and her boyfriend, one of the football players.

"Hey, what is this?" Andrei accused them.

Darren and Jenny turned toward the new senior guy and his goth girlfriend.

"I don't know," Darren said, a troubled look in his eyes. "I swear to God, I don't know!"

The crowd stopped at the edge of the parking lot as Joe stepped over the rear-view mirror he'd smashed to pieces. The mirror itself remained undamaged.

Joe sat back down in the driver's seat of the black Camaro.

Everyone waited, expecting him to turn the key and once again fail to start the engine.

Instead, there was a dull thud. The trunk of the sports car popped open.

Joe stepped out of the driver's seat and walked back, pushing the lid all the way up.

"This is what I did last night!" he announced to the crowd.

He opened up the football kit bag.

A pair of blue jeans sailed into the air, landing a few feet away. Some t-shirts quickly followed, along with shorts, boxers, and socks.

Joe Torelli flashed back to that night.

He remembered walking off the field as the John Muir High Mountaineers celebrated their victory, but it was not their voices that grinded inside his mind.

"This is your last chance Joe," the older voice derided him. "You want to prove yourself to recruiters? Show colleges you have any damn potential at all? Then you need to blow them all away. It's not just victories that matter, it's spectacle! You want history to remember you, then you have to do something big!"

Joe unzipped a hidden pocket of his kit bag. A small plastic bag with a variety of pills sat in there.

Joe took three or four of the different shapes.

"Don't give me that sass you little shit," the voice said again. "Blood, sweat, and tears are the price for greatness. If my knee hadn't given out, I'd have paid that price twice over by now!"

Several hours disappeared into the darkness.

"You come from good marble, son," the voice said, "but if you want someone to build a statue of you someday then you better be ready for the chisel!"

It wasn't until almost 4:00 a.m. that Joe had a sense of himself again.

Joe had driven the Camaro to the game, expecting to ride off in victory with Isabella. Instead, he had arrived home alone, the car coming to an idle stop in his driveway. It was still a few hours before sunrise.

Joe stepped inside the household of two. His mom had left with his sister years ago.

"The Torellis are great men!" the voice said again. "You're still here, because you are great too. Your mother never saw that greatness. If you think I'm hard on you, it's because I do!"

Joe pulled open the door of the master bedroom.

The crowd of Villa Vista students had formed a half-circle around the car, watching Joe empty his football bag onto the pavement, one item at a time.

Among the clothes were maps of Latin America, some jewelry, bags of cash, toiletries, some medicine bottles, and a variety of other "long-term vacation" supplies.

He was communicating his thoughts to them in a non-stop rambling sentence. He did not place any time frames or events at all. He hadn't actually said anything about what he did after the game. All he was saying was how much he hated his father.

A lone figure lay on the bed in the middle of the room, fast asleep.

An empty bottle of Hennessy Cognac was sitting on the nightstand.

Joe grabbed the man by the middle of his shirt, dragging him out of bed in a single swift motion.

The man stumbled backward into the armchair where Joe had thrown him.

Joe clicked on the television set in the middle of the room, turning the volume up to maximum.

"You want to know what I did last night?!" Joe yelled to the crowd.

He grabbed the final item inside the kit bag, which had been hidden under a false bottom.

The image was fresh in Joe's mind, the clearest memory from his entire eighteen years of life. Salvatore Torelli looked scared, truly scared, for the very first time.

Joe pulled out the eight-pound assembly of wood and steel, swinging it away from the trunk so that everyone could see.

With a single snap of his wrist, the action of the double-barreled shotgun closed with a satisfying click.

The crowd immediately ducked, with those in the back scattering or retreating inside.

Joe shoved the over/under barrels of the Browning Citori into his father's mouth.

"I fucking killed him!" Joe announced to the crowd, pulling the trigger.

The 12-gauge round exploded from the top barrel, bringing a swift end to Salvatore Torelli.

Darren and Andrei pressed Jenny and Blaire behind the planter. If they had the space to run, they might have, but the sound of the shotgun firing into the air stopped everyone in their tracks.

Joe sat on the edge of his father's bed, continuing to watch football highlights for several more hours. The elder Torelli's blood pooled on the floor around the armchair.

At one point a clip came on discussing the disastrous Giants/Bears game. The Giants' loss was almost solely due to the three interceptions thrown during the game, in the same way that the Coastal Classic had been lost because of the interceptions that Joe threw.

"You see?!" he yelled to the headless corpse. "Even Manning!"

Eventually, Joe got up and went to the shower.

For almost half an hour he sat under the burning hot water of the faucet until he was sure he'd washed away the dried layer of blood and flesh.

Joe knew he would have to flee the country. He had thought about killing his father for a long time, including the logistics. The only thing that surprised him was that he didn't do it earlier.

Having his cousin Tito's Camaro just meant he'd be able to get more money selling the car in rural central Mexico. From there, he'd continue on to Argentina.

Joe knew more Italian from his extended family than Spanish from a few years at Villa Vista. He also thought he might bump into Isabella's family down there.

A small long-term goal he had set out for himself, as fanciful as it might have been, was to make contact with her again after he'd settled in under a new name.

They might not have dated long, but they'd known each other for longer and Joe was really growing fond of her.

He had written a letter, a physical, paper letter to her, explaining his true feelings. He placed it in the outgoing mailbox, fairly certain she would get it by Monday or Tuesday.

By then she might know why he did what he had to do.

He didn't like having to break her heart at the dance, but it was the only valid excuse he could think of to cut out of the night early without anyone following him.

He wanted to go to the dance with her no matter what ... but he also had to make it to Mexico before someone found Salvatore's body.

Joe flipped on the air conditioning to max to keep the house nice and cool. The smell of rotting flesh would likely be what finally got someone to break down the door.

The two of them were always very noisy. Yelling often happened in both directions and the TV would play loudly at odd hours. He knew that the NFL game would be enough to mask the sound of the shotgun blast.

Joe just had to keep Sal hidden until someone from the school called the house on Monday ... when he didn't show up to Villa Vista.

Now everything had changed. Isabella was dead and so was he. Even though he was free from the American justice system, he was still apart from her.

Whoever killed Isabella needed to suffer and the two pussy sophomores weren't cut out for the job.

Joe had to take control.

From the same hidden compartment in his football kit bag, Joe revealed a bandolier full of fifty shells for the shotgun. He slung it over his shoulder.

***

Blaire and Andrei disappeared out of the door, leaving Elise and Rafael alone in the rehearsal room.

They promised to bring back breakfast of some kind, which sounded nice to Elise even though she wasn't really hungry.

She looked around the room, getting a better sense of where she was. The last thing she really remembered was seeing Ellen Taylor in the snack bar bathroom.

This ... this was the Choir & Drama room.

She looked back at what she had been laying on.

A bunch of chairs had been pulled together and some school musical costumes had been draped over the seats to form a sort of bed.

A second pile of costumes were lying beside the assembly of chairs. A third was spread out against the far wall by Mr. Richter's piano.

"I was out of it for a while, wasn't I?" Elise asked.

"It's been about ten hours," Raf said. "But we all needed a full night's sleep. The last one didn't really count."

"I'm sorry." She looked down at the floor. "It just ... it was just so terrifying. I'm having a hard time keeping it out of my head."

Raf sat down next to her, rubbing her arm.

"You can't listen to that girl," he said, referring to Ellen Taylor in the bathroom. "She probably had a lot of stuff going on in her head before any of this happened in the first place."

"Do you think we're really stuck here forever?" Elise asked.

"I don't know," Raf admitted. "To be honest I'm still coming to terms with the idea of an afterlife at all. Like, you hear all the stories, and maybe you believe in one thing or another ... but to actually wake up here is a lot to deal with."

Elise was silent, just feeling his hand on her arm.

"I know one thing for sure," Raf continued. "There are a lot of worse places we could be."

That seemed to strike Elise in a strange way.

"I mean, I miss my family, I miss my life, everything I didn't get to do. But to be stuck somewhere with you ... and to have Blaire and Andrei, and a few of our other friends too. I'm not complaining."

"But what about what might happen today or tomorrow?" She turned to him, welling up.

"We were at Homecoming!" she said. "It had been a wonderful night, you had been so great ... and just like that, we were dead."

"And it was horrible," Raf said. "But there are a million other horrible ways that night could have ended. Heck, we could have survived."

Elise was dumbfounded by that statement.

"Think about it," he said. "Years spent in hospitals, getting skin grafts and surgeries for our burned bodies. We could have been blind, paralyzed, we could have lost limbs, we could have spent fifty or sixty years in wheelchairs, and everyone else might still be dead."

Elise looked down, imagining losing Blaire or never recovering from the broken neck.

She felt caged now, she couldn't fathom the horror of being trapped within her own body ... unable to walk, unable to move her arms, maybe unable to speak.

Raf stood up, taking her hands and standing her up with him.

She still wore her pink tennis shoes. She could feel her toes flex as she found her balance.

"Tomorrow could always be worse," Raf said. "It could also be better."

He gave her a serious look.

"We have to make the most of the *now*."

Raf then let go of her hands and slid backwards in a pose.

Elise could tell a song was coming.

Raf broke out into the chorus of "Locked Out of Heaven" by Bruno Mars. He was getting much more into it than she expected.

"Okay, okay ..." she said, stopping him before he circled back to the saucier lines.

Elise was smiling again and that was all Raf cared about at the moment.

He slid down into one of the normal choir chairs, patting the seat next to him.

"Did I ever tell you about what happened after my cousin Pedro's wedding?" he asked.

"Did he die?" Elise asked, easing down into the chair.

"No, but I bet he wished he did."

"What?" Elise chuckled.

"He got food poisoning. But it didn't come on until later ... that night."

"Oh no ..." Elise cringed, imagining how bad that might have turned out for the honeymoon.

They talked for a long time. The funny stories shifted back and forth into more meaningful ones. The Herreras and Gosselins were big families; both teens had left a lot of people behind. Talking about them helped.

At one point, Blaire and Andrei returned with some muffins and orange juice, then they went back downstairs.

Raf assumed they were having their own one-on-one time somewhere, unaware of the conversation they were having with Niles and Laura.

Things had been nice. After an hour or so, he felt like he had finally pulled Elise out of the mindset she had been placed in by the crazy freshman girl.

That was the thing that had pissed him off the most last night. It wasn't just the fact that she could be the killer, but that everyone else's instability was wearing down on Elise so much.

For God's sake, there weren't any dudes with red skin and goat legs torturing them all, maybe they should count their blessings for a while before coming to pieces.

Raf didn't think this could be Hell anyway. To him it seemed pretty likely that they'd landed in Purgatory and had to chill there for a while until someone made a fat donation to the Pope or something.

That is when they heard the gunshot.

**

"So the cars don't work but guns do?" Darren thought to himself, his hands still covering Jenny's head.

Not only that, but Joe had brought ammo to spare. He hung a belt of 12-gauge shells off of one shoulder. It was completely full, covering his chest and back.

Even worse than realizing that Joe brought a fucking shotgun to a school dance was watching Blake's prediction come true in real time.

The new guy and his junior girlfriend were staring at Darren and Jenny like they had given the thing to Torelli as a birthday present.

"If we're going to find the person that blew up the school, *who took Isabella away from me*, then we have to be ruthless!" Joe said to his captive audience. "We have to do what's necessary."

He leaned the shotgun back across one shoulder.

"Who's with me?" he called to the crowd, extending a hand.

There was a long silence, everyone was still huddled on the ground too frightened or shocked to do anything.

Then the first domino fell.

Marcus Johnson stood to his feet and walked over to Joe. He took his hand, squeezing it hard.

"For Janice," he said, a cold emptiness behind his eyes. He stood next to Joe, facing the group.

Brendan Jensen was next to stand up, then Trey Devall. Sheena and Ashley followed them, but they looked much less certain.

Paxton Bannister was next, with Amanda Burke in tow.

"Dammit ..." Blaire whimpered. She could imagine Raquel and Dina following suit if the former wasn't helping keep the latter in a makeshift straight jacket.

Seeing the turning of the tide, Greg Henshaw and Chelsea Morton inched upward as well.

They stayed huddled on the periphery, clearly disturbed by what was happening, but also looking like they didn't have a choice.

Their submission was a turning point. Soon dozens of others were standing. Many of them looked much more excited, already growing drunk on the idea of revenge.

Darren and Jenny looked over at the next planter, where Jimmy and Camellia were huddled. Jimmy gave them a shrug of defeat and started to move.

"What should we do?" Darren asked Jenny.

"Either we go along with it or they'll find a way to blame us." Jenny's frown deepened, understanding Darren's feelings of guilt by association.

As one, they rose and followed Jimmy and Camellia next to the other varsity players.

"I'd rather not stand out either," Blaire whispered to Andrei.

He nodded and they matched the crowd.

A few of the other students, who had retreated inside the Murphy Center entrance, stepped outside, following the madness of the mob. The ones who didn't exit were the ones who'd already fled further into the building.

With the masses behind him, Joe began to march.

"First thing's first," he began. "If we're going to find evidence, proof of what happened, then we need to see for ourselves!"

From the moment the students of Villa Vista High woke up in this underworld, from the moment they looked in the mirrors and saw the horror of what had befallen all of them, a nightmarish fear had gripped their souls.

That fear was the column of black smoke pouring upwards out of the gymnasium. The cause of their death lay inside. Some otherworldly feeling warned that another death would come if they disturbed this place, that it was the entry to an even lower level of Hell.

Joe approached the construction fence in front of the gym, the Browning Citori shotgun in hand.

Signs on both sides of the gate displayed in big, stylized letters the acronym "MCL". The fine print at the bottom read: "Myers, Cline, & Leitheiser Construction Associates".

Joe tugged on the metal gate, the chain and lock were still fastened.

He opened the action of the shotgun, sliding another 12-gauge shell into the top barrel to replace the one he'd fired. He snapped it closed again, then toggled the barrel selector switch.

The dual barrels were raised only inches from the stubborn lock and chain in the middle of the fence.

Both barrels fired.

Pieces of chain and buckshot blasted against the brand-new glass doors of the lobby, shattering over half of the panels.

Joe pulled open one side of the fence and Marcus pulled open the other.

The rest of the massacred students of Villa Vista High stepped behind them as though they were entering a minefield. They were still terrified of this evil place.

Behind the glass doors was an entrance lobby. There were a number of trophy cases ready and waiting to show off the successes of the school's various athletic programs. The trophies had been in storage, waiting for the grand opening with the start of a Varsity Basketball season that would never come.

Marcus Johnson paused in front of the cases, knowing his name was on at least one of the missing basketball trophies. Janice was far from the only thing stolen from him that night.

Joe stepped sideways to a set of metal doors for the gymnasium itself.

The shotgun was freshly reloaded.

His scarred knuckles wrapped around the handle, pulling open the door.

SIXTEEN

ROAR OF THUNDER

"SHIT, THIS IS NOT GOOD," Rafael said aloud.

He and Elise had just watched Joe Torelli overthrow the stupid sophomore kids in some kind of coup. With a shotgun in hand, he led his new junta straight to the doors of the gym.

Elise pulled the make-up compact out of Blaire's purse.

Staring past the image of her dead self, she looked down at the dark smoke rising out of the floor of the gym.

They didn't see the masses approach its front doors, but as the people began to filter into the building, it almost looked like the flames around the bottom were growing hotter and brighter.

"What's happening to them?" Raf asked her.

"I don't know," Elise said, terrified, "but something's changing."

She looked at Raf. "It knows they're going inside."

As the students crept into the gym, Blaire and Andrei had a chance to make their escape.

However, as much as she wanted to flee, Blaire knew that the time for that passed long ago. They had already been swallowed up by the evil residing in that place.

Why had it warned her of its presence beforehand? Why had it chosen to reach into her nightmares, yet not reveal enough of itself for her to escape?

She had to see for herself.

Andrei had yet to have any real alone time with Blaire since they died. She still hadn't told him how she knew the explosion was coming mere moments before the fire consumed them. He could see on her face that she was still looking for answers herself.

They all wanted to know who killed them.

Blaire stepped forward, still gripping Andrei's hand. He followed her without hesitation.

Joe Torelli cracked open the metal door of the gymnasium but was stopped in his tracks by a strange sound.

He pulled open the door a little bit more and heard the sound again. It was a familiar sound, not unearthly or demonic.

He threw the door open all the way. The stopper fell down after the door was shocked by the recoil of the closer mechanism.

Joe walked into the gymnasium while Marcus touched the source of the noise.

Strips of duct tape had been layered over every crack in the door.

Marcus looked down, finding several more strips of duct tape and some wadded up paper towels lining the bottoms.

He stepped through the frame, looking right and left. All the doors on the west wall had been lined with duct tape to make the seals air-tight.

Joe crossed the brand-new maple flooring, stopping at center court. He could already see that the doors on the other side had also been made air-tight.

The other hundred or so Villa Vista students trickled into the pristine, new high school gymnasium. Even the ones who had scattered earlier were now stepping in at the back of the crowd. They too wanted to see the weapon for themselves.

On the east wall, facing every soul that entered this place, was a giant twenty-foot-tall mural of Jackie the Jaguar, sinking his claws into an orange basketball.

Blaire was taken in by the horrifying yellow eyes, which seemed to look at all of them simultaneously. She could understand the primal fear they inspired in Elise.

Despite her wishes to peer inside Pandora's Box, Andrei held Blaire close. Some dark voice inside him warned that if he ever let go of her again, they would be pulled apart for the rest of time.

Blaire's eyes drifted over to the south wall. On the other side of that wall, she and Andrei had been relaxing after a passionate kiss and romantic dance. That wall is where she heard the horrific whistling.

That whistling, so piercing and demonic that it had reached into her dreams, crossing time and space, was a fatal promise of what was to come.

Blaire could not see the wall itself, the visiting team bleachers covered most of it.

Since they didn't see anything on the empty basketball court, Marcus Johnson and Joe Torelli began approaching the home and away team bleachers respectively.

The crowd separated in two directions, following each of them.

Blaire and Andrei drifted to the right, following Joe toward the south bleachers.

Like other modern high school basketball gymnasiums, the bleachers on each side of the court could be collapsed, closing in on themselves like the drawers of a cabinet. In this case however, they were still extended, providing easy access to the walls from below the metal framework.

Joe walked into the thin forest of reinforced tresses, while the rest of the group peered in from the side.

Blaire looked at the wall itself. Her blood would have run as cold as ice water, if those rivers of life still flowed in her veins.

Along the bottom of the wall was a line of steel grates, covering a long mechanical chase. Each grate was bolted down by a number of sizable screws ... all except one.

That one grate, measuring roughly five feet by three feet, was completely unbolted and removed. It was just off-center of the bleachers, but still roughly lined up with the middle of the Murphy Center.

The dance floor lay just beyond that removed panel.

Joe approached it with wide eyes, a bit of fear seemed to be gripping him as well.

Dark curiosity overwhelmed Blaire and she stepped forward, entering the crawl space beneath the bleachers.

With a strong grip, Andrei tried to pull her back, but several others around them began moving too, overtaken by the same need to witness this for themselves.

Relenting, Andrei followed her, until they were soon side-by-side with Joe Torelli.

He gripped the shotgun as though he were staring into a cage, expecting a great black cat to leap out at them.

Behind the removed grate was apparently the main mechanical panel. There were a number of valves, switches, levers, pressure gauges, a digital readout, and a stack of papers showing what all of these components were for and how to operate them.

That manual was irrelevant though, because anyone could easily tell what valves had been operated.

Four large levers were pointing outward in such a way that the metal grate could not be put back in place without closing them. This was likely a design feature, preventing a careless operator from making such a simple mistake.

In large letters, all four valves were clearly marked "NATURAL GAS".

In addition to the labeling and warnings on the connection points, there were four locking mechanisms which could secure the valves with rather large padlocks.

All four of those padlocks had been cut and were lying on the ground beside the metal grate.

These switches and access points were clearly intended to be there though. They had been designed and installed for one reason or another. Even the natural gas connection points seemed to exist for a purpose, to support backup heaters or something. They were not gigantic pipes; each was big enough to maybe support a single barbecue grill.

Whatever the reason, they were meant to be there as part of the normal use of the building.

However, they were simply the background, the wallpaper giving color and contrast to the actual weapon used to massacre the students of Villa Vista High School.

A strange device sat in front of the mechanical panel.

It was built off of a small metal frame fashioned around a car battery. The battery sat on the floor itself. Just above it in the framework was a mess of wires and circuit boards attached to a small radio receiver. There was a readout display which resembled a digital clock. A few buttons were located between it and the radio antenna. Above that control apparatus were two large metal rods.

Blaire went pale, taking all of this in. The rods on top of the device reminded her of a tuning fork. She could only imagine the tone they would make when struck. It could only be the same tone which the natural gas spouts hissed at ... like a high-pitched whistling.

Joe Torelli reached down for the device, trying to pick it up. As he gripped the center, his thumb came into contact with a small red button. That button had been labeled "TEST".

In a flash, a large bolt of blue electricity arced between the "tuning fork" prongs. The spark was so bright and sudden, it might as well have been a lightning strike.

Blaire leapt backwards with a shriek. She and Andrei collapsed into the metal trusses of the bleachers.

Screams filled the gymnasium as several other students scattered, overwhelmed by terror as their minds replayed the events of that night.

Joe had dropped the device as it sparked, but it was not damaged in the least. It landed upright on the heavy car battery base, mocking its victims.

Several wails filled the room and the other half of the students ran to the south bleachers with Marcus to see what they had found.

It was clear to everyone what happened to the students of Villa Vista High that night. No one had placed a bomb inside the new gym. The gymnasium itself *was* the bomb.

This ignition device was the key to finding the bomber.

***

Rick Wallace dragged himself out of Bob Melkonian's classroom.

He didn't think he was really doing Bob much of a favor by giving him his chair back. Sleeping on it had been a painful experience in countless ways. His back groaned with every step.

Still, he could only imagine how much worse the dissection table had been for Bob. A few meager papers were not a cushion at all.

Aside from the physical pain, Rick had been plagued with nightmares all night. Every time he opened his eyes he replayed a memory from the past fifty years, a time when he came close to admitting his original sin to his beloved Mary.

In his negotiations, he hoped to convince Greg Henshaw and Chelsea Morton to let him have his couch as well. It wouldn't be for himself, but for Bob.

He didn't deserve a good night's sleep at all, even the chair had been too charitable to him. He expected to be forced onto a bed of nails eventually.

He was impressed by what the sophomore kids had been able to do. They were fairly well put together, both coming from good families. Neither of them had ever been brought to his office, doubled over in tears and anguish.

Rick had known a bit about Bob's rough childhood, but he did not know the gory details until Bob finally explained it all to him yesterday.

While Rick's life had been defined by an unatoned lust, Bob's had been defined by an unatoned wrath.

Some priests and scholars could try to draw a moral equivalence between the two of them in Scripture, but Rick had a hard time coming to terms with that idea. It was like the thought that a serial killer and unrepentant pagan deserved the same eternal suffering and torment.

Then again, considering their current station in the afterlife, the evidence seemed to be on the side of Scripture.

What he could not understand was why he and Bob shared a prison with so many of these lost children.

Not only were they victims of unimaginable evil, but they were good kids as a whole. Several of them were even part of his congregation at St. Dominic Savio Catholic Church.

He couldn't imagine that the murderer was still among them. They must be in some dark place being rightly delivered some unspeakable torment.

There was a chance they weren't anywhere near the explosion at all and a massive manhunt was happening somewhere above.

Rick realized that it had been almost a day and a half since his death. He was perhaps the oldest victim, with the least life stolen from him ... and among the most deserving of such an end.

His family probably mourned him as a great man, a kind father and grandfather. It was all so undeserved.

He wondered if Gillie Wisbeck had gotten word of his death. Of course, she wasn't even known by that name when their night of sin occurred. She had married a man named Arthur Turner, and probably had several children and grandchildren by him.

Considering their mutual shame, she had probably remained in England with her husband and the Turner family. She had a whole life a continent away, no one was the wiser of that one night in San Diego.

Rick had avoided that city for his whole life. After that night with Gillie, he had secretly nursed a bottle of ipecac, vomiting for the rest of the trip.

His dorm friends brought him home to Mary and he talked about how he must have gotten food poisoning from some bad fish.

That story became the cornerstone of his uncomfortable reactions whenever San Diego came up in conversation. He jokingly vowed never to return, and Mary never pressed the idea, not having any real reason to visit the city herself.

Rick successfully avoided the Southern California town like it was in the Chernobyl Exclusion Zone. His guilt and shame stayed buried, but the sound of his own "Tell-Tale Heart" never disappeared. When he was alone, when everything else was quiet, he could hear sounds from that night in the distance.

Part of him wondered if his death would change anything for Gillie. Would she be overwhelmed with guilt and confess to their infidelity?

In some ways that was the ending that Rick preferred, he wanted his name dragged, his memory sullied, rather than being remembered as something he was not.

But she hadn't revealed the truth after all these years either, why would she do so now? She probably only had another decade left herself.

Rick passed another batch of classrooms after walking through the ground-floor atrium. Lights were glowing under some of the classroom doors.

He could understand Bob's moral panic at seeing a bunch of teenagers shack up together. Bob was still stuck in the mindset of the living, trying to protect the kids' innocence and integrity.

Rick knew that Bob saw every one of them as Monika in one way or another. He loved his daughter more than anything. He was the father that deserved the kind of recognition Rick's corpse might be getting.

However, these kids were dead. For whatever divine reason that Rick could not understand, they were sharing this piece of Hell together. It was long past the point of worrying about their flights of passion.

In most cases, the kids were probably just seeking someone to hold. They were frightened, alone, and faced their own horrific, fiery death every time they looked in a mirror.

Rick finally reached the school's front foyer. Despite being supposedly three o'clock in the morning, an eerie daylight glow shone through the wall of white fog and the west-facing windows.

Rick looked left, expecting to see the kids settling into the Administration offices. The couch in his office was probably the closest thing to a bed on school grounds. They probably fought over who would use it.

Instead, the offices were empty, strangely empty.

Rick pulled open the door, it was still unlocked. Despite having to surrender *most of* his keys, Rick was still able to access the space.

After hearing the kids talk about turning the classrooms into dorms, and seeing how viciously they were turning on Bob, Rick had decided to hide his best key.

Barbara had given him a school master key in case of an emergency. It was not just the key to her office, which Rick had surrendered to the teenagers, this was a full master to the campus. She could have gotten in a lot of trouble with McDouglas or the School Board if they knew she had entrusted it to Rick.

Barbara was a good friend. She had been so incredibly helpful with certain students. Her own heart bled for some of the stories they told. Helping Rick with an occasional bit of group counseling seemed to be the most fulfilling part of her day-to-day work life.

After retrieving the bottle of Jack Daniel's whiskey from McDouglas' office, Rick decided to hide the master key. It was currently still taped under the arch of his left foot, concealed by the sock and dress shoe.

"Hello?" Rick called into the main office area. There was no answer, so he lifted the drop counter top and walked into the back area.

He stepped into the hallway, passing the bathrooms and entering his Guidance Counselor office.

The couch had one of its cushions pushed out of place. The other couch, which was the matching love seat, had an empty bottle of Coca-Cola lying on it.

Someone had clearly slept there the night before, which didn't surprise him. His odds of getting the couches in negotiation were pretty low.

The chair looked undisturbed however, it was still sitting at the strange angle Rick had left it when the posse of students had first come knocking at his door.

He grabbed the back of the chair. It was nice, maybe slightly better than other chairs in the office. It wasn't better than Fletcher's or McDouglas' though, so he hoped the kids wouldn't miss it.

He pushed it out into the main office space, then grabbed one of the spare swivel chairs that was sitting against the wall. He dragged that into his office, placing it at his desk as though it had always been there.

Rick put his hands on the back of his chair, ready to walk it to Melkonian's classroom. He hoped that the elevator in the hallway still worked.

He glanced back at McDouglas' office. Leonard had always been a good man. He'd been Principal of Villa Vista High School for over ten years. He was probably at peace with the Lord now.

Next to it was Ms. Fletcher's office. Barbara was among those who had been far kinder to Rick than he had ever deserved.

She was barely thirty-two, younger than any of Rick's kids. She had been seeing a very nice man recently and Rick hoped to hear wedding bells in her near future.

He wouldn't be there for such a joyous occasion, but he was eternally grateful to God Almighty that she would be.

Vice Principal Fletcher had not been one of the chaperones at the dance. She would probably be wrought with grief for the rest of her life from the loss of so many students and friends. However, Barbara herself still had a full life ahead of her and she deserved every minute of it.

Rick stared into her office for a long minute. His thoughts dwelled on how she might be dealing with the situation, imagining how the next days, weeks, and months of her life would play out in the wake of the massacre.

That's when something caught his eye. The top of Barbara's bookshelf looked unusually bare.

The giant packet of construction drawings was missing.

Barbara had thoroughly enjoyed the process of planning the remodels for Villa Vista High School. She was able to contribute a number of ideas and suggestions which ended up making it into the final design.

In a greater sense, she felt pride in the idea that she could help improve something that would be standing long after she was gone. At its core, it was the same drive that made her care about the students so much. She wanted to see all of them go on to live long, happy, fulfilling lives.

That packet of construction plans had been sitting on the bookshelf since they moved into the new offices two years ago. She would pull it down on occasion to compare the real-world construction to the plans she'd contributed to.

Rick walked away from his chair, pushing open the door to her office. The kids hadn't locked it.

He looked all over the office, pulling open drawers, cabinets, looking in odd spaces where it might have been moved.

The drawings were gone.

Nothing else in her office seemed to have been disturbed at all. Its absence spoke volumes. Why would someone move the remodel drawings?

Rick felt a crushing sense of dread coming over him as he began to consider what it meant.

That is when Rick heard a muffled boom and immediately turned toward the doors.

He recognized the noise immediately.

It was the sound of a shotgun blast.

***

Niles and Laura had been having a wonderful morning talking to Blaire Tidwell and her senior boyfriend. Even Liam and Melissa had been in a strangely upbeat mood. Death seemed to have improved their personalities. Perhaps they realized how petty a lot of high school things really were when it all came to an end.

Anne Kirkpatrick was handling things the opposite way, spiraling into depression and rage.

Laura came across her at one point and she shoved her away, almost as if she blamed Laura for what happened.

That was before Laura had come to Niles in the Lexus. Neither of them had seen her since.

After a few hours, more Villa Vista students had woken up and returned to the ballroom. Niles and Laura felt safer seeing others around after Joe Torelli had scared them. Plus, they were curious to see what was going on with everyone else.

One of the first things that Laura noticed was that a lot of the girls had taken off their heels and put on their P.E. shoes. That was a good idea, so she disappeared for five minutes to retrieve them from her locker.

She came back wearing a pair of Nikes, the black logo set against a fluorescent yellow stripe.

After that, they heard more about the details of Greg and Chelsea's school commune idea.

It occurred to them that they were now apparently homeless and/or living out of Niles' car.

As they were figuring out what to do, who they could talk to about rooming with, two unexpected people returned to their table, Liam and Melissa. They had apparently been spending some time together in the afterlife.

"Hey guys," Melissa had greeted them, absolute devastation in her voice. She looked like she'd been crying non-stop for the past thirty hours.

"Found this one on my way back from some private contemplation," Liam had said. He gave Niles a knowing look, but Niles didn't know him well enough to know what he was implying.

After that, Melissa had apologized for hitting Niles. They both sat down and just started engaging in conversation. They talked about movies, music, random stuff from the living world that they missed.

Niles wished that they had talked like this from the beginning of the dance. Homecoming would have been a thousand times better ... whether or not they still died at the end.

After things were trending toward the depressing side, Niles decided to invert the conversation. He proposed a game of basically coming up with as many good things about their current place in existence as they could think of.

That game had been even better than the conversation, so much so that Blaire Tidwell and Andrei Tutankhamun showed up to join in.

The discussion went on like that for a while. It almost felt like a regular school lunchtime, but everyone actually seemed happy to be there together.

Everyone was starved for a bit of real conversation. The whole situation had been stressful and emotional. That basic bantering gave everyone a sense of normalcy.

After a while, the rest of the students were awake and started filing into the ballroom. It seemed like Greg and Chelsea had decided to have some kind of school meeting.

Things were going fine at first. To be honest, Niles wasn't paying close attention. He had been thinking about the kiss with Laura since it happened a few hours ago.

He only started focusing on what was going on when people in the crowd began yelling. He realized that they were calling for Mr. Mel and Mr. Wallace to be arrested.

People were blaming them for blowing up the school? Seriously?

Then someone else in the crowd blamed Joe Torelli. That made a lot more sense to Niles.

Joe was actually there to defend himself though and walked up to center stage yelling right back at the kid. More people began blaming him and he suddenly said that he had proof that he didn't do it or something.

He started walking out toward the parking lot.

Niles looked at Laura. She seemed confused and curious too, shrugging.

Niles didn't really want to miss another meeting akin to "let's call dibs on dorm rooms", so they followed the crowd outside.

He and Laura were sort of near the back to one side. He wasn't sure where Blaire, Andrei, Melissa, or Liam had gone off to.

Joe Torelli was giving some kind of long-winded speech about how his dad was an asshole. It sounded really childish in Niles' opinion.

He had it better than almost anyone at Villa Vista. He was tall, handsome, popular, and athletic. He'd probably banged half the girls in his class. But no, here he was moping about how bad his home life was.

He even had this overnight bag packed so he could stay at his girlfriend's house.

Then Joe pulled out a shotgun.

"Shit! Shit! Shit! Shit! Shit! Shit!"

Niles grabbed Laura's wrist and bolted in the only direction that didn't have a crowd of people.

They ran past the entrance of the gymnasium when they heard it fire.

Niles grabbed her waist and dove into the decorative flower bed.

"Who'd he shoot?" Laura whispered as they army-crawled behind some bushes.

"I don't know," Niles said, trying to find a large enough gap in branches to get a better look.

The black sports car was in the way but Niles could still see part of Joe's head and arms. It helped that everyone else had crouched or dove to the ground as well.

The shotgun was aimed straight into the air. A thin trail was still smoking out of the barrel.

"I think it was a warning shot," Niles answered her.

"Mr. Wallace!" Laura whispered as loud as she could.

Niles turned his head toward her and saw Mr. Wallace standing on the sidewalk. He had apparently just come out of the main entrance.

He ducked down and got in the bushes next to them.

"What's going on?" he asked them, panic in his voice.

"Joe Torelli pulled out a shotgun and just shot into the air," Laura said.

"You kids okay?" he asked.

"So far," Niles said, not sure how this was all going to unfold.

"Can you hear what he's saying?" Rick Wallace asked. While his eyes were still good, his hearing was not what it used to be.

Niles focused as much as he could, the only words he could understand for sure was Joe saying "Who's with me?!"

"Is that Marcus Johnson?" Laura asked.

"Yeah," Mr. Wallace muttered.

It wasn't long until everyone was standing up, pledging their fealty to Joe Torelli.

"What just happened?" Laura asked.

"Change in management," Niles mumbled.

"Quiet, they're coming this way!" Mr. Wallace shushed them.

Joe walked up to the construction fence in front of the gym. He slid another shell into the shotgun, snapping it closed.

"So, it's a break-action," Niles thought to himself. "That means he only has two shots before he has to reload."

Niles was very familiar with shotguns ... in video games. He almost always picked one with some form of integrated or detachable magazine. Being limited to two rounds before reloading was a grueling, slow process.

Joe pointed the nose of the barrel at the lock on the fence.

Niles also noticed that he didn't shoulder the shotgun at all. He held it at arm's length, like it was a sawed-off zombie-killing shotgun.

He blew the lock away, his arm absorbing the recoil amazingly well.

Niles knew enough about real-life weapons handling to know that you had to be very strong to do something like that.

Joe and Marcus pulled open the fence, entering the new gymnasium.

"They aren't really going in there are they?" Laura questioned in a panic. She acted like the gym was going to blow up all over again.

It was an understandable feeling. Every mirror showed the fire in the gym still burning. It had been over a day since the bombing and nothing had changed.

That was proof to him that, like their dead reflections, it was meant to be a permanent loop from the moment of their deaths. By now the fire department or forest service would have quelled the real-world fire. Plus, the mirrors still showed a dark evening sky, even during midday on Sunday.

Near the back of the crowd filing into the gym, they saw Anne.

As she turned to pass by the fence, she stopped.

Niles stayed perfectly still. Had she seen them?

She then kept walking into the gym.

Laura breathed a sigh of relief, putting her face down into the flowers.

They waited for a long minute.

There was this intense energy in the air, like something was about to happen.

"You kids need to get out of here," Mr. Wallace said.

"And go where?!" Laura asked. "They've taken over all the rooms!"

Mr. Wallace thought for a moment, then shifted one of his legs.

"Go to the football stadium," he said. "There is an overflow storage room below the visiting team bleachers. Almost no one knows about it, and you can only see the door by looking directly behind the bleachers."

"Yeah, but there's no way that'll be unlocked," Niles said.

They watched as Mr. Wallace took off his left shoe and sock.

"What are you doing?" Niles asked, confused.

Mr. Wallace shifted his leg higher, revealing a piece of duct tape on the sole of his left foot.

He peeled away the tape, revealing a small key.

He gave the key to Laura.

"This is a master key to the whole school," Mr. Wallace said. "It'll unlock almost anything. Use it and hide wherever you can. Stay safe, at least until that gun is out of the picture."

"Thank you," Laura whispered.

But before anything else could be said, they heard dozens of screams from inside the gymnasium.

"Kids!" Mr. Wallace yelled. He jumped to his feet and ran toward the gym. His sock and shoe were left behind.

"Come on!" Niles said to Laura. "I know a shortcut."

Laura stood up and slipped the key snugly into the left cup of her bra.

Niles' mind stalled for a second before picking up again.

"This way!" he said, taking her hand.

They ran off at full speed, past the school entrance. They were in the open grass field which would have led to the middle school.

Without hesitation, they disappeared into the wall of mist.

***

Darren and Jenny felt like zombies, being dragged along by the mob into the gymnasium.

Jimmy and Camellia were just ahead of them. Jimmy chuckled nervously, as he usually did in uncomfortable situations.

Darren knew that shit stain Blake was one of the ones who ginned up the crowd against Joe in the first place. Oh, how the tables had turned.

Greg and Chelsea floated between the Varsity Football players and Varsity Basketball players. They gave off the energy of Menshevik leaders watching Leon Trotsky switch sides to the Bolsheviks.

Torelli had decided that he wasn't going to compromise on anything. He marched with a purpose. His rule was going to be absolute and total. Anyone who got in his way was going to stare down the business end of his weapon of choice. Not that it mattered, because the vast majority of the crowd seemed to whole-heartedly agree.

Blake had disappeared after Joe pulled out the shotgun.

A lot of people standing around him probably heard him publicly accuse Joe … big mistake.

Once the mob had opened the doors, they found duct tape covering every crack and hole.

In a pile between the entrances were half a dozen other large rolls of duct tape. They were apparently leftovers that the bomber had brought just in case.

Darren wasn't exactly sure what he expected to see in the gymnasium.

The image that had come to mind when he tried to picture the bomb going off was a giant pyramid of fertilizer bags stacked in the center of the basketball court.

However, Joe was now standing at center court. The only weapon there was the shotgun that he clutched in both hands.

He nodded to Marcus Johnson and then to the home team bleachers. At the same time, Torelli walked over to the visiting team bleachers.

Darren trailed behind. He figured he had to stay with the other guys for appearances. Considering how Joe had manhandled him earlier, the last thing Darren wanted was for that gun to point in his direction … or Jennifer's.

Joe walked below the bleachers and Darren lined up along the exposed edge right behind him.

To his surprise, the goth girl was the first one to follow Joe into the metal assembly. The new guy followed after her, but it looked like he was trying to hold her back a bit.

Brendan and Trey were the next to move forward, which of course meant that he and Jimmy were also in tow.

Within moments, they were all circled behind Joe looking at this exposed building panel. The cover had been set aside and there was some kind of device sitting right in front of the valves and readouts.

There were four valves in particular which said everything there was to say, "NATURAL GAS".

Jenny clutched his arm. He rested his hand over one of hers.

The tape on all the doors made sense now. Someone had turned the gymnasium into a giant gas tank.

The device sitting in front of the gas valves looked like a small bomb, it was covered in antennas and a timer, and had a car battery on the bottom.

Joe picked it up by its metal frame … but then a finger slipped.

Suddenly, a bright electrical arc surged between two of the antennas like it was a Tesla coil.

Everyone jumped backwards and people started screaming.

Joe was the first to compose himself, picking it up by a different part of the frame and exiting out of the other side of the bleachers. The rest of them scrambled out of the bleachers as well.

With the electrical device in one hand and shotgun in the other, Joe stood at center court.

"We have our first piece of evidence!" he announced to the crowd.

There was a disturbance near the back, by the doors. Someone was being pushed forward into the room. It was Rick Wallace.

A dark grin rose on Joe's face.

"And it appears we have our first suspect." He aimed the shotgun at Mr. Wallace.

Darren watched as Mr. Wallace raised his hands in surrender.

A dozen memories flooded back to him, sitting on the couch in his Guidance Counselor office, listening to music, doing homework, talking about how mad he was that Jenny wasn't talking to him anymore, telling him about the Niners game he went to with his dad ...

Joe guided the old man over to the front row of visiting team bleachers.

He then directed Brendan and Trey to get two of the spare rolls of duct tape and tie him up.

The crowd cheered ... Darren held back tears.

SEVENTEEN

A HELL OF THEIR OWN

"WE NEED TO GO check on them." Raf held Elise's shoulders with both hands.

"I know. I know. I know," she whispered back to him, repeating the phrase.

Raf had been trying to psych her up as soon as they watched Joe Torelli lead everyone into the gymnasium like he was the Pied Piper of the Underworld.

It had been more difficult than he hoped. He thought he had gotten Elise back to a better place, but the gunshot had sent a fresh surge of fear and anxiety through her.

He really didn't like the fact that Andrei and Blaire were swept in with the crowd. Something was very wrong … something other than Joe, obviously.

That is when they heard a chorus of screams coming from the gymnasium itself.

"Blaire!" Elise yelled, snapping out of her paralysis.

That seemed to be enough to do the trick. There was real, direct evidence that Blaire might be in pain at the moment.

Elise ran for the door and Raf followed right behind her. They pulled apart the door rigging and slipped out into the hallway.

At the bottom of the stairwell, a few students were hiding in the bathrooms or other dark spaces, popping their heads out at the sound of screaming.

Raf and Elise burst through the front doors of the Murphy Center and caught up with the crowd pouring into the gymnasium.

They saw another figure being forcibly pulled through the mass of students. Raf couldn't see who it was though.

They pushed their way past the others until they stepped through the doorway.

Elise heard a sticky sound on her foot. She looked down and saw that she was stepping on a strip of tape lying on the floor.

She followed the tape to see that it was layered over every door frame on that front entrance wall. There was even a pile of unused rolls of duct tape lying in the middle. Two of the football guys walked up and pulled rolls off of that pile.

That seemed strange, she thought to herself. Why would the football players be duct-taping the doors?

She turned her head and saw someone standing above the crowd. It was Andrei.

He met Elise's eyes, then bumped someone next to him. It was Blaire, they were okay!

She waved to Elise and Raf to come over to them. They were sort of stuck in the crowd by the away team bleachers.

Elise turned to tell Raf in case he didn't see them.

That is when she locked eyes with the yellow gaze looking down at her through the darkness.

The Jaguar leered down at her, hungrily. It must have been the size of a dinosaur. It approached her like the T-Rex approached the lawyer in the *Jurassic Park* movie. The mouth opened and darkness swallowed her whole.

Raf saw Andrei and Blaire waving at them, but before he could tell Elise, he felt her body go limp in his hand.

He caught her just in time before she dropped onto the floor.

She had fainted, blacked out completely.

"Whoa, hey, you okay?!" Raf exclaimed, trying to wake her.

He turned in the direction she was facing and saw the giant mural of Jackie the Jaguar, clutching the basketball.

"Fuck!" he yelled, stomping on the ground.

The crowd started cheering.

"You've got to be kidding me," he said, looking around.

They weren't focused on him though. The crowd was watching something happening on the court itself.

Raf shuffled with her along the wall.

Andrei could see his distress and started moving toward them. They would end up meeting in the far corner of the gym.

"Elise!" Blaire cried, taking her other arm.

They sat her down in the corner, between the walls.

"Please tell me the gym isn't going to explode again," Raf begged Andrei.

"I don't think so," he said. "If it was, that electrical device would have done it a minute ago."

"Electrical device?" Raf asked.

Andrei pointed through a gap of people. "The thing that Torelli is holding."

Joe Torelli gripped some kind of really messed up Unabomber-looking shit. In his other hand was the shotgun. It was aimed at Mr. Wallace as two of his flunkies were tying him up in duct tape.

"So, he's in charge now, isn't he?" Raf muttered.

"Yeah," Andrei said, quiet enough that no one else around them could hear. "Even without the gun, he really has people wound around his finger. They want to find the bomber and torture them."

"Jesucristo," Raf said, rubbing his eyes.

"Guys, what's he saying?" Blaire asked, as she tried to wake up Elise.

Andrei peered over the crowd.

"... without knowing exactly who is here, exactly who we're dealing with!" Joe said. "Which means we need to search everywhere, open every door, every vent, every crawl space. Everyone who ended up down here needs to be accounted for so that we can find the truth!"

There was another cheer from the crowd.

"I think we're stuck in the gym for a while," Andrei said.

"Paxton, go get the room assignments. We'll start there," Torelli said. "Jordan, you go with him."

Jordan Trainor, another member of the Varsity Basketball team, was dispatched along with Paxton.

The two disappeared through the gymnasium doors.

"Everyone else, get into the home bleachers," Joe demanded. "Sit according to your room assignments."

The crowd began moving, filling the stands.

Reluctantly, Andrei, Blaire, and Raf moved too. Raf once more carried Elise under her back and knees. They picked the top corner of the home bleachers, hoping to stay out of sight and out of mind.

"You four guard the doors," Joe motioned to Darren, Jimmy, Brendan, and Trey.

Darren and Jennifer began moving toward the closed set of doors when Joe barked again.

"I said ... *you four*!"

"But you said to stay with our room assignments!" Jenny yelled back.

Joe pointed the electrical device towards the stands. "Ashley with Sheena, Jennifer with Camellia."

There was an eerie silence as the crowd listened to the exchange echo in the dark gymnasium. The only light source was the single set of open doors by the home team bleachers. Brendan and Trey stood to either side.

Jenny gave Darren a very worried look, then went and sat down next to Camellia.

"Don't get her *too* hot and bothered," Jimmy called to Jennifer. "You're a tough act to follow."

There was some light chuckling from the crowd.

Darren stood next to Jimmy by the closed set of doors. They were in the darkest corner of the space.

Rick Wallace sat alone on the front row of the visiting team bleachers, tied up with several layers of duct tape around his arms and legs. He was being watched by nearly a hundred vengeful students.

"You think this is funny?" Darren whispered to Jimmy, barely containing his rage.

"You're right," he answered Darren. "What you're doing is a much better approach for helping the situation."

This only made Darren more furious ... because he was right.

Arguing with Joe was just going to piss him off more. Darren needed a real plan.

Joe was now talking with Marcus and Eric Schwartz, the fourth Varsity Basketball player that had appeared in this place.

They were having Eric write some notes down on a piece of paper.

"Since when did the basketball players get promoted above us?" Darren asked Jimmy.

"Well, it happened when you didn't suck Joe's dick hard enough," Jimmy quipped.

Darren sighed.

"Don't worry," Jimmy said. "I didn't either. Plus, it probably wouldn't have done much anyway. Trey and Brendan are on him like a leech and they're still just doing guard duty."

That actually made Darren chuckle a little.

"Part of it is the fact that they're too dumb to do anything else," Jimmy continued. "Joe almost broke Trey's jaw and he was still out there defending him to Principal McDouglas. I mean, maybe fighting back wouldn't have worked, but god, what a bitch move."

"Maybe we're all too dumb." Darren shrugged. "So Joe's recruiting the members of a non-contact sport to do the administrative work."

"Brains aren't everything," Jimmy replied. "If I was locked in a chimpanzee cage, I wouldn't pick the class valedictorian to help me in a fight, I'd pick the other chimpanzee."

Jimmy nodded to him. "That's *you* champ!"

Pfft, Darren spat.

There was a lull as they really took in the scene that was in front of them.

"Do you think it'll work?" Darren whispered.

"Do I think *what* will work?" Jimmy said, the humor gone from his voice.

"Do you think all this will actually get revenge on the true bomber?" Darren asked.

"I do," Jimmy said, but with a dark intonation to his words. "If you torture everyone, one of them is bound to be the bomber."

***

Niles and Laura materialized through the wall of mist.

They were standing in a small parking lot next to the tennis courts. This was the southernmost end of campus and also the southernmost point of their postmortem prison.

Laura walked forward a few feet, standing in the empty drive which led to the track around the stadium.

"Two and a half days ago," she said. "Two and a half days ago I was standing right here, fussing with the float."

She looked back at Niles.

"It felt like everything in the world, the only thing that mattered," she said. "Now we're dead and none of it really mattered at all."

Niles walked up and took her hand.

"I know ..." he said. "We can talk about it later. For now, let's stay in the fog as much as we can until we get to the hiding place."

Niles scanned around the empty tennis courts. He didn't think they were really alone.

Laura nodded.

They retreated back into the cover of the fog and followed its outline around the edge of campus. Following a bit of guesswork, they finally appeared directly behind the visiting team bleachers.

After checking both sides to see if the coast was clear, they ran toward the door. It was hidden in the shadow of the concrete overhang.

Laura retrieved the key from her bra and slid it into the lock of the door.

The knob turned and the door pulled open. They had to move it slowly, the underused hinges creaked and groaned with every inch.

Once inside, they reset the deadbolt and breathed a long sigh of relief.

The air was damp and cold. They were surrounded by concrete walls and structural supports for the seats above them.

The storage space wasn't being put to much use. The things that were in there didn't look like they were worth keeping in the first place. There were a few old football tackle dummies, pommel horses, and a giant container of unused Gatorade squeeze bottles.

Laura sat down on one of the football tackle dummies that was laying on its side. It was covered with dust and cobwebs. Laura pulled up her hand, looking at the broken strands of spider silk that were between her fingers.

She stood to her feet again and pressed on the dummy, rolling it over. There was a long, muddy patch of soil with an equally muddy spot on the bottom of the dummy cushion.

Laura turned her hand toward Niles, showing him the webs.

"Cobwebs, but no spiders," she said.

She then stepped near the muddy patch.

"Underneath an old thing like this," Laura continued, "this mud should be crawling with worms, beetles, and ants."

"It's not quite the spookiest thing I've seen today," Niles said.

Laura sat down on a different dusty tackle dummy.

"But, why?" she threw her hands up. "Why have the cobwebs, why the grass?"

"Set dressing?" Niles offered. "It's here because we expect it to be here ... because it was here in the real world. Either that or there's some Insect Heaven that's a lot more lenient."

"How does this figure in your 'video game lobby' theory?" Laura asked.

To Niles, it seemed like she wanted to talk about anything besides the violent mob of their former classmates.

"It fits pretty well actually," Niles said, sitting down next to her.

Laura turned to face him, happy for the indulgence.

"The reason video game graphics are the way that they are is because we want to see them, or because there is a functional need for them to be there," Niles began. "The fog outside makes sense because Alexandria gets really foggy from the ocean winds."

"That's easier to do than bending the school campus around some tiny globe?" Laura asked.

"I don't know if 'easier' is the right word," Niles replied. "I'd say it's more like the 'uncanny valley' effect. If something is similar enough to what's real, but not quite, it can be really disturbing. So, you noticing that there aren't any bugs around is that deep, subconscious recognition that this place isn't real ... well, whatever 'real' means. It's not the same as it was when we were alive."

"Then why make it look close at all?" she asked. "Why the school and not some recreation of the Greek Underworld with the River Styx and all that stuff?"

"Maybe some people did see that," Niles said. "And that's why they talked about it like that after coming back to life somehow or seeing it in a dream."

"Why would it be different?" Laura asked. "Wouldn't Hell look the same to everyone?"

Niles thought for a long moment. He wasn't sure if Laura was just distracting herself or she was looking for a real explanation. That's when Niles thought he had a good answer.

"What's the scariest movie you've ever seen?" Niles asked.

Laura thought for a moment.

"I don't know, maybe one of the *Saw* movies?" she replied. "Like, the first three."

"Why?" Niles prodded.

"I mean, obviously ..." She chuckled.

Niles waited.

"Well ..." she elaborated. "There's all the blood. It's very gory and over the top. The characters have to put themselves through so much pain and they almost always end up dying."

"So, a big part of it is the gore?" he asked. "Then things that would be up there for you would be like *Texas Chainsaw Massacre* and similar slasher movies?"

Laura shuddered. "Yes, definitely."

"What about now?" Niles asked. "Knowing that we don't bleed anymore?"

"Well, it still hurts," she said as though she were stating the obvious. "That's what the others were saying anyway."

"That's still a good answer," Niles said. "The physical sensation of pain is one of the most primal fears. Others would say the *Saw* movies too, not just for the torture aspect, but for the game aspect. There's always that dangling hope that if they suffer just a little more, they'll be able to get out and live."

Laura chuckled a little. "Yeah, but that almost never happened. It was pretty much a guaranteed death."

"But *they* didn't know that," Niles said. "That slim chance they had of success, before it was ripped away from them, probably hurt just as much as the physical pain."

"What's the worst horror movie for you?" Laura asked, curious where his line of reasoning was going.

"Technically, my question was 'What's the scariest movie you've ever seen?'" Niles said. "I'm not trying to be pedantic though. Mine's just not what you'd consider a conventional 'horror' movie."

Laura waited for him to continue.

"Some people fear movies like *Saw* for the same reason they fear things like *The Hunger Games* or *The Truman Show*," Niles began. "It's more of an existential horror, the idea that your life isn't your own. You're being toyed with, pawed around by some big monster, or just a piece on a chessboard. The last day or so must have been absolutely devastating for people like that, since it seems to be proven true."

"Is that how *you* feel?" Laura asked.

"Maybe a little bit," Niles said, "But I always assumed something like that was going on anyway. You toy around with enough characters of your own and it becomes hard to think that you're the one sitting at the top. *'It's turtles all the way down'*, but in this case, *'it's gamers all the way up'*."

Laura chuckled a little, thinking he was making a joke out of it.

Niles smiled, happy to distract her ... but he wasn't.

Laura picked up where he left off.

"So, *The Truman Show* then?" she asked. "That your whole existence is just for the enjoyment of someone else?"

"No," Niles said. "For others I'm sure, but not for me."

"What is it then?" she asked.

"Cast Away," Niles said, his eyes drifting to the far wall of the storage room.

"The Tom Hanks movie? I don't think I ever saw the whole thing."

Niles nodded.

"It's the one where he's stuck on the island?"

"No," Niles corrected. "It's the one where he's stuck *alone* on the island.

"I saw it in theatres when I was a kid because my mom loves Tom Hanks.

"There is an hour-long portion in the middle, all the years where he is on the desert island, where there is virtually no music or dialogue. There are no computers, no technology, no distractions beyond the things he has to do to keep himself alive.

"His mind is stretched so thin that he even has to create a character to talk to out of an old volleyball. It's his *only* friend for four years.

"But of course, it's not a friend, it's a psychological break. He never learns to be alone, he just continues filling the void with anything he can generate on his own until there's almost nothing left."

Laura was frowning at this point, seeing how serious Niles was being.

"He returned to civilization after 4 years," Niles continued, "but by that point the whole world had moved on without him. They buried an empty casket, the woman he loved married someone else and had a baby. Even delivering the package he held onto as some goal to keep him going had been pointless.

"Literally the only excuse he had to not end everything was the fact that he was able to come back. He could make new friends, he could start over, there was something beyond the void."

Niles looked at Laura. "It could have been 40 years. He could have died on that island. He could have ended things when he had literally nothing else left to put in that void."

"Niles ..." she tried to interject.

"What if he couldn't kill himself? What if instead of 40 years, there was the real prospect of it being 400 years or 4,000? What if you layer the *Saw* movies on top of that? The loneliness, the knowing that you're being toyed with, the physical, visceral torture?"

"Niles," she tried again, feeling him spiraling.

"And there's something else still," he continued. "Because what's the premise of the *Saw* movies? That each of those people did something to deserve it!

"Maybe not all of the reasons were justifiable or coherent, especially in the later movies, but what if the person had done something really, really horrible?

"You think anyone would show remorse or hesitate if they thought you'd killed 300 people, and most of them were teenagers? They would be the ones designing the game! Imagine what they'd do to us!"

Laura put her hand over Niles' mouth.

"Shh," she interrupted his panic.

She felt teardrops hit the top of her hand.

Laura pulled his head down, lying him on her lap like a pillow.

He stopped trying to talk.

She lightly tousled his black hair as he started to calm down.

She had been so petrified in fear, so shaken by the feeling of being burned alive, that she hadn't even considered how deeply Niles' pain might be rooted.

Worse still, she felt guilty that it had taken being accosted by Blaire and Andrei to even go looking for him in the first place ... and that was after passing out for a while.

If she had been with Niles at the table, or dancing with him in the ballroom, her death would have been near instantaneous. They would have had someone to cling to from the moment they'd awakened.

She had a lot to make up for going forward.

This very well could be their island lost at sea for 400 or 4,000 years.

No matter how long she mourned being apart from her family, Niles was right here.

He had been waiting the whole time.

***

Jennifer watched from her seat as Paxton Bannister returned with the classroom dormitory assignments.

Chelsea and Greg stood beside Joe, Marcus, and Eric Schwartz, watching as Paxton slowly began calling out people's names, tallying everyone in their census.

Camellia was sitting next to Jenny, fussing with her shirt as she usually did when she got nervous.

Over half of the girls and roughly a third of the boys had changed into their gym clothes. In a few odd cases, people were wearing shorts, jeans, or a regular skirt if they happened to have a spare set of clothes in their locker.

There were quite a few girls who remained in their dresses. Jenny assumed that they had decided to use their gym clothes as pajamas and changed back into their dresses before returning to the ballroom this morning.

Chelsea Morton was one of those girls. She was still wearing her bright apricot orange dress. Greg, like many of the guys, was wearing his suit but had removed the vest and tie.

The late Sophomore Class Princess had changed into her P.E. sneakers though. Almost none of the girls were still wearing their heels or dress shoes, except for maybe the rare, comfortable flat.

Chelsea had also let her hair down. It hung loosely to her shoulders. She didn't have the length or volume that Jenny did to justify tying it back into a ponytail, but the reasoning was the same.

The party was over.

Even those still dressed formally didn't look like they were attending a dance, they looked like they were at a funeral.

Jenny couldn't help but think of what everyone actually looked like. She'd caught a glance of maybe two dozen students in various mirrors. While there were some unique damaged features to people, such as the way Darren's limbs had been broken against the stairwell, most things were the same.

The way everyone had been literally broiled alive felt like their humanity had been stripped from them along with their souls. There was no amount of make-up or embalming fluid to fix what had become of them. Everyone that wasn't cremated (or rather, *fully* cremated) would have to have a closed-casket funeral.

Jenny had also found that she was not alone in having burns uncover private places. Several girls were in a similar situation to her, their dresses having been torn or scorched away by the blast of fire. She had also seen one of the guys have everything below his waist made bare by a chance situation, likely being in the restroom when the explosion happened.

She was feeling less uniquely exposed ... especially considering who would end up witnessing her that way.

In the living world, the only people who would see her body like that would be a firefighter and a coroner. Probably some kind of police investigator also, but that should be all of the strangers.

Jenny's parents would need to see her no matter what, to identify her. Hopefully they'd only be shown the left side of her face.

That wouldn't be enough for her mom though. She would want to hold her, even just for a moment, to say goodbye.

Jenny hugged her sides. She wished she could hold her parents too.

She wondered if they would end up moving. Jenny was the youngest in the family. With her dead, there was nothing really holding them in Alexandria.

Her dad worked down in the city anyway. He was the Maxwell of Maxwell, Moisen, & Associates.

Her older brother was getting his Law degree from U.C. Berkeley at the moment. He planned on joining the firm after passing the state Bar exam.

Her dad had really wanted Jenny to go into Law too, but it didn't really interest her. She wanted to do something more along the lines of contracting or sales, being a corporate negotiator. She thought she'd be good at that ... but it was a moot point now.

They'd probably rent the house and get a new permanent place down in San Mateo or Palo Alto. They'd be closer to the airport and about the same distance from the law offices. However, they wouldn't have to look at the ruins where Villa Vista High School used to be. Her dad wouldn't have to spend every day driving by the place where she was murdered.

That's what she would do if she were in their shoes.

Jenny also wondered where they'd bury her.

Their family ended up in the area after World War II. Her grandfather was in the Navy during the Pacific Campaign. He loved the Bay Area so much that he never left. He was buried in the Golden Gate National Cemetery with her grandmother.

Her parents hadn't been in the military, but they talked about starting a new set of family plots at Holy Cross Catholic Cemetery just up the road in Colma. It was long-term planning for themselves, but now it looked like Jenny would be the first Maxwell to be buried there.

She hoped so. She hoped they didn't bury her somewhere in Alexandria, then decided to move. Jenny didn't want to feel even more separated from them than she already was.

A small part of her was really hoping Darren was right about haunting. If the ruins of the school were turned into a memorial, and her parents visited, would she be able to see them? Would they be able to interact at all?

Maybe not, but just to hear their voices, to sit by them, would mean so much to her.

Jenny assumed every student was mourning the loss of their families to one degree or another, but how they were handling that loss is what frightened her.

Joe had obviously lost his mind even before they were blown up at the dance.

Considering the packed bag and the shotgun, she took him at his word that he had killed his dad after the game. Salvatore used to always be a harsh and demanding father. Jenny just didn't understand how abusive that dynamic must have been.

Even when he wasn't on Addys, Joe always had an intense personality. He was all testosterone all the time. Jenny had actually wondered if he'd messed around with steroids at one point. Then again, Joe had acted that way long before they all wound up in the Varsity Football clique. It was part of the core of his personality already.

Still, as intense as Joe had always been, she didn't see him as someone who would actually kill a person in a premeditated way. Either he killed his dad in a depressed rage, and the escape to Mexico plan was cobbled together after that ... or it *was* somewhat premeditated, and Joe was more shrewd and calculating than she realized.

If that was the case, maybe he did blow up the school. So far, he was the only one proven to have brought a weapon on school grounds.

All of this witch-hunting could be posturing. Maybe he expected Jenny and Darren to take Isabella home before the bomb went off? Maybe the drugs were still a factor and he couldn't remember?

Then again, the more Jenny stared at that electrical detonation device, the more it looked way too complicated for Joe. He had to have an accomplice if he was attached to the bombing at all.

Jenny looked over at Darren. He was stuck in the dark side of the gymnasium next to Jimmy.

Darren was already watching her, like he had been at the Homecoming game. He raised his hand in a subtle wave.

Was this really what the afterlife had in store for them? Being rank-and-file members of Joe's Stasi?

Paxton Bannister turned toward her and Camellia.

"Darren Clark & Jennifer Maxwell in Ziegler's room," He stated aloud, looking for confirmation.

"Yes," she spoke up in response.

Darren also called "Yes," from the far side of the room.

She hoped all this investigation would actually reveal the true killer just so it could all be over with. They could go back to the sophomores' little township idea.

Paxton continued: "Blake Samuels and Kyle Moreno in Jameson's room."

"Well, I'm here," a voice said from a few rows behind Jennifer.

Kyle Moreno was sitting next to some other friends of his.

When Jennifer was dating Blake, he never really talked about Kyle much. He must have really been trying to get under Darren's skin to weasel his way into a room next to them.

She couldn't believe she ever dated that scumbag.

"Where's Blake?" Greg Henshaw asked Kyle.

"I don't know, I haven't seen much of him all morning," he said, sounding sincere.

"Add him to the list," Joe said, referring to a short but growing list of those unaccounted for in the gym.

Then, Joe's dark eyes turned toward Jenny.

"Unless *someone* might know where he could have run off too?"

Jenny gave him a cross look, but didn't answer. From the corner she could see Darren fuming.

"Jennifer?" Joe said aloud, dropping all pretense.

"I don't talk to that asshole anymore," she said, before adding, "I try not to talk to assholes at all."

Joe smirked, then turned back toward the doors of the gym. The easiest way to snap back at her was by dragging Darren into this.

"What about you Darren?" he asked. "Keeping tabs on him?"

Jenny could see his knuckles clenched, but unlike Joe, Darren could keep from exploding impulsively.

"Have you tried looking in his shitty car?" he called from the shadows. "He was probably too cheap to get a limo."

Jimmy chuckled from the same shadow, amused by the contentious banter.

Joe took his suggestion seriously.

"Make a note," he said to Eric Schwartz, before expanding, "let's actually sweep all the cars first."

"Got it," Eric said, jotting in a notebook.

Joe turned back to Jenny once more. "That's why you're the Queen."

She felt herself close up again, crossing her arms as everyone looked at her.

"What the fuck does *that* mean?" she thought to herself.

She hadn't put on the stupid toy crown since she woke up ... and saw herself in the mirror. She hadn't tried to act like an authority figure at all, she'd barely talked to anyone besides Darren and the girls.

Jenny then noticed the way Chelsea Morton was eyeing her, which made her think ... "Did Joe just call me a 'whore'?"

She'd take a swing at him herself if she didn't think Darren would suffer consequences for it.

Joe wasn't one to talk anyway, he'd messed around with plenty of girls, including a few from the class below them.

Except for Darren and Blake, she'd only dated one other guy in high school, Peter Onassis, back in their sophomore year. Not only was that a reasonable amount, but also, she hadn't slept with any of them! Not everyone used Jimmy's house as a love shack, he just happened to be their friend.

Jenny thought that should be the last of the list, but Paxton mentioned an extra set of names on the bottom, something about the Choir & Drama room.

She recognized one of the names, "Andrei Tunnikov". Wasn't he the new guy from Pasadena?

A voice called from the far corner of the bleachers, one of the junior boys. "Yeah, we're all here."

He was wearing a white suit, which looked dirty, like he had been walking around outside since they woke up. He must have had a colorful vest on at one point, but that was gone, just like with the other guys.

Next to him was a girl in a pink dress. Jenny was pretty sure she was his date; she'd seen them dancing a lot during the banquet. The girl was completely passed out. Joe must have really scared her with the gunshot.

The junior held her steady on his shoulder. On her other side, she was supported by the goth girl.

She was wearing a black hooded sweatshirt jacket, but the hood was pulled back, exposing her wavy dark hair. She huddled close between the new senior guy and the girl in the pink dress.

She was staring at Jennifer with this frightening death glare.

Was it over what Joe said? Was it because they hid in the same planter earlier and she and Darren stood up before them?

Jenny sighed, they really were going to go down with Joe, no matter how things played out.

In the end, she knew that Darren was just trying to protect her.

That was another disquieting thing she hadn't quite come to terms with. Joe was *very* uncomfortable around the couples that ended up here.

Did he really miss Isabella like he said he did? Was it jealousy that he was alone and all the other girls were still here?

She'd seen him snap at Chelsea and Greg a few times too, even before his shotgun stunt. It wasn't *just* them, it was all the couples.

Jennifer feared that he would probably point that shotgun at her at some point to get Darren to do something ... and he would do it.

Maybe this really was Hell ... there were more than enough demons already.

EIGHTEEN

LOOSE THE HOUNDS

DARREN SHUFFLED FROM CAR to car, turning every few seconds to make sure that Jenny was right behind him.

He was surprised Joe had surrendered to the idea so quickly. Darren had straight up told him he wasn't leaving the gym without Jenny.

Torelli mainly seemed to agree because he didn't want the girls to glare at him. He was getting increasingly weird around them ever since he heard about Isabella. Darren was not going to leave Jenny with him and that shotgun.

After the Varsity Basketball Politburo determined who was and wasn't accounted for in the gym, Joe began forming teams to go out and retrieve those who were missing.

The varsity players, with their dates in tow, had to sweep every inch of school grounds to recover not only the students on the missing list, but a few more who had been seen but weren't present during the whole dormitories thing yesterday.

One of the junior girls in a blue dress had specifically highlighted a couple named Niles and Laura who weren't in the gym.

They must have really done something to piss her off for her to bring them up when no one else did.

Beyond that, the full search of their small little hellhole was meant to root out anyone else who was here but hadn't been seen the past two days.

After that stunt he pulled with Jenny, Joe had told them to start by going car to car in the parking lot.

They started with Torelli's car, or rather, the one he'd stolen from his cousin Tito. He said it included several other tools which would aid them in their manhunt.

Darren gripped one of them in his hands ... a crowbar.

Most of the cars were still locked, naturally. So, Darren had chosen the task of being the infiltrator. Being honest with himself, it was a big part of his skillset. While it played into a side of himself that he really didn't like, he preferred that over what the others were preparing to do.

Marcus and Jordan had returned from the cafeteria with every steak knife they could find. Using some of the duct tape the bomber had left in the gym and metal table legs from the ballroom, they had fashioned a collection of short lances.

Their intended use was essentially as cattle prods. The sharp points would coax the hiding teenagers into the gymnasium like they were livestock being driven into a slaughterhouse.

Just being the breaking and entering guy felt slightly less horrible.

If he had anyplace to run, he would have grabbed Jenny's hand and disappeared into the fog. They'd run for tens or hundreds of miles if they could actually get that far away from this place.

But instead, the demon which fashioned this cage for them was more calculating. They'd vanish into the fog only to reappear on the other side of the school. Those knives would end up at their own throats eventually.

So now, Darren was busting open windows and prying open trunks and other locked compartments.

To distract himself from his moral culpability, the main task Darren was focusing on was the search for the "trigger mechanism". It was the smoking gun that everyone hoped to find.

It could be a key piece of evidence in uncovering the identity of the bomber. It was something that should appear similar to the device in the gym. Where they might find such a trigger would connect that student to the bomb.

Unfortunately, studying anything related to a trigger or the electrical device was a puzzle in and of itself.

Joe had tried to find people who might be experienced enough to examine it, but no one came forward offering to help. They all rightly deduced that it was basically a Kafka Trap. If they admitted that they could understand how the thing was built, it would be used against them as proof that they could be the bomber.

So, the rest of Joe's enforcers had to just look at the thing themselves and see if they could find any clues based on their own limited knowledge.

Clearly the device was built for the purpose of generating a high voltage electrical spark. It was the fuse which ignited the natural gas in the gym.

Within the complicated guts of the circuit components, there appeared to be some kind of radio antenna built into it. While it also looked like it had a clock and timer, that radio antenna implied the bomber must have had some kind of transmitter to set off the explosion manually.

That suggested quite a few other things. Did they not have faith in the timer? Could the transmitter shut off the timer if they wanted to delay the explosion? Did they think the gas buildup would get discovered early and wanted to be able to set it off before anyone could escape?

All of those possible contingencies meant that the transmitter must have been on their person or somewhere close by when the bomb detonated. Of course, now that it had been a day and a half since the explosion, they could have hidden the transmitter anywhere.

But if the ignition device appeared here, in this netherworld, the transmitter had to be here also.

So that's what Darren was looking for, anything that might look remotely cobbled-together like that oversized spark plug.

He plunged the gooseneck of the crowbar through the window of someone's Mustang GT. He flipped the unlock button on the driver's side door, then pulled it open. Next to the stick shift, Darren pressed the trunk release button.

He walked around toward the back, keeping the crowbar in a defensive posture in case someone jumped out. He pulled the lid open. The trunk was almost empty, except for a backpack.

Jenny walked up next to him.

"I'll get this," she said.

"Thanks," he answered. He handed her the bag and pulled up the trunk bottom.

The spare tire looked like it had never been removed, and nothing out of the ordinary was stored around it.

He circled around, opening the passenger door to examine the glove box.

"It's Tom's bag," Jenny called from the back, opening up a notebook.

"Tom Sweeney?" Darren asked.

"Yeah."

Tom Sweeney was one of their fellow seniors. He was a pretty normal guy, not really a significant figure in one of the cliques or groups at Villa Vista High.

"Who did he take?" Darren asked, sitting down in the passenger seat.

Jenny leaned her head back, thinking for a moment. Darren watched her ponytail bounce in the mirror when it came to her.

"Penny Rymer," she answered.

Another senior, Darren could recall a few instances of him flirting with her.

He thumbed through the items in the glove box. There was the owner's manual, a flashlight, some gum, and not really much else.

"They're not here, are they?" Darren asked.

"No," Jenny said in a sad tone. "I'm pretty sure they made it to the other side."

Darren sighed, then pocketed the flashlight.

He opened up the storage area in the center console, then felt around in the various pockets, sleeves, and cup holders. After a casual scan of the back seats, he returned to the trunk with Jenny.

Tom Sweeney's things were scattered across the trunk. It was all books, notes, pens, and other generic school supplies.

"No transmitter?" Darren asked her.

Jenny shook her head. She was staring into the trunk, unmoving.

"Hey, what's up?" He touched her forearm.

"What if the bomber's not here?" she asked Darren.

"What?" he replied, a bit taken off guard.

"Doesn't matter where they are," she said. "They could be in a lower level of Hell getting tortured, or their crazy religion was the real one and they're in some kind of paradise, or they escaped the explosion."

"Could be," Darren said. "I don't think there's any way for us to tell. Not that we've seen yet anyway."

"Does that mean the 'search for the bomber' just keeps going?" she asked. "Is it going to be months or years of torturing everyone here until Joe decides who the bomber is, whether or not it's true?"

"I don't know," Darren said, his face downcast.

Jenny came in close and he held her there.

All around them was the sound of other windows being smashed, other cars being searched, other Varsity players equipped with sharp or blunt weapons.

The shotgun didn't matter at all, most of them agreed with Joe. Blood demanded blood, but since no one had blood left to give, they were determined to carve as much dust out of the killer as they could for all eternity … whether or not it actually *was* the killer wouldn't ultimately matter.

"What did we do to deserve this?" Jenny asked him.

Darren stayed silent, because his answer was the same. However, he added one thing, the only thing he could say with certainty.

"I will protect you no matter what," he promised.

They held each other for a few moments longer before a voice cut in from nearby.

"Next car."

They looked over … it was Marcus Johnson.

Just two nights ago they were laughing and taking pictures as the Homecoming King and Homecoming Queen. He hadn't even cared about being King. He was just nominated in the first place because he was so nice and everyone liked him.

Now, the happy-go-lucky guy Jennifer had played rally games with all of Spirit Week was totally and completely dead. There was no spirit left behind his eyes. He stood there like a wax mannequin, the hood of his Golden State Warriors jacket casting a long shadow over most of his face.

He clutched an L-shaped tire iron in one hand.

Jenny pulled away from Darren, walking towards him.

It was definitely not the right moment to try to talk to him, but this was the first time the three of them had been alone since they'd woken up.

"Marcus," Jenny began. "I am so sorry about Janice."

He said nothing, appearing to stare right through her.

She took a few steps closer to him, hoping to try to console him, at least a little.

He took a few steps forward, putting more distance between them.

"Next car," he said again, turning his face to walk away.

She turned back to Darren.

He gave a shrug, there was nothing else she could have done.

They kept walking, cracking open a few more cars. By the end, Darren had salvaged a handful of spoils. There was one item in particular he wanted to pass along.

Marcus still kept his eye on the couple as they worked, Darren had to get him to look away.

"Hey," he said to Jenny, stepping close to her. "Did I ever tell you how hot you look with a ponytail?"

"I don't know," she answered, somewhat confused but also receptive. "What did you say before?"

"I can't remember the words exactly," he said, putting his hands on her hips. "It might have been something like ..."

Darren shared a tender kiss with her.

Marcus looked away, his own pain making the sight hard to witness.

At first Jenny thought this was just a pleasant distraction from the job they'd been doing, but she quickly realized the calculated nature behind the moment.

She felt something poke her stomach, which was more than a little surprising. She didn't think the ponytail was *that* attractive.

Darren then turned the object sideways and she felt the flat metal surface of its side.

She shifted her hand inconspicuously and took it.

It was a switchblade.

Their lips separated, but their foreheads were still touching.

"Found it in one of the glove boxes," he whispered.

"Does this mean you don't like my hair?" she whispered back, crestfallen.

"I love your hair," he said. "I don't want anyone to be able to harm it."

She kissed him again, slipping the weapon on the inside strap of her gym shorts. It was hidden as well as it could be on the outfit.

"Alright, circle up," Marcus summoned everyone.

Darren and Jenny caught up to the group. Jimmy and Camellia were already standing beside him, along with Paxton and Amanda on the other side.

They faced the only vehicles which remained to be checked. The four limousines had been parked next to each other in the far corner of the lot, to keep from interfering with the other cars.

"Darren, Jimmy," Marcus began, "you'll be doing the sweep, the rest of us will be keeping the perimeter."

"You want the girls directly involved?" Paxton asked, a bit surprised.

"Why not?" Marcus said, an edge to his voice. "Since they're here anyway, they can make themselves useful."

Paxton looked over at Amanda.

"It's okay," she said, not wanting to cause trouble for either of them.

"See?" Marcus snapped. "Plus, we've got some strong girls among us, don't we?"

He shot a sharp glance at Jennifer.

With her arms folded, her biceps were very pronounced through the short sleeve gym shirt. That Marcus had used one of the last good moments of their lives as some kind of rhetorical weapon only made him seem more lost.

She didn't visibly react, beyond a look of pity on her face for what he had become.

"Yeah, that's great," Jimmy cut in, breaking some of the tension. "Some of us don't have a dommy-mommy fetish though. Can I get one of those pokers for Camellia?"

"He knows I'm good with a poker," she said with a wink.

"Ah-ah! Bite your tongue," he cut her off, smiling.

Marcus rolled his eyes.

"Hand 'em out," he told Paxton, vaguely motioning to all the girls.

Paxton reached into the modified gym bag slung over his back and slid out three of the steak knife and table leg lances.

Darren took it from Paxton and passed it over to Jenny.

"Thanks," she said, twisting her hips a bit. The knife he had given her was fully concealed. Even staring, and knowing where it was, he couldn't see it.

As cruel as he was becoming, Marcus was right about one thing. Jenny was very capable and strong on her own. Darren just didn't want her to face all the dangers of this place, supernatural or otherwise, without him.

"Welp," Jimmy said to Darren. "I think I know which one we should start with."

"Sure," Darren answered.

They walked up to the yellow Hummer H2 limousine, the very same vehicle the eight of them had taken to the fateful dance.

Darren brought up the crowbar, about to bust the window.

"Hold up," Jimmy stopped him.

He doubled back a few feet and approached one of the cars they had already checked. With the cross-shaped tire iron he was holding, he smashed the driver's side mirror off.

Jimmy picked up the unscathed mirror from the broken plastic pieces and flipped it around.

"Whew, look at that." He held the mirror up for them to see.

Camellia and Jenny came in close as well.

The Hummer limousine had its thick tires melted into the asphalt. The long body of the vehicle twisted in two directions. Both the front engine area and the gas tank below had exploded. The paint from all of the vehicles had been eaten away. The excess cushions and supplies inside the passenger cabins made easy kindling for the fire.

Not to mention, some chunk of the Murphy Center's wall had landed in the Lincoln Continental. It must have flown at least 1,000 feet.

"Enough," Marcus said, taking post on the opposite corner of the parked vehicles.

"Some people can't enjoy the simple pleasures," Jimmy said, approaching the passenger cabin door. "If you're in the Netherworld anyway, you might as well do some sightseeing."

Darren raised his crowbar, before feeling a slight hesitation.

This was the last vehicle they'd been in. It was the last good time they'd had together without Joe's murderous insanity in their presence.

He tried the door handle, wanting to do as little damage to the vehicle as he could.

The door popped open. It was a small blessing. Darren gave a non-specific "thanks" to the sky.

Someone must be listening to them, considering that they had gone through the trouble of trapping their souls in this strange hell.

The keys were still in the ignition, the driver must have been sitting in the seat when the explosion happened.

That gave Darren pause. He grabbed the rear-view mirror and twisted it around.

He could see the burned-out husks of the limousines ... but no bodies. There were no bones of the drivers. In fact, there were no bones of anyone else who had definitely died but didn't appear in this place.

"Why?" he thought to himself.

He shook his head. What was the point of even asking? It's not like they were getting play-by-play announcements from Moloch and Chernabog describing the rules of this new game of life they were playing. The deities above and below were as quiet as they'd always been.

Darren pressed the unlock button and heard Jimmy open one of the passenger doors.

He did a quick sweep of the driver's cabin. He didn't really expect to find a bomb transmitter, but it would definitely raise new questions if he did.

Nothing.

There was something surprisingly ordinary to be found though ... gloves. There was actually a pair of gloves in the glove box. They were nice too, made of fancy black leather with white fur lining.

Darren slipped them on.

"Hello there," Jimmy said in a curious voice.

Darren hopped out of the driver's seat, gripping the crowbar in the black gloves.

He pulled open the door and found Jimmy sitting in an empty cabin space. He was going through the storage containers under the snack bar.

Jimmy sat up, holding a large Butterfinger bar in each hand.

"They didn't tell us they had candy stashed down here." He slid a few bars into the interior pockets of his suit coat.

Glancing at Darren, he started to chuckle.

"What ya got there, Agent 47?" he asked, motioning to the new accessories.

The gloves and suit coat did give off a bit of a *Hitman* aesthetic.

"You're just jealous that I found them first," Darren said.

"I am actually," Jimmy replied. "Dibs on the next pair."

"Fine," Darren said, pulling a few candy bars out of the container.

They did a full sweep of the passenger cabin, but didn't find anything noteworthy.

"Guess Brendan isn't the bomber," Jimmy said, sliding through the door.

"Jury's still out on Trey if you ask me." Darren cracked a grin.

He walked up to the driver's side door of the white Escalade limo.

"Could you imagine either of them hovering over a workbench pulling that spark plug thing together?" Jimmy asked him.

The Escalade's door was locked, so Darren smashed the window.

"God no. No motive either. Unless one of them told you they wanted to die with their friends or something."

Darren slid into the driver's seat, unlocking the passenger cabin and doing a sweep of the front.

"Trey once told me he wanted to die on a beach surrounded by bottles of rum," Jimmy replied. "Of course, this was after we had watched *Pirates of the Caribbean.*"

Darren opened the glove box.

"You're in luck," he said, tossing a pair of black gloves over to Jimmy.

"There is a God," he said, sliding them on.

He then held the cross-shaped tire iron out in front of him.

"Ooh, that gives it a nice grip."

They opened the door of the passenger cabin and hopped in.

"See anything weird?" Paxton Bannister asked, stepping up next to the door.

"Not yet," Darren answered, before asking, "why, you expecting us to?"

"This was our limo," Amanda said, popping her head in next to him. "My parents paid for it actually."

"Generous," Darren said.

"Excuse me?" Jimmy added with a wounded tone. "I don't remember charging you or Jennifer for a seat."

"Yeah, but you were trying to get me drunk early on to steal my wallet." Darren smiled.

"Maybe you should try not being a lightweight then," Jimmy shot back.

The thought caused him to tilt his head.

"Has anyone tried getting drunk yet?" Jimmy asked. "I haven't seen booze around anywhere."

"Where'd Brendan stash his travel bottles?" Darren asked.

"Oh shit, that's right!" Jimmy said, having forgotten them after drinking too many of them. "They were with Sheena in her bag."

"So do you guys see anything?" Amanda asked again.

"Yeah, you left your panties under the seat," Jimmy dismissed.

She gave him a cross look.

"Amanda got a bad vibe from one of our passengers," Paxton explained.

"Who?" Darren asked.

"Andrei Tunnikov, the new, tall guy," Paxton said.

"He's quiet," Amanda said. "Like I get why Blaire would go for someone creepier than her, but it's not the same."

"Blaire's the one in all the black?" Darren asked.

"Yeah," Amanda confirmed. "She's always been edgy like that, but there's something else going on with that Andrei guy. He looks like he really wants to hurt someone."

"Does he also have a shotgun hidden somewhere?" Jimmy asked.

"I don't know." Amanda was very serious. "The limo got to Blaire's house before I did."

Darren hadn't had too many interactions with him. He knew Andrei was one of the Choir & Drama people and he was in Ziegler's Government & Civics class with him and Jimmy.

Jimmy seemed to like the guy. He kept trying to invite him to the afterparty in the weeks leading up to the dance.

The dude did have an intense look about him, but it wasn't manic like Torelli. He came across as more of a military type. It was the same look you might see on the guards at an Air Force base. Of course, Darren had a bit of a biased perception.

Rather than going to USF, his brother had followed a personal calling to join the Air Force. He was in some kind of special duty program to get a degree fully paid for after putting some years in with Uncle Sam.

He was stationed nearby, up at Beale Air Force Base, so Darren was used to the look of gate guards.

If Darren were being more charitable to the other position, he'd say that Andrei's hard Slavic features did give him a bit of a Russian Mafia vibe. He didn't even have an accent though. Except for the name and the look, he seemed pretty chill. He was from Pasadena for God's sake.

"He just weirds me out," Amanda reiterated.

Darren felt like he was only getting half of the story.

He slid an unopened bottle of cider out of the bar. It had been sitting in a puddle of melted ice.

"Amanda, you mind giving this to Jenny for me?" Darren asked.

"Oh yeah, sure." She walked off with the bottle.

Once she was out of earshot, he turned to Paxton.

"What do *you* think?" Darren asked.

Paxton shrugged. "I've got Calc 1A homeroom with him. Seems fine, he helped me with integrals a few weeks back. I don't know, Amanda just got a bit freaked out.

"I think part of it is that Blaire usually has Elise Gosselin as a counterbalance to her moods, but she's been pretty attached to Andrei since the beginning of the school year. Then on Saturday they were almost inseparable.

"She's just never seen Blaire like that before. Andrei is quiet too, so the two of them whispering in a way that no one else could hear got under her skin."

"Well, things look clean in here," Jimmy said, finishing his sweep. "So tell her to keep her panties on."

"Yeah, yeah ..." Paxton walked off. He clearly hadn't wanted to broach the subject in the first place. He returned to Marcus' perimeter line.

"Next," Jimmy said to Darren.

They circled around to the third car. There were only two limos left, a black Lincoln Continental and a charcoal grey Chrysler 300.

They did a pass through the Lincoln. They needed to smash the window to unlock it, but once they did, they found nothing strange inside.

Next was the Chrysler. The driver's side door was already unlocked.

Darren pressed the button to open the passenger cabin doors.

Jimmy listlessly tugged the handle and was tossed backwards as the door flung open at full force.

Darren snapped his head around, pulling up the crowbar and running toward him.

Two kids wearing black t-shirts and sweatpants burst out of the cabin and began running toward the football stadium. They didn't seem very fast; Marcus could have easily outrun them. Neither of them got that far anyway.

The skinny kid tried to duck through a gap between the others, but Jenny extended her lance sideways, clotheslining him.

The bottle of cider in her hand dropped to the ground, smashing to pieces.

The kid's legs flung into the air and he landed on his back on the asphalt.

"Stop!" Jenny held the bar sideways to try to keep him from getting up. "We just need to have everyone accounted for."

It was flowery language, and pretty far from the truth, but she was trying to be diplomatic.

The skinny kid tried kicking at her to scare her away. His shoe landed a pretty solid strike on her knee.

She turned the knife on him, holding it only a foot from his face.

He raised his hands back in surrender and stopped moving.

Marcus had thrown an elbow to the chest of the heavy kid, knocking the wind out of him. He leveled the tire iron at his chin.

"You wanna keep your teeth?" he asked him.

The heavy kid froze, biting his lips while putting his hands up.

Darren helped Jimmy to his feet.

Jimmy coughed out a mouthful of sand.

"Fuck!" he said, trying to spit out every last grain of dust. "It tastes like I took a faceplant on the beach. I'm never going to get used to that."

"Anyone else in there?" Marcus asked the heavy kid.

He shook his head.

"Are you lying?" Marcus warned.

He shook his head again.

"Speak!" Marcus yelled.

"No, I'm not lying!" the kid cried.

"You go first," Jimmy waved to Darren, wiping granules from his lips.

Darren looked in the Chrysler, but didn't see anyone.

Jimmy followed him in and they checked all the usual places. Nothing was out of the ordinary.

"Do you see anything that could be a transmitter?" Darren asked him.

"No," Jimmy said, rinsing his mouth with one of the water bottles.

They hopped out of the limo.

"Nothing," Darren told Marcus.

Jenny had the skinny kid standing up next to the heavy one. She pulled the blade away from him though, holding it upright like it was a Color Guard flag.

Darren could see how downcast her face was that she had to threaten him at all.

"Either of you have any fancy tech hidden around here?" Marcus asked them.

"No sir," the heavy kid muttered.

"What about *on* you?" Marcus asked. "Hand over anything you got. You don't want me to find it later."

Both kids pulled out keys, cell phones, and wallets.

"Give 'em to her." Marcus motioned to Jenny.

"I'll take them," Darren offered as he walked up.

"No, you won't!" Marcus snapped.

Jenny moved in and collected the items, not wanting to cause trouble.

"Alright. Let's take 'em in," Marcus said.

The group circled the kids as Marcus led them to the gym.

Darren and Jenny trailed to the back.

She flipped the wallets open.

The heavy kid was "Barry Owens" and the skinny kid was "Melvin Mueller".

Darren felt like he'd seen them around school before, but not often. They were like wallpaper, always hugging the shadows and staying away from social groups.

That wouldn't play well for them in Torelli's trials.

If they were social outcasts, they'd be easy prey for mob justice.

Unless, of course, they really were guilty. They looked soft enough that Joe could probably squeeze the truth out of them one way or another.

Then again, torture doesn't guarantee facts. Eventually the accused will just say anything that they think will lessen the pain, including a full confession.

Would that mentality still be at play now though? No one could die anymore. Would that change the way they reacted, or are they too used to that psychological framework?

Only time would tell. Besides, the court was already in session.

***

Bob Melkonian watched as the door of his biology classroom pulled open.

Trisha Forrester, his sweet sophomore student, wore an indescribably cold face.

She reminded him of the drug enforcement agents that swept the school after the Varsity Baseball Adderall scandal.

Bob heard a door stop get kicked into place. His door was propped open to its maximum swing against the wall.

Trey Devall and Brendan Jensen, two of the Varsity Football players, walked through first. Both of them held what looked like metal legs from the circular banquet tables in the ballroom. At the end of each table leg there was one of the steak knives from the dinner duct-taped in place, forming a kind of short javelin.

"They made weapons?" Bob thought to himself, more disturbed than he already was.

Jordan Trainor, one of the shooting guards on the Varsity Basketball team, was next to enter. He was balanced on the other side by Greg Henshaw, the Sophomore Class Prince. Both of them were also armed with steak knife weapons.

Chelsea Morton followed Greg, holding some kind of notebook.

"Robert Melkonian," Chelsea said, addressing him with his full name. It felt surreal coming from a student. "You are being summoned to testify as a suspect in the bombing of Villa Vista High School."

Not able to wrap his head around the situation, Bob faced Trisha again, repeating his question.

"Trisha ... where is Mr. Wallace?"

"His trial is already underway," Greg said.

Bob couldn't ignore this anymore.

"Trials? Summons?" he asked them. "This is insane. Kids, look at yourselves!"

He was hoping to see at least a hint of introspection in their eyes, but the response was even worse than he could imagine.

Jordan Trainor stepped forward, leveling the point of his steak knife at Bob's throat.

"We *have* looked at ourselves ... in the mirrors," he said without remorse. "That's why this needs to happen."

"Please don't resist," Brendan said to Melkonian.

Bob was speechless, looking at the senior.

He was one of the toughest guys on the Varsity Football team, the center on the offensive line. He took countless hits every game, and was often a key component in the Jaguars' play strategies. The Mountaineers had put two guys on him during the entire Coastal Classic and he held them back with ease.

Bob had never really been an athlete. The most noteworthy use of violence in his lifetime was when he left his father battered and bloody at age sixteen. That was a crime of passion more than anything, pure rage and adrenaline.

Otherwise, Bob had always been more of a talker than a fighter. His exercise routine included calisthenics and hiking with his wife. Really, he'd do any workout with Angie ... she looked incredible in yoga pants.

Unfortunately, yoga wasn't going to help Bob challenge four student athletes equipped with knife weapons.

He raised his hands, scooting off of the lab stool. He backed a few inches away from the knife Jordan still held at his throat.

"Just take me to Rick," Bob asked them, worried what the students might have done to him.

"Of course," Chelsea said. "You'll be able to speak in each other's defense."

Jordan pulled the knife away and began leading the group back into the hallway.

Brendan and Trey stood to either side of him while Trisha, Greg, and Chelsea walked behind.

They stepped down the stairwell toward the atrium.

As Bob put his hand on the railing, he noticed more dust settled on the metal bars than there had been the previous day. Was the dust getting worse? What did that mean if it was?

The kids led Bob down the main hallway, approaching the front entrance of the school.

He noticed that all of the teacher classrooms in that main hallway had been secured with door stops. Not regular ones either, but the old wooden wedges they had to stop using because they were a fire hazard.

All of the doors opened outward, into the hallway. Stopping them up from the outside like that meant you wouldn't be able to open them from the inside. After the renovation, the new doors had closer devices installed which could prop the doors open.

These old stops were solid wood, with rubberized faces for grip. If they were pounded into place, they could act like the wedge holding an axe head on its handle. People would be trapped inside.

That's when it clicked for him ... these were prison cells.

One in particular stood out to him. He wondered how Timothy Van Gaal would feel about his "Classics" room getting turned into a kind of Tartarus.

A small thought also crossed Bob's mind that the whole school, this place lost in the mist, was essentially Tartarus.

Bob expected them to stop in the front foyer, that some kind of interrogation room had been set up in the Administration offices.

As they exited the hallway, Bob looked left and saw that the offices were empty. No one was inside at all.

Melkonian looked forward, seeing that Jordan had opened one of the glass doors. He followed them outside.

Maybe he was crazy, but the fog looked thicker too. The metal fence outside of the school parking lot looked less visible than it did yesterday. Was this place slowly shrinking?

Jordan led them down the sidewalk.

Melkonian could see some students going through the cars, searching them one by one. Were they looking for someone ... or something?

Bob looked forward again and realized where the kids were taking him.

The gymnasium.

The great dark funnel cloud was ever present in every mirror. Beyond the corpse with Bob's crushed chest and burnt face, beyond the distant orange glows of the fires, a storm of black smoke was visible from almost every angle. All of that smoke billowed upward out of the gym.

Why had the kids gone inside? What had they found?

Jordan led them through the construction fence, then into the front lobby, where the trophies were meant to be displayed. The glass on the doors had been smashed open, several of the trophy cases were also covered in scratches and cracks. The pattern was strange, had the students thrown handfuls of gravel at the glass to smash it open?

The group then led him through the metal doors onto the basketball court itself.

The first thing Bob saw were the giant yellow eyes of Jackie the Jaguar looking down on him. He dug his claws into an orange basketball. The artist might have gone overboard on the mural, it was more frightening than he expected.

Bob heard a small cheer and thought he was hallucinating for a minute, like he had walked into the memory of an old basketball game he was announcing. But it wasn't a hallucination, a hundred or so students were sitting on the home bleachers, cheering at him being brought there under threat.

His eyes drifted to the right. The visiting team bleachers had much fewer occupants. All of them were tied up with duct tape.

There was a small selection of students, including one in particular which caught his eye.

Ellen Taylor was sitting in the front row. The silver duct tape stood out against her emerald green dress. There was a wrap just above her knees. A tear had been made in the dress so the tape wrapped around her legs too. It couldn't be slipped up with the dress. She leaned forward, her head almost touching her knees. Her wrists were bound behind her, and another wrap was made around her chest and just above her elbows.

Scattered in the two rows behind her was a small selection of other students that looked like a set of "usual suspects". They were the kinds of kids who didn't fit in, who gave off a perception of being weird or dangerous.

Mikey Gregor was one that didn't surprise Melkonian. Rumors had floated around that he was the one that started the fire in the school dumpster two years back.

The claim was that he had destroyed evidence of stealing and selling the answer keys for the PSATs. No proof ever turned up that he was responsible, so nothing ultimately happened.

After that incident, he actually seemed like he was turning his life around. He seemed like a happier kid at the end of his sophomore year. Melkonian remembered noticing the change in him over the course of the Spring Semester. The fact that he was at Homecoming at all was a big deal.

He had taken a girl from John Muir. She gave off the impression that she was from a skater clique. She'd pop up out around campus sometimes if Mikey had to stay late for one reason or another. Definitely eccentric in her own ways, but they seemed happy together, including at the dance.

She didn't wake up in this hollow shadow of Villa Vista High School.

Blake Samuels was also tied up on one of the rows. He must have done something particularly offensive, because his mouth was duct-taped too.

Besides Ellen Taylor, and a few kids like Mikey, there was no one else on the bleachers.

This didn't seem like a courtroom at all. This was a Colosseum.

Assuming the role of Caesar was Joe Torelli. He still wore the charcoal grey vest and red tie with the rest of his dress suit. The suit was far from pristine though, it looked like he hadn't changed out of it at all since waking up in this place.

It was not the suit which stood out though. The bandolier of bright red shotgun shells was what concerned Melkonian the most. It hung across his chest like a sash, a decoration of leadership.

Extending from Torelli's left hand was a long metal barrel resting against his shoulder.

"Where on earth did Torelli get a shotgun?!" he thought to himself.

The quarterback turned as the crowd began to cheer, smiling at seeing Melkonian brought into his hall of judgement.

Behind him, two of the large mirrors from one of the bathrooms had been brought in. They had been placed on chairs, resting upright in landscape orientation as they normally would behind the sinks. Instead of being flat, they were angled a bit toward each other, like mirrors in a changing room.

Sitting in a chair, just in front of the seam, was Richard Wallace. He was also bound in duct tape.

The chair was oriented in such a way that he was facing the two mirrors. On each side of him was a different crushed and burned doppelganger of himself. The corpses matched his sitting posture, like mimes floating in mid-air.

The mirrors were also the main source of light in this place.

While the gymnasium appeared as a column of black smoke to every mirror outside, from the inside it appeared as the source of that smoke ... a lake of fire.

Tendrils of fire climbed up to the ceiling on all sides. Giant holes and cracks in the maple wood flooring poured out flames like they were lava geysers.

Looking into the mirrors felt like looking into an industrial-sized smelting furnace. The red, orange, and yellow embers filled the "real" gymnasium with an appropriately hellish glow. The light seemed to reach into every shadow, trying to smother every trace of darkness.

"Mr. Melkonian," Joe Torelli said, quieting down the crowd. "You arrived just in time."

Rick Wallace turned in his chair to look at him.

A knife had been stabbed into his shoulder.

NINETEEN

THE NINTH CIRCLE

JENNIFER WALKED SLOWLY DOWN the path toward the football stadium.

All she could see was the fear in that Melvin kid's face as she held the knife to him.

The makeshift lance hung loosely in her right hand. Someone could easily pluck it from her grasp and stab her in the back with it.

She thought she deserved something like that right about now.

In her other hand was Darren's. His bare fingers were laced between hers. He had removed his right glove and placed it in his pocket.

This was perhaps the first time since they actually died that they truly felt dead.

He seemed to squeeze the crowbar in his left hand, like he was about to chuck it into the baseball field at any moment.

When they helped bring the two geeky boys into the gymnasium, they saw Mr. Mel sitting in the cross-examination chair.

Jenny hadn't yet seen the mirrors Joe had set up in the back. They frightened her more than her own reflection. She hadn't let go of Darren's hand since.

The two boys had begun crying when they saw the walls of fire beyond the glass.

And yet, despite all that fire, things felt colder now than ever before.

Darren had given her his suit coat to wear. The sleeves ran down almost to the knuckle of her thumb. It helped a bit, but she couldn't make up for the cold when she couldn't feel any warmth on the inside either.

Technically they didn't have blood, perhaps they weren't warm anymore at all. If someone put a thermometer in her mouth, she'd be surprised if it even broke 60 degrees Fahrenheit.

Darren still felt warm to her though. He was one of the only things that felt warm here.

Camellia and Jimmy seemed similarly disillusioned. He hadn't even been cracking any jokes since they turned over the two geeks to Torelli. He just walked silently, Camellia wrapping her arm around his.

The other team had finished their job of rounding up people on the list. Most of those too frightened by Joe's initial outburst had retreated to their classroom dormitories or hidden in one of the bathrooms or closets in the Murphy Center.

Chelsea and Greg were in that group, but Jordan was the one leading the pack. They went through the indoor spaces and dormitories, before finishing up with a sweep of the buildings between the baseball diamonds.

That is where they found Ellen Taylor, the late Freshman Class Princess. She was armed with a small pen knife, but they were quickly able to disarm and capture her.

Jennifer hadn't asked for any of the details, she really didn't want to know.

However sad or broken the girl was before the bomb went off, she looked much worse now.

Darren didn't want to stick around for whatever they were doing to Mr. Wallace and Mr. Mel. After a few minutes they were back out of the gym, going to complete their search of campus.

Since the other team had covered the baseball diamonds, Marcus was leading the final sweep of the football stadium and tennis courts.

Jenny realized that the last time she'd walked this pathway was with Darren and Isabella after the Coastal Classic, back when they were alive.

For all the drama, life seemed so much simpler. Joe was just having a bitch fit after losing the big game. Jenny was planning on talking to Isabella. She was going to suggest breaking up with him if he didn't shape up for the dance. She was excited about the vote for Homecoming Queen and thought she had a real chance of winning with one of the nicest guys in their class.

Now Marcus trudged so lifelessly that it felt like he was one of the coldest points in their small little world.

Winning Homecoming Queen seemed so trivial and pointless, especially now that a real system of power had arisen in their underworld and she was near the bottom of the hierarchy.

Isabella, like the rest of them, didn't survive the dance. Instead, she was burned to death by the crude machine of one or more psychopaths. At the very least, she didn't end up in this part of the afterlife, hopefully she was in some real paradise.

And of course, the biggest surprise was not that Joe had spun into rage and depression after losing the game. Instead, it was the fact that the loss would be the final straw of an abusive relationship with his father. Joe would go home at some point in the night and kill him with a shotgun. He then packed it with an escape bag to flee to Latin America.

If Joe really was involved in the bombing at all, she and Darren would suffer the consequences too. No matter how much they felt like they were under duress, none of the others would see it that way if the situation inverted and Joe became the one tied up in the chair.

Marcus stopped the group at the edge of the stadium bleachers.

"Alright, you four go through the locker rooms," he said, motioning toward Jenny, Darren, Paxton, and Amanda. "The three of us are going upstairs through the announcement booth and snack bar."

Everyone nodded wordlessly, splitting off.

They followed Paxton into the locker room entrance, starting with the boys' side.

Jenny was actually surprised by how clean it was. Somehow, she expected it to look a lot worse, with mud and old grime rubbed into the grout of every tile.

They went through all of the bends and corners. Darren drove the crowbar into the latch of one of the closets. After only a minor effort, he was able to pull the door open.

There was no one inside, just cleaning supplies and other miscellaneous janitorial equipment.

Soon they passed a locker and Darren stopped, approaching the dial. He spun a combination and the locker pulled open. It was empty.

Darren turned to her. "I always took my kit bag home after a game, to wash clothes and equipment. Plus, I just never liked leaving too much stuff behind."

He chuckled a little, tapping the crowbar on the locker next to his. "After freshman year I didn't like the idea of leaving anything in the school. I was scared I'd have to break in again to retrieve something."

He lowered the crowbar to his side. "Kind of ironic huh?"

"I wish I'd left more stuff in my lockers too," Jenny said. "There was no way to know we'd get to take some things with us."

Darren turned to the others.

"Paxton?" he asked. "Are we supposed to go through the lockers?"

Paxton was completing a more thorough search of the opened closets.

"No," Paxton said. "The sophomores are going with a group to open up these and the classroom lockers this afternoon, using the master keys. Joe's hoping to have a more refined search area by then, after the trials. This morning is all about people."

Jenny and Darren looked at each other with weary expressions.

"Okay," Darren acknowledged.

They moved over to the girls' locker room. The layout was a mirror image of the guys' side.

Darren went to the two locked closets and pried them open. Paxton and Amanda began their respective searches after no one was found inside.

Jenny led Darren as they walked through the sections, before stopping at her own locker.

She spun the number dial and pulled it open.

"Since I was on the float in that Victorian outfit for the game," she said. "I wasn't cheerleading on Friday."

She zipped open the duffel bag. There was a black, yellow, and white Jaguars Cheer uniform inside.

"Looks like your wardrobe count is up to three," Darren said.

"I'll have to try it on later," she replied, eyeing him suggestively.

A slight smile appeared on his face. Now she was the one trying the distractions.

"I think that's everywhere in here," Amanda said, breaking the moment.

"Alright," Paxton replied. "Let's cover the bathrooms then we'll meet the others upstairs."

"Duty calls," Darren said mirthlessly.

Jenny zipped up the duffel bag and slung it over her back.

The bathrooms were both empty, as were the two single-stalled "family" restrooms.

Having finished, they returned to the bleachers, waiting near the 50-yard line on the concrete sidewalk at the bottom.

After a minute or two, Marcus, Jimmy, and Camellia came walking down the center stairwell.

Marcus looked at Paxton, awaiting a report.

"Nothing," Paxton said.

"Us neither," Marcus said.

"There's about 20 gallons of nacho cheese sauce up there though," Jimmy said. He was back to trying to break the tension with humor.

"Alright," Marcus said. "What about the other bleachers?"

Darren and Jimmy locked eyes for a moment. Both of them knew about the old storage room underneath the stands. Neither of them said anything.

"It looks like there could be something underneath," Paxton said. "Maybe a crawl space."

"Let's go," Marcus said.

Paxton and Amanda followed first, with the four others trailing behind.

Jimmy and Darren shared a glance again. If anyone was hiding, it would be in there.

The group passed through the tennis courts first, completing their coverage area before reaching the smaller visiting team stands.

Darren, Jennifer, Jimmy, and Camellia covered the bleachers themselves, making sure there was no one lying underneath any of the metal benches. They exited using the other concrete ramp.

As they circled around past the shot put field, they saw Paxton and Amanda waiting near the back-center of the stands.

The four met up with them, then turned to see Marcus walking up to the old steel door concealed by a small concrete overhang.

Creeping silently, he put his ear to the door and listened.

After a few seconds, Marcus smiled.

He held up two fingers.

***

Bob Melkonian yelled out as soon as he saw the knife sticking out of Rick's shoulder.

"Rick!" he cried, ignoring Torelli's initial greeting. "Are you okay?!"

Rick said nothing. His face looked as hopeless as it did the first time they'd faced their dead bodies in a mirror.

"He's fine," Joe said. "But he won't be for long if he doesn't explain what was taped to the bottom of his foot."

Bob looked closer to see that Rick was propping his left leg on his right knee. A second knife was sticking out of the bottom of his foot.

"It's strange that he somehow lost a shoe, and has the residue of duct tape on his foot," Joe continued.

"Well, where did *you* get duct tape, Torelli?" Bob challenged him, motioning toward all the others seated in the visiting team bleachers. "You've tied up several of your classmates and now you're torturing Mr. Wallace?!"

He then turned his glare to the audience.

"And all of you are watching this? Cheering along?"

Most of the kids turned away, or didn't meet his eyes.

"Well really, we would like to hear him give us any answers at all." Torelli took a few steps closer to Melkonian. "For instance, one of our questions was 'have you ever seen this thing before?'"

Torelli picked up a strange looking device from a chair. It looked like a modern art sculpture built off of a car battery.

"Well, Mr. Mel?" Torelli asked again, expecting an answer.

"No, I've never seen that before. What is it?"

"This is what blew up the gym," Joe said, pressing the red "TEST" button.

A powerful arc of electricity surged between two metal rods on top of the sculpture.

Half of the audience flinched at the sight. Many covered their eyes or shook in fear.

"That's the bomb?" Bob's eyes opened in shock.

"No," Joe groaned, upset by how genuine Bob's reaction looked. "*This* is the bomb."

Torelli held out his hands like a ringmaster, motioning to the walls of the gym.

Bob said nothing, distracted by the dancing fiery glows.

Eric Schwartz, one of the Varsity Basketball small forwards, stepped closer to the two of them. He was holding a notebook and explained to Melkonian in more detail.

"From what we've found so far," he began. "It looks like the gym was filled with natural gas, then ignited with this device during the dance."

"Natural gas?" Bob asked, looking at him. "No, someone would have smelled something."

Brendan Jensen walked up with a large roll of duct tape.

"Hands behind your back," he muttered.

"Now you know where all the tape came from," Torelli said. "Just look at the doors."

Bob turned back to where he walked in and noticed the layers of silver-grey duct tape scaling all the cracks in the doors. A small pile of extra rolls sat against the wall just below the basketball hoop.

Brendan wrapped the tape around his wrists, then pulled several layers around his chest and arms.

"Why would Mr. Wallace do this?" Bob yelled, addressing the crowd.

Torelli stepped in again, shifting the gun into his right hand and grabbing the foregrip.

"The *real* question ..." Torelli said, also addressing the crowd more than Melkonian, "... is why *you* are speaking more in his defense than *he* is?"

"Because he thinks he deserves it," Bob answered, before adding, "for a personal sin, he did *not* blow up the school."

"Well let's see if you can get him talking," Torelli said.

Brendan walked Melkonian over to the chair.

Trey pulled the knife out of Wallace's shoulder, then the one in his foot. A bit of fine powder trickled out of both wounds.

Rick grunted, but otherwise bore the pain without a sound.

Jordan pulled him out of the chair while Brendan and Trey sat Bob down to face two reflections of himself.

Bob took a deep breath, watching the chests of the two corpses crumple inward. They had been crushed too much and failed to expand at all.

Rick was on his feet now, limping a bit, but facing Torelli.

"You've got a high pain tolerance," Torelli said. "You think it's higher than Melkonian?"

Trey plunged one of the knives into Bob's back.

He yelled, both in surprise and agony, gritting his teeth.

"No!" Trisha screamed, finally finding some courage to speak up.

"Stop this Torelli!" Rick pleaded.

"Explain the foot," Torelli demanded.

"I had a spare key!" Rick said. "I used it to get the chair out of my office. Before I could put my shoe back on, I heard the gunshot and came running."

Rick sounded very convincing. It was close enough to the truth after all. The crowd seemed to believe him too.

Eric Schwartz wrote down what he said, acting as the stenographer for the proceedings.

Rick then turned to the crowd.

"I think I know where there's evidence of the bomber, the *real* bomber," he said. "Because it isn't Melkonian or myself."

"Go on," Torelli said.

"When I was getting my chair, I noticed that the roll of construction drawings in Ms. Fletcher's office was gone," he said.

There was a minor rumbling among the crowd, not fully putting the pieces together.

"Ms. Fletcher had the full design blueprints for all of the renovations to the high school building," Wallace continued. "Those blueprints were the *only thing* missing from her office."

"What are you saying?" Torelli asked, fully engaged.

"I'm saying that the bomber is *here*," Wallace concluded. "There is evidence of their identity in the remodel drawings, so they took the drawings to keep from being discovered."

The conversation among the students got louder.

Greg Henshaw stepped in.

"Where would we find another copy of the drawings?" he asked.

"I don't know," Rick said. "If they aren't in here, and there aren't any more in the Administration offices, I wouldn't know where to look."

"What do you think?" Chelsea Morton asked Joe.

"Accepting you at your word, it could make sense," Torelli said to Wallace. He then turned to Eric. "Have everyone be on the lookout for more drawings."

"Now for the love of God," Rick said. "Take that knife out of Mr. Mel!"

Joe turned toward Trey and Brendan, nodding.

Brendan pulled the knife out and Bob groaned again through gritted teeth.

"Has anyone else actually seen these drawings?" Jordan asked. "Were there drawings at all or is this just a diversion?"

Torelli turned to the others.

"Since everyone's more talkative now, how about we get back to regular questioning." Joe walked closer to Melkonian.

"So, Mr. Mel," he said. "Where were you Friday night?"

More than a little indignant after being stabbed, Bob flipped the question back on him.

"Where were *you* Torelli?" he asked the reflection. Joe's corpse looked like it had been shredded with hundreds of razor blades.

"I was killing my father with this shotgun," Joe said nonchalantly, holding the Browning Citori so that Melkonian could see the full length of the barrel.

"You did what?!" Bob asked, just now learning of his admission.

"I'm not the one in the chair, Mr. Mel." Joe motioned to Jordan to bring a chair over for Rick Wallace.

"I was at home, with my wife," Bob said. "Rick walked out with me after the game, and I didn't return to campus until 5:30 p.m. on Saturday."

"It's true," Rick said, sitting in the second chair that Jordan pulled up. He was staggered a bit behind the "hot seat" that Melkonian was in.

"Torelli, what on earth have you done?" Bob asked again. "You're the only admitted killer here."

Joe walked in front of him, standing in the seam of the mirrors. He looked Bob in the eyes.

"I should have killed him a long time ago. If he were here with us, I'd keep killing him over and over again no matter how many times he got back up."

"Joe," Bob said, "you may not believe me, but I know what it's like having an abusive father. I beat him bloody when I left home and it left a permanent scar, separating me from my family."

"What a coincidence," Joe said sardonically. "We're all here because we've been permanently separated from our families. That's what this is about."

Melkonian had announced sports games for years. At least as far as athletics went, and from biology class, he knew Torelli well enough. He had never seen so much darkness in his face. The wall of flames behind him only accented the hateful fire that was inside of him.

"Joe why didn't you tell anyone?" he asked. "Really explained what was going on? We could have helped you, gotten you away from that environment."

"Hello?!" Joe screamed in his face. "I'm already in Hell. We're trying to find our murderer!"

Stunned into compliance, Melkonian answered. "I don't know anything about that! I would never hurt you kids and neither would Mr. Wallace. We cared about you, your welfare, your futures."

"What futures?" Someone called from the bleachers.

Melkonian turned to the crowd, not able to identify the voice.

"Fine, don't believe me," Bob replied. "What other motive would I have to kill myself in such a way? I love my wife, my daughter, and they both love me. There's nothing to gain financially in suicide, and with Angie's job and our savings I could have retired Monday morning if I hated the school or the people so much."

The crowd was quiet.

"What about you Rick?" he yelled, trying to get him to speak for himself. "Did you have some motive for killing a bunch of kids?"

"Absolutely not!" he said, finally with some passion. "I spent my life trying to help you however I could."

His voice broke and he began swallowing tears.

"I had a lot of reasons to kill myself," he mourned. "I would have never ... *never* hurt any of you in the process."

There was a concerned rumble in the bleachers about what he meant by that.

It was beginning to feel like Bob and Rick were winning over the crowd.

Eric Schwartz walked up to Torelli; Bob could hear him speak to Joe over the noise from the bleachers.

"Joe, maybe we should do the walkthrough of the lockers this morning," he said. "We could get a group looking for the transmitter and/or construction drawings at the very least."

Torelli looked over at the sophomore couple.

"Works for us." Chelsea shrugged.

"Alright," Joe said, also noticing the loss of popular support. "We can't let anyone leave until we do anyway, so we might as well speed things along. We'll see what strays turn up after Marcus wraps their search. Once we have everyone inside, we'll hit the lockers and dorms of the suspects first."

They spent a few more minutes discussing details. Then there was a sound at the door of the gymnasium.

Marcus walked in, leading their search group.

In the middle of the group were two junior students. As soon as they saw the wall of fire in the mirrors, they began whimpering.

Melkonian couldn't hear what Joe and Marcus were discussing, but assumed it was more of the same.

He was able to see Darren Clark and Jennifer Maxwell standing among Joe's enforcers.

As soon as he locked eyes with Darren, the Varsity Football fullback turned away. He grabbed Jennifer's arm and they walked to the far side of the wall.

Bob thought he recognized the two junior kids. He believed their names were Barry and Melvin. They were notoriously quiet, among the lowest rungs of popularity in the school. Even in schoolwork, they just did the bare minimum to pass and disappeared into the shadows. Bob felt bad that he couldn't even remember their last names.

Marcus Johnson walked back outside with his group. Brendan and Trey led the two boys to the mirrors.

"Alright, back to the bleachers," Joe said.

Jordan Trainor pulled them out of the chairs and guided them back to the visiting team bleachers with his knife lance. He sat Wallace down next to Ellen Taylor and Melkonian next to him.

Barry and Melvin were now in the staggered chairs, staring at their own corpse reflections. Both of their upper bodies had been caved in by falling debris. It was a hard sight to stare at. Barry in particular had taken a hit so directly, that his skull had been forced down into his ribcage.

Bob hoped neither kid remembered the pain of ending up that way. He was lucky that he couldn't really remember his own death either. He must have been knocked out upon impacting the wall.

"Well, I feel a bit awkward," Torelli said, circling the two chairs. "I have no fuckin' idea who either of you are."

He looked up at the crowd as a few laughs could be heard.

"No, seriously," Torelli said. "Does anyone know these geeks?"

"I do," A girl's voice came from one of the lower bleachers.

Melkonian could see a blonde stand up in a royal blue dress.

He definitely recognized her; it was Anne Kirkpatrick. She was the date of the Junior Class Prince, Liam Connelly. She made googly eyes at him all night and he seemed to mostly ignore her. Bob remembered finding that strange.

"I also know their motive," she said, walking down onto the basketball court.

"Anne, no!" Barry screamed. "It's not true, we didn't do it!"

To some extent, Bob felt like a lot of the kids had been swept into this current scenario by a sort of mob madness. They were being driven by their own sadness and thirst for revenge. Joe was channeling that energy into a very real and palpable witch-hunt with his own murder weapon transformed into their symbol of "justice".

For this girl, it seemed to be something else entirely.

For her, it seemed to be personal.

***

Rafael Herrera always tried to be a jokey and fun guy. His favorite thing to do in most social situations was to chat up his date or a group of partygoers, entertaining them with some story.

He was a natural fit for Choir & Drama, performing was a passion in his daily life.

That daily life was over now and he was getting really sick of the show he was a part of.

As soon as he saw the freshmen girl with the X-Acto knife, a suspicion of his was proven to be true.

They weren't stuck in some after school special, playing high school in Purgatory until someone prayed hard enough to get them out. There were real stakes, real weapons, and real threats at play. That was only further confirmed when Joe Torelli pulled a shotgun out of the trunk of his car.

People not being able to die made the situation a thousand times worse. There was no holding back now, you could be as brutal as you wanted to someone because you'd get put back together again like magic ... but the pain was the same.

Raf was glad that he was somewhat prepared.

When they retrieved stuff from their lockers earlier, he was sure to pick up some items of his that he usually kept under wraps. In the living world he could have gotten in big trouble for having them.

His uncle Arturo always wanted to make sure that Raf, and his brothers, sisters, and cousins, knew how to defend themselves. They needed to know how to fight and they needed to know how to use a blade.

He had shown these to Elise once before and taught her a few moves with the others he had back home. They were the first and foremost things he wanted to get from his locker. The right weapon could mean the difference between life and death, or in this case, capture and freedom.

However, Arturo Herrera was not some punk cholo getting mixed up in petty gang wars. His weapon of choice was not a cheap folding blade that any young thug might have lying around. Arturo Herrera was a U.S. Marine, who spent four years in the jungles of Vietnam.

Raf unscrewed the "extra" thermos he kept in his gym bag, pulling out a 13" long serrated Ka-Bar knife. He attached the sheath in such a way that it was concealed just below the nape of his neck, between the jacket and his dress shirt. He could slide it off his back at a moment's notice.

He then opened up the old biology textbook he kept in his locker, even though he wasn't in that class anymore. It was actually a spare he had turned into a concealed storage case. The second knife just barely fit diagonally in the large textbook.

They weren't normally in the same place. It was only during the gym construction that he began keeping his P.E. bag in his regular locker.

This knife was for Elise. She'd have an easy time concealing it. Raf had a leg strap which could be attached to either sheath, which she wore like a garter belt. In a full-length dress, no one had seen it, apparently not even Blaire or Andrei, even when he was carrying Elise. He assumed they would have said something if they did.

Raf leaned against the metal frame at the back of the bleachers. It pressed the outline of the sheath into his back.

Elise's head was resting on his left shoulder. He'd tried waking her a few times, but she was still out. Blaire sat beside her, helping to keep her steady. Then Andrei was in the far corner.

He wasn't sure where this little show trial was going, but Raf wanted escape options.

The only one who was perhaps more upset than him was Blaire.

After dating Elise for a good five months now, Raf had gotten used to the cold, penetrating glare Blaire could wield. It was genuinely terrifying.

She had the same look in her eyes all the time that Arturo did when he described the first time he killed someone.

It went beyond eyeliner, make-up, or attitude. Blaire looked like she'd seen the face of Death for a long time, and it still took him sixteen years to actually claim her soul.

She turned that gaze on everyone now. Occasionally she'd glare at Torelli, but he was too up-his-own-ass to notice. Mostly, her eyes seemed to fall on the strange device that now sat in the middle of the basketball court.

It was like something cobbled together in an automotive shop, at least on the bottom. The further up you moved on the gizmo, the more it looked like some kind of *007* shit. Really, the car battery was just there as a power supply. It was something easily sourced that wouldn't have been noticed by authorities.

Still, Raf wasn't sure what she could possibly be seeing in it.

Blaire had trouble taking her eyes off of the ignition device.

Without knowing the face of the killer, that was all she could focus her rage and hatred on.

She wasn't paying much attention to whatever nonsense Joe Torelli was doing. He was clearly deranged, and probably killed his dad like he said, but something about his own righteous fury seemed legitimate.

The way he was going about it was definitely going to lead to disaster though.

Paxton Bannister was going along with the little junta Torelli had pulled together. After Marcus Johnson folded into the cause, he seemed to drag the other Varsity Basketball players right along for the ride.

Blaire wondered what Amanda thought of all this. She was sitting in the front row along with the other dates and girlfriends of Torelli's terror squad.

In Blaire's opinion, a lot of the girls were airheads, including Amanda. They were the kind of bimbos that gravitated to the think-with-their-cock athletes in the first place. For the most part, the girls just took a number and got in line. They'd have a ride as arm candy for a few weeks or months then the next girl would be up.

Torelli was the ultimate example of this. Blaire was surprised there hadn't been at least one pregnancy scare rumor in the past few years.

There was one girl who didn't quite fit that mold though. She happened to be the girl that Joe was now berating.

Jennifer Maxwell seemed like she was cut from a different cheer uniform than the rest of them.

Her break-up with her last boyfriend, who wasn't a jock, was an ugly, public mess. Blaire didn't know much about either of them, but once it came out that he cheated and she caught him in the act, things seemed to make a lot more sense. He came off as really slimy to Blaire too.

Honestly, Jennifer had upgraded by moving on to a jock.

Darren Clark was now yelling about how the other guy was too cheap to rent a limo.

Darren didn't seem to be quite as much of a dude-bro as the others. Like party mansion Jimmy, he seemed unique. He didn't quite match the set.

For him, instead of playing football to flex and pick up chicks, he seemed more like he was trying to really prove something. Not prove something like Torelli was, that he was some unrecognized sports god, but prove something to himself.

Blaire couldn't imagine what it was, but it felt more meaningful.

Torelli said one more thing to Jennifer. "That's why you're the Queen."

Blaire looked down at her, everyone was. She began closing up immediately, trying to hide from their eyes.

Whatever Joe said was probably some kind of insult, but she had a better claim to being Homecoming Queen than most girls at Villa Vista. She'd probably make Blaire's Top Ten anyway.

Just by being in that jock and cheerleader world and not being a terrible person was quite an accomplishment.

Blaire heard her name being called by Paxton. He was taking account of their claim to the Choir & Drama Rehearsal Room.

Raf answered for them. "Yeah, we're all here."

Jennifer suddenly turned to look at them and they locked eyes.

She had all the outer bimbo qualities, blonde hair, blue eyes, big boobs ... but it felt surface level.

The other cheerleader types were like chocolate bunnies ... *Playboy* bunnies. They were processed sugar shells with nothing inside.

Jennifer was like a caramel apple. There was all the same heart-attack-inducing candy wrapped around the outside, but inside she actually seemed to have some substance.

Beyond her baby blue eyes, Blaire could see sadness. It wasn't the sadness that everyone now shared, as members of the recently deceased. It wasn't even the sadness of a broken heart. She really seemed to care about Darren Clark, much more than the other guy anyway.

Whatever that sadness was, whether it be conviction, self-awareness, or something else ... *that* was the apple. That was the endearing moral core that made her more than just another bunny.

Jennifer turned away from her, apparently ashamed. It was just more proof of the apple.

With everyone taking their focus off of them, Blaire could feel Andrei squeeze her hand.

She turned to look at him.

"We're going to get through this," he reassured her.

She smiled back and hoped he would believe it.

She wanted to trust him, but something else hadn't left her mind in the last hour.

The nightmare.

For all of its omens that had come true, there was one shadowy figure which had yet to reveal itself.

Blaire hadn't even found the chance to actually tell Andrei about the dream yet. She had no idea what he could be thinking, how he was interpreting those last moments of their lives.

When she placed her ear against that wall, and heard the whistling, she immediately knew it was a sign of danger. Little did she know it was the hiss of natural gas filling the gymnasium.

She knew to be scared because she'd seen a vision of her own death the night before. Unfortunately, it didn't give her enough clairvoyance to actually change the circumstances. Within seconds of putting the pieces together, the fire consumed them anyway.

In a way, it felt almost like a cruel joke. How many others foresaw their own death, but only realized it the moment beforehand? Was it a common thing? Did this just happen to Blaire by accident, or was it something else?

The lighthouse in the vision didn't even look like the one on Point Reyes. It was like an old New England lighthouse, something you'd find in Massachusetts or Maine rather than California. The setting reeked of nineteenth century nautical fiction. Blaire would know, she'd read dozens of stories from that era.

Worst of all, why did it show her grandpa up by the lighthouse beacon? Was he there just to watch her descend into fire and darkness? Was it more mockery, a reminder that even in death she was still separated from him?

Blaire's heart broke, darkness leaking into the back of her thoughts.

She tried her best to forget about that part of the vision. It wasn't really him anyway, just a cruel shadow. It was really no different than her own dead face that looked at her in the mirror.

Maybe people actually have a keener perception of the afterlife than most of the living realize. There actually could be something to the various stories of dreams and visions weaved into the world's religions.

Blaire thought back on some of the Biblical stories she was dutifully told in her own childhood.

"It's not fair," she thought to herself. "Joseph actually got to change things with his visions."

She looked down at her sleeves. The black sweatshirt jacket was far from an amazing technicolor dreamcoat.

After a bit more discussion among them, Torelli sent most of the jocks out the door in teams.

Darren engaged Joe in what seemed like a firm conversation. Eventually Torelli just threw his hand up in resignation and walked away.

From there, Darren grabbed Jennifer's hand and they jogged out the door. Jimmy O'Shaughnessy likewise took his girlfriend.

The other two football jocks left theirs behind. It probably hadn't even occurred to them to bring the girls along. They were the jocks that fit Blaire's stereotypical mold the best ... smooth-brain flunkies.

Of the basketball players, Paxton was the only person left who had someone down in Limbo with him. To his credit, he took Amanda on his way out too.

The way Torelli waved that shotgun around was more than a little worrying.

Blaire definitely wouldn't leave Andrei behind with him.

Chelsea and Greg exited with the jocks too. Greg was technically in JV Baseball, but perhaps he was too young to have been possessed by the machismo demon yet.

Despite all of the theatrics going on below, the slamming of the gymnasium door behind them had one very positive outcome.

Elise began to stir.

Blaire took her focus off of the meathead enforcers, turning to the sleeping redhead.

"Elise," Blaire said, shifting to look her in the eyes. "Hey, can you hear us?"

Raf was surprised by her sudden rousing and began searching around his person.

"Ah ... Andrei," he said, looking past the girls. "Do you have something we can use as a blindfold?"

Andrei began patting around, aiding the search, but by then it was too late.

Elise Gosselin opened her eyes.

In front of her were two sets of piercing, predatory eyes surrounded by black hair. One set was dull yellow, painted on an oversized mural adorning the back wall. The other set was greenish-brown, looking at her with concern.

She took in the image all at once, and seemed to hesitate for a moment, processing everything.

Then Elise began chuckling.

Blaire became more concerned.

"Is this a good thing?" Raf asked, really hoping the long-time best friend could reassure them.

Elise finally settled on the hazel eyes, a strange smile donning her face.

"You're scarier than Jackie," she said to Blaire.

Blaire tilted her head for a moment, not quite sure what she heard.

Once it clicked, Andrei was the next to chuckle, then Rafael, then they were all laughing. Blaire hugged her and the guys hugged them both. Elise was starting to seem like herself again. They soon separated, noticing a few errant stares looking at them.

"Please tell me you're okay now," Raf begged her.

"I mean, I'm not really okay," Elise joked, "I am dead after all."

Raf gave her an annoyed look.

She scanned around the room, seeing dozens of Villa Vista Jaguars P.E. shirts. So far, she was holding it together. Something about being exposed to the biggest one, while juxtaposed with Blaire, seemed to flip a different switch inside of her.

She still felt dread looking at the pictures of the jaguar. But being reminded about how capable her best friend was at inspiring terror was somehow comforting. It defanged the paralysis which had gripped her during the last two episodes. It was sort of like how someone who lived with big cats didn't fear wild ones in the same way regular people did.

Blaire was not a monster, she was a big, scary kitten. It made the other Jaguars look less like monsters and more like kittens too.

Elise sat up straight in the bleacher. She flattened out the odd creases on her dress, then pressed her knees together. She could feel the leather sheath between her thighs, the weapon still holstered.

She had to remind herself that she had to be pretty strong to live in the presence of Jaguars.

In a lot of ways, she was a Jaguar too.

TWENTY

PARADISE LOST

NILES FELT A BIT EMBARRASSED for freaking out. However, once he un-freaked-out enough to realize what was going on, he was in no rush to get back to normal either.

When he came out of the panic of imagining himself trapped on a desert island, getting tortured by a faceless demon for all eternity, he found himself in a more pleasant situation. He was lying on Laura's lap and she was stroking his hair.

He gathered his thoughts a bit and calmed down from the episode.

"Thank you," he finally said, keeping his eyes closed and enjoying the moment.

"You're welcome," Laura said simply.

They both realized that simple was what they needed right now.

The football tackle dummy was surprisingly more comfortable than either of them expected. They eventually shifted positions, each lying on half of the dummy. Their feet were resting on the ground at each end, and the tops of their heads were almost touching in the middle.

Niles could feel Laura's hair curls. They'd bounce occasionally when she talked or nudged her head.

They talked like that for a long time, speaking in a low whisper.

The one thing they could possibly do to hide more would be to stay completely silent and bury themselves in one of the tackle dummy cushions.

However, there was already evidence that the sports equipment had been moved recently. If anyone came looking for them, all they'd have to do was prod the dozen or so dummies and pommel horses to eventually find the couple.

The conversation mostly floated back and forth between the inane and things they might have done if they had lived longer.

"So, you really think you would have gone into Poli-Sci?" Niles asked Laura, transitioning out of another subject.

"I don't know," Laura said. "Really that was just a random thought of what a continuation of Student Council might be. I didn't like Student Council because of a power trip or anything, I liked it because I had an outlet to be creative. I could help plan events and games. It's not like we had any real power beyond that anyway."

They chuckled.

"As Class Treasurer, did they at least let you handle the money?" Niles asked.

"Nah, not really. They did let me contribute to the budget planning beforehand though ... little things that got us more food for our money, or cheaper concession prices."

"Oh really?" Niles asked. "Like what?"

"Well last year, when I was the Sophomore Treasurer, they were wondering what to do with a bunch of leftover chocolate bars from the Valentine's Day sale. Then for the Spring Formal, we were running thin on the dessert budget."

Niles sat up on an elbow.

"The Spring Formal?" he asked. "You mean *our* Spring Formal?"

She shifted onto her elbows too.

"Yup," she said, with a pleased look on her face.

"I don't remember seeing any chocolate bars there," he said, thinking back.

"Well, as you might remember," Laura continued. "The chocolate bars were one of the fundraisers that helped pay for Student Council events in the Spring Semester."

"Oh, I remember," Niles said. He then quoted the tagline. "'Do two good things for the price of one!'"

"Right," Laura said, shaking her head at the cliché. "However, we accidentally ordered way too many of the plain bars this year. Almost no one bought them, so they were just sitting in our storage room. I pointed out to the others that we have two problems that cancel each other out."

Niles finally put the pieces together.

"... but you couldn't just sell bars wrapped in Valentine's Day packaging, so you had to transform them into something else."

They said it together. "Fondue fountain!"

They chuckled.

"That was the best recycled chocolate I've had in a long time," he said.

"That was a really fun night," Laura said, thinking back on it.

"Who was that guy that Anne went with?" Niles asked.

"Oh Craig Allen?" Laura said, before giggling a bit. It was a pity laugh. "I felt so bad for her. I don't know why he agreed to go in the first place."

"Yeah, that's what I didn't get at the time," Niles said. "He totally split on us before we went over to the retro diner."

Laura shrugged.

"Anne's always had a habit of going after guys who weren't interested," she explained. She then rolled her eyes a bit. "... and the same thing happened with Homecoming."

"Yeah, Liam Connelly doesn't exactly scream 'commitment' to me," Niles said, before adding, "not that Barry would have been a better choice. He's got his own issues to work out, obviously. If they weren't at the school to prank *us*, he wouldn't have gotten himself killed."

"I don't know why Anne's so angry with me now though ..." Laura said. "When I finally found her, she looked at me like *I* set off the bomb. It was the weirdest thing."

"You, you didn't ... did you?" Niles asked, pretending to be scared.

"Yes," she said, playing along. "I felt so wronged over the float that the whole school had to pay."

They both laughed.

"For real though," she said. "If I really did want to blow up the school, which I totally wouldn't do, I know I'm creative enough to find a way to do it without getting blown up too."

"So, you think the bomber is still alive?" Niles asked.

"That'd be my guess," Laura said. "Why go through all that effort, especially when it's a gamble on how painful your death could be? The only 'smart' way would be to kill yourself before the bomb went off with like a pistol or knife or something. Otherwise, they probably escaped the blast and are hiding from the Feds in rural Nevada or Arizona."

"Damn," Niles said. "Well, if so, they won't be hiding for long. Something like this is going to have the whole world after them if they're still topside. They'd be lucky if the Feds got to them before some kind of angry mob carried out a 'citizen's arrest'."

Laura looked down toward the mud, dwelling on the other scenarios.

Niles decided to pull her back to something happier.

"So, what was the Prom theme last time?" he asked. "After we had the Spring Formal."

"Uhh, let me think ..." Laura said, shifting her focus. "You see, it's usually just the Junior and Senior reps that plan Prom."

She bit her thumb in contemplation.

"Oh, duh, it was the Mediterranean theme!" she remembered. "'A Night in Venice.'"

"Sounds fun." Niles nodded.

"The whole 'Venice' thing was just marketing," Laura explained. "There was Italian, Greek, Spanish, and French food, and a really generalized selection of music and decorations. They held it in some banquet hall near El Campo."

"What would you have done?" Niles asked, in a relaxed tone. "If things had been different, and *we* made it to Prom, what would you have planned out if they let you pick everything?"

Laura sighed, the emotions swirling within her.

"I would have done a cruise theme," she finally said, looking him in the eyes. "'Love at Sea.'"

Niles smiled.

"It would start out in the Bay; everyone would board the ship in Alameda or Richmond," she began. "It wouldn't be a massive ocean liner, but something cozy, luxurious. It'd be more like a large ferry or yacht.

"The night would be split up into three sections. Each section of the dance would set a mood based on where we were on the trip and what time of day it was."

Niles got more comfortable, watching her run off with it.

"When there was still daylight, we'd be passing lots of greenery around places like Angel Island," Laura continued. "The music would be a lot of pop and rock, really fun stuff. Then we would time things so that we pass under the Golden Gate Bridge right at sunset."

"*Ooooo,*" Niles said, impressed.

"Once we're out into open ocean, well, not open ocean, we'd probably hug the coast and turn around at Point Reyes." Laura was smiling, the details working themselves out as she spun the fantasy. She amended, "once we're past the bridge, the music would shift to classical. It would be peppier stuff at first as everyone ate dinner."

"What kind of dinner?" Niles asked.

"Seafood for sure," she answered, looking embarrassed. "A bit obvious, but the specifics are where it would shine. It wouldn't *just* be lobster; it'd be lobster thermidor. The vegan option could be coconut-mango quinoa. Another meal option could be seared scallops with hazelnuts and tomatoes."

Niles felt like he was getting hungry for the first time since they'd died.

"Once we ate, the music would slow down, it would be a lot of classical dancing."

"Like waltz?" Niles asked.

"Not exclusively," Laura said, "... but that kind of feeling. Only old-fashioned orchestras, very romantic."

"I like it," Niles said.

"Then for the final third of the night, as we're returning to the Bay, the music would shift into the electronic and club stuff," she explained. "It would be completely dark by then, and we'd have the whole San Francisco skyline lit up around the boat. It'd be more modern, cosmopolitan."

"It all sounds magical," Niles said.

It was a pleasant escape from where they were now. The couple wore crumpled, nineteenth century clothes, which were covered in mud and dirt from old sports equipment. The room around them was cold and damp, smelling like used mattresses.

"It would have been, I'd make sure of it," Laura said. "We would have had the greatest night."

Niles looked away from her as he asked something else.

"Laura, why did you agree to go to Spring Formal with me? And not only that, but really spend time with me, rather than disappearing like Craig Allen?"

She smiled. "Are you asking why I like you Niles?"

He looked back at her, not daring to speak.

"When you first wanted to group up with Anne and me for the Shakespeare project," Laura began, "I thought you guys were just looking for a way to boost your grades. I agreed because I felt bad, you always seemed miserable to be there. It didn't look like you enjoyed Mrs. Jefferson's class at all."

Niles blinked; this new information was reframing a lot of those early interactions.

"But as those weeks went on, I think I really started to understand," Laura said. "I expected you two to do the bare minimum amount of work and then disappear when the bell rang every day. I think I was right with

Barry, but not with you. Once we got assigned *Macbeth*, it seemed like you read the whole thing over that first weekend."

"Twice ..." Niles said, blushing.

"You knew more about the story than I did for all those early assignments," she said. "You impressed me."

Niles felt a surge of confidence rush through him.

"You weren't just trying to coast off of Anne and me, you put in your fair share of work, and then some," Laura continued. "I had misjudged you. So then for the rest of February and March, I started reexamining a lot of things you did."

The rush of confidence stopped.

"Like when you finished your section of the daily review, you would lean back in your chair and begin twirling your pen. I used to think that was apathy, but at least where our project was concerned, it wasn't. You had done the work you needed to do, more than your share, and you were able to relax."

Niles wasn't sure what to make of that line.

"You weren't burdened by worrying about the end of the project all the time," Laura explained. "You weren't freaking out about Grade Point Averages, or S.A.T.s, or colleges. You knew how to relax, how to have fun. You could stop and smell the roses when given the opportunity."

Laura sighed.

"I always struggled with that," she said. "As soon as I finished something, it felt like the pressure of the next thing was dropped on my shoulders. I didn't feel that way with you."

Niles folded his arms; she had thought about this more than he expected.

"When you asked me to the Spring Formal, I thought, 'This is a fun, silly dance and Niles is a fun, silly guy.' And it worked out just as I expected. You were a great date and a good friend. Then in all the times we talked over the summer, I could hear the things you cared about too. You could put yourself into a task and do great things and still 'take the scenic route'. You could enjoy life along the way."

Laura frowned slightly.

"You did such an amazing job on the float," she said. "It was everything I could have ever asked of you. When we lost, it was beyond our control. You let that go, you were ready to have a fun, relaxed Homecoming."

Niles put his hand on hers, stroking it with his thumb.

"I couldn't enjoy life on the last day I had of it," Laura said, shaking her head in disappointment.

"You still feel alive to me," Niles said.

She leaned in and they shared a tender kiss.

They lay silent for a moment, still facing each other on the football tackle dummy.

"Can *I* ask *you* something Niles?" Laura said. "Why do you like me?"

Niles took a deep breath, giving himself time to think. He wanted to be honest, but he didn't want to phrase it poorly.

"Well, from the start of the school year, when we had Mrs. Jefferson's class together ..." Niles began. "I first noticed you ... because you were beautiful, easily the prettiest girl in our class."

Laura blushed, looking away.

"And I'm sure that sounds really shallow, but everything else isn't, I swear," Niles added.

She looked back at him, smiling. "No, it's okay Niles. You can tell me I'm pretty whenever you want."

He chuckled, relieved.

"As the year went on," he continued, "I started seeing something in you that most of the *not-as*-pretty girls don't have at all ... passion. You had this zeal, this energy, that you put into everything that you did.

"It seemed like no matter what it was, you did it because you absolutely loved doing it. When there was a reading assignment, you got into it like it was the most important thing ever written. With friends, you talked to them like you were all on a desert island, and they'd be the only friends you'd ever have. With the Student Council, well, it's like what you just did.

"Immediately you could pour all of yourself into some fantastic and wonderful Prom theme idea. I'd die again just to get the chance to take you to that."

Laura sniffled, holding back a tear.

"That's what I really love about you," Niles said. "For you it seemed like life was a grand adventure and you were conquering it one quest at a time. I wanted to join you on those quests."

"Niles ..." she said, looking touched.

SHOONK.

There was a loud metallic sound. Niles and Laura panicked, hopping down behind the tackle dummy.

The old metal door of the storage space was creaking loudly in its frame. One particular sound screeched louder than all the others, as though it was struggling to hold itself together.

It couldn't hold on for long.

Within seconds, the metal latch wretched and twisted out of place until the door popped open. It pulled outward, no longer protecting the two of them.

Niles couldn't hear any voices, but he heard footsteps. At least three pairs of shoes stepped through the mud into the room.

He held up a finger to his mouth. Laura nodded in acknowledgement.

They were sort of near the back of the room, the light from the door didn't shine near them in particular. If they were lucky, the group wouldn't look too hard and just leave.

They heard kicking as the box of old Gatorade bottles was disturbed.

After a moment of silence, where Niles thought they might have made it, they heard one of them speak.

"Come on guys, we see you," a flat voice said.

The two continued to stay still, hoping the guy was bluffing.

That is when a steak knife duct-taped to the end of a metal table leg dropped down next to Niles' head.

He jumped, pulling Laura behind him as they backed into the concrete wall.

It was the senior guy from Blaire and Andrei's limo group. Behind him was Marcus Johnson, holding a tire iron. Finally, at the door was Something Clark, Jennifer Maxwell's boyfriend, holding a crowbar.

"What do you want with us?" Laura asked, irate.

"We're trying to find the bomber," Marcus said matter-of-factly. "Everyone's staying in the gym until we do."

"How come you're not in the gym?" Niles asked him.

Marcus gave one chuckle, then turned to Paxton. "Bring 'em."

"We didn't do it!" Laura exclaimed as Niles backed them away from Paxton's knife.

"Then I'm sure you'll be found innocent," Paxton said.

"What if we refuse to go?" Niles asked, testing their resolve.

Paxton stopped advancing, then turned to look at Marcus.

Marcus gave a subtle nod.

In a swift motion, Paxton shifted forward, plunging the knife into Niles' shoulder.

He screamed in pain and Laura screamed in horror.

"Paxton!" the Clark guy yelled from the door, apparently not expecting the attack either.

Paxton pulled the knife out. A trickle of powder poured from the hole, like he had stabbed a large bag of flour.

Niles pressed the wound with his right hand. His left arm felt weak; he couldn't lift it if he wanted to. Every time he shifted his left fingers, he could feel a jolt of pain pass through the throbbing shoulder.

"Are you okay?!" Laura asked, her hand on his good arm.

Niles looked back at Paxton. He had this deadpan expression on his face. Niles was afraid they'd start stabbing Laura too if the two of them fought back any more.

He had never been stabbed like that when he was alive, but the pain sure felt like he imagined it would. Even without blood, it was agonizing. He clenched his jaw to hold back any more screams.

There was no way he could fight off the three jocks, and they couldn't outrun them either. It's not like they had anyplace to run to anyway.

"Alright, we'll go," Laura spoke first. "Just don't hurt him anymore."

Laura kept a comforting hand on his back as they followed Marcus. Paxton walked behind them, the lance weapon still gripped in both hands.

As they passed through the door, they got a better look at Clark. He wore a very apologetic expression.

Laura sneered at him.

Once they were outside, Niles noticed Jennifer Maxwell and some other girl. They both looked equally horrified. They must have heard Laura's scream. They could probably see the wound too. Niles' hand was still covered in quite a bit of dust.

There was a third girl, but she looked much less upset.

Next to the three of them was Jimmy, the party house guy.

Without really thinking, Niles said the first thing that came to mind.

"Your party sucks." He groaned.

That seemed to cut Jimmy deep ... probably not as deep as a steak knife though.

Niles and Laura stayed silent the rest of the walk, keeping their eyes to the ground as they followed Marcus.

***

Andrei was very happy to see Elise awake and stable again. He needed Elise on her feet so they could all run as fast as possible when they needed to.

If the four of them could just get back to the Choir & Drama room, they could seal themselves inside.

Of course, Andrei wasn't sure how well their door blocking measures would hold up to the newly revealed weapon.

The situation was getting worse by the hour since their rude awakening that morning.

Now Joe Torelli had them all trapped in the gym wielding a double-barreled shotgun with a bandolier full of shells. A lot of people were beginning to think that he was the bomber.

Clearly Joe was planning on taking a more personal approach if the bomb hadn't gone off. He probably didn't know electronics at all and had no faith in the sparking device to actually work. It looked like he'd cobbled it together out of a toy car and a battery from some auto shop.

After failing to escape his own bomb, Torelli had now decided to torture them all in the afterlife, using his petty Cheka to enforce this show trial.

Andrei looked down at the white tennis shoes on Blaire's feet. Something she had said kept coming back to him.

"Well, I feel like I can run now ... if I have to."

Those words haunted him, almost as much as something else she had said not much earlier.

"Forget the purse, we need to go now!"

Somehow, Blaire knew the explosion was coming, but she didn't realize it until it was too late.

Andrei still remembered the expression on her face when it came to her.

They had just shared the most romantic moment in either of their lives, and all signs were pointing toward more to come. His mind was so removed from danger that when her countenance dropped it felt like whiplash.

Fear gripped her so suddenly and so overwhelmingly that he couldn't even comprehend her urging to leave until he sensed the wall rumble beneath his hand.

Even if she had slipped out of her heels, or he carried her, and they ran at full speed toward the exit, they probably wouldn't have even reached the glass doors before the fire swallowed them.

Andrei didn't understand what short and impotent clairvoyance Blaire had been granted, but from the genuine change in her expression, he didn't think she was the bomber.

Even if she was, it didn't look like she intended for either of them to die.

With Elise's PTSD somewhat under control, the main focus of their attention had shifted back to the actual show trial itself.

Torelli had decided that Mr. Wallace was one of the prime suspects. At the very least, he was the first one in their custody, so he was given the "privilege" of being the opening act.

Andrei didn't know the Villa Vista faculty too well; he had only been here for a few months after all. However, Mr. Wallace was one of the first adults he met and he had a rather long conversation with him.

It wasn't too common for a student to transfer to the school in their senior year, so Wallace sat him down to establish a baseline of his "hopes and dreams". Of course, he meant that as reference for college and career counseling which would happen in the coming months.

Andrei had given him a quick rundown of his background. His sisters had decided to pursue Business and Political Science majors respectively, but he was really interested in music. He explained their father's career and current work with the San Francisco Symphony.

Mr. Wallace had been ecstatic, more than happy to tout Villa Vista's performing arts program. He explained the late Lawrence Murphy and the contributions he'd made to the school's remodeled theatre hall.

Wallace also made sure that Andrei was signed up for the Choir & Drama class ... the place he would end up meeting Blaire.

Andrei felt her leg beneath his hand. She was wearing the P.E. shorts, so he was able to rest it on bare skin just above her knee. Her hand was on top of his. They had been like that since Elise woke up.

So much of Andrei's final days would have been different if he had not been in that class. A small realization had crossed his mind that they probably wouldn't have been his final days.

He and his dad lived fifteen miles from the school. There was no way they would have been harmed at all during the explosion if Andrei hadn't gone to the dance.

Blaire might not have gone to the dance either. If they still ended up together, it would have been with a different backstory entirely, finding each other in the tragedy of loss.

Probably three quarters of the Choir & Drama kids died in the explosion. They were on average more outgoing than the student body at large, by nature of being performers. Mrs. Donovan was at the dance too. She also perished. The surviving Choir & Drama kids might not even number two dozen. Would they have found solace together in such a small group?

Probably not, he decided. He and Blaire wouldn't have really known each other at all. If they had not ended up meeting the way they did, their paths would only end up crossing at a few horrible intersections, when the survivors of Villa Vista High School would need to gather for an event or memorial.

Andrei looked down at her, her dark hair danced from left to right as she said something to Elise.

They had essentially chosen to die by going to Homecoming together. Would he have made the same choice if given the knowledge beforehand?

Maybe he would.

Blaire was granted some kind of foresight and she was right there next to him against the wall. If she knew about the bomb, she probably would have stayed far away, at least for her own sake. Did he really mean that much to her?

Even if she helped plan the bombing, but got the timing wrong, was he really worth dancing that close to death with ... just for the sake of one night?

Andrei shook his head a bit. It was ridiculous of course. Blaire didn't blow up the school. It wouldn't just be for Andrei's sake; she would have gotten Elise and Rafael far away from there beforehand.

He turned his focus on the stage again.

Mr. Wallace hadn't said much of anything, and now they were all looking at the bottom of his foot.

Before Andrei could really catch up to what was going on, the doors of the gymnasium opened again and two of Joe's Cheka walked in with large bathroom mirrors held between them.

They were facing each other, so no one could see the reflections yet.

These were the next batch of props they'd brought in after the stack of chairs from the Murphy Center.

One of the two guys was a basketball player named Jordan. The second guy was the Jaguars' football kicker, Devall. The kicker also had a bag of some kind slung over his back.

The smaller basketball player, Eric, the guy with the notebook, pulled down four of the chairs. He set them up as stands for the mirrors to sit on.

When they pulled the two mirrors apart, everyone was shocked by what they saw.

Bright orange flames sat just behind the glass as though it were a window into some kind of metal foundry.

Joe Torelli seemed thrilled by the reveal.

They set the mirrors up to face Wallace, duct-taping the backs so they fit together at the seam.

The whole gymnasium glowed orange now because of the ambient light pouring through.

Blaire squeezed Andrei's hand in fear ... it was his right hand.

Andrei thought about how those were the same flames which had completely seared away all the skin and muscle from that hand, leaving little more than charred bones.

That is when Devall set down the bag he had slung over his back, revealing half a dozen short spears made out of table legs and steak knives. They seemed to have a few loose steak knives too.

Andrei squeezed Blaire's leg. They looked at each other, the same worried expression passing between them.

Raf and Elise seemed to shift uncomfortably at the sight, Raf rolling his shoulders and Elise tucking her hands between her thighs.

Andrei squeezed his left fist, then opened it flat.

He heard Katya's voice echo clearly in his head. It was as if she were right in front of him.

"When you strike at your opponent, you don't aim for them, you aim behind them, through them. If you have to fight, then you have to treat every move like your hand or leg is going to break them in half. You need to give those hits that kind of power if you want to stop them from hitting back."

It wasn't exactly formal training, but enough years of being Katya's sparring partner had taught him some moves, making up a well of experience to draw from.

If it came to that though, he would need to get a hold of one of those lance weapons.

Torelli and the subdued guidance counselor had a dialogue for a while, but Mr. Wallace was saying very little.

Eventually, the shotgun-wielding maniac grew unsatisfied with the old man's lack of cooperation. After a line of questioning regarding his foot, Torelli ended up taking one of the loose steak knives and stabbing him with it.

The crowd audibly groaned, but Wallace seemed to grit his teeth and bear it. Maybe it wasn't as painful as it looked?

Enough kids had tried to kill themselves in the last twenty-four hours that pain wasn't exactly debilitating. They had all been forcibly resurrected and now sat in the same audience.

Blaire squeezed Andrei's hand harder when Torelli put a second knife into Wallace's exposed foot.

Wallace was beginning to look like a Voodoo doll.

His lack of outward suffering was a bit disarming. None of this seemed real to most in the audience. The lack of blood added to that perception. Some dust poured from the two wounds like sand being poured through a sieve, but otherwise he looked unphased.

Questioning continued like that for a while longer and Wallace gave a few more curt or basic responses. He really wasn't fighting for himself at all. It almost seemed like he wanted to keep getting stabbed.

In between all of this cross-examination, the group of Cheka led by the sophomore couple returned with some various students who had been hiding elsewhere in the school.

One guy in particular with greasy black hair had his mouth duct-taped shut. He seemed to be the most scared of all those brought into the visiting team bleachers.

But while he was the most crazed and worried, the Freshman Class Princess, Ellen Taylor, was the most despondent. After hearing the story from Raf about what he and Elise had seen, Andrei wasn't surprised.

He knew almost nothing about the girl, except for her fall during the Spirit Week game last week. Since then, a good portion of the school were now calling her "Mudbra". Far too many of them were doing it to her face.

Ellen's head was hung low as the two football players basically carried her into the gym and placed her down on the other bleachers.

She said and did nothing except sit limply like a doll while they tied her up with the duct tape.

Elise took a very deep breath when she saw the girl brought onto the court, but otherwise was able to stomach the sight.

The girl's visceral wounds were all healed. At least from a distance, her arms seemed fine and her thighs were hidden under the dress. The football goons must have also confiscated the X-Acto knife she'd damaged herself with.

Raf seemed to think she was the bomber, based on the way he described what happened. To Andrei, it mostly sounded like he was angry that she had upset Elise.

Torelli didn't seem keen on interviewing any of these students yet, his focus was very much on Wallace. He was also waiting for the sophomore couple's search team to retrieve the other adult.

One of the girls from the audience went up to Greg and Chelsea, apparently asking to join them in the recovery for some reason. She seemed to have a personal interest.

Torelli had said a few times that people could speak in the defense of the accused if they so desired. No one in the crowd had taken him up on that offer until then.

At least where Wallace was concerned, no one was quick to come to his defense. It was very strange, and very much stood out, how he and Melkonian were the only two adults to appear in this place.

Andrei felt like he couldn't say anything either. He barely knew any of these people.

The only ones he had come to know very well were sitting next to him. He hated the fact that he couldn't even feel certain that Blaire wasn't involved in the bombing.

What could he say for Wallace? He didn't have an alibi for him.

After a while longer, Melkonian was finally brought in. Perhaps as could be expected, he had a lot to say. He put on his best announcer's voice to chastise the crowd.

Andrei found it hard to disagree with his indictments, but he knew there were only two ways to survive Soviet-style proceedings like this. You either escape someplace out of their reach, as Andrei's family had done a century ago … or you keep your head down until they destroy themselves, as the Communists had done just a few years before he was born.

One benefit of Melkonian's pleas for sanity though was the way he finally spurred Wallace to testify. Of course, Melkonian had to take a knife to the back in the process.

That knife actually sounded like it hurt, quite a bit, and the crowd were disquieted.

In order to save Melkonian from more suffering, Wallace revealed something which changed the nature of the investigation.

He claimed that the construction drawings for all the school remodels had been stolen from Vice Principal Fletcher's office. In his opinion, that was proof that not only was the bomber among them, but there was some evidence of their identity in the pages of the blueprints.

"Could that be true?" Blaire whispered to Andrei.

"It would make sense as to how they got into the gym," he supposed.

"That could be real proof," Blaire said. "We could actually find out who killed us."

Andrei shifted, putting his arm over her shoulder.

Most of the students seemed convinced.

Wallace's own emotional pleas really cemented his testimony. He tearfully promised that he would have never harmed any of the students, while at the same time admitting his own past thoughts of suicide.

Torelli and his cronies spoke for a long time, deliberating on this revelation.

As they did, the other group of Cheka returned with two more kids.

Andrei thought he might have seen them once or twice in the same hallway as Blaire's locker, so they were probably juniors. They were wearing black shirts and sweatpants for some reason, which immediately made them look suspicious.

They began whimpering when they saw the wall of fire in the mirrors.

Torelli suddenly seemed keen to interview them, satisfied by what he'd gotten out of Wallace and Melkonian.

One thing that surprised Andrei was how little anyone seemed to know about them. Torelli addressed the crowd saying the same thing. It was only then that someone stepped forward to accuse them.

"Anne, no!" the heavier kid screamed. "It's not true, we didn't do it!"

As Anne began to speak, the group which brought the two kids in left the gymnasium again, apparently continuing their search.

"Who's this?" Andrei whispered to Blaire.

"Anne Kirkpatrick," she said. "She's a junior, I had a few classes with her."

"These two are Barry Owens and Melvin Mueller," Anne announced to everyone, motioning to the heavy and skinny kids respectively.

"Okay," Torelli said, running with it. He then addressed the two. "Why the hell are you dressed like that?"

"We were jogging by the school," Melvin spoke up.

"No. No you weren't," Torelli retorted, poking Barry's stomach with the barrel of the shotgun.

"They were probably putting that thing in place," Anne said, pointing at the electrical device.

"How exactly do you know them again?" Torelli asked, turning his questioning back on her.

Anne answered him and the crowd as a whole.

"I was stuck in an English class group with that loser," she said, pointing to Barry. "After he didn't get the hint, I had to finally, openly tell him that I wasn't interested. Ever since then they must have been planning this little stunt to get back at me."

"No one gives a shit about you," Melvin spat.

That got the crowd chuckling a bit.

"Excuse me," Anne said, her knuckles on her hips. "I was at the dance with Liam Connelly."

She pointed to the crowd.

"She was?" Andrei asked Blaire.

Blaire shrugged in response. Anne's name hadn't come up at all in the nearly two hours they were talking with Liam.

The audience turned to where she was pointing.

Liam was sitting next to Melissa Levitt in the bleachers. He said nothing in response to the callout.

"You got anything to add, pretty boy?" Torelli asked him.

"No, I don't." He didn't make eye contact with either Torelli or Anne. "I don't know anything, man. I've got nothing to say one way or another."

"Fair enough," Torelli said, turning back to Anne.

"Do *you* have anything else to say?" he pressed her.

She looked livid.

"What else *is* there to say?!" she exclaimed. "They're a couple of loveless and dateless losers that must have done all this as their very own Columbine!"

The crowd rumbled in discussion.

"You clearly weren't at the dance," Torelli said to them, motioning to their dead bodies in the mirrors. They were wearing the same all black jogging getups that they still currently had on.

"We didn't blow up the school!" Barry yelled again, before continuing in a more level tone. "We were going to set off the fire alarm."

"What?" Torelli asked.

"The fire alarm," Barry continued. "I was going to trip the panel, so you would all have to evacuate the party until the fire department arrived."

"Well, that would have been really convenient," Torelli said. "Too bad the opposite happened."

"I had no idea about any of that!" Barry said.

"Hold on," Greg Henshaw asked from the side of the group. "Why were you going to trip the fire alarm?"

Barry sighed, looking more embarrassed than afraid.

"Anne did reject me, long before the dance, and I was upset about it," he admitted. Then, with more anger, he continued, "But despite the fact that she's a self-centered bitch who wants to make everything about herself-"

"Fuck you," Anne interjected, still standing on the edge of the court.

"-it wasn't about her," Barry said. "It was about my friend, or former friend, and how everything *did* work out for him."

"So Niles was involved!" Anne declared, as though she had just been proven right about something.

"Who the hell is Niles?" Torelli asked.

"Oh no ..." Blaire whispered to Andrei.

The rest of the crowd didn't seem to recognize the name.

"Niles Koh," Anne elaborated. "Another junior, like us ... but more specifically, another *freak*, like *them*!"

"Then why wasn't he stashed away with these two?" Torelli asked her.

"Because he actually convinced some stupid girl to go to Homecoming with him," Anne said with disdain. Before they could ask, she continued. "Her name is Laura Nakano. As you can see, they aren't here."

Laura Nakano was a more familiar name. After a quick set of glances, the crowd seemed to confirm that she was absent.

Andrei and Blaire looked at each other, asking the same question without speaking.

"Are they hidden well enough?"

"Where'd they run off to?" Torelli asked Barry and Melvin.

"There isn't a 'they'," Melvin said, with some perverse pleasure in his voice. "She dumped his ass at the dance."

Andrei and Blaire glanced at each other, then down at Liam and Melissa, wondering if they'd say anything.

They both remained silent.

"Well, they'll turn up sooner or later," Torelli said with confidence. "First, why don't you tell us how you were going to 'set off the fire alarm'."

"Yeah," Chelsea Morton asked. "Why didn't you just pull one of the levers by a door?"

Barry went on to explain that he wanted to slow down the alarm to the fire department so everyone would have to stay outside of the building longer.

He was diving into a lot of technical discussion about circuits and bypasses which made things look worse for him rather than better.

If these guys really were friends with Niles, they were pretty bad to be associated with right now.

Blaire turned to Andrei, speaking low enough that even Raf and Elise couldn't hear them.

"Anne used to be Laura's best friend," she said. "They would always hang out together, I don't get why she's so upset with her."

"Do you really think Niles could be involved with the bombing?" Andrei asked her.

"I don't know," her eyes drifted. "I really don't know him at all. I used to think his name was 'Neil'."

At one point, Barry seemed to realize talking about electronics was a bad idea. He moved on to the part of their story where he was an idiot and couldn't find the fire alarm panel in the first place.

It was a better defense to take, but it was already too late in the minds of many.

Andrei was starting to feel convinced too. A couple of obsessive geeks with non-existent social or romantic lives really fit well into the idea of bombing a school dance. All the red flags were there.

One thing he didn't believe though was that Niles and Laura were connected. Niles seemed like the kind of guy who went all in on asking out a girl he really liked and won the hand. He was a success story, admirable.

Thanks to a little help from Andrei and Blaire, the "happy ending" was working out after all. If they weren't dead, Andrei and Raf could have taken him out on a guys' night to celebrate.

Hell, if none of them were dead, there were so many better things Andrei would be doing right now.

It was Monday morning; it would have been a regular start to the week at Villa Vista High School. One of the AV kids would be kicking off the morning announcements and hoping everyone had a *very very* wonderful Homecoming.

Andrei probably would have waited for Blaire in the parking lot. Their parking spaces weren't too far from each other.

No matter how the afterparty went - which was something *else* he'd rather be thinking about right now - he would be kissing her and they'd be walking in through the front doors hand in hand.

He'd be avoiding nosy text messages from Katya, bugging him for details.

His dad, overall not very intrusive, would have asked some normal questions on Sunday about how the night was, then moved on. Andrei would have probably told him more than Katya, at least at first, because their dad wouldn't extrapolate the unspoken things.

Unfortunately, Katya had a way of digging the real answers out of Andrei one way or another. If things went well with Blaire, *really well*, there was a chance Katya could have eventually gotten the full truth out of him. After that, it would have only been a matter of time before Anastasia was texting him too.

Her line of questioning would be more motherly, a role she'd embraced all too well in recent years. He would be hearing a lot about "safety" and "protection". Every Health class lesson would be custom-curated specifically for him by one of the few people who knew him the best.

A cold splash of reality dampened the scenario Andrei was imagining when he heard Torelli yell about something.

What was he doing here in some high school hell with a 'roided-out quarterback swinging a shotgun at everyone?

He'd give anything to have his sisters pry and nag him about his teenage romance. Even to just hear them yell at him, and nothing else, would be so much better than this deafening silence of the grave.

Andrei pulled out his phone. There were no new messages, of course. He opened up the texting application anyway.

He still had a single reply from Katya highlighted:

September 28th · 1:38 p.m.

Ooh, she's cute ... congrats
Andrei! You better be on your
best behavior, treat that girl
right.

Andrei stared at the message for several long seconds.
Blaire must have noticed, because she put a hand on his arm.
"I miss my brothers too," she whispered in somber reflection.
He closed the phone app.
Blaire rested her head on his shoulder and he leaned his head against hers.

Of course Andrei would treat her right. If things were different, they would have seen it for themselves. His sisters would have quickly come to adore her.

In fact, Andrei would likely have had the opposite problem. There was a chance Katya would be able to start pulling gossip of their love life out of Blaire.

She wouldn't have divulged such things on purpose, but Blaire was not yet familiar with how crafty Katya could be.

She spoke three languages and she had a silver tongue with all of them.

Before Andrei could dive into another daydream of what could have been, a loud sound boomed through the gym.

The door was pulled open by Marcus Johnson.

Niles and Laura were being marched in behind him.

TWENTY-ONE

DIES IRAE

BOB MELKONIAN AND RICK WALLACE WERE dropped unceremoniously back onto the bleachers, while Torelli moved on to torment Barry Owens and Melvin Mueller.

What Bob didn't expect though, was how personally vindictive Anne Kirkpatrick was about the situation. She really seemed convinced that these two, in conjunction with Niles Koh and Laura Nakano, were responsible for the bombing.

Rick was still very emotional after Bob had finally gotten him to speak up to the kids.

Bob wasn't sure if he was serious about the evidence of the bomber's identity. He leaned closer to Rick, speaking low.

"Is all that true ... about the construction drawings?" Bob asked.

Rick took a deep breath, recentering himself.

"Every word," he replied. "Barbara looked at those drawings almost every day. If they're missing, that means something."

"That's insane," Bob said. "Who was the contractor again?"

"MCL," Rick said, before examining his own thoughts deeper, "Myers, Cline, & Leitheiser."

Bob's shoulders slouched. He didn't know kids by any of those names.

"It's a nation-wide company," Rick said. "They're probably based out of Delaware or something. I can't imagine anyone high up enough to have their name on the signs would even live out here."

"They'd have to steal a lot more than drawings," Bob agreed. "They'd need to take every sign and every photo someone took of the signs, as well as hope that people forgot an acronym like 'MCL'."

"It's gotta be something deeper," Rick said. "If their name is on a single page in the packet for one reason or another, that would be enough of a clue."

"Probably more than one place," Bob said. "Otherwise, why not just rip out the one page, not draw attention? Removing the whole packet obviously caused you to notice."

Rick shrugged through his duct-tape bindings.

"Unless another packet turns up, it looks like they'll get away with it," Rick said, before referencing his earlier definition of Hell. "Not knowing is part of the suffering."

Bob felt like he collapsed inward a bit. His own duct-tape bindings seemed looser as he turned sunken and hollow.

"I literally can't believe it," Bob said, a quiver in his voice.

Rick turned to him.

"If you're right, and the killer is here, and they took the construction drawings," Bob went on. "Then that means the killer is one of these kids."

Rick's gaze fell to the floor.

"Kids, Rick!" he exclaimed, though few could hear them over the theatrics of Torelli's yelling and Barry Owens' pleas in his own defense.

"Maybe a few are eighteen," Bob continued, "but some are as young as fourteen."

He scanned the students in the opposite bleachers, trying to guess the ages of those he didn't explicitly remember.

"The average is probably sixteen," Bob decided, with more quiet horror in his voice. "Rick, how could a sixteen-year-old do something so monstrous?"

Rick had nothing to say.

There had been a few high-profile massacres at schools in recent years. In most cases, the weapons of choice were firearms.

Rick's eyes drifted over to the small device sitting on a chair in the middle of the basketball court.

Unless Torelli was the killer, so far, no other student was found to have brought a gun on campus. Even then, no one had died from bullet wounds. The electrical sparking mechanism functioned as it was intended.

Perhaps if it didn't, Torelli meant to set off the natural gas with the shotgun. That would have been easy enough considering how saturated the gym must have been.

Motive is where things got muddier though.

Torelli seemed 100% sincere, and unapologetic, that he had murdered his father with that shotgun. From what Rick could remember of Salvatore Torelli, it wasn't exactly surprising.

Salvatore had been irritable in every situation Rick ever met him face-to-face. Half of those situations were when Joe had done something successful, such as winning playoff games, clutching a victory in overtime, or breaking Marin City High's impassible defense last year.

Salvatore always had an excuse for being less than thrilled. To him, these little victories were like celebrating at the end of the first quarter. The game was far from over and Sal was never satisfied.

Rick couldn't imagine what that was like behind closed doors, how much worse things must have been.

Perhaps that was another failing of his. He should have tried to gather more evidence, more justifiable cause to get Child Protective Services involved.

Did Torelli blame all of them for his suffering the same way he blamed Salvatore?

Despite all of the school massacres in the recent decades, the one that Rick still compared everything to was the one that happened in his own youth.

He was in his late twenties, his kids Georgie and Susan were still very young, and Mary was pregnant with their second son, Alex.

Rick had just completed his Master's Degree and credentials courses in counseling students, so he was only a year or two removed from college campus life.

That is when one late summer afternoon, horrific news broke of a mass shooting which had taken place from a tower building at the University of Texas.

Once the story came out, nearly twenty people had been murdered, including the perpetrator's wife and mother.

A number of reasons were given following the investigation into the events. Some blamed drug-induced psychosis for his rampage, others blamed the Marine Corps, trying to tie it into the culture of violence and politics associated with the escalating Vietnam War. The most disturbing explanation was one the killer himself suggested.

In one of his suicide notes, he requested an autopsy. He claimed a medical anomaly of some kind existed in his head which was filling his mind with violent and impulsive thoughts.

When doctors performed the requested surgery, they found a "pecan-sized tumor" inside the killer's brain.

It could never be fully established what effect the tumor actually had on his mental state. It could very well have been nothing chemical at all. He may simply have felt the anomaly and projected his dark and evil thoughts onto it as a way to excuse his own actions.

But what if he was right to some degree?

Several Christian denominations, and other religions, strictly police the use of alcohol and drugs among their flocks. The Bible was clear in its distinction of regular use of certain substances and crossing a threshold into "drunkenness" or "debauchery". Where that threshold was could very well be different for everyone.

Many recovering alcoholics Rick knew had decided that one drop was too many. In some cases, they had found God in their sobriety.

What could be said of them if they weren't imbibing by choice?

What if one of these otherwise innocent Villa Vista High students was being drip-fed feelings of anger and hatred by some biological malformation? Like a dam of poison, it could have been leaking into their thoughts until finally bursting one day.

Would that wash them of moral culpability?

No.

In the same way not every clinically-diagnosed sociopath or psychopath becomes a serial killer, that student's condition would not separate them from their sins.

Whether someone was pulling a trigger to fire a rifle or pressing a button to detonate a building-sized bomb, that action required a conscious decision. The soul is always given the choice. Unfortunately for so many hundreds at Villa Vista High School, that soul had chosen evil.

Rick came out of his contemplation, seeing that Torelli was still questioning Barry Owens.

His eyes turned to the others sitting on the visiting team bleachers with him and Bob.

All of these kids had struggles of one kind or another, whether or not they had ever come to seek help from Rick. What could have pushed one over the edge into doing something so heinous?

His gaze fell down to the student sitting right next to him.

Ellen Taylor had not moved the entire time she had been in there.

Rick could still vividly remember the conversation he'd had with her and Barbara Fletcher.

Bob must have seen him glancing at her, because he spoke up.

"You should talk to her," he encouraged.

"I'm sure she's heard enough from me," Rick answered, turning toward the court.

"She needs your help now more than ever!" Bob said, a little louder.

"I couldn't save her before," Rick said. "There's no way I can save her now."

"You might as well try," Bob replied, a judgmental tone creeping into his words.

Rick turned an eye to him.

"You can feel as guilty as you want for all the sins you committed," Bob said. "I'm sure you felt that way in life too. Nothing has changed. Your whole career, every kid you've ever helped happened *after* what you did. Those students' lives were improved anyway. The only sin you're committing now is giving up on those kids."

Rick looked away from him, feelings of guilt beginning to reverse their course.

He turned to Ellen Taylor, leaning a little bit even though his arms were tied up.

She had been sitting so motionless for the last hour, he wasn't even sure if she was sleeping or not.

"Ellen, can you hear me?" he asked her, in a voice loud enough that only she could hear.

"Ellen, please talk to me," he said again. "I don't know if there's anything I can do to help you feel better, but I want to try. I want you to know that I'm here to listen, just like before."

Rick noticed her head dip a bit. She seemed to have heard him, even if she didn't directly respond.

"Like I said to the others," Rick continued. "I'm not the one who did this to all of us. I hope that you believe that at least."

She didn't move.

"I don't think you did it either," he said, extending the same benefit of the doubt. "Whatever pain you were feeling before and whatever pain you are feeling now is real. If you had turned that pain into anger and used it against everyone else, you would not be sitting like that. You'd probably be wearing a fake expression of innocence or happiness, probably be sitting in the other bleachers."

She seemed to breathe a little deeper than normal.

"I don't expect you to open up to me without reciprocation," Rick said.

He paused, gathering his thoughts.

"I'll tell you why I'm down here," he began, giving a condensed version of his own story. "I've only told this to Mr. Mel until now. When I was young, still in college, I cheated on my sweet wife in the very first year we were married."

Ellen didn't visibly respond.

"I kept that secret for over fifty years," he said. "My whole life amounted to a lie, at least where our marriage was concerned. I never confessed my sin to her. If she had known, I wouldn't have expected her forgiveness."

She continued to sit motionless, her hair hanging like a curtain, covering the totality of her face.

"That is my deepest, darkest secret," Rick summarized. "It's the reason why I'm here. No matter what you think you've done, I promise you that it isn't as bad.

"You're a sweet, young girl. You didn't deserve what happened during Spirit Week, you didn't deserve whatever might have happened in the years before, and you certainly didn't deserve what happened to you at Homecoming."

Rick turned to face the basketball court again. He'd said all that he could, opened every door of conversation he could think of. He hoped she would open up to him eventually, especially before she was put at the mercy of Torelli and the other kids.

As the minutes passed, she remained silent.

Torelli continued his interrogation of Barry Owens, with Melvin Mueller speaking up only intermittently. He seemed to just be an accessory in whatever Barry was actually doing at the school on Saturday night.

That's when Marcus Johnson and his group of varsity players returned to the gymnasium. They had found and captured Niles Koh and Laura Nakano.

The kids met Rick's eyes as they were marched onto the basketball court.

They all shared the same defeated expression.

***

Blaire watched as Niles and Laura walked into the middle of the gymnasium.

For a moment, they were frightened by the fires in the mirrors, but they looked much more afraid of Torelli specifically.

Anne Kirkpatrick was there to celebrate the capture, even before the quarterback.

"Well, that didn't take long," she said.

"Anne?!" Laura asked, surprised to see her among the organizers. "You're part of this?"

"I never wanted to be!" Anne shouted, sounding more acrimonious than Laura was. "You were the one who got involved with this loser and brought a curse on all of us!"

Niles stepped in front of Laura.

"Anne, I don't know what your deal is," he began. "You can hate me all you want, but I did *not* blow up the school."

Paxton Bannister grabbed his arm when he stepped too close to Anne and pulled him away from both girls.

When Laura tried to get to him, Amanda Burke held her back.

"What the hell is with her?" Blaire asked Elise.

"I don't know," Elise said, disgusted by what she saw.

"How do you girls know her again?" Andrei asked them.

"Middle school," Elise answered. "It started with a class group or something ... Amanda was nicer back then."

"Then she became *Ms. Nouveau Populaire*," Blaire said, simmering.

"A lot of boys asked her to the Spring Formal in our freshmen year," Elise explained. "Ever since then, it's kind of gone to her head and she's been more focused on looks and status. I really didn't think she'd get involved in something like this though."

Joe Torelli approached the couple while Paxton and Amanda held them six feet apart.

"So, you're the third Musketeer?" Torelli said to Niles. He waved his free hand over the outfit. "You do look like you fit the part."

Niles gave him a hard stare.

"Where'd you find them?" Torelli turned to Marcus.

"Under the visiting team bleachers," Marcus said. "There's a little storage room in the back."

"There is?" Torelli asked him. "I didn't know that."

"He's the quarterback and he didn't know that?" Blaire whispered to Andrei.

He chuckled.

"It must have been locked," Torelli said, processing the information. "Coach wouldn't leave something like that unsecured, no matter how obscure or hidden it was."

Torelli looked at them.

"One of you must have a key," he concluded.

Paxton raised his lance to Niles again.

"No!" Laura yelled.

"Turn out your pockets," Paxton demanded.

Niles did so, giving him the same look of hate that he gave Torelli.

Torelli looked at Mr. Wallace sitting on the bleachers.

"Take off your shoes and socks too," he said.

Niles complied, showing them to be totally empty, including the bottom of his feet.

"Your shoes too," Torelli said to Laura.

She did so, slipping off the sneakers and socks. There were no keys to be found anywhere.

"We'll have to search them," Torelli concluded.

"No need," Anne Kirkpatrick spoke up again. "I bet I know where it is."

She walked up to Laura, facing her almost nose to nose.

"How could you do this?" Laura asked her.

Anne said nothing. Instead, she reached down Laura's dress.

There was a stunned gasp from several people, including Laura, who was horrified by the violation. It was happening in front of over a hundred students and two adults.

After a moment of fishing, Anne pulled her hand out. A small silver key was pinched between her thumb and index finger. Laura's cheeks turned red as she hid her face from the crowd.

"They used to be friends?" Andrei asked Blaire.

Blaire said nothing, but Elise added her own take.

"I would have kneed her so hard in the groin." She shook her head.

Raf chuckled next to her, imagining the scenario.

"What is it?" Torelli asked the sophomore couple.

They walked up. Greg held the keychain they'd taken from Mr. Wallace while Chelsea took the key from Anne.

"It looks closest to the one for the Vice Principal's office," Chelsea concluded.

Torelli looked over at Mr. Wallace.

"Well, that's one mystery solved," the quarterback observed.

He plucked the key out of Chelsea's hand before she could add it back onto the keychain.

Torelli pocketed it.

Niles looked furious about what they'd done to Laura.

"For all we know," Anne spoke up again. "They used that key to set up the bomb before the dance."

"That's not true!" Wallace shouted from the bleachers. "Torelli was right, I gave that to them just this morning, so they could hide when the shooting started."

Torelli looked down at the Browning Citori, checking to make sure it was fully loaded.

Paxton Bannister still gripped Niles' arm. He held the lance in the other.

"So, these two were getting the key for those two?" Paxton asked, pointing the weapon at the couple, then Barry and Melvin.

"Niles wasn't with us at all!" Melvin Mueller yelled from his chair. "Barry and I have barely talked to him in months. We were there to mess with him and that girl, nothing else. If they blew up the gym, we didn't know about it!"

"Fuck off Melvin!" Niles yelled at him.

Torelli looked over at Laura. "You were at the dance together?"

"Yes," she said, pushing past her embarrassment. "We were having a great time."

"No, you weren't," Anne corrected, her arms crossed.

Laura didn't look at or acknowledge her.

Blaire and Andrei glanced at each other. She was right to some extent.

"The annoying kid said you two broke up at the dance," Torelli added, pointing the shotgun in Melvin's direction.

Laura's face looked guilty, she turned down toward the floor.

"We just had a small fight," Niles interjected. "We patched things up afterwards."

"After what?" Anne asked. "After you blew up the school?"

"We did not blow up the school!" Laura yelled, to the crowd more so than Anne.

"Is that true?" Torelli asked Anne. "They're back together?"

"I guess." Anne shrugged. "I saw them talking in the ballroom earlier with Liam and Melissa ... and two other students."

"Oh God, no ..." Blaire whispered, a chill running down her spine. The same sense of foreboding crept over her as when she heard the whistling noise in the wall.

Anne turned to the crowd, quickly spotting them.

"With them," she said, pointing, "the new senior guy and the goth girl."

Raf and Elise turned to them, confused. Then everyone else in the gymnasium turned to them as well.

Joe Torelli locked eyes with Blaire, walking over in their direction.

"What?" Blaire asked. "We were just having breakfast."

"Just breakfast?" Torelli asked them, his eyes squinting.

"They were playing some kind of game," Andrei added. "Things in life that sucked, and everyone was glad to be done with. We were just looking for something lighthearted and positive to do."

"That's them!" a shrill voice screamed from one of the chairs by the mirrors.

Everyone turned toward Melvin Mueller, who was now standing on the metal chair, his arms still duct-taped behind his back.

"They were talking about the bomb earlier," he announced to everyone. "They knew about the gym before it exploded!"

Blaire's whole body went cold as ice ... cold as the deepest depth of Hell.

She glanced at Andrei and even his stoic expression was cracked and horrified by the charge.

Melvin had heard them talking by Blaire's locker.

Suddenly, another voice raised from the basketball court.

"I knew something was up with him!" Amanda Burke added. "I could feel a bad aura from that guy ever since the limo."

Blaire's horror refocused on her, transmuting into anger.

"You two, get down here," Torelli demanded, pointing his finger at the ground.

"We had nothing to do with the gym!" Blaire yelled, trying to focus on the absolutes.

Everyone seated in the bleachers near them had turned to face them.

"Go down!" one of them said. Blaire couldn't tell who.

"It wasn't us!" Andrei yelled.

One of the students in the bleachers approached them, her hand reaching out to grab Blaire.

She was maybe a foot away when her arm suddenly stopped in place.

A thick, black knife blade exploded upwards out of the girl's forearm. A thin dusting of sand fell in the area around them, trickling off of Blaire's jacket.

The girl began screaming in pain and quickly pulled her hand away.

Blaire followed the tip of the weapon down. At the bottom was a hand with salmon-colored nail polish on the fingers. Just below it, the floor length dress had been pulled away somewhat, revealing a leather holster wrapped around the inner leg.

Blaire looked at Elise, who wore a familiar, devious smile.

"Shit," Raf said, quickly pulling out a second knife from his back.

At the sight of the knives, the rest of those near them began scooting away. They moved quicker once they saw Torelli aim the shotgun at the group.

"All four of you," he yelled. "Down. Now!"

Andrei and Raf shifted in front, protecting the girls.

They started moving to the floor.

"We're innocent!" Blaire began pleading to the crowd. "Homecoming was the best night of my life; I would have never ended it like that!"

"Maybe not you, but what about him?" Amanda Burke retorted, pointing at Andrei.

"I didn't do anything!" Andrei announced.

"Amanda, how could you?!" Blaire said, the betrayal cutting her deep.

"Tie them up," Torelli told Paxton.

He approached the group, moving toward Blaire first.

Andrei looked Paxton dead in the eyes.

"If you lay a finger on Blaire, I'll kill you with my bare hands," he growled.

Paxton hesitated ... then took a step backwards.

Torelli's other goons were looking at the large knives Raf and Elise were wielding. They put the steak knives to shame.

"On your knees!" Torelli yelled. He stepped closer to Andrei, aiming the shotgun at his chest.

Neither he nor Blaire were armed at all. Their only chance was to get the gun away from Torelli, turn the tables on him and this whole abomination of a courtroom.

Andrei shifted his stance, then swung a leg into the air. The heel of his left shoe made contact between the barrels. The kick would have shifted the gun away from him and Blaire, possibly sending it flying out of Torelli's hands.

The shotgun fired.

The crowd screamed at the deafening sound as it echoed around the gymnasium.

Andrei was launched backwards seven feet, sliding along the polished maple floor of the court.

The only thing louder than the shotgun blast was his scream that followed it.

Large pieces of Andrei's leg had been blown off of him. Most of his calf, thigh, and a good portion of the skin were torn away and scattered along the floor behind the four of them. Roughly thirty pounds of flesh now lay between them and the east wall of the basketball court. A dusting of fine powder trickled down between all of it.

Miraculously, the leg was still attached to him. The bones seemed to be undamaged. They could see for themselves. The femur, tibia, and fibula were exposed to the air, since most of the meat and muscle that concealed them were now gone.

Andrei was in unimaginable pain.

Following his first scream, he bit into his sleeve as tightly as he could. More howls of suffering escaped his lungs through the gritted teeth.

Blaire cried out also, moving down next to him while Raf and Elise shifted positions to protect them.

Torelli himself seemed surprised that the gun had gone off. He pulled his finger off of the trigger.

After their initial shock, the crowd were now dead silent. Their eyes were fixed on the gaping holes in Andrei's leg and the massive amount of torment the wounds were causing him.

Blaire tried to tend to him, holding him steady until the fits subsided.

Rafael was the first to break the silence.

"Are you all satisfied yet?!" he yelled at the crowd, pointing the knife at them. "There's a lot more of that on the way, for each and every one of you! All it's going to take is for one or two assholes to accuse you of something and they'll see you tortured for it!"

People in the stands shifted. Close to a dozen of them decided that they wanted to leave and began descending the flights, jogging toward the doors.

Torelli snapped out of his stupor.

"What are you doing?!" he yelled at them. "No one can leave until we've found the killer!"

"You already said you were the killer!" a glib retort called from the crowd, drawing chuckles.

Torelli couldn't even focus on petty revenge for that statement, he had to quickly mobilize his true believers into securing the gym.

"Marcus, Jordan, Brendan, Trey, get the doors!" he said. They moved into position.

The rest of the crowd didn't like the look of the dozen or so students being stopped from leaving.

Guys and girls alike tried to zig-zag around them and burst through the doors. Brendan was holding them back as he did to players on a defensive line. Marcus and Jordan juked from side to side, using the basketball court as it was intended. Trey was the one most out of his element in the spontaneous scenario. He would be the first one to stab a student.

Once one scream was heard, the others took action as well. Guys and girls cried out as the four of them pierced and struck those trying to escape Torelli and his shotgun. The lances were very effective at crowd control.

After enough pain had been dealt, those trying to flee cowered and returned to the stands. There was a mixed ruckus in response. Close to two dozen people aligned with them began giving their own alibis and objections to the cruelty and violence.

Torelli turned from the crowd, overwhelmed by the noise.

After Paxton and Amanda had shifted their focus to Blaire and Andrei, Niles and Laura were able to move back together. They held each other close.

Blaire was now supporting Andrei's back, holding him sideways while he continued to writhe in pain.

"What do we do?" Elise asked Raf.

"I don't know," he said, glancing at Andrei. "It's gonna take at least two of us to carry him. We'll never make it back to the rehearsal room."

Torelli was facing the direction with the least amount of people. His free hand was balled up into a fist in front of him. He stared at the knuckles as he opened and closed the hand.

Darren Clark and Jennifer Maxwell walked up to him.

Elise and Raf couldn't tell what they were saying.

After they talked for a minute, Torelli looked over at Eric Schwartz, who was also standing nearby. He nodded his head in agreement to whatever the couple told Torelli.

Darren stepped away from them, approaching Raf and Elise. He was carrying a crowbar.

They took stances with the military knives, ready to attack.

"Wait, wait!" he said, holding up his hands. "Listen, just quickly get into the visitor stands and sit quietly ... no tape, keep the knives."

"Or what, bitch?" Raf said. "Bet I can take more pieces off of you than he can off of me."

"Look, we're trying to help," Darren whispered. "Just get the other two into the bleachers and you'll all be left alone for a while."

Raf and Elise looked at each other. It was probably the best deal they had on the table.

Elise nodded and the two of them backed up toward Blaire and Andrei.

Darren walked away from them, approaching Niles and Laura.

Elise and Raf knelt down by Andrei.

"How is he?" Elise asked. She could see all the other pieces of him scattered across the floor. They looked like slabs of meat being left out in the sun to dry age.

Andrei was lying on his right side, partially supported by Blaire behind him. He couldn't really sit or lie down normally, quite a bit of his gluteus was gone too.

Blaire looked exhausted, like she had just been awake for four days in a row.

"He stopped screaming," she said, "but the pain is still there, I think he's in shock."

A thought crossed Elise's mind whether you can have shock without blood ... but then again, they all had a pulse, still felt a heartbeat, and had other gooey sensations inside of them, so who the hell knows?

She could see what Blaire meant anyway. He didn't look like he was fully awake. He was non-responsive, staring into the distance and shivering. He clutched his arms to his chest like he was freezing to death.

"Listen," Raf said. "Darren and Jennifer talked to Torelli; we can all just sit in the bleachers. No getting tied up and we can keep our knives."

Blaire glanced at Torelli, then at Raf's knife.

"Got any more of those?" she asked.

"Sorry," Raf said.

Jennifer Maxwell was looking at Blaire and the rest of them from across the court. Her arms were folded up in front of her. With one hand, she motioned them toward the bleachers. She seemed to have a sense of urgency on her face.

Blaire sighed, feeling the same lack of available options.

"Okay," she said. "Raf, get his waist, but watch the wound. Elise, can you keep his feet together?"

"Yeah," Elise said, as the two of them got into position.

"Babe?" Blaire said, getting close to his ear. "We need to move you really quick, then we can rest."

She shifted his arm and put the bite of suit coat back in his mouth. Then, she adjusted her grip to get a more stable hold around his shoulders.

"Okay, one ... two ... three ... lift!" Blaire counted out. They lifted all 6'-8" of him into the air.

As soon as he felt the shift, he bit down again, grunting with every jostle of his body.

Niles and Laura were in the bleachers already, guiding the four of them into a section with lots of empty space.

They laid Andrei down on his stomach over a stretch of seats.

"Okay, all done," Blaire told him, folding his arms under his head.

His eyes were squeezed shut, wincing occasionally.

She sat one row down from him in the foot rest. She leaned back so her face was right next to his.

Niles came up next to them, holding a medicine bag. In his other hand, he offered her a small pile of pills.

"Ibuprofen 800s," he explained. "It's not a lot, but it might help."

"Thank you," she said with sincerity. She put the pills into Andrei's mouth and got him to swallow.

Blaire kissed his cheek, then moved her mouth by his ear. She hoped a bit of extra encouragement would help him somehow.

"You need to get better," she whispered seductively. "We still have an *afterparty* to throw."

Andrei didn't seem to respond.

Blaire couldn't tell if her words were getting through to him. She'd have to keep trying until he came out of it. She wanted him awake, she wanted him talking to her.

Elise and Raf sat down nearby, on the row in front of Andrei.

"Did Darren talk to you too?" Laura asked them. She and Niles sat down also.

"Yeah," Elise said.

Raf glanced at Torelli. He no longer held the Citori in front of his chest or over his shoulder. It hung limply at his side, parallel with his leg.

"Great job with that knife by the way," Laura said, referencing Elise's surprise strike.

"Thanks, it felt really good." She smiled.

Elise hiked up the cut away on her dress. She flipped the leather sheath around to the outside of her thigh, then tucked the dress behind the leather strip so it was easier to access. After that, she holstered the knife.

Raf kept his in hand, at the ready.

"I sure wouldn't mind seeing one of them getting stabbed," Laura said. "They stabbed Niles earlier."

"Damn, they did?" Raf asked him.

"Yeah, right here," Niles said, pointing to the spot on his shoulder. It didn't really hurt anymore; the sand must have patched itself already. Niles was actually working on a theory about that.

Before he could elaborate, he felt the spot on the coat where the knife went in. There was no tear, no damage to the coat.

Niles pulled the coat off of his shoulder, inspecting the dress shirt. There was no puncture mark there either.

"My *clothes* healed," Niles said, perplexed.

Laura felt the spot herself.

"That's so weird."

"I think it's a common courtesy," Elise mumbled. "Since most of us only have like two things to wear anyway."

"A courtesy from who?" Raf asked.

None of them answered.

"I guess that's good news for Andrei," Elise added, looking at the wound.

Andrei's dress pants were more damaged and tattered than the pair his dead body wore in the mirrors. A good portion of his boxers had been torn away also, revealing some of his pelvic bone.

The wounds were heavily saturated in white powder now. The exposed bones were almost covered.

Blaire was stroking his hand and whispering to him as he rested.

"How long do you think it'll take to heal?" Laura asked.

"A lot of the suicides seemed to be back on their feet in like ten minutes," Raf said.

"That's a bit of a different circumstance," Niles responded. "None of them were dismembered, they just jumped and broke their necks, or cut up their arms a bit."

"What do you mean 'just'?" Elise asked, remembering her own mortifying death.

Laura looked at him curiously too.

He had to explain.

"Think about it," Niles began. "When someone gets stabbed, besides the pain, the only physical damage is just a bit of powder that trickles out. It's not like the threat of losing a gallon of blood. Obviously, we're not exactly human anymore. We're like stuffed animals or ragdolls."

None of them liked the comparison, but they couldn't find a way to disagree.

"So, if you stabbed a teddy bear for some reason, and a small clump of stuffing came out on the knife," Niles continued, "all you have to do is put that clump back and sew it up."

"Okay," Raf said, agreeing with the basics.

"What if your dog got to the bear instead?" Niles proposed. "The tears are larger and most of the stuffing is gone. It's going to take more time to go to the store, buy more stuffing, put it in the bear, and then sew it all together again."

"What's the store in this scenario?" Laura asked.

"It doesn't matter," Niles said. "Just, look over there."

He motioned toward the pieces of Andrei still lying against the wall. They had begun dissolving into powder, slowly getting absorbed into the atmosphere around them.

"The more stuffing you lose," Niles summarized, "the longer it'll take to repair you."

Elise shivered, reminded of her first encounter with gore and dust.

"So, what you're saying," Raf added, "is that a shotgun is probably the worst weapon Torelli could have, rather than, say, a pistol."

"Right," Niles said. "I actually think that's why it took us so long to wake up."

"What do you mean?" Laura asked.

"After we died," he explained, "we didn't wake up again for like twelve hours. We probably started out looking the way we do in the mirrors, until this place slowly put us back together, including our clothes."

Laura hugged her shoulders, feeling sick. She pictured a timelapse of the dust settling onto her skeletal remains until she was whole again. She couldn't imagine anyone else witnessing that process before she woke up on the lawn of the baseball field.

"Hopefully it doesn't take twelve hours," Raf said, glancing at Andrei and then at Torelli. "I don't think we have that kind of time."

TWENTY-TWO

THE PALE HORSE

DARREN AND JENNY WATCHED as Niles and Laura were led to the center of the basketball court to be dressed down by Joe and the others.

The girl who'd first mentioned their names seemed thrilled by their capture.

Jimmy returned to the gym doors he was originally set to guard. He dropped the cross-shaped tire iron on the ground unceremoniously, sliding his back down against the wall.

"Give me a minute," Darren said, turning to Jenny.

She nodded, then walked over to Camellia.

They all stayed in the empty quarter of the gymnasium, between the visiting team bleachers and the southwest doors next to them.

Darren slid down the wall next to Jimmy, dropping his crowbar beside the tire iron.

"This is so fucked, man," Jimmy groaned. "Why the hell are we doing all this bullshit?"

"I guess because we're all scared of Joe," Darren answered.

"What that kid said is right." Jimmy motioned to Niles. "I mean, dead or not, there are a thousand other things we could be doing right now. This *should* be an afterparty … drinking, orgies, breaking shit all over campus … not some fuckin' lynch mob."

"Guess that's why they call it 'Hell'." Darren sighed. "We don't get what we want, no matter how close it seems to be."

"Which of course is why Joe is so fucked up," Jimmy said. "Without Isabella, he's gone all to pieces. Although if I lost Camellia in all this, *I* wouldn't be keeping everyone else hostage over my own fucking depression."

"Jenny doesn't think the bomber is even here," Darren admitted.

"She's probably right," Jimmy said. "All I know is, once we're out of this gym, I am done being a dancing monkey for Torelli. I'm going to take Camellia and we are going to sit somewhere until Joe is out of shotgun shells, or he forgets we exist."

Camellia walked up to the two of them.

"Trade you," she said to Darren.

"Yeah, sure."

He pat Jimmy on the shoulder, then picked up the crowbar.

Camellia slid down next to Jimmy.

Darren gave them some space, returning to Jenny.

She still had one of the knife lances hanging from one hand.

"How is he?" Jenny asked Darren.

"Same as us," Darren said.

"Well, we did what Joe wanted us to." She shrugged. "Everyone has been stuffed in here like chickens on a factory farm."

"We're all going to end up as nuggets and Joe still won't know the killer's identity." Darren sighed.

"I've been thinking about that too," Jenny said.

Darren looked at her, curious.

"Joe's outburst earlier, about killing his dad, was full of holes," she noted. "Those holes might not even be lies."

"What do you mean?" Darren asked.

"I mean maybe enough years of Oxy and Addy abuse has carved up his brain like Swiss cheese. Maybe he did help bomb the school, thinking he would escape. He could have assumed that we would have left with Iz. Maybe he thought our limo would be gone by then to set up for Jimmy's party."

"There's no way Joe built that spark plug thing," Darren said, motioning to the electrical device.

"That's what I'm saying," she reiterated. "How do you get away with mass murder?"

Darren looked at her like she was making some bad joke.

"You find a fall guy," Jenny elaborated.

"So, Joe's just a patsy?" Darren asked.

"What if Joe was pissed about the game," Jenny began. "Someone went up to him as he's punching trees or whatever, and said they had a plan to get back at the school for screwing things up for him. Doesn't matter how they phrased it, just that they blamed Villa Vista instead of Joe for the loss, and he believed it because he wants to believe it.

"They could have gaslit Joe into thinking the school cares more about the basketball program than football. They did just build them a brand-new gymnasium, while the stadium is still older than some of our parents.

"They give Joe some bolt cutters and the car battery thing, and tell him what to do. They say it's going to toast the paint of the gym and delay the grand opening, totally screwing up basketball season.

"After the gym exploded, all the evidence of the electrical thing would have vaporized. They'd probably assume it was just an alarm clock or something. But all the security tapes and fingerprints and everything else would show Joe. Heck, maybe they got Joe all worked up to kill his dad too. Have *you* ever seen that shotgun before? Where did he get it, where'd it come from? Maybe someone had been planning to set Joe up for a long time."

Darren took in Jenny's new theory with quiet contemplation. He'd never heard Joe talk about going hunting or shooting before.

"That's them!" a shrill voice screamed from the center of the basketball court.

Darren and Jenny turned, focusing on whatever was happening in the gym.

The Melvin kid that Jenny had subdued with the knife lance was now screaming at the crowd.

Everyone was focused on the far corner of the bleachers at Andrei and Blaire.

"I knew something was up with him!" Amanda Burke added. "I could feel a bad aura from that guy ever since the limo."

Jimmy and Camellia ran up next to them.

"The fuck is going on?" he asked them.

"I don't know," Darren replied.

Suddenly they heard a scream from the bleachers.

The kid in the white suit pulled out a large black knife. His girlfriend in the pink dress had one too.

"Shit," Darren said.

"Are those Ka-Bars?" Camellia asked.

"We're innocent!" Blaire pleaded to the crowd. "Homecoming was the best night of my life; I would have never ended it like that!"

"They're not giving up those knives without a fight," Jimmy said.

Joe was moving in closer to the four of them, now that they were down on the court. He had the shotgun aimed right at Andrei.

Darren and Jenny couldn't see too well though. The glow from the mirrors was very bright and distracting, plus there were like ten other people standing around the court blocking their view.

Suddenly, the shotgun fired.

"Fuck!" Jimmy yelled, as Camellia pulled him down behind the bleachers.

Darren and Jenny dove with them.

Once the ring of the 12-gauge round subsided, they heard loud, deep-throated screaming.

"Shit, that's the new guy, isn't it?" Jimmy asked them.

"Are you all satisfied yet?!" they heard the junior kid yell at the crowd. "There's a lot more of that on the way, for each and every one of you! All it's going to take is for one or two assholes to accuse you of something and they'll see you tortured for it!"

"He's got that right," Camellia said, holding Jimmy below a metal frame.

Darren peeked his eyes above one of the bleacher seats.

"The crowd's panicking," Darren told them. "They're trying to leave."

Brendan and Trey appeared within view, blocking the southwest doors to the gym. A few people tried to run past them. There was another yell as Trey drove his lance into a guy's stomach.

"We didn't do it, let us out!" the girl next to him screamed.

Brendan also took a stab at someone, nicking their arm. Eventually, they were able to drive the runners back to their seats. It didn't even seem like they noticed Darren, Jenny, Jimmy or Camellia.

Jenny looked at Darren.

"We need to stop this before it gets worse," she told him.

He nodded his head in agreement.

They walked out from behind the bleachers, taking in the scene.

Brendan and Trey continued blocking the doors. Marcus and Jordan were posted on the northwest doors. Close to twenty people were yelling at Torelli from the stands as he stood facing the back corner of the gym.

The white suit guy and pink dress girl were still armed with their knives, standing in front of Andrei and Blaire.

Andrei was on the ground; half of his leg had been blown off. The pieces on the ground looked like stew meat.

"Oh my god," Jenny whispered.

Blaire was holding him at an angle, trying to keep pressure off of his mangled leg.

They walked up to Torelli.

"Joe, what happened?" Darren asked, keeping his eye on the shotgun in case he moved it against them.

"I, I don't know," Joe said.

He was staring at his fist for some reason.

"Joe, listen," Jenny said. "We need to deescalate the situation; the others are panicking. If we don't cool things now, they're going to rush out of here in a mob. How many more people are you willing to shoot to stop that?"

"I only want to shoot the person that killed Iz," Joe mumbled.

"Did that guy kill Iz?" she asked, motioning to Andrei.

"I don't know," Joe said, squeezing his fist in frustration.

"Then we really need to keep from shooting people until we do," Jenny replied calmly.

Torelli didn't answer her.

"How about we get them sitting in the benches. If we let them keep their knives, I'm sure they'll comply," Jenny said, reasoning with him. "They can't go anywhere with their friend hurt like that anyway."

Joe turned his head. Eric Schwartz was standing nearby, still holding the notebook with all of their investigation proceedings.

"She's got a point," Eric agreed, nodding. "If people bolt out of here in a mob, you'll never get their support back. We'll have a dozen separate gangs fighting each other and we'll never find the bomber."

"You should tell the others to ease it with the stabbing too," Darren added. "Once this is all over, we have to live with these people, probably forever."

"We could move on to searching rooms and lockers," Eric offered. "Send out mixed teams, let everyone cool down."

"Yeah, fine," Joe said in resignation. "Just get everyone in the bleachers."

"Thank you," Jenny answered.

They walked away from Torelli, approaching Andrei and the others first.

"Stay back a bit," Darren said to her, "they might take a swing at us."

As expected, when he got close, the knife-wielding couple took stances, ready to lunge.

"Wait, wait!" Darren said, holding up his hands. "Listen, just quickly get into the visitor stands and sit quietly ... no tape, keep the knives."

"Or what, bitch?" the guy responded. "Bet I can take more pieces off of you than he can off of me."

"Fuck, Torelli," Darren thought to himself. "Could you have made things any worse?"

"Look, we're trying to help," Darren whispered to them, motioning to Jenny behind him. "Just get the other two into the bleachers and you'll be left alone for a while."

For a moment it looked like the couple might still take a stab at him, but finally the girl nodded her head in acceptance.

Darren sighed, walking back to Jenny.

"Okay, now let's get the others away from Paxton."

Paxton and Amanda were standing away from all the action that had just happened. They pretended like they didn't get involved because they were watching Niles and Laura.

"Joe said we can move them to the stands for a while," Darren said to Paxton.

"They're not going in the chairs?" Amanda asked.

"Not right now," Jenny said.

Paxton hesitated.

"You can ask Joe to confirm, if you want," Darren offered.

Paxton put a hand up in resignation, walking off with Amanda.

Niles and Laura weren't exactly happy to see them.

He stood in front of the Student Council girl.

"Stay back!" Niles shouted.

"Relax," Darren said, holding the crowbar as non-threateningly as he could. "We were able to get Torelli to cool down for a while."

They didn't move, not believing him.

"Please," Jenny said. "We're not going to tie you up. Just sit tight in the stands. Hopefully the others will find more clues in someone's locker and this will all be over."

She motioned to an empty space on the east side of the visitors' bleachers. It was out of the direct light of the fires burning behind the bathroom mirrors.

Niles and Laura shifted away from them, keeping their eyes on the weapons until they got to that place in the stands.

Jenny turned toward Andrei, Blaire, and the others.

"Come on, get up there," Jenny whispered, motioning. She was afraid Joe would change his mind if they didn't settle in quickly.

Finally, they lifted Andrei and carried him into the stands by Niles and Laura.

"Good job," Darren told Jenny. "Joe wouldn't have listened to any of us like that."

"Let's get the last two away from the mirrors," Jenny said.

They walked over to Barry and Melvin.

Jenny saw her corpse reflection in the approach and crossed her arms, covering her chest. She stepped out of direct line-of-sight of the mirrors.

Darren approached Melvin.

"What the hell?!" he said, indignant. "How come none of them are tied up?"

"Shut. The. Fuck. Up." Darren snapped. "You've caused enough trouble."

Melvin withered in fear, not saying anything in response.

Darren pulled Barry out of the other chair.

"Just find a seat in the bleachers," he said. "I'd like a few hours not dealing with this shit."

They complied, skulking toward an empty corner of the visiting team stands.

Melvin happened to cross eyes with Blaire as they walked.

The glare she gave him was sharper than the two knives her friends were wielding.

Melvin snapped his head away and they retreated to their seats.

As Darren and Jenny turned to face the other varsity players again, Torelli had taken center court.

"Alright everyone," he announced to them. "We've had enough interrogations for now. We know what we're looking for, so sit tight while we send search parties out to go through the lockers, starting with theirs."

He motioned to the visiting team bleachers.

There was no clapping or positive response at all, just a few more mixed interjections about wanting to leave.

"We *will* find the bomber," he promised.

After gathering everyone up again, he organized the search team.

The sophomores, Greg and Chelsea, would take the group locker to locker and room to room, searching for construction plans, transmitters, and any hand-written notes which may have drawings of the electrical device.

Marcus, Jordan, Paxton, and Amanda would be among the search party. Joe would keep all the Varsity Football players in the gym with him.

Darren wasn't sure what to make of that decision.

Eric Schwartz was remaining as well, Joe wanted to talk about all the findings and theories they had so far.

Paxton took the student roster and the locker manifest they'd found in the Administration offices. They would hit the lockers and living spaces of the accused first, then those of the students currently in this slice of Hell, then everyone else.

Torelli pulled the chairs away from the mirrors, then set down two more from the stack.

Eric Schwartz took one of the seats and Joe took another.

"Go on, sit," Joe said, motioning to Darren and Jenny. "It's going to be a while."

Darren and Jenny hesitated.

"What about the door?" Darren asked him.

"Camellia's got it." He waved a hand.

They glanced back and saw that Jimmy and Camellia had taken post by the door. Jimmy gave a small wave in acknowledgement.

"Asshole," Darren said under his breath.

"Don't worry, she'll be fine," Joe said, laying the shotgun across his lap. "Did you know her dad's a Marine?"

Darren and Jenny eased down into their seats.

It was going to be another long day.

***

Pain. So much pain.

Andrei could feel nothing but constant signals of fire and electricity surging up his spine from his left leg.

His mind wandered, searching for something to retreat into as a means of escaping the indescribable and relentless pain.

Andrei knew that kick was a risky move.

He was a bit out of practice since they moved to Alexandria and Katya moved into a UCLA dorm with a girlfriend. She wasn't throwing one-two punches for him to block in the hallways anymore.

It was actually kind of nice living with just his dad for a few months. They were able to get some quality time in without Katya or any other women around.

To be honest, they had been a bit loose with the cleaning and upkeep too. His dad had focused on making sure all of his parts were memorized perfectly, to impress the SF Symphony during this first Fall Season. It was one reason why Andrei hadn't invited Blaire over to his house yet.

He planned on getting things cleaned top to bottom once they had decorated for Christmas. Then he'd invite her over in December some time, probably when Katya and Anastasia were in town for the holidays.

There really was no rush before then. It would just be her, him, and his father otherwise, and his dad was not very talkative at family dinners.

Often Katya and Anastasia would run the conversation, while Andrei and Vasily would provide quiet intermissions between their topics of discussion.

Andrei wasn't sure how much Blaire even cared about such things. She didn't seem to be in a rush to sit him down with her parents and brothers.

Chris and Tommy were literally kids, so they wouldn't have much to say beyond regular kid questions. Andrei already thought he could keep them entertained with stories from Southern California, like the time his friend Bill broke his leg when he tumbled halfway down Mt. Baldy.

With her parents, he thought he'd handled things pretty well when they met at her place for the limo. He'd be able to easily fill a few hours of conversation with stories from his dad's concerts and stuff about his sisters. For instance, he could tell the story about how Anastasia met Jacob, his brother-in-law, by tripping on the sidewalk and sending both of them into a puddle of mud.

Yeah, he could have easily handled dinner with her family.

He'd want her to meet his family eventually, if nothing else than as a way to vaccinate her, by introducing them in small doses. He also figured that December would have had his sisters on their best behavior. Anastasia loved the holidays, so she was always cheery at the end of the year. Katya would be too busy watching him and Blaire interact to pester her too much with personal questions. Those were the "one-two punches" he could take later on to protect Blaire.

A few more months before some big family gathering would have worked out better anyway.

Andrei had been fairly focused on his own music in recent months. While his father used the grand piano in the living room, he was in his bedroom with closed-ear headphones plugged into his Yamaha.

It took him three weeks to compose just the right piece for Blaire to ask her to Homecoming.

He really felt like he won her over with "The Seasons, No. 10", so he used that as a starting point for something that would turn more romantic as the music went on.

He was fairly proud of it. It was the longest piece he'd composed in a year or two. Otherwise, he'd mostly been playing and learning classical works, the kind that you'd be expected to know starting off in a fancy music college.

The real feeling of success came when she asked him for a recording of the piece. That's when he knew that she actually liked it, rather than just appreciated the gesture.

He recorded the piece several times, eventually deciding the fourth take was the best. Then, he added a few effects to help it sound warm and full in playback.

He didn't want to title it something too pretentious or strange, so he simply named the file *"For_Blaire.mp3"*. Once he was satisfied, he emailed it to her.

He wondered if she'd listened to it at all; he hadn't heard her mention it since. She was much more moved by that picture Elise was able to take, which Andrei could totally understand. A picture's worth a thousand words and it was much easier to enjoy at a glance rather than a three-minute-long piece of music.

There was a change in the pain. Andrei could feel shifts in the electricity surging up his spine. He also felt like he was floating.

That's when he realized there were hands on him. He was being moved.

They set him down on some kind of plastic. It didn't feel as hard or as cold as the basketball court. It was a small improvement anyway.

They gave him something to swallow too. They were probably sleeping pills.

From what he could remember of the other kids who hurt themselves, it took time for them to heal. He'd rather not be present for most of that. He had a very long damnation ahead of him already.

Andrei wasn't even sure how much of his left leg remained. Would he be an amputee for all eternity? Where was he going to find crutches or a wheelchair to use if that were the case? Would he need to build one? At least there was a chance the elevator would keep working.

Before his mind could stray any further down that depressing route, he was given a much more pleasant distraction.

"You need to get better," Blaire whispered seductively in his ear. "We still have an *afterparty* to throw."

Was he dreaming, or was that really her? Did she mean what he hoped she meant?

It wasn't the only thing she would say either. She continued whispering kind words and sweet nothings to him until the sleeping pills took effect and everything faded into black.

When Andrei finally came to, he found himself lying on his stomach. The pain in his leg was down significantly compared to what it was before. It was no longer so intrusive that it stripped him of all awareness and reason.

He could feel something soft and warm wrapped around his left arm, stroking it gently.

That's when he heard Blaire's voice right next to him.

"... stop it, I did not!" she said in a playful tone.

Elise was nearby, answering her.

"*Almost* every day then," Elise relented. "And when Ms. Martinez did ask her why she was late, because it was more than a few minutes, she gave her these big puppy dog eyes and said 'I had some *girl stuff* to deal with.'"

Laura laughed nearby.

"Ugh," Blaire groaned. "It was just so boring. I'd already read all of those books. Freshmen English was too casual."

"Which is how *I* got straight A's in the class," Elise chirped. "Because Blaire could tolerate all that old-timey Brontë-speak, and tell me what they were saying."

Five voices chuckled around Andrei.

"Still not as bad as Shakespeare," Laura groaned. "I had to get one of those modern translation side-by-side versions, because otherwise it felt like I was reading another language."

"Not only that," Niles added. "But our book was *Macbeth,* so that language might as well have been Old Gaelic."

"My group did *Romeo and Juliet,*" Rafael said. "Simple, familiar, no surprises. I didn't want to mess with something obscure or weird."

"I made our group do *Twelfth Night,*" Elise said. "Because I absolutely love that *She's the Man* movie with Amanda Bynes and wanted to see how close it was to the original."

"Ooh, that is a good movie," Laura agreed, before apparently pivoting to Blaire. "Were you in her group too?"

"No," Blaire said. "We had different periods for Sophomore English. My group did *The Tempest.*"

"Is that the one with the fairies?" Raf asked.

"I'm pretty sure there's at least one fairy," Laura offered.

"Yeah, Ariel," Blaire said. "What you're thinking of is-"

A Midsummer Night's Dream," Andrei whispered, stopping everyone in surprise.

"Hey!" Blaire turned to him with a soft tone. "How are you feeling?"

"A bit better," Andrei groaned. "Still hurts a lot though."

"I bet it does," Elise said. "You're still missing quite a few pieces."

"Pieces?" Andrei asked, opening his eyes.

"Yeah man," Raf said. "You took that 12-gauge round point blank. Most of your leg was gone."

"We could see the bones," Niles said. "None of them were broken though, so good job on the vitamin D."

"Most of it is healed," Blaire reassured him. "It's just your calf and a bit of skin left to repair."

"Good thing the pants are back too." Raf chuckled. "Talk about being half-assed."

"Raf ..." Elise chided him.

"My pants were gone?" Andrei asked, feeling embarrassed.

Elise gave Raf a harsher look.

"There was a lot of damage," Blaire whispered. "Everything from your ankle to your beltline was just torn away ... both your pants, and you."

"And you found new pants in my size?" he asked, still confused.

"No, the pants stitched themselves back together too," Niles explained. "Apparently the dust fixes our clothes the same way it fixes us."

"Really?" Andrei said in surprise.

"Yeah!" Raf said. "I'd show you in a mirror, but, you know."

Andrei looked around the gym. It didn't seem like much had changed, except for the fact that no one was getting questioned in front of the mirrors, and some of the varsity players were gone.

"How long have I been out?" he asked.

"Almost ten hours," Blaire said, still stroking his arm.

"Guess that's one of the perks of being here," Laura said, quoting their earlier conversation with Liam. "'Damage recovery.'"

Andrei pushed upwards on his right arm, shifting to a sitting position.

"Whoa, easy," Blaire said. She stood up, following the other arm.

Andrei gingerly swung his left leg outward, setting the foot down on the bleacher seat in front of them.

"It doesn't hurt?" Raf asked.

"Nope, sitting is fine," Andrei confirmed, pressing his hands down to lift on and off of the seat.

Blaire sat down next to him.

"I can fccl that calf though," he said.

Everything below the knee was flat and raw. All roundness and definition of the muscle was still missing. It looked like it had been shaved off with a dull carving knife. Enough dust had layered on top the wound that the bones were no longer visible.

"It looks like everything healed from the top down," Niles observed. "Even though your calf took the worst of it, we apparently still have some kind of 'core' or essential center. I wonder if that's the head or the heart."

"Even your clothes were repaired that way," Elise observed.

Andrei felt the edge of the missing fabric just behind his knee. His dress socks had only stitched together up to the ankle.

He turned down to Blaire, who still had a look of concern on her face.

"Thank you," he said, hugging her and kissing her cheek.

While he was down there, he whispered in her ear. "I heard what you said earlier too."

When he sat upright, she was blushing, a conspicuous smile replacing the worried look.

"Thank you guys too," he said to the others. "Raf, Elise, where did you get those knives?"

"My Uncle Arturo," Raf said, angling the Ka-Bar around so everyone could get a good look at it. "I think we outgun them in everything except the actual gun."

"Did anyone else get hurt?" Andrei asked, looking down at Blaire.

"We're fine," she said. "Torelli's goons stabbed a few other people who tried to leave the gym though."

Andrei scanned the room. Everyone else had noticed him wake up.

Darren and Jennifer were looking directly at him, apparently relieved to see him alright. Torelli only glanced from his periphery, then turned away.

"You slice any of them?" Andrei asked, looking at Raf.

"Not after what Elise did!" he said proudly. "They were too scared to come close."

She pulled the knife from its sheath, mimicking the motion of stabbing the girl in the crowd.

"And you said *I'm* scary," Blaire teased her.

"You are," she answered. She held up the knife like a telescope, 'staring daggers' back at her.

"Why isn't Torelli talking to anyone?" Andrei asked. "Are we waiting for something?"

"After you got shot the crowd started panicking," Laura said. "People tried to leave but they got stopped."

"It almost became a mob, but then Jennifer Maxwell and Darren Clark worked out some kind of deal with Torelli," Niles said. "He stopped interviewing people, we didn't get tied up, and they started sending out search parties to check the lockers for clues to the bomber's identity."

"You mean the construction drawings that Mr. Wallace mentioned?" Andrei asked.

"Yeah," Raf said. "As well as bomb parts, a remote trigger, basically anything they think could be a clue. They don't want anyone to leave and destroy evidence before they can do their searches."

"Who's gone exactly?" Andrei asked. Most of Joe's Cheka seemed to still be there.

"Paxton and Amanda," Blaire said with a snarl. "I'm sorry we ever went in her stupid limo ... heartless bitch."

"Also, Marcus Johnson and that Jordan Trainor guy," Raf added. "They're doing the stadium lockers right now. The sophomores came back when they finished with the school lockers."

Andrei could see Greg and Chelsea sitting in chairs beside Torelli and Eric Schwartz.

"Did Amanda say anything to you earlier?" Elise asked him.

"No," Andrei said with a shrug. "I had no idea she felt that way. Paxton seemed fine when we were talking at the dance."

"It's true," Raf said. "He seemed normal back then ... *pfft*, 'back then' ... it hasn't even been two days, has it?"

Andrei pulled out his phone.

Monday, 4:10 p.m.

Blaire sighed. "I just want this to be over."

As she spoke, a bright flash of blue electricity lit up the room. The amber-colored flames pouring through the mirrors completely disappeared for a moment.

Several yelps could be heard throughout the gymnasium as everyone turned their eyes to the source of the lightning.

It did not come from the bomber's detonation device.

***

Bob Melkonian was glad some of the kids were able to escape being tied up. It mostly looked like it was due to the intervention of Darren Clark and Jennifer Maxwell.

They were good kids; they really didn't look like they wanted to be mixed up in all this.

The rest of them were still tied up though.

Bob's back got sore after a while, so he shifted to lie sideways on the bleacher seat.

Rick had sunk backwards, propping himself against the row behind them. It seemed to be comfortable enough, because he'd sat that way for the last few hours.

They had made various petitions to talk to the other kids scattered on the visiting team stands. They weren't allowed to stray too far from where they'd originally been placed though. One time when they did, Torelli stood up and demanded that they return to their seats.

Since then, he and Rick had been passing the time by talking about their families and reflecting on past holidays. Most of those stories were about times that the Melkonians had gone over to the Wallace household. On the rare occasion when it was just Rick and Mary in town, they came over to Bob and Angie's. Monika usually had one or two school friends over as well, so she didn't get bored to death by the adults and their "old people stories".

"Hey," Rick said, interrupting their conversation. "That Tunnikov kid is awake."

"He is?" Bob asked, sitting upright to see for himself.

Andrei was sitting normally on the bleacher, surrounded by his friends and girlfriend. He kissed Blaire on the cheek and they said something to each other.

Bob remembered seeing the way they were at Homecoming ... mostly because he thought he would need to intervene at some point.

Those two were probably having the best night at the dance. Bob had never seen Blaire Tidwell light up like that before. She was elated in a way she'd never been on the grounds of Villa Vista High School before. While Andrei seemed like a hard and focused kid normally, he spent the night smiling at Blaire like Charlie Brown smiled at the Little Red-Haired Girl in the *Peanuts* comics.

The idea that either of them were responsible for blowing up the school was crazy.

"Thank God he's okay," Bob said to Rick, looking at the couple.

"Why?" a small voice said close to the two of them.

Rick glanced down at the curtain of brown hair. It hung draped over the emerald green dress.

The head finally pulled upwards, off of her knees.

A single greyish-green eye looked at Rick between the parting layers of hair.

"Why should he thank God?" Ellen Taylor asked. "What is there to be grateful for, returning to this hell? How many more times does he need to be shot?"

Bob was stunned into silence. Rick answered her in a calm voice.

"You're right. That probably isn't the right phrasing," Rick said, going into Guidance Counselor mode. "I think what Mr. Mel means is that Blaire Tidwell seems to be happy he's back."

"Of course she is," Ellen said, "she didn't have her leg blown off."

"Mr. Mel and I will do everything in our power to protect you from something like that," Rick said, trying to be supportive or reassuring.

"What power?" Ellen mumbled in bitter words. She glared at him. "You're tied up just like the rest of us."

"Ellen," Rick said. "I'm sorry ... I'm sorry I couldn't save all of you from the killer."

She started chuckling.

Rick wasn't sure how to respond to that.

"I would have been dead either way," she said.

"What do you mean?" Rick asked her.

"I was already bleeding out when the school exploded," Ellen admitted.

"Oh, Ellen ..." Rick shook his head.

"I was really hoping I'd win Homecoming Queen," she continued. "Then when you all came looking for me, you would have found me like that ... hopefully dead already."

"Why, Ellen, why didn't you tell Ms. Fletcher and I what you were feeling?" Rick asked.

"It wouldn't have made a difference," she said with certainty. "My parents never cared and the kids in my class always made fun of me. You didn't have the power to change any of those things either."

Tears trickled down her face.

"I just wanted them to leave me alone," Ellen whispered. "I just wanted to get away from everything ... now I can't."

The girl was leaning forward again, almost slouching back down to where she was.

"You went to my church, didn't you?" Rick Wallace said, recognizing her face.

"Yeah," she said.

"I'm sorry Ellen," he said again. "I'm sorry that I didn't have the power or discernment to help you earlier, when it might have changed something."

She nodded slightly, at the very least recognizing what he said, whether or not she believed it.

There was one more thing Rick thought he could do for her now.

"May I pray for you?" he asked her.

There was a hesitation, but eventually she nodded, accepting his request.

Rick closed his eyes.

He spoke aloud the only prayer he could think of that fit this circumstance.

"God Almighty," Rick began, "You called us forth from the darkness. Your providence lights our way. And as You design, we return to dust."

Bob's eyes were closed too, even though he didn't recognize the prayer or its significance.

"Lord," Rick continued, "those who died live anew with You. Their lives have changed but will never end. I pray forever for my family, relatives and friends. That alive or dead, they are at peace at last."

Ellen did recognize the prayer and whispered along with Mr. Wallace.

"Together with Christ," Rick concluded, "who died so we may live. May they be fulfilled as one in Paradise, where sin and pain are washed away. Unite our family in our final home, to exalt Your name forever and ever."

"Amen," the three of them said together.

Rick opened his eyes.

A slight smile had returned to the young freshman girl's face.

"Thank you," she said. "I actually do feel a little better."

That is when Rick was almost blinded by a brilliant blue arc of electricity. It surged down the girl's arms like they were the conduction rods on the bomber's horrible machine.

Ellen brought her hands forward. She looked at her bindings. The electricity had burned through all of the layers of duct tape, cutting her free.

Another arc flashed between her palms. Dust trickled out of both hands.

More lightning surged between her head and arms, between her legs and stomach, between her elbows and knees.

"It doesn't hurt," Ellen said, her face glowing blue from the constant surges of energy.

The fine powder ran off of her on all sides, her body was dissolving away.

A high-pitched scream came from the basketball court as everyone in the gymnasium watched this take place. The imperious blue light washed away the orange and red pouring through from the fire beyond.

Within seconds, the last flash of lightning forked upward, connecting with the metal ceiling of the gymnasium.

Ellen Taylor, and all that she was wearing, had disintegrated into a pile of sand. Only the strips of duct tape remained.

She was gone.

TWENTY-THREE

RAPTURE

Dear Isabella,

If you're reading this letter, then you probably know what I did.

I really don't know what to say about that except that it had to be done.

It would have only been a matter of time before the police came after me, but even then, I still wanted to go to Homecoming with you. You've been one of the best things in my life lately, I had to risk it all to spend one more wonderful night with you. I hate the fact that I had to hurt you at the end.

Whatever I might have said or done, I didn't mean it. I'm sure Darren and Jennifer were able to get you to Jimmy's party, or at the very least back home afterwards. They probably told you how much of an asshole I am and that you should stay away from me. In some ways they're right, but you don't have to do anything, because I'm the one that can't stay.

However you feel about me now, knowing what I did and why I had to leave you that way, I hope you know that I love you. I really love you, Isabella. I care about you more than almost everyone in my family, almost everyone I actually share blood with.

To be honest, that goes for most of you. Please tell the others that I'm sorry too, that I'll miss them.

If you want to give me another chance, if you want to see me again, I'll be at the place we talked about going for a year before college. You should remember ... "Where we can look out over the whole world."

I love you Iz, I really hope to see you there. I'll be spending that year there no matter what, thinking of you.

~ Joe

***

Joe Torelli thought about his letter every time he thought about Isabella, and he hadn't stopped thinking about Isabella since he learned of her demise.

She never got to read it.

Whoever blew up the school killed Isabella before she could know the truth. Her last memories of Joe were him acting like a crazy jackass who made her cry.

She didn't see the dance for what it was, Joe risking his own life and freedom to have one last evening with her. She wasn't able to understand the night's conclusion for the ruse it had to be. He was keeping Isabella away from him so he could escape and she would be ignored as an accomplice.

Joe had his left hand in his pocket. His fingers continued to twitch involuntarily, squeezing and releasing the empty Ziploc bag. He'd run out of the pills hours ago.

Once Joe sent Marcus out to run the search party, he had Eric read through the roster of students. One by one they reviewed every piece of information they had about everyone present and what their possible motives could be.

At one point, Jennifer proposed the idea that someone was gaslit into planting the device by the real bomber. That the kid might have thought it would only burn the gym or set off the fire alarms ... property destruction, not mass murder.

It was a good idea, but Joe didn't pursue it too far. If they didn't have the real killer down here, then what was the point of knowing?

Of course, they would find that sacrificial lamb either way if they had enough clues to pin the evidence on someone.

One problem though was that the evidence was thin. Joe was really hoping a set of construction drawings turned up.

If Wallace was telling the truth, that could be the "smoking gun" they needed.

Either way, someone had to pay for what happened to Isabella.

Darren and Jenny sat dutifully with Joe Torelli and Eric Schwartz. All three of them entertained Joe's review of the existing information for all the hours it actually took to discuss it.

They went through over a hundred names, spending several minutes on each. They talked about who the kid was, who they went to the dance with, if that date was still down here, if they were dormed up together, and what possible reasons they might have for blowing up the school.

When they came across one of the accused suspects, the people sitting in the visiting team stands, they spent more time deliberating. Everything concerning their capture, words, and actions in the gymnasium were analyzed thoroughly for every relevant detail.

Nothing new seemed to stand out, they were still missing that one vital piece that connected all of the disparate parts together.

Joe finally gave up, sitting back in his chair and waiting for a while.

Eventually, Greg and Chelsea returned to the gym. Their search of the school lockers revealed nothing, so they let Marcus and the others continue the search of the football stadium lockers.

The sophomores pulled up chairs and joined them as they waited for the search to finish.

At one point, the conversation drifted onto the subject of guns. Greg was talking about times he'd go shooting with his dad and brothers. It was the opportunity Darren had been looking for.

"Speaking of clay pigeons," Darren began. "Where did you get that thing Joe?"

Joe shifted the Browning Citori in his hand, staring at it for a few seconds.

"It was my grandfather's," he answered. "He used to hunt with it, deer, elk, stuff like that."

"Your dad's dad?" Darren asked. Did he kill Salvatore with his own gun?

"No." Joe chuckled, finding the idea amusing. "My mom's dad, Vincent Pacelli. We used to call him 'Grandpa Vinny'."

Jennifer saw Joe looking at his knuckles again.

"He had a cabin up by Bear Valley," Joe continued. "We used to spend weekends up there with him, go hunting or just do generic nature and camping stuff."

Joe slowly broke open the action of the gun. The two unspent shells stuck out a bit from the barrels, having been partially ejected.

"He loved this gun," Joe said. "He always preferred these simple double-barreled designs."

A strange smile donned Joe's face. Jenny could only guess it was nostalgia.

"Grandpa Vinny used to say *'Life will usually give you a second chance ...'*" He let the words hang in the air before finishing the quote. *"'... but never a third.'"*

Joe pressed both 12-gauge shells back into the barrels and closed the action.

"After Vinny died, my dad must have used up his second chance, because that's when my mom split with Nicole," Joe said. "I always figured she'd gone back to 'Pacelli', but maybe not. I wasn't able to find them. I don't think she wanted me to find them."

Greg and Chelsea were terrified, sitting in dead silence. Neither of them were going to risk saying the wrong thing regarding this set of topics.

They probably figured that Jenny and Darren knew more, but the truth was ... they really didn't. Most of this was new information, beside the fact that his mom had left with his sister back in middle school.

Joe never forgave his mom for leaving him alone with Sal. In fact, if Joe did know where they were, he probably would have killed her on Saturday morning just like his dad.

He loved Nicole though. Joe could be angry and explosive with so many people, including Darren and Jenny, who were by all other measures some of his closest friends.

He was never like that with Nicole. In fact, it was almost adorable how much he used to dote on her. She was six years younger than them, so whenever they'd cross paths in the elementary and middle school lunchroom, he would switch into protective older brother mode. She'd give him a hug and he would ask her very directly if any of the first-grade boys were being mean to her.

No one knew what a seventh-grade Joe would have done to a first-grade boy teasing the baby sister. It didn't matter, because the fear his presence inspired was enough to deter any such incidents from happening in the first place.

Darren and Jenny's friendship went deeper, because of all the one-on-one time they spent together in the carpool. However, at school they saw Joe quite a bit between classes. They were all "Lifers", kids who'd been going to Villa Vista since kindergarten, so they had a lot of history with each other no matter what.

Joe was only twelve when his mom left. Stealing Nicole from him probably did more damage than her abandonment and Sal's abuse combined. His mean streak became much more pronounced after that.

Darren didn't see much of him between eighth grade and junior year, when he joined Varsity Football. Jenny only saw him sporadically, when he would hit on her cheerleader friends … often successfully. He never did that to her though. When she was dating Peter Onassis and later Blake, he respected those boundaries.

"So, is that where you went after the game?" Jenny asked him. "Your Grandpa Vinny's cabin?"

Joe searched his thoughts. Her prompting, along with detoxing from the pills, was causing him to actually recall the details of late Friday evening.

After the game, he grabbed his kit bag and walked straight to the Camaro.

He knew he'd done something bad by leaving Isabella behind. However, his mind had already refocused so closely on its new goal, that her importance was minimized.

In retrospect, he had already considered the implications of her being in his presence for what he was about to do.

He took the Camaro to the highway, thinking about how Tito and the other Torellis did jack shit to balance out Salvatore's rage over the years.

If he didn't already have the rural Mexico plan in the back of his mind, he probably would have sent the Camaro flying off of a cliff into the Pacific Ocean, destroying the car just to spite Tito.

He arrived at Grandpa Vinny's cabin just before midnight.

He ripped off his football pads with the jersey on top of it, ditching them in the trunk.

Wearing only the shoes, pants, and undershirt, he approached the door of the cabin.

"Yeah, I did," Joe answered Jennifer. "Grandpa Vinny always kept a key hidden nearby."

Joe ran at full speed, smashing through the old wooden door of the cabin.

There was no one inside, the cabin hadn't been used since Vinny died. Whichever Pacelli inherited it must have left it alone. Changing the lease or legal paperwork would have threatened to reveal the new identities and locations of his mom and sister.

God forbid.

So, they just paid the taxes and fees, letting the cabin get filled with cobwebs and dust. It was now a mausoleum to his dead childhood.

"I hung out there for a while," Joe said to Darren, Jenny, and the others. "I needed to get away from all the noise and just think."

Joe clenched his fists and started throwing punches at everything he saw. Every piece of furniture, every cobweb, every picture frame, every decoration was smashed to pieces if it was structurally weaker than the bones in Joe's hand.

Drops of blood trickled wherever Joe walked.

Once he finished the main room, the bathroom, and the two small bedrooms, he went into the master bedroom. Vinny's things were still there, exactly where he left them between hunting trips.

Joe destroyed everything he could using only his fists and feet. The football cleats protected his bare skin from bloody abrasions, unlike his gloveless hands.

Vinny's things probably didn't deserve this level of punishment, but Vinny's death was the instigator in a lot of ways. His passing coincided with the end of things for Joe.

Once everything else was thoroughly beaten, Joe pulled the gun box out from under the mattress where Vinny left it. Vinny never put a lock on it. He figured the mattress concealed its location enough for thieves, and when he stayed in the cabin, he wanted ready access to the gun in case of bears.

Joe pulled the Browning Citori out of the decorative hard case. He snapped the two pieces together, connecting the barrel assembly to the stock and trigger assembly. Then he picked up the bandolier, which Vinny also kept fully loaded with shells. The shells might have been seven years old, but they still felt dry and undamaged.

They would get the job done.

"Then eventually you took the gun with you?" Darren asked.

"I mean, obviously," Joe answered with a glib tone. "I got home around four in the morning and finished Sal off as soon as I stepped in the door. It was the best I've felt in years."

Greg and Chelsea continued to sit in silence, their eyes shifting between random places in the gym.

Before Darren and Jenny could go any further into psychoanalyzing Joe, Eric spoke up.

"Hey, I think that Andrei Tunnikov is waking up," he said, nodding toward the visiting team bleachers.

Darren and Jenny watched as he sat upright, swinging his leg around to sit on the bench in front of him. From the motion it was obvious that there were still pieces missing that hadn't been restored yet.

"Good," Joe said, glancing toward Andrei for only a brief moment. "The others should be more cooperative again."

Jenny and Darren looked at each other.

"Joe, a lot of people got stabbed trying to leave the gym," Darren said.

"Yeah, and they're all fine," Joe said, dismissing the point.

"They were all screaming in pain," Jenny said. "It doesn't matter if they physically healed, that really damaged any hope of things working out smoothly."

"It doesn't have to work smoothly," Joe retorted. "It just has to work."

"What if we don't actually find definitive evidence of the bomber's identity?" Greg Henshaw asked hesitantly.

"Then we keep looking," Joe said, his eyes lingering on the electrical sparking device.

They had this evil machine that the bomber built with their own two hands. There *must* be proof of their identity somewhere.

Suddenly, Joe saw a bright flash of blue electrical current ... and it didn't come from the device.

He turned his head, seeing another bright arc of lightning surge between the hands of Ellen Taylor, the Freshman Princess girl.

Chelsea screamed at the top of her lungs as the electricity began to envelop Ellen Taylor, breaking down her body into powder wherever the lightning struck.

Ellen's dress and shoes also atomized as the blue energy swarmed around her until everything was a pile of fine sand ... everything except for the duct tape.

A final bolt of lightning shot up from the pile, terminating in the roof of the gym.

Half of the gymnasium began screaming.

As Joe looked at the remains, he saw Melkonian mouth something to Wallace.

Rick Wallace had been sitting right next to her.

Joe stood up; the shotgun aimed right at his head.

"What did you do?!" Joe yelled at Wallace. "Where did she go?!"

"I ... I don't know," Wallace admitted. Fear filled his eyes, but not from the presence of the shotgun. "All I did was pray for her!"

"We hadn't even interviewed her yet!" Joe said, pressing the barrel into Wallace's forehead. "What if she was the bomber?!"

"Torelli stop!" Melkonian yelled.

Joe moved the gun in his direction.

"This is your fault too somehow!" he decided.

"He killed her!" someone yelled from the crowd. "Wallace brought back death!"

"What?!" Wallace and Melkonian said in confusion.

"All I did was pray for her!" Wallace shouted to them, but by that point the crowd had already stood to their feet in a sort of mania.

Many of the kids now looked at him like he was the Grim Reaper. However, a significant portion of students seemed to be relieved.

There was a way out of this place.

The students massed together in a mob, rushing to flee the Villa Vista High School gymnasium for one reason or another.

"No, stop!" Joe yelled, then turned to the four at the doors. "Stop them!"

Jennifer could see Jimmy and Camellia step aside while half of the crowd poured through the southwest doors.

Darren watched as the other half of the crowd pushed Brendan and Trey right through the egress, regardless of where they shoved the lances.

Panicking, Joe turned the shotgun on the visiting team bleachers.

"Stay where you are, all of you!" he said to the suspects.

Joe then turned to the other four standing at center court.

"That's it, we're moving them to the rooms!" he announced. "We'll interview them one at a time afterwards."

Greg, Chelsea, and Jennifer had their own lances, while Darren still had the crowbar.

The others stood beside Joe, ready to help usher everyone into the makeshift prison cells they'd prepared.

Darren and Jenny found themselves staring at the six students they'd helped earlier.

All six of them stared back in hatred, just like they did with Torelli.

***

Niles watched in stunned silence as Mr. Wallace appeared to totally destroy the Freshmen Princess girl with a Tesla Coil's worth of electricity.

Whatever he had done, with the help of Melkonian or the girl herself, had completely freed her from this place.

Ellen had been the first person Laura saw after waking up in the afterlife, following her own reflection in the bathroom mirror. Laura's skeletal appearance, and Ellen cutting herself into a pile of sand, had deeply frightened her.

He could feel that deep unsettling fear as he watched the freshman dissolve completely.

Niles could only assume this is what happened to all the others while they slept. Rather than their bodies slowly rebuilding, they were violently dissolved into powder. The energy, the lifeforce, was completely separated from the crude matter, leaving behind the atmosphere of dust they still walked around in.

Either Mr. Wallace had discovered some secret no one else was aware of or that girl was finally ready to move on.

The crowd in the other bleachers were not lost in their own forms of contemplation though. They were going crazy.

This was the first instance of someone who had been restored after hurting themselves being totally deconstructed and freed.

No matter what any of them individually thought, as a mass of people they were scared shitless and immediately bolted for the gymnasium doors.

Niles thought of grabbing Laura and running too, but it took the mob nearly a minute to force their way through the available exits.

Before Niles could make a decision, Torelli had already deployed his flunkies to keep watch over them. In the case of the six of them, it was Darren and Jennifer doing the guarding.

Andrei tried to stand on his own, but as soon as he put weight on his left leg, it buckled. Rafael had to catch him, at which time Blaire switched to Andrei's left side to replace him.

He wasn't going anywhere on his own.

Raf and Elise had decided to stick with them. They were either going to leave together or stay together.

Niles observed that his indecision turned out to be a moral good. He looked at Laura and then they looked at the other four.

Maybe they didn't know them too well, but Niles was not about to believe Melvin's accusations that Andrei was the bomber. He also *definitely* wasn't going to believe the girlfriend of the guy that had stabbed him.

When Niles had asked Laura if they should help Andrei and the others get settled safely in the stands, she was quick to agree.

He couldn't quite decipher the look on her face. They seemed to have similar reasons for wanting to help, but there was something more involved for her. She was feeling really betrayed by Anne.

Now, after all these hours of talking to Blaire and Rafael and Elise, the conclusion felt pretty obvious. These were the only friends they had left. All the others had either abandoned them or turned overtly hostile against them.

"Joe, everything's falling apart!" Jennifer Maxwell yelled at Torelli. "We don't need the rooms; they can't go anywhere anyway!"

"Are you kidding?!" Joe snapped back at her. "Wallace just sent one of them away. He could be the bomber! They all could! We will keep them contained here no matter what! They need to pay!"

"But Joe!" Jennifer pleaded again.

It is then that Torelli turned the shotgun on her, aiming it right between her eyes.

She stepped backwards at the shock, dropping her knife lance to the ground.

"Do it!" Niles heard Melvin Mueller shout from the other side of the stands.

Darren Clark stepped in front of her.

"Don't you fucking dare, Torelli!" he yelled, raising the crowbar in the air in a threatening stance.

"Then do your jobs, Darren!" Torelli said, the Citori aimed through both of their heads.

Jennifer grabbed Darren from behind, pulling him back, away from the gun.

"Don't. Please ... don't," she said to him.

Niles figured she was reminded of what happened to Andrei after facing the gun.

"Torelli, please stop!" Mr. Wallace said. "It's me you want, let these kids go."

Brendan and Trey ran back into the gymnasium.

"Jimmy and Camellia are gone!" Trey said. "They disappeared into the crowd!"

"We'll find them later," Torelli said. "Help us get all of them into the cells."

"Right," Brendan said.

"Well Darren?" Torelli said to him.

Jennifer was holding him from behind, more of a hug than keeping him from attacking.

Darren turned up toward Niles and the rest of them.

"Please," he muttered. "Please just come to the rooms."

The six of them were the only ones not tied up. The others even had a set of bindings above their knees, keeping them from running.

Torelli turned the gun from Darren and Jennifer, aiming toward them again.

They were all backed up together in a tight cluster.

"Okay!" Blaire said from the middle of the cluster.

"You guys go," she whispered to the four of them, "run to the choir room when you get the chance."

"Are you crazy?" Elise said, the Ka-Bar knife in her hand. "We're not leaving you."

"We'll be okay," Andrei said through the pain. "Get away from him."

"Well?!" Joe yelled.

The six of them moved down onto the basketball court.

Trey, Brendan, Chelsea, Greg, and Eric herded the other captured students as well as Wallace and Melkonian. Darren and Jennifer walked beside the six of them as Torelli held the shotgun to their backs.

Niles could hear Andrei groan with every step. He was essentially just hopping on his right foot. Blaire did her best to support his left side, holding his chest as he put his arm on her shoulders.

The barrels of Joe's gun were too close to Niles and Laura. They couldn't get away even if they wanted to abandon the others.

As they walked, the group was led into the main entrance of the school building. They could already see half a dozen bodies lying on the ground of the front foyer. They were all completely motionless. Most of their heads were in a million pieces, smashed open like hourglasses full of fine sand.

There was a line gathered around the railing above the foyer, people were taking turns.

"Hey guys," a familiar voice said above them.

They looked up to see Liam standing on the metal railing.

"Looks like it's finally going to work this time," he said, a disturbing serenity to his words.

"Don't!" Laura screamed, but it didn't matter.

Liam jumped, diving down the forty-foot drop head first.

Laura buried her face into Niles' jacket. Blaire and Andrei turned away as he hit.

Niles watched the powder explode outward, the body going totally limp.

He realized that no one's skulls were damaged when the students tried this before. It was similar to how Andrei's bones remained undamaged also, even though Joe's shot should have shattered several of his bones to pieces.

The worst that happened before were "disconnections", such as neck vertebrae temporarily coming out of alignment.

This was real ... these kids were double-dead.

Where did they go this time?

"Keep moving!" Torelli yelled from the back.

Brendan and Trey forced the students into the classrooms in that main hallway. There were only eight rooms in total, so they were doubling people up.

Wallace and Melkonian were shut away into a room too, leaving only the six of them left.

"Drop the knives," Torelli demanded of Elise and Raf as they were all pressed up against the open door of a classroom.

"No fuckin' way," Raf spat back, standing in front of the rest of them.

Torelli aimed the gun at Elise. It made Raf shift positions, moving in front of her, but he did not drop the Ka-Bar.

That is when a lance came flying through the hallway like a javelin, landing where his appendix would be. The blow was shocking and painful, enough for him to lose focus.

Torelli bashed his head with the back of the shotgun, knocking him out.

Before the rest of them could react, Brendan shoved Andrei and Blaire into the room, slamming the door behind them.

Trey moved in, separating Niles and Laura from Elise.

The person who threw the lance closed in on them ... Jordan Trainor. Close behind were Marcus, Paxton, and Amanda.

Elise dropped her own knife to pull the lance out of Raf. Both of the Ka-Bars were kicked away as they were all surrounded. Trey Devall picked both of the knives up, sliding them in his back pockets.

"In the room," Torelli said, pointing to a different open door.

She grabbed Raf's arms and pulled him carefully through, before being trapped inside.

Brendan and Trey secured their room with wooden doorstops, the same as they did with Blaire and Andrei.

"You're out of rooms," Laura said.

"Oh no." Torelli smiled. "We're keeping the Musketeers together."

Trey opened a door, revealing Barry and Melvin inside.

Jordan moved his knife lance toward Laura. Niles pulled her away.

They slowly backed into the room.

The four of them were sealed in together by Torelli and his varsity goons.

***

Jennifer finally understood what it meant to watch your life flash before your eyes.

When she actually did die, that didn't happen to her.

She still wasn't sure if she'd fallen asleep on Darren's shoulder. She was emotionally exhausted, but the adrenaline of Torelli being thrown out and comforting Isabella had her too wired. Even Darren had said he remembered talking to her up until things went black.

Her new theory was that when the gym exploded, she was burned alive too quickly. The blood in her brain probably boiled before she could register the memories, let alone roll the clip show of her seventeen-ish years of existence.

Ironically, Joe Torelli had given her a second chance to experience it.

As he pointed that gun in her face, she looked down the top barrel and watched all of those moments flood into her mind in an instant.

She could see her three-year-old self sitting on her dad's knee at the law office. He pretended to be a judge while she argued a case for one of her dolls.

She could see her seven-year-old self walking with her brother along the sidewalk. He began taking a right on the street, heading for the high school, while she still had to go left toward the elementary and middle school.

She could see her twelve-year-old self in the carpool with Darren after her brother graduated and couldn't drive her to school anymore. She couldn't even tell what they were talking about, she was just glad to be talking to him. Darren was fun and really nice to her; she was glad they had that extra hour of time together every day.

She could see her fourteen-year-old self in the passenger seat of her mom's car. She was lost in thought. Just because she left the carpool, why had she also stopped talking to Darren? Why had starting high school torn them apart like that?

She could see her sixteen-year-old self watching Darren walk out onto the field for the first time in his full football gear. He was so much older and more mature now. But instead of ogling him like some of the other girls were, she felt sad. She could still see twelve-year-old Darren sitting next to her, but she couldn't see any of the years in between, even though they'd crossed each other in hallways and shared classes together.

She could see her seventeen-year-old self cheering at one of the Varsity Football games. They finished up their halftime set. Darren had watched her, and only her, for the entire set. Rather than go up and point that out to him, she watched him, and only him, for the rest of the second half. He definitely noticed.

She could see herself two days ago, taking off her Homecoming Queen crown as they confessed their love for each other in the hallway. It was ten minutes before they were murdered together in a fiery explosion.

Then, finally, she could see the back of Darren's head as he stepped between her and the barrel of Joe's shotgun.

It all happened in a brief moment, but it felt like she lived her life all over again.

It reminded her of everything she lost and everything she still had.

She wrapped her arms around his chest, holding him from behind.

"Don't. Please ... don't," she begged him. The images of Andrei Tunnikov's body, torn to pieces, were burned into her mind.

Jenny was glad she had kept him from attacking Joe. They walked through the main atrium of this hellish recreation of Villa Vista High School. Close to two dozen dead bodies were scattered around the floor. Each of them had jumped from the second-floor catwalks above. None of them were coming back.

Eric Schwartz reached down, feeling the wrist of one of the bodies.

"No pulse," he said. "Also, he's cold ... colder than we are already."

Joe and Marcus talked in the middle of the atrium.

"What's going on?" Marcus asked him. "Why aren't they gettin' up?"

"Wallace did something," Joe said. "He vaporized the freshman girl and somehow brought death back."

"He did what?!" Marcus yelled in anger and confusion. "She was probably the bomber!"

"I know," Joe answered through gritted teeth.

"Or how about all of these?" Marcus said, motioning to the bodies. "One of them could be the bomber."

"I know!" Joe said again.

"Are you telling me they're going to slip through our fingers like fucking sand before we can confront them?!" Marcus asked, his eyes straining.

"They could be going someplace worse," Torelli offered, trying to give himself some closure too. "Honestly, it's like things were before. It's just another mysterious wall of death."

"I don't just want them dead; I want to kill them like they killed her!" Marcus yelled.

"Look, if they haven't offed themselves yet, then the bomber is still here for some reason," Joe figured. "So just ... wait. We'll find out who's gone, check their shit again, and then go from there."

Marcus shook his head in hopeless disbelief. He had no power to stop the bomber from disappearing, just like he had no power to stop Janice from disappearing. He stumbled out of the atrium and walked toward the ballroom.

Eric Schwartz had the notebook ready. The others started tallying up the dead.

"Let's get out of here," Darren whispered to Jenny.

She nodded.

They slid away into one of the stairwells, heading toward Mr. Ziegler's room.

Jenny was happy to not see Blake lurking outside of Mr. Jameson's room next door. If Kyle Moreno was inside, he had turned off the lights to hide. She didn't think she'd seen him among the dead.

Blake had pushed too far, pissing off Joe like that. As soon as Joe saw that he wasn't in the gymnasium and Brendan had ratted Blake out as one of the instigators, it was all over. Joe ordered him to be gagged with duct tape and brought back as a suspect to stand trial.

There was no justifiable reason for this, Joe just wanted revenge.

Blake fell near the bottom of Jennifer's list of suspects. He was far too narcissistic to kill himself for any reason. He would want to survive and revel in the enjoyment of having killed Jenny and Darren, assuming that was his primary motive.

Taking the younger girl to the dance instead was much more in his character. He was flaunting the sophomore in Jenny's face all night. He probably would have followed them to Jimmy's place too.

Luckily, Jimmy would have likely thrown them out on sight if Camellia didn't threaten them first. They were good friends, real friends.

She didn't know where Amanda and Sheena had disappeared to in all this. Brendan and Trey seemed to have totally forgotten them while getting swept up into this mafia enforcer mindset.

Darren punched in the door code, letting them into the classroom dorm.

Jenny closed the door behind them, making sure it latched securely.

When she turned back around, she felt Darren pull her into a close hug.

"I thought I was going to lose you again," he said, holding back tears.

She returned the embrace.

"Me too," she whispered.

"I don't want to go yet," he said. "Who knows what's on the other side?"

"I know," she agreed. "We've only had a few days. It's not enough."

Darren took a deep breath, gathering his determination.

"We're going to outlast Torelli," he promised. "We're going to have that time."

***

Andrei felt completely useless as he hobbled down the main hallway of the school. He might as well have been an amputee missing his knee and everything below it. Without the various muscles and tendons in his calf, the leg just buckled whenever he put weight on it.

Blaire had literally become his other half, propping him upright so he wouldn't collapse onto the stone floor.

Worse than that was realizing that his other fear may be coming true. All of these students were taking the easy way out and it seemed to be working. Maybe the rest of his leg would never heal at all now. He needed to find or make a permanent crutch.

Torelli marched the six of them in front of an open classroom door.

Andrei found himself and Blaire to be at the center of this pod of people. He hated the feeling; he should be the one protecting them.

Torelli demanded that Raf and Elise drop their knives, which Raf unsurprisingly refused.

Unfortunately, none of them saw the reinforcements arrive to help the football players. Jordan Trainer tossed a knife lance through the hallway. It stabbed into the side of Raf's gut, causing him to let go of the Ka-Bar. In a quick follow-up, Torelli bashed him in the head with the gun, knocking him out cold.

Elise was distracted, moving to reach Raf. Niles likewise pulled Laura away from the danger. With an opening made, Brendan Jensen stepped in to act. He shoved Andrei and Blaire, sending them stumbling backwards into the classroom.

Just like that, the door was slammed shut.

Blaire scrambled to her feet, rushing at it, but found that the handle on the inside had been broken off. Because the door swung outward, they couldn't even shove something into the doorframe to pop open the latch.

They could also hear the sound of pounding as wooden wedges were placed along the bottom of the door, barricading them inside.

This was their prison cell now. Perhaps it should be called their own personal Tartarus, because they found themselves in Mr. Van Gaal's room.

Blaire listened against the door as the last of the action wrapped up outside.

Andrei grit his teeth as he sat against one of the walls. He lifted his left knee and propped up the foot to take the pressure off of his calf.

"I think everyone's been put in separate rooms," she said.

"I hope Raf's okay," Andrei replied. "I don't know if the healing thing is happening anymore."

"He wouldn't die from that, would he?" Blaire asked.

"A gut wound is usually fatal from bleeding out or sepsis," Andrei said. "Neither of those are really a factor anymore."

"That's good," Blaire breathed in relief. She couldn't imagine Elise having to watch him die, all alone. The pain would be unbearable.

"Even still, if healing is back to the way it used to be, when we were alive," Andrei said, "it's gonna take a lot longer to come back from."

Blaire realized what else he was implying by that theory.

The lower portion of Andrei's leg was still little more than bones and skin. If the calf muscles didn't miraculously restore themselves from the dust in the air, then Andrei could be crippled permanently.

"I might need to find a leg brace and a good cane." Andrei chuckled.

"I'm so sorry," Blaire said, sitting down next to him. She chose his right side to avoid bumping the open wound.

"This is all my fault," she mumbled, folding her arms on her knees. "I should have told you as soon as we woke up."

"I shouldn't have brought it up by the lockers, where we could be overheard," Andrei said, taking part of the blame.

He glanced down, looking in her sad eyes.

"I have to admit though," he said, "I am curious."

Blaire turned away from him, staring over her knees.

"I don't even know how to start," she said.

"How about ... at the end?" Andrei asked in morbid reflection.

She sunk down into her sweatshirt jacket.

"When we were leaning against the wall," Andrei began, "correct me if I'm wrong, but you looked like you were having as great of a time as I was."

"Yes ..." Blaire said, taking his hand, "absolutely I was."

"But while we were talking about what we were going to say to Raf and Elise," he went on, "you just froze in fear. Then suddenly you were trying to pull us out of the building."

"I didn't know what was going to happen," Blaire whispered, "I just knew that it meant death."

"What do you mean 'it'?" Andrei asked. "What did you see?"

"It wasn't what I saw," she said, moving her hand to hug her shoulders, "it was what I heard. When I put my ear against the wall, I heard this high-pitched whistling sound."

"The natural gas valves," Andrei said.

"Yes," Blaire replied. "But I didn't know that's what the sound was. I only found out when you and I saw it for ourselves under the bleachers."

"Then how did you know that the sound meant death?" Andrei asked.

She took a deep breath, then finally spoke it aloud.

"Because I'd heard it once before," Blaire said, "in a nightmare."

"A nightmare?" Andrei asked.

"It wasn't even twelve hours before the gym exploded," she said. "That's how I was woken up Saturday morning, I heard that sound and I died in the dream."

Andrei was quiet, letting her go on.

"I used to dream quite often," Blaire began, "But I seldom had nightmares. My dreams used to be a lot more pleasant than real life ... at least, that's how I used to feel."

"Have you dreamed since then?" Andrei asked.

"I wish," she mumbled.

"How did things happen?" he asked. "Did you see the school, the dance?"

"No, none of it," Blaire said. "I was on this old-fashioned wooden ship. The ship was just sitting anchored in some harbor. The only light in the sky was from the beacons of a lighthouse."

"Point Reyes?" Andrei asked.

Blaire shook her head.

"It looked like New England," she said. "The air was very cold. I was wearing a Victorian-era dress and this really tight corset. I tried to cut it off, but I couldn't find anything that could do it. I stumbled to the railing of the boat and looked up at the beacons."

Blaire looked up at the corner of the room.

"I thought I saw my grandpa by the lighthouse," she said.

Andrei knew exactly who she meant. She had told him more about Edward Tidwell than any of her living family members.

"I wish I could see him now," Blaire whispered, her face looking even more downcast.

Andrei put his hand on hers. She turned her palm over, lacing their fingers.

"That's when I heard it," she said, her eyes opening in fear as they had that fateful night. "Instead of cannons, the ship had all of these giant tea kettles and every one of them was whistling. I went down below deck to try to quiet them, and that's when I saw that the whole ship was on fire. There was nothing I could do to stop the fire, or the whistling, or the-"

Blaire paused again, stunned into silence as she put one final piece together.

"Blaire, what is it?" Andrei asked quickly, putting his other hand on her knee.

"On the ship," she said, looking at him with quiet horror. "There was dust everywhere."

She reached up with her free hand and brushed her hair. A small puff of powder trickled down out of her hand.

"The dust covered everything," she said, "just like now. When I woke up, I thought it was ash, but it wasn't. It was this ... it was *people*."

Andrei looked down at the thin layer of powder covering the wound on his leg.

"I saw it all Andrei," Blaire said, her voice cracking. "But I didn't know what it was, I didn't know until it was too late. I swear ... I would have saved us if I knew."

"I know, I believe you," Andrei said, trying to calm her down.

"And Elise, and Raf, and all the others," she muttered. "If only I had figured it out."

"There was no reason to believe that any of that was a vision," Andrei said. "It was just a bad dream."

"And the corset," she said, "that was how I died. The corset kept pulling tighter and I couldn't breathe. It was just like at the dance, I was lying there and I couldn't breathe and then everything went black."

She was sobbing into his shoulder now. All of the memories and pain and death were flooding through her. He kissed her head as he held her there.

Blaire had alluded to that earlier, but Andrei hadn't really thought much about those final seconds of their lives. She must have either suffocated on the smoke and ash, or the fire had scorched the inside of her lungs and she could no longer pull oxygen out of the air.

In Andrei's case, he remembered them landing against the stage apron, but very little afterwards.

His last memory of life was a shockwave of sensation. The pain in his right hand rolled back over his fingers, then his wrist, then his elbow, until the only actual pain left was creeping over his shoulder. All the nerve cells in his arm had died as the fire burned deeper into his flesh.

The next memory after that was Blaire calling his name and waking him up.

It was a crazy story. Andrei considered what he might have thought if he were still alive, and it wasn't Blaire saying this. He wouldn't take it at face value at all. He would think the person had spent a night partying a little too hard and hadn't shaken off the paranoia yet.

Things were a bit different now. They actually were dead. Her premonition turned out to be true. How was she supposed to know it was anything more than some bad football stadium food manifesting itself into a scary dream?

Of course, she could have been coming up with this story over the past two days as a way to explain her actions. That's definitely what Torelli and his Cheka could accuse her of, if she was sat down in front of that wall of fire.

Andrei did believe her though. As the only person to see her reaction first hand, it all made sense to him. Even if her story was less convincing, he might have still believed her anyway.

Andrei was dead, separated from his family completely. He didn't see himself going anyplace better if he died here. If this was Limbo, there were many more Circles of Hell they could drop down to, each worse than the last.

Blaire was all he had left now. He wanted to cherish these moments of togetherness before they sunk lower into the hellfire.

He was not going to let some petty dictator take her away from him. He was going to stay by her side no matter what. He had to be there to protect her.

With Torelli and the others losing so many of their potential suspects or witnesses, they were going to get desperate.

Desperation always brings out the worst in people.

TWENTY-FOUR

JUDGE, JURY, & EXECUTIONER

RICK WALLACE AND BOB MELKONIAN found themselves in Hana Novak's Student Council and Psychology classroom.

The Student Council only had one class period in the mornings, so for most of the school day the room existed to give kids a basic introduction to the study of the human mind.

Mrs. Novak often used each of her two subject areas to improve the efficiency and function of the other. For instance, she would use the psychology classes to run polls on what kind of event themes the student body might be interested in for the next Prom, or Spring Formal, or Homecoming. She would present the information to the student representatives from each class and see how they would react to the results.

How the student leaders made use of the opinions of the masses was a psychology lesson in and of itself.

Of course, she never explicitly painted a target on the back of her Student Council kids by announcing that they had rejected an idea a lot of students found compelling. Her testing had enough layers of obfuscation that they couldn't draw such conclusions one way or another.

She sort of enjoyed the Game Theory to all of it. It was her belief that it would make the Student Council kids better leaders. It would also help the Psychology classes get a deeper understanding of their own interests and why they liked them in the first place.

Hana had a strange reaction to the kids' decision to use "High Society" as a banquet theme.

When she first mentioned it in the faculty lunchroom one day, Bob and Rick thought that the appeal seemed pretty straightforward. What better theme for a Homecoming dance than to make it fancy galas from other time periods?

Hana's fascination lay in the specific time periods each class had selected to represent them.

The Freshman Class reps had chosen the American Roaring Twenties, often better known as The Jazz Age. The most noteworthy depiction of the era, arguably one of the greatest novels in American literature, was F. Scott Fitzgerald's *The Great Gatsby*.

The novel was about how hollow and empty all the wealth and splendor really was. By the end of the story, the titular Jay Gatsby lay dead. He spent his whole life pursuing the green light across the bay, representing the simple love and happiness which always glowed just out of his reach.

The Sophomore Class reps had chosen a more remote time period for one specific and obvious reason; the Italian Renaissance was the setting of *Romeo and Juliet*.

All of the sophomores spent their English 10 class imbibing in the sixteenth century literature of the historic English playwright. It was perhaps Shakespeare's greatest work, the most famous story about love ending in tragedy of all time.

The Junior Class reps had chosen Bourbon Restoration France. While French literature is famously saturated with love and romance, the students were particularly inspired by the recent film adaptation of the *Les Misérables* musical.

The only love story that worked out well there involved Cosette and Marius, and that's only after so much bloodshed and suffering and misery. Not to mention, the musical paints a much rosier picture of Marius than the original Victor Hugo story. Most students were only familiar with the Marius of film and stage, but at the novel's end, he is much crueler to Valjean than most would be comfortable with.

The Senior Class reps had chosen Victorian England. While it was arguably one of the highest societies that ever existed, holding imperial control over most of the world, it also fell short in the ways of romance. The most famous work of Victorian literature, that the Villa Vista High School students were all familiar with, was Emily Brontë's *Wuthering Heights*.

Brontë family literature was part of the junior year English curriculum. It would have been fresh in mind for the seniors. Needless to say, things had not gone well for the novel's most famous character. Heathcliff is known for turning cruel after the loss of his beloved Catherine. He exerts his suffering as rage and vengeance on all the other characters of the story until his pain finally consumes him and he dies. Only in death is he rejoined with Catherine.

Hana Novak dug into the rationale for why the students would have chosen such things as inspirations for a school dance.

On one hand, Bob Melkonian remembered feeling dismissive of her allusions to "love". This was a high school dance; these kids didn't know what love was. To him, love was waking up every day next to Angie and knowing that she was still right there next to him, despite all of his flaws and failings. Real love isn't understood until you've spent years in that kind of commitment.

She retorted, saying that the kids didn't know anything else. Asking that girl or boy they had a crush on to a formal affair, explicitly framed around the idea of romance, was the closest thing to love they would understand. Even then, she pointed out that for many of these kids those feelings were years in the making. While maintaining the fire was necessary, you don't get love without that initial spark.

Rick, fully versed in his own areas of psychology, pointed out that most famous love stories are tragedies. It wasn't about the specific stories the students might have read, it was about the nature of love and death itself. You only feel warmth because everything else is cold. Those stories ring true in so many because the love felt most real when cloaked in the shrouds of separation and death.

That conversation with Hana Novak weighed very heavily on Bob's thoughts, now that he stood in this room.

Rick Wallace was rubbing his duct tape bindings against the sharp edge of her teacher's desk.

"Rick," Bob asked him. "Was Hana at the dance?"

Rick looked up at him, then glanced around the room, seeing what he meant.

"Mrs. Novak? She's always at the dances, it was a Student Council event after all."

The bindings on his wrists snapped. With his hands free, he began tearing away at the tape near his biceps.

Bob finally remembered seeing her. She spent a lot of time in the media booth making sure all the music and lighting played out dramatically with each part of the evening.

The media room was in the catwalk on the north side of the Murphy Center. That room would have been one of the first places destroyed by the explosion of the gymnasium.

"She's gone too, isn't she?" Bob asked.

Rick walked up to him with a letter opener.

"I'm afraid so."

He made perforations in the tape until Bob could pull himself free.

"Rick," Bob asked, "what if a teacher was responsible for all this?"

"You mean Hana?" Rick dismissed him. "No, absolutely not. She had a husband and two boys at home."

Rick also recalled the conversation they'd had in the faculty lounge.

"Are you thinking about what she was saying with the class themes?" he asked. "You do remember what she said about the 'Tropical Getaway' theme, right? The students were 'looking for their own escape from the storms and tumult of life'. Come on Bob, she always talked like that."

"Okay, yeah, you're right," Bob conceded.

They sat down in the office chairs on each side of her desk.

"But that's something the kids haven't really considered either," Bob said.

Rick looked at him in disbelief.

"Bob, that's the *first* thing the students considered," he said flatly. "That's why we're locked in here."

"You worked here for decades," Bob said, "you would know better than anyone. Is there someone, a faculty member, a teacher, a janitor, *anyone* who might have had a reason for doing all this?"

Rick Wallace sank back in his chair, slowly replaying all forty-six years of his career at Villa Vista High School.

"Probably the biggest grudge I could think of," Rick began, "was a teacher named Matt Summer."

Bob drew a blank, the name didn't sound familiar at all.

"Yeah, you probably don't remember him. I think he was gone before you even got here," Rick said, swiveling a bit in the chair. "He taught World History, long before Nordquist."

World History was a mandatory requirement for the Freshman Class.

"So, what happened?" Bob asked.

"He was accused of sleeping with a student." Rick rapped his fingers on the desk.

Bob winced in disgust. He didn't kill his abusive father, but he absolutely would have killed anyone who preyed on Monika like that.

"I know," Rick said, seeing his reaction. "It was only his second or third year teaching. As you might figure, it was also his last. The school quickly called the police once the accusation was made."

"So, he *was* arrested?" Bob asked.

"Yes," Rick nodded, "and tried, and convicted."

Bob looked relieved.

"He did six years and was listed as a sex offender for the rest of his life."

"Just six years?" Bob sat upright.

Rick nodded again.

"His wife left him and he never saw his own young daughter ever again. He was in his early thirties when the scandal broke."

"Filthy predator," Bob spat.

"That's how everyone felt." Rick closed his eyes. "Everyone except for him. He claimed he was innocent the entire time, that he had never touched the fifteen-year-old girl, let alone slept with her."

Bob's expression changed.

"Why would the girl lie?"

"Summer claimed it was revenge for giving the girl bad grades," Rick said. "Supposedly she was on track to fail the class. The girl claimed that he had forced her into intimacy as a quid pro quo. He would have only passed her if she slept with him."

Bob felt dirty all over just talking about the subject.

"What happened to him?" he asked.

"Well, he could never work around children again," Rick said. "His career was dead, family had left him, society in general saw him as a monster. He spent the years afterwards doing odd jobs wherever he could."

"No, but where is he now?" Bob clarified.

"He killed himself in 2001." Rick paused, letting the finality hang in the air. "He left a suicide note continuing to claim his innocence, reiterating everything he'd said at the original trial back in 1993. He also left some harsh words for his ex-wife for not believing him, and some sadder words for his daughter who would have been in high school herself by that time."

"Well," Bob said, not sure what to feel, "he's long dead, clearly he didn't blow up the school over a decade later. Why bring him up?"

"Because once news of his death circulated," Rick said, "the girl that accused him came forward. She was in her twenties by that point. He was telling the truth."

"Oh my god," Bob whispered. He felt even dirtier than before.

"It could have been worse," Rick said. "That girl could have taken the truth to her grave. Not that her confession did anything for Summer. Most people who remember the scandal don't even know that she recanted her story."

"Why?" Bob asked, thinking back to 2001. "How come no one was talking about it at the time?"

"Because it was uncomfortable," Rick said. "It didn't just shift the blame onto the girl, it shifted blame on the school, the faculty, his ex-wife, and everyone else who'd abandoned him.

"I remember that story because it was well documented from start to finish. How many stories like that didn't even make it to the papers? How many grudges could be out there?

"Even if they'd never heard of that scandal, a lot of the kids probably think you or I have some hidden hatred just like that, some real reason to turn our anger onto the school."

"But, the girl confessed." Bob placed his hands on the desk, working out the details. "So, there must not have been evidence that he'd done it, if she admitted she was lying. How did he get convicted in the first place?"

"Because sometimes it's easier to fight the monsters we expect to see, rather than the *true* demons hiding in their shadows," Rick said. "As far as the court goes, all it takes is *Twelve Angry Men*."

Bob realized that he might as well have been one of those men. He looked down at the sticky duct tape residue still clinging to his wrists. He was now more or less in Matt Summer's position.

The children could convict him as guilty of blowing up the school. They could even torture and execute him. If the real killer said nothing, they would be none the wiser. In fact, they'd feel fully vindicated in their righteous judgement.

Bob pictured himself beating someone like Matt Summer to death, only for Monika to tell him that she'd made the whole thing up because she was failing World History. The absurdity of it somehow made the tragedy that much worse.

For the real girl, she could have stopped the madness at any time, when he was arrested, when the police filed charges, when the news spread, at the trial itself. Sure, Summer's name may have been tarnished, but he would at least be exonerated in the eyes of the law. He might not have lost his wife. He might have had a normal relationship with his daughter.

Even after real damage was done, that girl could have come forward when he was in prison, or when he was released. Why wait to tell the truth until it was too late for literally any redemption? Did it take that long for her conscience to finally wear down on her? Did she pay a price at all? Did she wait until Matt Summer was in the ground just so she wouldn't have to face her own demons?

"What did his wife and daughter think of the revelation?" Bob asked.

"I don't know," Rick said. "She moved away after the trial, most likely changed her name. Who knows if they even found out? That little girl's entire life with her father was stolen from her by a teenager protecting herself and a compounding pile of lies."

Rick looked Bob in the eye. "That's why I don't think it was a teacher that blew up the school. They may be young, but these kids are capable of a lot more greatness and terror than they're ever given credit for."

Bob was reminded of seeing that Tunnikov boy's leg get blown off by one of his classmates. No matter how big or terrifying he or Joe Torelli could be, they were still just teenagers.

"I guess they can actually kill us now," Bob said, referring to the students. "None of the ones who jumped seemed to be getting back up anymore."

Rick was silent, images of blue electricity flashed before his eyes.

"Rick, what did you do?" Bob asked. "Where did Ellen Taylor go?"

"I don't know," Rick muttered, just as baffled as Melkonian.

"What was that prayer you said?" Bob asked him.

"It's nothing special." Rick crossed his arms on the desk. "It's one of the common 'prayers for the dead'. Ellen went to my church. Our priest said it sometimes ... she would have recognized it."

"So, does that mean this is Purgatory?" Bob asked.

"No," Rick said, still certain of *his own* judgement. "It just means we're dead and I couldn't think of anything else to say. I was just trying to make her feel better."

"Well, it worked, obviously."

Rick didn't reply, but he wore a face of disagreement.

"Well, where else did she go?" Bob challenged him. "You can't honestly think somewhere worse?"

"I don't know."

"Well," Bob said, "she wanted out of here, and it happened for her."

"And what about all the other kids?" Rick said. "They're not coming back at all. There's no lightning, no fanfare, no chorus of angels. They're just dust and corpses."

"If not Purgatory, then what else would a prayer like that be meant for?" Bob asked.

Rick furrowed his mustache and leaned back in his chair

"One idea is that it's meant for the souls facing final judgement," Rick said, "like the Rapture, End of Days."

"Well, do you think the Rapture started an hour ago, just as you were praying for her?"

Rick said nothing.

"Rick, we don't have to know the mechanics," Bob said. "We just have to know that it works, it delivered Ellen Taylor out of this place. We've got to try again."

"What?" Rick asked, "you mean you?"

"No, not me … the kids, Rick." Bob took a deep breath in contemplation. "What if that's why we're here? To set them free."

"We're here as punishment," Rick said. "Bob, I don't mean to be cruel, but you sound like you're still in the 'bargaining' phase."

"Maybe you're wrong about this being Hell," Bob said. "Don't you remember how much suffering happened in the Bible to 'good' people. That's the entire book of Job! Satan was allowed to put him through a great deal of suffering as a test of his spirit."

"Job wasn't dead," Rick said. "The test is over."

"It's not 'over' until we've tried that prayer on every single one of the kids still stuck here. God has used much worse people for much more extraordinary things before."

"What do you mean 'we'," Rick smiled. "I thought you were Orthodox?"

"Well then I'm in luck," Bob retorted, "because according to you this isn't Purgatory."

Rick's smile faded.

"They'll probably kill us before we even get the chance."

"Maybe," Bob agreed.

He then sat forward on his chair, facing Rick like a teacher.

"Now, repeat the words again."

***

Elise Gosselin pulled Raf through the door of the classroom as carefully as she could. Quite a bit of powder was trickling out of the wound on the right side of his stomach.

Once they were inside, the footballers slammed the door and started blocking it up on the bottom.

Elise sat Raf upright so his chest would put pressure on the wound and close it.

He groaned a bit at the feeling, which was a good sign.

She looked at the wound on his head, where Torelli had butted him with the shotgun. There was a bit of a break in the skin, but nothing serious.

"Raf, honey, can you hear me?" Elise asked, trying to hold his head upright.

"Ugh," he groaned again, before muttering, "Holy shit, that hurts so much. I can't even imagine what Andrei was feeling."

"Just rest," Elise said, trying to keep him from squirming. "I think we'll be here a while."

"Which one of them stabbed me?" he asked.

"That basketball guy named Jordan," she answered.

"I'm gonna stab him back," Raf grunted, "as soon as I get my knives back."

Elise chuckled.

"You can stab him too if you want."

"I will," she agreed.

She sat down next to him against the wall.

"What'd they do with Blaire and Andrei?" he asked.

"They shoved them into Van Gaal's classroom and locked the door." Elise sighed. "They wanted to separate all of us."

"Where are we?" Raf asked her, trying to get his eyes to adjust.

"Mr. Guzmán's room," Elise said.

"Oh shit, Algebra? I hated that class. Guzmán was a dick."

Elise smiled, snuggling closer to him. "So, I guess we're stuck here until they decide to interview us."

"I don't know what the hell they expect," Raf quipped, "we didn't do anything."

Elise looked away from him.

"What do you think that boy meant?" she asked him. "That Blaire and Andrei knew about the bomb?"

"Who knows," Raf dismissed. "That Melvin kid's probably the killer, trying to pass the blame off on anyone he could in Torelli's kangaroo court."

"He seemed so certain though." There was a nervous tone in her voice. "I didn't research Andrei at all. I don't know where he came from or if he was dangerous or what he was like in his old school."

"Elise, stop." Raf put a hand on her arm. "We've spent so much time with him and Blaire over the last few months. Do you honestly think either of them would blow up the school?"

Elise said nothing.

"Let me rephrase that," Rafael said. "Do you think Blaire would murder you?"

"No, never!"

"Do you think she would get involved with Andrei at all if he were a threat to any of us?"

"Well, no," Elise said, "but she's got a lot of hormones clouding her judgement right now. She hasn't had a relationship like this before, *at all*. I almost thought she was going to maul him on the dance floor."

Raf chuckled a little, picturing her tackling him to the ground and getting down to business.

"Isn't that more reason that she wouldn't blow up the dance?" Raf pointed out.

"Yeah," Elise admitted. "But you yourself said that you can't read Andrei's mood at all. We don't really know what he's thinking."

"Yeah," Raf said, "but that's the way everyone else feels about Blaire too. When she's not getting all hot and heavy for Andrei, she looks like she's wishing death on everyone."

Elise looked away from him, considering it.

"You're used to it, and I'm more used to it now," Raf said, "but even you admitted today that Blaire is scary. Andrei is more or less the same way, but with some subtle variations. That's why they work so well together."

"You're right," she said, feeling ashamed for suspecting him.

"And if you're wondering about what Amanda said," Raf added, with a bit of ire in his voice, "I'd also like to point out that the bitch said nothing when Torelli had his gun pointed at us. There was nothing like 'guys stop it,' or 'Raf and Elise are innocent.' We defended them at first instinct, and instead of trying to persuade us, she just sat quietly like we were co-conspirators."

"I know." Elise shook her head. "Amanda hasn't been the same since freshman year."

"We can't turn our backs on Blaire and Andrei now."

"I wasn't saying that!"

"I know, I know," Raf assured her, "I'm just saying ... they're the closest thing to family we have left. Torelli and his cholos *want* to pull us apart. That's why we're separated like this. One of them is probably the bomber, but they want us to turn on each other. Even if they aren't the bombers, what they're doing with all this prison gang bullshit is bad enough. We *can't* let them break us."

They heard a distant thud somewhere outside their door.

"How many do you think have jumped?" Elise whispered.

"I don't know," Raf mumbled, not even hazarding a guess. "I'm more curious why their bodies aren't breaking down."

"What do you mean?" Elise asked. "You don't think they're dead, or, twice dead?"

"No, I think they're definitely gone," Raf said. "But I don't think they went someplace better."

"What?!" Her eyes were wide.

"I mean, it looked like that freshman girl was praying with Wallace and Melkonian. Then she got this really angelic looking exit with lightning shooting up into the ceiling."

"You mean," Elise pieced it together. "Because they jumped ..."

"Let's just say," Raf said. "That if I had jumped like that back when we were regular alive, and there was a mess of blood rather than sand, I wouldn't get buried near my abuelos. If you take a leap like that, the only way out ... is down."

"Oh god." Elise covered her mouth with a hand. "But what if they die some other way now? Like some accidental way? Are you saying that if they don't get all that electricity, then their soul goes to a worse level of Hell?"

"I don't know," Raf said. "All I'm saying is that I'm not jumping at any point. Because wherever they're going, it all seems to be in the same direction."

***

Niles and Laura sat in a far corner of Mr. Harold Jackson's Calculus classroom. They were at the furthest point away from Mr. Jackson's desk, where Melvin and Barry were sitting.

Things had been quiet in the room for a while.

Barry and Melvin whispered to each other as they cut loose their duct tape and sifted through supplies in the desk. Niles and Laura had likewise searched through the cabinet in their back corner.

Both of them wanted to find some kind of weapon to help defend themselves. They didn't quite expect to turn up any hidden Ka-Bars, but literally anything would be better than nothing.

Inside the cabinet, Laura found a large architectural compass. One end had a nut fixture so a pencil or pen could be screwed into place for drawing circles of various sizes. On the other end was a sharp metal point which would rotate in place on a sheet of paper.

It wasn't exactly a weapon, but the metal point and compass were both made of stainless steel. Laura could stab someone several inches deep if they approached her. One person in particular was fresh in her mind, her former best friend.

If she could go back in time, Laura would have immediately thrown punches at Anne for trying to reach down her dress. Even if she had to fight that Amanda bitch too, she would have.

Niles found something he thought he could put to good use, a claw hammer. He had spent hours swinging a hammer last week, while working on their Junior Class float. He was well practiced. Luckily, he had work gloves at the time, because the wooden handle was starting to splinter.

This hammer in Mr. Jackson's classroom was made of forged steel, with a comfortable rubberized grip. He could swing it a lot more easily and accurately.

Once they were satisfied with their weapons, Niles and Laura arranged two of the desks into a defensible position and sat down.

The conversations stayed isolated for a long time. Niles actually tried his best to just ignore them. He and Laura went on talking about old stories when they were younger, good times long before any of this. Niles found it difficult to summon to mind stories that didn't include Barry or Melvin, but he found a few.

Eventually, the two ran out of topics. Laura was the first one to bring things back to their current predicament.

"What do you think they're talking about?" Laura whispered to Niles.

"Probably just the same shit they were saying in the gym."

"How long have we been in here?" she asked him.

Niles checked his phone.

"A little over two hours."

"You think they're done with us for the day?" she asked. "Maybe Torelli and them are just going to go to bed?"

"Maybe," Niles said. Then he joked, "Torelli probably sleeps like a vampire, standing wrapped in the stage curtains like Nosferatu."

Laura chuckled, a little harder than she intended. Barry and Melvin turned at the sound.

"Yeah, laugh," Melvin said, loud enough for them to hear. It was the first time they'd acknowledged each other since the door was closed. "I'm sure this is all a real show to you."

"We weren't laughing at you," Niles said, matching his volume.

"Really," Laura said in agreement. "There was this weird thing with Torelli earlier that-"

"Whatever," Barry said, trying to cut her off and end the exchange.

The silence didn't settle well between the two groups, the tension in the air was thicker than the wall of fog that surrounded the school. It was too uncomfortable now. With the ice broken, they were going to have to talk to each other.

Laura decided she would try a joke as an olive branch.

"At least Anne's not here," she said aloud, mainly in Barry's direction. "She turned out to be a real bitch."

Barry chuckled a little.

"It takes one to know one," Melvin muttered.

"Fuck off Melvin," Niles muttered in response, repeating what he'd said in the gym.

"Where am I going to 'fuck off' to Niles?" he snapped. "Unless you have some underpassage exploit, none of us are going anywhere."

The *Intrepid* game had been present for a sizable portion of their mutual friendship. It might as well have been a second language that the three of them spoke, like hardcore *Star Trek* fans had with Klingon.

An 'underpassage exploit' was more or less exactly what it sounded like. The way the ships were modeled, you could get your characters to reload below the floor of the deck they were currently on. It had become known as the 'underpassage' and was a way to pass through walls and barriers. The developers would keep patching the exploits, but players would discover or forge new ones wherever they went.

"You know what I don't get, Melvin," Niles said, sitting upright. "Is why the hell you're here at all ... in Hell. Sure, Barry at least had some motive to fuck with us, and the dance as a whole, but why are you here?"

"You seriously have to ask that question?" Melvin said through a disgruntled expression. "Maybe because I'm actually a good friend and decided to help him with something he wanted to do."

Niles turned away, facing a distant space on another wall.

"I know you remember," Melvin continued. "Your head might have gotten crushed like a Fin-Yll egg, but you haven't forgotten the past decade. Why wouldn't I be here with Barry, when we've always done *everything* together?"

"Oh, come on!" Niles raised his voice. "It's not like I went AFK, we did a ten-hour raid just a few weeks ago."

"We sure did," Melvin groaned. "It was the first one in months, and only because it was Barry's birthday."

"I was there, wasn't I?" Niles said. "Yeah sure, I haven't had as much time to just burn, but I was there for the big stuff."

"Just admit it, Niles," Melvin said. "You got one whiff of pussy and abandoned us to chase after it."

Niles was shocked and apologized to Laura for him. "I am so sorry that he is such an *asshole* sometimes!"

Laura ignored what Melvin said. She was looking at Barry, who had been silent for most of the exchange.

"Barry, be honest," she asked in as diplomatic a voice as she could, "if things had gone down differently, if Anne had said yes, wouldn't you have gone to Homecoming too? Wouldn't you have been at that table with us?"

"Yeah," he responded, before continuing, "and there's another timeline where I was Marcus Johnson, and stood on stage as the Homecoming King."

"There's probably a timeline where we don't die at all," Melvin said, glaring at Niles. "A timeline where you fucked things up just the same as you did and she would have never spoken to you again."

That cut Laura worse than his other comment.

"You would have come crawling back to us." Melvin chuckled. "And you know what we would have said to you? 'Fuck off!'"

Laura felt like she should say something else. After all, this whole argument was indirectly about her. However, it seemed like anything she added might only make it worse. She had to leave it up to Niles, he was the only one who might understand how they were feeling.

"No, you wouldn't," Niles responded to Melvin. "You didn't tell Barry to fuck off over the summer, after Anne didn't work out. You didn't say it to me a few weeks ago, you invited me to the raid! You weren't just stringing me along so you could pull off the fire alarm thing. In fact, you could have gone totally no-com for the last four months and still tried to trip the signal the same as you were doing."

Neither of them responded.

"I mean, come on guys," Niles said. "Just because I happened to find someone to click with first you decide to Karnekov me, drag me back down into the singularity because you can't get out at the same time?"

They still said nothing.

"Barry," Niles addressed him, "if things were reversed, I wouldn't have brought Melvin here to pull something like this. Yeah, I would have been bitter, but I wouldn't have actively tried to sabotage it for you. You were doing the same shit to me as Anne, just from a different angle"

Barry slouched over in the desk chair. That line felt quite poignant.

"We wouldn't have ditched you," Melvin mumbled.

"Yes, you would have!" Niles said. "Remember when you asked out Samantha Palmer? Are you telling me on a Saturday night if you had the choice between going to dinner with her and doing just some ordinary raid with Barry and I, that you would choose the raid?"

Melvin said nothing.

"In fact, we probably wouldn't have *let* you join," Niles said. "We would have told you to wise the hell up and call her."

"Fine, Niles," Melvin said in defeat, just trying to end the conversation. "You won anyway. You got the girl and we all died. It's game over. We weren't even able to pull off the plan anyway. We never found the stupid fire alarm panel."

"The men's locker room," Barry whispered.

"What was that?" Laura asked him in a soft voice, trying to encourage him to engage.

"The fire alarm panel," Barry said louder, "it's in the mechanical closet, in the men's locker room, in the gym."

"What?!" Melvin sat upright, looking pissed.

"You knew where it was?" Niles asked him.

"I planned it all out last Wednesday," Barry said, confessing the whole story. "It was short notice, but it wasn't slapped together.

"Each of the three sections of the building have their own fire alarm panels. I didn't want to bump into you by accident, because you would have definitely found it suspicious. So instead of tripping the Murphy Center panel, I planned on shorting the one in the gym section instead.

"I also didn't want to actually dress up in a suit like we were at the dance. It hurt too much to even consider. So, I thought if we wore something plain like this, we'd look like staff just unloading supplies outside.

"I think it worked. We made it to the building and no one stopped us. Then we used Reynolds' key to enter.

"We thought we were alone in the classrooms section, but that's when a couple came through from the gymnasium hallway. We had to wait for them to leave before we could approach the lockers."

"What couple?" Laura asked him.

"It was Jennifer Maxwell and Darren Clark," Barry said. "I figured they were just walking around the atrium to find someplace to fool around, but they didn't. They went to the freshmen lockers for some reason and were just talking. They almost looked sad.

"They weren't just some cheerleader and varsity jock making out in a hallway. They were really hashing something out. That got me thinking about you two also."

Laura and Niles glanced at each other.

"Laura," Barry said. "You have no idea how hard Niles worked to win you over. I mean, maybe you have some idea, because he did, but it was months of effort. Since this time last year, when we were first put together in Mrs. Jefferson's class, he's been doing all these little improvements on himself to try to impress you."

Laura rested her hand on Niles' leg. She was subtle enough that the other two didn't notice.

"You're right Niles," Barry said. "I felt like shit. I spent two hours second-guessing myself, running all these scenarios on whether you would do it to me or not."

"So, you were just wasting my time?!" Melvin blurted out.

"I honestly thought I'd 'wise up' and we'd do it eventually," Barry said to him. "But every time I felt close to committing, I didn't do it."

Melvin scoffed in disbelief.

"So, it's your fault I'm dead. That's what I get for trying to be a good friend. You spun your wheels long enough that we got fucking crushed in a bathroom."

Melvin kicked at the ground, rolling his chair away into a third corner of the room. Now every corner was filled with someone, except the one with the door.

"Melvin, come on!" Barry said. "I didn't know about the bomb ..."

"Oh really?" Melvin challenged him. "How'd you find out so much about the fire alarm panels then?"

"I found the old drawings online," Barry said. "The ones that were like fifty years old, for the original 'new' combined building. They wouldn't move a fire alarm panel during a remodel, they'd have to reroute a bunch of wires and pipes."

"Are you saying that anyone could have found old drawings online," Laura asked, "including the bomber?"

"I guess," Barry said, "but obviously there must be something else to the remodel drawings if the bomber removed the new ones like Wallace claimed.

"Almost every building has a fire alarm panel. It wouldn't have been too hard to find in a new building if it were built to regulation. They wouldn't have had to break into the construction site around the gym if they were only messing with the fire alarm."

Niles said nothing, but this was the kind of talk that drew so much suspicion to Barry and Melvin when they were tied up in front of the mirrors.

"I can't believe you were lying to me," Melvin muttered.

The way he looked at Barry was the same way Anne had been looking at Laura. He seemed pretty convinced that Barry was the bomber now.

Barry gave up trying to persuade anyone of anything.

"Look, Niles, Laura, I'm sorry, okay? I was still at the school because I was still thinking about doing it, but I just wanted to tell you that I felt bad enough that I didn't."

Laura took him at his word for the sake of making peace.

"Thank you, Barry," she said. "I wish things didn't end like they did. Next year you two could have been there with someone also. All six of us could have had a great time with other friends."

"Yeah, well now any other friends we might have had want to kill us!" Melvin snapped. "Congrats Barry, you're probably going to get us killed a second time."

"I didn't know about the gym!" he repeated again.

The four of them heard a hard slam against the stone floor outside.

"I don't know if there's going to be anyone left to kill us," Niles said. "We might need an underpassage exploit regardless ... if no one's alive to let us out."

"They wouldn't all kill themselves, would they?" Laura asked.

"Is it even suicide at this point?" Melvin mused. "Does double-death send you to double-Hell? Why not just roll the dice again? You can keep making leaps through lightspace until you find a world worth sticking around in. I sure as shit am not staying here in 'Villa Vista High, Remastered Edition'."

"Maybe it's a good thing," Barry whispered. "They can't torture us endlessly anymore, shoot pieces off of us like they did to that Andrei guy. At least we have death as an option again, a way out of here."

Niles and Laura looked at each other uneasily.

Considering what happened last time, they were in no hurry to die again.

***

Blaire and Andrei were still sitting against the wall in Mr. Van Gaal's classroom. Blaire felt very comfortable where she was, huddled under Andrei's right arm. She didn't want to move him anyway.

After all the exertion when they were transferred to the classroom, Andrei's calf was in a lot of pain. He winced occasionally as they talked.

Blaire wished she had her purse on her. She didn't have any ibuprofen, like Niles had given her, but there was something close enough. She could have given Andrei some of the Midol she kept for period cramps. It's not like she had *that* to worry about anymore.

It had been hours, but the dust layer on his leg hadn't changed at all. No more muscle had restored itself. Compared to the way things had healed before, he should be halfway there by now.

Whatever happened to Ellen Taylor had changed things for good.

After telling Andrei about her prophetic dream, Blaire slowly kept replaying it in her head. Maybe there were other details that she might have missed, things that could help them now.

She tried not getting too lost in thought though. Her first priority was distracting Andrei from the pain with conversation. She thought a good way was to have him tell her more about his old high school.

Eventually, Blaire set up a scenario by essentially reversing their life paths. What if her dad had gotten a new senior corporate accountant job down in L.A., and Blaire ended up at Pasadena North High?

Andrei found it entertaining.

"Okay," he began. "So, you would join the ranks of the Thunderbirds."

"That was your mascot?" she asked in disbelief.

"Oh, it was awful," Andrei said. "Most of the images of it were way too cartoony looking. It was like a knock-off *Pokémon*, rather than some fearsome mythical beast."

Blaire chuckled.

"What were the colors?" she asked.

"White and orange," Andrei said.

"Ugh," Blaire groaned. "So, the choir still looked like traffic signs?"

"I'd say we looked more like Coast Guard boats," Andrei proposed. "But most of the time we had black suit coats. The orange would make its way into the vest and ties, then we had our regular white dress shirts."

"And the girls?" she asked.

He had to think back for a moment.

"Oh, that's right," he remembered. "They had black skirts, white blouses, and orange sort-of-ascot-looking ties. It felt like a very 1950s look."

"Not bad," Blaire said, picturing herself in such a getup. Even a rustic orange would have been way too vibrant for her taste though.

"Do you think you still would have ended up in the choir though?" Andrei asked. "Without Elise?"

That was a very relevant question. Truthfully, in such a scenario she would have felt horribly alone for quite a while. At Villa Vista she always had Elise there with her at the very least.

"She might have convinced me to join Pasadena's choir," Blaire imagined. "As a way to 'network' ..."

Blaire then shifted the speculation back onto him.

"What about *her*?"

Andrei had told Blaire a slight bit about his old girlfriend, Clarissa. He hadn't hidden her existence from Blaire, but at the same time he didn't want to talk much about her for numerous reasons. The foremost of which was that he didn't want Blaire to feel uncomfortable or jealous, because the truth was, he had no feelings for Clarissa at all. She had gone through a similar transition to the one Amanda Burke supposedly went through.

Clarissa was cool back in their freshman year, she could be a friend and just hang out whenever neither of them had anything else going on. Eventually, they were exclusive enough that they just called it a relationship for simplicity. It really wasn't some hot, impassioned romance like what he had with Blaire. Clarissa was the friend he could rely on to be a date for all of his dad's various concerts and fancy gatherings.

It wasn't until their junior year that he noticed she was enjoying the black-tie events more than she was enjoying Andrei's company. He was starting to realize that rather than going with him for the fun of it, she was coming to bask in the atmosphere, to rub shoulders with anyone who seemed famous or powerful.

He'd kissed her on the cheek a few times, but never a *real* kiss. As their junior year went on, he was getting more and more sick of the way she was acting. They barely even talked as friends anymore. She'd only call or text him when she was fishing for information on the next fancy, formal event.

"As I've told you," Andrei began, "I would have dumped her by August no matter what. She became a parasite."

"Okay," Blaire accepted his answer. Then she challenged him, "so how do *we* meet?"

He thought for a moment. She was clearly setting him up for some kind of clever answer, he just had to think of something romantic.

"You mean, how do we meet without Elise and Raf aggressively playing matchmakers?"

Blaire smiled, turning to hide a blush.

"Well," Andrei began. "At some point in the first couple of weeks, just passing in and out of class, we would have locked eyes."

Andrei rested a hand on her cheek. She covered it with hers.

"Even though so many others would turn in fear. I'd have trouble taking my eyes off of you. I'd have to think of the right excuse to come up to you, just so I could look a little longer."

That must have been a good enough answer. Blaire kissed him for several long seconds.

As they separated, he began to chuckle a little.

"What?" she asked, still blushing.

"I just can't imagine you down there surrounded by all the valley girls."

Blaire smiled. "I guess that would have been one benefit of the traffic. They stay locked outside and we cruise wherever the road takes us."

Andrei liked that answer.

"Where would you want it to take us?" he asked her. "After high school, after college, where would you want to live if we could choose anywhere?"

It didn't take her long to make a decision.

"Denver," she said.

"Really, Colorado?" Andrei asked.

"I like the mountains and the snow. But it's a large city, so you're not isolated in the wilderness like it's rural Alaska." Blaire met his eyes. "I'd need someone to teach me how to ski."

"Oh, wow," Andrei rested his hands on his knees, "that's a lot to ask. You can't just learn how to ski in a few weekends. It would take *many years* of practice."

"I think I could commit to that."

They snuggled a bit closer together.

Each of them pictured how such a future could have unfolded.

After a moment, Andrei said, "I'm pretty sure my dad and Katya would both follow us there."

Blaire frowned.

"I don't think my family would follow me," she whispered.

Andrei was caught off guard by the mood shift. "What do you mean?"

Blaire took a deep breath.

"With me at a distance, my parents could focus on Chris and Tommy," she said. "I wouldn't be there as some aberration anymore. Then again, I guess that problem is already solved."

"Hold on," Andrei matched her serious tone. "Your parents definitely love you. I'm sure they're devastated by what happened to us."

Blaire didn't answer him ... because she didn't believe him.

"Blaire, you cannot think that way." Andrei took her hand again.

"I never fit in with them," she said. "As soon as my grandpa died, I was alone again, out of place in a family that wasn't like me at all."

"Being different from them doesn't mean they loved you any less than Chris and Tommy."

She said nothing.

"I've told you how different I am from my sisters," Andrei reminded her, "how much more they took after our mom and I took after our dad. None of that meant we didn't care about each other."

Still, Blaire said nothing. He recognized that she had felt this way for a good portion of her life, long before he showed up.

"We don't get to choose our family," Andrei said, trying another tactic. "But we do get to choose our friends. How long have you been friends with Elise?"

Blaire eyed him, not following the tangent.

"At least ten years," she said, "since like kindergarten or first grade."

"Do you think Elise hates you?" Andrei asked her.

"No, of course not," Blaire said without hesitation.

"Why?" Andrei asked.

He didn't want her to mistake his intonation, so he continued on his own.

"Because if she did hate you, she could have stopped being friends with you at any point over those years," he said. "She could have stopped after we died, or after we were accused by Amanda and that nerdy kid. They didn't have to defend us. They could have sat there and done nothing, but what did Elise do instead?"

Blaire smiled a little.

"She stabbed that girl who tried to grab me."

"That's right." Andrei chuckled. "Now, how come you are still friends with Elise?"

"Because we've been friends for basically forever," Blaire said. "She's like the sister I never had."

"That's an interesting choice of words," Andrei said. "Because when you introduced me to your mother, Elise was the first person she reminded me of."

"Really?"

"Blaire, your parents love you for the same reason Elise loves you," Andrei said. "It's the same reason your brothers love you. It's also the same reason Katya and Anastasia love me. It's not that you don't fit because you're not like them. You're the piece of them that's missing."

Nothing Andrei had said was particularly profound, but the fact that he was the one saying it carried a lot of weight for Blaire. It wasn't just that she had strong feelings for him, he was so similar to Blaire in so many ways. That was one of the things that attracted her to him so much. It felt like he already understood her so well, because his soul had walked so many similar roads as hers.

She sat there, thinking about what he said. Andrei continued talking about some other stories from his old high school. It seemed like he was trying to lift her spirits, but her thoughts felt so heavy with doubt and regret.

Blaire was the one who died, but her family felt like the ghosts, haunting her wherever she went.

Would it always feel that way?

Leaks of sadness filled the back of her mind, despite Andrei's best efforts.

After not much longer, Blaire and Andrei were startled by a sound at the door.

One by one, the wooden stoppers were pulled away from the bottom. The missing handle did not turn, but its counterpart on the outside did. The latch clicked and the door pulled open.

Andrei stood to his feet, pressing his left arm against the wall when the calf refused to carry weight.

"Stay behind me," he whispered to her.

Joe Torelli stepped through the door frame.

He looked up at Andrei, who stood nearly half a foot taller than him.

"Looks like that leg isn't pulling back together anymore, is it?" Torelli mocked him.

He held out the shotgun, aiming at Andrei's chest just the same as before.

"You probably can't pull off another kick like that in your condition," Torelli quipped. "But I would love to see you try."

Blaire peeked out from below Andrei's left arm, taking the same position that she had earlier, to help walk him to the room.

"What do you want?" she demanded.

"You," Torelli said.

"Well, she isn't going alone," Andrei replied.

"We stay together," Blaire agreed.

Torelli cocked his head to the side.

"Do I look like I have a wheelchair?" he asked. "Besides, this is a solo interview. We're going to see just how well your stories line up."

"Then bring me some earplugs," Andrei said. "Ask all the questions you want and then we'll swap, but she's not leaving my sight."

"How good is your sight?" Torelli asked, raising the barrel between Andrei's eyes.

"Stop it!" Blaire shouted.

"Uh, Torelli?" Eric Schwartz asked from beyond the door. "Maybe we should consider his idea. I could get some headphones; we can play loud music."

"What's the point anyway?" Andrei asked. "We've been talking for hours. If it weren't already completely obvious that we didn't do it, we would have had plenty of time to come up with a matching story."

Torelli's mouth turned into a snarl.

Andrei was right, with all the time that had passed since the gymnasium alone, not to mention the two days since they'd died-

The Browning Citori fired.

Time slowed to a crawl.

Blaire felt the way that she did when the wall of the gymnasium began to break apart and come toward them.

A bright orange cone of fire reached forward out of the top barrel of the gun.

It was just an arm's distance away from Andrei's face.

The buckshot concealed within the glow of gunpowder sailed forward in a tight group.

Even if Blaire had stood directly behind Andrei, she might have avoided harm completely. In a way, Andrei's height had saved her from meeting the same fate.

Blaire watched as the cone of fire wrapped around Andrei's head. When the glow finally passed, there was no head left behind. Everything above his Adam's apple had been blown away.

She heard the horrible sound of sand spraying across the back wall of the classroom.

Andrei's left arm went limp and his right leg buckled.

His lifeless body fell past Blaire, collapsing to the ground.

Andrei was gone.

A cry of pure anguish escaped Blaire's chest.

TWENTY-FIVE

COLLAPSE

AFTER AN AGONIZING DAY of acting as Joe's enforcers, and being put under his gun, Darren and Jenny were doing everything in their power to forget about all of that.

"Oh, I have one," Darren said to her, continuing their conversation.

"Okay, go." Jenny was holding one side of Ziegler's dry erase board.

"Casper." Darren wrapped duct tape around the stacked student desks and the other corner.

"You want to be a 'friendly ghost'?" Jenny asked doubtfully.

"I mean, I don't want to be bald," Darren conceded, "but as far as ghosts go that was a pretty good interpretation."

"Well, what does he *do*?" Jenny asked. "All I remember is seeing him look cute and talk to Christina Ricci."

"You say that like those aren't two very positive outcomes," Darren said, finishing his side of the whiteboard.

He walked up to her, grabbing the other corner.

"If you're jealous, I would be more than happy to share Christina." Darren smirked.

Jenny rolled her eyes and stepped away, inspecting the back side of their construction project.

"That movie came out in the nineties," she said. "I'm pretty sure she's older than my brother."

"That doesn't sound like a 'no' to me," Darren pointed out. He wrapped the duct tape around the final support point of the makeshift wall, securing it to the rest of the framework.

"Okay, besides the chance of flirting with your childhood crush," Jenny said. "Why else would you choose *Casper* as a good interpretation of ghosts?"

"Well, for one thing, they could interact with the living world," Darren said. "Talk to people, touch people, and to top it all off you've got a machine that can resurrect the dead. We just need to find a genius inventor dad, who lost his son, and a few dozen bottles of his magical primordial elixir."

He smiled in a goofy way, imagining the scenario actually playing out for the two of them. Jenny smiled a little too.

They might as well enjoy the fantasies. Just to savor the "what ifs" was enough to keep their hopes up a little bit. So much had changed in the last few days. They had to believe in even the slightest chance that something might change for the better too.

"Alright, your turn," Darren said.

Jenny stood there thinking as he put some final reinforcers on their privacy vestibule.

They had taken the dry erase whiteboards off of Ziegler's wall and mounted them to the stacked student desks, blocking the door to the room. A hard framed map of the United States formed the final piece. While it wasn't as tall as the whiteboards, even turned on its side, it ended up forming a sort of 'saloon door'.

"I don't know, I think we've covered them all," Jenny said, referencing their other favorite ghost mythologies. "Most of them aren't exactly happy endings, they're just restless or evil spirits terrorizing the living."

"I think it's done," Darren said, stepping back from the duct tape hinges fixed on the framed map.

Was it a perfect separation? No. But at least they had some semblance of privacy now. Neither Joe, nor the sophomores, nor anyone else with a master key could barge into their room without at least a little warning.

"It's great," Jenny said, grabbing his arm.

Darren had taken off his suit coat before they started work. She squeezed his bicep beneath the thin dress shirt material.

"At least it feels a bit more like a home now," Darren said.

She didn't answer him with words. Instead, she grabbed his other arm, pulling him into a kiss. Darren kissed her back, but she didn't stop pulling.

They had been friends for years, including much of their childhoods, long before puberty. Now they were high school seniors and a lot had changed over the years. Darren had become strong and rugged, while Jenny had become toned and voluptuous.

The shift in their relationship from friendship to romance was really only a few months old. Most of that romance had involved expressing long dormant feelings they'd had for each other, processing old regrets. They really hadn't moved into new territory up until that point.

With a second chance at life, Jenny felt like she was ready to remedy that.

She led them to the far corner of the room, the one which benefited most from the privacy wall. They eased down onto the air mattress. It was still fully inflated, more comfortable than probably ninety percent of the accommodations the other students had at their disposal.

They made out for a short while, but Jenny took things a step further. She slowly slid her gym shirt up past her navel until it was bunched just beneath her chin.

Darren gladly followed her lead. He inched his hand up from her hip and past her ribcage. The sensation seemed to feel as good to her as it did to him. She moaned softly in his ear, telling him to keep going.

And like all good things, their rising passion came to a swift and unexpected end.

A loud explosion echoed through the classrooms section of the building.

Their small little world was nearly silent. There were no cars and no sounds of distant highways. There was no wind. The fog which surrounded them was motionless and still, draped like a great curtain. Only the soft hum of the lights, electricity, and ductwork cycling the air made any sound at all.

Every interruption of that silence of the grave could be heard very easily. However, nothing announced its presence more than the lone instrument of death found in that place.

Joe had just fired the shotgun.

The couple went from pawing at each other to facing the entrance of their room. The sound shocked them both, as it had everyone else.

"Shit!" Darren yelled in frustration.

The feeling of anticipation manifesting inside of him had been violently shifted to one of dread and foreboding.

He looked down at Jenny. The same was true for her. She wore an expression of worry and apology. Even if she didn't, he knew that he couldn't just ignore whatever fresh madness Joe was unleashing.

"We have to go see what happened," he bemoaned.

"I agree," she whispered.

She lowered her shirt as Darren walked over to grab the black leather gloves and crowbar.

Darren decided he'd have better flexibility to swing the blunt weapon without the suit coat. It's not like it would do anything to protect him from stabs or gunshot wounds anyway.

Jenny grabbed her knife lance and they stepped through the door.

Following the gunshot, a loud, grieving cry carried upwards out of the foyer and atrium.

Jenny suspected that she already knew what had happened.

Dozens of other heads popped out of their various classroom dorms as Darren and Jenny quickly descended the stairs for the first floor.

The bodies which had jumped from the railings of the atrium still sat cold and motionless where they landed. Hours had passed and they were still dead.

Probably a third of the students of Villa Vista High had taken their own lives to escape this Limbo they were all stuck in.

Only one student's life had been taken against his will.

"Just block it up!" Joe yelled at Trey Devall. Trey used his Varsity Football kicker leg to press the wooden doorstops into place as well as he could.

Brendan Jensen and Eric Schwartz stood by, doing nothing but watching as Trey re-secured the prison cell that used to be Van Gaal's classroom.

The gun hung from Joe's right hand, pointed down at the stone tile floor of the hallway.

Jenny could see the fingers in his left hand twitching open and closed. Joe must have run out of Addys and Oxy.

He glanced over when he heard the two of them reach the hallway.

They all looked at Darren and Jenny, but none of them said anything.

"Well?" Darren said. "What happened?"

The haunting wails continued to list out of the classroom.

Jenny knew for sure now. It was Blaire Tidwell, the girlfriend of the guy Joe had shot earlier.

"Joe?" Darren stared at the quarterback. "Why isn't *he* screaming too?"

Eric Schwartz made a subtle motion, pointing one of his index fingers right between his eyes.

"Are you fucking serious?!" Darren snapped.

Joe Torelli said nothing. He faced the glass windows that covered the front entrance of the school, looking away from all of them.

A row of bodies lined the ground of the foyer, illuminated by the even daylight seeping through the fog.

"They were going to be taken individually for questioning," Eric explained when no one else spoke up. "They refused to be separated. And after that ..."

Eric gave a slight shrug, not exactly sure why Joe had shot him.

"That's great Joe," Darren growled. "You better hope he *was* the bomber. Otherwise, why else would he deserve the same fate as Salvatore?"

Joe balled his left hand into a fist, but didn't turn to face them.

Darren backed Jenny out of the hallway, just in case Joe did decide to confront them or go into a full massacre mode.

"Hey Brendan, Trey," Jenny said as they moved away from the group. "How are Sheena and Ashley doing? Do you even know? Do you even care?"

They both gave a slightly worried look. It was almost like they'd totally forgotten about them.

Darren and Jenny disappeared from sight, slipping down the other hallway.

***

Following their imprisonment, Elise and Rafael's conversations had drifted back to memories of their families.

"You can't be serious," Raf said.

"No, things were really starting to look good," Elise said with a Machiavellian grin. "Trust me, I've known both of them their whole lives. The seeds of interest were definitely there. They just needed some tending."

Elise had been explaining to Raf her master plan for the next few years ... had things worked out differently.

While Elise had many cousins between her dad's four siblings and her mom's three siblings, both of them had decided to stick to a smaller family plan. So, they chose to stop with only the two children. Elise was sixteen and her sister Yvonne, whom she called Yvie, was fourteen.

Her baby sister was the same age as Blaire's brother Chris.

Once Elise began her informal practice as a "love doctor", she began hatching a plan for the two of them.

Of course, she explained to Raf the disclaimer that she wouldn't push them any more than anyone else. If there was truly no chemistry between them then Elise would let it go.

But ... they weren't even old enough for accurate chemistry to be measured yet.

With both of them starting in Villa Vista as freshmen, Elise was going to get the wheels turning for them as soon as she found someone for Blaire.

If things had continued working out with Andrei, she planned to recruit him and Blaire to begin influencing Chris.

They were already basically friends. The families had known each other since Elise and Blaire had met, so Chris and Yvie had been around each other since they were toddlers.

Blaire had been less enthusiastic about the plan when Elise first proposed it a year ago. It was not an insult to Yvie, but more of a protective fence.

She said that Yvie was too sweet to have to deal with a spaz like Chris. Tommy kept him acting a little more kiddish than he should be at his age. He needed another few years to calm down before Blaire thought he'd be ready for any kind of real long-term relationship.

Blaire was not an accurate bellwether for fourteen-year-old boys though. Even when she and Elise were fourteen, Blaire acted more mature for her age.

Boys were always a year or two behind girls in maturity, at least in middle school. By the time the two siblings were fifteen or sixteen, Elise thought there could be real potential there.

Of course, this long-term plan had many long-term benefits. Elise felt like a queenmaker in Medieval Europe. She would unite their two Houses and bring Clans Tidwell and Gosselin together for good. She would literally make a sister out of Blaire ... or sister-in-law at least.

"I know Blaire would have totally gotten on board with the plan if things worked out with Andrei," she said. The levity fell when Elise admitted, "but I guess the odds of all that are pretty low now. Our families will probably end up drifting apart. Yvie isn't going to want to hang out with Chris. Every time they saw each other they'd only think of their dead sisters. Now Yvie's an only child."

Yvie was fairly shy, quite different from Elise. So, like Chris, she had also decided to pass on Homecoming that year.

Elise had said many silent prayers since waking up in this place, but that one was the most common.

"Thank you, God. Thank you for saving Yvie."

There were moments when she felt much less gratitude, demanding answers for why any of them had to die at all, why they had to suffer like this. However, when those moments passed, she would still send one more mention of thanks.

If it was all just mindless balancing of cosmic scales, she would have traded her life for Yvie's every time.

"I am very sorry it worked out that way," Rafael said.

Elise turned to him. He sounded like he was trying to be comforting, but there was a distance to his words. He was distracted by something else.

"What's wrong Raf?" she asked him, placing a hand on his.

He swallowed a little. It didn't look like he actually wanted to answer.

"It's nothing," he said, dismissing his own feelings. "Honestly, I should be happy."

"What are you talking about?" Elise asked, confused.

He leaned his head back against the wall. He'd held in this particular grief pretty well since he'd died, but this stretch of the conversation had bubbled those feelings over the top. Once Elise noticed, he knew he had to tell her. She wouldn't stop asking about it otherwise.

"Well," he began. "For your sister, it's going to be painful being alone. You were her *only* sister. Without you, a big piece of your family is gone. Your parents lost half of their children."

She frowned. Why was he measuring things up like that?

"Your parents are going to know you're gone, your sister is going to know you're gone," Raf said. "Your loss is really going to mean something, carry weight."

Elise wasn't sure what to say, she still didn't fully piece together where he was going with this.

"For me, not so much," Raf said. "Danilo graduates from Irvine next year, Rosa is getting settled in at UCSF ..."

Elise squeezed his hand tighter. It was beginning to dawn on her.

"Maria starts high school next year," Raf continued, choking back a few tears. "God knows where, probably John Muir unless my parents move. Then there's Carlos, who just started middle school."

"Raf," Elise said, taking him into a hug.

Raf was always such an amicable and talkative person. Elise seldom thought about the reasons why he was that way in the first place.

With two brothers and two sisters, Rafael was the middle child among middle children in the Herrera family. A lot of his personality manifested from a place of needing to make himself known, to announce his presence to a crowd. There was a constant fear of sitting in obscurity.

His older siblings were both in college, but even growing up Danilo and Rosa fought constantly. The few meager years he spent as the "baby" in the family were overshadowed by their antics.

Following him, Maria and Carlos were both known among his cousins and extended family for their respective talents.

Maria was very adorable. Since she was two, their mother had been able to get her into child modeling gigs. There was a small stack of magazines on a shelf in their living room of Maria dressed in various clothing brands. She was still modeling even now, slowly turning her natural beauty into a lucrative profit stream.

Carlos was very smart, taking heavily after their dad's dad. He was very good at tinkering and could also do the math behind it all. He was guaranteed to become very successful in some kind of science or engineering field.

Then there was Rafael, right in the middle in every way.

He was moderately smart, a straight B student. He enjoyed singing and theatre, but he didn't have enough natural talent to make any kind of career out of it. He had a small hobbyist interest in botany. It stemmed from a time in his youth, when an aunt showed him the inside of an Aloe vera leaf.

"They're not even going to notice I'm not there," Raf said, squeezing her tight. "All they're going to remember me as is the one who died in the bombing. They're not going to remember my life, only my death."

"That's not true," Elise said, rocking him slowly from side to side. "They'll never be the same without you."

Elise began feeling very guilty. Raf had been there to help her through all of her own trauma. She hadn't paid nearly enough attention to his feelings in all this.

She settled in closer to him. There had to be a way to help him realize how much they would miss him for who he was, that he was not just part of a set.

"Remember that time where Danny took you to San Diego on a whim, because he wanted to get away from Rosa?" Elise asked.

"Yeah," Raf muttered.

"You told me that you spent half the trip stopping at random roadside attractions just to kill time," Elise continued. "It was just the two of you on that trip, without you, it doesn't happen at all."

Raf had told her so many stories about his family. She had to show him how empty those stories would be without him in them. Those memories were going to mean so much to his siblings whenever they thought about their brother.

She went on like that for a while, and it seemed to finally start cheering him up. They were shifting back into what was going to become of their families.

"... and he's gonna be a mad scientist or something," Raf continued. "As soon as he's in college, Carlos is gonna have Danny strapped into one crazy machine after another like a lab monkey. Maybe he can finally develop a deodorant strong enough to actually work on Danny."

They chuckled a little.

"Raf," Elise said again, becoming more serious. "Please talk to me whenever you're feeling down. I am here for you always, I promise."

"I will," he whispered, "thank you."

They shared a tender kiss.

He continued with what he was saying.

"And all of them better keep their shit together to watch out for Maria," he said, with a worried look on his face. "When she goes from being 'cute' to being 'hot,' they need to keep their eyes on those scumbag modeling agency types. The worst thing ever would be if-"

Rafael was cut off in mid-sentence by a loud boom just outside their door.

He and Elise heard a heart-wrenching scream.

"Blaire!" Elise yelled. The voice was unmistakable.

She ran up to the door and tried to turn the latch. A few broken points of metal stuck out from where the lever used to be. Sand trickled out of her hand as she cut herself trying to operate it anyway.

"Watch out!" Raf shouted.

Elise stepped aside and Raf started running at the door. He threw his shoulder against it with the full weight of his body. The door didn't budge at all. The latch was still secured and at least three wooden block door stops were wedged along the bottom.

Blaire continued to wail.

After his fourth hit, Raf slid down to the floor. He'd opened up the stab wound in his side again.

Elise started running against the door in the same way.

"Elise," Raf said. "It's no good. Save your strength."

"She could be hurt!" Elise said.

"Elise ..." Raf looked up at her. "She wouldn't be screaming like that for herself. We'd be hearing another voice too."

Raf's eyes were steady, certain. She searched them and did not like the answers within.

"No ..." Elise said in disbelief. "It can't be."

They began to hear other voices outside the door.

Raf got to his feet again, leaning next to her, both with their ears to the door.

Darren and Jennifer were talking to Torelli's goons. One sentence explained everything to them.

"That's great Joe," Darren said from another part of the hallway. "You better hope he *was* the bomber. Otherwise, why else would he deserve the same fate as Salvatore?"

"No, not Andrei." Elise squeezed her eyes shut.

Raf hugged her as the grief swept over them.

They had really grown to care about Andrei. That had only intensified after their deaths. Where was he now, what was beyond the second veil of death?

Whatever sorrow they felt, it paled in comparison to the pain they could hear filling the air around them.

Elise pounded on the door.

"Let us out!" she demanded. "Let me go to her you fucking murderers!"

There was no response.

They made a few more requests in a similar vein, with similar results.

Blaire's cries carried on for what felt like an eternity.

Elise desperately wanted to hold her, to comfort her, but she couldn't.

Blaire suffered alone, but every lost soul still lingering in Villa Vista High could hear her grief.

***

Niles and Laura were back to just talking amongst themselves when the shotgun blast rang out. They dove under their desks. Barry and Melvin did the same in their respective corners of the classroom.

They all heard the soul-chilling wail seep through the cracks of the door.

"That's Blaire," Laura said.

"I don't hear Andrei," Niles added.

Andrei had a powerful set of lungs. After he was shot, the whole gym could hear his retching in agony from the pieces of leg that were blown off.

Blaire's cries were not ones of physical pain at all. Her suffering came from a much deeper place.

"Oh god ..." Laura said, covering her mouth. "I think they killed him."

"They probably found proof that he did it," Melvin quipped from his corner of the room.

"Shut up Melvin!" Niles shouted.

"Look, I don't care how much you two played nice with him." He stood to his feet. "Him and that goth girl were talking about how they knew the gym was about to explode before it happened.

"Everyone already accepts that the bomber was probably one of the students. So clearly someone must have been lying to everyone, pretending to be innocent.

"You can be sad all you want, but this means it's over."

Melvin strolled over to the door. He knocked hard against it.

"Hey!" he shouted, sounding impatient. "Great job on finding the bomber. You are our heroes! Now can you please let the rest of us out?"

They all waited a minute, seeing if anyone would actually answer him.

When enough time passed, he tried again.

"Um, hello?" Melvin reiterated, pounding harder. "That's it, 'Mission Accomplished!' You can let the rest of us out now."

He only waited a few seconds for an answer this time.

"Oh, come on!" he yelled, kicking the door as hard as he could. "Let me out, you found your guy!"

Still, there was no answer.

"I don't think it's over yet," Barry said, pointing out the obvious.

"Fuck!" Melvin screamed in frustration.

He walked back to his chair and rolled it over by the door.

When no more gunshots followed, Niles and Laura sat back down at their desks.

With Melvin no longer yelling, they could hear Blaire's howls of sorrow pouring through the walls again.

Laura took Niles' hand.

"He wasn't the bomber," she whispered to him. "I don't believe it."

Niles put his other hand on top of hers.

"I don't either," he agreed. "And I don't think Torelli will stop with him."

***

Jennifer and Darren walked slowly into the Murphy Center ballroom.

Blaire's crying could be heard all over the north side of the building. They had to get away from that.

"I feel sick," Jenny said. "How did it all come to this?"

"I don't know," Darren said, his voice tired. "At this point I don't even care who the bomber is, I just want all this to stop."

Jenny rubbed her stomach; the emotions of the situation were manifesting as nausea.

"We could check the cafeteria for some 7 Up," he offered.

Jenny nodded her head.

Once inside the old lunch room, they were surprised to find as much food as they did. A lot of banquet meals were still there, and they didn't look spoiled.

Jenny walked over to one of the soda refrigerators and pulled out a 20 oz. bottle.

After taking a sip, she turned to Darren.

"How many rounds does Joe have left?" she asked him.

"Of the 12-gauge shells? At least forty."

"So, he could kill over half of the people left," Jenny said. "And if the bomber was here at all, they probably jumped to their death after Ellen disappeared."

"We should have tied him up the first chance we could after he pulled out the shotgun," Darren said.

"When exactly?" a voice called out from the other side of the cafeteria.

The two of them flinched. They thought they were alone. Luckily, the voice was not a threatening one.

"Hey Jimmy," Darren said, annoyed by his sudden appearance.

"Don't get bitchy," Jimmy responded, "we were here first."

"Shouldn't you be in your room, with Camellia?" Jennifer asked, also wishing he would leave.

Darren and Jenny walked over to where the sound was coming from. They found Camellia sleeping on an assortment of seat cushions piled loosely on the ground.

"I'd love to," he said. "But our room got turned into one of the gulags."

Jimmy was sitting in the doorway of the walk-in refrigerator, letting the cold air pour into the room.

"This is some premo real-estate though." Jimmy motioned his hand toward the fridge's cooling unit. "We're getting Ninth Circle air conditioning for First Circle prices!"

They stared at him without responding.

"Anyway ..." Jimmy was annoyed that they weren't in a bantering mood. "When exactly were you going to take the shotgun from Joe?"

"We weren't," Jennifer said, a nervous expression climbing her face.

"Jenny, please," he said. "Do you think I, of all people, am going to narc on you? Come on."

Jimmy reached into a box, fishing around for something. It looked crudely organized, like he had been gathering items in his own personal shopping cart.

"What I mean ..." Jimmy continued, "... is that Joe hasn't slept once since we got flash-fried. I don't think he's going to be doing so anytime soon either."

"I think he's already run out of Addys," Jennifer said. "He'll crash hard in a few hours."

"It ain't the Addys." Jimmy wagged a finger.

"What do you mean?" Jennifer shrugged. "What *is* he taking then?"

"Around 120 Volts?" Jimmy quipped.

When they still weren't making the connection, he pointed up at the ceiling lights.

"You ever considered the fact that maybe it isn't just our phones maintaining a hundred percent battery life?"

"We've all slept at some point," Darren said. He then motioned to the cushions. "Camellia's sleeping *right there.*"

"Yeah, but headspace tired is different than body tired," Jimmy replied.

He pulled an apple out of the grocery box. It was a relatively nice-looking green Granny Smith.

He took a big bite out of the side, then tossed it to Jennifer.

"Have a taste."

"Is this some kind of Adam & Eve bit?" She raised an eyebrow.

Jimmy looked disappointed, then motioned to Darren. "Would you ... please?"

Darren sighed, then pulled the apple from her hand, taking a bite. He chewed it a few times and swallowed.

"What? It tastes fine, maybe a bit tart." Darren tossed it back to him.

"Pretty wild that Hell has fresh produce don't you think?" Jimmy prodded again.

He took another bite.

"It doesn't even turn to ash in my mouth!" he said while chewing.

"Look, enough bullshit," Darren said. "Just spit it out."

Jimmy leaned back against the walk-in refrigerator door, turning the apple in his hands.

"This isn't Hell," he said.

"Have you looked in a mirror lately?" Jennifer waved a hand.

"I never really expected to leave a pretty corpse." Jimmy looked her in the eye.

"Then where are we?" Darren asked. "Purgatory? Limbo? A cosmic elevator?"

"Do I look like a priest to you?" He chuckled.

"You're acting as haughty as one," Jennifer snipped back.

Jimmy laughed bigger. "See, that's funny."

He took another bite of the apple.

"And what's crazy is," he swallowed, "I've spent a good chunk of my afterlife right here in this cafeteria. I died right over there after all."

Jimmy pointed to the soda fountain. The gym had exploded when all of them were getting ice for Trey's jaw.

"And after all these days, how many people have come through to start grabbing for food? About thirty ... and it wasn't even hoarding. It was random things, like one dude thinking 'I want a pizza.'

"No one's hungry! They probably aren't thirsty either. They don't really have to sleep unless they need to hit the psychological pause button for a while."

He leaned over and stroked some of Camellia's hair.

"She really misses her family."

Darren and Jenny really thought about those implications. Could that change at some point? What happens when food does run out, then will people start starving? Was the Devil's long game just waiting for them to kill each other off and move deeper down the Circles?

"There's another reason that I know we're not in Hell," Jimmy added.

"Really, what is it?" Darren asked, expecting another round of banter.

"Because if this were Hell, my mom would be here."

Both Darren and Jenny shifted uncomfortably. Jimmy almost never talked about his mom. The only thing most people inferred about her was that she had left when Jimmy was young.

"My mom was a professional whore," Jimmy began. "Not like the strip clubs or Nevada brothels kind of whore, mind you. She was someone who used her body to pump riches out of business professionals.

"At the time, my dad was just some lower management pissant at ... Oracle, I think.

"Mom shows up, it's all love at first sight, wild times, parties, long weekends, then ... whoops! Condom must have broken.

"What she didn't expect was how receptive pops was going to be to the whole family idea. Suddenly he was game for a Vegas wedding and everything.

"Luckily for him, wedding bells weren't part of the program.

"That was never what mom was looking for in the first place. She wanted to keep climbing that corporate ladder. Little Jimmy was an anchor holding her down.

"She grabbed all the money she could and disappeared, not wanting to waste any more of her 'climbing' years on us.

"Pops was a bit fucked up over it. He decided to bury himself in work. After that, the money came pouring in.

"He may have never been 'Father of the Year', but he didn't dump me at, like, St. Paul's Orphanage or some shit. He fed me, clothed me, and put a pretty fuckin' big roof over my head. I was luckier than most would be in that situation.

"Hell, I was lucky she didn't just vacuum me out in the first trimester.

"Most people have a fucked-up past. They should have the right to bury that past however they want.

"That's why I tried to keep my place open to everyone who *understood that*. They need some booze to feel better, ecstasy, weed, Percocet, Vicodin, or just someplace to bang their girlfriend? That was fine by me. Hell, if you're lucky enough to find someone who cares about you ... enough to *stay* with you ... then make the most of it."

Jimmy stroked Camellia's hair again.

For all the fame and infamy that Jimmy had accrued over the years, Jennifer had never heard anyone accuse him of being a cheater. He'd dated Camellia for the last two years and she'd never once said she suspected him of fooling around.

Darren and Jenny were stunned at listening to his emotional unraveling.

"Jimmy, man, I'm so sorry," Darren said.

"Mom would have screwed with the wrong suit eventually," Jimmy whispered. "He would have put her through a windshield, or to the bottom of a lake. There's no way she lived longer than me."

He looked up at Darren and Jenny, taking another bite out of the apple.

"That's how I know we're not in Hell," Jimmy said, without a trace of doubt. "She's dead, and if she's dead, she's in Hell. If I haven't bumped into her by now, it's not Hell."

"Are you ... okay?" Jennifer asked, showing concern. "Do you want us to sit with you?"

"*Pshht*, no, no, I'm good." Jimmy straightened out the sleeve on Camellia's shoulder. "You kids go do your own thing before any more of Joe's screws come loose."

Darren and Jenny glanced at each other. Jimmy definitely wasn't in a good headspace right now.

"Did you hear the commotion earlier?" Darren asked, sliding down to the floor across from him.

"Oh yeah," Jimmy said. "That gun is fuckin' loud. He actually kill someone this time?"

"Yes," Jennifer said somberly, sitting down next to Darren. "He killed Andrei."

"What?" All humor dropped from his face. "Are you serious?"

"Yeah," Darren confirmed. "That Blaire girl has been crying ever since."

"Oh, don't fuckin' tell me that." Jimmy shook his head with a pained expression. He tossed the apple core as hard as he could out into the ballroom.

"You know what the last thing I said to him was?" Jimmy said. "Back before we got cooked, I ran into him in the bathroom and made sure he knew about my afterparty."

"That was nice of you," Jennifer said.

"You know what he told me?" Jimmy went on. "He said that the girl had already invited him over ... his girl, that girl! I know she's been here for years. She *knew* what she was doing."

"*She* invited *him*?" Jenny asked, understanding the implications.

"Yes!" Jimmy said. "That guy was gonna have the night of his life in the clutches of that freaky goth girl. There's no way he was the one who blew up the gym."

"We don't think he did it either," Darren said.

"Then why the fuck did Joe kill him?!"

"It might have partially been an accident," Jennifer said.

They both turned to her in surprise.

"Remember when he shot Andrei before?" Jenny asked them. "He was all freaked out like he didn't mean to. Ever since then, I've noticed that his hands have been twitching a lot. I think he's having withdrawals from the pills."

"Maybe he shouldn't be pointing that shotgun at everyone then," Jimmy said. "Or leave his fingers off the trigger like someone should have taught him from the start."

"I'm not saying it's an excuse," Jennifer said. "I'm just saying it's a factor."

"He aimed that gun at you *after* he shot Andrei in the leg," Darren fumed. "And that was after Ellen disappeared too! He didn't learn his lesson the first time, when Andrei could be put back together. He had his chance."

Jimmy shook his head in grief.

"We can't let this go on," Darren said.

"There must be something we can do," Jenny agreed.

"We just need to find the right opportunity," Darren pondered.

"Obviously, you have our blessing," Jimmy said. "Just make sure the stars align before you make a move. Don't risk another bad end, unless you think you can really pull it off."

Jimmy began chuckling.

"Fuck man," he said sardonically. "I don't know whether or not I'm happy that death is back on the table. Is that all we have to look forward to now, new and mysterious hereafters, each one more fucked up than the last?

"You think everyone goes back to high school? Are we fuckin' ghosts haunting the ruins? What is everyone else seeing?"

"We've been wondering that ourselves," Darren said, looking over at Jenny.

"Hell, we think things are bad here," Jimmy said. "The living must be going crazy by now."

Sadness swept over Jenny and Darren. It had been hard enough processing their own grief and loss. The families they all left behind must be devastated.

TWENTY-SIX

DREAMS & DARKNESS

Welcome back to NEWS10 Alexandria.

We continue with our coverage of the worst tragedy which has ever struck our dear town.

State Department officials have released a statement that they have found no evidence connecting the Villa Vista Bombing to any foreign-based extremist organizations. No groups of interest have claimed any responsibility for the attack.

As of now, the FBI are investigating the event as an act of domestic terrorism carried out by a "lone wolf". They claim that the attacker is likely someone who harbored a grudge against the student body or the school as a whole. With no clear motives otherwise, it is believed that it may have been perpetrated by a current or former Villa Vista High student.

Experts say the school gymnasium, which had been undergoing renovations at the time, was made air-tight and filled with natural gas over the course of at least 12 hours, perhaps longer. A single timed or remote trigger mechanism was likely used to ignite the gas within the sealed gym.

Class action lawsuits have already been filed against Pacific Gas & Electric for negligence in monitoring the inordinate gas usage. A similar suit is being prepared against MCL Construction, the contractor performing the renovations. That suit claims they are not only negligent, but potentially complicit. It calls for a criminal investigation of every employee who was connected to the project.

Due to the scale and nature of the situation, recovering victims from Villa Vista High School has been a slow process. There are currently a confirmed 258 dead, ninety percent of which were teenage students, and more are being unearthed by the hour. As of now, there are no confirmed survivors. Federal officials are expediting the investigation so that they may release the bodies to loved ones as soon as possible.

Many among the NEWS10 family join you in loss. Our prayers are with you, as they are with each other.

***

It was a cold, foggy morning. It had been cold and foggy ever since the explosion, as though all sunlight had disappeared from the world.

The whole town heard it as soon as it happened. The whole town died that night.

Jack Tidwell stood in the study at the back side of the house.

He had been drinking the thick, boiling hot coffee around the clock since Saturday evening. It was the only thing which gave him any warmth at all.

Despite what the news reports had said, Jack rushed at full speed to the school as soon as he could see where the smoke was coming from. He nearly drove through a police cruiser which was blocking the evacuation perimeter.

The National Guard showed up around midnight, they began setting up a bunch of medical emergency tents.

Milly had stayed home with Chris and Tommy, making phone calls to anyone she knew who may be more informed of the situation.

Jack spent the night staring at the orange glow from a distance. He was going from cop to soldier to federal agent to try to get closer. He wanted to dig through the rubble himself.

He was almost arrested for attempting to bribe a U.S. Marshal.

He gripped his cell phone tight, answering calls from Milly all night, communicating their mutual updates back and forth to each other.

He held on desperately to hope that Blaire would somehow materialize out of the smoke, that she had been away from the building and just been knocked out ... that he could take her in his arms and never let go of her again.

He prayed for that all through the night, prayed that God would give him back his little girl.

Only when the FBI set up the fence was he forced to retreat back to their home.

After crying with Milly for a few hours, Tommy had spent the past few days sleeping. He'd get up once or twice a day to use the restroom or grab some small bit of food from the pantry, but that was it.

Like Jack, Chris didn't sleep at all. He mostly sat in his room, wrapped in the largest sweatshirt jacket he owned. He wore his good headphones, pumping the loudest music that he could tolerate into his ears. Anything to drown out his thoughts.

Milly had slept in Blaire's room the few times she did sleep. She just wanted to lay on top of her covers, surrounded by her things ... the lavender walls of her room, the floral headboard, the scent of her shampoo on the pillows, the perfume she usually wore, the pictures she had scattered on her dresser, the pile of old laundry in her hamper, the side of the closet with her favorite tops, the art books and old diaries she kept hidden in the bottom drawer.

Jack had literally not slept at all. If he rested, it was seated in the large chair in the study that Edward favored. Across from it was a smaller chair, which pre-teen Blaire would sit in and listen to her grandfather tell stories.

Edward was an excellent storyteller. He could read copy from a dozen different news organizations and spin a compelling narration of the events within a few minutes.

Jack stared at the smaller, empty chair for hours. He could imagine how Blaire looked up at Edward, captivated. He remembered walking in on them occasionally.

Edward's intense eyes would rise to meet him, wordlessly. Then a nine-year-old Blaire would pivot in her chair, her own stare piercing like needles.

Jack mostly left them alone when they had moments like that. He knew how much Blaire treasured those times with Edward. In an unfortunate way, absence was the best thing he could give her.

Milly had felt the same, outside of the dynamic with Edward.

At some point on Monday, she had found Jack in the study, staring out at the ocean.

He was sipping from the mug of coffee, no longer watering it down.

"Did she feel like this all the time?" Milly had said, observing the way they now crept through the house, smothered in a shroud of despair. "Was this Hell for her?"

Jack set down the coffee and held her.

"Is she happier without us now?" Milly cried. "I just wanted her to be happy."

Jack did his best to comfort her, but he didn't have a real response. The same questions haunted his own thoughts. They would probably haunt him until the day he died.

***

Blaire lay on the ground clutching Andrei's lifeless body for a long time. Only when she stopped crying did she make the decision to move him.

She wasn't going to let him just lay in the doorway, to be disgraced by those wicked demons.

She covered what remained of his head with her sweatshirt jacket, then slowly slid him back behind the teacher's desk.

Andrei's neck and torso were now somewhat concealed by the table top, at least from the view of the door.

She then carefully refolded the sweatshirt to cover him down to his shoulders.

Blaire sat against the side of Mr. Van Gaal's desk, hugging her knees. She held Andrei's hand, feeling every last bit of warmth it would offer.

"No splitting up," she whispered ... but there was no response.

She decided that she would not leave his side. She would wait for the demons to return and end her just the same as they had done to him.

Elise would be okay without her. She would have Rafael ... she would have everyone. In every way that Blaire was abrasive, Elise was agreeable. She would find fellow travelers and kindred spirits wherever her soul was carried.

Deep inside, Blaire's wall of darkness had collapsed, and a thousand painful memories flooded through her like a bursting dam washing away a city.

There was a time when she was six years old. Her parents had taken them to a park. Her brothers were having fun, playing in the sandbox and going on the swings, but she sat in the shade of the tree, annoyed that they had dragged her out there.

There was a time when she was eight years old. Chris was pestering her to go swimming with them because they needed more people for Marco Polo, but she said no.

There was a time when she was ten years old. She had found out that Tommy had been scribbling in her diary with crayons, "adding his own pages". She yelled at him until he cried.

There was a time when she was thirteen years old. Her mom wanted to have a "girls' day" while her dad took the boys to a birthday party for one of Chris' friends. Blaire preferred to stay inside, finding all of her mother's ideas boring.

There was a time just last year, when she was fifteen. Chris wanted to ask her for some advice on how to talk to girls, but when the time came, she flaked on him.

Blaire covered her head with her free hand, gritting her teeth.

How could she have been so horrible to all of them? What was the matter with her? Why had it been so hard at the time to be there for them, when she actually could be?

But those were not the most painful memories.

The ones that would make her heart bleed ... if she were still able to bleed at all ... were part of a smaller, more precious set of experiences.

There was a time when she was six years old. She held a purple crayon in baby Tommy's hand, guiding it while they drew animals in a forest.

There was the time when she was eight years old. Chris broke one of their mother's vases. She was able to use her art glues to patch it up without her ever noticing.

There was a time when she was ten years old. Her dad sat down to join her and her grandfather in the study. They talked for hours, and her dad seemed to be genuinely enjoying himself around his dad ... which was a rare occurrence in itself.

There was a time when she was thirteen years old. Her mom was laid up in bed for a few days with a really bad flu. Blaire curled up beside her in a nightgown and read ghost stories to her.

There was a time earlier in the year. Chris had a cute sort-of-date with his friend Sarah. Blaire helped him pick out the best smelling cologne.

She wondered if they remembered any of those times. Was her short life spent too often as a thorn and not enough as a rose? Why did it feel so hard to connect with them?

When their spirits were high, hers were low. When they were overjoyed and expressive, she was serene and closed-off. Why did things so seldom fit together at the same time?

She squeezed Andrei's hand tighter.

Why, when she found someone to love, to really love, was their time cut so short? Why, when she found someone who understood her on such a deep level, were they then condemned to a fiery death? Why, when she found a kindred spirit in every way that mattered, in mind, body, and soul, was he stolen from her before they could be joined as one?

Now her only future was to descend even further into the abyss, without Andrei, without her dad, without her mom, without her brothers, and without her grandpa.

She sat huddled in this way for a very long time. At one point she must have slipped into some form of sleep, because she was surrounded by darkness once more.

"Blaire," a voice called forth from the veil.

It was familiar, a voice she'd heard numerous times in the past.

"Blaire," it called again, begging for her response.

Her spirit was weak, she was so tired.

"Sweetheart?" a second voice spoke with it.

She looked up, a small flicker of hope lighting her from within.

***

It was just before sunrise on Tuesday morning.

Jack Tidwell pulled his car up to the edge of Mitchell Avenue.

The official entrance to the disaster site was a block over at the intersection with Westmont. A large makeshift memorial had been assembled near there. Thousands of candles, photos, trinkets, and crosses were placed along the sidewalks around the entrance.

This particular intersection only featured a straight piece of fence.

On the other side of the fence was U.S. Marshal Tom Morgan, whom Jack had attempted to bribe to get closer to the school. Mr. Morgan had rejected the cash offer, but he was also nice enough not to report the grieving father for what was technically a crime.

This was the third time Jack had stopped at this part of the fence while running an "errand".

It was the closest he could get to the school, the closest he could get to Blaire.

Tom Morgan nodded, then stepped a few paces down the fence, giving Jack some privacy.

He stood there, statuesque, with his thermos of coffee. He stared at the last trails of smoke that trickled out of the rubble.

His right hand gripped the fence. Like his father's old cane, he needed it just to stay standing. He felt as though his knees could give out at any moment.

For this trip, Jack brought with him something new.

A small gold cross necklace hung between the fingers that were clutching the fence.

It belonged to his mother, who had left it with Edward after she passed. It took hours on Monday to dig it out of the storage box with his father's things.

But now he had it, and with it, he prayed.

He prayed all the prayers his mother had taught him as a child, he prayed passages that he could remember from his old Sunday School, and after all that, he just said anything.

Jack was pretty sure his dad loved him, but the worst thing about his childhood was how hard it was for him to feel that love from him.

Edward was a cold man; his expressions of affection were subtle and dependent on context.

One example happened on Jack's fourteenth birthday. His father bought him a stereo, which his mother swore until the day she died really was Edward's idea.

Even with headphones, noise pollution from such a device was a threat to solace.

Edward was a quiet, contemplative, methodical man. When he did seek out music for pleasure, it was often some form of small symphony orchestra, mainly being led by a single grand piano.

Jack being given his own stereo, with a built-in cassette deck, was Edward's unspoken permission to play Rolling Stones and Van Halen music when he wanted ... within reason, of course.

Still, the gesture was meaningful, Edward had gifted him part of his own peace and quiet for Jack's enjoyment as an angsty teenager.

It would take him a decade to truly appreciate that sacrifice.

He wondered if he had ever truly communicated to Blaire how much of her own childhood he had sacrificed so she could spend those years with Edward.

His father had passed just as she was becoming a teenager, where normal teenage rebellion came into play. Jack gave up a lot of those last daddy-daughter years so Blaire could make the most out of the only other Tidwell cut from the same coarse cloth as her.

Tears trickled down Jack's face.

What he would give to have Blaire back at her worst. To see her again in her most closed-off, doom-and-gloom teenager mood would be better than anything he could imagine.

"She's with you now, Dad," he said aloud. "Please take care of her for me."

Jack broke down. His knuckles loosened and he dropped to his knees. His forehead rested against the metal grates as he sobbed quietly.

He was there for a long time, longer than he intended. At some point, the coffee could provide no more energy and Jack fell asleep against the fence.

When Jack opened his eyes, there was an infinite plane of darkness all around him. He stood up, looking in all directions, but found nothing but inky abyss.

He pulled off his glasses, wiping them as hard as he could, but nothing he did could bring light back to this place.

He needed help.

A glow beckoned above him, but then quickly disappeared.

It lit up white again, then once more faded.

Only with enough rotations did enough light fill this place that the island was fully visible.

Jack walked forward on grass, crossing an open field to reach the tower.

Two opposing beams pushed back against the darkness as the lighthouse beacons turned.

With each rotation, a familiar silhouette at the base of the structure would gain more detail.

Jack was afraid, but he continued to move forward.

A wizened face looked down at him. The figure stood several inches taller, as he always had. He wore a longshoreman coat, which Jack had never seen him wear when he was alive. But the sharp, penetrating eyes looked at him as they looked at everything else, with all of his focus and attention.

"Dad?" he asked, feeling a breeze drift past them.

"Jack ..." Edward said, taking him in a tight embrace.

Jack was sure he was dreaming now; he only remembered a handful of times Edward ever showed affection like that.

"What are you doing here?" he asked him.

"My duty," Edward said succinctly, sounding much more like the man Jack remembered.

The wind was becoming stronger now and Edward looked out sideways.

Moving over the black abyss was a white blanket of fog, coming in like the evening mist from Drakes Bay.

"She was caught in a storm along the way," Edward said. "I'm here to help guide her to shore."

"Blaire ..." Jack said, following Edward's eyes toward the fog bank.

"I'm sorry Jack," Edward said, an uncharacteristic tear welling up in his eye. "I didn't think I'd be out here until the day you were arriving."

The fog slowly rolled over the island, the white mist enveloping them.

"Please, take me instead," Jack begged him. "She has her whole life ahead of her!"

"No, son," he said. "She has eternity ahead of her."

"Blaire," Edward called into the mist.

Jack saw nothing.

"Blaire," he called again.

That's when a silhouette began to appear.

"Sweetheart?" Jack asked the spectre.

The small black form was huddled on the ground, holding her knees, but Jack's words caused her to look up.

"Dad?" she answered, her voice full of uncertainty and doubt.

Jack ran closer. The shadow stood up and began to solidify.

He took her in his arms, experiencing a warmth he thought he'd never feel again.

He kissed her head, squeezing her so she could not slip from his grasp.

She was as perfect and lovely as she looked when she had left that fateful night.

"Dad ..." She said, grief stricken. "Dad, I'm so sorry ... I always loved you ... I always loved Mom, and Chris, and Tommy. I'm sorry that it was so hard to say."

They collapsed onto their knees, a shapeless white aether beneath them.

"And we always loved you Blaire," he answered her. "And we always will."

Jack could feel her relax from hearing his words, a weight drifting away from her.

"Please!" Jack begged Edward. "Take me instead!"

"No!" Blaire interjected, dread filling her words. "You don't deserve my fate."

"Yes, he does," Edward replied.

Blaire stared back at her grandfather in horror.

"He just needs to wait a while longer," Edward said.

"But ..." Blaire sputtered. "But I'm ..."

Jack could feel her body quiver in fear.

Edward finished her sentence, "... you're in a ship not meant for either of you."

The white fog thinned, revealing the deck of a historical wooden schooner. It was a sight all too familiar for Blaire.

"Is Andrei here too?!" Blaire straightened up.

"No," her grandfather said. "He's waiting for you down below."

"What?" she asked, hope lifting her spirits.

"You were brought out here against your will," Edward said. "You and so many others."

Faint shadows appeared on the edges of the fog.

"There is no salvation for such a crime." Fire burned behind his eyes. "The captain will go down with their ship, alone, and their suffering will be never ending."

"Who?" Blaire asked him. "Grandpa, who did this to us?"

"I don't know their name," Edward admitted. "That you'll have to find out for yourself. But sooner or later, everyone else will make it to shore, and they'll succumb to the deep."

"Will I see her again?" Jack asked him, holding her close.

"Yes," Edward said, without hesitation. "But you have your own duties to attend to."

Three faint glows appeared just beside them.

"Tell them that I'm sorry," Blaire said. "That I love them."

"I will," Jack said, kissing her cheek and holding her one last time.

Edward came and knelt down, wrapping his arms around both of them.

"I love you both so much," Edward said to them.

"I promise I'll take care of her, son," he told Jack. "We'll be waiting for you."

"I love you Dad," Blaire whispered one more time.

Jack Tidwell opened his eyes.

He was kneeling against the fence, as he had been before.

He pulled the glasses off of his face, sobbing fresh tears, harder than he had the past several days.

As painful as the feeling was, at the end there was hope.

"Thank you ... thank you ... thank you ..." he mouthed to the heavens.

***

Blaire opened her eyes.

She was staring at a painting of Mount Olympus. It hung on the wall of Mr. Van Gaal's classroom.

Tears trickled down her face.

"Thank you, Grandpa. Thank you for letting me see him again."

She replayed the meeting in her mind several times. It was one of the precious memories, one she'd never forget ... no matter how long eternity really was.

She regained sense of herself, huddled on the floor by the desk. How long had she been asleep?

Andrei's hand still felt warm.

She squeezed it.

It squeezed her back.

The response startled her so much that she jumped away from the desk, landing near Andrei's feet.

Slowly, Andrei began to sit up, supporting himself on one elbow. With his other hand, he pulled her sweatshirt off of his face. A fine white powder covered Andrei's entire head. He brushed along his hair and face until all of the dust had puffed off of him.

He shifted his left leg too, seeing that his calf, and the dress pants covering it, had been completely restored.

"Andrei," Blaire asked, "Is it really you?"

"My head hurts ..." he said, a wry smile forming.

Blaire jumped on top of him, kissing his face and clutching his chest.

"I thought I'd lost you," she whispered.

"I wasn't ready to go," he answered her. "'No splitting up.'"

She laughed through tears of joy.

They sat upright against the wall behind Van Gaal's desk.

"How long has it been?" Andrei asked her.

Blaire slid the phone out of her gym shorts.

Tuesday, 6:16 a.m.

"Has Torelli bothered you at all?" he asked her.

"No," Blaire said. "After he shot you, he quickly left and sealed the exit again."

Andrei looked over the edge of the table at the door. Thin shadows of the wooden wedges were visible below.

"I don't think they've heard us," he said in a low voice.

"The whole building must have heard the shotgun," she answered him in a quiet tone. "And after that, I was crying pretty loudly. They probably figured that if they tried anything else the others would revolt again."

"Well right now we have the element of surprise," Andrei said. "We need to think of the best way to use it."

"Oh!" Blaire exclaimed, "speaking of surprises, I had another dream."

"You did?" Andrei asked, happy to see the joy in her face.

"I got to talk to my dad, and my grandpa too!" Blaire said. "That's why I had the dream before."

"What do you mean?" Andrei asked.

"My grandpa knew what was coming," she said. "He was sent to help me."

"Does he know who the bomber is?" Andrei wondered.

"No," Blaire said. "But he told me it was only a matter of time. We were all going to get out of here and the bomber was going to pay for what they did."

"Well, that's encouraging." Andrei smiled. "Let's hope your visions prove to be true like last time."

Blaire was smiling too, looking off distantly. Andrei could tell there was more.

"Did something else happen?" he asked.

"I was able to say goodbye to my dad," Blaire said through bittersweet tears. "I said I was sorry, that I always loved them ... and he said that they'd always love me."

"Of course they will," Andrei said, holding her.

"Grandpa said I'd see them again one day," she finished.

A lump formed in Andrei's throat. To see their families again would be the greatest blessing of all.

"Come on," he whispered to her.

He stood them both up, planting his left leg surely on the floor before finishing.

"We need to make this look good."

***

"Yeah man, of course it sucked," Brendan Jensen said, leaning against the wall of the main hallway. "Joe wasn't too happy about it either."

"He's still the one that pulled the trigger," Darren said, trying to reason with them.

"Look, Darren," Trey Devall said. "I get what you're feeling, but we need to get this done. The sooner we can find the bomber, the sooner we can punish them and this will all be over with."

"Yeah, but we already have at least one casualty!" Darren said. The three of them stood between the makeshift prison cells. "And that's not even counting the freshman girl or everyone else who jumped because of her."

"You can't put that on Joe," Brendan retorted. "If you ask me, that's more proof that Wallace and Melkonian are the murderers."

"We're getting closer," Trey reassured him. "Joe's been talking with the others, trying to find the holes in some of the testimonies. Who knows, maybe it'll turn out that Andrei guy *was* responsible."

"Alright, fine," Darren said in defeat. There was no changing either of their minds.

"Just get some sleep," Brendan said to him. "I have a good feeling about tomorrow."

Darren walked away from them without saying anything else.

Jenny was waiting for him by the gymnasium hallway.

"How'd it go?" she asked him.

"Like I expected," he said. "They're sticking with Joe to the end."

Jenny sighed. She looked like she was really hoping for better news.

"How'd things go with the girls?" Darren asked her, already anticipating her answer.

"Well, Sheena kept me for almost an hour," Jenny began. "She was talking about this big fight she had with her sister that she can't apologize for now. Then Ashley just seemed kind of shell-shocked. She was too emotionally drained to care about what Trey was doing or why. I think she's just been sleeping this whole time."

"Damn," Darren said. He thought Jenny would have been able to convince them. If she could have flipped Ashley and Sheena, they could have flipped the guys. They'd have much better odds of carrying out a mutiny against Joe if they could all spring a surprise attack on him.

"Where is Joe now?" Jenny asked him.

"He walked by Brendan, Trey, and I earlier," Darren said. "He was talking with Eric, Jordan, Paxton, Amanda, and the sophomore couple. I think they've all been in the gym looking at the sparking device."

"What about Marcus?" Jenny asked him.

"I haven't seen him since he walked away earlier."

Jenny shifted her eyes in thought.

"Which room was his again?" she asked.

They listened to the door of his dorm, seeing if they could hear him inside. The lights were on, so he must not be sleeping.

"Marcus?" Jenny called inside, rapping her knuckles on the door.

There was no answer.

"We wanted to check on you," she continued, "we haven't gotten to talk at all."

"There's nothing to say," a tired voice said from inside the room.

"Please, Marcus?" she asked. "Just a minute?"

There was a pause, then they heard the clicking of the door lock.

Jenny pressed the handle and the door opened into the room.

Marcus sat on top of one of the side tables along the wall. The L-shaped tire iron rested next to his leg.

Darren checked his grip on the crowbar, but held it in a non-threatening way.

"How come you're up here and not in the gym?" Jenny began.

"It's all over." Marcus shook his head a little. "We ain't never gonna find the killer. They're probably out there lying on the floor below the atrium."

"Could be," Jenny said. "I'm afraid of what might happen if the others don't agree though."

"It was wrong," Marcus said, looking past the shadow of his hoodie. "Joe shouldn't have put that gun to you. You're not the reason why we're here."

Darren stood by, letting Jenny do the talking.

"I mean, why would you?" Marcus said. "We won! Homecoming King and Queen! Everyone cheering for us, taking pictures with my goofy ass and *your* goofy ass."

He motioned to Darren.

"You were looking great in your dress," he went on. "And Janice, she was just dazzling. The whole package top to bottom. Shit, she could always outdress me. I thought she'd tie me up in Gucci and Chanel if I didn't keep my threads fresh."

"You could pull off Gucci," Jenny said with a smirk.

"Oh, stop it, now you're sounding like her," he said, a slight smile finally donning his face.

"Would she really want you to feel this way?" Jenny asked, becoming a bit more serious.

Marcus said nothing, considering her words.

Jenny continued, "If it were her stuck here instead, what would you want her doing?"

He looked down, picking up the tire iron.

"Not this shit," he mumbled. "All these people getting stabbed and beat on, locked up, and we still have no damn idea who did it."

He rested the iron in his lap.

"How about that Andrei guy?" Marcus asked them. "He finally on two legs again?"

Darren and Jenny looked at each other.

"Didn't you hear all that noise a few hours ago?" Jenny asked him.

Marcus looked confused.

"Well yeah," he said. "It sounded like Joe started pulling scare tactics and that girl freaked out."

"Marcus," Darren said. "That was Blaire, Andrei's girlfriend. Joe shot him again, in the head. The guy's dead."

His eyes opened wider in shock.

"What the hell, why?" Marcus asked. "Was he the killer?"

"No one knows." Jenny shrugged. "They were going to question him and Blaire, then there was some arguing, then Joe just shot him."

"Shit!" Marcus said, getting off of the table. He rubbed a hand over his head, his shoulders dropping.

"Didn't think it would be like this," Marcus said. "I just wanted to put thing's right for Janice, but that can't happen with Joe in charge. That dude's got way too much of an itchy trigger finger. Someone else should be holding the gun."

"I agree," Jenny said. "We've got to get it away from him when we have the chance."

"Shit," Marcus said again, but quieter. "I should have stopped him from waving that thing around so casually."

"Us too," Darren agreed. "We can't turn back the clock, but we can do something now. Can we count on you ... when we make a move?"

"Yeah, I'll help you," Marcus said, with new conviction. "This can't go on anymore."

"Thank you," Jenny replied.

She then stepped up and hugged him. It was the first time they'd been this close since the dance. Marcus had been so tucked away in his own darkness that he hadn't let anyone else in.

Jenny couldn't let the moment end without mentioning one more thing.

"I'm so sorry about Janice," she said. "She was very kind. I'm sure wherever she is now, she misses you terribly."

Marcus put his free hand around her.

"I hope so too," he said.

Once they let go, Darren shook his hand.

"Thank you for your help."

Marcus pulled the hood off of his head.

"Welp," he said. "Let's go see what they're up to."

***

Bob Melkonian and Rick Wallace had been sitting casually in Hana Novak's classroom.

The prayer that Rick had recited to Ellen Taylor was not very long at all. Bob was able to memorize it in a few minutes.

Even Rick's spirits seemed lifted by Ellen's miraculous departure. He was able to start talking about his family again, without the added mention of his original sin.

"... but Mary will make sure they still get plenty of nice gifts for Christmas and such," Rick said, wrapping up discussion of his grandkids. "She never needed me for that anyway. I always figured she'd live longer than me, but I thought I'd have another decade or so."

"I'm grateful that I lived long enough to raise Monika," Bob said, "to see her into adulthood with all the support and love I could offer. I just wish I could have been there for so much more, to walk her down the aisle, meet my grandkids, see *them* grow up."

"You did good, Bob," Rick said. "She's a wonderful young woman, and she'll have a long and happy life thanks to having you as a father."

"You know," Bob said, transitioning back into old family stories. "This one time when we took her to Disneyland, one of the costumed-"

A loud explosion rang through the door.

Both men jumped to their feet, looking at the source of the sound.

A girl began crying in absolute sorrow.

"Oh god, they shot someone else!" Bob said.

Rick walked over, putting his ear to the door. Bob joined him.

It wasn't long until Darren Clark's voice could be heard in the hallway too.

"He's dead?" Bob asked him, wondering if they heard right.

Rick looked down, forlorn. He slid down the wall to the floor. "Torelli, what have you done?" he whispered.

Bob remained standing. He lay his palm over the middle of the door.

"God Almighty," Bob began, "You called us forth from the darkness. Your providence lights our way. And as You design, we return to dust."

Rick looked up, meeting his eyes. He began speaking it with him.

"Lord," they continued, "those who died live anew with You. Their lives have changed but will never end. I pray forever for my family, relatives and friends. That alive or dead, they are at peace at last."

The wails of anguish gave the prayer a haunting feel. It also carried much more weight to them, considering what happened last time.

"Together with Christ," they concluded, "who died so we may live. May they be fulfilled as one in Paradise, where sin and pain are washed away. Unite our family in our final home, to exalt Your name forever and ever."

"Amen," they finished.

Bob looked down at the shadows underneath the door. There were three distinct impressions where the wooden blocks were placed on the other side.

He held his breath, waiting to see the bright blue glow of electricity. The glow never came.

"I don't understand," Bob said. He then asked Rick, "Did I say it right?"

Rick nodded.

"Was it because he was already gone?" Bob asked. "Was he not a believer?"

"Maybe they have to say it with us," Rick said, "or at least agree with it in spirit."

Bob's faith was clearly shaken, so Rick set his own doubts and pessimism aside.

"Maybe it's not the words that matter at all," Rick said. "We couldn't free his soul because it was already taken from him."

"Then what happens to him?" Bob said. "Is he just in another place like this, but alone?"

"'Maybe we don't have to know the mechanics,'" Rick said, quoting Melkonian from earlier.

Blaire Tidwell's cries continued to fill the school building.

"How can they cause so much pain and seem to feel nothing?" Bob asked, sliding down to sit against the door.

"The boy's in God's hands now," Rick said. "We need to focus on the kids that are still here."

They listened to Blaire's weeping for nearly an hour, until it finally died down.

Both men had returned to their chairs, making themselves as comfortable as they could, considering the circumstances.

"I think the poor girl's finally fallen asleep," Bob said.

"I think I might turn in also," Rick replied, yawning. "Could you get the light?"

"Yeah," Bob answered. It *was* pretty late, considering everyone had woken up around three in the morning.

Rick was already leaning back in the chair, propping his legs on Hana's desk.

Bob stayed up for a little while longer.

He pulled out his cell phone, which he couldn't believe still worked in this place. The seemingly infinite power available meant the phone could stay on all the time without charging. It didn't have a lot of uses without an Internet connection, but it still had what was stored on the memory card.

Bob scrolled through a large folder of images which had accrued over the years. He had thousands of pictures of Angie and Monika to look at, in case he ever felt like he was forgetting them.

TWENTY-SEVEN

DEMON DANCE

DARREN, JENNIFER, AND MARCUS joined the others in the gymnasium right around 9:00 p.m. on Monday night.

Of course, that time distinction was almost totally meaningless. Everyone's cell phones just so happened to remain in sync, telling them what time it was in the living world. Otherwise, there was no night to speak of, just the even, overcast daylight that poured through the unceasing continuum of mist that surrounded them.

Despite the Sabbatical the three of them had taken from the Varsity Politburo, nothing new had come up. There were no discoveries or clues and no more construction drawings had been found anywhere. It wasn't like they had an Internet connection to try to hack the information off of a website.

Everyone avoided talking about Andrei at all. If he came up as a suspect, it was without the added note that he was already dead.

Perhaps the most surprising thing was Torelli's own conclusion drawn from the day's events. With his hands still twitching occasionally, Joe announced that nothing had changed. They would be moving forward with the interviews.

Following that, he said everyone could get their rest. They would meet again in the gymnasium at 9:00 a.m. on Tuesday morning.

The way he bid them good night made the proceedings sound like a day job. Joe intended this to be like a regular 9-to-5 work schedule. He had already internalized the mindset of going about interviewing people in an almost bureaucratic kind of way, a more banal approach to the evil nature of the investigation.

He would slowly milk drops of information out of each of them until he was satisfied enough to remove them as a suspect. How long that could last was anyone's guess. But with an infinite amount of time to fill, there was no sign of it ending anytime soon.

Darren and Jenny returned to their room. The moment of romance had long since passed, so they kicked off their shoes and fell asleep on the air mattress.

Darren was surprised that they'd slept all the way through to his 8:30 a.m. alarm. Maybe there was something to Jimmy's theory of "headspace tired".

They did what little morning routine they could, considering the materials they had available.

Jenny knocked on the door of the girls' bathroom. When it turned out to be empty, Darren followed her in.

The only toiletries they had between them was the small kit that Jenny kept in her cheerleading bag.

Once Jenny finished brushing her teeth, she rinsed her toothbrush and offered it to him.

Darren washed his face with water from the sink, then sniffed his armpits.

"What are you doing?" Jenny asked, scrunching her nose.

"I usually shower in the morning," he said. "It's been a couple mornings since the dance, but I don't really smell anything."

"No body odor?" She smelled the corners of her own shirt and was pleasantly surprised.

"Have you had to ... you know?" Jenny motioned toward the stalls.

"I took a piss on Sunday," Darren said. "Apparently I'm well hydrated, but nothing since then."

"Maybe Jimmy's right," Jenny said. "This place is too weird to be Hell."

They stepped casually down the stairwell, then turned to walk through the prison hallway. Brendan and Trey were still at their stations. They were talking and laughing loudly about some old football stories.

"Have you guys been here all night?" Jenny asked them.

"Yeah, we're doing alright," Trey said. "Joe said he'd be figuring out a more concrete guard rotation in the next day or two."

"I'm not all that tired," Brendan agreed. "We can keep an eye on things until he has the plan together."

"Alright," Darren said, not arguing. "Guess we'll see you guys later then."

Darren felt like their lack of exhaustion only validated the "headspace tired" theory. What was there to be tired from when they were letting someone else do all the thinking for them?

He and Jenny continued on to the gymnasium.

Everyone returned to their seats in the circle of chairs set up the night before. Joe Torelli sat in the most prominent position, shotgun in hand. The bomber's device was perched on the chair just in front of him.

To his left was Eric Schwartz, followed by Jordan Trainor, Paxton Bannister, and Amanda Burke.

To his right was Marcus Johnson, followed by Darren Clark, Jennifer Maxwell, Greg Henshaw, and Chelsea Morton.

"Alright," Joe began, once everyone had quieted down. "Today we're going to start out by interviewing the Blaire Tidwell girl."

"Seriously?" Chelsea asked in disbelief.

"Are you sure that's appropriate after yesterday?" Greg asked him.

"She's already alone in there," Joe responded to them, "This just makes the process easier."

Even Amanda, who had very publicly accused Blaire and Andrei, looked uncomfortable with the idea.

"Maybe we should save her for last," Eric offered. "She is not going to be cooperative."

Joe paused for a moment, even though his mind was clearly made up.

"Her anger works to our advantage," he muttered, "she won't hold back. She'll put everything out on the table and we can evaluate what she says."

He looked around at the rest of them.

"Any more questions?"

They stayed silent, knowing how pointless it was.

"Good," Torelli said. "And be sure to bring the duct tape."

"Awful," Jenny whispered under her breath to Darren.

All ten of them slowly marched out of the gym, the giant mural of Jackie the Jaguar roaring at them as they exited. He and the bomber's evil machine were all that remained inside.

Marcus stepped past the empty trophy cabinets, partially blown to pieces by buckshot damage.

They exited through the covered chain-link fence. The "MCL Construction" sign was still mounted prominently on the front.

They moved along the sidewalk in front of the main parking lot. Glass was scattered all over the asphalt. Almost every car had its windows broken during the search yesterday.

Entering the front doors of the school, the group had to step past several dead bodies which still lay around the foyer, below the walkway. Joe hadn't even opened the floor to ideas of what to do with all of them.

They reached the entrance of Van Gaal's classroom.

"Open it," Joe said to Trey Devall. He then sighed. "Let's get this over with."

Trey pulled away the wooden blocks and punched in the code to unlock the door. Brendan Jensen stood on the other side, ready to catch her if she tried to run.

Darren and Jenny watched as Joe held the shotgun at the ready. At least he had the sense to keep his finger off of the trigger this time. It rested against the side of the barrel, pointing forward.

Trey opened the door, revealing the state that Blaire was in.

She lay curled up on the floor in a fetal position next to the body. She was more or less exactly where Joe had left her the night before. Her hood was pulled back and her dark, wavy hair covered much of her face. The hours of crying had left long streaks of eyeliner on her cheeks, like spider webs.

She had covered Andrei with some kind of decorative rug which Van Gaal kept as a display piece.

Darren had spent a few months in his Classics period, but he couldn't quite place what civilization it was from. Van Gaal had a lot of artifacts like that which he put to use in his lectures.

Joe kept the gun aimed just slightly off of her as he stepped through the door. It looked like he planned to check her with the wood and metal frame of the gun if she leapt up to attack him. She was a head shorter than him, and half his weight, it wouldn't be much of a struggle.

But before Torelli could say a single word, a metal chair flew in from the side of the classroom and cracked Joe along his left temple.

"Crack" was the proper word, because it was the sound all of them heard when it hit. A spray of dust shot out through the black, curly hair.

The chair seemed to float away after making an impact.

The shotgun dropped out of his hands.

In sudden, swift movements, Blaire jumped forward and took hold of the Browning Citori.

Torelli fell to his knees, trying to reach for the weapon. His whole body was beginning to convulse. That head wound had done some kind of serious damage.

In his frantic searching, he pushed at the rug covering Andrei. Some pieces of ancient-style pottery had been arranged in such a way to make the necessary bumps in the thick carpet. It was enough to look like a body.

Blaire stood to her feet.

She shoved the barrel of the gun into Torelli's mouth.

"Fucking monster!" she screamed, then pulled the trigger.

The entire exchange happened so quickly that Darren only had fractions of a second to pull Jenny away from the cone of fire.

Joe's head exploded through the doorway into millions of pieces. Dust trickled into the corridor.

His body went limp and dropped onto its back.

Blaire leaned down and slipped the bandolier of ammunition off of his arm. She tossed it over her shoulder. Nearly four dozen bright red shells of 12-gauge buckshot remained on the belt.

Her furious glare at the rest of them was frightening enough, but then something else stepped into view from the left side of the door.

It was Andrei Tunnikov.

He was alive, ambulatory, and fully healed. Both shoes were firmly planted on the ground. His body almost totally filled the seven-foot-tall door frame.

His eyes were cold and fearless.

In his hands, he held the metal stackable chair. It was one of the heavier kinds, like the one Darren used when trying to check on Isabella in the single-stall bathroom.

Andrei leapt through the frame in a very purposeful movement and swung the edge of the metal chair into Trey's face.

He dropped his knife lance and stumbled backwards to the floor.

Andrei let go of the chair, picking up the lance like a bow staff.

"Joe, Trey!" Brendan yelled, thrusting his knife toward the revived prisoner.

Andrei blocked the blade with the bar, then used his weapon to fling the lance out of Brendan's hands. However, he lost his own lance in the process.

Darren turned to Jenny. This was their chance. She nodded and they both glanced at Marcus.

Darren's grip on the crowbar tightened. He slammed it into Paxton's elbow. He grunted in shock, not expecting the hit, but still maintained his hold on the lance.

Darren hooked it with the gooseneck and pulled it from his hands. The sharp weapon bounced along the stone tile floor.

Marcus likewise pivoted and swung the tire iron down onto Jordan's lance, breaking it free from his grasp.

Seeing Paxton engaged, Amanda turned to attack Jennifer.

Jenny was able to block the attack, but they both took hold of each other's lances. After a moment of struggle, Jennifer was the one disarmed.

Amanda leaned forward, driving the steak knife toward her stomach, but Jenny was able to twist out of the way.

Jenny reached into her gym shorts, fumbling with the backup weapon still concealed on her person. The switchblade flipped open.

Amanda's lunge had exposed an opening under her right arm.

Jenny pressed the blade into Amanda's ribs.

She began gasping in pain and dropped the knife lance.

Jenny kept the switchblade at the ready, moving back-to-back with Darren to defend each other.

Jordan scrambled to pick up a weapon as Marcus pivoted around him like they were on the basketball court. Marcus kept one eye fixed on Eric, who was not engaging either of them.

Instead, Eric was watching Andrei.

With Brendan disarmed, Andrei balled up his fists, throwing hard punches into his liver.

Katya's words about fighting echoed in his thoughts. He punched like he was reaching for Brendan's kidneys and the liver was just in the way.

As an offensive lineman, Brendan was strong and tough. However, most of his strength was oriented around field sports. He had the most experience stopping full-body ramming by defensive tackles in gear.

Andrei didn't know much else about the lineman, what other skills he might have for them to face. When Andrei and Blaire strategized fighting their opponents, he would have to work off of the assumption that his reflexes and reactions were still going to come from a football mindset.

That is why Andrei opened with fast, precision liver punches. While he wasn't sure how much anatomy still applied to their current bodies, he knew that pain was still very real. Liver punches were very painful.

Brendan doubled over, gripping his stomach to keep any more strikes from making contact.

That was when Andrei kicked the side of Brendan's leg. The varsity player stumbled down to his knees. He was now exactly where Andrei wanted him.

Andrei spun back and slammed his elbow hard into Brendan's temple.

The lineman collapsed face first onto the floor, totally knocked out.

By this time, Trey was back on his feet. Dust trickled from a large gash in his nose and forehead. Even still, he made an attempt to stop Andrei. He flung his foot toward Andrei's rib cage, using all the force his Varsity Football kicker leg could muster.

Andrei caught his shin and gripped the leg.

Trey was unbalanced, hopping momentarily on one foot.

Using the advantage of his long arms and the length of Trey's leg, Andrei pivoted his whole body, building angular momentum. He slammed Trey against the wall with a great deal of force.

Trey twisted on the ground, even more dazed than before.

With the two immediate threats neutralized, Andrei took stock of his surroundings. He was surprised to witness the power struggle taking place among the others.

While the other varsity players engaged their comrades, Andrei saw Greg and Chelsea run away at full speed. They disappeared into one of the side hallways, just trying to escape the situation. It was a panicked retreat from the shotgun blast.

They had reason to be scared.

Blaire Tidwell stepped through the door frame. She had loaded a fresh shell into the Browning Citori to replace the one that exploded Torelli's head.

The action closed with a practiced click. Joe wasn't the only one experienced with firearms.

"Freeze!" she yelled, sweeping the shotgun back and forth among the remaining goons.

All of the melee engagements did indeed stop cold in their tracks. They stood like deer, staring down the headlights of a big rig as it barreled toward them on a highway.

"Wait, we were trying to help!" Darren said, pulling Jenny behind his back.

"Drop the weapons!" Blaire yelled at them.

Darren and Jenny loosened their grips. The crowbar and switchblade clattered to the floor.

Everyone else still holding something also surrendered them, then lifted their hands into the air.

"Where's Elise and Raf?!" she demanded.

"Blaire!" a voice yelled through one of the doors.

Andrei grabbed Trey by the collar, lifting him a few inches off of the ground.

"What's the code?" he demanded.

Trey barely processed the question, his vision still swirling like a carnival ride.

"9947," he mumbled.

Andrei's cold eyes turned to Darren and Jennifer.

"Open it," he said, dropping Trey back against the wall.

They complied. Darren pulled away the wooden blocks and Jenny punched in the code.

As soon as the door opened, Elise ran out and wrapped her arms around Blaire. She nuzzled Elise's neck in relief. The red hair and pink dress were a welcome sight. Even with the hug though, Blaire still had a firm grip on the Citori.

"Man, it is so good to see you." Raf walked out after her. He gripped Andrei's hand and pulled into a hug.

"It's good to be back," Andrei replied.

"We thought you were dead," Elise said, still holding Blaire on one side.

"So did we," Jennifer said with relief.

Raf spotted his Ka-Bar knives sticking out of Trey's suit coat pockets. The blades were sitting upright. If Trey had fallen the wrong way, they could have stabbed him right through the ribs.

"Give me those, dumbass," Raf said, snatching them back.

Elise let go of Blaire and took the knife Raf handed her. They stood beside their friends once again.

This time, Raf kept his eyes glancing left and right down the hallways, watching for flying weapons.

The other students of Villa Vista High had gathered at each end of the corridor, watching the exchange take place.

"How about Niles and Laura?!" Blaire shouted.

"We're here!" Laura's voice came through a different door.

Darren and Jenny pulled away the blocks and punched in the code.

Niles and Laura crept out, keeping their eyes on their former captors. With the exception of Darren and Jenny, they all still had their hands in the air. It felt good to see.

"Holy shit, you guys are incredible," Niles said, patting Andrei on the shoulder.

Laura hugged Blaire and Elise, happy to see them okay.

That's when Melvin Mueller and Barry Owens appeared in the doorway too.

Blaire's eyes fixed on Melvin and she tightened her grip on the shotgun.

Melvin almost stepped backwards into the room.

"Hey man," Barry murmured in Andrei's direction, "glad you're okay."

"Thanks," Andrei replied.

Everyone else was dead silent, the tension in the air was almost smothering.

"May ... may we go please?" Melvin asked in a submissive voice.

Andrei glanced back at Blaire.

She thought for a moment, before finally nodding.

The hallway was whisper quiet as their shoes clapped against the stone floors. They slipped through the crowd in the main atrium.

Elise was the first one to break the silence.

"What are you holding?" she asked Laura.

"Oh, uh ... a weapon?" Laura shrugged. The steel mathematics compass looked goofy the way it was gripped in her hands, with the sharp end pointed forward.

"You need something better than that," Raf said.

"Grab the steak knives off of the floor," Blaire told them. "In fact, keep whatever you want, just get them away from *these assholes.*"

Blaire motioned to the former leadership class.

Andrei glanced over at Paxton Bannister. The bag he'd used to carry the spare lances was still slung over one shoulder. He'd kept it as a holster for himself and Amanda.

"We'll take the bag," Andrei said.

Paxton nodded, slinging it forward on top of his own lance.

Amanda was still holding the wound in her ribs, a few grains of dust trickling out. Since the attention was turned on them, she decided it was the right time to try to engage Blaire and Andrei.

"Guys, listen-" she began, but those were the only words she'd manage to get out.

"Shut. Up. Cunt." Blaire spat, venom in her words.

Paxton put a hand on Amanda's shoulder, shaking his head to tell her to be quiet.

Niles walked up to Paxton, trying to hide a smug look as he grabbed the bag and both of their lances.

He and Laura then gathered up all the other weapons on the floor. Niles slipped the hammer into his belt and took a knife lance as his main weapon. Laura chucked the math compass back into the classroom and did the same.

Niles handed the collection to Andrei, who slipped out a lance for himself before slinging the bag over his shoulder.

"Open the rest of the doors," Blaire demanded.

Darren and Jennifer went classroom to classroom, freeing the other suspects. They were the other students who fell under suspicion for one reason or another. They stuck their heads out of the doors, not sure what was in store for them.

"It's okay," Blaire said, "you guys can go."

Relieved, they all ran off, pushing through the gathered crowds.

Mikey Gregor was among that bunch.

"Thank you," he said to Blaire and Andrei before leaving.

Also among the captives was Blake Samuels. He glanced at Darren and Jenny as he exited the prison.

He didn't even muster some kind of smug or satisfied expression at the changing of fortunes. Darren and Jenny's fates were already sealed together, regardless of his scheming. He also had enough sober self-reflection to realize that his chances with Jennifer were more dead than he was.

He turned tail and slipped away as well.

The final classroom contained Rick Wallace and Bob Melkonian.

They were right by the door, having been listening since the shotgun was fired again.

The first ones to greet them at the door were Darren and Jenny.

Darren swallowed a lump in his throat at the sight of the guidance counselor.

Rick Wallace had mentored him through one of the toughest times in his life, yet Darren had completely abandoned him. He had sat idly by, too scared to act in his defense.

"Mr. Wallace," he said, "I'm so sorry. I should have stopped Joe earlier. I should have kept them from tying you up, or the knives and the mirror ..."

Darren continued to mumble through sorrow and guilt.

Rick looked at the boy. Darren Clark was one of the toughest players on the Varsity Football team, but Rick still remembered him from those troubling freshman and sophomore years. He had come so far since then.

Here he was standing next to his old childhood friend, finally together. Drifting apart from Jennifer Maxwell had been one of the biggest causes of his problems back then. He had lost one of his closest friends, a girl he'd even said that he loved, and he didn't understand why. The breakdown of their relationship had caused him to question everything about himself, lashing out at the world when he couldn't find the thing that was broken.

It had taken careful work to guide Darren through all that, and the boy had come out of that valley whole again. He was able to make it through that dark passage of his life. Then, on the other side, he found Jennifer, having crossed through her own dark valley.

Rick Wallace hugged him.

"It's alright son," he said to him. "I'm okay. I know things were difficult."

Following his lead, Jenny hugged Mr. Melkonian.

Bob accepted the embrace. These kids had been through a living nightmare in this place, a nightmare mostly caused by their own classmates. All of it had been hard on Bob too. At that moment, he couldn't help but picture that it was Monika hugging him.

The kids stood next to them, and Rick and Bob turned to address the others.

"Thank God you're okay!" Bob said, looking at Andrei. A small part of him was hoping the prayer had worked in some way.

Rick's eyes were fixed on Torelli.

Joe's body was lying just inside of Van Gaal's classroom. The top of his head was visible for all to see. It was mere inches from the door frame as the door was propped open along the wall.

The lower jaw was still loosely attached, as was his tongue. Everything above them was gone though. The top ring of his spine stuck out at the end.

Joe Torelli had decided to live by the "sword". It was little surprise that he died at the hands of that same "sword".

Rick looked up at the girl now holding the shotgun.

He had never needed to set up any extended sessions with Blaire Tidwell. There was a particularly sad aura to her, the way she normally carried herself. However, she'd never needed counseling for any specific emotional incidents like what happened to Ellen Taylor.

Her regular expression made reading her moods difficult. She usually wore a cold and melancholic countenance on her face. Right now though, there were some very obvious shades of fury and vengeance.

"So, what happens now?" Rick asked her.

"Now, we tie them up," she said without hesitation.

"Wait a minute, who are you referring to?" Bob asked, not liking the idea of this becoming a cycle.

"You don't want to repeat their mistakes," Rick said, taking on his guidance counselor voice.

"No offense Mr. Wallace," Andrei interjected. "But they arrested us on baseless accusations without evidence. We've *all* seen what they did."

"For instance," Laura spoke up, pointing at Paxton. "He stabbed Niles."

"And he would have stabbed Laura too if we didn't comply," Niles added. "Wouldn't you?"

Paxton flinched at the attention. Amanda stood silent beside him.

"That was back when everyone healed quickly," he responded, "and I would have gotten it myself if I didn't bring you in. Marcus gave the order."

Everyone glanced over at Marcus Johnson.

Few could forget that he was the first one to stand beside Joe after his violent ascent to power. Even without the shotgun, he and Joe were two of the most physically intimidating people in their corner of the Underworld. Marcus could have been someone who led the charge against Joe from the beginning.

After only two shots, Joe would have been relatively defenseless. He would need to reload the simple double-barreled shotgun before continuing a rampage. A small mob of people could have overpowered him, even if two of them were shot in the process.

At that point in time, death was off the table.

Marcus' capitulation had little to do with fear of the gun, or what pain it might inflict. He had been driven by the same bloodthirst that drove so many others to consent to Torelli's rule.

"He's right," Marcus said. "I've got no excuse. I was in a dark place and I'm very sorry. Do whatever you gotta do. I just want peace."

"Besides," Rafael spoke up to the adults. "If we wanted vengeance, I would have stabbed this motherfucker by now."

He pointed his Ka-Bar at Jordan.

Jordan glanced at Marcus, seeing him submit. He then turned to Eric, looking for support.

"I didn't attack anyone," Eric said to the others. "I just took down the notes."

He shifted his shoulders, sliding off his backpack.

Not expecting the sudden movement, Blaire aimed the shotgun at him.

"Wait!" he said. "It's in there, everything we found during the investigation."

Laura was standing nearby. She picked up the backpack and opened it.

"Yeah, it's just a bunch of notebooks and loose papers," she confirmed. She then slung the backpack over her own shoulder.

Blaire took the gun off of him.

"And he helped us talk Joe down after shooting you the first time," Darren added, although he wished that he had phrased it better.

Andrei turned back to Blaire.

"Alright," she said, "but if we see you touch a knife or weapon of any kind, you're getting tied up too."

"Thank you," Eric said, relaxing the tension in his shoulders.

"Now, grab the duct tape and start wrapping up Torelli," Andrei said.

"You're tying *him* up?" Rick asked.

"Well yeah," Andrei said, motioning to himself. "Obviously the gun isn't a permanent solution."

"It could be because we prayed for you," Melkonian offered.

"You did?" Andrei asked. He didn't remember hearing any voices when everything was dark. He just had a sensation that he needed to wake up, that he couldn't leave Blaire behind.

"What about the ones who jumped?" Laura asked, did you pray for them too?

"Not specifically, no," Melkonian said.

He turned to Andrei again.

"I was expecting something to happen like it did to Ellen Taylor," he admitted. "When it didn't, I figured that we needed to be closer."

"Or maybe," Rick added. "It didn't work if you were already gone."

"Well he's *not* gone!" Blaire snapped at them.

"I didn't *want* to go," Andrei said, before smiling back at her.

Rick and Bob glanced at each other.

"Maybe others do though," Bob said. "That was all Ellen cared about, she just wanted to leave this place. Then Mr. Wallace prayed for her and she disappeared."

"That's how it happened?" Niles asked, working the information into his own theories about their confinement.

"Maybe it is a lobby," Laura whispered to him.

Niles took her hand. They both felt a sense of hope and relief.

"We'd be willing to pray for anyone!" Bob announced to the students on both sides of the hallway. "Isn't that right Rick?"

Rick still looked hesitant, but he agreed.

"That's right. Nothing's changed from before, I'm here for you kids."

A soft rumble of conversation came from both sides of the hallway.

"That's fine," Blaire said, "but first, we take care of *them.*"

Eric dragged Joe Torelli's body out of the classroom.

"He'll be back by the afternoon," Andrei guessed.

"Now do them," Blaire said, motioning to Brendan and Trey. "Then we'll get to the rest of you."

"Can I say something?" Marcus asked them.

Andrei and Blaire turned to look at him.

"I fucked up bad," he began. "I deserve to be benched for a bit, but you gotta give Darren and Jenny a chance. They were doing everything they could to temper the crazy."

The two shifted their gaze to the Homecoming Queen and the varsity fullback.

"It's true," Jenny said, "we kept trying to talk Torelli down. You saw it for yourselves, he put us both under the gun too. I thought he was going to kill us."

She took Darren's hand.

"It was after what happened to Ellen," Darren added. "We thought it would be permanent."

"They *are* the ones who kept us from being tied up earlier," Niles mentioned from the side.

Blaire glanced over at Jenny; she had a pleading look in her eyes. She then looked up at Andrei. It was clear in his expression that he wanted to give them a chance.

"Okay," Blaire said, "same deal as Eric."

"Thank you," Jenny said.

"You can start by tying up Paxton and Amanda," Blaire said.

"Fuck you," Amanda said under her breath.

"Her mouth too," Blaire added.

Bob and Rick didn't exactly sanction this new arrangement, but these kids weren't torturing anyone for information yet, so it was still a net improvement.

"Please don't tell me we're going back to the gymnasium too," Melkonian said as Torelli's goons were wrapped up.

"No," Andrei said, "we're going to the Murphy Center."

"The Murphy Center?" Wallace asked.

"Well unless you want to stay here with all the dead bodies," Blaire said, "then yeah, I'd rather get out of here for a while."

Marcus, Jordan, Paxton, Amanda, Trey, and Brendan were all bound in duct tape around their upper bodies. Their wrists were tied and their fingers were wrapped too, so they couldn't pull hidden tools or weapons out from anywhere.

Darren, Jenny, and Eric ended up at the front of the pack, leading the group back to the ballroom. The crowd in the main atrium separated as Eric approached them. Jenny was a step behind him, staying close to Darren. He alone had decided to take on a specific responsibility.

He had fashioned a length of duct tape into a rope which then split into a "Y" shape. He attached each point of the "Y" to Joe Torelli's shoulders. With the rope draped over his own shoulder, he dragged his old friend behind him. Joe had always been a burden for him. He felt like he had to do this after failing to stop this fate from playing out.

Watching Darren pull the body, Jenny couldn't help but remember the warning that Joe had passed along from his grandfather:

"Life will usually give you a second chance ... but never a third."

Following the quarterback was Marcus, the only one of the group who agreed to his own arrest. Like the others, he had let his own anger consume him. But it was okay, he could do his time. He wasn't imprisoned by his own rage anymore. He had done the right thing and he knew Janice would see it that way if she could still see him somehow. He had Jenny and Darren to thank for snapping him out of it.

Rafael and Elise marched on one side of the group, keeping watchful eyes on the captives. Niles and Laura observed from the other side, though they felt much more assured being matched with the other two. Raf and Elise clearly knew what they were doing with those military knives.

As the group passed through the atrium, Niles and Laura saw a very familiar royal blue dress among the bodies. Even though the head was gone, they could tell it was Anne Kirkpatrick.

Laura's face twisted in pain as she looked away.

Niles took her hand. No matter how complicated her feelings were about the situation, it still hurt to see. They had been friends for so many years, even before Laura came to Villa Vista. Having it all end like that was difficult to deal with.

At the back of the group, Andrei and Blaire kept their eyes on the whole gang. Blaire held the Browning Citori at a low angle, pointed at the back of Brendan's knees.

She had no intention of killing any of them. She was pretty sure Torelli would be back in the same way as Andrei in a few hours. That's why he was wrapped up with several more layers of duct tape than the others. However, crippling legs would be the easiest way to stop them if they caused any more trouble.

Behind them walked Rick Wallace and Bob Melkonian. They both prayed that the violence was truly over.

As the group passed into the crowd, the students of Villa Vista High wore very different expressions than they had a few days ago. They no longer looked at Bob and Rick with hostile intent. The men were no longer school bombers making a slow walk toward the gallows.

The crowd followed Wallace and Melkonian. The kids looked apologetic and tired. They didn't want vengeance, they wanted rest. They desperately wanted to be free of this place.

TWENTY-EIGHT

LAST RITES

BLAIRE WALKED SLOWLY BEHIND the line-up of varsity goons. Joe Torelli's headless body led the pack, being dragged in front of them.

Now that her own rage was beginning to subside, she felt strange clutching the shotgun in her hands. For one thing, it was the same terrifying weapon which had been used to seriously maim and then basically kill Andrei.

She looked up at the tall figure walking beside her. He had come back from the clutches of death just for her.

Andrei noticed her looking at him and put a hand on her shoulder, hugging her as they walked.

He still held a lance in his other hand, with a bag of other weapons strapped to his back. They had taken control of everything used against them and their friends in the recent days.

This world had quickly become a unique form of Hell, casting the wayward souls as demons. However, all of that violence was ultimately unleashed by a single spark. Like the bomber's evil machine, Torelli's weapon had become the thing which ignited everyone's vengeance and sorrow.

It had turned so many kids into something horrible. Blaire thought of the girl who reached for her in the bleachers, trying to drag her down to face this very shotgun. Luckily, Elise was there to save Blaire with a hidden knife.

Torelli's anger was something which had clearly festered for a long time. He had sought out this weapon back before the fire consumed all of them. He had forfeited his own life and future when he enacted his own vengeance against his father.

Blaire could imagine all the ways his dad might have been evil, all the reasons Torelli might have been justified in shooting him. Even if those reasons were enough, Torelli's anger didn't die with his father. That same rage had outlived both of them. It formed the backdrop of everything that had happened, like the wall of fire in the mirrors that now stood in the gym.

The group reached the ballroom of the Murphy Center.

"Where are we going?" Darren called to Blaire and Andrei.

The two walked forward, then motioned to a spot along the east wall.

"Sit them down there," Blaire said.

They were all placed in a row below one of the large windows. They were seated with their legs crossed.

"Make sure they don't go anywhere," Andrei said to Darren, Jenny, and Eric.

He then walked off to speak to Blaire and the others.

"Ha-ha, I knew it! Who's my favorite chimpanzee?!" Jimmy O'Shaughnessy said, walking out of the cafeteria.

"Hello Jimmy," Darren said, rolling his eyes.

Camellia was right behind him. The four friends hugged close now that the madness was over.

"What did you do?" Camellia asked them.

"It wasn't really us," Darren said, motioning to Andrei and Blaire.

"Holy shit, he's alive?!" Jimmy said.

"It surprised us too," Jenny said, "but it was Joe who really wasn't expecting it."

They all glanced down at the one motionless body. Joe's tongue and lower jaw hung limply in front of his gaping throat.

Jimmy didn't even have a quip for the situation.

"Yeah, that seems about right," he muttered.

"Are *you* okay?" Camellia asked Darren. "You knew him the longest, right?"

"I guess so," Darren said, not realizing that fact until she pointed it out.

For all the terrible things Joe had done in the last few days, there were still a lot of good memories Darren could recall. They had all been close once, on and off the field.

"Maybe if I kept a tighter leash on him after the game, none of this would have happened," Darren mumbled. "If he didn't get the shotgun, didn't kill his dad, maybe he wouldn't have been tweaked out on pills, he wouldn't have fought with Isabella."

Jenny put an arm around him.

"This isn't your fault," she said. "There wasn't anything we could have done. Joe was the one who made the choices for himself. He seemed pretty set on them regardless of what we said."

"Who knows," Jimmy said. "Maybe he's with Isabella now. She can kick his ass for a few months until he pays off his penance and puts things right with her."

As those four spoke amongst themselves, Elise came up to Blaire and pulled her to the side a few feet.

Blaire could finally relax her grip on the shotgun. She wrapped her arms around Elise, squeezing her tightly.

"Oh Blaire," Elise said, rubbing her back, "I was so scared for you. I just wanted to hold you when I heard what happened."

"Me too," Blaire said, her voice cracking a bit from the memory. "It was so horrible. He was just lying there where he fell. I thought that was it, I thought I'd never see him again. Even if they came back and did the same to me, who knows where we would have gone?"

Elise's face winced in pain as she held her.

"You shouldn't have even been *here*," Elise said.

"What?" Blaire asked, confused.

"If I hadn't pushed you so hard with Andrei, maybe things would have gone slower." She sniffled. "Maybe you two wouldn't have been at the dance. Maybe you'd still be alive."

"No, no." Blaire stroked her hair. "Elise it is *not* your fault that we're dead. Without you, I might not have talked to him at all. We might not have really found each other."

Andrei and Raf watched as the girls held each other, talking for a few minutes.

"So," Raf said, "were you like him then?"

He motioned to Torelli. Even without blood, the sight was horrific and gruesome.

"I guess so," Andrei said. "I can't even imagine how hard that was for Blaire. Being stuck with me, looking like *that*."

"I'm just glad to see you upright again," Raf said. "Hell, without you two toppling the cholos, who knows how much longer Elise and I would have been locked up."

"To be honest," Andrei said. "I'm surprised it worked."

"What do you mean?" Raf asked.

"I woke up about three hours ago," Andrei said. "We had a lot of time to brainstorm and set up the fake body. We had worked out all these possible situations, about others trying to enter the room. Whenever someone would have approached the rug, she was going to freak out and try to scare them back.

"The worst-case scenario was that they'd send multiple people in to restrain her. Then I'd have to spring in and we'd try to make due with whatever weapons we could recover."

"Not to mention those fast hands of yours," Raf joked.

Andrei chuckled.

"Neither of us thought Torelli would be the one to return so soon and be the first one in the room," Andrei said. "It was just so shameless and heartless; I can't believe he actually did it."

"The dude clearly has his own demons to worry about," Raf agreed. "Whether or not he comes back here, he's got a lot of shit to answer for."

With the varsity players settled against the wall, Wallace and Melkonian approached Blaire and Andrei.

"How long are you going to leave them like this?" Rick asked them.

"We'll figure something out when Torelli wakes up," Andrei said. "It'd just be nice to have a few hours without needing to worry about them."

The men seemed satisfied by that answer. They truthfully didn't mind the easing of everyone's tensions either. Without Joe Torelli ginning up the mob like a demagogue, things felt a lot more peaceful.

"Looks like you'll be busy in the meantime anyway," Blaire said, motioning behind the two late faculty members.

The crowd of students were waiting in a loose arrangement near the back of the ballroom. They seemed desperate, but frightened.

While some of the students had slept in prison cells, many others had been free to come and go from their personal classroom dormitories. However, even when Blaire's wails of grief had subsided the night before, they were still haunted by the bodies of dozens of their former classmates every time they left their abodes. None of the students in the atrium or foyer had decomposed at all, nor had they resurrected like Andrei.

The pieces of Andrei's leg that were blown off of him in the gym had broken down to fine powder in less than an hour. By the time Ellen disappeared, the particles had been almost completely absorbed into the air.

The kids who hadn't jumped resisted the temptation for many reasons. One fear that they all shared was the feeling of eternal uncertainty. They could tell there was something wrong with the end that the others had chosen. They were hoping for another way out.

After a minute of stirring among the crowd, one girl finally came up to approach the two teachers.

"Hi Mr. Mel," the sophomore mumbled.

"Hello Trisha," Bob said to his former student.

"Did you mean what you were saying earlier?" she asked him. "Even after what we did?"

"Yes Trisha," Bob assured her. "Is there anything you wanted us to pray for first?"

The girl began going through a few things that had been on her heart over the last three days. She prayed that her brother Johnny would forgive her over what happened to their family dog. She prayed that her parents would be okay and remember her for the good times. She prayed for some of her friends who weren't at the Homecoming dance. Finally, she prayed for the students that disappeared afterwards, the students who didn't wake up in this place at all. She prayed that whatever happened to them was better than what happened here.

After all that, she seemed to finally be at peace.

Bob hesitated before the next part, glancing at Rick.

"Take it away," Rick said to him, letting Bob lead.

Robert Melkonian took a deep breath, praying a short prayer of his own that God would guide them all.

He put a hand on Trisha Forrester's shoulder and began to repeat the prayer that Rick had said over Ellen Taylor.

The whole ballroom fell silent as they watched the exchange take place. The actual prayer was much shorter than any of them expected. After only a minute or so, Rick Wallace unclasped his hands.

Nothing happened.

"Thank you, Mr. Mel," Trisha said, her shoulders dropping in disappointment.

"You're welcome Trisha," Bob said, equally saddened.

There was still a pang of guilt on her face.

"Mr. Mel?" she asked him.

"What is it?"

"Earlier, I said that I was going to speak in your defense at the ... trial," she had a hard time actually saying the word. Only now did she understand how horrible it had turned out to be.

"But I was a coward," she said. "I was too scared of Torelli to say anything until it was too late. Can you ever forgive me?"

Bob sighed.

"It's surprisingly easy to get swept up in feelings of anger sometimes," he whispered. "We can all find ourselves in moments of weakness like that, and let that anger cloud our clear judgement."

She didn't respond, not understanding what Melkonian was saying.

"It's happened to me too," Bob elaborated. "Nothing could have prepared you kids for any of this. None of you should be dead in the first place ... of course I forgive you."

Trisha smiled.

A bright arc of blue electricity trailed off of her back.

"It's happening!" she exclaimed. "Thank you, Mr. Mel! Thank you, Mr. Wallace!"

The whole ballroom watched in amazement as the energy continued to trail over Trisha's body. Dozens of bolts danced over her skin. Each strike of lightning dissolved more of her until nothing was left behind except a pile of fine powder.

Jenny and Darren still felt unsettled by the sight. It was hard for them to picture anything besides the single-stall bathroom, filled with what was left of Isabella Carrizo.

A final bolt of lightning forked upward into the ceiling.

The students broke out into applause like they had just watched the finale of a Fourth of July fireworks show. The hope and joy and relief that filled the room was palpable.

"It's incredible," Laura said to Niles. "Instead of four years, it might not even be four days."

"It wasn't the same anyway," Niles said. "We weren't trapped here alone."

They kissed, then bounced up and down in anticipation.

Rick also looked happier than he had been in the last three days. He put a hand on Bob's shoulder.

"You did good," Rick said. "I wouldn't have even tried this without you."

"Come on," Bob replied, "let's move someplace better."

He and Rick went to the front of the dance floor. A loose queue formed, folding between the stage apron and the wall adjacent to the gymnasium. They began talking to the next student who approached them.

In his case, he confided for nearly ten minutes before the lightning finally began to flash. At this rate, it would take several hours to get through everyone.

There was a certain amount of unburdening each of the kids needed to do before they moved on. They had to be ready, nothing left unsaid, nothing left undone.

Blaire and Andrei looked at each other, smiles forming.

Now was the time.

They had spent a lot of time discussing what they hoped might happen if they were ever free of that makeshift prison. Now that they were, they finally had a chance.

The two of them approached the group watching over the captive varsity players.

"Okay, things seem to be working out with them." Blaire motioned to the teachers. "But still, make sure all the others go first. Only once the rest of them leave can these guys get brought over to Melkonian and Wallace."

"Gotcha," Niles said.

"Make sure they don't get up and cause any trouble for the process either," Andrei added.

"No problem," Jenny said, looking at Darren. "We're not in a hurry."

Blaire then turned to Elise. She presented the shotgun to her.

"What are you doing?" Elise asked.

"Take it," Blaire said.

Elise looked at Raf, then holstered her knife. She accepted the gun from Blaire.

Blaire then slid off the bandolier and gave that to her also.

"Can you keep an eye on things down here for a while?" Blaire asked her.

"Sure," she said, still hesitant. "Where are you going?"

"We had to keep quiet in the room," Blaire said. "So, Andrei and I are just going to talk for a while."

"Get away from all the noise for a few hours," Andrei added.

"Okay, yeah," Elise said, but her nerves didn't ease.

"Don't go without us," Blaire asked her, nodding towards Wallace and Melkonian.

"Same," she agreed, her eyebrows furrowing in worry.

"It's fine, you guys go chill," Raf said, putting a comforting hand on Elise's shoulder. He then flexed the Ka-Bar a bit. "We'll keep things under control here."

"We appreciate it," Andrei said. He pulled the bag of weapons off of his back and handed it to Raf.

Then, Blaire grabbed his hand and led him off toward the stairwell.

Elise frowned at Raf. She was afraid they'd disappear without them.

"They'll be fine," Raf assured her.

Elise took a deep breath. She was happy with that last heart-to-heart she shared with Blaire. She could be okay if that was the last time they ever saw each other.

"Whew, I gotta say," Raf mentioned, looking at the shotgun up close. "That is pretty fancy."

As things carried on down below, Blaire and Andrei continued to the top floor, back to where it all began.

They had spent three days trapped in this strange afterlife, adrift in the great black ocean of eternity. So much had gone on in such a short time. They were thrown from the fires of death into damnation and depression. Their wayward souls were put under the torment of other lost spirits. Their new bodies were maimed and destroyed as they experienced whole new levels of grief and mourning.

All of this had stood between them. Their spirits were restless. They simply could not move on before resolving one last piece of unfinished business.

Blaire and Andrei stepped into the Choir & Drama Rehearsal Room, closing the door behind them. It had been undisturbed since Raf and Elise left it yesterday.

Andrei pulled the parts of their barring mechanism back together, double-securing every piece of interlocking metal. The rumble of the hallway air conditioner died down now that they were behind the room's sound paneling.

Blaire's heart had been racing since all of the action that happened earlier. Though it moved no blood in this temporary form, the feeling was a sign to her that in some way they were still very much alive.

She and Andrei had passed beyond one threshold of death already. There was no telling what lay beyond the next. Wherever the released souls were disappearing to was as much a mystery as the last time.

The dream of her father and grandfather was as vivid as anything else she'd experienced in this afterlife. She'd shared every detail with Andrei in those quiet morning hours. There was still no guarantee how long it would take her to get back to that place, how many more Circles of Hell she would have to descend before reaching her final destination.

She was not risking another opportunity.

Andrei had done all he could to the door. It was all but welded shut. The bomber would have to destroy the school all over again to disturb them now.

That is when Andrei began hearing soft piano music filling the room.

He turned, recognizing the melody instantly. It had taken him days to be satisfied with it.

Blaire rested her phone down on a table, letting the speaker play it for them.

Andrei smiled. "I wasn't sure if you liked it."

"I *loved* it." Blaire met his eyes.

She slowly unzipped her hooded sweatshirt jacket.

Too much had been taken from them, an entire life they never got to experience together.

Andrei slid off the suit coat, dropping it to the floor. They approached each other, meeting in the middle. One by one, Blaire undid the buttons on his dress shirt.

They would never know years of dating, of college, of marriage, of children.

The dress shirt dropped to the ground and Andrei pulled off the sleeveless undershirt after it.

Blaire lifted her gym shirt, tossing the once-threatening face of Jackie the Jaguar into a crumpled pile against the wall.

They continued in this way, removing pieces from each other until they were each fully stripped.

With every last layer shed, they embraced.

A lot had been stolen from them in the last three days ... but not this. They would not lose this chance to be together in the face of yet more uncertain eternity.

Time disappeared. They loved each other as if it would be their only chance. In this divine tragedy they were at the mercy of, it very well could be.

Eventually, the young lovers found themselves lying beneath a nondescript black cloak. The pile of costumes against their bare backs had been spread between the wall and the edge of the piano.

"Heaven. This is Heaven."

That was all Blaire could think as her head lay against Andrei's chest. It sure didn't feel like they'd been dead for three days.

Andrei stroked her shoulder with his hand. It was the same comforting gesture he'd done after they had faced their burned bodies in the mirror.

"This is the way Homecoming should have ended," she said to him.

"With this many costumes?" Andrei smirked.

Blaire chuckled.

A silence passed between them as they rested.

"You know," Andrei began. "If we had died that night, truly died, and disappeared into empty annihilation, it still would have been worth it."

Blaire looked up at him.

"That was the best night of my life too," he said. "Even without this."

They shared a tender kiss.

"What do you think happens next?" Blaire asked. "Where are they disappearing to?"

"I think we already know," Andrei said. "So far you have a perfect score in clairvoyant dreams."

Blaire chuckled, making light of the idea to conceal her own doubt.

"Does that mean our next life is spent as Netherworld pirates?" she asked.

"You just want more costumes to add to the pile," Andrei retorted.

She slapped his chest, harder than he expected. He wrapped both arms around her to prevent any more strikes.

They lay there in loving embrace for a long time, knowing that as soon as they got up again there was no telling what would happen.

Down below, what was taking place in the ballroom was nothing short of a miracle.

The lightning strikes were almost happening like clockwork now. According to their phones, it was after noon on Tuesday. Half of the students had been released from this place. Dozens of piles of dust were slowly being absorbed into the atmosphere.

All of the students were broken in one way or another. Most of them apologized immediately upon approaching the two adults. They still pictured the knives stabbed into the teachers' flesh. Even once they were forgiven, there was much crying. Many weights held down their spirits. The largest of all was ... "why them?" Why had something so horrible happened to so many who were so young?

Bob and Rick gave the best answers they could. Neither of them were priests or theologians. They were just semi-regular churchgoers who found themselves in a grave position. In most cases, the kids simply needed to confess. They needed to give voice to those emotions before they could move forward.

One other common find was that most students had already given up their burning desire to face and punish their murderer. They still did not know if the killer was among them. However, the sight of Joe's headless body, and the knowledge that bloodlust had utterly destroyed him, was enough to sour the thirst for vengeance in their own hearts.

There were also a handful of students in the crowd who had unfinished business with those against the wall.

Ashley Stillwell approached Rafael and Elise.

"Can I please speak to Trey?" she asked them.

Elise glanced back at the football players on one end of the row.

"Okay," she said, walking her over.

"Ashley," Trey said, whimpering. "Ashley, I'm so sorry."

"I know you are," she said to him, "but I can't take the chance of this happening again. I can't stay if you're here for Joe, or the sophomores, or someone else."

"What are you saying?" Trey asked her, tearing up.

"I'm going on ahead," she said. "I'll be waiting for you, but please don't make me wait long."

"I won't," he said, despondent. "I promise."

Ashley looked up at Elise, seeking approval.

"As soon as everyone else has had their chance," Elise said.

"Thank you," Ashley responded.

She knelt down and kissed Trey.

He stayed with her lips as long as he could before she pulled away.

It wouldn't be long until Sheena Gilquist made a similar request to Brendan.

Jimmy, Camellia, Darren, and Jennifer watched the exchanges take place from a few feet away. They were standing near Joe Torelli's body.

It had been over three hours now and Torelli hadn't changed at all. None of his head had grown back. He sat cold and lifeless like all those on the floor of the atrium.

"I was sort of expecting we'd get a chance to say something to him," Jimmy said to Darren. "But it looks like wherever he's gone, he's staying there."

"We might go get in line," Camellia said.

"That's alright," Jennifer said. She gave her a hug, then Jimmy.

"We'll get the party started for everyone," Jimmy said, patting Darren's back. "Fingers crossed we end up at my place next."

"We won't be late," Darren said, looking at Jenny.

As the two of them walked off, Elise and Raf noticed a few other faces in the line. Mark, Raquel, and Jeremy were standing together. They had Dina in between them, and she was looking a bit better. They all waved or nodded goodbye. Elise and Raf returned the gestures.

"Come on," they heard a voice from the floor, "you really going to leave us like this?"

It was Paxton.

"You'll have your turn soon enough," Raf answered flatly.

Amanda had licked at the duct tape over her mouth and pushed it away from her lips.

"What did we ever do to you?" Amanda asked them.

"I don't remember you speaking up when Torelli had the gun on us," Elise snipped back.

"Well, none of them did either," Paxton said, nodding to the other four.

"They weren't down on the basketball court," Raf retorted. "They weren't armed."

"And they weren't the ones who accused us in the first place," Elise added, her eyes staring hard at Amanda.

"Look, you can think whatever you want about Blaire," Amanda said. "I get that you've known her forever. But *none* of you know that Andrei guy. You're letting your friendship with her distract you. There is something up with him!"

"Enough," Elise growled. "One more word about them and we'll put fresh tape on your mouth."

She glared back at Elise, but said nothing more. Instead, Amanda turned to Paxton and they whispered to each other to pass the time.

As the afternoon dragged on, a few other students appeared in the ballroom. They were all those who had run or scattered following the explosive confrontation with Torelli.

Barry and Melvin were among those students. They watched what was going on for a few minutes until witnessing one of the students being broken down by electricity. There was a rather large pile of dust between the teachers and the stage. After each student, they would shift to one side and eventually step forward, forming loose rows.

Niles watched them as they took in what was happening.

Next to him, Laura was slowly sifting through all of the investigation notes. Eric had good handwriting, so she was able to easily read from the pages.

He was over on the far side of the line, talking to Marcus. Laura didn't want to disturb them, since they obviously couldn't find anything definitive anyway. She just found it fascinating to look at. Whenever something interesting was mentioned, she would read it to Niles.

"Oh wow," Laura said, coming across a surprising entry.

"What is it?" Niles asked.

"They found a box of 9mm ammunition in Kerry Mercer's locker."

"Really?"

Kerry Mercer was a junior like them. He didn't run in the same circles as Niles, Barry, and Melvin, but he wasn't that popular either.

"I don't think I saw him here anywhere," Laura said.

"I don't even think he was at the dance," Niles added. "Did they find a gun too?"

Laura looked deeper through the pages.

"No," she said. "Just a new box of ammo."

"God," Niles said. "So, the gun is probably in his backpack. The ammo they found was just for backup."

The search had also turned up over a dozen switchblades. After seeing Jennifer pull one out to stab Amanda, Blaire had been adamant about taping up all of their fingers and thumbs. Not to mention, even Blaire and Andrei were surprised by the Marine knives that Rafael and Elise had hidden on them.

So many students at Villa Vista had their own secrets. There were hundreds of kids who survived the explosion because they skipped Homecoming for one reason or another. There were another hundred or so who didn't appear in this ghostly game lobby at all. They were dust from the start. Without being around to interview, it just seemed more and more likely that the bomber never showed up in that place at all.

"You think Kerry would have gone on a shooting spree?" Laura asked him.

"I didn't really know him," Niles said. "He never talked to us either."

Laura sighed.

"He was in my U.S. History period with Reynolds," she said. A sense of finality settled over her. "Were we meant to die in the school no matter what?"

Before Niles could think up something to comfort her, Barry and Melvin approached them from across the room

"Hey," Barry said. "So, it looks like Wallace and Melkonian finally figured out the 'jump equation'?"

The *Intrepid* reference seemed to be intentional. It was an olive branch, a reminder of old times.

"Not a moment too soon," Niles said.

"We're going to go," Melvin said, "but first, we wanted to say goodbye."

He turned to Laura, holding out a hand.

"I'm sorry," he said, not wanting to elaborate the details. "I'm really sorry."

"It's alright." She shook his hand. There was no point belaboring the past.

"So am I," Barry said, switching places with him. "I should have just been happy for both of you."

"It doesn't matter now," Laura said with a bittersweet tone. She would love to undo what happened, see a better life play out for all of them, but it was beyond their control.

They both stepped up to Niles and the three of them hugged.

"We'll 'clear the space' for you two," Barry said to him.

"We won't be far behind," Niles answered.

The friends parted ways, finding their place in line. They hoped that the next world they were loaded into held a more promising future.

TWENTY-NINE

THE FACE OF EVIL

ANOTHER FEW HOURS DRIFTED BY and Elise was beginning to get worried again.

It was almost four in the afternoon. Blaire and Andrei still hadn't returned.

Only two or three students remained in the crowd. The entire dance floor was covered in the fine sand.

"We have to go looking for them," Elise said, becoming more fretful with every passing minute.

"We will," Raf assured her, "as soon as the teachers finish with the others."

"What if they've already disappeared?" Elise asked him. "What else could they be doing?"

Her mind was so weighed down with all the stress and disorder of the past few days, that Elise had completely forgotten about another set of possibilities. Those possibilities all flooded back into her mind as soon as she saw the two of them reappear in the ballroom.

Blaire and Andrei were walking hand in hand. Blaire's face was glowing in a way Elise had never seen before.

"Oh!" Elise said, the realization hitting her like an exploding wall.

"'Oh' what?" Raf asked her. He then followed her eyes. "Oh hey, there they are!"

As soon as Blaire locked eyes with Elise, she looked away, tucking her head into the neck of her hoodie. Blaire's face puckered up like she had bitten into a lemon, but her cheeks were tomato red.

Blaire was a terrible liar, especially when it came to Elise.

"What?" Raf said, noticing an odd look on Elise's face.

"Play it cool," she said to him.

"About what?" he asked.

"Hey," Blaire said, once the lovers reached them. "Wow, they've really freed just about everyone."

She motioned back to Melkonian and Wallace, trying to force a different subject.

Now that Raf was close enough, he could feel the vibe from them too.

"Aw shit, are you telling me?" he thought to himself.

He needed confirmation.

"Pretty *amazing* ... isn't it?" Raf said, giving Andrei a knowing look.

Andrei glanced over at the teachers, then back at Raf.

"It is," he said, with a sly smile.

"My man!" Raf thought to himself, trying to hold back a congratulatory grin.

"Any problems down here?" Blaire asked, still trying to stifle her embarrassment.

Elise stared back at her with her pale blue eyes, tilting her head ever so slightly.

"Shit, she knows, she definitely knows," Blaire thought to herself in a panic.

"No," Elise answered, while her face said a dozen other things. "In fact, things have been *better than ever*. No *action* going on down here. They've just been *doing their thing* ... like a *marathon*!"

Now Andrei was blushing too. Blaire's expression was begging Elise to keep quiet.

Luckily, the others in the ballroom were distracted by the last of the departures.

Blue glows filled the Murphy Center again as someone broke down to dust. A final arc of lightning connected with the ceiling. They had disappeared into the next life.

"Hey guys, what's up?" Niles asked, walking over to the four of them.

Laura was next to him, her eyes focused on a notebook in her hands.

"Nothing much." Andrei shrugged. "We talked for a while, then I took a bit of a nap. The dead sleep last night wasn't exactly the same."

Blaire showed a grateful glance to Andrei. He was so much better at playing things off.

In truth, they hadn't slept at all.

"I hear that," Niles responded, remembering how he felt when he woke up at their dinner table.

"What are you reading, Laura?" Blaire asked, grasping for an alternate conversation.

"Oh, I've been looking through the notes that the others had gathered," she answered.

"It's everything from their investigation," Niles said.

"Anything interesting?" Andrei asked.

"Well," Laura began, "if the bombing didn't happen, it looks like two unrelated school shootings were being planned."

"Oh my gosh," Elise said, her wide grin dropping to an expression of horror.

"Who were the two people?" Raf asked.

"Kerry Mercer and Bill Friedkin," Laura answered.

"A junior and a senior," Niles elaborated. "They didn't appear to know each other at all."

Andrei looked down at Blaire.

"You know the names?" he asked her.

"No," she said. She turned to Darren, Jenny, and Eric. "Hey guys, come here."

The three of them walked over.

"What's up?" Jenny asked.

"Do you know Bill Friedkin or Kerry Mercer at all?" Niles asked.

"Sorry," Jenny said. "I don't."

"I might remember Bill," Darren said. "I don't think he came to Villa Vista until our sophomore year."

"Oh yeah, the ammo boxes, right?" Eric asked. "We're pretty sure neither of them were at the dance. Unless they snuck in like those two other guys."

Eric motioned to Niles and Laura, referencing Barry and Melvin.

"Then again," Eric said. "The antenna on the sparking device looked like it had a pretty good range. If it was one of them, they probably sat in a car up by the gas station. It would be so easy to trigger it, then 'drive off in a panic' when they saw the explosion."

A bright blue burst of lightning filled the gym.

Everyone glanced back at the person disappearing, then returned to their conversation.

"So, you really don't have anything else?" Raf asked. "After all that stabbing and questioning?"

"Honestly," Eric said. "I don't think the bomber is dead."

Rick Wallace and Bob Melkonian walked up to the gathered group.

"Hey kids," Bob said.

"Is everyone else gone?" Elise asked them.

"I think so," Rick said, a smile on his face. He then motioned to their group against the wall. "It's just us left."

"Thank God," Niles said.

"I don't think the real bomber is dead either," Jenny said, continuing their discussion.

"Plus," Darren added, "if it was one of us here in the ballroom, they would have to say it before they disappeared. They would have had to confess. Isn't that right?"

He looked up at the two faculty members.

"Now kids, I thought we dropped this," Bob said. "It's all over now, we're leaving this place. You need to let go."

"Do you think he's right though?" Laura asked Mr. Wallace. "It probably wouldn't work for them if they didn't confess."

Rick said nothing, but the look on his face seemed to confirm it to everyone.

"Well then!" Raf said, stepping over to the captives sitting on the floor. "You morons hear that? If the bomber doesn't fess up, they, ironically, aren't going to ride the lightning out of here. So why don't you just come clean now? Otherwise, we'll find out anyway."

"We don't know if that's how it works," Bob said, intervening.

The whole group of them were standing in front of the captives now.

"I don't think that's gonna happen," Marcus spoke up from one end of the group. "We already got our answer."

"What do you mean?" Jenny asked him.

"Just see for yourself," he said, nodding to the other side of the row. "Torelli's been gone for seven hours now and hasn't changed a bit. He ain't coming back like Andrei."

"No ..." Darren said. "I don't believe it. Look, I know Joe fucked up badly, but there's no way he would blow up the school."

"Look, no offense," Raf said, "But that dude didn't have the brains to build a machine like that even before they got blown out."

"Maybe he didn't know what he was doing," Eric said. "Maybe Jenny was right about him being a fall guy. Heck, maybe someone else was used that way too."

"Kids, you really should drop this," Bob said, looking at Elise ... and the shotgun. "This will only lead to doing trials and other horrible things again. Now please, let us continue."

"Mr. Wallace doesn't seem to agree," Elise said, turning her cunning eyes on him.

Rick flinched as everyone glanced over.

"It's the packet of construction drawings, isn't it?" Andrei asked him. "You can't get past that."

Rick furrowed his brows.

"They were here," he said. "At some point, the bomber was here and they took those from Ms. Fletcher's office."

"Rick?!" Bob said, using a scolding parent voice. "We need to move on."

"Who could have built that thing?" Darren asked the group, referencing the machine.

"I mean, it looked pretty complicated," Niles said.

"Yeah," Raf agreed. "My brother is really good with that kind of stuff and it even looked beyond him. You got to be at least decently experienced with electronics to build something with all that wiring. Maybe not an engineer or mechanic, but at least a good handyman."

Blaire thought back on the first time she had seen that evil machine, sitting in front of the mechanical systems panel. She remembered how she and Andrei had jumped when Torelli pressed the button on the device, causing it to spark. How everything was propped open, with-

"Oh my god," Blaire said aloud, her eyes darting back and forth as she recalled the memory.

Following the deep horror felt from her dream, Blaire had been transfixed by the image of the opened mechanical chase. Every little detail was part of the tapestry of their death.

"What is it?" Andrei asked. Everyone else was looking at her too.

"I think I know where we can find a clue," she whispered.

"Wait, seriously?" Elise asked.

Blaire grabbed Andrei's hand. "Come on!"

Andrei stumbled behind her as she led him away.

Darren, Jenny, Niles, and Laura followed.

"Blaire?!" Elise called after her. She gave chase, shotgun in hand.

"Shit," Raf said. He then turned to Eric Schwartz and handed him a knife lance from the weapon bag. "Watch them. If they get out, it's on you."

"No problem." Eric nodded.

Raf followed Elise.

Rick looked at Bob, then the kids.

"They're not going anywhere," Rick said, then jogged after the group.

Bob sighed, then caught up to him.

Blaire and Andrei rushed past the giant pile of dust covering the dance floor. Almost all of the students of Villa Vista had been set free of this place.

They pushed through the glass front doors of the Murphy Center. Andrei thought for a moment that she was leading them to Torelli's car, but instead she took a right and they ran for the gymnasium.

The large "MCL Construction" sign remained on the fence where it had been from the beginning. They stepped over the broken chain which once secured the gate.

She led them through the entrance, past the empty trophy cases and through the metal doors. There was a sticky sound as the bottom of her tennis shoe pressed against a strip of duct tape then pulled away from it.

The others were close on their heels, filtering out onto the maple wood floor of the basketball court.

Elise paused when she glanced up at the giant mural of Jackie the Jaguar. He was still sinking his claws into the orange basketball. Elise stepped through the doorway. With the shotgun in hand, she could probably take on a real, live jaguar right now if she needed to.

The rest of them stopped on the court as Blaire led Andrei under the visiting team bleachers.

Andrei stepped carefully, watching his head like he had to before. The last time they were there, Blaire was following Joe Torelli. It was right after he had begun his day of wrath, which ended with Andrei lying dead.

"Blaire, please say something," Andrei asked her.

"It's got to be here," she said.

"What? Torelli took the machine with him, it's out there on the court."

"Not the machine ..."

They reached the mechanical panel. The metal grate still sat to the side, where they had found it originally. The four natural gas valves were still left open, making it so the grate could not be put back in place without closing them.

Around the valves were a number of other levers, switches, pressure gauges, other valves, a digital readout ... and something else.

It was something that seemed so irrelevant at the time, so irrelevant that Blaire had barely stored its existence to memory at all. She had only seen this place once, when she first witnessed the source of their deaths. Only with deep introspection, reliving the memory, did that last forgotten detail return to the front of her mind.

Blaire reached toward the panel, her hand passing by the four natural gas spouts. She placed her fingers on top of the digital readout, then slid down a small stack of papers.

"What is that?" Andrei asked her.

She held the booklet for both of them to see. The cover read: "OPERATIONS & MAINTENANCE MANUAL."

Below it was a subheading.

"Prepared by: Waters MEP Engineering."

"What's 'MEP'?" Andrei asked. "I thought 'MCL' were the ones who did the construction?"

Blaire opened the booklet to the first page.

"'Waters Mechanical, Electrical, & Plumbing Engineering of California.'"

"A subcontractor?" Andrei asked.

They turned the page ... and found a short list of names.

Daniel H. Waters P.E., CEO
Dean S. Christian P.E., Mechanical Designer
...
Laura W. Sawyer P.E., Plumbing Designer

One engineer in particular stood out above all others.

They quickly turned to the related pages. His name was all over it.

Blaire and Andrei looked at each other.

"Does that mean?" Andrei asked, his body freezing cold.

"All this time," Blaire said, clutching her sides. She could feel the corset wrapped around her again.

"And we ... and they?!" Andrei stammered.

The events of the previous few days were forcibly replayed through their minds. It was as though they were strapped to chairs, being made to witness everything all over again. Only now, they knew the face of their killer. Every appearance sent pain shooting through them.

Andrei could feel the fire searing through the flesh of his right arm once again.

Blaire collapsed into his embrace, hyperventilating, gasping for air she thought she couldn't pull in.

"It's okay, it's okay," Andrei said. "I'm here."

He gently stroked her hair, trying to get her to calm down, but he himself had to concentrate to keep from shaking.

After everything that had happened ... why? Why in the name of God Almighty would they do this?

"Blaire?!" Elise called under the bleachers. The shotgun was gripped in her hands. She turned a critical eye at the six others, still waiting on the basketball court.

She and Raf were at the end of the stands, just now noticing their reaction.

"What did you find?" Raf asked.

Both of them were waiting for some kind of signal in case the bomber was in the gym with them.

The other six of them were standing at the edge of the court, watching Elise and Rafael.

"Has anyone else been back there?" Darren asked Jenny.

"Not that I remember," she said.

"Mr. Wallace?" Darren asked him. "Since you were here most of the day ..."

"I don't remember seeing anyone go back there," he said. "You kids had already pulled out that spark device when I got here."

"That's where the natural gas came from, right?" Melkonian asked.

"Yeah," Jenny said, her own memory of the sight fresh in mind.

"Laura," Niles whispered to her. "If it was Barry or Melvin, I swear ... swear ... I had no idea."

"I believe you," she said, taking his hand.

Blaire and Andrei held each other for a few more moments until they both calmed down.

Raf and Elise glanced back and forth at each other, their nerves fraying at the reaction.

Finally, they began stepping away from the mechanical panel.

"Is it one of them?" Raf whispered, nodding to the court.

Andrei shook his head.

They breathed a sigh of relief, then backed up, giving the couple room to step out.

Blaire and Andrei walked onto the basketball court. The sadness inside of them was beginning to flash boil, a righteous fury quickly replacing it. The large bathroom mirrors at the back of the gymnasium glowed with the bright orange flames that they could feel inside themselves.

"When Torelli shot through the construction fence," Blaire announced to everyone, cold rage in her words, "he did so because he had to. The lock was still there, the gate was secured."

"Yeah ..." Jenny nodded.

The rest of them followed Blaire and Andrei as they approached the center of the court.

"Joe didn't have a key, and no one had cut the lock already," Andrei continued, a similar undertone of fury in his voice.

"Which means someone had a key to the construction site beforehand," Blaire said.

"So, they didn't break in?" Darren asked.

"Well, they still had to cut those giant locks off of the gas valves," Andrei reminded him.

"Because they didn't have the keys to unlock those," Blaire continued.

"They had a key to the fence but not the gas valves?" Laura asked, confused.

"Yes," Blaire said. "Because their dad wasn't the plumbing engineer ..."

Andrei reached for the evil machine and pressed the red "TEST" button on the device.

A bright blue arc of lightning surged between the prongs.

"He was the electrical engineer," Blaire concluded.

She and Andrei held up the company information page in the Operations & Maintenance Manual.

The name in the middle immediately drew everyone's attention.

"Dear God ..." Melkonian said, stumbling backwards.

Wallace held his head, unable to comprehend the sheer level of evil, now that they had a face to the massacre.

Laura began crying, gripping Niles' coat. Her body felt like it was on fire all over again. Niles was too stunned for words.

Jennifer went pale, crossing her arms over her chest. She pictured her right side being melted away.

"No," Darren said, holding Jenny close. "Fuck, they were just stringing us along?!"

The shotgun rattled in Elise's grasp as she began to shake in fear. A sharp pain manifested in her neck. Every throb felt like her spinal cord snapping all over again. She could feel the fire on her back, dress and flesh searing away, exposing bone and muscle.

Raf had dropped his knife to the floor, collapsing to his knees with Elise as they embraced each other.

The truth was painful. It made them relive all the memories again as the pieces fell together.

Blaire and Andrei stepped up to Wallace and Melkonian.

"Are they gone?" Andrei asked them.

"N-No," Bob said, only now realizing. "They never came to the ballroom."

Blaire glanced down at Darren and Jennifer.

"Where are they?" she demanded.

"They probably ran off to their dorm," Darren said.

"Kids ..." Bob eked out. He intended to complete the sentence with something along the lines of "we're jumping to conclusions," or "there must be another explanation."

Instead, Bob finished the sentence: "... how could they? They're just kids."

"Elise," Blaire said, once everyone was on their feet again. "Give me the shotgun."

***

As soon as Trey Devall pulled the door open, Greg Henshaw could tell that something was wrong.

He felt like he had a pretty good sense of picking up when something had a bad feeling. It had gotten him a lot further in life than a lot of his peers.

Van Gaal's classroom opened to reveal Andrei Tunnikov's body lying in repose underneath a sort of decorative carpet.

It almost seemed like Blaire Tidwell had held some kind of private funeral for him. She still lay curled up by his arm.

"Fuck," he thought to himself. "Torelli is going to get us all killed with his stupid bullshit."

It was right around that time when a chair seemed to fly in from a far corner of the classroom and strike Joe right in the side of his head.

The shotgun fell out of his hands and Blaire immediately jumped into action to grab it.

"Shit!" he yelled. "Come on!"

He grabbed Chelsea's hand and they ran at full speed through the hallway.

They were barely ten feet clear of the door when he heard the shotgun blast. Out of his peripheral vision he could see Joe's headless body drop to the ground.

"We've got to lay low for a while," Greg told her.

"Okay," she said, a worried expression on her face.

Chelsea looked over her shoulder, seeing Andrei step through the doorframe, miraculously resurrected. It surprised her, but gave her hope.

She and Greg hopped over some bodies in the atrium as they pivoted sideways for one of the stairwells.

They reached the second-floor Sophomore Class hallway. After passing Melkonian's Biology classroom, they reached the door across from their own lockers.

They slipped inside Mrs. Jefferson's English 10 classroom.

Greg bolted the lock, then pulled out two of the wooden door stops that they had smuggled up to their room. He kicked them both into place as securely as he could against the industrial carpeting.

He then flipped off the overhead fluorescent lights, using the flashlight on his phone instead.

"Let's stay here for a while," Greg whispered to her. "Once they're through with each other, we'll talk to whoever's left."

"At least maybe we can get back to the way things should be," Chelsea said, nestling her face into his neck.

"Don't worry Chels," he said. "I'll protect you no matter what."

They each had their knife lances.

They walked over to the couch on one side of the room.

The student desks had been cleared away and stuffed in a corner. The only exception was a set of eight desks arranged in two rows of four. They faced each other like a dining room table.

Mrs. Jefferson would often sit on her couch and read while the students were working on their own various assignments. Other students were welcome to use it if there were only a few of them in the room, in between classes or something like that.

Greg laid the knife lance down next to the couch, then lay down across the three seats. He kept his shoes on, in case they had to spring into action.

Chelsea laid her lance down next to his, then crawled on top of him, resting her head on his chest.

They had been a couple for almost two years now, though they'd been friends for much longer. They had officially started dating just before Christmas of eighth grade.

He really cared about Chelsea. Middle school was hell for so many people, but with her it seemed almost magical. It really did feel like they were made for each other.

Over those years, they had kissed many times, but it hadn't moved beyond that. Things changed after a bit of bad news happened over the summer. Chelsea suddenly became much more affectionate. She wanted to take their relationship to the next level, so that they would be able to make it through any storm life threw at them.

One night, back in July, her dad had to run to his office for a while for some kind of meeting.

As soon as he was gone, Chelsea pulled Greg into her bed. That was the first time they were together … the first of many. Greg had remembered talking to her beforehand, making sure she was really comfortable with this, considering what might happen.

Not long after, she was lying against him in the same way. The difference this time was that they were still wearing clothes.

He wore most of his original Homecoming suit, except for the vest and tie. Most of the guys around the school had dropped those items. It had given them a strangely uniform look. Chelsea, on the other hand, wore her orange dress during the day.

They had been wearing their gym clothes at night as pajamas.

It was a lot to get used to. It seemed like every hour they learned something new about this strange afterlife which had taken the shape of their school.

She really liked his idea of the classroom dormitories. They had both thought of Mrs. Jefferson's classroom when they proposed it to everyone. Her couch was one of the best beds available.

"I still think Wallace's couch is more comfortable," Greg whispered. They had tried those out for a while after looking around the Administration offices.

"Maybe," she agreed. "But I don't know if we can get away with taking the love seat too. Swapping this out would make the set mismatch."

It had been almost half an hour. They were illuminated by the flashlight on his phone.

"I think they only shot the gun once," Greg said in a soft voice.

"Good," Chelsea said. "That must mean Torelli and the numbskulls won't shove people around anymore. We'll knock on doors and check on the others tomorrow. I think we should just stay here for the rest of the day."

"Yeah, I'd be alright with that," Greg said.

They shared a passionate kiss.

"Maybe tonight?" Chelsea offered, "once they finish all their couping and go to bed?"

"Why not?" Greg said. "After all, we've broken it in already."

She giggled.

Greg listened to the distant sounds in the hallway for what felt like another hour, but at some point, he must have fallen asleep again.

When he woke up, he saw Chelsea sitting behind Mrs. Jefferson's desk. She was typing on her phone. The main lights were still off, so the glow only illuminated her face.

"Hey," he said. "Sorry, I must have fallen asleep on you."

"I think *I* was the one sleeping on you," Chelsea joked.

"What time is it?" Greg asked her.

"A little after four," she said nonchalantly. "I actually wasn't that tired at all. I just wanted to let you sleep."

Greg had noticed that too. For whatever reason, he lost his energy a lot faster than her.

Before they died, Chelsea was the one who usually ended their nightly texting or phone calls. In recent days however, he hadn't seen Chelsea sleep at all. He was out first between the two of them and she woke up before him.

He was close to breaking open the vending machines and raiding them for energy drinks.

"I've been working on another idea actually," she said.

"What is it?" Greg asked her.

"Well, now that Torelli is gone," Chelsea began. "I thought we could begin working on more long-term plans."

"Like what?" Greg replied, sitting across from her.

"Well," she said, "there seems to be a lot of fresh food left in the big refrigerators, so what if we planted them?"

"Planted them?" Greg repeated.

"Yeah!" she chirped.

She showed him what was on the screen of her phone. It was a text document list of all the foods she remembered seeing the last time they were in the kitchen.

"We could set up a sort of garden on one of the sports fields," Chelsea said. "We could grow some apple trees, orange trees, tomatoes, potatoes, and whatever else we can find in there. It would give the others some added purpose, something to work for, plan for."

"Do you think anything would actually grow?" Greg asked, trying to reign in her expectations. "We don't really understand how anything works yet. Does the glow in the fog really count as daylight? Are there seasons? I haven't seen any bugs either."

"Well, I think it's at least worth trying," Chelsea said. "We can't give up until we've tried *every* possibility."

"Everything's just so weird," Greg said, resting his chin in his hand. "I actually think we should put some samples underneath one of the microscopes, different kinds of foods, maybe some skin or hair from a student.

"I mean, it almost seems like we're just animated sand bags at this point. For all we know, there isn't even like cells or microbial life anymore.

"Everything just seems kind of fake, like props used for a stage play."

"Well, nothing about us is fake." Chelsea put her hand on his. "And the others are very real too, otherwise their 'sand bags' wouldn't keep getting stitched back together."

"What about those in the atrium and foyer though?" Greg pointed out.

"Maybe they just need more time," she replied hopefully. "That Andrei guy seems to have come back. We just have to believe."

Greg pulled out his own phone while she worked on that.

That was one odd blessing of this afterlife. For whatever reason, they had infinite, omni-present power.

Greg pulled up a basic puzzle game.

"Here's another idea," Greg said. "We should get a kind of Underworld Internet going. We could pool all of the different files and games that are on people's phones together."

"Ooo, I like that!" she agreed. "We could involve the school computers too, maybe set up some kind of local network."

They discussed that idea for a while, imagining what kind of files might be available, what they might have at their disposal, and what they could build.

Near the end of the conversation, Chelsea brought up another point.

"Eventually, people will probably write their own books too. That would be something else we could work towards, look forward to. Who knows what they might write, what they might be able to imagine!"

A small click broke the relative silence.

Greg's eyes darted in the direction of noise, but the room was mostly dark. He quickly fumbled for the flashlight on his phone. By the time it was on, a much louder sound broke their serenity.

A hard slam pounded at the door. The wood blocks slid on the industrial carpeting. They didn't have the same level of friction, couldn't grip it like the smooth stone floor of the main hallway.

There was another hard slam, and the door moved another few inches.

A final hard slam pressed the egress to its widest extent.

A long, shadowy leg dropped down from the center of the door, where three distinct prints remained. A collection of silhouettes were behind it. The attached arm floated over to the light switches and clicked them on.

Andrei Tunnikov stood in the doorway and he was not alone.

***

As they marched up the main hallway of the school, Andrei picked through the bag of weapons that Raf had returned to him.

He stepped surely behind Blaire, who now led the pack for their final confrontation.

A crowbar appeared out of the modified gym bag. Andrei swung it behind him, presenting it to Darren, who was close on his left side.

"Thank you," he said.

Next in his hands were a knife lance and switchblade, which he held out to Jennifer.

She took them without a word, still more shocked than furious.

He then pivoted the bag to Rafael, who marched just to his right.

"Take what you want, pass it back," Andrei said.

"I don't need a steak knife on a table leg," Raf mocked. "I'm used to fighting with this alone."

He passed the bag to Elise, who likewise was satisfied with the large Ka-Bar.

The bag ended up between Niles and Laura, who were each already equipped with a makeshift lance.

Niles turned the bag behind them.

Mr. Melkonian was mumbling to himself, not paying attention. His mind was breaking a bit, as it had when they first woke up.

Mr. Wallace took the bag from Niles. He stared at the weapons again. The steak knives themselves were fixed to the table legs with the very same duct tape used to contain the explosive gas in the gym.

Once the juniors had turned away, Rick pivoted the bag in one hand and dropped it into a trash can as they crossed hallways.

There were a dozen things he wanted to say to the kids. He agreed with a lot of the warnings Melkonian had said earlier. Vengeance belongs to God, after all.

But while those thoughts stewed deep inside of him, a thousand other questions floated to the surface. They were the same questions that now muttered from Bob's lips in a kind of quiet horror.

Once they were on the second floor, the group passed Melkonian's classroom.

Blaire pulled a key from her pocket, handing it to Andrei. It was the same one she'd taken from the lifeless body of Joe Torelli. It was the same one Torelli had taken from Chelsea and Greg before it could be added to their key ring. It was the same key Anne had forcibly removed from Laura. It was the same key which had sheltered Laura and Niles, at least for a short time. A key which had been given to them by Rick Wallace so that they would be safe from the ensuing gunfire. It was the same key that Rick had kept hidden from the mob of students when they evicted him from his own office. It was the same key entrusted to him by Vice Principal Barbara Fletcher.

She was Rick's boss, but also his assistant. In many ways, he saw her as a friend, almost thought of her like a daughter. Rick Wallace had been working as a guidance counselor at Villa Vista High School since before she was born, yet her presence in recent years had helped countless kids, and girls especially, open up to him.

However, neither she, nor Rick, nor anyone else could have ever suspected who all this destruction and death would ultimately come from.

The group reached the door of Mrs. Jefferson's English 10 classroom.

Blaire rested her ear against the door.

Andrei looked down at her. Striking hazel eyes searched the door as she listened. Her dark hair framed a pale but loving face. For all the beauty he saw, he couldn't help but see flashes of that face as it was in the mirrors, lifeless and burned. Even in his protective embrace, she was torn violently from the world. There was nothing he could do to stop it at the time, but now he had the opportunity for some retribution.

He shifted his grip on the lance.

After a moment of listening, Blaire nodded.

Andrei turned the school master key in the lock. It made a satisfying click.

He pressed on the handle, but faced resistance. He looked down, feeling the strain coming from the floor. The impedance ignited the anger which had already been boiling inside of him.

He reared back, and with practiced form, kicked the center of the door like he was kicking the chest of an opponent.

The door slid open a few inches.

Andrei kicked it again, and again the door relented to his assault.

The final strike pressed it all the way against the wall, save for the wooden blocks in between.

There were two faint lights illuminating the dark room.

Andrei clicked the switches beside the door.

There they stood.

"What is the meaning of this?" Greg lowered his phone.

Andrei stepped forward into the room, moving between the sophomores and the couch. Their knife lances still lay on the ground beside the cushions.

Blaire was right behind him, shouldering the Browning Citori and aiming it squarely at them.

"Whoa, whoa," Greg said, stepping between Chelsea and the gun. "Take it easy. We're glad Torelli is gone. We never wanted any of that to happen."

Rafael and Elise were next in the room, both of them with knives drawn.

Raf tossed the rolled-up booklet of papers onto the "dining table" in the center of the room.

"Page 3," Blaire growled. "Who is he?"

Greg looked confused, inching forward with his hands in the air.

He opened up the booklet.

The name was right there in the middle of the page.

Walter B. Morton P.E., Electrical Designer

"Chelsea's dad?" he asked, lowering the booklet.

He glanced back at her, but she wore an almost blank expression. It was as though her face had been unplugged from her brain, showing literally zero emotion.

Greg looked at the front of the booklet, then flipped through the pages.

"You didn't tell me your dad was working on the remodel," he said.

A moment of silence hung in the air. The implications began to dawn on him.

He turned to face her again. Still, she seemed to look right through all of them.

Greg took a step backwards, standing in the middle of the room.

"No ..." he said. "It's not possible. She would never do that."

Greg turned to face the others.

Beyond the door, Rick Wallace and Bob Melkonian watched the exchange take place in total disbelief. They looked the same way they did when Greg first approached them on the stage, back before they'd seen themselves in a mirror.

He looked at the couple standing just inside of the door frame, Niles Koh and Laura Nakano. They had interacted quite a bit with Laura in recent weeks. As part of the Student Council, she was heavily involved in organizing all of the Spirit Week events and the float parade. He didn't really know Niles at all, but perhaps he didn't have to. Both of their faces were full of pain and anger.

Standing a few feet in the classroom were Greg and Chelsea's rivals, of sorts. Jennifer Maxwell had competed against them just a few days ago in all of the rally games. She had ridden beside them in the float parade at the big football game. After a close competition, she had ended up beating them as the Homecoming Queen, alongside Marcus Johnson as King.

She clutched her knife lance, holding it over her chest in a strange position, like she was blocking a blow. Her eyes looked past Greg's shoulder.

Next to her was her boyfriend, Darren Clark. He had been drawn into Joe Torelli's junta, but that was only after he had helped Greg and Chelsea get the dormitories established. Originally, Greg thought he was going to be the best one of the "hall monitors" to keep the peace. He seemed to be the most honest and level-headed. The only reason Torelli ranked higher at first was because he was more enthusiastic about establishing some kind of order to the chaos they had woken up to. Obviously, that had turned out very poorly.

Now, Darren stared directly at Greg. His black leather gloves gripped a crowbar. He looked like he wanted to break every bone in Greg's body and probably wouldn't stop there.

Beside them were Rafael Herrera and Elise Gosselin. Greg knew very little about the couple, only that they were juniors and that both of them were very extroverted. They were always laughing and chatting up people in the hallway, almost as much as Greg and Chelsea used to.

Only when violence unfolded in the gym did Greg start to see another side of them. He had no idea where they had gotten the large military knives, but they were really good with them. When he heard Darren and Jennifer talk Torelli down after shooting the new guy, he was relieved. Just trying to disarm the two of them would have been a battle in and of itself. Joe would probably have to shoot more of them, and that might have been enough to start a coup right then and there.

Both Rafael and Elise were frothing with rage, ready to carve them to pieces.

Finally, there was the last couple. The new guy himself, Andrei Tunnikov, had the most cause to overthrow Torelli and the violent trials he had begun. He had suffered the most under that temporary suspension of peace. He stood nearly a foot taller than Greg, readying the lance to gut him like a fish.

Beside him was Blaire Tidwell. Greg remembered seeing the two of them embrace on the dance floor. He knew very little about Blaire, except that she usually seemed way too upset to ever show love like that to anyone. She normally had a grim look on her face, but the intense wrath filling her eyes now was something else entirely.

She intended to fire every one of those shotgun shells until they were reduced to shallow piles of sand.

Greg didn't understand it at all. All of this anger, all of these accusations, it was just like Torelli, it was crazy!

It was odd that Chelsea hadn't mentioned that her dad was working on the renovation, but why would she? Her dad didn't tell her about every project he was working on. His company did MEP engineering for numerous jobs all over Northern California. There was just no way this was related to what happened to the school.

"You knew," Blaire growled at Greg, breaking his momentary retrospection. She took a step closer to him, the shotgun aimed at his chest. More accurately, it was aimed *through* his chest, and at its real target on the other side.

"I don't know anything!" he said. "This is ridiculous, why would Chelsea blow up the school?"

"For us," she whispered.

An air of dread filled the room, as all of the anger burning inside the victims ran cold.

Greg was perhaps the most horrified now. He met her eyes; she was no longer staring past all of them.

Chelsea Morton stood behind Mrs. Jefferson's desk, wearing her bright orange Homecoming dress. The peridot earrings still hung from each ear, matching her bright green eyes. Her sable-colored hair hung down to her shoulders.

All ambiguity had fallen away with that simple admission of guilt.

Chelsea Morton was the Villa Vista Bomber.

Only one question remained in everyone's mind.

"Why?"

THIRTY

FAUSTIAN BARGAIN

IT WAS A LITTLE AFTER 4:30 p.m. on Friday afternoon.

This was the perfect window of time. Pretty much all of the regular students, even those with some kind of after school class or detention, had gone home.

A lot of the football players and cheerleaders would have left for a little bit too, not returning until after 5:30 p.m. for warm-ups. The game wouldn't start until 7:00 p.m., so there would be almost no attendees either.

Chelsea Morton parked her car in one of the aisles right in front of the main construction fence of the gymnasium. All the regular cameras were oriented around the other doors for the buildings and the main gates of the parking lot. Her car was roughly in the exact center of the lot. It was a blind spot.

Part of the Scope of Work for the renovations was upgrading the security cameras of the gymnasium. According to the project schedule on her dad's laptop, the wiring had been installed, but the software wasn't being patched into the school's system until the following weekend. For the moment, the gymnasium cameras might as well have been scarecrows, dummies to discourage trespassers.

Chelsea wasn't a trespasser though; she had a right to be there.

She was wearing something plain, one of her larger VVHS sweatshirt jackets, jeans, and generic looking tennis shoes. She also had an official

Jaguars Baseball cap. It was one of the spares that Greg had given her after joining the JV team. He was always so thoughtful like that.

She had the peridot earrings in her pocket and she couldn't wait to put them on.

Also in her pocket were a pair of thin gloves, which she put on immediately.

In the trunk of her car were two duffle bags, nearly identical. She grabbed the one on the left and closed the trunk.

She walked toward the high school building with the gym bag slung over one shoulder. She had tucked her hair into the baseball cap, so at a glance, passersby might mistake her for a boy. She stopped at one of the trees a good distance from her car and leaned against the trunk, pretending to text on her phone.

Chelsea glanced around in all directions, looking for faces in the windows, bodies in the other parked cars, other people walking on the sidewalk. The key things she watched for were those she might bump into, especially if they recognized her. There were also those who might see her from a vantage point out of a second-floor window.

When she felt that the coast was clear, she briskly walked toward the construction fence. She already had the key in hand. As soon as she reached the gate, she undid the padlock and pulled the chain from one side. Once she slipped into the construction site, she threaded the chain back through the gate so it looked undisturbed.

With that done, she quickly approached the glass doors and pulled one open as quietly as she could. The new locks wouldn't have cores installed until the same date as the camera activation next weekend.

Enough people had been in and out of the site over the previous weeks that her shoe prints weren't even noticeable. She had bought new shoes anyway, with cash, and she'd be throwing away this new pair after tonight's game.

Once she stepped onto the fresh maple wood of the basketball court, a jolt of electricity seemed to pass through her body. Everything was so fresh and new. To actually be standing there was exhilarating. A lot of planning had gone into this.

A giant mural of the school's mascot, Jackie the Jaguar, greeted her. The beast was squeezing a basketball, just like it did to all the other sport logos.

Chelsea thought every iteration of it looked tacky, but this one was like twenty feet tall. Good thing no one else was going to see it. She'd be doing them a favor.

The gym was a bit dark, so Chelsea clipped a flashlight onto the brim of the baseball cap. With a much better view, she approached the visiting team bleachers along the south wall.

She stepped carefully through the metal framework until she reached the correct grate in the middle of the passage.

Unzipping the duffel bag, she pulled out the right size wrench to unscrew the bolts. Once they were off, she slid the grate to the side and set it against the wall.

Everything was exactly where it was supposed to be.

She clicked on the digital display, then flipped over to the HVAC system controller. The exhaust fans were running at full speed. They had been venting the paint fumes, and had mostly completed their task.

Chelsea opened the cover, exposing the wires running into the controller's circuit board. She counted the wires until she reached the correct one. Once she was sure she had it, she used a stripper to pull the rubber coating away, exposing the metal. She spliced in the small component she had put together, which effectively inverted the circuit's signals.

Once the component was in place, she heard a faint hum slow down to nothing. It then started up again, but at a slightly different pitch.

The exhaust fans were no longer pulling air out of the gymnasium, venting it through the roof. Instead, the modified circuit had the fans run in reverse. They were now pushing air in from the outside, creating a downward pressure.

Natural gas was lighter than air. This added modification meant that the pressure from the powerful exhaust fans would keep the natural gas inside the gymnasium. They would help build up a high gas density to be contained within.

Chelsea did have to make sure there weren't any leaks on the bottom though.

She pulled out the new pack of a dozen rolls of duct tape, as well as some paper towels and a pair of scissors. This would be the most time-consuming part.

She set down the rolls along one wall, and slowly went from door to door, sealing every crack with several layers of tape. This was tape literally purpose-built to seal air leaks. The positive pressure against the rubberized face would make that even easier.

The same had to be done for all of the "intake" grills along the walls, which would now act as exhaust vents if she didn't contain the pressure. They could allow natural gas to escape. The artificial scenting agents would alert people to what was happening. It would have been a lot easier if it were pure natural gas, which was completely odorless.

After using half of the rolls of tape, she was satisfied.

One door, the one she would leave through, was slightly propped open. She had to build a bit of an extra web of tape around that one so it would seal properly when she pressed the door closed into the frame.

Chelsea returned to the mechanical systems panel.

Inside the duffel bag was something that felt like a beach towel wadded up. She had wrapped it thoroughly to protect it, as well as deter suspicion. The towel sat within two garbage bags, to make it look like dirty laundry. A bit of dirty laundry had been placed on top of the towel wrapping just for good measure.

She pushed all of that aside, and unwrapped the towel. The spliced circuit component only took an hour or so of assembly and soldering. This device was something else entirely.

Chelsea had worked on it for several nights after her dad had gone to bed. She had to cut off phone conversations with Greg on a few occasions, but she knew he would forgive her.

If this worked, she'd have an eternity to make it up to him.

Most of the machine was stuff that was already lying around in her dad's garage workshop, including the spare car battery. Some stuff she did have to purchase though.

She kept all the pieces in the duffel bag anyway, and her dad was so messy he wouldn't notice stuff getting moved around or used. He really didn't notice much of anything.

Chelsea's mom had died in a car accident a few years ago. After that, her dad had retreated somewhat and tried to fill the void in his own love life with online dating and some various hook-ups in the area. Between that and work, there wasn't much he saw eye to eye on with a teenage girl.

He mostly let her do things on her own, taking a very hands-off approach to parenting. Case-in-point, while Chelsea didn't even have her learner's permit yet, he sometimes let her drive a car by herself, so long as she stayed within Alexandria and didn't go on any freeways.

Greg had actually been the one to be there for her after her mother died. That was when she started seeing him as more than a friend. Just over a year later, they would be officially dating.

One of the ways her dad tried spending time with her was by teaching her electrical engineering. Sometimes, when he had the opportunity and she had the free time, they would build random things in his shop.

Besides that though, he wasn't good at connecting with her. He did make an attempt though, and because of that, she didn't want him to be caught up in what happened.

That's why she tried to keep everything clean of evidence, so it couldn't be led back to him after the fact ... or led back to her if something failed.

Chelsea sat the device down in front of the mechanical systems panel.

She pressed a button on the side and the digital display came to life. A small LED light illuminated next to the word "READY".

Below that was the "TEST" button, which she had already put to use several times when building the circuit board.

Instead of pressing the button, Chelsea pulled out her cell phone. There were two "Calculator" applications. One of them had an icon identical to the other, but it was black and white.

She pressed the black and white one and a very basic grey screen appeared.

Nestled within the device were the guts of a disposable "burner" cell phone. It wasn't a smartphone, but it was advanced enough to send and receive text messages. With a slight user interface design, she was able to use that messaging protocol to build this basic controller application.

On the grey screen were a few buttons and displays, which more or less matched the physical ones on the device itself.

One of the buttons on her touchscreen also read "TEST".

She pressed it.

With only a few seconds delay for the text to be sent, a high voltage arc of electricity jumped between the metal rods.

Below the "TEST" button was a clock timer. The burner phone was already synchronized with hers.

She typed "10192030" into the module, then pressed "SYNC". The digital clock on the device blinked "10:19" then "20:30". It was now programmed to go off on October 19th at 8:30 p.m.

That would be just right. Chelsea wanted to enjoy basically the entire dance with Greg. Even the early people didn't start leaving until after that half hour mark. Almost everyone should still be present when it ignited.

With the tape in place and the machine fully tested, it was time to begin.

Chelsea pulled a large set of bolt cutters out of the bag. One by one, she cut the locks off of the natural gas connections.

She flipped the first valve.

A high-pitched whistling sounded from the nozzle. It wasn't loud enough to be heard through the walls though. Even if it was, the other students would just think it was some kind of water pipe or air conditioning refrigerant line.

Most people thought of walls as solid. They seldom consider all of the pressurized pipes and live wires and gas connections flowing inside. The average electrical amperage surging through a residential home could kill all its occupants at any time. All you need to do is close the circuit. There were devices to protect people, like ground fault circuit interrupters, but all it takes is for enough protections to fail and you might as well be dropping a toaster in a bathtub.

There was a certain harmony to nature. The same kind of equations that governed forces of electrical energy had cousins and equivalents which governed pressure and fluid dynamics. This flow of explosive hydrocarbon filling the space was no different than trickle-charging a large battery. In the end, it was all just stored energy.

Chelsea wanted all the energy that she could summon.

She flipped the other three valves, creating a small ensemble of whistling nozzles.

The smell was beginning to bother her, so she picked up the duffel bag and headed for the door.

Once she was out of the gymnasium, she carefully pressed the door like it was a refrigerator, making sure everything was sealed. To be sure though, she added a few layers of duct tape to the outside.

Only then did she realize that she had left her other spare rolls on the floor against the wall.

Whatever, they would be vaporized in twenty-seven hours anyway.

Everything was in place; the pressure began to build.

Chelsea took the flashlight off of her cap and pulled it lower on her face before opening the glass doors.

It was after 5:00 p.m., but the school should still be mostly empty.

She peeked through the cracks in the construction fence before inching open the gate and slipping out.

She re-secured the chain and padlock so it looked exactly as it was before.

After that, she briskly returned to the tree. She stayed there for about ten minutes, glancing around to see if anyone was watching her. Even if they had only noticed her momentarily, she wanted to create a gap in time that they would have stopped paying attention or left.

Only once that time had passed did she walk up to her car and open the trunk.

She pulled off the shoes she'd worn and deposited them in the bag on top of the bolt cutters. They were replaced with a pair of Converse. After that went the gloves, then the jacket, then the cap.

Her hair fell to her shoulders. She was wearing a bright orange top which draped down to the middle of her thighs. It was part of her other outfit for the evening.

She pulled the peridot earrings from her pocket and put them on. After zipping up the first duffel bag, she grabbed the second one.

Chelsea closed the trunk and began casually walking toward the football stadium.

It had worked, she hadn't been caught. It was just another sign that this was meant to be.

That's how she felt over the summer too. After learning about what was going to happen with Greg, her dad had randomly mentioned that he was doing the electrical design for her school's gymnasium.

Knowing him, he probably thought he had mentioned it before at one point, but actually didn't. He was very scatter-brained like that.

Chelsea was not though. She took this opportunity as a sign. This was her chance to make everything right! The whole plan weaved itself into her brain over the course of that evening. Research and planning began the next night.

Once she crossed the bleachers, Chelsea reached the far parking lot by the tennis courts.

All four floats had arrived for the parade that night.

Only a few people had shown up with each float. For the most part it was just the drivers of each tug car and the Student Council kids who'd worked on their respective floats.

Chelsea passed the Junior Class float.

"Hi Laura!" she chirped. "Wow, you guys did a great job!"

Laura Nakano turned to answer her.

"Hi Chelsea," she said. "Thanks, it's everything we could do with everyone we had available."

The "everyone" was standing on the float. It was Laura's date, Niles Koh. He gave a slight wave as he was reattaching props, now that the float was off of city streets.

In truth, their float was easily the worst of the four. That should impact the juniors' chances of beating them as a class. It would also damage the odds of Melissa Levitt or Liam Connelly winning Homecoming Queen or King.

Chelsea then went on to greet her own classmates and waited for Greg.

There were so many wonderful things about him, but timeliness was not one of them. He said he'd be there by 5:30 p.m., but didn't arrive until almost 6:00 p.m. Once he did, however, she gave him a big hug.

It wouldn't be long now.

"Do you have everything?" Greg had asked her, pointing to the duffel bag.

"Yup!" she said, unzipping the top.

Inside was the Italian Renaissance costume she'd be wearing when the parade happened during halftime. It looked ridiculous. As much as she loved the stories set in that era, the "period appropriate" clothing looked too silly for her.

That was fine though, because what elevated stories was not the set dressing, but the timelessness of their messages. That's why Shakespeare still rang true centuries later, and why others continued to find inspiration in his works. It was the same way he had found inspiration in the Classics that preceded him.

Once they had checked in with all the right people, she and Greg found a place on the bleachers with some of their other friends.

Greg's parents couldn't make it tonight, so it made things that much easier for Chelsea to convince her dad not to come. He was really busy with some other work projects that weren't related to the Villa Vista gymnasium anyway.

At least *her* dad showed some interest in going though. Greg's parents were so much worse.

It was *their* fault things had to happen this way in the first place.

She couldn't live without Greg ... and she couldn't die without him either.

Chelsea had considered possible ways of pinning the explosion on them somehow, but things were too precarious as it was. Absolving her dad of any involvement was more important.

She and Greg ate dinner during the first quarter of the Homecoming game. They were careful not to spill anything, even though their costumes were still packed away.

During the second quarter, they went downstairs to dress into their proper attire.

They each emerged from the single-stall bathrooms at the same time. They would have probably shared one of the bathrooms if there wasn't a chance they could get caught.

"You look fantastic." He grinned.

"It's okay," Chelsea responded, "I know it's terrible."

"Oh, I know," he said. "The costume is whatever, but *you* look fantastic regardless."

She smiled seductively at him.

When Greg first broke the terrible news to her, she felt like the world was ending. However, even before the plan was conceived, she wanted to make the most of their time together.

She made love with him at the first available opportunity.

Besides the obvious physical pleasures, the intimacy had an added benefit as well. Greg wasn't one to pry too much into her business or snoop around her things. However, the few times he had come close to discovering her machinations, she was able to distract him with something most teenage boys couldn't resist.

They had gone on a "full" date the previous weekend. Then, after the Homecoming dance, they were planning on attending Jimmy O'Shaughnessy's afterparty. Unfortunately, Greg would have to wait a little longer for them to spend the night again. She wasn't exactly sure how things would unfold afterwards.

Once she and Greg returned to the floats, the other princes and princesses were there too.

That Ellen Taylor girl was wearing a "flapper" dress to fit their 1920s theme. She didn't seem all that thrilled to be there though.

After her incident in the Spirit Week games, she wasn't a serious competitor to win. She was just a sideshow. They were calling her "Mudbra" for crying out loud. Even nice boobs won't win you points if they become the butt of the joke.

Melissa Levitt was there, looking as unapproachable as ever. For a French-themed float, they should have put her in a guillotine. That would have at least drawn a laugh.

Then there was Jennifer Maxwell, the senior. She was the only real competition.

She and the senior boy, Marcus Johnson, had done really well during the games. They had definitely racked up more points than Chelsea and Greg.

Luckily, she and Greg's relationship was a big selling point. No matter how regal and elegant Jennifer looked, Marcus was a bit of a goofball. He was nice, but she and Greg were nicer.

Chelsea looked at her phone and realized that it was 8:30 p.m.

Exactly twenty-four hours remained.

After the float parade, Chelsea didn't pay too much attention to the game. She just focused on talking to Greg, spending the most time with him that she could. There was still a chance that something would go wrong, and it wouldn't work out like she expected.

In the last seconds, the stupid Jaguars quarterback threw an interception and lost them the game.

Afterwards, she shared a long kiss with Greg before they departed in their separate cars.

On the way home, she stopped by a gas station. As her car was filling up, she bought a few snacks inside. Once she dumped the snacks in her trunk, she picked up one of the duffel bags and walked it over to the dumpster with some other mixed garbage.

The bolt cutters and other remaining evidence would disappear into a landfill before anyone could put the pieces together.

The Homecoming dance itself began just perfectly. She and Greg rode in a limo along with some other friends. It dropped them off before leaving. It was intended to return at 9:00 p.m. to take them to Jimmy's, but it definitely wouldn't be arriving.

There wouldn't be any place to return to.

As Chelsea walked through the doors of the Murphy Center, she couldn't help but keep glancing at the gymnasium.

There was no odor and there was no alarm. After over a day of pressurizing, no one seemed to have noticed anything out of the ordinary.

Chelsea had tried running a few numbers on how much energy would be stored in there, but there were too many variables that she couldn't quite resolve. In her broad estimates though, if things unfolded as designed ... there was going to be nothing left.

She and Greg danced, they had dinner, they took pictures, and they went on stage as the Sophomore Prince and Princess to make one final petition to the audience.

With a kiss on his cheek, which the crowd uproariously loved, she thought they had the win guaranteed.

That was the first thing to go wrong.

Because Jennifer and Marcus were such meatheads, their athleticism in the Spirit Week games put them over the top to win Homecoming Queen and King.

Chelsea was devastated.

Greg had been very nice in trying to cheer her up, but it was the one major blemish on an otherwise perfect evening.

Eventually, Chelsea settled down. Jennifer wouldn't even have her little victory for an hour. Then, a whole new royalty would emerge.

As the minutes got closer, she and Greg shared a few romantic slow dances. She savored each moment as much as she could, but it was hard to keep her eyes off of the clocks.

Then, one of her favorite recent songs came on. They had to dance through it to the end.

Chelsea pulled out her phone.

It was 8:28 p.m.

Chelsea updated the clock, pushing out the activation time by four minutes.

All she had to do was press the "SYNC" button to transmit it to the machine.

Just below that was a smaller button which read "STOP".

That was, ironically, her kill switch. If pressed twice in a row, it would turn off the device and format or destroy all the data and memory components. That would erase the electronic evidence, including the message history from Chelsea's phone.

She paused for a moment. This really was the last chance to back out.

Chelsea looked at the wall by the back doors. There were fire alarm pull stations by every main exit, as was mandated by law. All she'd need to do was stop the device and pull one of those to evacuate the school.

After that, she could make an anonymous bomb threat from a payphone at the gas station to alert the fire department.

She would need to be careful in the weeks that followed, but there was still a road of return.

She could still stop this.

Chelsea glanced at the north wall of the ballroom.

Blaire Tidwell was leaning against the side of the gym talking to her date, the new senior boy. She had been making out with him only a few minutes earlier, hogging the center of the dance floor and all the attention of the others.

A flash of anger surged through Chelsea. The center belonged to her and Greg *alone* ... no one else! It made her happy to know that Blaire and Andrei would be among the first to die.

She pressed the "SYNC" button and the clock updated in the ignition device.

The first verse of the favorite new song came on.

"Who was it?" Greg asked, referring to her "text message".

"My dad," Chelsea answered. "He's turning in early, which means we have all the time we could ever want."

Greg kissed her and they danced out the rest of the song. It ended just a few seconds after 8:33 p.m. The next song had barely made it through its own first verse when it was silenced forever.

The wave of fire hit Chelsea so suddenly that it took her by surprise, even though she was the only one expecting it. After that, everything seemed to go black in an instant.

At first, a thought occurred to her that it had all gone horribly wrong. There was only blackness, oblivion. Then, she began to wake up.

She was not anticipating to still be in Villa Vista High School. In fact, the chants she had repeated had petitioned for something else entirely.

Greg was still asleep next to her.

They had been blown off of the dance floor completely. They were lying in the center of the stage, surrounded by over a hundred of their classmates.

"Where are the rest of them?" was one of the first thoughts that crossed her mind.

Somehow, nearly two thirds of the others didn't make it through, but why? There's no way that many survived.

She pulled out her phone, realizing that nearly twelve hours had passed.

To be safe, she pulled up the "Calculator" application again and double-tapped the "STOP" button. That should wipe the memory. Chelsea then deleted the application, erasing it from her phone completely.

After Greg woke up, they began to take in the details of their surroundings.

Chelsea wouldn't think to look in a mirror until they heard the screams.

That was when she truly felt the finality of what she had done.

Both of their reflections were severely mangled. The explosion had thrown them sideways against the short wall of the stage apron. Their opposite arms had struck the edge of the platform and the force pivoted them, slamming their heads against the floor of the stage.

They must have both been knocked out instantly, which is why they didn't remember anything. The opposite sides of their heads had horrible impact craters, like they had been killed by a sledgehammer.

Chelsea was not expecting to see herself as a corpse in the mirrors, but at least she was not alone. Everyone saw themselves and each other like this. The reflections revealed the way that they died.

As Greg processed some of his own emotional pain, Chelsea put on a matching show for how she was supposed to feel.

After that, she was able to convince Greg that they needed to reach out to the others. The students loved them, trusted them, they needed to help bring some order to this strange chaos they were now living in.

As the hours passed that Sunday, Chelsea was able to develop a deeper understanding about their circumstances based on everyone else's stories and perspectives.

It was not what she expected, but she could work with it.

Later in the day, Greg was really taking on the leadership role he was made for. His classroom dormitories idea was brilliant, as was his suggestion for their personal room.

Despite some missteps, things were beginning to fall into place. There were just a few loose ends she needed to tie up.

Then Torelli happened.

His personal crusade was an impediment, but as Chelsea expected, he burned himself out quickly.

He'd barely held power for a day before someone else took the shotgun from him and put him down with it.

They just needed to bide their time, play the long game. They had all the time they could ever want.

Chelsea only needed to wait for the others to process their personal grief and accept their new stations in their new lives.

***

As soon as Andrei had flipped on the light switch, and Blaire saw her face, she was sure that Chelsea was the bomber.

Upon meeting Blaire's eyes, she seemed to know that she'd been found out. Her face went completely blank.

Blaire wanted to begin shooting them right then and there, but she remembered how much the pain had affected Andrei.

She didn't want them passing out and she didn't want them dying ... at least not yet.

Their short exchange with Greg surprised Blaire a bit. She suspected Chelsea to be the mastermind, but she also expected Greg to have been in on it.

Only when the killer finally said something, did everything change.

"Chelsea, what are you talking about?" Greg asked her.

Something about actually hearing words come from her mouth brought a wave of absolute dread over Blaire. She didn't feel like she was holding the shotgun as an executioner anymore. She felt like a scared housewife, hearing the voice of a serial killer walk up a stairwell.

Chelsea Morton had killed more people than any serial killer Blaire could bring to mind.

Despite all the emotions she felt at the moment, Greg Henshaw seemed to be feeling twice as many.

"They were taking you away from me," Chelsea said to him.

"What is she talking about?" Elise asked.

"You mean the move?" Greg said.

"Explain, asshole!" Raf demanded, stabbing at the air with his Ka-Bar.

Greg blinked, overwhelmed by the situation.

"M-my mom works for SoftBank," he began. "She got a big promotion over the summer, but it requires her to work from the headquarters. We were going to move to Tokyo over Christmas. I told Chelsea it was a long way and it was a long time. If she wanted to date other people in high school that was fine by me. Maybe we'd reconnect in college.

"I gave her those peridot earrings to hopefully make her feel better ... it was the least I could do."

Jenny and Darren looked at each other.

"I had to find a way to fix it," she said. "A way we could be together forever."

Laura was beginning to sob again. Niles held her. The lance in his hand shook as they listened.

"The night was almost perfect," she continued. "Homecoming would have been the last dance that we deserved ... if not for her."

She turned her empty gaze toward Jennifer.

Jennifer flinched and was too afraid to speak.

Darren shifted his gloves around the crowbar.

"But still," she said. "The ritual worked!"

She took a step closer to them and Blaire stepped closer with the Citori.

"We were reborn into our own world where we could be King and Queen!" Chelsea exclaimed.

"What?!" Melkonian said in disbelief from the hallway.

"We only had to outlast the savages and their little trials," she continued. "I knew Torelli would destroy himself quickly. This world wasn't meant for him."

"The construction drawings ..." Greg mouthed.

"They're in the garbage can in the girls' gymnasium bathroom," Chelsea answered. "After what happened Sunday morning, everyone was too afraid to go in there. I washed everything out with acetone I got from Mr. Moll's room. The other set of drawings, from McDouglas' file cabinet, are also in there. I was sure that I'd erased everything."

"You were wrong, you fucking demon," Blaire whispered, tears streaming down her face.

"Chelsea ..." Greg said, but he couldn't even fathom the words for this situation.

"Eventually Torelli would have gotten bored or the crowd would have turned against him after torturing enough people. Heck they could barely stomach seeing some totally new guy get shot." She motioned to Andrei.

Blaire's eyebrows furrowed in rage.

"They would have come back to us," Chelsea said. "They loved us, we helped them."

"You _killed_ them," Niles said, shocked by her dissociation.

"But then we lost our power," she said. "All because of _you_, old man."

The killer shot a glance at Wallace.

"Less souls mean less power and a smaller world in the afterlife," she explained. "If everyone showed up like they were supposed to, they would have had to listen to us unquestioningly."

"What the fuck are you talking about?!" Jenny yelled, incensed.

"It couldn't just be us," Chelsea told Greg. "'The dagger is happy when its sheaths are many.'"

"Oh my god ..." Blaire said in astonishment, the shotgun lowering slightly. "You can't be serious."

"Did she just say what I think she did?" Elise looked dumbfounded at Blaire, their horror and anger was interrupted by mutual bewilderment.

"Girls, could one of you please explain?" Andrei asked.

"You psycho bitch, that's a ghost story!" Elise screamed, sounding manic.

"What is?!" Raf asked, confused.

"The Harbinger of the Happy Dagger," Blaire elaborated. "It's an anonymous Internet story about a mysterious stranger who gives a magic dagger to Romeo and Juliet. Angered that they can't be together in life, they slowly kill off their families with it, then themselves. In the afterlife they become the heads of their combined family. 'Only in death do our fortunes reverse.'

"It's the kind of trashy amateur horror story thirteen-year-old girls read at a slumber party!"

Blaire spat the last line, feeling completely unsettled by this revelation.

Everyone was speechless.

Niles was the first to break the silence. "You killed us over fanfiction?"

Unfortunately, this wasn't the first significant instance of violence inspired by works of fiction. The J. D. Salinger novel, *The Catcher in the Rye*, had several famous shootings supposedly based on its messages. Similar charges had been placed on the works of Friedrich Nietzsche.

Even in recent history, the *Doom* video game series had been blamed directly or indirectly for certain major acts of violence.

The Harbinger of the Happy Dagger was not even the first story to spawn from Internet culture to be tied to an attack of some kind. However, there had already been a handful of murders associated with that particular tale.

Blaire knew of certain online forums where people took dumb creepypastas like that way too seriously. She just had no idea that *she* would end up dying because of something so absurd.

Except, it wasn't really because of some dumb story.

"You felt like love was being taken away from you, so you decided to steal it from all the rest of us?!" Blaire whispered.

"Everything had worked," Chelsea said, full of conviction. "But some people must have slipped through the cracks. We didn't have all the power we were supposed to, so Torelli and Marcus and others like them became unbalanced."

"You're going to judge people on being 'unbalanced'?" Andrei asked, still in utter disbelief.

"Chelsea," Mr. Melkonian said, standing in the door frame. "Wherever you think you are right now, you're wrong. This isn't some fantasy land where you get to play princess for real. You murdered hundreds of people!"

"This place is better than home," she dismissed. "We don't need to eat, drink, or sleep. Until Wallace ruined it, we didn't even die! You would have gotten used to it. This is Paradise."

"Paradise?!" Jenny screamed. "This is Hell! Every mirror shows what *you* did to us. We're cut off from our families and friends forever."

"Then go," Chelsea shooed them. "Take your exit one way or another and leave us in peace."

"Us?" Greg Henshaw whispered. "Chelsea, you're … a monster. You *killed* me and so many others. I never want to see you again."

After maintaining a sociopathic composure throughout the conversation, Chelsea finally broke.

"What?! Greg, no! You don't understand!"

Greg took a step away from her, but before he could step any further, the group felt a powerful rumbling beneath their feet.

There was a deafening noise as all the glass in the school seemed to shatter at once.

"An earthquake?!" Andrei shouted, covering his ears.

He wrapped an arm around Blaire, but before he could pull them through the door, the floor gave out.

With the exception of Melkonian and Wallace, who were still in the hallway, the rest of them fell down into the classroom below.

Greg recovered quickly and ran through a hole in the wall. Chelsea sat up and followed after him.

"Stop them!" Elise yelled, alerting everyone to their escape.

Andrei and Blaire crawled out of the rubble and gave chase. They followed her bright orange dress as she tracked Greg through the atrium.

"Where are the bodies?" Blaire asked Andrei. All of those who had jumped to their death in the atrium were gone.

"What's happening to the school?" Andrei added.

The ghostly recreation of Villa Vista High School was falling to pieces. Thick black smoke poured out of several rooms.

Wallace and Melkonian reached the bottom of the stairwell as the others entered the atrium

Andrei and Blaire passed through the double doors into the hallway adjacent to the gym.

Black smoke was pouring out of those doors too, but not a volcanic funnel cloud like they'd seen before.

"Where is it coming from?" Blaire thought.

The walls to their left began to crumble. Cinder blocks were cracking away and sinking into the ground like melting ice cubes.

They could see inside the gymnasium bathrooms.

The couple stopped in their tracks.

The black smoke was pouring out of the mirrors ... every mirror. Shattered glass covered the floor in front of them. The mirrors were like windows which had been smashed open.

The smoke wasn't the only thing coming through.

They watched as a skeletal right arm reached out of the frame, grabbing the edge of the sink counter.

It pulled itself past the threshold, bringing two long legs down onto the ground.

It was Andrei ... his corpse reflection.

Its left hand reached back into the mirror. As it pulled, another hand came with it. The corpse wore a black dress with a rose lace pattern burned into its skin.

It was Blaire.

The unburnt Blaire shouldered the shotgun, while Andrei backed them up.

The others caught up behind them, witnessing the doppelgangers step through the door frame into the hallway.

Blaire aimed at the corpse couple, but she was too frightened to fire.

Rather than actually being reflections, both bodies had flipped, accurately portraying the fatal wounds the couple had suffered.

Blaire's corpse looked at her with its torn left iris.

She winked.

"Oh god," Blaire uttered in fear, the shotgun shaking in her grip.

With its black, skeletal hand, Andrei's corpse beckoned them, motioning for the group to follow. Then, the dead couple began walking toward the Murphy Center.

Andrei looked down at Blaire.

"What do we do?" he asked, uncertain.

That's when they heard a scream from behind them. It was Laura.

"Keep moving!" Niles yelled. "They're coming!"

Blaire tried to steady her aim, guiding them forward. They crept through the hallway, watching every doorway and plume of black smoke.

Eventually, they were out the other side.

To their left, a row of corpses lined the wall, standing like dancers relaxing between songs. To their right was the same thing. They stood against the north-facing wall, adjacent to the gym.

In the place where they'd left Eric, he was gone. Those who were tied up were also gone. Only piles of dust remained, as well as the strips of duct tape which once bound them.

The Blaire and Andrei corpses waited for them, standing just in front of the column of tables.

The rest of the group followed, Elise and Raf huddling close behind the real Blaire and Andrei.

"Oh shit, oh shit," Raf panicked. "This is Hell, this is really Hell."

Things were beginning to make sense. From the beginning, many of them had been questioning what exactly this place was. If it truly was Hell, then where were all the demons?

Now they knew. The demons had been there the entire time, staring at them from behind the mirrors.

Blaire's corpse maintained eye contact with her. Even with dead eyes, the piercing glare was frightening to behold. For a moment, a thought crossed her mind, "Is this how everyone else feels looking at me?"

The corpse lifted her hand, making an "out with it" motion.

That's when the words seemed to come to Blaire.

"This ship isn't meant for us," she announced to the group.

"Ship?" Elise tilted her head in confusion. Then, she screamed.

Elise's corpse walked up next to Blaire's, followed closely by Rafael's.

Darren and Jennifer saw their dead selves walk in from the crowd as well. Jennifer's corpse stood behind the left side of Darren's, covering the part of itself that was exposed. It smiled at her.

"Th-thanks," Jenny said in a delirious voice.

A charred black skeleton followed them, laced arm-in-arm with a corpse whose head had been crushed.

Niles and Laura stared at them.

Melkonian and Wallace were startled by their reflections, as they took position to the far-left side of the group.

Just as they had appeared in the mirrors, every dead body wore the same clothing and accessories that it did at the moment of death. They were all still dressed for the Homecoming dance.

The Murphy Center was filling up quickly. It was not just reflections gathering in the ballroom, it was the corpses of everyone.

Principal McDouglas walked by Bob and Rick. His body had been crushed by some kind of falling debris.

Timothy Van Gaal moved up next to him. His round head was unmistakable, even without the shock of ginger hair.

Andrei flinched as two more familiar sights walked by him.

Joe Torelli and Marcus Johnson passed the huddled group, approaching the stage.

The corpses of Melkonian and Wallace walked off, disappearing into the crowd.

"Where are they going?" Bob asked Rick.

The sudden appearance of their dead doppelgangers had temporarily caused everyone to forget their original chase. It wouldn't matter anyway, there was no place to run and there was no place to hide.

Villa Vista High School continued to crumble. It was not explosive, as the fate of the original. It was a subtle deconstruction, the rubble returning to its place. Fires raged all around them and black smoke filled the sky. It fell back down onto the surface around the original edges of campus.

They were inside the mirror world now. The fog had been a temporary vacuum, which was now fully breached by the Hell contained within.

"It looks more or less the same as what happened," Andrei observed. "Except for us still walking around, of course."

Blaire understood what he was saying.

"You think if Chelsea had killed everyone in a different way, it would *look* different too?" she wondered aloud. "Like if she had filled the building with chlorine gas, would that be the extent of everything, four walls and a green haze?"

"Who knows?" Andrei said.

It had been phrased in a rhetorical manner. However, Andrei's corpse turned around to face the two of them. It pointed at itself.

They had an answer.

After a moment of fear, Blaire addressed her other self.

"You're not actually *us*, are you?" she asked. "Like, our bodies?"

The Blaire corpse shook her head.

Andrei asked his opposite, "Then why do you look like us?"

The Andrei corpse tugged at its one remaining lapel.

"Clothing?" Blaire asked.

Her double smiled wider, then winked at the Andrei corpse.

It reached into the coat with a skeletal hand and pulled out a black tricorn hat. It looked like something one might wear with a pirate costume.

Blaire suddenly blushed, stepping behind Andrei to cover herself.

The Andrei corpse pushed the hat back behind the lapel. It disappeared into a void.

The Blaire corpse made a motion, zipping her lips.

"I get it," Andrei said. "Everything in the afterlife is dressed up to our expectations, what we know, what we want ..."

The Andrei corpse raised his skeletal hand, rolling the bony wrist.

"... or to our fears, what would bring us the most suffering," Andrei finished.

Both corpses smiled darkly.

Demonic music began booming up from the ground. The speakers had been blown away in the explosion, but whether or not they produced the sound didn't seem to matter. The noise was coming from everywhere.

The music was staticky and distorted, out of tune, with a floating tempo and pitch. Every instrument sounded like it came from a different suffering creature. Each note was a scream, a wail, or whimpering.

Despite all of this, it still sounded loosely like one of the pop songs they might have heard at the Homecoming dance.

All of the corpses in the ballroom faced the stage.

They began to hear an individual scream, distinct from the evil music.

Blaire raised the shotgun to her chest again.

None of the corpses reacted. They didn't seem to acknowledge or care about the Citori at all.

Joe Torelli and Marcus Johnson walked out to the center of the stage. They each had hands firmly grasped on the arms of the star of the show ... Chelsea Morton.

She flailed and kicked wildly, her orange dress fluttering over the stage like a Color Guard flag.

The Melkonian and Wallace corpses walked down the center of the dance floor, a path having been made for them.

Greg Henshaw, the real Greg Henshaw, stood between them.

"Greg!" Chelsea screamed. "Greg, sweetie, help me!"

"What do you want *me* to do Chelsea?" he asked, frightened by what surrounded them. "Look around, look at all these people you killed. Obviously, this is your punishment."

"I did this for us!" she wept. "So that we could be together!"

"You could have moved to Tokyo after high school," Greg said. "Or I might have gone to college back in the States."

He concluded with the likely possibility.

"Maybe we would have fallen in love with different people," he said. "High school could have been something nice we looked back on when we bumped into each other every few years.

"Instead, you did something so unbelievably evil. It'll affect the living world, everyone we knew and cared about, for at least the rest of their lives, probably longer."

He began tearing up.

"And what about our lives Chelsea?" Greg asked her. "You stole those from us too. Maybe we would have gotten back together, done the whole thing ... marriage, kids, etc. You destroyed that possibility for us and so many hundreds of others."

Chelsea was crying now, not even answering with words.

"I don't know if you're crazy, or a literal psychopath or whatever," Greg said. "But there's no getting away from this. Even if you only have to pay back a year for every one you stole, that's like 60 years from 300 people."

Greg did the math.

Niles whispered the number along with him.

"18,000 years, Chelsea," he said. "That's not even eternity. You better hope something else changes at some point."

That is when another set of corpses walked onto the dance floor, replacing Melkonian and Wallace.

It was Greg and Chelsea. Both of their skulls had been smashed in on one side.

The Chelsea corpse was holding the electrical ignition device.

The real Chelsea began screaming, kicking harder at the Joe Torelli and Marcus Johnson bodies which held her in place.

"No! No! No! Stop it! Stop it! Stop it!"

The other group of living souls watched all of this in silence. They clung to their lovers, held close to their friends, and prayed as hard as they could that they would not find themselves on a similar stage at some point.

The Chelsea corpse pressed the red "TEST" button.

A bright arc of blue electricity jolted between the metal rods, then jumped from the device onto the real Greg Henshaw.

The lightning surged over his body, as it had done to every other soul freed from this Hell of Chelsea's creation.

Greg was reduced to dust. The last spark of the soul inside shot upward, disappearing into the smoke-filled sky.

Chelsea broke completely, her cries becoming an incomprehensible wail, her body jerking in emotional pain and torment.

The Greg corpse kicked at the pile of sand, then stepped in to take its place.

He then began to laugh.

It was not a human laugh. It was not even an animal laugh. It was guttural and deep, yet throaty and pitchy. It sounded like one unearthly creature being swallowed alive by another.

Every other corpse began to laugh in the same way. Chelsea's wails, and the inhuman music, were quickly drowned out by their demonic cackling.

The souls pulled tighter together.

While the other demons continued to ignore them, the ten doppelgangers turned from the stage to face the wayward spirits.

No longer laughing, they circled the group, aligning with their opposites. They were standing barely out of arm's reach.

Blaire hadn't even bothered to raise the shotgun. She had dropped it to the ground, holding Andrei as tightly as she could with both hands.

They were all weeping and moaning, waiting for something horrible to happen.

That is when their ten dark reflections folded their hands in front of them. They all turned their heads toward Wallace.

One by one, the souls opened their eyes, following the gaze of the corpses.

They were all looking at him now.

"Rick ... do it," Bob whispered.

Rick's own deceased face nodded at him from a few feet away.

He took a breath, then began.

Everyone closed their eyes, putting everything they had into that final appeal to the Almighty.

"God Almighty, You called us forth from the darkness. Your providence lights our way. And as You design, we return to dust.

"Lord, those who died live anew with You. Their lives have changed but will never end. I pray forever for my family, relatives and friends. That alive or dead, they are at peace at last.

"Together with Christ, who died so we may live. May they be fulfilled as one in Paradise, where sin and pain are washed away. Unite our family in our final home, to exalt Your name forever and ever."

"Amen," they all said together.

EPILOGUE

This is NEWS10 Alexandria coming to you with breaking news.

The FBI have just released a report claiming to have positively identified the Villa Vista Bomber.

Following a rigorous internal investigation, MCL Construction detected irregular login hours from an account associated with one of their subcontractors, Waters MEP Engineering. After alerting the FBI of their findings, a joint task force carried out a raid early this morning.

The project's electrical engineer, Walter Morton, was found to have accessed site plans and drawings past midnight on multiple occasions. It was seemingly the only account to do so. Following a thorough questioning of Walter Morton and comprehensive search of his residence, it was determined that the bombing was planned and carried out by his daughter, fifteen-year-old Chelsea Morton.

Chelsea was a sophomore at Villa Vista High School. She was in attendance at the dance and perished during the attack.

The investigation of her personal computer has also brought to light a motive. There were numerous recently deleted files on her hard drive relating to an amateur horror story called *The Harbinger of the Happy Dagger*.

NEWS10 Alexandria reported on a related incident last year which took place in Kenosha, Wisconsin. A high school girl took revenge on her boyfriend after an act of infidelity, killing both of them as well as the girl he had supposedly cheated with.

The story in question is based on Shakespeare's *Romeo and Juliet*. It is themed around saving lost romance in the afterlife through the sacrifice of those who wronged the couple.

How exactly this may have contributed to her motives has not been clearly established. However, according to federal officials, there seems to be no question now who was responsible.

We will continue to provide more updates as soon as they become available.

We here at NEWS10 hope this revelation can bring some peace to those who have suffered from this loss.

Finally, we would like to remind the bereaved that the memorial service is scheduled for this Friday morning, November 1st. It will be held on school grounds for the families of victims.

***

It had been almost two weeks since the bombing.

The pain hadn't really lessened at all, but at least it wasn't the only thing Jack Tidwell was feeling.

The vision that Jack was shown in his dream was so incredibly real. He could still feel the warmth of holding Blaire in that strange void. He knew it must have been some kind of divine gift.

Jack had never abused drugs to any degree, shy of trying a bit of weed in college. So, unless his grief had caused him to have some kind of psychological break, he really, truly believed that he was given a last chance to see his sweet baby girl.

The short interaction he had with his father had also brought a bit of comfort to his mournful spirit. Blaire would not be alone. At the very least, her grandfather was there with her, guiding her to the beyond.

Edward had thankfully passed peacefully in his sleep one night. Jack was afraid he would begin losing mental function, becoming a confused shell of himself at the end. Not only did he not want his dad to go out like that, but he didn't want Blaire to see such a sad end for him.

Even still, Edward had been particularly warm in the weeks beforehand. Perhaps he had his own vision of what was coming. Jack felt like he had the chance to say everything he wanted to him; he didn't pass with anything left unspoken.

That is one of the many reasons why Blaire's death had been so difficult, especially in those first few days. He felt like he wasn't able to say goodbye to her at all, not until that vision anyway.

He would treasure that meeting for the rest of his days, but he couldn't think of any way to share it with Milly or the boys. Even if they believed that it happened as literally as he did, it would only sadden them if they were not given a similar opportunity. Jack couldn't do that to them.

Instead, when he got home, Jack brought all four of them together, and spoke in much more vague and emotional terms.

He didn't want them to suffer in silence or isolation anymore. They were going to talk about Blaire together, they were going to remember her together, and they would mourn her together.

He spoke from a position of authority, reminding them how much Blaire cared about each and every one of them, even though it may have been hard to see sometimes. He related similar stories of his own childhood with his father.

While Jack didn't explain his divine encounter, the family felt the conviction in what he was saying. It helped Milly the most, which is what he wanted more than anything.

Of course girls always fight with their mothers in their teenage years. Milly had been a handful with her own parents, not as someone dark and brooding, but mischievous and rebellious. It was never out of any sort of hatred of her parents, she was just a kid.

After a few more conversations between the grieving couple, Jack finally felt like he had gotten through to Milly. They could begin to heal, as much as was possible for parents who lost a daughter.

It hadn't been a moment too soon either. By the end of that first week, the FBI contacted them to receive the body.

The Gosselins were kind enough to watch the boys while they made their way toward the school campus. Jack and Milly would watch poor Yvonne the next day when they were summoned to transfer Elise.

The boys were so young, Jack didn't want them to see their sister like that. He wanted them to remember her as she was, alive. He was already terrified enough of what *he* would see.

They parked in one of the spaces along the road just off of school grounds.

It seemed like every single federal law enforcement agency had some kind of detachment set up near the attack site. With the National Guard providing medical tents and other support structures, it felt like Alexandria was under military occupation.

The FBI agent that greeted them looked like he was barely out of the Academy, in his mid-twenties. People of all ages, from all over the country, had been brought in to deal with the situation.

He seemed like he tried to be sympathetic, but there was a certain dissociation to the way he spoke. All of the agents and military members were acting in a similar way, masking their own trauma of having to clean up such a horrific tragedy.

The agent brought Jack and Milly to one of the medical processing tents. There were a dozen stations around the sides, only barely being isolated by thin privacy curtains. The middle of the tent contained computers, tables, and lab supplies.

The agent led them to the back. There was a fully uniformed guardsman with some kind of medical insignia on his collar. He was standing beside one of the privacy curtains.

The agent tried to prep the two before seeing her. He gave the explanation that because of how quickly everything happened, she didn't feel any pain. It was just sudden, like a light switch.

It sounded like a canned line, something they were telling all the parents to make them feel better. The agent almost said it like a prayer, trying to convince himself that it was true just as much as he was trying to convince the family members.

The Tidwells took a deep breath, then stepped in.

Milly could not look long before she began weeping as she did the night of the explosion.

Jack wanted to believe it was quick also. He desperately hoped that Blaire hadn't felt any of the injuries that covered her from head to toe.

She was in a clear plastic box, which had kept her refrigerated as the investigation was carried out. She was still wearing what was left of her Homecoming dress. She looked more or less the way they found her.

Milly asked if they could touch her, and the guardsman nodded his head. He stepped over and unzipped the top of the clear plastic box, folding the side open also.

They held Blaire's good hand and kissed the less damaged side of her face.

The reunion meant more for Milly, who was saying her own goodbyes. Jack was still comforted by the vision he had been given. That was the Blaire that he still felt in his arms.

He stepped back, giving his wife a moment alone with her.

The FBI agent could see how relatively well Jack was handling things and saw it as an opportunity to speak more frankly with him.

He explained in hushed words how much worse so many of the others looked. As hard as it was to see Blaire like this, many of the students had been crushed, or were in pieces, or mostly skeletal. They too would have to be positively identified by the parents before being released.

Looking through the case file on her specifically, he explained that Blaire was found on the dance floor. She was relatively less damaged because she was in the arms of someone else. The description given explained who that someone was. As the agent had put it, Andrei had taken the brunt of the flames trying to shield her.

Jack removed his glasses, covering his face with a hand to hold in a fresh wave of grief. He wished he had been nicer to the boy before they left. He had been there for Blaire up to the very end.

After leaving the tent, they followed the agent to his work station. They contacted the funeral home and did the transfer paperwork.

That first week had been a whirlwind of activity outside of the private sorrows of the families.

Many people wanted to leave, they wanted to go away on holiday to someplace where they couldn't see the smoke or the ruins of the school ... but they couldn't.

While the joint investigation was carried out, everyone was confined to the city. The feds couldn't risk a suspect or witness fleeing the scene.

Early on, there was talk that the school's football quarterback, Joseph Torelli, may have been involved in the bombing. After trying to contact the family, they found his father's body at their home with his head blown off.

Joe's body had been found sitting in the car he drove to the dance. His trunk was full of supplies showing that he had planned to flee the country to Latin America. Among the luggage was the hunting shotgun he had apparently used to kill his father.

He was the leading suspect, and international news had speculated endlessly about the details and motives. Then, a physical letter he had mailed to his girlfriend was found in her parents' mailbox. The details of the letter made sense in the context of killing his father, but not in the context of the bombing. Both he and the girlfriend died in the explosion. The letter was written in such a way that it anticipated none of that, let alone an explosion at all.

That is when the public at large were beginning to have their doubts. It wasn't until Saturday that the FBI released their new report following a thorough shakedown of the construction companies involved.

Jack was not sure how to feel about the revelation.

Chelsea Morton was *younger* than Blaire by about a year. How a single teenage girl could be so evil and do something so horrible was beyond most people's comprehension.

Most had decided to place the blame squarely at her father's feet, considering he was the only one left for them to focus their anger on.

He was still in federal custody. At the very least he was being charged with gross negligence for letting his company laptop and credentials be used by an unapproved party. Of course, the trial would likely last for years, and they would try to add everything they could to put him away forever.

The real negligence was clearly in raising his daughter. There were dozens of opportunities where her plot could have been foiled if he simply paid more attention.

Jack had a fleeting moment of imagining himself in such a situation. If he had found out that so many people had been murdered because of his own failing as a father, he probably would have killed himself by now.

One way or another, Walter Morton would face justice.

What really mattered was that it was all over, all the questions had been answered. However, Jack would struggle to accept the sheer madness of the motives for why his daughter had to die.

Following a totally ignored Halloween, the Tidwell family returned to the site of Villa Vista High School. Chris and Tommy were with them as well.

They checked in with someone at the front to gain entrance. Even restricted to just the direct family members of the victims, there were thousands in attendance.

They were each given a black and yellow ribbon to pin to themselves. The school colors had been incorporated into the remembrance symbols. In the place where the ribbon ends crossed, there was a small circular pin containing the number "337".

It commemorated the 337 victims of the bombing. Among those numbers, there were 34 faculty and adult staff. The other 303 bodies were teenage students in attendance, most of whom were from Villa Vista.

However, there were a few students from John Muir and other schools who were the dates of some at the dance.

There were no survivors found in the rubble. The main school building was too compact, and the ballroom was right next to the gymnasium. Those in the houses around the campus were able to escape with only minor injuries. Over twenty homes were also destroyed in the ensuing fire, as well as the football stadium, some storage buildings, and the baseball snack bar.

Jack led his family through the crowd.

Along with the ribbons, they as a family had been given a single white lily on a stem.

A temporary memorial wall had been set up near the main entrance to the campus. They were gathering on an unburnt section of lawn between the middle school and high school.

Villa Vista as a whole was shutting down. The undamaged middle school and elementary buildings were going to be used as overflow storage for the school district. No one wanted to work there anymore.

For the high school, there were already plans in the works for how the site would be transformed into a permanent memorial.

One of the early ideas was spearheaded by a surprisingly meaningful discovery made after the attack.

Two of the adults who perished in the blaze were the professional photographers hired to take the official pictures of the students. The photos they had taken that evening were uploaded immediately to their company website. That way the students could view them on their phones throughout the night and decide how many prints they wanted to buy while the passions were still fresh.

What had been intended as a bit of advantageous marketing, instead became a time capsule.

The Tidwells walked along the temporary memorial wall.

A much larger, more elaborate wall was being planned, with those photos intending to be the centerpiece of the site.

It showed each student dressed in their finest clothes, in one of their happiest moments at the height of the dance, before everything ended in such tragedy.

The Tidwells stopped. They found the picture of Blaire.

The photography company had given each family all the pictures taken of their respective students.

Every one of the pictures taken of Blaire and Andrei were beautiful. She looked happier than ever. It had been another moment of comfort for all of them. She had been blessed with a wonderful final night at the end.

They were having all the pictures taken of her printed and framed for her room, including the group picture with Elise and her other friends.

The shot selected of her and Andrei for the memorial was the most "standard" pose. They wanted as much uniformity for the wall as they could. It was meant to remember the students as a whole.

Jack personally preferred the other two pictures. The sillier ones with the young couple showed just how close the two had become in recent months.

A glass vase sat in front of the framed picture. Milly carefully placed the white lily for Blaire into the vessel. There was already one lily there.

On their way down from the wall they bumped into many of the other families they'd come to know over the years. Alexandria was not a big town after all.

One of the parents was Jonathan Maxwell. He was an attorney that had helped Jack process some of the legal issues tied up in his father's estate.

Jonathan had also lost a daughter, Jennifer. She was a senior, just one grade ahead of Blaire.

They spoke for a minute about how they were handling things. Jack mentioned that they had buried Blaire by her grandfather. There were quite a few Tidwells in that section of the cemetery already. She wasn't alone.

Jonathan and his wife were planning something similar. They'd purchased a new set of family plots down in the city. His dad was buried in a nearby veteran's cemetery and he wanted all of the family to be close by. He explained that he and his wife were going to be leaving Alexandria, to move closer to his dad and Jennifer.

It was a sentiment most of the parents shared. It was hard enough to bury a father or mother; how do you bury a child?

It seemed like almost every victim's family was there in the crowd, with a few notable exceptions.

There were no Torellis left to mourn the passing of Joseph. One of the news reports noted that his mother had gone into hiding after an abusive relationship with the father. If she had surfaced, the media hadn't told the rest of them.

Walter Morton wasn't in attendance, of course. The devil he had spawned was the 338th body found in the rubble. It was presumably also in federal custody. Who knows what they'd do with it? Jack thought they should study the brain, see if they could find what had gone wrong to make someone so indescribably evil.

Almost no one spoke of the bomber or the upsetting motives. Most simply chose not to think about it at all. This memorial was about the kids, not their killer.

After what Edward had told him in the vision, Jack felt confident that the killer was facing the punishment she deserved.

There was another family notably not in attendance though ... the Henshaws.

Greg was the only victim without a picture on the memorial wall. Every picture taken of him that night also had her in it.

The FBI didn't seem to attribute any blame to the boyfriend, but his family had gone into hiding anyway. They were already in the process of moving to Japan and simply accelerated their schedule once the government allowed them to leave.

Most of the other parents were happy he didn't appear on the wall either. The strange nature of the killer's motives had tainted him as well. He probably wasn't actually involved in any way, but most basically considered him an accessory to her horrific crime.

The Tidwells found a place in the crowd next to the Gosselins. They greeted Howard and Patricia.

The boys began talking with Yvonne, making inane small talk to distract themselves from the circumstances. Chris hadn't spoken much since it happened, but he'd talked to Yvie every chance they had. The kids looked like they needed each other now more than ever.

Elise had been buried near Patricia's parents.

As heartbreaking as it was, none of them wanted to leave Alexandria. Many of their families had lived there for generations. Both couples had decided to transfer their kids to John Muir.

A few of their administrators were in attendance with the families of the John Muir student victims.

Their principal had given a short but touching speech. They had brought the "Coast Board" trophy with them to donate it to the memorial. He said that they wished they could have played a thousand more games with Villa Vista.

It was very bittersweet, especially for the families of the football players.

There were a few other speakers, but the final one seemed like she was having trouble keeping it together.

Just to the side of the stage, she spoke with someone before they called her name. He kissed her forehead trying to give her the courage to make it through the speech.

Finally, she approached the microphone.

It was Vice Principal Barbara Fletcher.

Aside from all the students, two dozen teachers and faculty had died in the bombing. One of those was long-time Principal Leonard McDouglas. Another was the oldest victim of the bombing, the school's guidance counselor, Richard Wallace.

In many ways, Ms. Fletcher was the only administrator left. She began her speech saying as much.

Most of her words were as positive and reflective as they could be. She mentioned how wonderful the students were, how bright, and smart, and talented, and sweet they had all been to her. She gave a few examples without naming names. She wanted her anecdotes to apply to all of the victims, representative of the meaningful qualities inside each of them.

She then gave some words of remembrance for the teachers who had perished, as well as Principal McDouglas. One of the hardest personal losses for her was Mr. Wallace. She reflected on how she had talked with him more than any other faculty, how grateful she had been to help students with their problems wherever and however she could.

She concluded by saying that the students were in a better place now and that they deserved nothing less.

Once she was done, the crowd slowly began to disperse.

The Gosselins invited them over for dinner that night, which they were more than happy to accept.

After they left, Jack began walking his family toward the car. That is when he heard a raspy older voice call his name.

"Excuse me," it said. "Are you Jack Tidwell?"

He turned toward the voice and found a balding man with round glasses and a partially-greyed goatee. He recognized the face instantly from the background check he had performed.

"Yes," Jack said, extending a hand. "I'm sorry I haven't had a chance to contact you earlier."

Between everything that had happened in recent weeks, he hadn't really thought about Andrei's family in all this.

"It's not a problem," the man said. "I'm sorry we are only now meeting like this."

Milly and the boys were a bit confused, so Jack elaborated.

"Milly, this is Andrei's father, Vasily Tunnikov," he said.

Jack suddenly felt like he needed a better reason for already recognizing him.

"Blaire showed me a video of one of your performances at the Symphony," he explained.

"Ah, yes," Vasily answered as he shook Milly's hand. He gave Jack a look.

It was reasonable that Jack had looked into him a bit before letting his son date Jack's daughter. They would have arranged for a meeting of some kind beforehand, but the kids were very private in their own ways.

At first, Andrei was just a new friend in Blaire's choir class. Then, all of the sudden, he was taking her to Homecoming.

Blaire liked keeping her affections to herself.

She even kept Andrei and his dad away from them at the football game, afraid her parents would say or do something to screw things up with Andrei before the dance itself.

That wasn't even really a Blaire thing, that was a teenager thing. Her relationship with Andrei was much deeper than Jack had realized at the time. It was her first *real* dance with her first *real* boyfriend. She was probably nervous enough; she didn't want her parents to get too parental and scare him off.

Vasily stepped to the side, presenting the rest of his own family.

"This is my oldest, Anastasia, and her husband Jacob," he said.

A couple in their mid-twenties greeted the two.

"And this is my daughter Katya," he said, resting a gentle hand on her shoulder.

She was a college-aged girl with light brown hair and blue eyes. She smiled for a brief moment, but could not look at the two of them. She clutched her arms as though she were freezing, and her face was just as pale.

Katya had been crying the most out of all of them.

"I apologize for not yet retrieving Andrei's car," Vasily continued. "The girls just arrived a few nights ago and we have been busy with the arrangements."

"It's perfectly fine," Jack said. "Take all the time you need."

There were a few other cars still parked around the Tidwells' driveway. They had all converged together for the limousine, but the limousine and the children never returned.

They had more than enough room. Jack wasn't going to bother any of the parents for something so trivial so soon after what happened.

"What 'arrangements' are you making?" Jack asked him. "We've laid Blaire near my father. It's a very nice funeral home if you're still looking."

"Oh, thank you," Vasily said. "We are actually taking Andrei back to Pasadena. There is a place near our old house, where my wife is buried."

"Of course," Milly said. She would want the same for herself. She and Jack had already reserved the plot right next to Blaire.

"I am actually returning there as well," Vasily said. "Katya has a few years left at UCLA, and I don't feel like staying up here, so close to ..."

Vasily trailed off, gently rubbing Katya's back.

It would be better for both of them to have someone to mourn with.

"That's what I would do," Jack said, "stay close to family."

"We're looking for jobs in the area ourselves," Anastasia said.

"We work in finance," Jacob elaborated, "it should happen quickly."

Most of the crowd was gone now and the two families could see the entire stretch of pictures along the memorial wall. Blaire and Andrei's picture was right in the middle.

"The photos were lovely," Vasily said. "Andrei cared about Blaire very much."

"We know he did," Milly said.

She pulled out her cell phone.

"I found this on Blaire's computer." She tapped the screen.

A gentle piano melody flowed out of the speakers.

Katya recognized it immediately. Andrei had sent her the final version to spot check before sending it to Blaire.

She buried her face into Anastasia's shoulder, muffling her sobs. Anastasia held her close, tears trickling from her cheeks.

They let the whole piece play through to completion. It ended on a chord being tapped pensively several times, but differed from its original live performance. A short outro followed, resolving the music in a harmonious end.

"Blaire was very fond of him too," Jack said. "I think they might have stayed together for a long time."

"So do I," Vasily agreed, "which is why I wanted to reach out to you."

He pulled out an index card with all of his contact information on it.

"While I am returning to Pasadena, I will only be a short flight away," he said. "If you need anything at all, please feel free to reach out to me. If you are ever around Los Angeles, my home is open to you."

"Thank you," Jack said, taking the card.

"The same goes for you," Milly agreed. "Whenever you come by to pick up the car, please stay for a meal. We would love to get to know you better."

"I would like that." Vasily smiled.

The two families walked away from the ruins of Villa Vista High School.

They would return there many times over the years, often together, to visit the proper memorial park which was erected in its place.

While horrible tragedy had torn away at the loved ones of the victims, many of them found solace in new friendships. They were now connected together by this dreadful shared experience. More so than not, they needed each other to fill the holes in their hearts. They were all missing the same pieces.

They kept alive the memories of their children. As painful as the loss was, the families had to have faith that they were in a better place.

***

"Amen," the lost souls said together.

Blaire could feel a tingling on her skin, her hair standing on end.

She was too afraid to open her eyes. Instead, she focused on what she could feel.

Andrei's strong but gentle hands were wrapped around her. His black suit coat was still there beneath her fingers. He was still warm.

After a few moments, the tingling stopped.

Blaire Tidwell opened her eyes.

Andrei Tunnikov opened his as well.

They were staring at each other. They were still there, still together.

They kissed and squeezed each other tightly. The lovers fell to their knees, chuckling in relief.

There was a slight creaking sound below them. They looked down to find that they were on some kind of wooden dock.

On one side of them was a wall of white fog. On the other side was a great black ocean which seemed to go on forever.

"This is it!" she said. "This is where I came in my dreams!"

Blaire felt down around her waist. There was no corset. However, she was wearing her Homecoming dress again, jewelry, accessories, corsage, and all.

Andrei was fully dressed as well.

Their hair was perfect and their skin was unburnt and unblemished.

They were whole.

"You look incredible," Andrei teared up.

"So do you," Blaire replied, resting her head on his chest.

They were kneeling at the end of the dock, the only section extending out beyond the white wall of fog. Several more docks reached out from the mist in both directions. A spinning lighthouse could be seen in the distance.

Just beyond the lighthouse, floating alone in the great black ocean, was an old wooden schooner. The ship was on fire, burning bright orange. Its nose sank more and more into the water with every passing second.

Blaire and Andrei stood to their feet.

Andrei was wearing his fresh, polished dress shoes. Blaire, on the other hand, was surprised to find her white tennis shoes with the black stripes. She wore ankle-length socks between them and her nylons.

"That's weird." She twisted her ankle from side to side.

"Probably easier to walk on wooden planks," Andrei guessed.

They turned toward the wall of fog. Only about twelve feet of walkway separated them from it.

"What if it just spits us out on another dock?" she asked.

"Then we keep trying, together." Andrei offered his hand and she took it.

"No splitting up." She smiled.

"Never," Andrei replied.

They walked into the white curtain of mist.

The wooden dock was narrow, but it was just wide enough for both Blaire & Andrei.

The fog never got so thick that they couldn't see their feet and a few paces of dock in front of them. It wasn't like the first time they crossed the intersection at the school, where everything went white before they were cast out in front of the baseball diamonds.

They walked peacefully, a relaxing stroll. One thing they could tell for sure was that time meant nothing anymore.

Would they still have to wait to see those they left behind? Yes. But 40 years or 80 years compared to 80,000 seemed like nothing at all. They could feel no anxiety, no unease, only anticipation for seeing those loved ones again.

The three days they spent passing through the Hell of another would become a blink in time.

It was a memory worth recalling, a memory worth passing on to the living should they ever be given the chance to do so. It would be a potent warning, a vision of things that could be if those people ever tried to cut away at the souls of others for the sake of their own.

Not all of those days were entirely suffering either. In fact, when weighed on the scales of time, more good came out of those three days than bad. And that was only the start, there was so much more to come.

The fog began to thin and the two could see the vague outline of some mountains. It was a bright, sunny day, the kind of day Blaire used to greet with scorn. Somehow though, this was different.

There was the distant sound of people ... lots of people.

Once the fog thinned completely, they found a surprisingly familiar sight. It looked almost like Alexandria.

The ocean below was no longer black, but a cool, clear, and refreshing blue. It rolled along a shoreline made of bright white sand, with pink specs sprinkled throughout.

Everything was vivid, as though the trees and landscape were painted with colors Blaire had never seen before. They were not pastels that polluted the cool, dark atmospheres she used to surround herself with. These colors were like auras, glows in the darkness which gave depth and breadth to those atmospheres.

She thought of the great black ocean lying behind them. This whole place, this Paradise, was the aura. It was the glowing star in the void of space. It was the pale blue dot of life in a dead universe. It was the sole oasis in a barren desert. It was the vein of gold in a wasteland of stone. It was the lone tropical island in a tempest sea.

Blaire could smell food in the air, pizza, burritos, ice cream, sandwiches, and smoothies. She had a feeling that if she looked hard enough, she'd find anything that could ever be found on a beach, and so much more.

As vibrant as the trees were, the colors, the smells, the sounds, one of the most awe-inspiring things on the landscape was the thin line of light tracing the top of the mountains. It occurred to her that despite finding it difficult to imagine eternity, she was already starting to get the idea.

Eternity only seems long when you run out of discovery, when you run out of experience, when you no longer have things to fill the void. In fact, there was no void at all anymore. The void was behind her.

She could feel content sitting on this beach forever. But *so much* lay just beyond that coastal mountain range, she just knew it. She wanted to see it all ... she wanted to see it all with Andrei.

Blaire and Andrei were almost to shore.

At the end of the dock was a familiar figure. He was standing statuesque, waiting for them.

No longer playing the role of lighthouse keeper, he was dressed in something more casual, something he actually used to wear on weekend trips and vacations. He looked healthy and strong, as he did before he got sick and had to come live with them. There was no cane in his hand.

Once his form was fully visible, Blaire ran up and hugged him.

Andrei approached as they loosened their embrace.

Blaire returned to him, slipping her arm through his.

"Andrei, this is my grandpa." She had dropped all pretense of formality. In a way, they already knew each other well.

Andrei extended his hand and they shook.

With a smile on his face, Edward Tidwell said to both of them, "Welcome Home."

Beyond the three of them, the beach was very busy today ... busier than most days, unfortunately.

Hundreds of deceased students of Villa Vista High School lined the shoreline. Beyond them lay thousands more ... family, friends, and loved ones.

But one group in particular, the lost ones, were especially familiar to Blaire and Andrei.

They had been pulled into a storm beyond their control and against their wills. Some of them had to survive together to the very end ... when demons circled them, wearing their faces.

Those six other students were also on the beach, having finally made it to shore.

So many of them had been lost in the great abyss, but they were sent shepherds to guide them Home.

They were lost no more.

Just beyond the edge of their dock, off in the distance, Andrei saw someone he hadn't seen for a very, very long time. She was waiting for him on the edge of the sand.

A tear came to his eye, he thought he'd never see her again. He had so much to tell her and they had so much to tell Blaire.

"What do you think?" Andrei asked her, wiping the tear away.

"I love it," Blaire said, squeezing his arm.

They followed Edward, stepping off of the wooden dock onto the beach.

This was their new start, their new future, their new forever.

AFTERWORD & ACKNOWLEDGEMENTS

This story was roughly thirteen years in the making. That is around the time that my creativity was really beginning to manifest in my senior year of high school.

After puberty, when my voice settled in, I joined my school's performing arts program. Having grown up on many of the animated musicals of the 1990s, it was a short transition for me to fully embrace the world of musical theatre.

My foray into writing began in college. In my first semester, I had a G.E. class in English 1A. Our professor was very encouraging. "Write every day and believe in yourself!" was the essential thesis of her class. I credit her for kicking off my interest in writing prose and fiction. Although my degree is in Mechanical Engineering, she's probably the professor that had the single most impact on my life.

There are many inspirations for this story from some of my favorite writers and composers. However, I'm sure it's not surprising to say that some of my own high school experiences made it into the pages as well, especially the various banquets and dances … like the Homecomings.

While some descriptions of Villa Vista High School and its students may seem similar to real life classmates, there are no direct "shadows" of people in this tale. These are characters and do not reflect real life personalities at all, especially the antagonists. Overall, I had a wonderful high school experience. Attending my class's ten-year reunion was actually one of the main catalysts that finally drove me to write *Homecoming*.

When I say this story was thirteen years in the making, I'm referring to one very specific event. Our school had an *accidental* incident involving natural gas which could have easily become a situation similar to the one I describe. I had to sit in the bleachers of my own high school's football stadium. We spent all day waiting for the fire department to bleed the gas pockets built-up in our school building. It was then that I wondered how it might have gone differently … if it wasn't an accident and if we didn't escape. That is where the seed of this story was planted.

As for Acknowledgements, I'd be remiss not to mention God Almighty, considering the subject matter. The first chapter literally came to me in a dream on Christmas morning, 2020. I'm not sure if it was "divine inspiration", but it sure felt like it. After that, I had the first draft finished in three months.

I also mainly owe my gratitude to my loving parents. I was blessed to be born into a clever and artistic family, including my brother as well. It was because of their support that I have been this successful at everything in life, from career, to performing arts, to creative writing. They were always there to offer me words of encouragement as I honed my skills and confidence to the point of finally being able to bring *Homecoming* to life as I always intended.

Frank Winter
Northern California
July 2021

For news, updates, upcoming novels, & other info, please visit:
www.frankwinterfiction.com

www.ingramcontent.com/pod-product-compliance
Lightning Source LLC
Chambersburg PA
CBHW071332020726
47502CB00001B/71